Until You

TRILOGY

Joseph and Samantha's epic love story

Until You Series Books 1-3

D.M. DAVIS

Until You SET ME FREE

An Until You Novel

Book One

Playlist

Say Hey (I Love You) by Michael Franti & Spearhead

Little Things by One Direction

Birthday Cake by Rhianna

Let me Love You by DJ Snake (featuring Justin Bieber)

Birthday Sex by Jeremiah

Then There's You by Charlie Puth

I Get to Love You by Ruelle

Kindly Calm Me Down by Meghan Trainor

I Miss you by Adele

Mercy by Sean Mendes

This Town by Niall Horan

She Will Be Loved by Maroon 5

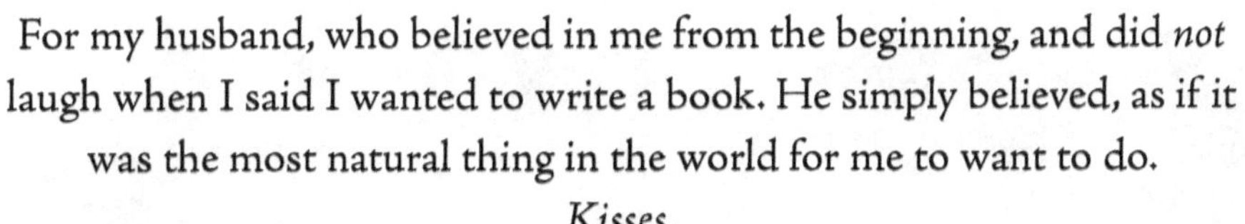

For my husband, who believed in me from the beginning, and did *not* laugh when I said I wanted to write a book. He simply believed, as if it was the most natural thing in the world for me to want to do.
Kisses.

Until You SET ME FREE

PART 1
GIVING THANKS

NOVEMBER

One

OUTSIDE MY CHEM CLASS WINDOW THE SKY IS Caribbean blue with tranquil clouds. An easy breeze makes the leaves rustle like waving hands to the passing cars. The sun is high in the sky, shining like a hot summer day rather than the chilly fall day it is. I'd prefer to be out there than in here. It's the last day of school before Thanksgiving break, everyone is distracted and impatient for the day to end. Yet, I'm distracted and anxious for a whole other reason. My brother, Jace, is coming home to Dallas from the University of Texas at Austin—with his roommate, Joe.

What's Joe McIntyre like? Will he be approachable and talkative, or stuffy and terse? Will he treat me as an equal or as a kid? I know what he looks like. Anyone with a television, computer, or smart phone knows what the McIntyre brothers—heirs to the multi-billion-dollar technology company, McIntyre Corporate Industries—look like. They come from corporate-billionaire-handsome-rugged-GQ type sturdy stock. And the youngest of the three is coming home to stay for the week-long break.

"What are you going to say? Are you nervous?" A soft whisper and tap to my shoulder draws my attention.

Margot has known me since second grade and should know the answer to that is *hell yes, I'm nervous.*

"I'll probably just stumble all over myself either verbally or physically." Being awkward with the guys in my school is bad enough, but god, I'll die if I actually trip in front of Joe.

Great. Now, I've probably just jinxed myself.

"I don't understand it, Sam. You're the smartest person at this school." She wags her finger, imploring me with her light brown eyes to accept what she's saying.

I roll my eyes. She's just as smart as me. We're both in the running for valedictorian of our senior class when we graduate in May.

Ignoring my obvious protest of her pep talk, she continues. "You're also smoking hot."

"Shh." I scowl, glancing around the classroom in case anyone overheard.

"Seriously? You think they don't know you're smart and beautiful?" She laughs. "You're a lost cause, Sam. Truly. How are you so shy and insecure when you have a brother like Jace—who's also crazy hot and smart, by the way. Y'all are gifted. I mean, jeez, you come from doctors and lawyers. There's not a bad gene in your family tree."

I can't help but laugh. "Margot, stop. You're working yourself into one of your rants. I appreciate it. I do. But I don't need you to try to build me up before I meet Joe McIntyre. I know who he is. I know who he will be. He won't give me the time of day."

I turn back around to face the front of the classroom. "I'm seventeen, for god's sake. What would he want with me when every college girl on campus is probably throwing herself at his feet?" I murmur more to myself than her.

After school, I rush through the door, excited to see Jace. Dropping my bag on the stairs, I move toward the baritone voice coming from the kitchen.

"Jace?" I holler.

"Is that my favorite sister I hear?"

"It's your only sister, jackass."

"Jackass?" His smiling face greets me at the entryway. "Is that any way to greet your favorite brother?"

I leap into his arms. "You're my only brother, Jace."

He stumbles back from the force of my lunge, stopping us from toppling over. His arms wrap around me, swinging me around, laughing at my exuberance.

I shut my eyes, trying to still the ache of loneliness. It's been too many months. "I missed you," I whisper.

He sets me down, his blue eyes piercing mine. "Missed you, too."

The kindness in his voice steals the tears from my eyes.

"Hey, no crying."

I nod and wipe my damp cheeks, sniffling. *God, I've missed him.*

He hugs me again. "We have a whole week together." His words hold promises I hope he can keep.

Releasing me, his hands remain on my shoulders as he searches for signs of more of my "girly emotions," as he calls them.

Satisfied the waterworks have stopped, he puts his arm around my shoulder and turns me to face the island where, lo and behold, sits the most beautiful man I have ever seen. My breath catches as I take in his dark hair, chiseled features, and skin that glows with sexiness. Or maybe I just had an aneurysm. That must be it. It's affecting my vision, because I swear he's glowing like a beacon. And my body responds as if he's calling me home.

What. The. Hell?

"Sam, this is my roommate Joe," Jace introduces the god in front of me.

How could I have missed him sitting there?

The beautiful man rises from his seat, his eyes glued to me. My gaze continues to rise as he comes to his full height. He has to be six and a half feet of solid muscle. His faded blue jeans and white t-shirt, tucked in at the waist, only accentuate his ripped torso visible under the thin fabric.

Holy mother of god, I can't breathe.

He moves closer, towering over me, his emerald-green eyes flickering across my face. "Samantha, it's lovely to meet you."

Lovely? Did this gorgeous hunk of man-cake just say it's lovely to meet me? Is he from the seventeenth century? I'm thrown off balance; my thoughts, my body, are in a whirlwind of sensory overload.

Somehow, I manage to take his outstretched hand. "It's Sam, and it's *lovely* to meet you, as well."

His slight grin spreads into a full smile with, *oh dear god,* dimples. They're not oh-aren't-they-cute dimples. Oh no, these are

I've-got-a-dirty-secret-and-I-just-might-whisper-it-in-your-ear-as-I-fuck-you-senseless dimples.

He slowly lifts my hand to his mouth and kisses it. His sultry lips linger before he lowers our joined hands, still not releasing me.

The warmth of his touch sends shivers up my arm and down my body.

Danger is all I can think as my body screams *yes, please.*

"No one as beautiful as you should ever be called Sam, Samantha," he says seriously with just a bite of condescension.

I don't quite know what to think. He gives me a great compliment, calling me beautiful, yet makes me feel childish for loving my boyish nickname. I think it's sassy and free of pretension.

"Well, *Joseph*, perhaps you should get to know me before you decide my name doesn't fit."

He drops my hand, humor gone, but his eyes still hold mine. "No."

"No?"

He nods. "No. I don't need to know you better."

Wow. "Alrighty then." I turn to Jace, giving him a some-nice-guy-you-brought-home look. I guess Joseph's going for stuffy and terse and treating me like a kid instead of an equal. That's a shame.

Jace laughs, bumping me with his shoulder. "Joe, man, ease up. She's only seventeen. Sam suits her just fine."

"Nearly eighteen," I remind him, my chin rising in defiance.

He laughs again. "More like seventeen going on thirty-five."

He says it like it's a bad thing. I can't help it if I'm an old soul.

Joseph's still focused on me, sizing me up, I suppose. His face is unreadable, void of any emotion as he takes his seat back at the counter. I'm disappointed—I don't measure up. Then again, I already knew I wouldn't, so I shouldn't be surprised. If past experience drives future expectations, then I already knew I could never measure up to the likes of Joseph McIntyre.

"What are you doing tonight?" Jace draws my attention as he takes a seat next to Joseph. "Got a hot date?"

I scoff. "No. I'm working."

He knows better than to ask. As much as I notice boys, they rarely notice me. There was one, once. For a brief moment in time, someone noticed me, but I don't even try anymore. I throw myself into my studies, working on my AP college level classes that will allow me to graduate high school with an Associate's Degree in a mere six months.

"When do you get off?"

"Late. Eleven." I still feel Joseph's eyes on me, and it takes all I have not to glance his way and give him the satisfaction of knowing he's the reason my heart is pounding as my scattered thoughts ping around like a pinball machine. I wouldn't be surprised if my eyes gloss over and an out-of-order sign pops out of the top of my head.

I need to disappear for a while. Regroup. Take a cold shower. Run a marathon. Get laid. *Like that's gonna happen.*

Jace's face scrunches up, not liking my answer. He's overprotective, thinking I work too hard. He'd rather I was a carefree teenager instead of focusing on my future all the time. I don't work because I have to financially; I work because I want to. I need the experience. By nature, I'm an introvert. I prefer small gatherings, one-on-one interaction, to groups or parties. For my career aspirations in the corporate world, I need to be able to converse and interact with all types of people. I can't hide at my desk and hope someone notices my work. Technology is my passion, and the industry moves at the speed of light. I want to be at the head of the pack.

"What about tomorrow night?" Jace counters.

"I can't. I've got a term paper I need to work on."

He blows out a punch of air. "Sam, seriously, it's Saturday night. The weekend. You don't need to try to graduate college at the same time I do. You can be a kid, you know. You don't always have to be the most responsible person in the room."

"Says the boy who's in his junior year of college after only two years," I retort.

"Yeah, but I didn't start bustin' my ass until after high school." He motions to his roommate. "Joe, help me out here."

Joseph takes us in, running his hand through his wavy black hair, messing it up in that I-just-got-outta-bed kinda way.

I want to touch it, tame it.

"Come out with us, then you can work on your term paper on Sunday.

Your brother just got home. He missed you. Spend time with him before you bury your nose in homework."

I didn't expect that. I thought Joseph didn't want to get to know me better, much less want to hang out with me. I can't focus on that dangerous territory. I don't have time for romance or a shattered heart, and Joseph McIntyre is an unrequited love-fest. He would eat me up and spit me out without a second glance, not because he's cruel, but because he's on a different level and wouldn't even notice the ant he just crushed as he walked by. *I'm the ant, by the way.*

Ignoring the angst in my stomach stirred up by Joseph's comment, I focus on Jace. "You really missed me?" He said it earlier, but only after I said it to him first, like an obligatory response.

Not missing a beat, he jumps up, making his way to me. "Don't start. You know I did." He squeezes my arm. "Come on. Come out with us tomorrow. I'd tell you to ditch work tonight, but I know you won't."

No, I won't ditch work. "What are y'all doin' tomorrow?" I shouldn't be considering this.

"We thought we'd go eat and then go to The Club, get our dance on, see who's home from college." He shrugs. "You know, see and be seen."

"I can't get in there. You know it's eighteen minimum age, and I don't have a fake ID."

He smiles. "I love that you don't. But Tommy's workin' the door and he already told me he'd get you in if you come with us. I promised him we'd only drink sodas. Plus, he's always had a thing for you, you know."

I grimace at the thought. "No. He's like…no." Tommy's like a brother, a silly, dopey brother. I nudge Jace, scowling. "You're just saying that. He does not have a thing for me."

Jace laughs. "He does—not that I'd let him touch you, but…well…" He shrugs, leaning against the counter. "It'll get you in. Come with us. Don't make me beg." He pulls out his big blue puppy-dog eyes.

"Are you gonna dump me to pick up women?" Jace is a manwhore, and has left me in the dust when I didn't have a backup plan to get home.

"Nope. Promise. Just you, me, and Joe here. No women. Though, you are a pretty good wingman," he teases me.

There were a few times I helped him seal the deal. I'm not proud of it. But honestly, if those girls don't know what they're getting into with Jace, I'm not going to be the one to break it to 'em. He's tall, dark, and handsome with those mischievous blue eyes woman fall for.

He's good to 'em. He just doesn't stick around for long.

He's young, sowing his oats, my dad says.

The apple didn't fall too far from the tree, according to my mom.

Apparently, my dad was the original manwhore until he met my mom. He says his heart didn't start beating until the day he laid eyes on his Eleanor.

They met at UT, in the quad. She was sitting under a tree studying, when my dad saved her from an errant football about to take off her head. He still lights up when he talks about that day, like she was sitting there and a ray of light shone down from Heaven leading him to her.

Mom tells it a little differently. Of the two of them, Dad is the romantic, fanciful one. And she's the down-to-earth realist.

They can't keep their eyes or hands off each other. I've come into a room more than a few times and had to turn around to keep from seeing more parental PDA than any kid should be subjected to.

I want that someday. I want a man to look at me the way my dad still looks at my mom. Like his life begins and ends with me. Like his next breath is tied to mine.

Someday. I hope. But for now, I can't live my life as a hermit, and I'll never meet anyone if I never go out.

"Is that a yes?" Jace asks.

"Yes, but I'm taking my own car. I don't trust you not to leave me in the lurch if you get a better offer."

Joseph laughs. "She knows you well, man." His eyes meet mine. "I won't leave you in the lurch, Samantha, but I'd appreciate the ride home if he dumps us both."

"Y'all suck," Jace growls, throwing his arms up and stomping out of the room.

He's not really mad, just sensitive about us not believing he won't leave us for a piece of ass.

Shrugging, I start to head out of the kitchen, but then feel bad for leaving Joseph. I turn around. "Do you need anything? Did Jace show you the guest room?"

"No, not yet. We came in the kitchen to eat as soon as we got in. I haven't even gotten my stuff out of the car."

When his eyes lock on mine, I swear I feel a zap of electricity running between us. His nostrils flare, and his chest rises. Am I affecting him as much as he is me? He looks at me as if he can read my thoughts, knows my desires, and can hear the quickening of my pulse.

He truly is a god of a man with his purely masculine features, thick wavy hair, and eyes that see things they probably shouldn't. He makes me feel things I know I shouldn't.

"Come on, Joseph, let me help you get settled."

His smile lights up his face and does crazy things to my body. "I'd like that, Samantha."

Two

Samantha

I MAKE IT TO WORK WITH PLENTY OF TIME TO SPARE. I didn't exactly sneak out of the house, but I did make a point to be quiet as I left my room and descended the stairs, hoping not to run into Joseph. He's on my mind enough as it is; I didn't need the added distraction of seeing him just before I left.

I love my job for two reasons. One: I don't have to focus on my future here. I don't have time to think about school work or what needs to get done for me to keep my high grade point average. This place is always busy, and I just have to focus on being friendly and making the few moments I interact with the customers as pleasant as possible. And two: I get to wear black. All black. Every day. All day. I feel comfortable in black. I feel safe. Secure. And even sexy. Sometimes.

"Hey, Sam." Trent, my friendly and on-spot boss, greets me as I put my purse away and clock in.

"Hey. How's it going tonight?" I'm sure he got here a few hours ago, even though he tries to keep his evening hours to a minimum for his family. That's a hard thing to do in the restaurant business when nights are where the money is.

"It's a good night. A bit slow for a Friday, but hopefully it'll pick up." He turns to leave. "Oh, there's a guy at the bar. He was asking for you."

My hand pauses midway to setting my time card back into its slot. "A guy? For me?" I hate the surprise in my voice. It's not likely a guy would be asking for me, but I don't have to make it so obvious.

He laughs. "Yes, Sam." His inflection is firm. "Take your time. Becca's got the hostess stand covered." He waves over his head as he slips out front.

As I near the bar, the air thickens and sizzles. And then I see him. Sitting there with his back to me, facing the door and the hostess stand.

Somehow, he senses me, turning as I approach.

That sizzle I felt a moment ago morphs into a full-fledged roaring inferno when his eyes lock on me. I stutter in my steps and trip into his side. He catches me in his capable arms as he pivots on his stool in one smooth, graceful move. Completely unlike me, who tripped over thin air simply because of the intensity of his gaze.

"You okay, Samantha?" He studies my face and rights my body, still holding me tightly around the waist against his solid chest, locked between his massive thighs.

Jesus. Fuck.

"I…uh…yeah." My hands splay across his perfectly-formed chest.

"Samantha?" His voice is low and powerful, like its pure frequency alone could produce enough energy to power a small town.

It's making my heart beat a million miles a minute and my brain foggy. "Hmmm?"

His smirking mouth knows too much. "You okay?" He clasps my cheek and encircles my waist, holding me securely in place. His green steamy gaze eats me up.

"Yes, I'm fine." I push away from the inferno that's Joseph McIntyre. "I'm sorry." I run my hands down my blouse and skirt like they need to be ironed out.

His hands release me slowly, as if reluctant to let me go. A chill courses through my body as the cool air hits the places he warmed with his touch.

If he notices, he doesn't let on. "No need to apologize. I'm just glad I was here to catch you." His eyes twinkle with mischief.

"I wouldn't have needed catching if you hadn't been here in the first place." I'm not clumsy by nature, but this man throws me off, keeps me off balance. Literally and figuratively. I knew I'd jinx myself worrying I'd trip in front of him.

He laughs. He actually laughs.

It's a nice round and robust sound. I can't hide my smile.

"What are you doing here anyway, Joseph?" I scan the bar. "Where's Jace?"

His smile drops. "He had a date."

I scoff. "Yeah, right. A *date*," I say with air quotes.

He shrugs, not confirming or denying. "My family's out of town," he says simply, as if that explains why he's here instead of at home or at a real bar hanging out with friends.

We stare at each other for a moment. It should be uncomfortable, but, strangely, it's not.

"I have to get to work."

"Have dinner with me," he says at the same time.

"What?" The word escapes before I can fully process what he said.

He looks chagrined. "Have dinner with me, Samantha."

I start to protest, but he raises his hand to halt my objection. "I know you're working." He motions around the restaurant. "They're not too busy. Perhaps they could spare you for an hour."

Ignoring my speeding pulse, I notice it might be possible, but really, it's just so unexpected. Why would he want to have dinner with me? I spot Trent watching us. He's amused, and I'm sure I'll hear about it later.

I step back. "I'm sorry. I can't." I make my way to the hostess station before Joseph can respond or change my mind.

Samantha

"Sir, I assure you we will seat you as soon as a table fitting your party's size becomes available." I shoot my co-hostess a look for assistance in re-assuring this guy. He's offended we've seated others who arrived after his party and doesn't comprehend, or care, that the smaller parties he's refer-ring to are easier to accommodate.

What group of eight men come to eat at the Cheesecake Factory, anyway? Go to a bar for god's sake.

Thankfully Becca smiles and assures him it shouldn't be much longer. I give her a nod of thanks.

"Well, honey, you're so sweet you make the wait worthwhile." He oozes with false charm, making my skin crawl.

"Thank you, sir." I reply half-hoping he was speaking to Becca.

He stays at the hostess stand, talking to his friends standing near the bar, but still within ear shot. "Pete, isn't she the sweetest? I think I should take her home."

Seriously? He's talking about taking me home like I have no say in the matter. I try to ignore him and scan the room, praying for a table to open.

"Yeah, man. Maybe she's got a friend or two who can join us," his friend replies.

I lean in to Becca and lower my voice. "Can you find Trent? Tell him we have a potential problem? If you don't find him, tell Bruce. He's big enough to scare them off."

Becca nods and flees. I wish I were the one leaving this uncomfortable situation instead of her.

"Where's your friend going, honey?" He doesn't seem to miss a thing.

I step to the side, keeping the hostess stand between us. He's making me uncomfortable, but it's nothing I haven't experienced. My customer service skills tell me to remain nice, until nice is no longer appropriate. I've just about reached the tipping point. However, I'd rather Trent be the one to make that call.

"She's going to check the tables," I offer, trying to busy myself so perhaps he'll back off and give me a break. Unfortunately, they're the only group waiting at the moment.

He moves closer and grabs my arm before I can respond. He reeks of beer and cigarettes, making my stomach churn. "Why you hiding back there, honey? You should come out here and have a drink with us." His fingers dig into my skin as he pulls me from behind the hostess stand.

I gasp and try to jerk my arm free, but he's got a death grip on my upper arm. "Let go of me," I demand, working to steady my breathing and not give in to my rising panic.

He steps into me. "Not until you agree to have a drink with me."

"That's not going to happen." Joseph's deep voice comes from behind me. His arm wraps around my waist, and I instantly start to calm. "I suggest you do as the lady asks and release her arm." The menace in his voice cannot be missed by this guy, even if he's had one too many drinks.

"Find your own female. I saw her first," he spits back at Joseph, squeezing my arm tighter.

I whimper as his fingers dig into my flesh as he tries to pull me out of Joseph's hold. "You're hurting me." My voice trembles. *Shit.*

"I warned you." In a flash, Joseph has a death grip on the guy's wrist while he peels his fingers off my arm. I think if it weren't for my arm being attached to the guy, Joseph would have taken him down by now. But since I could be collateral damage, he's taking it easy until I'm free of his grasp.

Trent and Bruce show up with Scott, who's as big as a house and one of our head chefs. He puts his hand on Joseph's shoulder with a nod of solidarity.

Joseph releases the guy with a small shove, allowing Scott to step in.

Trent crosses his arms. "Sir, I'm going to have to ask you to leave the premises."

I'm not sure if it's Trent's words or the appearance of three more guys to defend me, but whatever it is, I'm thankful as the guy finally steps back. Joseph guides me back from the line of fire and into his side.

Trent, Bruce, and Scott step in front of us, forming a protective wall. His friends don't seem to want a fight, but the guy is not backing down and starts to make more of a scene.

Joseph walks us farther away before turning me to face him. "You okay?"

I nod. "He scared me. I'm fine."

I'm shaking. Why am I shaking?

He pulls me into his arms, and I don't resist. His hand cups my head to his chest as he holds me tightly. "You're okay, Samantha. I've got you."

I relax into him, feeling safe in the comfort of his arms.

With my eyes clamped closed, I'm lost in the feel of him holding me, soothing my body with his hands and gentle words. As I start to come down from the frenzy of whatever that was, my breath steadies, but I'm still off-kilter.

"You okay, Sam?" Trent asks from behind me.

Joseph pivots so I can see Trent without moving away from his embrace.

Trent's brow rises as he takes us in, making me self-conscious. I pull away. Joseph slowly releases me but captures my hand, keeping me close.

"Yeah. I'm fine." I nod toward the hostess stand. "Sorry about that."

Both Trent and Joseph snort in unison.

"You have nothing to apologize for. He's an ass," Trent says.

"I could have handled it better. Put an end to it sooner before he was even able to get close enough to grab me."

"Sam, stop. You handled the situation professionally and with class, which is more than I can say for him," Trent insists.

"He was trying to show off for his friends and too drunk to listen to reason, Samantha. Don't second-guess yourself." Joseph squeezes my hand.

Trent motions to Joseph. "If you're hungry, I can set ya'll up at the bar. Then take Sam home. She's had enough excitement for one night." He stops my protest. "I don't want to see you back here until the Friday after Thanksgiving."

"Trent, I have shifts on the new schedule. I can work. I don't need the time off."

"You won't be out any money if that's what you're worried about. You'll be paid for your shifts. But I think it's a good idea you take the week off. When you do come back, no walking to your car alone. Understand?"

"Yeah, I got it." I don't have it in me to fight. If he wants to pay me for not working, I'm not going to argue. At least not tonight.

"Good. It's settled. Order whatever you want; it's on the house."

He shakes hands with Joseph and gives me a quick hug before Joseph leads me to the bar. "Looks like you're having dinner with me after all."

I shake my head in mock disapproval. "Don't look so smug about it."

He throws his head back and laughs. "I can't help it. I like it when things go my way."

"Yes, I'm quite sure you do."

He looks at me pointedly with fire burning in his eyes. "Count on it, Samantha."

Three

Joseph

I'VE PRACTICALLY HAD A HARD-ON SINCE SHE WALKED into Jace's kitchen. Her sass, her confidence, and angelic face knock me clean over. And Christ, those blue eyes, long auburn hair, and red, pouty lips. She's Jace's sister, and she's only seventeen, but fuck me running backwards with a dog in my arms, she's something else.

Not like I'm thinking of her in that way.

Who am I kidding? I'm totally thinking of her in that way.

And don't get me started on loving how much she loves her brother. They have a great relationship. It's fun, but it's also genuine. They know each other and love each other anyway. Jace can't shut up about his kid sister. When my parents announced they were going skiing for Thanksgiving, I took the standing invite from Jace to spend the holiday with his family. I had no idea what I was in for. It probably would've been smarter to go with my brothers to Cabo. I can't say I regret it, though.

I can't get involved with Samantha. I know this. But as she worked the hostess stand in that fitted black skirt, simple black blouse, and nearly CFM black pumps, I can't seem to remember why. My mouth goes dry, my heart rate increases, and my thoughts go places they shouldn't. Not just because of my career priorities. Not just because she's Jace's sister. Not just because she's young, inexperienced, naïve, and has her whole future ahead of her.

It's all of those things that should make me run the other way as fast as I can. And yet, here I sit like a lonely sap, aching for a girl who looks like a goddess and is genuine to the bone. There is no pretense. What you see is what you get. If she's flustered, it shows. If she's mad, put off, it shows. If she's turned on, Christ Almighty, it shows.

Her fingers lazily skim the rim of her glass of iced tea. Her lower lip, captured between her teeth while her middle finger circles over and over again. It's sexy as hell, and my cock stirs at the sight.

Fuck.

"Are you sure you're okay?"

With a shy smile and minimalistic nod, she breaks the seduction of her iced tea, taking a deep drink.

Damn, if that's not sexy as hell too. *Double fuck.*

Maybe this wasn't such a great idea. Not dinner per se, but showing up at her work. Period. For the life of me, I don't regret sitting here in companionable silence. I don't give a shit if she doesn't say a word, I'm just glad she's okay after that man…I shake the thought away, lest I track him down in the parking lot. I can see her mind working, her face reacting in the smallest of ways to whatever's going on in that head of hers. I wish she would share. Particularly those thoughts that make her bite her lip and blush.

Christ. She takes my breath away.

"Tell me about your brothers. I know Fin is the oldest, and then Matt is your middle brother, but I don't know much else."

"Like you said, Fin is my oldest brother at twenty-five. He's great at his job, but he's an even better brother. He's single and looking, but he's more dedicated to the job than the search for *the one.*"

"Isn't he named after your grandfather? Finley McIntyre founded MCI with his brothers, right?"

More surprises from the auburn-haired beauty to my right. "Yes. That's correct." I turn to face her. "What else do you know about MCI?"

She swirls her straw in her drink, not meeting my gaze. "McIntyre Corporate Industries was founded by your dad's dad, Finley, and his brothers Maximus and Gabriel. Your father, Hugh, is the current CEO. Fin is the VP of Accounting and Finance, and Matt's the VP of Marketing." She glances sideways. "And you're going to be the VP of Product & Technology."

The last part, about me, was said with a pout, as if it makes her sad. "You've done your research."

She rotates on her barstool toward me, her lips drawn in contemplation. "I've met your brothers."

"Really?" Why didn't either of them mention having met Jace's sister? And more importantly, "Where?"

"They were really nice. Surprisingly down to earth."

My hand goes up. "Wait. Why do I feel like you're trying not to tell me something?"

Her crooked smile is endearing and draws me further into her spell. "Because I am."

I wait her out, arms crossed, one brow raised, with a smirk that trumps hers.

She breaks. Finally. "Okay…okay." Her blue eyes sparkle with mirth as her hands gesture in supplication. "Fine. I'll tell you. I'm actually surprised you don't already know. I interned at MCI this past summer—"

"What?"

"—I plan to return this summer and then apply for a job after college." She cringes like she's getting ready to give me some bad news. "And… apparently, you're going to be my boss."

Are you fucking kidding me? I've been groomed for the job by my father, grandfather, and uncles for as long as I can remember. I know everything about my department. I run my hand over my face and pin her with my stare. "Seriously? How did I not know this?"

"I don't know, really. Fin and Matt approached me last summer as I was leaving for the day. They introduced themselves, which was completely unnecessary. I was shocked they were approaching me." Her face lights up as she laughs. "I thought I did something wrong—that they were coming to fire or reprimand me."

"They never told me this."

"They said they'd heard Jace's sister was an intern and if I needed anything, to let them know. But…"

I lean closer. "But what?"

"I asked them not to treat me any differently. I want my abilities to stand on their own. I didn't—I don't—want any special treatment because of Jace." Her eyes sadden as her gaze roams my face. "Joseph, I didn't know you were Jace's roommate, not then. It was only a few weeks ago, when you decided to spend Thanksgiving with us that Jace told me his roommate Joe was…you. *Joseph McIntyre.*" She sighs in resignation. "Imagine my surprise."

"I don't have to imagine it. I'm feeling it right now, Sweetness."

"I'm really sorry. I don't expect anything from you. If it'll be a problem…I'll…" Her voice breaks, and she quickly glances away, but not before I notice her eyes welling up.

I can't see her tears, but her hands dash them away quickly.

Christ, this girl. "Samantha." I grip her shoulder. I can't let this upset her. She's had a hard day as it is. "We'll figure it out. It's not worth getting upset over." Not, now, anyway.

She nods, still not meeting my eyes. "I could go somewhere else," she says so softly I nearly miss it.

A surge of pride swells through me that my family's company means so much to her. "It means a lot to you, doesn't it? MCI?"

Unshed tears glisten in her eyes, yet there is a fire inside them that burns deeply. "MCI is on the cutting edge of technological advancements. It's all I've ever envisioned for myself. Everyone said I was too young to know what I really wanted, but I knew as soon as I saw that story about MCI developing a software program for the space shuttle—I had to be a part of a company like that."

"That was years ago." I think back. "I was only thirteen or so. Jeez, you would have been…ten?"

"Yep." She beams brightly.

Christ, she sounds like me. Discovering what she wants so young. Just knowing, in your gut, when something was right, but more than that— actually pursuing it the way I've done. I stare at her, study her face, her shy smile and blush that creeps up her neck as I don't let up. "You're remarkable." I finally breathe out.

I'm not sure I actually said it out loud, until her blush deepens.

"No," she says incredulously. "I…" She shrugs on a sigh. "I just knew."

She doesn't have to say any more. I get it. I totally get it.

Our food is delivered, and we return to our companionable silence.

My mind is anything but silent with racing thoughts about this unexpected woman beside me. I've never been a partier, even in high school. When most of my friends were out drinking and getting laid, I was focused on technology and the future of MCI. Now, I see the woman next to me is not any different than me: streamlined, proficient, voracious focus with little time or interest in typical teenage carousing ways.

Her hand lightly brushes my arm, and I glance up to see her eyeing me expectantly. Shit, I missed what she said. "I'm sorry, what?"

Her smile unforgivingly pulls at my heart. "I asked about Matt. Are you closer to him since he's only a few years older?"

"You'd think so, but, no. Fin and I are cut from the same cloth. Matt and I look alike, but Fin and I are twins on the inside. He calls me nearly every day, keeps me on the straight and narrow. He's my sounding board, friend, and mentor." I take a sip of water.

Understanding glows in her eyes. "That's nice. What's Matt like?"

"Matt is twenty-three. He's actually like Jace. Personable, well-liked. Entirely too popular with the ladies."

Her eyes light up as she laughs. "Ah, another manwhore?"

"I was trying to have more tact, but yes. He's incredibly intelligent, easily bored, needs new challenges. I've often wondered if that's the reason for his womanizing ways."

Mischievously, she leans over and bumps my shoulder. "Or, he just really likes the ladies."

I chuckle. "Or he really likes the ladies."

"How is it you'll go from being a college student to being a Vice President? How does that work exactly? I mean, doesn't the current VP resent you swooping in and taking his job?"

"This has been in the works for a long time. I started training for the job when I was thirteen. Worked my way through the different departments, different jobs, different responsibilities. Once I decided on the technology wing of the business, my focus was…" I shrug, not wanting to come across a smug. "…razor sharp." I couldn't get enough, still can't.

"My Great Uncle Max, Maximus, will retire once I take over. I attend key meetings and keep up with the quarterly reports, meet with him weekly to stay abreast of what's going on. Plus, he'll remain as my mentor for a few years, before he fully retires." I pause for a drink. "He's looking forward to retirement, as is my Great Aunt Vi. She says he works too hard and is looking forward to traveling."

"Wow, it sounds like you're already working full-time for them."

I push my plate away. "Nearly. I don't have much time for anything other than school and work. It's been my single-minded focus for so long. I'm not sure I remember a time that it wasn't."

"That brings up an interesting point." Her blush is back, and her eyes evade mine.

"And what is that?"

She surprises me when her eyes boldly lock on mine. "Why are you here?"

I study her for the briefest of moments. "I don't really know, to be perfectly honest. I'm having a hard time staying away, even when I know I should."

She nods, breaking eye contact to scan the bar.

I'm not sure what that reaction means. "But I'm glad I was here." I touch her hand, squeezing lightly to bring her attention back to me. "I'm sure Trent and the other guys would have handled that asshole customer without my help." I duck my head to catch her eye. "But it makes me sick to my stomach thinking of you here, shaky and upset with no one to comfort you."

She leans against my arm. "I'm glad you were here too. Though, I feel like I wouldn't have been nearly as upset if you hadn't been here."

I scowl. "Why? I made it worse?"

"Not…worse. There's something about you, Joseph. It's like you make it okay for me to be vulnerable, instead of keeping it in. Because you were here, I was able to feel the weight of it by acknowledging it."

"You say it like it's a bad thing. You don't always have to be strong and stoic. It's okay to rely on others for support, comfort."

"I've just…never had that."

How can that be possible? She comes from a great family. Why does she feel she has to be an island unto herself?

"Why is that, Samantha?"

With a shrug of her shoulder, she looks away. "I guess I've always been rather self-reliant. People—my family—expect it of me now. It's become a given. They assume '*Sam can take care of herself*.'"

Christ. "Just because you can, doesn't mean you should."

"Maybe. Or maybe because I can—I should." Her eyes search mine as if seeking some sort of affirmation from me.

"I'll never agree to that. We all need support, especially from our family. Do you ever ask for help?"

She laughs, but there's no joy in the sound. It's a sad laugh that twists my heart. "No, Joseph. I don't. They have enough going on in their lives; they don't need any of my teenage drama."

"What about tonight? Will you tell them about that guy grabbing you?"

"No." She scowls at me. "And neither will you. It will only make them worry, needlessly."

"Samantha."

"No," she says more firmly, then picks up her tea and finishes it off as if it's the last of a desperately needed beer. "We should go."

What happened? I thought we were having a connecting moment, and now I feel relegated to the backseat of the car like a child. A child who needs to mind his own damn business.

We'll see.

PART 2

THE BLOOM

Four

Samantha

THE MORNING LIGHT STREAMS IN FROM THE GAP in my curtains, like laser beams cutting through the fog of sleep and igniting the memories of last night. It's not every day I get rescued from an asshole and have dinner with my hotter-than-sin rescuer, who in all likelihood will be my boss if I'm lucky enough to get a real job at MCI. Not to mention the fact that he's a future vice president and millionaire.

"For all I know, he's already a millionaire," I mutter to the floating dust particles dancing in the beam of light as if they too just woke up. They seem much more alert than me.

He held me in his arms. Joseph McIntyre not only rescued me, but then comforted me like he'd known me forever and it was his *place* to protect me. His right. I wish it were. I wish he could see me for the woman I hope to be and not this teenager who's more geek than beauty queen.

"God. Sam, get a grip," I mutter, rubbing my eyes. "He was just being nice. He'll never see you that way."

I roll to my side and flinch. "Ow." I forgot about my arm. I lie on my back and examine it. Finger-shaped bruises mar my skin. I guess I won't be going sleeveless tonight.

On a sigh, I sit up. Should I even go tonight? Maybe I could talk Margot into going with me. I could use a buffer between me and Joseph. Or rather, between me and my desire for Joseph.

I send her a quick text to call me when she wakes up and then head to the bathroom. I throw on some yoga pants and an oversized t-shirt, grab socks and shuffle to the kitchen for some much-needed caffeine.

With my mug and phone in hand, I slip out to the back patio and curl up on a lounger by the pool. The temperature is chilly but the morning sun and my coffee should keep me warm enough.

My black gold is half-gone and cooling off faster than I'd like when my phone rings with Margot's "Single Ladies" ringtone.

"Hey."

"Hi. I'm sorry I didn't call you sooner. I went for a run and just saw your text."

"You're crazy, girl. The sun's barely up, and you're out running."

"I like to run in the early mornings best. And why are you up? You like to sleep in on Saturdays."

"I don't know. I woke up early for some reason."

"I hear birds. Where are you?"

"I'm in the backyard by the pool, having coffee and talking to my friend Margot."

"Smarty-pants."

"I know, but you love me anyway," I tease.

"I do. To what do I owe this early morning phone call?"

"I wanted to see what you were doing tonight. Jace and Joseph want me to go out with them, and I was hoping you'd join us."

"Aww, I can't. The Dubois women are getting ready to leave for our day of pampering and evening of debauchery. Well, as debauched as it gets with my sister, Mom, and Grandmother." She laughs.

"So, you're going to a strip club then?" I snicker at the thought.

"You know it. I've been saving up my singles so I can shove them in the male stripper's g-string using only my mouth."

"Eww. That's a visual I'm not sure I can ever scour from my brain. Thanks for that."

"You're welcome, Sammykins."

I laugh at her silly nickname for me. "Have fun."

"You too. I want all the juicy details about tonight!"

"Uh, I doubt I'll have any details to share." Or none that I'm ready to admit to.

"We're still doing movie night sometime next week, right?"

"Yeah. Monday or Tuesday?"

"Monday would be better. We start cooking for Thanksgiving on Tuesday," she suggests.

"Okay, let's plan on it then."

"It's a date."

I head inside for a fresh cup of coffee and to start breakfast, but the smell of bacon wafts in the air. Someone beat me to it. Mmm, one of my favorite smells. I freeze at the doorway when I spot Joseph at the stove flipping pancakes and turning over bacon. *That's a beautiful sight.*

"Good morning, Sweetness." His voice is gruff from sleep.

"Good morning." I refill my cup. "Would you like some coffee?" I spot a mug on the counter. "Or a refill?"

"A refill would be great."

"Shouldn't we be cooking for you?" I refill his coffee and add sugar and cream to mine.

He glances at me and then returns his focus to the stove and the tasks at hand. "I figured it was the least I could do for crashing here all week. I could stay at my parents' house or Fin or Matt's, but I'd rather be here than alone at their places."

"I can understand that, but solitude is nice too, sometimes."

He places pancakes and bacon onto two plates and hands me one, his forehead creased as he pins me with his eyes. "I think you spend too much time alone."

I take both plates and move to the kitchen table. "I don't mind being alone. I'm not one of those people who can't stand the silence of their own thoughts. I rather enjoy my company."

Our coffees in hand, he joins me at the table, sitting across from me. "I rather enjoy your company too." He pushes the butter and syrup my way.

"I rather enjoy your company," I whisper back, afraid even that simple truth is too big of a confession.

"That's good, 'cause we're gonna see a lot of each other this week."

I grab the milk and two glasses, pouring him one without thinking.

His disarming smile sends my heart racing as I hand him his milk.

"How'd you know I wanted milk?"

I shrug. "Who doesn't want milk with pancakes? Or anything sweet for that matter."

"True."

The house is all too quiet for a Saturday morning. "Where is everyone?"

"Your parents went to the gym, but said to save them some food and they'll eat when they get back."

"When did they leave?"

"You were on the phone when they left."

"Oh. And Jace?"

"I haven't seen him, but his car's not out front, so I assume he didn't come home last night."

I nod as I dig into breakfast. "Thank you for this, by the way."

"You're welcome."

"I was talking to my friend Margot earlier, and she'd just come home from running. Now my parents are at the gym." I point to our food and back at him. "I feel like I need to go exercise after this."

He pauses mid-sip. His forehead furrowed, considering my statement. "I could go for a run."

His mischievous green eyes and smirk stop my chewing. "What?" I murmur around my bite of food.

"Wanna come with me?"

"Sure, why not."

Why not? I can think of a million reasons why not, but all of them escape me at the moment as my sense of daring clouds my better judgment.

Joseph

That evening, Jace and I visit with his parents while Samantha gets ready to go out. I've met Daniel and Eleanor a few times. Daniel is a successful plastic surgeon who specializes in reconstructive surgeries. He primarily focuses on birth defects and traumatic injuries. He has quite a large military clientele.

Eleanor specializes in corporate law. My dad has tried to lure her to come work for MCI for years, but she's happy in her current gig. She and my mom serve on several charities together. Our parents were friends before I met Jace at UT. Oddly enough, we don't hang out together as families. My mom swears we all met when we were just kids, but I truly don't remember. If I had met Samantha before, no matter my age, I would have remembered her. She's captivated me from the moment I set eyes on her, and after our dinner last night, she's burrowed her way into my thoughts and won't let up.

Samantha trots down the stairs, hotter than any seventeen-year-old should be. I thought nothing could be hotter than the shorts and tank top she wore for our run.

I was wrong.

She's a classic in black jeans, black heeled boots, and a black sweater that nearly hangs off her shoulders, accentuating her curves. She's the epitome of understated sexuality. To top it off, her auburn hair flows down her shoulders and back in sensuous waves.

If I didn't know better, I would think she's the older sibling instead of Jace. He has the same strength and confidence of character, but comes across more as a good-time Charlie, whereas Samantha has a fierceness burning inside her, dying to break out and blaze a trail across everything she encounters.

With her looks, personality, and most definitely her quiet strength, it's no surprise guys her age aren't chasing her. She's intimidating as hell. They wouldn't know what to do with her if they caught her. She's not someone to take lightly. Her waters run deep, and if you're not a powerful swimmer, you'll surely drown.

She needs a man who's not afraid to let her be the woman she's meant to be, to let her stretch her sizable wings, giving her space as she takes off, and then wait and watch her soar, praising her heights and accomplishments. She needs a champion, a guardian who will stoke those flames, give her strength when she needs it, and be her safe place to land.

I stand when she descends the last stair, her smile lighting up when she notices. She motions for me to sit down as she kisses her parents hello, and then makes her way to sit on the edge of the couch where I'm sitting. I take it as a compliment, her choosing to sit next to me instead of on the other couch with Jace. Pride swells. I want to beat my fists across my chest in display of my manhood, of my possession of her.

Christ, alpha much? Tamp it down. This is Jace's sister. She's seventeen. She's not ready for you.

Not now, but maybe someday, she will be.

"Hey," she whispers over her shoulder. The soft curve of her lips and the mischievous twinkle in her eyes make my cock stir.

Holy hell, not yet.

"Hey," I reply, nearly short of breath, my fingers twitching to touch her, pull her into my side, under my arm. Safe. Secure. Protected.

Five

Samantha

THE BEAT-BEAT-BEAT OF THE MUSIC THRUMS through the walls and floors and into my chest. A mash of wall-to-wall bodies sway and bob in continuous motion either to the music or to the bump and grind of those around them. The lighting is low and sensual, yet bright and exhilarating at the same time, constantly changing with strobe and spotlights in never-ending motion. There is no stillness, no solitude, no sanctuary from the constant assault of the senses.

It's fucking amazing!

"This way, Sweetness." Joseph's lips brush my ear as his warm hand envelops the curve of my waist, ushering me through the throng of people.

He glances down at me, and the flash in his eyes sets my pulse racing. We follow Jace to an upper level corded off with red velvet ropes. Joseph takes my hand and my elation blooms as he leads me up the stairs. His hold on me is firm, protective. There's something about his large hand engulfing mine that makes me feel safe with him.

Jace speaks to the large bouncers guarding the entry through the velvet ropes. After a moment, they shake hands with Jace and Joseph, waving us in, giving me a friendly nod as I follow. We're shown to a private sitting area with three couches set in a U-shape with end tables and a glass coffee table in the center. Jace selects one end of the center couch. Joseph sits next, pulling me to sit between them.

Only once I'm seated does he release my hand. I bring my newly-freed hand to my lap, touching it lightly to see if it feels as hot as it seems. My skin is enflamed from his simple, possessive touch.

I'm taken back to last night, him coming to my rescue, protecting me from the overly aggressive customer, then comforting me in his embrace, ensuring I was okay.

I was fascinated and entranced by his enthusiasm for being part of MCI. He talks about it like it's a Mom-and-Pop operation when it's one of the largest technology companies based in the United States, definitely the largest in the South.

I hope to return there after I graduate from UT, but having a crush on the future VP isn't going to do me any favors. I don't want any special treatment. I want my every achievement to be because I earned it, not because the heir apparent twice removed is my brother's roommate and friend.

…and apparently has the power to make my girly parts come alive.

"Sam." Jace's voice brings me back to the VIP lounge. He motions to the waitress. "What do you want to drink?"

"Oh uh, a Coke, please." I tune out again as they order their drinks.

The view from up here is even more spectacular. The entire club is five stories high, with each level open to the main atrium dance floor area below. People are hanging out over the ledges, peering down at the lower levels and those on the main dance floor. The vibrations are just as strong up here, but the music is not nearly as loud. It's actually possible to carry on a conversation.

Joseph bumps my leg with his. "Are you okay? You're awfully quiet."

I barely glance at him as I answer—I'm more focused on the ladies they've attracted who have taken up residence on the other two couches. "Yeah, I'm just taking it all in." I wonder if he'd be hitting on one of them if I wasn't here.

Get over yourself, Sam. He's going to pursue who he wants whether you're here or not.

Our drinks arrive, and Jace and Joseph continue talking over me. Sometimes to me, but mostly to each other and the ladies vying for their attention. It's uncomfortable. I feel awkward and like the odd man out.

I lean forward and scan the room. How many hundreds of people are actually in here? I can't imagine how much money this place brings in each night. There is no single-women-get-in free discount, at least not on this hopping Saturday. Although, technically, we got in free, as Tommy let us slip in after tagging Jace and me as under twenty-one.

I want to get a closer look at the atrium and the other floors, but mostly, I want to escape feeling like the ugly duckling in a sea of swans. I stand up, barely making it to my feet before a hand captures mine. I know that hand. He's only touched me few times, but it's a touch I could never forget.

I peer down at Joseph questioningly.

"Where are you going, Samantha?" His voice is commanding, stirring things inside me I shouldn't be feeling for someone like him. I can't forget who he is. Who he will be. Despite last night's events and our remarkably relaxing dinner, I'm not the woman for him. Maybe one of these women are future VP wife material. But it's not me. He only represents heartache for me.

I motion to the ledge. "I just want to get a better look. This place is amazing." I glance from Joseph to Jace, whose focus doesn't shift from the woman nearly sitting on his lap. Veronica. *Shit.*

Joseph releases my hand. "Don't disappear on us." The concern on his face makes me think he really means "don't disappear on *me.*"

Stop. It. Now! Don't go there.

I force a smile. "I'm not going anywhere, Joseph." Except away from here…and *her.*

Skirting around the women, who've slowly crowded in closer, I move toward the ledge and grip the handrail for support.

It's no big deal. They're in their element. You're the one out of place.

"Let it go," I chastise myself as I scan the dance floor. It's an incredible effect seeing the entire floor vibrate with moving bodies in time with the music. It's choreographed chaos. I'm entranced, giving myself over to the rhythmic beat of the music and the swaying bodies. I close my eyes and tip my head back, taking a deep breath. I can feel his eyes on me, or I imagine they are. It doesn't matter, the effect is the same. I shiver. My skin pricks with goosebumps, and my nipples harden.

"Have you been here before?"

I'm pulled from my reverie by a voice to my right. It's one of the bouncers.

I shake my head. "No. It's incredible." I'm sure my face shows my awe. I hope it doesn't betray my inexperience.

"I didn't think so. I'd remember seeing you," he says sincerely.

I laugh out loud. "Right. In this sea of people, you'd remember me?"

He studies me intently, his eyes landing on my lips before returning to my eyes. "Yes, I most definitely would." He reaches out his hand. "I'm Paul."

"Sam." I shake his hand. "It's nice to meet you, Paul." I survey the club. "Is it always this packed?"

He laughs. "The night is still young. We're only at fifty percent capacity." He points up to the top levels. "See, there's hardly anyone up there. Give it a few hours and you won't be able to find yourself, it'll be so full."

I giggle at the notion. "I had better not lose myself then, huh?"

"Best not to, but if you do, just come find me, and I'll help you find yourself," he says with a teasing gleam in his eye.

Warmth covers my back and a strong arm wraps around my waist. Paul looks up into the face of whom I can only imagine is standing so close to me, blanketing my entire back. His scent fills the air around me, and his hard body presses into me. Joseph.

I tilt my head to meet his eyes, those green orbs that tell me so much, but instead I see a sternness in the set of his jaw and coolness in his eyes, not so much for me, but for Paul, I think. I'm not sure what that look means, not at first, but Paul backs away, nodding to Joseph, almost in supplication to his authority.

His authority over me?

"Do you do that often?" I look away, hiding my smirk and elation that he came after me.

"Do what, Sweetness?" His voice tickles my ear, his arm still firmly wrapped around my waist.

"Take ownership of things that don't belong to you?"

He chuckles in my ear, his chest rumbling against my back. "Perhaps I just took ownership of what needed to be taken."

Holy shit.

My heart races like a train getting ready to jump the tracks and pulses between my thighs. I need to get away from him. "I need to dance." I step out of his embrace.

"Not alone, you don't." He lets me move away, but only slightly, his hand resting on my hip to keep me close.

Behind him, the couches are now full of women glaring at me. "Where's Jace?" And Veronica?

"He spotted someone he knew." His tone is flat.

"You mean a *woman* he knew?" I don't know why I have to drill home the point.

"Yes." I see an apology on his lips.

"That took less time than usual." I shift, sweeping the club, wondering if I can spot him.

"He'll be back. He hasn't left you." His voice sounds so sure, as if he knows something he has no clue about.

My gaze slowly meets his. I want to touch his face, run my fingers through his hair and kiss those lying lips. "You sure about that?"

He moves closer, pressing against me. "No." The need to apologize for my brother is back on his face, but I know the score. When it comes to choosing hanging with me or getting a piece of ass, the ass wins every time.

I turn away from Joseph, not wanting him to see the thoughts I can't hide. "You don't have to babysit me," I say over my shoulder, not even sure he can hear me.

He moves in front of me, lifting my chin. "Samantha."

I close my eyes, jerking my head away. "Really. I can take care of myself. Go, have fun. Find your own woman. I'll see you before I leave."

Run.

I walk away, but only make it two steps before he captures my hand.

Joseph

"Not happening, Sweetness." I pull her back to me. "I'm no babysitter. I'm here because I want to be."

I don't let her avoid my eyes. I hate the pain I see there. She puts on a brave front, but it obviously hurts her when Jace dumps her to chase a girl. I bet Jace has no idea he crushes her spirit just a little each time he does it. Each time he shows her she's not a priority to him. She, on the other hand, is always there for him whenever he needs her. I hear him on the phone with her, texting her, emailing her. She's always there, quick to reply. Available to him, always.

I scan the room. Dancing is not my favorite thing. I prefer dancing in private, the horizontal kind of dancing, where you only need a partner and no spectators, and music is completely optional. But she likes to dance, and at the moment, I would do anything to lift the sadness from her eyes.

I wrap my arm around her. "Stay close." I head for the stairs.

She peeks up at me, her eyes wide. "Are we leaving already?"

Would she leave if I asked her to?

I stop in my tracks, running my thumb across her jaw, wanting more than anything to kiss those pouty lips. "No, beautiful, we're going to dance."

The smile taking over her face makes my heart jump.

"Really? You'll dance with me?"

I chuckle. "You might not call it dancing, but I'll try my best."

On her tip-toes, she wraps her arms around my neck, giving me a quick hug and a kiss on the cheek, scorching my skin. "Thank you."

"Don't thank me yet."

I let her lead us as we weave our way onto the dance floor, letting her decide where she wants to do this.

As she stops and turns toward me, someone bumps her from behind, shoving her forward into my chest. Instinctively, I wrap her in my arms, swinging her around so my back is to the offending person.

"I'm sorry." She breathes across my chest, her hands resting on each pec. A pink flush creeps up her cheeks.

"Don't be." I loosen my grip and move to the music. It's a fast song, but we sway slowly, in half time to the beat. She doesn't push away, and I'm in no hurry to relinquish her.

I want to hold her close, like I did last night after that asshole dared to touch her. It took everything I had not to rip the hand touching her from his body. But her boss and the other guys had it handled, and she needed comforting more than me acting like a caveman. And I needed to be reassured she was alright.

As the music morphs into a slow song, Samantha's bumped again, and this time I pull her flush against my body, my arms around her back protectively, in an effort to cocoon her from further threats.

"Did you just growl?" Her amusement twinkles in her eyes and in the curve of her need-to-be-kissed lips.

Shit. Did I?

"Possibly," I simply reply. Though there is nothing simple about how I feel about this woman. Before I'm ready to lose the feel of her in my arms and the warmth of her touch, the slow song ends, and we're back to the club mix. The positive note? I get a close-up view of her gorgeous body as she works it to the music, finding her own rhythm to each song. I try to keep up, hold my own, but truly I'm just along for the ride—and what a beautiful ride it is.

She gets lost in the music, her shyness forgotten, her body leading instead of her brain. Passionate. That's what she is when she dances. It's intoxicating to watch, but I don't want to just watch. I want to be a part of it. I want to be consumed by her fire. I want to burn with her.

Fuck. I've got to get a grip.

Two more songs, and I convince her to take a break. Back on the couch, catching our breath, the waitress is quick to hand us two bottles of water. I spot Jace on the far side of the dance floor, grinding with that girl from the couch.

"Do you know her?" I point in their direction.

Samantha follows my line of sight and quickly diverts her eyes when she sees them. "Yep. Not a fan."

Her fidgeting hands and the way she chews on her bottom lip hint that there's a story behind her dismissive tone.

"What'd she do to you?"

She inhales sharply, pinning me with her eyes. I've hit a sore spot, nailed the crux of the issue.

"Nothing worth talking about." She motions toward the stairs. "I'd like to go up to the top and check it out. Would you come or would you rather stay…and…" She glances to the women surrounding us on the couches. "…find another dance partner?"

Another dance partner? It's the second time she's insinuated I might prefer someone else's company to hers. "Why do you think I don't want to hang out with you?"

"I'm going up." She ignores my question, finishes her water, and walks over to the bouncer who spoke to her earlier.

He points to a particular staircase as he whispers in her ear, standing too close for my comfort. Samantha smiles at him and nods, glancing back at me as I join her before she exits the VIP area.

"What was that about?" I try to hide my irritation.

"Paul was pointing out the quickest way up to the top, but you need special access. He said he'd tell them we're coming." She stops her progress, glances over her shoulder. "Are you coming?"

Man, I'd love to. *Crass, man. Not cool.*

"Lead the way." I press my hand to the small of her back, needing the contact.

We have no problem gaining entry to the roped-off stairs; we're even given passes to the terrace lounge on the roof, which is more elite in its admittance. I try not to stare at her ass as we climb the stairs, but it's impossible when it's right in my face. The sway of her hips, the brush of her hair across her back, and her little glances back at me to be sure I'm still here captivate me.

The stairs are empty, so I could climb next to her. I don't for two reasons: one—she could have a misstep in her boots, and I'd rather be behind her to catch her, and two—why would I give up the best view in town?

We stop halfway to take in the expanse of the atrium and dance floor below. It really is a nice place, all four sides surrounded by the upper levels, looking out over the atrium and across the way to connecting platforms surrounding each level.

I glance at Samantha, but her attention is elsewhere. She's spotted Jace on the dance floor with that girl grinding against him. The pensive look is back.

"What happened, Sweetness?"

With a quick half-hearted smile, she dismisses my question again and moves away from the ledge, climbing up the stairs to the roof. Whatever it is, she obviously doesn't want to talk about it, but I'm not sure I can let it go that easily.

At the top, we give our passes to the gatekeeper, entering through the double doors, and still as the cool breeze hits us to take in the roof-top opulence. There's a glass surround along the entire edge. The seating is broken up into different areas, each resembling an outdoor living room with lush chairs and couches surrounding a fireplace. Some sitting areas accommodate large groups, while others are smaller, intimate and private. As a backdrop, there's a maze of trellises with greenery and lighting woven throughout.

I lead her to a more private area, situated away from everyone else. She moves closer to the glass, gazing out over the Dallas skyline. "It's beautiful."

"Yes, it is." Though I'm referring to the beautiful woman reflecting back at me. I'm lost in her. She doesn't notice my preoccupation. She has no idea what she does to me.

I wave off a waitress, not wanting to be disturbed.

"Tell me," I prompt again.

She shakes her head *no*, but her whole body stiffens.

I brush her cheek with the back of my hand. "Come sit by the fire and talk to me."

I'm relieved when she agrees, and I'm able to pull her to my side on the couch with my arm over the back, resting behind her, itching to touch her.

"What classes do you have this semester?" She tries to sidetrack the conversation, but I'm not letting this go. It obviously bothers her, and the fact that Jace has ditched Sam for this woman is concerning to me. I need the facts before I decide whether to mention it to him or not.

"Tell me."

Her big blue eyes shimmer in the firelight, piercing through any pretext I still harbor that I will not, one day, make this woman mine.

Mine. The thought resonates in my head like a bell.

"I'd really rather not talk about this, not with anyone, but especially not with you."

Her body is riddled with tension, her face is cautious, guarded. Her walls are up, and instead of letting it go and giving her respite, I want—no, need—to charge forward, knocking down any barrier between us. I can't explain it.

I don't normally have to try so hard, but mostly, I don't really care if they let me in or not. Sex has been the guiding force of all my relationships. I'm not interested in serious. I'm focused on the goal—graduating top of my class and sinking my teeth into MCI. It's not just a job. It's my future, my birthright, my focus. But this face, this woman, makes me want more.

More.

Everything.

I try not to balk too much. "Why not me? Do I seem disinterested, like I don't care?"

"No, that's not it." Her eyes cast down at her hands clasped in her lap.

Christ, I can feel her emotions burning her up inside. *Let me help, Sweetness.*

"Then why?" What's so wrong with me, for fuck's sake?

She sighs in exasperation. "Maybe because I don't want you to look at me like I'm a loser."

I lift her chin. I have to see her eyes to gauge her responses, her feelings. But mostly because I want to be seen by those remarkable soulful eyes. "That could never happen."

She laughs me off and tries to move away, but I still her with my arm around her shoulder.

"You don't know me well enough to say that, and you already made it quite clear you don't want to get to know me. Remember?"

What was last night, then? Why the fuck does she think I was there? For the cheesecake?

Christ, fuck. What are you doing, man? She's not ready for you.

She sighs. "My name."

"I should have cleared this up last night. I didn't make myself clear." I lay my hand over hers. I'd draw her onto my lap if I thought she'd let me. "I never meant that. I just meant, knowing you better wouldn't change my opinion about your nickname. I'll never believe *Sam* is suitable for someone such as you."

"*Such as me?* What does that mean?" Her brow furrows.

She has no idea of the storm she stirs in me. "It means, Samantha, I believe you are far too exquisite to go by a boyish name such as *Sam*. Your beauty requires a more suitable name." I squeeze her hand. "Maybe even Goddess. You're blushing. Have I embarrassed you?" I want to see how far her blush goes.

She meets my eyes. "How can you be so comfortable saying such things? You're older, sophisticated, good-looking, and well-bred. You're not supposed to notice a girl like me."

What the hell? She's from a good family. She's beautiful, exquisite even. How could I not notice her? "For the record, I don't agree. But, for now, I'll just say, I do notice you, and you are no girl. You might be three years younger than me, and perhaps more naïve in certain areas, but you are no young girl to be dismissed, not noticed, or not taken seriously."

She smiles at me genuinely. "Thank you, Joseph. That might be the nicest thing anyone has ever said about me."

Christ, I hope that's not true. This girl needs consoling from a heinous lack of compliments.

"Now, tell me what she did to you." *I'm not letting this go.*

She settles a little more under the crook of my arm. "She dismissed me. Negated my importance. She takes great pleasure in taking things away from me."

I still. That's not at all what I thought she'd say. "What's her name, anyway?" *If she's hurt you, I need her name.*

"Veronica Hamm. She's a year older than me. Honestly, I don't really even know her. I don't think I'd actually had a single conversation with her before she showed her distaste for me. She truly dislikes me, and I haven't a clue why."

"What did she do?" This Veronica is pissing me off. How could she not like this angel in front of me?

"The first time I met her, she was hanging on Jace's arm, glued to his side. She's a *clinger*."

"A clinger?"

"Yeah. Girls who latch on to a guy, all fake, all boobs, no brains or pretend to have no brains, feeding the guy's ego, and lashing out at any perceived competition." She stares at me. "I imagine you've known a fair number yourself."

I laugh. "Yes, maybe a few." I know exactly the type she means, and I don't stand for it. If a girl shows her claws, her cattiness for no apparent reason, she's gone. Jealousy is one thing, but being purposely mean and snotty is another.

"She didn't like me talking to Jace or the fact he stepped away from her the minute I said I needed to talk to him. She got all rude and in my face afterwards. When he wasn't around, of course. In front of him, she's all fake smiles and pretense. It didn't matter to her that I'm his sister. Time was time, and she wanted all of his."

"I can't believe Jace would put up with that." I've seen him dump girls for less, and I can't believe he would ever put up with anyone being mean to his sister.

"As I said, he didn't know."

"You didn't tell him?" For fuck's sake.

She cocks an eyebrow like I'm an idiot. "I'm the kid sister of Jace, the pussy whisperer. You think Veronica is the first, last, or only bitch to give me shit?"

"Such language." I try not to laugh at her spirited delivery of a very sad fact.

"I'm sorry. It's frustrating." She sighs. "I love him. I'd do anything for him, but sometimes the reality of the bimbos he tends to go for is just too much to put up with. I mean, Jesus, will he ever grow up, grow a pair, and have a real relationship with a grown woman who doesn't think a blow-job is synonymous with a handshake?"

"Wow, that's a pretty apt description of Jace's type." Sad to say, it's spot on.

She's gone quiet, staring at me, studying me, it feels like.

Does she see me? Does she see the man—or does she see what my future can do for her?

She's not like that.

"Is that your type too?" she whispers, almost apologetically, like she doesn't mean to offend me if that's the case.

"Fuck, no." I scowl. "Listen, I don't disagree with anything you've said. But just because we're friends doesn't mean I roll the same way he does. Jace is a sprinter. I'm more of a marathoner, in it for the long haul."

Well, once I find the one I want. And, Sweetness, I want that girl to be you.

She nods, seemingly accepting and relieved by my answer, which I find quite satisfying. "Explain to me how this Veronica is different from the way all the other *clingers* treat you."

She pauses, contemplating. I can actually see the moment she gives in to me. The moment she lowers her wall, just a fraction, to let me peer over.

That's right. Let me in, baby.

"There was this guy, Roger. We went out. Dated. Hung out at school, had lunches together, talked in the halls. Everyone knew we were kind of an item, new, but still, something was there. It wasn't a secret, or just in my head. He openly pursued me in school and out."

A secret?

What's going on with the dumbfucks in her life? She's elated from my compliments and has to point out that a guy actually liked her in public and didn't keep his attraction for her a secret.

She shifts on the couch. I sense her discomfort, and I imagine it's because of what she's going to say next.

I pull her closer to me. "I've got you," I say softly. "It's just a memory, but I'm here to help any way I can." Thankfully, she relaxes into my side.

"One of his friends stopped me before last period telling me Roger wanted to meet after school by the football field." She looks up through her lashes. "I thought it was kinda sweet, like a secret rendezvous."

Jealousy rips through me. Though I can't be with her right now, I sure as fuck don't want anyone else to have her. Not even a taste.

Mine.

"When I got there, I couldn't find him, not right away. It was off-season for football so there were only a few people milling around." She squirms again in her seat, leaning forward this time, putting distance between us. "I found him eventually. Well, I found *them*, under the bleachers, of all places. Such a cliché. Veronica was on her knees, giving him a blowjob. I just stood there, shocked, unable to move. But, then it got rougher. He was pumping into her. Hard. Holding her head in place with his hands. She was gagging…choking." Her voice cracks with emotion.

I place my hand on her back, needing to touch her. She glances over her shoulder long enough for me to see shame mixed with unshed tears in her eyes.

I want to break Roger and Veronica for hurting her like this.

"I've never…I didn't know…" She stumbles over her words. "I was actually afraid for her. I moved closer. Despite who she was. Despite who he was, and what they were doing together, I feared for her safety. I thought he was hurting her. Until I heard him say *'Take it deep. Show me what Sam will never give me. Fuck, that's right, all the way, babe.'*" She cringes, shuddering from the memory.

Christ, the idea of talking to Samantha about taking it deep would've turned me on under any other circumstances, would have made me *hard*. But not this. The idea of these two getting it on in front of Samantha, contaminating her with their vile act while talking about *Samantha* taking it deep or not, actually turns my stomach and flips my protective instincts into high gear.

She stands up and moves to the edge, placing her forehead against the glass. "This is humiliating. Why would you ever want to know this?" she says so softly, I never would have heard her if I hadn't followed her.

Like I could have stayed away.

Mine.

I place my hands on her shoulders, squeezing slightly. She's trembling, and my chest hurts for her.

"He's a fucking idiot, and she's a royal bitch." I kiss the top of her head. "This betrayal is not about you. I mean, it's not a reflection on you. You have no reason to be humiliated, embarrassed."

She wraps her arms around herself. "I call bullshit on that." She takes a staggered breath. "Anyway, she must have heard me, saw my movement or something, as her eyes locked on mine, and the vitriol in them almost knocked me over. Her hands gripped him, and whatever she did with her mouth pleased him greatly by the sounds coming out of him.

"It hit me then. She did it on purpose. She wanted me to see, to find them, to put me in my place, to take him from me. Though, he obviously wasn't mine to begin with." She sighs, shaking her head. "It took another second, but I finally turned and walked away. I'd only made it a step or two when she called, '*Where you goin', Sam? You're gonna miss the best part.*' Then I heard Roger's voice, '*Goddammit. Fuck. Sam! Get off me, you bitch. You did this on purpose. Sam, wait!*'"

"I didn't look back. I didn't stop. I just kept walking."

Six

WE NEVER DID SEE JACE WHEN WE LEFT THE CLUB shortly after my rooftop confession, my humiliation laid bare for Joseph to witness.

Why did I share that? And with him of all people?

The humiliation.

The rejection.

The shame.

He looks at me as if he really sees me. It's unnerving and exciting, all at the same time.

But nothing can come of it.

I can never be his.

It's probably all in my head, anyway. He doesn't really see me. Am I so desperate to be seen that I'm projecting my desires onto him? Joseph McIntyre would never want a girl like me. Not for a night, much less forever.

Not me.

Joseph drives my car home. I feel shaky and too lost in my memories to drive, and he kindly offered. He's just being nice, watching out for Jace's kid sister.

As soon as we get home, I head to the stairs, Joseph hot on my trail, only a few steps behind me. I grab the banister, pausing before taking the first step. His footfalls stop. I don't look back, but I can feel his nearness.

"Thanks for tonight. I…uh…I'm tired. G'night," I force out in a rush and bound up the stairs as quickly as I can.

Hide.

"Samantha." His voice is closer than it should be, he must have taken the stairs two at a time.

Shit. I freeze at the top of the stairs. "Yes?"

The steps creak as he moves to stand directly behind me. I close my eyes, my heart pounding in anticipation of his touch, but it doesn't come, not in the way I expect. I thought he might grip my shoulder or arm. Instead, his whole body presses against my back, his warm breath skirting my neck.

I glance back only to come face to face with his lips. *Fuck, those lips.* He's a step below me, still taller than me, but his lips are dangerously close in proximity to mine.

He brushes my hair off my shoulder, sweeping it to the other side. His fingers graze my skin and make me shiver. "Are you okay, Sweetness?"

No. Hell, no. Please kiss me. Make me forget Veronica and Jace, and that damn embarrassing story I told you.

"Yes," I chirp, my voice way too high.

His fingers trace the curve of my neck. My breath catches and automatically my head tilts, giving him better access.

"Why is it I don't believe that's true?" His words trail down the same path as his fingers, and my knees nearly buckle.

Jesus, I have to get out of here before I make a complete fool of myself.

I step forward, immediately missing his warmth. I turn, nearly facing him, unable to make eye contact. "Other than dying of embarrassment, I'm just fine." I dare a selfish glance, aching to see his face. I need to see the truth of this moment.

He ascends the last of the stairs and stops right in front of me. "Don't." His deep voice resonates between my thighs. "Don't give them that power over you."

Yes, he's right.

I simply nod and slip away down the hall.

"Samantha."

His plea doesn't slow me down. I keep going. Shutting my bedroom door behind me. Shutting him out. Shutting out the possibility of what would have happened if I had stayed in the hall until things progressed. How long would it have taken for him to walk away? Instead of finding out, I walked away first.

I strip as soon as my door clicks closed and head for the bathroom, turning on the shower. Feeling undone from Joseph and covered in the memories of Veronica and Roger, I need the comfort of the hot spray on my body.

I wash every inch of me. Twice. Even my hair, despite having just washed it a few hours ago.

By the time I get out, dressed, and dry my hair, it's late, after one. I should go to bed, but I'm keyed-up, revitalized by the shower.

I head to the kitchen for a drink of water and a snack.

Finishing my last strawberry, I hear a sound behind me. I turn.

Standing in front of me is the sexiest man alive, in just a pair of black workout pants that sit low on his hips. His upper body is even more cut than I'd imagined, and of course he has an eight pack, because a six pack would be too common. He's tan with the perfect amount of hair on his chest and abdomen.

His happy trail.

Jesus.

He's the perfect male specimen.

If I were a painter, a sculptor, he would be my muse, my model.

If I were a composer, I would write a symphony about him.

If I were more experienced, I would drop my panties and beg him to take me places I'm convinced only he can take me.

My eyes travel up his body, taking longer than they should. When I finally reach his face, his jaw is clenched, his eyes are burning hot, and his chest rises and falls with each breath. He seems pissed.

Why's he pissed?

"Hi," I say softly. My voice, my face, my body betray my lecherous thoughts, I'm sure.

He silently stalks closer, giving me the same perusal I just gave him.

It'd be funny, if it wasn't so sexy. My heart pounds faster with every passing second.

His eyes latch onto my breasts, and it's only then I realize what I'm wearing, or the lack of what I'm wearing: black boy shorts undies and a white cotton camisole. No bra. And to top it off, I can feel how hard my nipples are, which grow painfully harder from the realization he's seeing me in my underwear.

"Shit." I fold my arms over my chest, clutching my forearms.

Some sort of animalistic sound emanates from his chest as he steps closer, looking as if he wants to devour me.

Devour. Me.

"Too late, Sweetness." His voice betrays him as well. He licks his lips. "I've already seen those delectable nipples."

Shit. Shit. Shit.

I squeeze my thighs together and tighten the grip on my arms, trying to contain the rage of lust he's released throughout my body.

He moves closer, placing his hand on my hip. "I'm going to kiss you." He scans my face, landing on my eyes. "If you don't want me to, you need to tell me now."

Shit.

I don't respond. I can't even keep his gaze, much less form any words.

He unfolds my arms, his eyes locking on to the handprint-shaped bruise around my arm. "Son of a bitch," he hisses. His fingers gently explore the marks. "Does it hurt?"

The concern in his voice is enough to unhinge me. The lump in my throat prohibits my answer.

He bends down and brushes his lips across the bruise. Slowly. Reverently.

It's such a tender gesture that seizes my breath and sends a torrent of chills through my body. "Joseph," I whisper.

He rises to his full height, cupping my cheek. "I want to kill him for hurting you, Samantha." His other hand continues to caress the bruise. "He marred you. He hurt you. He manhandled you." He's getting worked up, and not in a good way.

"I'm okay. You were there to save me. You protected me. You stood up for me." I choke on the last part. No one's ever stood up for me.

His eyes flash, catching on to the gravity of my words. "I would never let anyone hurt you. Ever."

My head spins from the words coming out of his mouth, the tenderness of his touch, and the desire on his face. *How will I ever survive you, Joseph McIntyre?*

I don't say anything. I just nod.

He runs his thumb across my lips. "I'm going to kiss you."

My breath hitches again. I picture those same lips that were just grazing my arm doing the same to my lips.

"Samantha?"

I'm stunned. I can't move. I can't even think.

His thumb traces my lips again. "If you don't want me to kiss you, you need to tell me."

Isn't my non-answer telling him what he needs to know?

His head moves closer, his lips grazing my cheek, then his nose nuzzles my ear. "Cat got your tongue, beautiful?"

Jesus.

The shudder his voice and warm breath produce has me wet and weak in the knees. There's no way he didn't feel my body quake.

I nod.

He smirks, humor and lust dancing in his eyes. "Well, at least your head works. Let's try this. If you don't want me to kiss you, shake your head *no*."

I nod my head *yes*.

His emerald eyes stare into mine; his thumb continues to caress my bottom lip. "Is that a *yes* you understand, or a *yes* to kissing you?"

I think I'm going to die if he draws this out any longer. "Jesus. Fuck. Kiss me already."

He growls.

This time I heard it for sure. He fucking growled.

"Such language," he whispers against my lips. "I've tried to resist you, this pull between us. I…it's stronger than I am."

"Joseph," I warn.

"Impatient much?" he teases me. "Anticipation, Sweetness."

"I think if I have to endure a second longer, I'll explode." I start to back off.

He grunts his disapproval and pulls me flush against him, closer than before, securing me with an arm around my back. "We can't have that." His lips brush across mine, and then his tongue runs the seam of my lips. "Fuck me, you taste like strawberries."

"Such language," I chide.

"Give me those lips."

There is no more teasing, no more anticipation, just raw desire. His warmth, his taste, his need overwhelms me because it matches mine.

His hand holds the back of my neck as his lips move slowly, tenderly, arousing every inch of me to his touch. The clean spicy scent of him and the remains of his cologne engulf me. The hand on my back moves lower over my ass. He squeezes and then pulls me closer still.

I gasp as his erection pushes against me. His tongue slips past my parted lips, slaking his desire, consuming my mouth.

My hands move in opposite directions, one to his ass and the other into his hair. I've been dying to touch his silky black mane, and his tresses do not disappoint. He moans as my fingers grip his hair, ensuring our kiss does not end too soon.

His hands slowly lower to the back of my thighs, lifting me, placing my legs around his waist. The kitchen counter is cool against my ass as he sets me down, like a fresh breath against my heated skin. He settles between my thighs, his embrace pulling me flush against him, pelvis to pelvis, chest to chest.

"Better," he breathes across my lips. I pull him back to my mouth; he doesn't resist, but he does chuckle. "My greedy girl."

"More," I whisper before his lips return to their rightful place—against mine—in a deep soulful kiss.

His growl reverberates through my chest before it reaches my ears. My nipples ache, wishing his hands, his lips would search them out. No man has ever touched my breasts, much less kissed or sucked them. I moan at the thought, which only spurs him on, kissing me feverishly.

As if he can read my mind, his hands relinquish their current positions and take residence along my waist, moving slowly up to the bottom swell of my breasts. I arch toward him. His hands squeeze lightly.

Touch me, take me, make me yours!

When his thumbs finally graze my nipples, I whimper from the immediate pleasure that shoots between my thighs. I want more. No. I *need* more.

He does it again, and again. Gently at first, and then lightly pinching and pulling, making me crazy with lust, with need, with things I don't even have the words to express.

His.

He pulls away, his breathing heavy. His needful eyes scan my face as his thumbs continue their teasing. "Has anyone ever touched these beauties before?"

As soon as I answer. This. Will. End.

If I affirm my innocence, he will feel guilty for touching me.

If I say he is not the first, he will feel guilty for continuing my corruption.

I lose either way. I lose him, no matter what I say.

"Sweetness?" he prompts as he kisses the corners of my mouth.

"I don't want you to stop." Jeez, I sound desperate.

On an exhale, his head lowers to my shoulder. His warm breath tickles my neck as he draws air in and out of his lungs in long, stuttered breaths.

His hands still.

My head falls forward to rest against his shoulder, and I close my eyes. A tear skates down my cheek. "Please don't regret kissing me," I murmur into his bare skin. My heart's heavy at the idea of him regretting touching me.

I knew it was too much to hope for.

I know better.

I'm a fool.

His head rises, and his warm hands capture either side of my head, lifting my face to his. His thumbs swipe my tears away before his lips press to each makeup-free eyelid and then down my cheeks, following the tears' trails.

His lips brush mine before he pulls away. "The only thing I regret is our circumstances, our timing. If we were both in a different place in our lives, I would not hesitate to make you mine, in every way."

His.

I smile and nod, liking that.

I take comfort in knowing he feels the same pull for me, and for now, that's enough.

Maybe someday it can be more.

I can only hope.

"Come on, let me walk you to your room. It's late and I need to get my beauty sleep." He grins.

Holding my hand, he laces our fingers together as we silently walk up the stairs to my bedroom.

At my door, I face him. He leans in, and softly presses his mouth to mine and then whispers, "Someday, Sweetness."

He steps back, our hands still joined, fingertips to fingertips, barely holding on, not wanting to let go. That wisp of a smile is back on his lips. "So, answer me now. Was I the first to touch them?" He nods at my breasts.

"Would it make you happy if I said *yes?*" The dimpled smile that spreads across his face is answer enough. "Yes," I whisper.

He nods, understanding what that means to both of us. He slowly moves away, forcing our hands to part. "Goodnight, beautiful."

I wrap my arms around myself to keep from reaching out to him as he backs down the hall. "G'night, Joseph."

I watch as he makes it to the end, his eyes meeting mine before he enters his room. With a final nod, we back into our respective rooms and close our doors.

Seven

Joseph

I WISH I COULD SAY I HAD A RESTFUL NIGHT. IT started out that way. Peaceful, full of promise of a future with the amazing creature just down the hall from me.

But then my thoughts turned back to earlier in the evening. Jace abandoning her. The treatment she endured from his passing hookups, and lastly the horrific vision of Samantha coming upon Roger and Veronica. I could still see the shame on her face when she imparted the details to me, and to think, Jace was probably with that witch as I lay there steaming.

I did eventually fall asleep, but it was fitful at best. I wake in the morning in time to greet Samantha and her parents as they make their way out the door. My gaze lingers on Samantha, as does hers on me, before the door closes.

Someday there will be no more doors between us.

I make my way to the kitchen to feast on the food Eleanor promised was warming in the oven. I text Jace and tell him to get his ass home, pronto.

An hour-and-a-half later, he finally graces me with his presence.

"Jace, you dumbshit, I've got a few things to talk to you about." I motion to the fridge. "You'd better get us a couple of beers; you're gonna need it." I don't care that he's underage at the moment. We're in his parents' house, and we're not going anywhere.

He joins me on the couch, handing me an open beer. "What'd I do now? Is this about last night?"

"You're a fucking asshole for leaving your sister last night, especially when you made a point of saying you wouldn't, and even got all pissy when neither of us believed you. But the reason I'm pissed off is larger than last night."

I take a long draught of my beer and rest it on my knee, trying to retain control of my rage. "You're gonna have to forgive me. I've had all night and part of the morning to get all worked up over this. This is probably going to blindside you, but there are things you need to know. Things you need to take control of. Fix."

"Jesus, Joe, what the fuck's going on?" He glares at me as he takes a drink of his beer, waiting.

"Did you at one time tell someone, or get the word out, about your sister being off-limits?"

His eyes flash with guilt.

I guessed right.

I sigh and roll my eyes. "What the fuck did you do, man?"

His hand snakes around the back of his neck, rubbing it, embarrassed. "There was this asshole a few years ago. I don't even remember his name. I caught wind about him talking about Sam. Me and a few friends cornered him one night and confronted him. He confirmed what he and his friends were saying and thinking about Sam."

His blue eyes glisten with sadness, making me think of Samantha's last night. "She was fourteen, Joe." He stands and starts pacing. "It kills me to think of what they were saying about her. Fucking fourteen! Barely out of playing with dolls and shit, and these guys were talking about getting balls deep in her. Fuck!" With a sigh, he faces me. "And that was the nice shit they said. Anyway, I beat the crap out of him and told him to pass it along to his friends that Sam is off-limits, then, now, forever. My buddies did the same." He sits down, finishing off his beer.

"I understand why you did it, and I'm not sure I would have handled it any differently, but maybe you should have told her. Not what they said about her, but about you putting the fear of God in them, that she was hands-off."

"Why's this coming up now?" His voice is solemn, calm, but still on edge.

"She thinks she's a leper or something. No guys talk to her, or hit on her, and if some guy does show her any attention, she's so shocked, she eats it up like it's her last fucking meal. You meant well, Jace, but she needs to know she's not undesirable. She's fucking beautiful and doesn't deserve to be alone because you and your friends put a ban on her."

"You think my sister is beautiful?" His protectiveness comes on full-force again.

I sigh. "Man, I think she's more than that. I think she fucking hung the moon, and it breaks my heart she doesn't see it. And before you get all in my shit, I know she's seventeen. I'm not going to conquer her, if that's what you're worried about. But I do see her, and what I see is amazing. I can envision a future with her, when we're both older, more mature, out of college. But not now. I can't give her what she needs now. I can't be the one to help her see how incredible she is.

"She needs you, Jace. She needs her older brother to let her spread her wings and dip in the dating pool before she becomes an old spinster because she shut herself off from everyone, thinking she wasn't worth anyone's time or effort."

His eyes widen in shock. "She really thinks that?"

Dipshit. "Jace, her own brother dumps her for another woman at every turn. You're showing her how guys are supposed to treat women. Your pump 'em and dump 'em mentality is setting the precedent for what she can expect from men in her life. She called you the pussy whisperer and said that you only date, and I'm using the term *date* very loosely, women who don't know the difference between a blow job and a handshake." He flinches. "Is that how you want guys to see your sister?"

"Fuck, no." He runs his hand down his face.

"Well, then maybe you need to man up and stop chasing every woman who's an easy lay. Plus, you need to tell Samantha about the injunction you put on her. She needs to stop thinking there's something wrong with her."

I actually really hate saying that. I don't want her to date anyone. Anyone other than me, that is.

"Okay. I'll talk to her." He gets up, taking our empty beer bottles, and comes back with fresh ones. "Anything else?"

"Yep, there's two more things."

"Two? Fuck me. I think I'm gonna need some tequila."

I laugh. "Nope, there's no way I'm letting you get shit-faced. It's bad enough I'm sitting here drinking beer with you. But honestly, I need it after the last twelve hours."

"The fact that you, man of steel, are upset, is not making this any easier. If it's got you riled, then it's gotta be bad."

"It is. I'm just gonna rip the band-aid off, alright?"

He sighs, his head falling back, studying the ceiling. "Yes, please just make it quick."

"The women you *date*, again using that term lightly, treat Samantha like shit."

He sits up. I have his full attention now. "What do you mean?"

"They're all nice to her in front of you, but when you're not around or not paying attention, they're mean to her, catty, cruel. Some even use her to get to you, and once they've got you, they turn on her."

"Shit. Well, things just keep getting better for me all around," he whines.

"Hey, asshat, this isn't about you. It's about your sister and your ignorance in not understanding, or being aware of how your actions impact her." I motion to his beer. "Drink up. We're moving on to number three."

"Shit." He takes a long pull of his beer.

I take a sip and set mine on the coffee table. "The chick you were with last night, Veronica Hamm, she's some nasty work. Is she who you disappeared with?"

"Fuck, the fact you know her name at all tells me this is really bad. And yes, she's the one I was with last night, many times actually. She's a wildcat."

"Yeah, well, I sure hope you double bagged as she seems to get around, and just might have some shit that'll make your dick fall off." I'm half-kidding, trying to make him feel bad for his poor choices, but on the same hand, there's no way I would stick my cock in that woman, even tripled bagged.

"Jesus." He withers into the couch a little more. "I was safe, man. Just tell me, what did she do to Sam?"

I'm impressed he at least put two and two together. "Did you know Samantha was seeing some guy named Roger earlier in the year?"

He's back on the edge of the couch. "What? No, she would have told me."

I give him a you're-a-dipshit look. "Really? You talk about guys a lot, do you? Who she has a crush on? What she's been doing on the weekends for the last two years you've been away at college?"

"Fuck me. I'm a total idiot. We talk all the damn time, but…not about guys. I kidded with her yesterday, knowing she didn't have a hot date. She never dates. Yeah, I scared everyone away, but she's all about school and graduating early from college anyways." He puts his head in his hands. "I didn't think she cared about dating."

This sucks. He loves his sister, probably more than anyone else in his life. But he also loves himself a whole lot too, and self-involvement blinds him from seeing what's right in front of him. They don't discuss boys, ever. In his mind, she's his kid sister. He doesn't see her as the sexual creature she is. Though admittedly, if I had a sister, I wouldn't want to think of her in that way either.

Samantha needs him, though. He's her best friend, and if she can't tell this kind of stuff to her best friend, then who is she going to tell?

Nobody. And she deserves better than that.

I do the best I can to ease the news of what happened with Roger and Veronica, but Jace is beside himself, kicking his own ass for having spent the night with such a woman, probably doing the exact same thing she did to Roger, and more.

Much.

Much.

More.

PART 3
ASCENSION

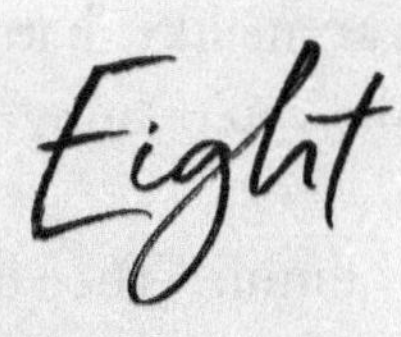

Eight

Joseph

"**D**O YOU EVER SLEEP IN?" I CLOSE THE BACK DOOR.

"Jesus! Joseph." She jumps and nearly spills her coffee. "You scared the crap out of me."

Chuckling, I join her on the double lounger by the pool. "I'm sorry, I thought you would've heard the door open."

"Apparently not." She eyes me sideways under her lashes before setting her mug on the table next to her.

I capture her hand in mine, relishing the warm softness of it. "Let me make it up to you by taking you to lunch."

I didn't get to spend any time with her yesterday. After confronting Jace, we ended up hanging out all day. I've barely even seen her or had a quiet moment with her since we kissed Saturday night, or I guess early yesterday morning.

I need to be sure she's okay. I'm not even sure I'm okay. The vision of my future seems skewed and not nearly as set in stone as it was before. Before meeting Samantha.

"Lunch? You're not hanging out with Jace today?"

"I'd like to hang out with you."

"But…what about Jace?" she persists.

"Do you want me to invite him?"

"I…uh…yes?" She frowns. "No. Actually, I don't."

I brush my lips across the back of her hand. *So soft.* "Good. I don't want to invite him either."

Uncertainty still shines brightly in her eyes. "Won't he wonder…"

"Wonder what? That I'm going to lay you out on the table and make love to you at the restaurant for all to see?"

"Jesus." She gasps and swallows hard as her skin pinkens.

"Sweetness, don't look at me like that. I'm trying to be good here, but when you look at me like you're hungry for me to do just that—I have no hope.

She pulls her hand out of mine. "Then don't say things like that. Put all these ideas in my head. It confuses me."

Confusing is too tame a description for what it's doing to me.

"You're right. I'm sorry. I was trying to make light of the Jace concern. You don't need to worry about Jace. He knows I see you as more than just his sister, but he also knows I respect you enough never to take advantage of you or your age, or your innocence."

She cringes. "Seriously? I'm not some child who doesn't know her own mind. If I wanted to be out getting laid in a restaurant or anywhere else—I would be."

She moves to get up, but I stop her with a gentle hand on her thigh. "Please don't go. I—"

"You and Jace don't get any say in the matter of my *innocence*."

"I know, and it's not what I meant, exactly. But I hope you won't be doing that. You deserve better than meaningless, casual sex."

"What, it's good enough for you and Jace, but not for me?"

Christ. I scrub my face with my hand. Where did I go wrong here? "Stop. I don't want to fight. I was simply trying to say that Jace trusts me not to lead you astray." I grip her leg. "Stay. Enjoy your coffee, and let's find something else to talk about."

She does as I ask, but I can feel her seething next to me. I'm not sure how to make it better. I just know I need to try. "I'm sorry. Don't be mad."

"I'm not mad." She bites.

My smile is inappropriate at the moment, but I can't help it. She's adorable and sexy when she pouts. "You are. I've offended you, and that was not my intent. Forgive me?"

She softens before my eyes, filling me with relief. "Forgiven. I'm sorry I got upset." She bumps my shoulder.

A wink and a dimpled smile have her smiling back at me. I lean over and kiss her behind her ear.

Her breath catches, and I savor the moment. "Can we just enjoy this for what it is and not have expectations of what it means?"

She shakes her head, raising a brow. "You said I shouldn't do casual."

Fuck, this girl is smart. She could run circles around me.

"You got me there. I'll be honest. You've thrown me for a loop, and I'm a mass of contradictions when it comes to you."

"As long as we're equally off-kilter, I'm okay with that. Let's just enjoy this week with no expectations of more."

I agree, but I fear neither one of us is capable of keeping that promise.

Nine

Samantha

STOLEN GLANCES, COVERT CONTACT, AND SECRET desires have me in a tizzy. My mind is reeling; my heart racing, and I'm aching in places I didn't know I could. For the last hour Joseph has been torturing me.

Pure. Evil. Torture.

It started out sweet and innocent enough. Margot and Jace picked the movie, or movies, to be more precise. We're having an *Aliens* marathon, apparently. Jace and I have seen all of them, but never back to back. We're on the second movie, and somewhere between when the first one ended and the second started, Joseph scooted closer to me on the couch, the sides of our bodies touching from my shoulder, down my arm, to my hip, and the length of my thigh. His hand moves to touch my hand resting on my thigh. Just the barest of touches, and it sends my heart thundering, more so than the terrifying alien that just ripped apart that poor actor on the screen.

Joseph links his pinkie with mine as he presses the entire side of his hard, warm body against me.

I glance up at him, his stare heating my skin even further.

"You okay?" he whispers a hair's breadth from my mouth.

I nod, swallowing stiffly as he licks his lips, his gaze focused on my mouth.

"You sure you don't need anything?" His lips brush my ear. "Anything at all?"

Jesus.

"I'm fine." I keep my blurry gaze trained on the movie, not seeing anything but the vision of his pouty lips too close to mine.

For the next hour, his hand moves to caress the top of my hand in slow circles. Then he places my hand on his thigh and his hand on my thigh, where he continues that same slow circling motion. All the while we remain facing forward. Jace and Margot are on twin recliners turned toward the TV, oblivious to the torture taking place behind them.

And now he slings his arm over the back of the couch, his fingers running along the curve of my neck and down my shoulder as far as he can go and still be touching my skin around my scoop-neck t-shirt, and then back up to the ridge of my ear and to my earlobe. Over and over again he tortures me. My mind is addled with wanton need and my panties soaked beyond repair.

Unable to take a moment more, I pop up off the couch, making Joseph jump. "Popcorn! I'm going to make popcorn. Anyone need anything?" I scurry off to the kitchen, barely giving them a chance to give me their drink requests.

Instead of tackling the task at hand, I pause at the kitchen window. The pool shimmers in the moonlight with aqua ripples as the pool genie glides through the water, silently doing its job to keep the water clean and pure. It's soothing, and I find myself taking deep, relaxing breaths.

A shiver runs up my spine, tightening my already sensitized nipples. My body alerting me to his presence before I'm cogently aware.

His lips graze my neck, taking the same path as his fingers did mere moments ago. His arms engulf me as his body molds to my back.

My head naturally falls to his chest and my eyes roll closed as he grazes my nipples with his thumbs. His lips pay homage to my neck and jaw, and finally my mouth as he pivots enough to consume me.

I'm lost in him, too lost, too consumed.

Before either one of us can come to our senses, I hear a gasp from behind him.

Joseph grumbles as his lips separate from mine.

Margot stands in the doorway, her eyes wide with shock. "I'm s... sorry," she struggles to speak and starts to back out of the kitchen.

"Don't go," Joseph says.

He kisses me with a soft *smack*. "Never enough, Sweetness." He then saunters out of the kitchen in the opposite direction of the den.

I wonder if he's going to go jerk off. For a split second, I consider joining him.

"So, I guess it's safe to say Joe doesn't see you as Jace's kid sister." Margot draws my attention back to her smiling, gloating face.

"Don't. It doesn't mean anything," I whisper for fear of Jace joining us in the kitchen.

"It sure looks like it meant *something*." She fans her face. "That was hot."

It was. It truly was. I sigh and grab two bags of microwave popcorn from the pantry. "It's not going anywhere, though. So, I'd rather not analyze the hell out of it."

She grabs a bag from me, pulling off the plastic wrapper and placing it in the microwave to pop. "That's not like you, Sam. You speculate and consider things from all angles. *Analyze-the-shit-out-of-things* is your middle name."

God, I love her. I wrap her in a hug. "We're just going to enjoy it while it lasts. It's just now. Nothing more. Okay?" I release her, avoiding looking at her.

She spots my watery eyes anyway and gently touches my shoulder. "Bull winkles, Sam. You really like him."

I place the popcorn bowl on the counter. "I do."

"You're gonna get hurt," she says softly.

I tap my temple. "I'm trying to keep it up here…" I then touch my heart. "…and keep it far away from here. I refuse to fall off the deep end and swoon like a silly teenager over my big brother's college roommate, who also just happens to be the future VP of the company I'd die to work for, and will apparently be my boss if that dream comes true."

"Holy nut cracker," she exclaims, her mouth agape and her large brown eyes even larger, if that's even possible.

"Yep, that about sums it up. I'd rather not think about it." I hand her the bowl of popcorn. "Take this, go back in and watch the movie. I'll be in, in a minute."

She nods, still in shock. "I love you, Sam."

I hand her her drink with a large smile. "I love you too. Now go act like you know nothing."

"Got it." With a quick nod, she departs the kitchen.

I grab the other drinks and take them to the den, setting them down, and then hurry upstairs for a fresh pair of panties.

I exit my bedroom as Joseph is about to descend the stairs.

He stops when he spots me. "Hey, what are you doing up here?" He looks flushed and guilty, like I caught him with his hand in the cookie jar. I may have hit the mark on my assumption.

I motion over my shoulder to my room. "I…" *Shit. What do I say?*

And now that I'm floundering, his interest just piqued. "Don't smirk at me. It's your fault I had to go change my panties."

He groans. "Christ, Samantha. Don't tell me that." He stalks closer, backing me up to the wall.

"And what exactly were you doing?" I press my hands against his chest to keep him from touching me, but it's a lost cause.

His hands fist my shirt at my waist, and his forehead lowers to mine. "Exactly what I'll have to go back and do again if you tell me I made you wet enough to require a change of panties."

His voice is thick and deep with need, causing my stomach to flutter. I lift up and press my lips to his. "Did you think of me?"

"Fuck," he grinds out, pressing me against the wall. "With every long, hard stroke I thought of only you."

Shit.

He cups my breast and holds my jaw. "Will you think of me as you touch yourself later? Will you picture my mouth sucking your nipples, as my fingers slide through your wet pussy, teasing and circling your clit until you cry out my name and come for me?"

Holy hell, that's the hottest thing I've ever heard, and I'm not sure if it's the words, his gravelly voice, his erection pressing against my stomach, or the fact that he just jerked off thinking of me, and now he's hard again. But whatever it is, I'm going to need another change of panties.

"If I wasn't going to before, I'm definitely going to now." I'm shaking with need and want nothing more than to ask him to do all of that to me right now.

Instead, I bust out laughing.

He drops his hands and edges back enough to see me fully.

"Did you really just masturbate thinking of me? And are seriously considering doing it again?" I press my hand to my mouth to try to silence my laughter, but it's of little use. I slide down the wall as my legs can't support me in their weakened state.

"Yes, I did. And yes, I was planning on doing it again, but now that you're laughing at me, it's kinda killing the mood." He slides down the opposite wall, staring at me.

"I'm sorry." I giggle.

He reaches for my hand, squeezing it tightly. "It's okay."

"Don't get me wrong. It was really hot. It just struck me as funny and maybe a little sad." My laughter finally abates. "We can't keep doing this, Joseph. We're just going to frustrate each other to no end." I glance down the hall towards the steps. "You were driving me crazy on the couch, such little touches, but what they did to me—there was nothing little about it."

His graces me with his sexy dimpled smile. "It was driving me crazy too. That's why I followed you into the kitchen. I just can't seem to stay away. It's like a live wire that keeps pulling at me, beckoning me to you."

"That's crazy sweet, and it's the same for me. But I think we need to try to resist it. Margot busting us is bad enough. What if it had been my parents, then what?"

"Agreed." He stands up, offering his hand, and pulls me to my feet and then into his arms. His lips brush across mine with one final kiss, as if to seal the deal. "But make no mistake, I'm still going to get off thinking of you."

"I find that oddly complimentary." I giggle.

"Good, you should." He releases me and starts down the hall but stops when he realizes I'm not following. "Are you coming?"

I raise a brow at his double entendre.

He laughs when he realizes what he said. "You know what I mean."

"Yes, I do." I motion to my bedroom door. "I'll be down in a minute." I bite my lip to stop from laughing again.

"Christ. You're gonna kill me with this panty thing."

"Hey, it's your fault."

He chuckles. "And I'll gladly take credit for it." He comes back and kisses me, sweet and tenderly. "I'll see you downstairs, Sweetness."

Joseph

I shuffle through the house Tuesday morning, trying to avoid Samantha. Margot spent the night, and I don't know if she's still here. But, if she is, I should leave them to that girl bonding time woman seem to like so much.

Jace and I head out to the gym and catch a late breakfast at our favorite diner near the hospital. It's open 24/7 and is popular with the hospital staff, college kids, and anyone with the munchies or hangovers.

"Margot's a trip. She likes to give you shit." I take a bite of my loaded egg scramble. "I like her."

Jace chuckles, adding more syrup to his stack of banana walnut pancakes. "Yes, she does. She has a younger brother at home, and they rib each other in the same way." He downs his orange juice. "She's good people. Had a bit of a hard start in life, but she doesn't let it get her down."

"What do you mean?"

"She had some health issues when she was a kid. She's fine, but she's one tough cookie. She's got a backbone of steel, that one." His gaze remains on his empty glass thoughtfully. "She's good for Sam. She brings out Sam's silly side, doesn't let her be so serious all the time."

"I've noticed that about Samantha. She's rather introspective, self-reliant. Has she always been that way?" I'm curious on his take on why she's so *together*.

He forks a mouthful, making me believe he's going to eat instead of answering, but he sets his fork down and meets my stare. "I don't really know. I think she comes by it naturally from Mom. But Sam takes it to another level. She's always been a loner, never really *seemed* to need anything or anyone. When she was old enough to read, she'd disappear for hours. When it came to birthday parties, she'd shy away from being the center of attention. I think her tenth birthday was the last party she had. She begged my mom to stop throwing them. She only wanted to celebrate with family, quietly at home."

He takes another bite of food, his forehead creased. I believe he has more to share.

I eat and patiently wait.

It's a few more mouthfuls from each of us before he speaks again. "She's shy, and yet she's not. She's truly bold when she has something to say. It's not that she can't talk to people or have fun…it's more like…she chooses not to. I've wondered if it's my fault. That I was too large and over the top, too busy being the center of attention, sucking all of the oxygen out of the room and leaving none for her." His eyes sadden as he looks at me. "I've been a shit brother to her."

I wish I could say I disagree, but I find much of what he says is probable. "It's not too late to change your dynamic. You'll always be bigger than life, and there's nothing wrong with that. She'll always be the steady rock behind you, but you can help her shine."

"Yeah." He smiles. "I could do that. I don't want her to feel like what she has to offer isn't enough and try to change. And I'm worried I've done just that with my ignorance and self-importance."

Yep, couldn't have said it better myself.

When we get back to their house, I pause at the bottom of the stairs. Music is blaring from somewhere on the first floor.

Jace continues up the stairs. "Sam must be in the library working." He looks back at me as I follow, in need of a shower. "She listens to music to clear her head. It helps her focus."

"How can she focus with it that loud?" I muse, looking over my shoulder as if I can see through the walls to the library.

He laughs. "She only listens to it loud until she feels her creative juices flowing, and then she turns it off."

Ah. Okay, that makes sense. Kinda.

After my shower, I brave the pelting onslaught of music still coming from the library. My laptop bag in hand, I slowly open the library door, feeling like an intruder in her private space.

I slip inside and close the door. It takes me a second to spot her in the back of the room in front of rows and rows of built-in bookshelves made of mahogany. The color reminds me of Samantha's hair, which is currently pinned on top of her head. Tendrils escape their confinement as she bounces, sways, and…grinds to the reggae song currently playing.

My lips curl in an unfettered smile as I lean against the nearest wall, watching in amused enjoyment. She does love her music. I knew that from dancing with her last Saturday night, but this right here is something entirely liberating. I feel bad for watching such unabashed freedom coming from a woman who is normally self-conscious of all things about herself. I should turn away, but I can't. I'm transfixed, mesmerized by the sway of her hips, the flow of her arms, and the utter joy on her face. She. Is. Beautiful.

One foot in front of the other, on instinct, I find myself drawing closer, like a honeybee to its amber pot of liquid gold.

Her movements slow as she turns, coming to a complete stop when her eyes lock on me in complete horror.

I grab hold of her upper arms, pulling her to me. "Don't freak out." I speak into her ear, ensuring she can hear me. "Don't you dare feel embarrassed. That was the sexiest thing I've ever seen. I enjoyed every second, every movement, every last breath and beat of your passionate heart. And I want to experience it again and again." I stand straight and breathe in relief to see a smile on her lips that sparkles in her eyes. "Beautiful."

"Thank you." She grabs a remote off the bookshelf and turns down the music.

"What song is that, anyway?"

"It's 'Say Hey' by Michael Franti & Spearhead. Do you like it?"

"I love it. I'll have to download it immediately."

She moves to the desk where her laptop sits and downs a large gulp of water. "What are you up to?"

I retrieve my laptop from the floor near the door. "I thought I'd join you, if you don't mind. I have some work to do for MCI and thought we could keep each other company. I assume you're working on your paper?"

"Yeah. I'm nearly done. I was taking a break, clearing my head."

I smile at that. "Yes, Jace told me you use music to do that."

"I do. It helps me get out of my head and find a creative space that allows my thoughts, words to flow more freely." Thankfully, there's not an ounce of remorse in her voice or manner.

"I can see how that might work. I may have to try it sometime."

"Good. Then I'll get to watch you dance and lose yourself to the music." She beams.

I shake my head, chuckling. "I'm afraid you far exceed me in grace, skill, and pure passion."

She rakes me up and down with her eyes. "I don't believe that for a second."

"Someday, we'll compare notes," I promise.

I set my laptop up at the table across the room from her. I'd like to share her desk, but I need to make a phone call to my Uncle Max, and I don't want to be overly intrusive on her space. She digs back into her paper, fingers typing away, and I peruse the reports my uncle sent me.

Five reports reviewed, two phone calls, and an hour later I look up as Samantha sets a Coke on the table next to me.

"Thank you." I take a cool sip.

"You're welcome." She points to my laptop. "Do you have much longer?"

"I'm finished actually. How about you?"

She leans against the table. "I'm done for today. I was thinking of making dinner and wondered if you wanted to keep me company. Unless you have plans tonight."

"Nope, no plans." I shut my laptop. "I'm all yours. What'd you have in mind?"

"Okay, don't laugh. I thought it might be fun to make pizzas and have a game night: board games or cards, nothing electronic. My parents love that sort of thing, and secretly, so does Jace. Are you up for it?"

I'm up for anything this girl offers me. "Absolutely."

Ten

Samantha

I STILL AS I ENTER THE DEN, NOT REALIZING JOSEPH is on the phone or in the room at all. I thought he was upstairs hanging out with Jace. I start to back out of the room when he glances up and stops me with a radiant smile. He holds up one finger, asking me to wait.

"Yeah, I will," he says, going silent as his eyes peruse me from head to toe and he listens to the person on the other line.

I squirm under his examination, but his frown stills my fidgeting.

"I talked to them earlier. They're having a good time, but no, I'm not sorry I didn't go. I've had a great time with the Cavanaghs. I've enjoyed getting to know Samantha and their parents better. Yes. Yes, she is." His smile turns sultry as he stands and stalks closer, changing to speakerphone. "How come nobody ever told me how beautiful she is?"

"You noticed?" The male voice on the other line says, followed by a deep chuckle.

"How could I not?" Joseph cups my cheek. "She's amazing," he nearly whispers.

He's talking to someone about me? About. Me? My heart skips a beat as his head lowers to mine. "I have to go, Dad. Give Mom my love. Tell her I'm sorry I missed her."

"I love you, son."

Joseph's lips feather across mine. "I love you too." His eyes burn with things unsaid.

I fight the panic exploding inside me. I know he's talking to his dad, but the look in his eyes seems like he's saying it to me. Impossible.

"You look beautiful," he says as he ends the call and slips the phone into his pocket. "Like an early Christmas present I want to unwrap."

"Joseph," I plead for him to not be so nice to me. To not get my hopes up that this is more than it is.

"I know. Give me a kiss. Help me make it through the day without your lips on mine."

He doesn't wait for my reply. He didn't need to. His lips crash into mine with the force of the gods, or so it seems. My knees go weak, and he moans as he steadies me in his strong embrace, his mouth savoring me like the Thanksgiving meal we are about to consume.

A deep voice clears their throat from behind me.

Shit.

"Sir." Joseph nods with a smile over my head.

I turn to see my dad smiling at us. "It's time to eat, pumpkin." His eyes flit between the two of us, and then with a wink he's gone.

"Shit," I say out loud this time. "Why the hell are you *smiling?*"

Joseph kisses my cheek. "It's okay. Your dad and I talked."

"What?" I'm completely horrified.

"It's okay, Samantha. He knows there's something here, but that we *choose* to not pursue anything right now."

If that's supposed to make me feel better, it doesn't. He told my dad he likes me, but not enough to be with me, like I'm some chick he's diddling on his break from college.

I push away and stomp to the kitchen, furious for letting myself think I was otherwise.

Joseph

That didn't go well. I don't understand why she's so upset. She'd probably be really pissed if she knew what I really thought and what I'm planning. I thought being upfront with her father was the best way to go. To speak my intentions for the future. I was trying to smooth the way for us, own it, instead of continuing to slink around like two lust-riddled teenagers, though in truth that's the way I feel when I'm near her. Which was even more reason to be sure her father understands I'm not here to mess around with her, to use her and leave her high and dry.

"I can see you have an inkling of the kind of woman Samantha will be. It's important to me that she fulfills her dreams. She has a passion for what she wants, but at the same time, she's afraid to want it—to believe it's possible. She's a contradiction unto herself. She needs a man strong enough to stand beside her and not in front of her," Daniel said to me as we grocery shopped yesterday while Samantha and her mom stayed home making pies and preparing for today.

"I understand, Sir. I would never want to stand in her way or be the reason she doesn't become who she's meant to be. That's why I want to wait to pursue anything with her until she's out of college. Two and a half years, if she finishes by her timeline. I need that time too, to focus on graduating and assume my role at MCI."

It's the perfect plan. But it's a plan I can't share with her. I don't want her to put her life on hold for me. She needs to get out there and experience life. If I tell her about my two-point-five-year plan, she'd wait for me, and I don't want that. I want her to date, get to know what she likes, who she is so she comes to me because she wants *me*, not because I'm the first guy who came along. She knows who she is when it comes to school and her career, but she doubts herself as a woman. She needs to find her footing. She needs to experiment. Find who she is beyond the 5.0 GPA high school student, or the dean's list college student, or the stellar MCI employee she is destined to be. Who is Samantha without those things?

I see her, but does she?

I grip the back of my neck and squeeze. "Fuck." I sigh as I follow Samantha into the kitchen to see what I can do to soothe her hurt feelings, but everyone's ready to eat and I don't get the chance to speak to her.

"Sam said you spoke to your family. How are they enjoying their vacations?" Eleanor asks me after we sit down to eat.

"My brothers are out on a boat today, deep sea fishing. Having a blast. They'll be having fish, or whatever they catch for dinner." I glance at Samantha on my left. She's picking at her food, barely eating. That just won't do. I slide my hand to her thigh and grip it firmly.

She tries to dislodge my hand, but I grab hers instead and hold it tightly. She needs to hear what I'm saying and stop listening to the devil in her head. "My parents are enjoying skiing. I only got to talk to my dad as Mom's having a spa day while he hits the slopes. There's a big dinner at the lodge tonight."

"Ah, that's nice," Eleanor exclaims. "Do you miss being with them for the holiday?"

I squeeze Samantha's hand. "I thought I would, but it's been so nice here." I look around the table at each of them. Samantha meets my gaze as I stop on her. "I've really enjoyed this week. It feels like home too," I say to her, and I hope she hears me.

"We've enjoyed having you, son," Daniel says as he serves himself more turkey. "Eleanor, my love, you've outdone yourself. This turkey is nearly as succulent as you are."

"Dad!" Sam blushes.

"Ugh, seriously!" Jace exclaims with a groan and a roll of his eyes.

Daniel winks at his wife with a laugh, and then holds up his wine glass. "To the most amazing woman I know, the love of my life, the mother of my children, and the keeper of my heart." He clinks glasses with her and all of us, but then his eyes return to his wife. "I love you, woman."

Eleanor's eyes glisten, and she leans forward, meeting his lips halfway. "I love you more than life itself, Daniel. Thank you for this life, every day passed, and every day yet to come."

They take a drink of their wine, never taking their eyes off each other.

Christ. That's some love affair they have. I feel like we should leave the room.

Samantha leans over. "You'll get used to it." She smiles at me, but her eyes are sad and filled with tears she's fighting to tame.

Someday, Sweetness, is all I can think as the lump in my throat keeps me silent. I simply nod, squeeze and then release her hand so that she can eat.

I never dreamt I'd find a woman who's so obviously made for me. Perfect in her imperfections I have yet to discover, but whole-heartedly can't wait to unveil.

PART 4
BEST INTENTIONS

Eleven

Joseph

IT'S BEEN AN AMAZING WEEK. JACE AND I LEAVE IN A few hours to drive home to Austin for school starting back tomorrow. I'll be sad to see Dallas in my rearview mirror because this time I'll be leaving a girl who's held me captive for the last nine days…and forever, if I play my cards right.

I stalk through the house searching for her, finding her where I should have checked in the first place, in the library. I've come to realized it's her "office" as such. Her study pad. Her think tank. Her sanctuary. She's at home here, at peace among the shelves of books, cozy couches, with her laptop buzzing along as her nimble fingers stroke each key succinctly and with lightning speed.

The door is open, so there is no noise to announce my presence as I stop at the threshold to take her in. As happens every time I draw near, the air between us thickens and sizzles, coming alive as if it's a third party in the room, not a barrier between us, but a bridge, a direct connection from my soul to hers. If I could see energy, I imagine the air between us would be as colorful as our auras themselves, an extension of us, linking me to her, reflecting our moods, our emotions, our passion. She lights me up at the mere sight of her. If fire were an aura, it would be mine when I'm in her presence: hot red, yellow, orange, blue flames dancing around my body, licking the air, eating it up between us, consuming the oxygen, drawing her to me so I. Can. Breathe.

Her fingers slow, coming to a halt as she senses me. Her face lifts from the screen, zooming in on my location.

My breath hitches, and my blood races to the part of me that wants to claim her.

Down, boy.

"Joseph." Her silken lips move. I don't hear the word so much as I feel it.

My body's in motion before my brain even makes the command. *Need.* I close the distance between us before it grows in the hours ahead.

She stands. Her hand lifts to her chest, and she backs away. There's no fear on her remarkable face. All I see is her desire reflecting mine, and it's the sheer force of it hitting her before I physically touch her. It's the same for me except it draws me to her, eliciting proactive motion to her reactive stance.

"Sweetness." My lips clash with hers as my arms envelop her.

She wraps around me in sweet perfection.

Mine.

Hers.

Yin.

Yang.

One.

Christ, I can't even make sense of my feelings, much less the depth of my words as they swirl in my head as our tongues touch…captivating the other. Our kiss is focused, drawing each other in, in hypnotizing passion.

Her hands scorch my skin as they move along my back and then up my chest to take root in my hair. A slight tug elicits a growl from me, forcing me in motion again. I cup her ass, lifting her, and like my true other half, she wraps her legs around me as I walk us to the secluded couch away from the door I should have shut when I entered the room.

Seated with her straddling my lap, I pull her close. My kisses slow to savor instead of devour. I need to concentrate and focus on remembering the feel of her, the smell of her, the all-consuming essence of her.

"Joseph," she moans against my lips, and I can hear the ache in her heart.

She's with me. She feels it too.

Thank god.

She's kissing me as much as I'm kissing her, taking and giving, beginning and ending, unhinging and completing.

Mine.

She grinds against my hard-on, her need taking over her senses and nearly overriding mine. Nearly.

"Christ, Samantha." My hands grip her hips to stop her movements. When she stills I kiss her one more time, my hand sliding to her nape, holding her close as our lips separate.

Pressing my forehead to hers, my breaths are harsh with need. "We need to talk."

She sighs, trying to pull away, but my hand keeps her in place.

"Nothing good ever comes from those four words."

I chuckle at the truth of that statement. "I'm hoping we can find some good in them. Maybe not immediately, but down the road, we will be better off for having spoken them."

Her hand wraps around my wrist. "Okay, but can you let me go?"

"No, Sweetness, that's just it. I can't."

"That's not what I meant," she says softly.

I release her, and she slowly sits back, my grip on her thighs ensuring she doesn't move any farther. "I know what you meant." The sadness on her face matches the sorrow in my heart which has a death-like grip on my chest. "We've been skirting this all week, playing with fire, but it's time we speak the truth and the reality of the situation."

"I got it," she says hoarsely, trying to stand up. She's sliding her walls back into place. I can't blame her. She needs to protect her heart as much as I have a need to protect her.

I grip her tighter. "Please don't pull away. Stay with me." I turn her face toward mine with a hand on her jaw so I can kiss her, remind her of what I'm feeling, open her back up for just a few moments more.

She sighs and relaxes in my arms, giving herself over to me once again.

This time when I end the kiss, I pull so her head rests on my shoulder and mine in the crook of her neck. "Don't shut me out just yet. Let me say what needs to be said before you disappear back into yourself."

The sound of anguish meeting my ears guts me. Her grip around my neck and shoulders tightens. I can feel her trying to rein in her emotions, stopping any further sounds from escaping. Yet, I can feel the warm tears on my neck. I hold her tighter, running my hand along her back, trying to give her comfort when I know I'm the cause of her pain. "I'm sorry. If I were a stronger man, we wouldn't be in this boat, but as it stands I'm trying to do the right thing, for both our sakes."

She nods, her voice shaking when she speaks. "I could have resisted you. Been stronger. But I didn't want to."

"I said I'm sorry. And I am sorry for making you cry, but I'm not sorry about you not resisting me. I've never felt this connection before. It's fast and intense. We need to think and put things in perspective. We're both intelligent people, we need to use our brains and not our hearts at the moment."

My girl takes a deep breath, and slowly releases me, sitting up to wipe her tears and sniffle. She's adorable and sexy all at the same time. I cup her cheek, running my thumb along the dampness. "I don't want to hurt you. I don't want to be a distraction for you. We both have school to focus on, and our careers."

She takes another deep breath, letting it out slowly and nods her agreement.

I lean in to kiss her. One. More. Time.

Samantha

He's only been gone six hours, but the longer he's gone, the more my mind falls back to old ways and disregards the words he said, the emotions he expressed. My mind twists the intention of us not pursuing a relationship into him not ever really wanting me.

I try to hold on to his words, the intent of his words, but it's like a dream that fades the longer I'm awake. I remember what the dream was about, but I can't verbalize it in any concrete way, and the more I think about it, the more muddled it becomes.

What stays true is the memory of the feel of him against my body. The way I felt in his arms. Safe. Desired. Home. Free.

I didn't have to pretend with him or feel I had expectations I had to live up to. I could just be me. The me who's confident in my skills, in my studies, and in my ability to do what is needed to get a task done and get it done correctly. But I was also free to be the uncertain me, the one who's vulnerable and doesn't always want to be the most responsible person in the room.

But that's all a dream, and the dream has ended.

It's time to focus back on school and my career aspirations. I'll allow myself a fantasy or two of Joseph being my first, of giving him my body. That should turn me on, but it makes me even sadder to think of what we had as only physical and nothing more. I want him to want me for more than just the pleasure my body can give him.

In an effort to shake it off, I head to the kitchen for a snack and then back to the library to work on my term paper. It's done, but it could always use another read-through to catch any details missing or grammatical errors.

Everything, no matter how much it's worked on, can always be improved upon.

Except Joseph. He's perfect the way he is.

I'm doomed.

I sigh and try to shake him from my thoughts.

On my way back to the library, I stop at the entryway to the den. My parents are cuddled up on the couch watching an old movie, the same couch Joseph had me tied up in lusty knots on only six days ago during our *Aliens* movie night. A fire is burning; the lights are low, and they're cocooned under a blanket. Mom nuzzles under Dad's chin. He gently cups her face and kisses her head. He whispers something to her that makes her smile and sink in deeper.

That.

Right. There.

Is.

My.

Dream.

PART 5
UNTIL YOU
DECEMBER

Twelve

Joseph

'M A MESS. I'M A FUCKING MESS.

Until I met her, I never had trouble concentrating. Keeping my head in the game. Keeping my goal of school first, play second.

But since spending Thanksgiving with Samantha, my head is all scrambled. My heart is all tied up. My thoughts are not my own.

I try.

Christ, I try to push her to the back of my mind, busy myself with school work, working out, drinking.

Way too much drinking. I have to knock that shit out.

Plus, when I drink, my resolve to not call her, text her, see her, starts to crumble.

Many times I've had to leave my phone in my car, just to reduce the temptation, make it more difficult to give in.

Jace isn't helping much, either. He doesn't know what's tying me up inside. He doesn't know what happened at Thanksgiving, that his sister and I kissed, touched…had a thing. My cock gets hard just thinking of it. Thinking of her.

In general, Jace knows I can't afford to get involved right now; my focus has to be school and my career at MCI. He knows I see his sister as someone in my future, potentially, but I haven't confided in him about my plan to wait until after she's out of college and then come for her. Hell, maybe he thought I was speaking in generalities and that I meant someone *like* Samantha would be perfect for me. I'm not correcting that assumption. I can't take the chance that he'll tell her.

It's not that she won't fit into my life. She will fit in, perfectly. It's all about timing, and ours sucks balls. She needs to finish high school and college. She needs time to experience life—to find herself as a woman. I need to finish college.

She'll be heading to Austin, and a year later I'll move back to Dallas to work with my family at MCI.

We're out of sync. And it won't be changing anytime soon.

Two and a half years. Then I'm coming for her—no holds barred.

Just because I've made my choice doesn't mean I'm not tempted to reach out to her. It's a daily struggle, and it sucks.

Just as I'm about to give in to temptation to see how she is, just to hear her lovely voice, there's a knock at the front door.

I tuck my phone away and answer the door. "Fin? What are you doing here?"

He laughs. "It's good to see you too, brother."

"Shit, I'm sorry." I step aside. "Come in."

I follow him to the living room. "It's good to see you. I'm just surprised, that's all."

He shrugs. "Yeah. I thought about giving you a heads-up, but I knew you'd come up with some excuse for me not to come."

He's right, I would've blown him off, made up some school project, downplayed my heartache to wallow alone in misery.

"Where's Jace?"

I take a seat on the couch, motioning for Fin to do the same. Not like I need to make him feel at home. He lived in this house before me. "He's on a date."

Fin's eyebrows shoot up. "Really? Like a real date, or is that a new euphemism for dinner and a blowjob?"

"A real date. He's trying to turn over a new leaf since Thanksgiving. Less manwhoring. More…dating."

"Huh." He contemplates the idea. "Well, good for him." His eyes circle the room before landing back on me. "And you? Are you dating?"

I let out a breath and sink down into the couch. "You know I'm not."

"Because of Sam." He straightens his tie even though it's not even a millimeter out of place.

I sit forward, my elbows resting on my knees. "I told you—the timing is off."

"Hmm." He nods. "But you're not dating anyone else either."

"I don't want anyone else, Fin."

I've talked to him about Samantha. He knows the score, how I feel about her, what I see as our future.

"So, you're what? Going to be celibate for the next few years then?" He shifts to settle into the couch more, like he's getting comfortable for a drawn-out conversation.

I'm not up for that. I scrub my face with my hand. "I don't know, Fin. All I know is she's the only girl I want. Now. Tomorrow. Ever. It would feel like I'm cheating on her."

Cheating myself.

He observes me dryly. "*You* don't want to commit to her. You don't want *her* to commit to you. But you don't plan on dating other people." His eyes narrow with skepticism. "Isn't that commitment?"

Fucking Fin. Leave it to him to point out the obvious.

I don't respond. What would I say? *Yes?*

We head out for dinner at one of his favorite hangouts, nothing fancy. Good burgers, good beer, and good music.

"You never did say. What brings you to town?" I take a bite of my burger and wash it down with the last of my beer.

Fin has a way of looking at me like he loves me, but I'm not necessarily the smartest cracker in the box. It's a *we're-just-thankful-he-dresses-himself* kind of look. "I came for you, dumbass. Why else would I be here?"

Really?

I feel like I can breathe a little easier with him here to help me pass the time. The weekends are the hardest. It's been three weeks since I've seen Samantha. Three weeks too long, and yet time is not passing fast enough. I don't know how I'll survive another week of this, much less years. At this rate, I'll go crazy before we're both out of school and free to pursue a relationship.

I shrug. "Honestly? I didn't think you'd come here for me."

His open hand whacks me on the side of the head. "You're smarter than this. It must be the blue balls affecting your brain function. You need me to get you set up with some porn and a cock-sucking toy?"

I laugh out loud. "Cock-sucking toy? Will it be from your own personal collection?"

"Fuck, no. It would be from Matt's. I don't have any need for that shit."

I scoff. "What and Matt does? That boy gets so much action there's no way he jerks off, there aren't enough hours in the day."

We both nearly double over in laughter.

Damn it feels good to laugh.

After our laughter dies down and another beer is consumed, I decide to bring up an issue that's been bothering me for weeks now, but I didn't want to discuss over the phone. "Why didn't you tell me Samantha interned at MCI last summer and has plans to return next summer, and to get a job with us after she graduates? She wants to work in *my* department. Don't you think I should have known that?"

Usually composed Fin flinches as if I punched him. "I knew this was going to come back to bite me in the ass." He sighs, putting down his beer. "You're right. I should have told you. Trusted you enough to handle it with decorum. But the other side of that coin is—you aren't VP yet, and Uncle Max agreed, given your friendship with Jace—and Sam's request to fly under the radar—that perhaps there was no harm in letting it slide."

My same green eyes stare back at me as I contemplate. "I can see your point. But it still pisses me off."

He nods. "I know, but would you be nearly as pissed if you didn't care for her like you do? If it were just one of your other friends' kid sisters, would you be so upset?"

He has a point. "No," I admit.

"Plus, Jace asked us not to tell her who you were either. According to him, she's dreamed of working for MCI since she was just a kid. It meant the world to her to have gotten the internship. He didn't want her to think he or you had anything to do with it. Admittingly, you two being roommates and Sam being head over heels for MCI is already an amazing coincidence on its own. Add in the fact she got an internship at sixteen, ahead of other older candidates, makes it difficult to believe.

Though, all true. It was a cluster-fuck of secrets all woven to be sure she got no special treatment."

I think back to the look on her face when she told me about her dream of working for MCI since she saw that news story when she was just ten years old. She lit up like a kid on Christmas morning, a look that makes my heart ache for her even more. "She loves MCI like it's her family heritage too."

Fin nods. "Maybe it's supposed to be. She wouldn't have needed the strings anyways. She was a rising star, received rave reviews from her manager, and was instrumental in getting two of our new key products out of research and development and into production."

I feel a wave of pride in hearing that.

Fin shakes his head. "She even has a couple of phone apps she developed and sells."

I knew she was smart and technology-minded, but not to the level Fin describes.

It irks me that I didn't know. But in the end, I understand the need to do things on her own. If I had known Jace's sister was working there, I would have searched her out and helped her in any way I could.

"Are we good, brother?" Fin asks.

"Of course. Just don't keep things from me again, especially when it comes to her."

"Understood."

Another round of beers and another hour of laughter later, Fin nods to a table in the corner. "I think you've got an admirer. The dark-haired chick over there can't keep her eyes off you. It's too bad. She's more my type than yours."

"You're in luck then, as I'm off the market."

He takes a sip of beer. "You're going to have to tell her that. She's on her way over here, and she's brought a friend." His smile is devious.

Great. Just what I need.

"Joe?" A soft voice greets me from behind before coming to stand beside me.

"Margot?" My insides light up. Samantha's not here, but I can't help feeling a little closer to her at the sight of Margot. "Hey. How are you? What are you doing in Austin?"

I only met Margot once over Thanksgiving when she busted Samantha and I kissing. Other than the cockblocking, she seemed like a nice person. It was obvious they've all known each other for a long time with how well she fit into their family dynamic. Especially how she busted Jace's balls like the rest of us do.

"I'm good. I'm here visiting my sister." She gestures to the woman standing next to her. "Jenny, this is Joe. He's Jace's roommate and Sam's… uh…hmm…friend, too."

I cringe at that introduction, but understand her uncertainty. It kills me she can't introduce me as Samantha's boyfriend.

I stand, sticking my hand out to Jenny. "It's nice to meet you. This is my brother Fin."

Fin's transfixed on Margot, giving me pause before I continue. "Fin, this is Margot. She's a good friend of Samantha's."

He's already on his feet and shakes hands with Margot and her sister. "It's nice to meet you both."

His eyes wander back to Margot.

Too thin for my tastes, but right up Fin's alley. She's quite pretty, with delicate features, except her huge light brown eyes are almost too large for her face. Her sister has similar features, but is curvier with green eyes.

"Would you like to join us?" Fin and I offer at the same time.

I can't wait to give him shit about this later.

Samantha

"You did what?" I screech on the phone and cringe at the volume of my voice.

"When I was visiting Jenny. We actually had drinks with him and his brother Fin."

I'm shocked. I knew she was going to visit her sister this past weekend, but I never thought for a second she would run into Joseph.

Why didn't she tell me sooner? That was a week ago!

I have a million questions I want to ask. But I can't go there. I can't afford to think of him more than I already do. It's been difficult since he and Jace headed home to Austin after Thanksgiving. I miss him. I miss Joseph. We spent almost every day together. We tried not to give in to the invisible pull making us gravitate toward each other. Even when I wasn't looking at him, I could feel him. I could feel his presence. His eyes on me. His desire for me.

Me.

Like. I. Was. His.

There was a tether between us that grew tighter with distance and eased when we were close. It seemed to correlate to the tightness in my chest and the knot in my stomach. When he was near, all was good. When he was not, I felt like I was coming apart at the seams.

My body started to rely on his to feel at peace. To function properly.

Crazy. Beyond. Crazy.

Now, nearly a month later I still ache. My body craves what it can't have. My mind wanders to what my heart wants, what my soul desires, what my essence can't seem to ignore. When we said we weren't a permanent thing, I'd meant it…I tried to mean it, but a part of me hoped he'd call and tell me he'd made a mistake and wanted more. When that didn't happen, I'd hoped for even a flirty text. He didn't even bother giving me that.

Joseph will only break my heart. I need to move on.

"Sam?" Margot's voice cuts through my musings.

"Sorry. I'm here. So, how is Jenny? Did you have a good visit?"

The line is silent for a moment. Is she contemplating whether she should tell me what she wants to, even though I'm obviously avoiding the whole "ran into Joe" comment?

"She's really good. She keeps trying to hook me up with guys. I shouldn't expect any different, I guess."

I sigh in relief. "No, probably not. Something would be wrong if she wasn't trying to get you laid."

"I know, right?"

Margot is a year older than me. She was sick as a child and ended up having to repeat a year, which put her in my second grade class. We've been friends ever since. I've been working to get closer to her over the last few months, trying to let her in, to trust her and let her be more than just the good-time friend she's been in the past. Not by her doing, but mine. I've kept a part of myself locked away from her, from everyone.

Until Joseph, I never wanted to let anyone in, let them see all of me.

The good.

The bad.

The dark.

And the light.

Until him.

But it can't be him. For my own self-preservation, it cannot be Joseph. I need to move on like he so obviously has.

I continue to visit with Margot as I finish getting ready for work, and as I get in my car and drive to work. We talk about anything and everything, except Joseph. He's not open for discussion.

That doesn't exactly go toward my whole *letting-her-in* endeavor, but I can't talk about him. I'm trying the whole *he-doesn't-exist* tactic to see if my heart and my head will follow suit.

We hang up when I arrive. Work has been calm for the last few weeks, no more customers manhandling me. I get a little flirt now and then, but they're just being nice or trying to get a better place on the waiting list.

"Sam, that guy is back again." Becca tilts her chin to the bar.

I follow her line of sight. There's a guy who shows up a few nights a week, orders a drink or two and then leaves.

"Is it him? I can't tell from this angle." He's in a different seat than he normally sits in, but the bar is full for a Thursday night.

She rolls her eyes. "Seriously? It is so totally him. You need to tell Trent he's here again."

The guy's my dad's age. Trent and Becca say he stares at me when he's here, but I've never noticed. Every once in a while, I get a feeling like I'm being watched, but I can never nail him staring. A little staring seems harmless in comparison to the guy who grabbed me, so as long as this guy stays away, it's no big deal.

I hang out in the back during my break. Scott made me my favorite pasta dish. It's not even on the menu, or it's a combination of things on the menu he throws together to make improvised magic. He knows how much I like fettuccine alfredo, but it's too heavy and too many calories to eat very often so he lightens up the sauce and adds in lots of veggies with the grilled chicken or shrimp. Today it's big, plump shrimp.

"God, Scott, this is so good. Why is this not on the menu?" I don't understand it. There's gotta be people out there like me who want more than a light olive oil but less than an Alfredo sauce.

He chuckles. "You're easily pleased, Sam. Not everyone likes that mutt sauce with all those vegetables." He points to my bowl. "I think you're a rabbit with the amount of vegetables you like in your pasta."

"Oh man, the crisp veggies are the best part. And this shrimp too. You even pull the tails off for me so I don't have to get my fingers dirty."

He laughs again. "See, you're easily pleased."

"I just appreciate good food when I taste it." I glance at the clock. "Shit, I'm gonna be late." I hop off the table, and he takes the bowl.

"I'll put some in a to-go container for you and maybe your favorite cheesecake." He winks.

"Are you trying to fatten me up?" I don't need any help. I have enough curves at it is. I don't need any more.

"Sam, you enjoy your food. I'm a chef. We like feeding people who enjoy our cooking. It's ingrained in our blood or something."

I wipe my mouth and quickly put on lip gloss. "I'm glad me enjoying your food makes you happy. Because eating your food makes me happy. It's a win-win." I head for the door to relieve Becca.

"Sam." Scott's booming voice halts me before I reach the door. "Don't leave without me tonight. I heard that creep is out there again."

I roll my eyes. They're so overprotective since that guy grabbed me. I wish they'd relax. "I'll be fine." I turn to leave. "Besides, he's never even talked to me."

"Sam." His voice is firmer this time.

What is it with these dominant men and using their voices to impart their will?

"Yes?"

"I'll cut you off if you leave without me escorting you to your car. No more pasta. No more cheesecake. No more food of any kind."

"Well, now you're just being mean." I flip my hair as I spin around and exit the kitchen.

His deep laugh follows me as I walk away.

When it's time to leave, I don't wait for Scott. I clock out and slip out the door. I don't want to inconvenience Scott or anyone else by walking me to my car when they have better things to do. Besides, the guy they're concerned about left hours ago while I was on break.

I click the key fob to unlock my door. As my hand touches the door handle, the hairs on my neck stand on end.

"Sam," an unfamiliar voice calls from behind. I can't place his accent.

My hand stills for just a second too long when a hand touches my shoulder. I stiffen, but don't turn around. It feels safer to not turn around. To not see his face. But it also means I can't see to defend myself. I should have waited for Scott.

I square my shoulders as I slowly turn.

His hand drops, and he steps back.

That has to be a good sign. If he was going to hurt me he would have grabbed me quickly, taking me by surprise.

"You need to tell your father about me," he says matter-of-factly.

"What?" I step back, moving to put my car between us. "Who are you?"

He doesn't try to stop me. "Tell him you saw me," he says succinctly.

I shake my head. "I don't under—"

"Sam!" Bruce and Scott run toward me. *Thank fuck.*

"Get away from her, you motherfucker!" Scott bellows menacingly.

The man lumbers to a car parked an aisle over. "Tell him," he says again calmly. Too calmly. He doesn't seem concerned with Bruce or Scott rushing our way. He's not panicked. He moves like it was simply time for him to leave.

By the time Scott makes it to me, a few seconds before Bruce, the man has driven away. I slump against my car, bending forward, my hands on my knees. *Breathe.*

Tears prick my eyes as the weight of what just happened, what could have happened, crashes over me.

"Sam? You alright?" Scott's hands grasp me firmly, pulling me upright. "Shit. Don't cry." He pulls me into his tight embrace. "Did he touch you?"

I shake my head. "He just touched my shoulder. He didn't do anything."

"Why didn't you wait?" His voice is harsh, full of censure. Tears skate down my cheek, and he rubs my back. "Fuck, Sam. I'm sorry."

"I'm sorry. I really thought it was no big deal. Don't be mad." I couldn't stand it if these burly guys were mad at me. They're like big, protective teddy bears.

Bruce pipes in. "We're not mad, Sam. Just concerned. What if we hadn't shown up? What would have happened? Did you get his license plate?"

"No. I don't think he wanted to hurt me. He seems to know my father."

That gets their attention. I fill them in on all the guy said, which wasn't much.

I promise to not walk out by myself again, and convince them to let me drive home without an escort.

Scott kisses my cheek. "Don't scare me like that again." He chucks my chin. "Let me know when you get home safe."

"I will," I promise. "Thank you."

Scott squeezes my arm. "Anytime, Sam."

"Yeah, be safe getting home," Bruce chimes in.

I pull out, wiping at the tears starting to fall again as I turn away.

What did the stranger want?

What could have happened if they hadn't shown up?

The ache in my chest for Joseph grows stronger than ever before. All I want to do is climb onto his lap and find comfort in his warm embrace and gentle words.

Until I met him…I never wanted to find comfort outside of myself. I was strong and independent. Self-reliant.

Now I feel…

Unhinged.

Unmade.

Undone.

Maybe needing someone isn't such a bad thing, but needing someone who doesn't want you back is.

Joseph

I T'S ONLY A FEW DAYS TILL CHRISTMAS. IT'S BEEN A month of hell. I've managed to keep my promise to myself not to call, text, or email her, but the closer I get to her house, the harder my heart argues with me.

Be with her.

Not now.

Those eyes.

No.

Those lips.

Man the fuck up.

Strawberry kisses.

No.

The feel of her in your arms.

Mine.

I'm hopeless. Fucking hopeless.

I pull into the driveway, picking up Jace at his parents' house. It's cold for a Texas December. It feels like snow is coming. I slip on my jacket as I trudge up the stairs and knock on the front door. I could have met him at a bar, at my parents' place, at Fin's. I could have stayed in my car and honked for him, but no, I'm here standing at Samantha's doorstep, picking up Jace, hoping I'll get a glimpse of her.

A sliver.

I'm a masochist.

Anything to hold me over. To either confirm she's nothing to me and I have simply canonized her memory, or to solidify she is, in fact, the goddess of my world.

There's mistletoe hanging above the door. My heart slams inside my chest. *Has Samantha kissed anyone under this mistletoe?*

The door swings open at the same time I hear the hum of the garage door opening.

"Joe, hi. Come in," Mrs. Cavanagh greets me with a huge smile and a kiss on my cheek.

"Hi, Mrs. Cavanagh. How are you?" I step inside.

"I'm good. It's great to see you. We've missed having you around since Thanksgiving."

"I've missed being here. It meant a lot to me to spend the week with y'all." The Cavanaghs have always been nice to me, but it was a great week, and not just because I spent so much time with Samantha. It was her family as a whole, making me feel welcome, a part of their family.

A flash outside catches my eye and I see Samantha driving off through the open front door.

Fuck.

She must have been the one who opened the garage a moment ago. It could be a coincidence, but I doubt it.

My stomach knots in the realization she doesn't want to see me.

Mrs. Cavanagh shuts the front door and continues to make small talk, unaware of the turmoil going on inside of me.

Jace trots down the stairs. "Hey, man." He's happy and oblivious as well.

"Hey." I nod, trying not to act like someone just shot my dog.

We say goodnight to Jace's mom and head out to my car.

"What's wrong with you, man?" he asks as I start the engine.

"Nothing." My irritation doesn't bode well for the evening's enjoyment.

I can feel his eyes on me, but he doesn't say anything, and I'm grateful for that at least.

"I need a drink. You good with driving home?" I don't plan on getting shit-faced, but I just might.

He glances at me, frowning. "Sure, man. You want to talk about what's crawled up your ass?"

"Nope."

"Okay."

♡

Samantha

I can't believe I just snuck out of my own house. My stomach twists as the reality of my action settles. Did Joseph see me leave? What's he thinking? I drive through my neighborhood faster than I should, trying to expand the distance between us—and that of my dignity I've left behind.

It's Christmas break from school. I have to keep myself busy, and, most importantly, I need to stay away from him.

At the last minute, Jace told me Joseph was on his way over. I barely had any time to text Margot and make a dash for the garage as Joseph pulled up out front.

I suck.

I know.

It's not one of my most shining moments. But desperate times call for quick escapes.

Self-preservation.

Not seeing him or hearing from him has been like enduring the third level of hell. I've been doing better lately. Seeing him, hearing his voice, knowing he's right there in my home but not being able to be with him would be excruciating.

He's made it clear he doesn't want to pursue anything, so I'm not going to throw myself at him like a lovesick puppy, and if that means running away, then fine, I'm a coward.

I was actually looking forward to just relaxing at home and not having to be social. I guess I could have hidden in my room, but there was no guarantee I wouldn't see him. Maybe they were leaving right away, but

I didn't have time to discuss the particulars of their plans before I made my impromptu escape.

Margot meets me in her driveway before I even pull to a stop.

I roll down my window as she nears. "Hey." My tone is apologetic for showing up like this.

"Hey." She bends down, leaning in my window. "I was thinking. Why don't we go to that place near the SMU campus we like? We can watch the college boys, get some good grub, listen to music…" She shrugs and gives me a soft smile. "…talk, if you want to. Or not. But, it'll be decidedly more fun than hanging out here." She wrinkles her nose and adds, "Dad's not in the best of moods. So, it's a win-win. We'll get to scope out hot college boys, and we don't have to listen to my dad whine about work, or the news, or my mom," she says the last part even more sadly.

Things must not be going well with her parents. They've had a rough couple of years, but it got worse when her dad lost his job last year. I don't really know all the details, but I know he's not happy with his current "temporary" job, as he refers to it.

I respond before I can overthink it. "Sounds like a great idea, actually." I motion to the passenger seat. "Hop in."

The place is packed, but we luck into a parking space near the entrance and snag a high table in the bar area just as another couple's leaving. It must be a sign we're supposed to be here.

My shoulders finally start to relax halfway through our burgers and a drawn out discussion on *Outlander* vs. *Game of Thrones*. I'm the *Outlander* fan, as it rocks, of course. She's *Game of Thrones* all the way.

We must have gotten too loud, too animated, as a sinfully sexy voice chimes in from behind me, "*Walking Dead.*"

Mid fry to my mouth, I stop and face that voice.

The guy it belongs to has beautiful blue eyes, highlighted by his tanned skin and black hair. Unusual features, delicate and yet masculine at the same time. Pretty. He's definitely a pretty boy, also tall, lean, and overly confident.

I cock a brow at him as he comes closer. "Excuse me?"

His devious smile crooks further. "*The Walking Dead.*"

He and his buddy come to stand next to our table. He sticks out his hand. "Sebastian." He motions to his friend. "Bobby."

So far, he's said seven words, none of them in complete sentences. His English teacher must be so proud right about now.

I take his hand firmly. No wussy handshakes here. "Sam," I simply reply before nodding across the table. "Margot."

"Pleasure," he says, meeting my eyes.

I can't help but laugh at his abbreviated speech. "Are you capable of speaking in complete sentences or are you going for the *less is more* approach?" I pull my hand out of his, seeing as how he doesn't seem inclined to release it on his own.

His head falls back, and a carefree laugh escapes his perfectly formed lips. Shaking his head, his eyes meet mine. "You're feisty, Sam. I like that."

He leans intimately closer and whispers, "I'm more than competent with my mouth, but wouldn't you feel bad if I were shy or had a speech impediment?"

I smirk. "Yes, actually I would. But, thankfully I don't have to apologize for being too candid."

"No, I suppose you don't. But you should probably apologize to the other women in this room."

He's lost me. "Why?"

"Because you're the most beautiful woman in here, and they don't stand a chance."

I scoff. "Seriously? Does that line actually work?"

"You tell me. I've never had a reason to use it before."

I almost buy it—he actually seems sincere. "Laying it on a little thick, don'tcha think?"

"I'm only calling it as I see it." His hand rests on the back of my chair as he snags a fry, giving me a devious smile and a raise of his eyebrow.

After a few more minutes of me rebuffing him, he dials down his charm a couple of decibels and ends up being a really nice guy. Margot and Bobby seem to be hitting it off, and the four of us delve into the topic that brought them to our table in the first place: the fact that Sebastian believes *The Walking Dead* is a far superior show to my *Outlander* chick-flick-kilt-wearing-time-period drama, or Margot's *Game of Thrones* kill-off-any-character-you-like-blood-bath-athon. In his humble opin-ion, of course.

"So, tell me, Sam. If I were to ask for your phone number, would you give it to me?" Hope glimmers in his eyes.

My heart pings for a man who's ever-present, yet strikingly absent from my life.

Sebastian is crazy good-looking and nice. I'm flattered, truly, but he's not Joseph.

I lower my gaze and my voice, hoping he hears my sincerity. "I'm not looking to get involved with anyone, Sebastian."

He nods in understanding. "I could use a friend. How about you?" His smile is sweet and genuine.

"They say you can never have too many friends."

His smile grows to show his perfectly straight white teeth. "Yes, *they* do say that." He places his phone in front of me. "Friends." He acquiesces to my limitation of our involvement.

I take his phone and wake up the screen, scold him for not having it password protected, then enter my number and name as *Sam My Super Cool Friend*. I then proceed to walk him through the steps to add a pass-word to his phone.

He laughs. "You're such a dork."

I shake my head. "You have no idea how much of a dork I truly am."

We spend the next thirty minutes talking about the cell phone apps I've developed. He insists I pull them up so he can download them, pay-ing for each without complaint. He even promises to recommend them to all his friends and family so they can do the same.

It's late by the time the four of us head out. The boys walk us to our car, pausing for a quick goodbye. I get a small hug and chaste kiss to my cheek. Margot gets a full kiss on the lips. I snicker when their kiss continues.

Sebastian nudges my shoulder. "Hey, I won over the prettiest girl in the room tonight. She even agreed to be my friend. I'd call it a stellar night."

I laugh and blush from the compliment.

We say goodnight again, and I slip into the driver's seat, starting my car, and wait for Margot to end her lip lock.

My phone dings with a text message from an unknown number: *Goodnight, beautiful Sam.*

I peer out my window and see Sebastian sitting a few cars over in a black sports car, waving at me.

I add him to my contacts and text back:

Me: *Goodnight, Sebastian of the Walking Dead.*

Sebastian: *LOL. Sweet dreams, Sam of Outlander.*

I turn my screen off, but continue to stare at it. I've gone years with no attention and now two of the hottest guys I've ever seen have given me the time of day. Joseph wanted me…at least enough to fool around with. Sebastian asked me out, but he's not Joseph.

Maybe I should give Sebastian a chance.

Maybe I could do casual.

Maybe if I see what else is out there, Joseph won't seem so perfect any more.

Fourteen

Joseph

CHRISTMAS AND NEW YEARS CREEP SLOWLY BY. I'VE been home for two weeks. Two long weeks of hanging out with my parents, brothers, and friends. No women. None. I can't have the only woman I want, and she haunts my days and my nights. I've been to Jace's four times and each time Samantha wasn't there.

Jace, of course, is being Jace, and giving me shit about pining over his kid sister. He's uncharacteristically harsh about it even though I told him I'd keep my distance from her. I'm not exactly sure what's bugging him: the fact I'm attracted to his sister, or me being a baby about it.

"You're such a pussy," he says as we step off the elevator, having arrived at Fin's penthouse aloft MCI Towers.

I halt in my tracks, making him stop to avoid running into my back, and pivot to face him.

"Why exactly is that, Jace?" I grab the back of my neck and squeeze to alleviate the tension building there. "Because I care for your sister? Because I respect her enough not to lead her on, making promises I'm in no position to fulfill?" I step closer, towering over him. "Would you rather I fuck her and leave her?"

He steps back, appalled. "Jesus, no."

I press forward. "Am I a pussy because I prefer not to fuck every skirt that looks my way in an effort to forget her?"

"No," he says solemnly.

"So, I'm a pussy because I physically ache for her, like I left a part of me behind the day we left your house after Thanksgiving break?"

"No." His eyes slowly rise to mine. "Well, maybe. You're just not yourself. It's like you can't function without her," he says in disbelief, unable to fathom what that would even be like.

I sigh and step back. "You're right. I'm not myself. And I'm pissed about it. I'm distracted, unfocused." I sigh and pin him with my gaze. "I feel undone, incomplete, with no end in sight."

"Yeah, like a pussy," Jace says again, only laughing this time.

I chuckle, feeling some of the tension leave my body. "Don't let Samantha hear you say that. She'd be offended you're using a reference to the female anatomy with a derogatory connotation."

"No shit," he agrees.

Most women would find it offensive. I'm disheartened we continually use terms related to women as derogatory putdowns toward men.

Fin opens his front door. "You pussies gonna come in or stay out in the hall gabbing like a bunch of women?"

Jace and I bust out laughing. I can't even catch my breath to explain why as I walk past Fin.

We're greeted by my brother Matt, who shakes our hands as our laughter wanes and we compose ourselves.

"Hey, Joe." Victor greets me with a smile and a pat on the back. He's MCI's head of security, who doubles as Fin's driver much of the time.

"Hey, man." I return his pat as he shakes hands with Jace.

A familiar face turns the corner. I grin. "Michael, it's been ages. How are you?"

"I'm good. I hear you're hung up on Jace's sister." He graces me with a rare smile.

I just shrug and head to the kitchen for a much-needed beer. The guys follow, picking up the drinks they left behind to meet us at the door.

Fin stands next to me. "I was getting ready to open the door when I saw you turn and nearly pounce on Jace. Was that about Sam?" He keeps his voice low so only I can hear.

I keep mine equally low to be sure Jace can't hear me. "Yeah, he called me a pussy, and I lost it for a minute." I take a pull of my beer. "We're good now."

"Hmm, but you're not really good, are you?" He's perceptive as ever.

I exhale. "Let's just play some poker and give me something else to focus on, yeah?"

He squeezes my shoulder. "You got it." He eyes my beer. "If you need to stay the night, you know my door is always open."

I nod, grateful. "Thanks, brother, but I'm done drowning my sorrow."

"Fair enough." He turns to razz the other guys in the group. "Should we get this game started? Or do you just want to hand over your money now?"

"In your dreams," Matt replies.

"Not happening, asshole," Victor pushes back.

He and Fin have a tight bond that goes beyond boss and employee. They met in high school. Victor's a few years older, but they remained in contact as Fin went to college and Victor went into the military—where he met Michael—and then did a stint in the FBI. Michael and Victor have become a part of our tight-knit group, *The Six Pack* as my father dubbed us when Jace joined a few years ago. Jace is the latest member, but you'd never think he wasn't one of us all along.

As Fin and Matt's younger brother, I was included even though I was entirely too young for most of their antics, but they looked out for me, kept me clean and out of trouble. Though, I did get more than a few beers before I was of legal age. Like tonight, Jace gets two beers, no more. Fin is a stickler for that rule. If anyone has more than two drinks, they stay the night, no discussion. Fin isn't as tall as me, or as thick, but he's strong as shit with a menacing glare that brooks no arguments from any-one. Not even Victor and Michael with their military backgrounds push Fin. He's calm, cool, and collected 99% of the time, but it's that 1% that makes grown men quake in their shoes.

With boastful pride, we take our seats as Fin exchanges our money for chips.

"So, Fin, you getting any, or are you still hanging onto your virginity for dear life?" Michael locks eyes with Fin.

"Fuck off, Michael. You know your mother was my first."

The four of us not in this conversation bust out laughing.

The gleam in Fin's eyes tells me he's not done. "But you were my second, Michael. And to be honest, I'm not sure who was the better fuck." Fin doesn't skip a beat as he deals the cards.

"Fuck, Fin," Michael exclaims. "You had to go there, always have to one-up me." He takes a long drink of his beer. "Jesus, those are two images I'll never get out of my head now. Thanks, man."

"Anytime, lover." Fin winks at Michael.

"Knock it the fuck off, Fin." Michael stalks to the kitchen and comes back with six shot glasses and bottle of Crystal Skull Vodka.

Shit. Fin was just kidding, but Michael's a hard ass of the highest degree. Kidding around about his sexuality is not something he takes lightly. I glance at Fin to get his beat on the situation.

"Michael, man," Fin says softly. "You know I'm just kidding, right?"

Michael pours a shot and throws it back before responding. "Yeah. I know."

"Besides. You're the best fuck I've ever had," Fin throws out with all sincerity before he winks. "Here, let me get you another one." He pours Michael another shot.

Michael throws it back muttering, "Fuckface."

Fin takes a shot himself, then prompts our big and small blinds. "Ante up, boys. It's time for this *'fuckface'* to take your money."

The laughter slowly dies down. The shots of vodka continue, and even Jace partakes, which means he's staying over. I resist the hard stuff and switch to soda after my first beer. I've had enough of drinking for a while. I'm done trying to lose myself in a bottle to avoid thinking of Samantha.

We stick to Texas Hold'em for the next hour or so. It's a serious but friendly game, meaning we play by the rules, but we still give each other shit.

I'm up a hundred bucks, which is impressive with these guys. It's not like playing a bunch of college boys. These are some seriously talented players.

Just to goad me, Michael tries to distract me with questions about Samantha.

By the third one, Jace has had enough. "God, can we not talk about

Sam tonight? Please," he grumbles from across the table. He keeps his eyes on his cards before he sets them face down and raises Victor. His glare narrows on me. "Besides, man, she's on a date tonight. You need to get over it."

I slump back in my chair as if he physically slapped me, though it feels more like a punch in the gut.

Goddammit.

"Jace," Fin barks at him.

Before they can get into it. I stand up, throwing my cards on the table. "Fold."

I scrub my face with my hands, stumbling back. *Fuck.* I'm going to be sick, physically sick. "Deal me out," I mutter as I head to the living room, but I don't stop until I make it to the nearest bathroom.

I splash cold water on my face, leaning against the counter.

I've lost her. She's moving on.

My gut revolts, saliva coating my mouth. I swallow hard, breathe deep, and rinse my mouth with water from the tap, hoping it will help. I didn't want to tie her down before she got to experience more, but I didn't expect it to feel this awful.

"I can't lose her," I mutter, standing to dry my face and hands.

A knock at the door startles me. "Joe, you okay, man?"

"I need a minute, Fin."

I need more than a minute. I need two-and-a-half years to have passed so Samantha has graduated early from college. I'll have graduated and settled into my job. She'll be twenty, and I'll be twenty-three, both more mature with our futures in hand. There'll be nothing to keep me from pursuing her.

But fuck, that's not the case. The reality of waiting all that time to be with her falls on my shoulders like a lead vest. Who's to say she won't fall in love with this asshole and forget all about me?

Of course she's not going to fucking wait on me. I never asked her to wait, but I'd hoped that she would.

Mine.

The thought creeps in and won't leave, tightening like a vise around my chest.

Mine.

I pull my phone out and dial her number before I can stop myself. As it rings, I lean back against the counter.

"Hello?" Her voice is uncertain. It's taken balls of steel not to call her every fucking day even though I've had her number all this time.

My dick goes hard from the simple sound of her voice. "Sweetness," I croak out.

"Joseph?"

I hear so much in that one word. Surprise. Hope. *Mine.*

"Are you alright? You don't sound alright. What's wrong?" Her voice jumps up in volume as her concern escalates.

"Where are you?" I don't have time for small talk, and I'm most definitely not alright. There's noise in the background and a man's voice.

"I…um…I'm out."

"Where are you?" I ask more firmly.

"Houston's." She pauses then adds, "What's wrong?" Her voice is soft, her concern apparent.

Despite my absence, her efforts to avoid me, and the fact that she's out with another guy, she still cares.

My heart pounds in my ears. "I just…need to see you." I ache for more, but it's a start.

"Now's not a good time. I can call you later."

Later? Well, at least she didn't say never.

"Promise?"

"Yes, I promise. I'll call you back in a few hours. When I get home."

I take a deep breath and let it out. "Okay. Later, then."

"Okay." Her relief is apparent.

"Samantha?"

"Yes?"

Don't move on without me. I don't say what I want to and struggle to find something of importance that won't freak her out. "Be safe," I eventually say. *That was lame.*

"Safe?" she questions.

"Yeah, don't do anything…foolish."

She giggles. She must think I'm ridiculous. "Okay. I'll stay safe and won't do anything foolish. I promise." She covers her phone and then comes back. "I have to go. Our food just arrived."

Fuck. *Their* food.

"You'll call?" I press.

"Yes, I said I would." She reassures, not scolds. "Goodbye, Joseph."

"Till later, Sweetness…never goodbye."

Her breath catches.

Fuck. She likes what I just said.

"Later, then."

Her words hang in my head as I pace the bathroom a few times.

I make a decision, probably rash, but one I will in no way regret.

I glance in the mirror. Finding myself acceptable, I shrug and open the bathroom door. I can hear the guys continuing their poker game in the dining room as I slip out the front door and send Fin a quick text:

Me: *I'm heading out.*

Fin: *U OK?*

Me: *I gotta go see about a girl.*

Fin: *Pussy.*

Me: *Yep, but only for her.*

♡

Samantha

I hang up, take a calming breath, set my phone in my purse, and sheepishly meet Sebastian's gaze. "I'm sorry about that."

He agreed this wasn't a date, but it was still rude to answer my phone. I normally wouldn't have, especially for an unknown number, but I felt like I needed to answer it.

I'm glad I did.

It was good to hear Joseph's voice, but he didn't sound quite right.

Sebastian smiles. "Was it him? The one who's locked down your heart?"

Has he? "Yes and no. It's not like that. We're not together. We're… not in love."

He nods as he forks a bite of food. "Yeah, I gathered as much from what you've said so far." He points at me. "And the sadness on your face when you think of him."

I guess I'm no good at hiding my misery.

We sit in silence for a few minutes as we eat, him more enthusiastically than me. I've lost my appetite. This is my favorite place, and I'm letting Joseph ruin my dinner with Sebastian. It doesn't matter why Joseph called—he and I are never going to be together.

I try to get Sebastian and me back on track. "So, Dr. Cole, tell me what it's like to be a Resident in the ER."

He narrows his eyes at me and frowns. "No." He dismisses my question, setting down his fork. "What's the deal anyway? Why can't you be together? Is he an ass or something?"

I push my food around my plate. "No, he's not an ass. It's just…we need to focus on graduating and our careers, and not get into a relationship." I lean back and take a long drink of iced tea. "Neither of us wants or needs the distraction. Plus…" I look away, not wanting to finish that thought.

"Plus what? He's an ass? See, I knew it," Sebastian jokes.

I laugh. "No, he's not an ass." Wiping my mouth, I set down my napkin and lean forward. "It's just who he is, or rather who he's going to be. He needs someone else…not…me," I huff.

"He said that?"

I shake my head. "He didn't need to say it. So…what's the point?"

"Let me get this straight. This guy you're longing for, missing, you don't see a future with, and yet, you're holding out for him. Not dating anyone else, for what? Forever?"

"I'm not trying to wait for him." I shake my head. "It sounds stupid, I know. But just because the timing isn't right for us now, doesn't mean I don't want it *now*. And just because he doesn't see me with him for the long haul, doesn't mean I don't want it all the same."

"That's so sad, Sam."

I nod and have to bite my lip to keep from crying. "It is. It truly is."

He studies me for a few minutes as I pick at my food.

"You're beautiful. Too beautiful and nice to spend your youth pining for some guy." He waves his hand in dismissal. "You shouldn't be alone." He leans forward. "And you're miserable."

I force a smile and nearly choke on my words. "I'm not miserable."

He lets out a small chuckle. "Ah, Sam. You are, baby." He lays his hand over mine and squeezes. "You don't have to be, though. Spend time with me. I'll help you forget. Help you get over him."

I pull my hand away. What he says is sweet and kind, and may be just a ploy to get in my pants, but he seems to honestly care. Still, I don't want to give Sebastian the wrong idea. "That's just it. I don't *want* to forget him."

The back of my neck prickles, and I feel that familiar buzz in the air. My breath catches when I see Joseph approaching our table.

"Samantha," he says simply, but there is nothing simple about the need in his voice or the heat in his eyes.

"Joseph." I'm surprised he's here, and yet I'm not. He said he needed to see me and sounded desperate on the phone.

His greedy eyes pin me to my seat before slipping across the table to Sebastian. A curt nod is all the greeting Sebastian gets. "Could I speak to you for a moment?" Joseph holds out his hand.

"I…" I peel my eyes off Joseph. Sebastian eyes are wide, his lips tight. "I'll be back."

I don't wait for his reply before I take Joseph's hand and slip out of the booth.

Joseph laces his fingers through mine and pulls me past the bar and kitchen, dodging staff and patrons as we go. I thought he would head outside, but there's a dark alcove between the men's and women's restrooms. He stops there and whips me around so I'm flush against the wall near the corner.

My breath catches. "What are you doing here?"

He moves in, hovering over me. One hand rests against the wall above my head, and the other is clutching my waist, pressing me to him, holding me tightly, protecting me from prying eyes. His head lowers to mine. "Sweetness," he breathes out before his lips crash into mine.

My entire body comes alive as he presses forward, pinning me against the wall. His arms, wrapped around me, hold me as if he can't get me close enough.

He groans into my mouth when my hands move along his body, holding him just as tight so he can't escape. I don't want him to let me go. Ever.

I'd not forgotten the taste of him, the smell of him, but I'm still overwhelmed. It all comes flooding back. His kiss softens as his tongue plunges deep and undoes all my work to forget him over the last few weeks. I pour all my pent-up frustration and desire for this man into kissing him back.

That small tender reprieve ends the moment his erection presses into me and I moan. He doesn't let up. Instead he ratchets up the tension when he moves between my legs. My flowy skirt gives him all the access he needs to press his jean-clad thigh between mine. His urgent, possessive kisses return as he swallows every bit of passion I have to give, his hand squeezing my ass, grinding me against him.

I gasp as he hits that spot, and it only fuels the fire.

He groans, his need as apparent as mine. He rocks me against him again and again as his mouth devours me.

My fingers dig into the taut, strained muscles of his back as I begin to tremble, reaching for release. The tingle starts in my legs, working its way up, growing like a bubble as it moves up my body, consuming me, rising higher and higher, expanding, until the tension is so tight it can't grow any more.

"That's it, Sweetness," he says a second before my orgasm bursts forth like fireworks, and I cry out as I come. Joseph swallows the sound, supporting me as I quake in his arms.

His kisses soften and move to my face, my jaw, and my neck.

He nuzzles into my hair, his breathing strained, his heart pounding in his chest, matching mine. "Don't go out with anyone else," he whispers in my ear. "Wait for me, Samantha."

My insides clench, sending another wave of shudders through my body.

"That's right, beautiful. Give me every bit of your pleasure."

He pulls a chair sitting only a few feet away over to our darkened corner and sits down, cradling me in his lap, my head buried in his neck. We're tight in each other's embrace.

"Only me." His voice is strained. "Don't give yourself to him or any-one else." He cradles my cheek. "I don't deserve you. But please, Samantha, wait for me. Please."

His pleas rip a hole in the wall I've put around my fears, my desires, my hopes surrounding him. The tears start to fall, as much as I try to hold them back. He didn't call or text or talk to me for over a month until he found out I was on a date. He doesn't want me—or does he? He's here right now…surely that means something, but I can't think with what he did to my body a moment ago.

"Shh. Don't cry," he coos into my hair and continues to comfort me as I recover from my orgasm and the emotional turmoil that is Joseph McIntyre.

I'm sure I'll be embarrassed later for what's happening right here near the restrooms, but at this moment, I feel cocooned and safe in his arms.

"You're so sexy, Samantha. That was hot as fuck." His smile warms me.

I'm so confused. "Why are you here? You made it clear you don't want a relationship with me. You never called or anything, but you want me to ignore Sebastian? You can't have it both ways."

He holds me tightly as he gently wipes my tears away. "Just because I didn't call doesn't mean I wasn't thinking of you every day. I need time to figure things out. Can you give me that?"

Can I? I touch his face, peering into his worried eyes. "Sebastian and I are just friends."

He searches my face for confirmation of my words, then nods, pull-ing me closer, burying his head in my neck. "My girl," he whispers.

My heart aches as his words echo in my head. I am his girl even though I tried not to be.

Once composed, I slip into the restroom to freshen up and gain some perspective.

I head to the nearest stall. I can't believe I just made out—and had an orgasm in public. Granted it was a secluded corner, but anyone could have walked by and witnessed my undoing. Luckily, that didn't happen.

He came here for me. Why?

I don't trust that I'll remember what it felt like to be in his arms hours from now. I close my eyes and relive every second, focusing on his touch and his words.

Time. He asked for time.

When I exit the restroom, I'm disappointed that Joseph isn't there waiting for me.

Maybe he's in the men's room. I wait for a few minutes, then decide I should get back to the table. What will I say to Sebastian? Some form of the truth, but most definitely not all of the truth.

I stop in my tracks when I see Joseph sitting in my spot, talking to Sebastian. Their conversation is intense, their expressions serious and locked in on each other. Joseph is talking and Sebastian is nodding. I can't make out any words, but it's obvious Joseph is laying something out, and Sebastian is in agreement.

With a final nod, Joseph stands, shaking Sebastian's hand. He turns and walks toward me, as if he knew I was here the entire time. Maybe he can sense me too.

He pulls me into his arms and kisses me tenderly, his tongue just barely brushing my lips. "You're mine."

He starts to pull away, but I grab his shirt and pull him back, kissing him fiercely. His hands grip my sides, tightening their hold as he kisses me back.

When I pull away, I say quietly, but firmly. "I'm not yours. I'm nobody's."

His dimpled smile weakens my knees. "You aren't nobody's." He kisses me one more time and steps back. "I just need time." He winks at me as he releases his hold and slips out of the busy restaurant.

I watch until he is out of sight and then join Sebastian.

"You alright? You're flushed," Sebastian says once I'm settled on my side of the booth. My seat is still warm from Joseph.

"Yes, I'm fine." I take a bite of my grilled chicken salad with renewed hunger. Even though I'm more confused than ever, I feel better for having seen Joseph. Knowing that our attraction is still mutual. Real. He said he thought of me every day. I feel a sense of power that I didn't feel before. He's jealous—crazed by the idea of me being with someone else.

We may not be together, but we're not with anyone else either. And that's something.

Is it enough? No. Though at the moment I'm high on endorphins and quite elated that he came after me and claimed me so intimately and publicly for anyone to have seen. I want to call Margot and scream over the phone that Joseph gave me my first orgasm. Well, first orgasm by someone other than myself. He asked for time. Does that mean he wants to be together? He wouldn't ask me to wait forever…

I don't want to analyze the shit of this. Not yet, anyway. I just want to bask in the glow of his touch, his desire for *me*. His jealousy over *me* being out with another guy. I've never felt so wanted, and I try to hold on to that feeling for as long as I can before my natural inclination to logically dismiss it all overrules my euphoric state.

PART 6
FAMILY TIES

FEBRUARY

Fifteen

MOM AND DAD ARE LEAVING FOR VACATION TODAY, and I'm in the driveway helping my dad load their luggage in the car. Mom packs like they'll be gone for a month instead of seven days. Dad doesn't complain, though; that's just Mom. He says packing heavy helps her relax and feel prepared, and he would rather she be relaxed than fight about the contents of her suitcase.

My dad's a wise man. He dotes on Mom and loves her more than I've ever seen a man love a woman. He doesn't sweat the small stuff. He gives her the freedom to be who she is and indulges her idiosyncrasies. She does the same, but he doesn't seem to have many.

This isn't the first time they've left me alone since Jace has been at college, but it's the longest time they'll have been away. I'm fine with it. Spring Break is in a month, and I have a project due before then. I'll spend my time focusing on that.

Mom finally makes it outside after checking and double-checking she has everything. She gives me a big hug. "Be good. Have fun but not too much fun." She kisses my cheek and moves to the passenger door where she stops and faces me. "I know you will, but I have to say it for my own peace of mind. Be responsible. No boys. No parties." She lets out a deep breath, and her shoulders relax now that she's said her piece.

I laugh. She's nervous. "Mom, I know the rules. I'm too busy for parties and boys, anyway."

Besides, there is only one man I want, and he's four hours away at college, living with my brother. Probably dating girls his own age. No, not girls. Women.

Shit. I had to go there.

Joseph said he's not interested in dating anyone else, but still, he's twenty-one and a sexual male. I don't expect him to go without. There might not be *dating*, but I don't imagine his bed is empty either.

I shake my head, trying to dismiss those thoughts.

Dad lays a kiss on my cheek. "She's just nervous about leaving you for a whole week. We trust you, Sam." He gives me a quick hug. "Don't disappoint us."

There it is. He had to get in his parental gibe as well.

"Geez, you two, I got this. I'm not gonna have a party, go to a party, have boys over, drink, or have sex. I'm going to attend school, work, hang with Margot, and maybe Sebastian, but mostly, it'll just be about school and work." As usual.

Feeling satisfied with that answer, Dad turns to Mom. "Come on, gorgeous, we've got a plane to catch and a bikini for me to get you out of."

OMG! I groan.

"I heard that, Sam. I'm a man. I still love your mother. Get over it." He winks at me. "Love you, pumpkin. Call if you need us."

With a final wave, they back out of the driveway and head to the airport.

I'm not even fifteen minutes into my solitude when I get a text from Jace.

Jace: *Freedom! Whatcha gonna do with it?*

Me: *Have an orgy and burn the house down around me, of course!*

Jace: *Ah, that's my girl. I've taught you well.*

My cell phone rings. "What, you can't stand that you might be missing out on the fun?" I tease.

"Well, hello to you too, sis." Jace chuckles. "I figured I could call you instead of texting."

"I'm sorry. Hello, dearest brother, how are you?"

"Alright, smartass. Enough of that." There's muffled discussion in the background, then his voice is back. "Sorry about that. Joe says *hi.*"

I laugh even though my insides ache at hearing his name. "And you seem overjoyed to be telling me."

He sighs heavily. "Look, I don't know what went on with the two of you, and I prefer not to know, but he's been a miserable ass since Christmas." He huffs. "Actually, I take that back. He's been a miserable ass since he met you at Thanksgiving. Maybe you two should talk."

My head swims with too many ways to respond. I'm both happy and sad that Joseph is in knots just as much as I am. "He's not asking to talk to me, is he?"

It's been radio silence for two months now. No contact at all. The incident at the restaurant feels like a perfect, weird hallucination. I thought he'd change, start calling or something after claiming me as his in that way…but nothing happened. He wants me to wait for him, but then doesn't freaking talk to me. It's like he wants me to be miserable. I don't get it, and maybe I don't care to. "He could have called if he wanted to talk to me."

"No, that's my suggestion. But it's obvious to me that you want to talk to each other."

"There's no point, Jace. He doesn't like me like that."

"I don't think that's true, not by how he's acting."

"When have you known him to not pursue something he really wanted?"

Jace sighs. "Never. He's the most determined guy I know."

"Exactly." My throat burns at the truth Jace just admitted. "If he wanted to be with me, he would."

"You could talk as friends."

"No." I have to take a few deep breaths before I can continue. "Tell him I said *hi*."

He sighs again before he continues, "Just so you know, he's not dating or anything. There's no women."

"That should make me happy, but it doesn't. Even though he doesn't want me enough, I don't want him to be alone. He's too great of a guy." I wipe a tear away and try to curb the emotion in my voice. "I can't do this with you, Jace. I appreciate your concern, but we can't talk about this anymore. I don't want to know if he's dating anyone or even if he's not.

Because one of these days, you're not going to tell me he's not seeing any-one, which will mean he is, and it'll break my heart."

Fuck. Stop crying, right now!

"Please don't cry, Sam." He lets out a long breath. "I hate this."

"Yeah, well, it is what it is. So, listen, I've got this crack-pipe calling my name and that orgy to get to, so if there's not some more heartbreak-ing stuff you'd like to discuss, I've gotta hop on that dick waiting for me."

"Jesus, Sam. That's not even funny." I can practically see him grimace.

"Yeah, it is. Just a little." I laugh as tears fall, and I cover my mouth to stop a sob from escaping.

I hate this. I hate this so much. Why can't I tell him how much it hurts? Why do I have to pretend I'm okay, when clearly I'm not?

"Okay, maybe just a little, because it's not true. But don't talk like that. It's so raunchy. I understand you're just trying to lighten your mood and stop your girly emotions, but you don't have to drum up degrading images to do it."

I take a deep breath and clench my fist, digging my nails into my palm. "Desperate times call for desperate measures. Anyway, tell me what you're doing today."

"I've got homework, and then tending bar later this afternoon. If I didn't have such a busy schedule, I'd come home and spend the weekend with you."

"It's okay. I've got a lot of homework to do, and then work tonight."

In a quick rush of words, he apologizes for what happened when he was home for Thanksgiving. He also shares the news of the ban he and his friends put out on me when I was fourteen and reinforced at every turn. It actually makes me feel good. I'm sure he thought I would be upset with him, but, I said, "Honestly, it probably was a good thing."

"Yeah?" he asks, surprised.

"It allowed me to keep my focus on my education instead of being sidetracked by boys and all the messy stuff that comes with teen love and heartache."

Kinda like what you're going through now?

"I also told Veronica to go take a flying leap and never darken my or your doorstep again."

I'm sure his actual words were much more colorful and less diplomatic. I wish I could have heard it. "Really?"

"Joseph went with me for backup, just in case I fell prey to her wanton ways. I ended up doing just fine."

"I can't believe you did that for me."

"I love you, Sam. You're the best person I know. I want to be just like you when I grow up."

"Shit, Jace. Are you trying to make me cry again?"

He laughs. "No. But I have to say this, and then we won't talk about it again, at least not until the timing is better. Joe is the second-best person I know, and if you two can make it work, I'm behind you 110%. Anything you need, I'm there for you, even if it means not talking about the elephant in the room."

"I love you, Jace. I'd do anything for you too. You know that, right?"

"Well, what's not to love?" he jokes.

I'm thankful for him turning the heavy back into light again. "Exactly. Okay, go rock your life, kick ass, and take names."

"You too. Bye, sis."

"Bye, bro."

An hour later I get a text:

Joseph: *Sweetness, I heard you were crying today. I'm sorry I'm not the one to dry your tears. I'm YOURS. There's no one else. No women. No one but you. Remember that. We just need time.*

Time.

I plop down on my bed, trying to think of a response. A million things run through my mind, but none of them are appropriate for the type of relationship we're trying to maintain. All of them tell him how much I miss him. How much I hate the distance between us, both physically and emotionally. All of them open my heart up even more to the brokenness I fear is inevitable.

I need to stay focused on school and not get sidetracked with the what-ifs. The bottom line is these are just words, and his actions say he doesn't want me as I am today, not enough to fight for it. Who's to say he'll want me enough in the future? How much time does he want and to what end? And why the hell won't he even talk to me if I'm supposed to be waiting for him?

Before I can come to any conclusion on what to say back, my phone chimes with another text.

Joseph: *Tell me you hear me.*

Me: *I hear you. You're saying you're MINE.*

Joseph: *Yes. And YOU. ARE. MINE.*

His. But not in any tangible way. Not in a way that soothes my ache and comforts my thoughts.

Words.

All he's given me are more words. A throwaway text after two months of nothing.

Easily broken.

Easily forgotten.

Easily left behind.

Joseph

Dad and my brothers are flying in to have a family meeting with me. I'm concerned. They've never done this before, and I'm wondering what's so urgent it couldn't wait until I'm home for spring break next month. Dad insisted taking a few hours out of his Saturday to fly in was no hardship, and I haven't been home since New Years, so it'll be good to see them, but I'm worried all the same.

Jace is at the library studying and then works tonight. I have the house to myself and have been anxious since Jace's phone call with Samantha this morning. I tried not to listen, but when I heard him tell her not to cry, my resolve broke, as did my heart. The idea of her being alone in that big house crying nearly had me driving to Dallas to be sure she's okay. If my family wasn't flying here, I would have already driven there and had her in my arms by now. I'm so close to breaking all my plans, just to be near her.

I'm trying to be mature by staying away from her, but it's never been more difficult than it was this morning. I felt a modicum of peace after texting with her. She was reserved in her words, but I believe she's just trying to protect her heart. I don't blame her. I'm trying to protect her heart too. I'd do anything for her, and if it means staying away from her and reducing contact as much as possible, then that's what I'll do.

I screwed up that night at the restaurant, but the thought of her on a date with someone else…I had to see her, damn the consequences. And the memory of the way she looked, smelled, the sounds she made when I made her come…it's enough to keep me going.

It shouldn't have happened, and I shouldn't have slipped and told her to wait for me. It's obviously made things harder, more confusing for her. But if she knew the timeline, it would basically press pause on her life.

My career is important, my family is important. I'm not sure I can say they are more important to me than her anymore. My own happiness is not more important than hers. She needs time to find out who she is, live her life, and finish college. She needs to be sure I'm the one for her, because once I decide to go for it, once I have her—nothing's going to stand in my way.

But it's taken everything I have in me not to break down and call her every fucking day.

A sharp knock at my door alerts me to my family's arrival.

I swing open the door, happy for the interruption of my pondering and the familiarity of my dad and brothers.

"Hey, Dad." I give him a hug as he walks in.

"It's good to see you, son." He pats me hard on the back and moves on to the living room.

"Hey." Matt gives me a big hug. He's a hugger, gets it from our mom. He has a soft heart like her too, though he does a good job of hiding it.

"Good to see you," I say after he releases me.

Fin steps in last, giving me a hug and a manly kiss on the cheek. He's always been affectionate with me, maybe more so than with Matt. He doesn't judge me for my feelings for Samantha. He's supportive, though I don't think he truly understands the depths of my feelings.

"Brother," he says.

"Fin," I reply, getting the distinct feeling I'm not going to like this visit much.

He nods as if to confirm my suspicions.

I follow them into the living room, my heart pounding. It feels like the time I snuck out of the house and took Mom's car. I lost my virginity that night. Managed to make it home without anyone finding out, or so I thought. Dad cornered me in the kitchen the next day insisting I tell him where I'd gone and what I'd done. The high from experiencing sex for the first time came crashing down with Dad's reprimand. Matt sat at the kitchen table snickering over his bowl of cereal. Fin called me later, from college, to congratulate me on getting grounded and laid all in one fell swoop.

I told him it was totally worth it.

I wonder if my argument today will be the same.

More as a delay tactic than being a good host, I ask if they'd like anything to drink or eat.

"Joe. Sit." My dad is a man of few words. He believes in direct communicating with no frills to distract from the message.

I sit in the only remaining chair, waiting for what I'm positive is going to be an unpleasant conversation.

After a few moments of blaring silence and pointed glances between me and my brothers, I break. "What's going on, Dad?"

He clears his throat, something he always does before he dons his *boardroom* voice. My brothers and I were too young to know what he really sounded like in the boardroom, but it was something our grandfather had said one time and it stuck. Whenever it was discipline time, Dad brought out the boardroom voice, and we knew shit was getting serious.

"How are you doing?" Dad asks, not using his boardroom voice at all.

I'm shocked and thrown off now, unsure what to expect. "I'm fine."

He nods slowly, understanding *fine* is not at all how I am.

"How's Sam?" He surprises me again.

He's showing me his hand, going about it gently instead of power-housing me. But either way, if he wants to talk about my relationship with Samantha, this is not going to go well. I crack my neck and stand up. I'm taller than all of them, particularly my dad, who's closer to Jace's height at six-two. I may not have the financial or business backbone he has, but I have my height and pure determination to not let him or anyone else intimidate me.

I take a step closer to him, not hiding my distrust of this line of questioning. "Why do you ask?"

He chuckles and sits back in the chair with the air of a man who doesn't have a worry in the world. "It's a simple question, son. It should have a simple answer."

"She's fine," I bark.

He laughs again, and it pisses me off. I glance at Fin and Matt, who both look like they'd rather be anywhere else but here right now.

"What's this about?" I'm not one to beat around the bush either.

"I'm concerned for your future. Your determination to focus on your career, to focus on MCI." There, he finally got to the point.

"Nothing has changed, Dad. I'll graduate next year and then head up the tech side of MCI," I say flatly. "I've stayed in contact with Uncle Max, as usual." Well, maybe I haven't been *exactly* as on top of things—I drank heavily for a while after Thanksgiving trying to forget her, but I'm back on track. "Nothing's changed," I reiterate.

He leans forward. "*Nothing* has changed?" His eyebrows nearly disappear under the sweep of hair on his forehead.

"No." I try to steel my words with the conviction I'm not necessarily feeling.

"Son, I recognize a man in love when I see one. And you're sick as a dog who got hold of a rat poison-laced bone. You can't see straight. You're not eating properly, and you can't concentrate for shit. She's got you all tied up in knots inside and out." He stands and moves to me, placing his hand firmly on my shoulder. "Have I missed anything?"

I slump, the air in my sails deflated. "No, that pretty much sums it up."

He smiles and pulls me into an unexpected hug. "Love is the greatest gift you'll ever receive, until it's not. It can rot your brain if you let it." He pulls back, placing both hands on my shoulders, holding me at arm's length. "This can go one of two ways, son. You let your love for this woman make you stronger and more determined than ever to reach your goals, so you can be the man you are destined to be and the man she deserves. Or, you let this love sidetrack you, turn your brain to mush, and sour your future and hers." He releases me and returns to his chair. "You've moped around long enough over your situation. You need to take the bull by the horns and show it who's in control."

I sit down, stunned by his words. "You're not telling me to forget her?"

His face softens with a warm smile. "Joe, she's a wonderful girl. She's bright, determined, comes from a good family, and she's already a part of the MCI family. She wants a future there. You want a future there. You like each other—maybe even love each other. I have no doubt you two will make a powerful team, if you can just get out of your way long enough to focus on what needs to happen to make a successful run at it."

"You like her?" I'm still surprised by his support. I thought for sure he'd tell me my life has no room for love right now.

He chuckles and points to Fin and Matt sitting like bumps on a log. "You're the youngest, but maybe the brightest of your brothers. You've already figured out there's more to life than a successful career. It took me a while to figure it out, but your mother is the best thing that ever happened to me. *She* gives my life meaning. And you boys." He shakes his head at Matt, who's pulled out his phone and tuned us all out. "To answer your question, yes, Joseph, I like her a lot. I can't wait to welcome her into our family. *After* you two graduate from college." He leans forward. "Stick to the plan, son. Find a way you two can coexist and still function to make that happen."

I flop back in my chair with a stupid grin on my face. It's one thing for me to plan on a future with Samantha—it's another to have my family's support. It's a boost that shows me I'm making the right decision even though it's a hard one.

Dad stands up, scanning us. "Now…" He claps his hands, rubbing them together. "I'm hankering for a steak your mother probably won't approve of, and a few too many dark ales I *know* she would not approve of."

He heads to the door with Matt in tow.

Fin comes over and offers me his hand. "You alright?"

Clasping his hand, I let him tug me up. "Yeah, just surprised."

I collect my keys, phone, and wallet, then turn to him. "You could have given me a heads-up."

He slaps my back, harder than necessary. "Now, where would the fun be in that?"

"Asshat," I mutter.

He laughs. "Hey, you know if it was going to be bad news I would have had your back, right?"

"Yeah, I know. But you didn't have to enjoy my stewing so much."

"Ah, stop being such a pussy."

With that one glorious word, my mind goes back to Samantha. I've been called a pussy a lot in relation to my feelings about her. I don't even give a shit anymore. I take it as a compliment, because if she makes me softer, kinder when it comes to her, then I'm all good.

Now, I need to stop being such a whiny ass and take control of our situation. I need to be proactive in my approach instead of being reactive.

Dad said love. I wasn't sure if I was there yet, but now I have no doubt I am.

I love her.

Now, I need to be the man who deserves her.

Sixteen

Samantha

"HEY, DAD, WHAT'S UP?" I ANSWER MY PHONE, STILL in bed.

"My morning surgery was canceled, leaving me with a little extra time I'd love to spend having breakfast with my daughter. Meet me at our usual place?"

He probably called my mom first, but she had an important meeting this morning. I don't hold it against him. It's my dad, and everyone takes second fiddle to my mom—him, his job, and even us kids. "Sure." I hang up and rush around like a madwoman so I can meet him and not be late for class. Luckily, I have a free period this morning, so if I'm late it's not the end of the world.

It's just a perfectionist thing in me. I'm never late, at least not since I've been in control of my schedule. In elementary school I was late a few times due to my parents running behind. They quickly realized I didn't need their help to get ready and turned their efforts toward Jace and themselves, knowing I'd be in the car waiting for them. And I was, every day, until I was old enough to drive myself.

I manage to make it out the door in under fifteen minutes. I don't have any makeup on, but most days I only wear mascara and lip balm, and I can do that in the car on my way to school.

Ten minutes later I'm pulling into the diner parking lot. I find my dad's car right away, but there's no parking spots near him. I continue to the back of the lot, park, grab my purse, and rush inside.

I spot him in a back corner booth. "Hi, Dad." I give him a kiss on the cheek. His skin still holds his tan from Hawaii a few weeks ago.

"Hi, pumpkin." He gives me a quick squeeze before I sit across from him. "You made good time." He studies me for a moment, his smile softening into a tender look of love. "You're beautiful. You remind me so much of your mother when she was your age."

My mother is a beautiful, sophisticated woman. She is all the things I don't feel I am. "Dad, you didn't know mom at my age."

"Psshhh, I saw pictures. And I knew her a few months after she turned eighteen. You're nearly eighteen. Practically the same age."

He motions the waitress over so we can order. "Where has the time gone?" he asks wistfully. "It's hard to believe you're basically the same age she was when I fell in love with her."

"You mean when you *both* fell in love?" I tease.

His laugh warms my heart. "I fell before your mother. It was pretty much love at first sight for me. She needed a little more convincing." He takes a drink of coffee. "I had a reputation back then—she doubted my ability to commit to her."

I love hearing Dad talk about how they fell in love. His eyes light up and shimmer in a way they only do for her.

"And you? You didn't doubt it?" It sounds like he's talking about Joseph and me. Joseph is my father, and I'm my mom. The similarities are striking, except the whole lover boy reputation is not Joseph's reputation.

"I've never doubted it for a second, Sam. I'm telling you, the minute I laid eyes on her, I was done for. I only had eyes for her from there on out. I still feel the same way. There's no one else. There never will be."

The smile on his face says it all, how happy and content he is. It must be a wonderful feeling to be so certain and feel so loved.

"I love that about you, Daddy. The way you love Mom. The way you never shy away from telling her or anyone else." I avert my eyes. I don't want him to see them fill with tears.

"*Daddy.* You haven't called me that in a long time. I've missed it." He smiles. "What's to be shy of? It's not weak to love a woman. In fact, it takes tremendous strength to love and commit to another person for life. I want that for you, Sam. Based on what I saw over Thanksgiving and the avoidance I've seen since, I think you've found it. A little earlier than your mother and I did, but not by much. I sense you're afraid, but you don't need to be. I see the man Joseph is, the man he will be. I see the way he looks at you, the way he treats you. He'll make you a good husband."

"Daddy! We're not even seeing each other," I admonish.

Stop! Just Stop. I don't need you feeding my hopes and dreams. I do it enough on my own.

"Don't let fear stand in your way, pumpkin. You'll be eighteen in a few weeks. Old enough to make your own choices, not that you're not mature enough now, but people tend to listen more when your age equals your maturity. But you've always been more mature than, well, all of us, I think. Don't let your mature ways scare you off from what's right in front of you. Have a little childish hope and belief left in you to see the life you could have with him."

I'm thankful when our food arrives. I brush my tears away and focus on eating and enjoying these precious moments with my dad. The rest of our conversation is more lighthearted as he tells me about an interesting case of a child he operated on yesterday. I get lost in his passion for his job and his patients. If you'd never heard him talk about my mom, you'd think *this* was his first love, but it's a close second. Though, he'd say it's Mom, me and Jace, and then his job. In that order—no arguments.

When we finish it's nearly 8 AM. I've got thirty minutes to make it to class. I excuse myself to brush my teeth and freshen up in the restroom before heading to school.

Dad's waiting for me by the door when I come out. He gives me a big hug. "I'm glad you made it, Sam. It's good to have this time to catch up."

"Thanks for inviting me." I decide not to mention I know he probably invited Mom first. There's no point in making him admit it. Plus, there is nothing wrong with him inviting Mom before he did me. It's the way it should be.

Someday I hope to be someone's first choice.

As we exit, he heads toward his car, and I point to the back of the parking lot. "I'm over here. I'll see you when I get home from work tonight."

"Alright, have a good day. Kick ass, Sam."

I just laugh and shake my head. "You too, Dad."

"Hey, what happened to '*Daddy?*'"

"I grew up." I keep walking to my car.

"You're never too old to call me Daddy, pumpkin," he hollers across the lot.

"Goodbye, Daddy," I yell back, ending this ridiculous conversation. I chuckle to myself as I approach my car. As the humor wanes, my mind wanders back to what he said about Joseph. I'm surprised by his observations and that he's telling me to go for it instead of telling me to focus on my education. I guess he wants me to have what he and Mom have.

My key fob in hand, I unlock the car.

"Sam."

My motion falters as a familiar bone-chilling prickle raises the hairs on my neck and sends shivers down my spine. His German-but-not-exactly-German accent is too distinctive for it to be anyone else. The same dreaded voice from months ago.

Before I can turn around, something hard presses into my back. This time I don't hesitate. I hit the panic button on my remote, setting off my car alarm.

"Stupid bitch," he hisses in my ear, too close to be drowned out by my car alarm.

He spins me around. I'm not surprised to see the man who used to sit at the bar at my work and approached me months ago in the parking lot.

He backs away from my car, motioning me to do the same. He's holding a gun pointed at my chest. "You never told your father. Why not, Sam?"

He's right. I never did. My dad was out of town when it happened, and by the time he was back, my panic had subsided. I decided to wait and see if I saw him again. When he never showed, I assumed it was just some bizarre prank.

"Sam!" My father's voice booms from behind me. I don't take my eyes off of the man with the gun.

"Ah, Daniel, so nice of you to join us." He points the gun at my father.

"No! Please, don't shoot him," I plead.

The man laughs. "I don't intend on killing him, Sam." He redirects his aim at me. "Now you, on the other hand, are a different story. Daniel…" He glances over my shoulder. "Step closer so I can see you, but not too close."

We're in the back parking lot, secluded between two buildings. It's not very likely anyone will come upon us unless their car is parked here.

My dad comes into view to my right.

"It's okay, Sam," he says softly.

No, it isn't. My palms are sweaty, and my pulse pounds in my ears. I'm determined to remain strong and not be a distraction or a hindrance to my father dealing with this man.

"Roderick, let her go. She has nothing to do with this." Dad's voice is full of conviction.

Roderick laughs again. "Daniel, Daniel, Daniel, you should have listened to me. It's too late for bargaining. You should have given me what I asked for. Now you have to choose between protecting your patient or your daughter."

Dad moves closer to Roderick, putting himself between us. "She's just a kid. Let her go. I'll give you what you want, but you need to let her get in her car and drive away. I'm not helping you as long as she's in danger."

I don't think I've ever heard my dad's voice be so commanding. If I were this man, I'd do as he says.

Roderick shakes his head. "You're still trying to manipulate me, Daniel. There are no negotiations here. You will go to your office and get me what I want. Then I will release your daughter."

Dad steps closer. "No," he says firmly.

Roderick's face turns hard, impassive. He cocks the gun still pointed at me. "No? I will shoot her, Daniel. I have killed those more important to me than her. Don't push me."

Dad steps closer. "Roderick, I will help you. I said I would. You don't need to threaten my daughter's life." His eyes flick to me quickly. "Sam, get in your car."

"Daddy," I whimper, my gaze teetering between him and Roderick.

"Do as I say, Sam." His voice brooks no argument, but I can't make my feet move. I'm pinned in place by fear.

"Move and I will shoot you and then your father," Roderick barks.

The threat is evident, yet instead of feeding my fear, it bolsters my confidence. I step forward, grabbing my dad's hand. "You won't have time to shoot both of us. If you shoot me, my dad will be on you so fast you won't know what hit you. If you shoot him first, then I'll be on you just as fast. I may not be as strong, but you won't take me easily."

My dad squeezes my hand tightly in a show of solidarity. But all I want to do is wrap myself around him and disappear.

Roderick's face twitches into a twisted smile. "You have balls, girl. You should be proud, Daniel. I've watched her for many months. She's a good girl, strong, independent, but maybe not so smart."

"I am proud." Dad slowly pulls me behind him. "I couldn't be more proud of her. Please, Roderick. Let her go."

"Hey! What the fuck?" A deep voice comes from the side of the building.

I chance a glance as a burly man comes into full view rounding the corner.

Roderick pivots quickly, his gun follows, pointing at the man.

I want to yell at the guy to *look out*, but before I do, my dad yells, "Get down!"

The gun jerks in Roderick's hand a split second before the shot rings out, echoing as if in slow motion, hitting the side of building, barely missing the man's head as he ducks behind a parked car.

"Sam." Dad's face encompasses my vision as he abruptly turns, diving to cover my body with his.

His face and my name on his lips are last thing I remember before the gun goes off again.

PART 7

THY WILL BE DONE

Seventeen

Joseph

A RINGING PHONE JERKS ME AWAKE, MY HEART pounding as if it was a siren blaring in the room. I arrived home from class and laid down to rest my eyes for just a few minutes. An hour ago. I guess I was more tired than I thought.

I stretch as I reach for my phone on the nightstand. "Hey, Dad." I stifle a yawn. I don't want to sound like a total slacker.

"Joseph." His use of my full name has my attention immediately. He only uses it when I'm in trouble or he's about to be terribly serious.

I also hear the strain in his voice. "What's wrong?"

"I just got off the phone with Eleanor," he says solemnly.

I sit straight up in bed, my gut filling with dread. "Mrs. Cavanagh?" I clarify. Maybe he means a different Eleanor—not Jace and Samantha's mom.

"Joseph—"

"Fuck, stop calling me that. You're gonna give me a heart attack. Did something happen to Samantha?" It can't be Jace. I just talked to him before I laid down.

"I don't have all the details…"

Fuck. Fuck. Fuck.

"…Sam was having breakfast with her father. Some man pulled a gun on them—"

"Christ, no!" I stand up and pace. "Please, Dad, tell me she's okay." Panic surges through my body.

"She's okay, son. Or she's going to be—"

"What the fuck does that mean?" I throw my bedroom door open and charge into Jace's room just to be sure he isn't here. He's not.

"Joseph, I know this is hard, but let me get this out before you jump to conclusions."

"Yes, okay. Sorry." I stop in the living room and sit on the edge of the couch.

"Both she and her father were shot."

Oh Christ. Jesus. No!

I squeeze my eyes shut, waiting, just waiting for him to finish.

"Sam's in surgery. They expect her to recover."

I let out a breath and open my eyes, seeing stars for a moment. "And her father?"

"He died, Joseph, I'm sorry to say." Dad's in tears.

It's my undoing. I start to cry even though I need to hold on tight and get to Dallas to my girl.

"Dad," is all I can manage.

"I know, son. It's a horrible situation. But Sam's going to be okay. That's something to be thankful for." His voice is comforting, and I wish I were already home.

"Does Jace know?" Dread fills me thinking of his reaction.

"Eleanor was calling him as soon as I hung up with her. She called me because…well, she wanted to get you boys home as quickly as possible. It's a tough situation. She needs to be strong for her kids, but she also just lost the love of her life. We're going to help get them through this," he says with absolute certainty. "Listen, the jet is on its way to you. You and Jace just need to get some clothes together for a week or so and get to the private airport. It'll be there waiting for you. It's faster and safer than you two driving home."

"Thanks, Dad. I appreciate it. Do Fin and Matt know?"

"They just walked in my office. I'll fill them in. I wanted to tell you first, get the ball rolling with getting you both home."

I'm in a daze, not sure how to proceed.

After a moment of silence, my dad's voice interrupts my thoughts.

"Joseph, you need to get a move on. The faster you get your stuff together, the faster you'll get to see Sam."

"Yes, you're right."

"I love you, son. And I'm really sorry about this. We'll get through this together. All of us."

"I love you too."

After we hang up, I sit for a moment envisioning the conversation he's having with Matt and Fin. Then I think of Jace. I hope his mom is able to reach him. If I don't hear from him in fifteen minutes, I'm going to call him. I need to give her a chance to be the one to tell him. Sometimes we need that connection from a parent we just can't get from friends, no matter how close we are.

I'm in the middle of packing when my phone rings. "Jace. I'm so sorry, brother."

"Joe." His voice cracks, struggling to keep it together.

"I know, man. We'll get through this. Focus on getting home to pack. My dad sent the jet. It'll be waiting for us."

He lets out a sigh of relief.

"We'll take it one step at a time. You're not alone. I've got your back. *We've* got your back."

I finish packing and start getting some of Jace's stuff laid out on his bed. He's not going to be thinking straight, so I'm trying to think for him.

I've done all I can and start to pace in the living room. Watching the minutes tick by is pure torture.

I call Fin.

"We've got you. Matt and I are almost to the hospital. Victor will meet your plane." He rattles off the facts like a to-do list, which is surprisingly comforting.

"Samantha…" I choke, not able to tell him what I really want to say.

"Joe, man. We've got her," Fin says.

"Concentrate on getting home. Let us focus on what's happening here in Dallas," Matt chimes in.

"I'll text or call with any news," Fin reassures.

"Thanks."

"You're welcome, brother."

I hang up, still anxious. I need to get home to my girl.

My Sweetness.

Joseph

Jace and I were a mess on the flight home. He more so than I. I was only stressed over Samantha. Jace was dealing with the loss of his father, his sister getting shot, and a mother who's even more of a mess than he is. I tried to console him, be his rock. But I was lost in my own thoughts most of the way here.

A herd of cattle couldn't have kept me away from Samantha once we reached the hospital. Thankfully, no one tried to stop me. We were greeted by my dad and brothers as soon as we walked through the waiting room doors.

Dad takes Jace in his arms as soon as he's within reach. Jace buries his face in my dad's shoulder and starts to cry. My dad just holds him tighter. "It's alright, my boy, let it out."

I sigh in relief. Dad thinks of Jace as his fourth son, which is exactly what Jace needs right now.

I move to Fin and Matt, hugging both of them close, taking a moment to remember how important they are to me. I fill with a sense of peace and thankfulness for my family being here. They're a deep well of support, not just for me, but for Samantha, Jace, and Eleanor too.

Fin fills me in. Our moms are keeping vigil by Samantha's bedside—she's out of surgery, but hasn't regained consciousness. With the blood loss and sedation, they don't expect her to fully wake up for a while. They haven't seen her yet, but it's good news she's not in the ICU.

Deciding to give Jace the time he needs with my dad, I make my way down the hall to Samantha's room. I knock on the door but don't wait for a response before I open and close it quietly behind me. Mom is sitting next to Eleanor, holding her hand. They're just sitting, too deep in thought to hear me knock.

Mom sees me first and relief spreads across her worried face as she takes me in. "Joe," she sighs. "I'm so glad you made it." She meets me half-way across the room and wraps me in her arms.

"Nothing could keep me away." Though her head hits me mid-chest, she is the one hugging me, comforting me. I hold her tightly.

Eleanor stands, shakily, and makes her way to us.

I release my mom with a quick squeeze. "Mrs. Cavanagh, I'm so sorry," I choke out before enveloping her in my arms.

"Thank you." She pats me softly. "Sam will be so happy to see you. She woke up earlier and asked for you."

My heart soars—even in her sedated state she's thinking of me. "Does she remember what happened?"

Mom comes back to my side. "She wasn't awake long enough for us to determine what she remembers. She said your name and fell back asleep. The nurse said it could be hours before she wakes up for any length of time."

I release Eleanor and steel myself for my first good look at Samantha. She's lying in the hospital bed. Her head and knees are elevated, IVs in her left arm, oxygen tube in her nose, and machines at the head of the bed where all those tubes seem to connect. Her hair's spread out over the pillow as if she's peacefully asleep. Pale, but still beautiful.

Sitting on the side of the bed, I hold her left hand in mine. "How is she? I mean, where is she injured and what did the doctor say?" I need all the details so I know what we're dealing with.

Eleanor moves back to her chair and rests her hand on Samantha's leg, but only closes her eyes instead of answering my question. She's heart-broken, obviously.

My mom sits back down and gives me a reassuring smile. "She was shot in her right shoulder. Miraculously, the bullet only nicked her collarbone and passed straight through, missing any major arteries. There's tissue damage and she'll have scars, but both should improve over time."

Samantha's right arm is in a sling, her hand resting on her chest. I touch her hand lightly and trail my fingers up to the top of her hospital gown. I can just make out a bandage under the neckline. I pull it back enough to see more of the bandage covering her shoulder. I study it for just a moment before covering her back up, continuing to trace my fingers down her jaw, and then cupping her soft, warm cheek.

My Sweetness.

I close my eyes, trying to compose the mixture of emotions rising in me. I want to cry for her loss and anguish over the death of her father as well as her own trauma. I want to get on my knees and thank God for sparing her life. I want to crawl in bed with her and never let her go.

"Eleanor, why don't we go see Jace and leave Samantha in Joe's care? He'll let us know when she wakes up. You've had a long day and need to get some rest yourself. There's a chance she may not even wake up tonight. You should get some rest while you can," Mom suggests.

Eleanor only takes a moment to study Samantha and then me. "Yes, she's in good hands." She nods and gets up.

My mom meets my eyes. "I'll send Fin in to answer your questions."

"Thank you."

I promise to contact them the moment she wakes up or if I have any additional news.

Not even a minute later, Fin comes in the room followed by Jace. I study Jace for a quick moment as he settles into the chair his mom vacated. He's haggard, worn out.

Fin comes closer. "The doctor said the surgery went well. She lost a lot of blood, but she's young, in good health. They expect her to recover fully."

I have questions. I don't want to make this harder on Jace than it already is, but it can't wait. "What happened? Tell me everything."

Fin sits next to Jace. "An eye witness says he came upon them in the parking lot. A man was pointing the gun at Daniel, who had Samantha behind his back."

Protecting her. He was protecting her.

I look at my sweet girl and squeeze her hand. I can only imagine how scared she was.

"The witness yelled out and the guy turned and shot at him. He didn't get hit, but he dove behind a car and didn't see what happened next. He only heard the second gun shot. By the time the assailant ran off, the witness found Sam on the ground with her father in her arms. She was busy caring for her father, as were the EMTs when they arrived. No one checked her out. They all assumed the blood on her was from Daniel. It wasn't until she passed out they realized she'd been shot too."

Christ.

"Until the police obtain the video surveillance and Sam wakes up, we won't know any more details, unless another witness comes forward," Fin concludes.

Jace leans forward, his eyes locked on Samantha. "The witness said he heard a *second* shot, assuming one more. If he only heard one, how did both my dad and Sam get shot?"

I was worried he'd shut down on us. I'm happy to see him present and thinking.

"The working theory is that given your father was shot in the heart—his left side, and she was shot on her right, the police believe your dad turned to face Sam just as the other shot was fired. The bullet hit him first and then continued into Sam. With their height difference it's a reasonable conclusion."

"Do we know…" Jace chokes back a sob.

Fin puts an arm around him. "It's alright, man."

Jace shakes his head, as if he's trying to dispel his emotions. "Did my dad die immediately?"

Fin nods with a grimace. "The EMTs said he was already gone by the time they got there." His eyes lift to mine before continuing. "He was shot in the heart. It would have been pretty instantaneous." He seems to ponder for a moment before continuing. "He didn't suffer long, if that's what you're concerned with."

"That's something, I guess," Jace mutters.

My eyes focus back on sleeping beauty. "She saw her father die." My voice is low, almost a whisper in reverence for what those words hold.

"Yes," Fin's reply is nearly as soft as mine. "The police said the EMTs had to pry Daniel from her arms. She was holding him tight, rocking him against her chest."

"Jesus," Jace vocalizes my sentiments.

I smooth her hair from her forehead, caressing her face as gently as possible. "She's gonna be a mess."

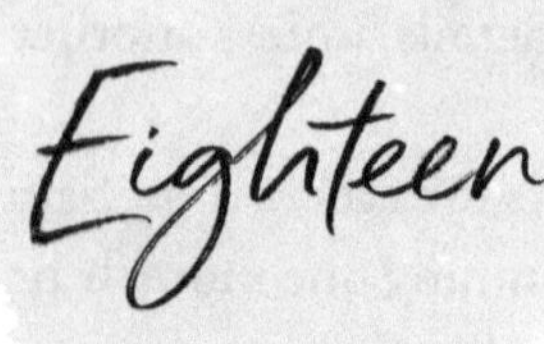

Samantha

I BLINK MY EYES IN THE DIMLY LIT ROOM. MY HEAD pounds like little coalminers are trying to dig their way out. My entire body hurts, even to breathe. It takes me a minute to clear the fog from my brain. I look around slowly, my head rioting against any quick movements.

Jace is lying in a bed a few feet away on his side facing me, sound asleep. Peaceful.

I scan my body, noting I'm lying in a bed similar to the one Jace is in, but there's a weight on my legs. My heart lurches at the sight of Joseph asleep with his head in my lap. My hand is resting on his cheek. Did he place my hand there or did I? Did I need his comfort, the contact, even in my unconscious state?

Joseph.

Jace.

Why are they here?

I survey the room, needing more clues.

Damn fuzzy brain. *Think!*

I've got nothing.

I hate to do it. I hate to wake him up. I flex my hand on his cheek. His stubble tickles my palm. If I weren't so groggy, I might have giggled.

"Joseph," I manage to croak as I run my fingers along his silky dark mane.

"Hmm?" he mumbles, opening his eyes, blinking up at me. "Sweetness." He immediately sits up. "You're awake." He seems relieved.

Shakily, I touch his face. I'm so weak. He places his hand on top of mine, holding it securely against his face.

"I'm so happy to see you." The pained emotions behind those words are apparent, but he doesn't really look happy.

Why?

"Why are you here?" I peer over at Jace and then back to him. "I don't…" My thoughts fumble for the reason I'm here.

Joseph captures my hand in his. "It's alright, baby. You've been asleep. Give yourself a minute to wake up. Adjust."

"Where?" I manage.

He nods. "You're in the hospital, Samantha. Do you know why? Do you remember what happened?"

His smooth voice is comforting and melodic. I close my eyes for a moment before opening them. "Talk…to me."

A small, sweet smile dons his lips. "You want me to talk to you?"

I nod, grimacing as my head revolts.

"Are you in pain?"

"Head. It's my head." I close my eyes, thankful for the dark.

I hear the beep of an intercom and Joseph speaking to someone on the other end.

Panicking, I open my eyes to confirm he's still here, to focus on him. I squeeze his hand. "Don't go."

My eyes slip closed despite my desire to keep them open.

Soft lips brush against mine. "I'm not going anywhere, Samantha. Rest. A nurse will be here in a minute to help with the pain."

I mumble my response, at least I think I do. I'm not sure.

I'm starting to drift.

A soft female voice and a gentle touch wake me up. I open my eyes to kind gray eyes watching me.

"Ms. Cavanagh, I'm Charlotte, your night nurse."

Nurse?

I nod, though I'm not sure why. It feels like I should acknowledge what she's saying even though I don't really comprehend what it means. Why would I need a nurse?

She asks me a list of questions about my physical state. I do my best to answer.

On my right, Joseph stands, watching me. "Joseph."

He smiles. "Yes, Sweetness."

"You're here."

He chuckles. "Not going anywhere. You can stop being so surprised each time you wake up to see me here." He moves closer, touching my cheek before his lips press to my nose. "I'm not leaving you. I promise."

Thank, god. "Good."

"Ms. Cavanagh." The nurse brings my attention back to her. She's holding up a cable with a button on the end. "This is for your pain meds. You can push it every fifteen minutes—more than that and nothing will happen. I would recommend you use it so you stay ahead of your pain. At least for the next twenty-four hours, I wouldn't wait until you're hurting to press it."

She holds up her hand. "I brought you a pill to help with your headache. Do you think you can swallow it?"

"Water," I croak.

She smiles and holds up a cup with a straw, bringing it to my mouth. I take a drink and then swallow the pill, finishing off the water.

She leaves with the promise to bring me back a tumbler with ice water along with some chicken broth.

Am I hungry?

Joseph gently massages my temples, running his thumbs across my brow, down my cheekbones, along my jaw and back to my temples. "Rest, baby."

He does it over and over again, slowly, tenderly, with just a hint of pressure.

I succumb to his healing touch as my eyes flutter closed.

"Samantha." Joseph's deep voice pulls me from sleep, his hand gently caressing my cheek.

I open my eyes to him sitting on the bed at my side. My eyes are still heavy, it's hard to keep them open.

"I'm sorry to wake you." He holds up a mug with a plastic lid. "The nurse brought some broth. I thought you might like to try to drink it while it's still hot."

"Kay," I manage with tremendous effort.

He punches a straw through the lid and takes a quick sip, making a satisfactory nod of approval. "Not bad."

Pressing the straw to my lips, he offers, "Small sips. It's hot, but not too hot."

I take a tentative pull on the straw, relishing the warmth as it coats my raw throat, which feels like I swallowed sandpaper.

Joseph continues to feed me, alternating between drinks of water and chicken broth until I've had enough.

I notice Jace is gone from the bed he was sleeping in before. *How long ago was that?*

"I sent him home." He smiles, grabbing hold of my left hand. "It's just you and me tonight." He bends down and kisses my forehead. "How's your head? Better?"

It takes me a second to remember why he's asking. I nod. "It's better." My voice is smoother but still crackling with the effort.

He frowns. "Your throat's sore, isn't it?"

"Dry. Scratchy."

"I'll get you some throat lozenges. It should help."

Pulling out his phone, he steps away and quietly asks someone to bring some lozenges, cough drops, or hard candy, anything to help my throat.

He hangs up, watching me watch him, and returns to my side. "Fin's going to bring you something for your throat."

I frown. "No. Don't trouble him."

"It's no trouble. He's here anyway. He brought me dinner and was just hanging out a while in case you needed anything." My confusion must show on my face. "I ate while you were sleeping."

Sleeping. The thought prompts a yawn I try to stifle.

He gives me a knowing look, bending down to kiss me. His lips are soft and tender against mine. Pulling back, he seems sad, his voice chock-full of emotion. "Rest."

He kisses me one more time, then moves to solemnly peer out the window into the night sky. His jaw clenches, and his hands are tightly fisted at his sides.

"Joseph," I call to him.

His eyes meet mine over his shoulder. "Rest, Sweetness. I'll still be here when you wake up. Promise."

"No."

His brow arches and then softens into a true smile as he stalks closer. "No, huh?"

"What's wrong?" I'm nearly in tears, and I don't know why.

His cups my face, his thumb caressing my skin.

"Shhh." He leans down capturing my mouth once again. "You can hardly keep your eyes open. Rest, Samantha. I promise to not leave you, but I need you to sleep now." He kisses my forehead, then sits on the side of the bed. "Close your eyes."

Reluctantly, I do as he asks. It won't take long for me to sink into slumber.

His warm, strong, capable hands begin to massage my face and head as he did before. But this time with no additional pressure, just light tender soothing touches that have my shoulders relaxing and thoughts drifting off…

Joseph

It didn't take long for her to relax under my hands and fall asleep. Fin arrived shortly after, having bought lozenges for her throat in the gift shop. He stayed for a while to visit, keeping me company, and helped me move the extra bed to the other side of hers. I want to be closer to her, but not block access to her injured shoulder, as the nurses will continue to come in and check on her through the night. In the end, I settled on her left side, my bed nudged right up to hers.

I intend it to stay there until someone tells me I need to move it.

I settle in, having brushed my teeth and changed into shorts and a t-shirt. I lie here watching her, her hand nestled in mine, her breathing soft and content. Her face is lax and has more color than it had when I first arrived. Her right arm is bound by the sling resting on her rising chest. She's a dream, an angel, and a heartbreak waiting to happen.

She's been too drugged to remember, to comprehend what's happened. She seemed to accept she's in the hospital and is apparently happy to have me by her side, which boosts my confidence tenfold for being the one to stay with her. Jace wanted to stay, or he felt like he needed to stay, but his mom needed support too.

I, on the other hand, *wanted* to stay almost more than I *needed* to.

My need is far different from Jace's, though. While we both love her in different ways, his need comes from obligation as her brother and now being the man of the family. My need comes from a much deeper and perhaps darker place. Mine comes from the need to protect what's *mine*.

Part of protecting her is to be here in any way she needs me to be, and if it's as her nursemaid, then give me scrubs and sign me up.

Mine to protect.

Mine to hold.

Mine to comfort.

Mine to heal.

Mine to love.

Mine.

I close my eyes as that word races through my mind, filling every empty thought, empty craving, empty promise, empty memory. Thoughts of her fill me to near capacity. I fear I will detonate from the sheer force of all those empty *everythings* being expelled from every cell of my being.

Mine.

Hers.

Hers to protect.

Hers to hold

Hers to comfort.

Hers to heal.

Hers to love.

Hers.

I. Am. Hers.

I'm roused from sleep by screaming, my hand gripped in a vise.

"No!" my girl screams.

Adrenaline rips through my body with as much power as her next scream. "Daddy, no!" She's still asleep.

"Samantha," I call to her, moving as quickly as I can, half-lying on my bed and hers, pulling my covers, still tightly wrapped around my legs, with me.

"Wake up," I plead with her thrashing, whimpering form.

With another jarring move she screams in pain as her injured shoulder takes the brunt of her escapades.

I move closer, wrapping her in my arms, avoiding her right arm and shoulder as much as possible.

"Samantha, wake up," I say firmly and sigh in relief when she starts to relax in my hold.

"Joseph." The pain in her voice guts me to my core.

She remembers.

My girl remembers.

"I'm here, Sweetness." My tears fall, mixing with hers as she sobs in my arms. "I'm here."

I'm here.

I'll always be here.

Nineteen

Samantha

THERE'S A SOLEMN MOOD COATING MY WAKING state. Tears are never far from my eyes. I feel up-ended and drained physically, mentally, and emotionally.

I remember.

I remember it all.

I should be sad. I should prefer not to remember, but I can't bring myself to feel that way. Those were the last moments of my dad's precious life, and it's a burden I will gladly carry. It should be *my love* carrying them and not the murderous heart of the man who took his life.

The police have come and gone. They accurately surmised most of what happened. I filled in the rest.

If they know who Roderick is—they aren't saying.

If they understand his motive, what information Dad had that the killer wanted—they aren't saying.

They aren't saying much, actually. They want me to give and give so they can take and take.

I stand for it. I allow it, as if I have a choice. It's the only hope we have for answers. For a reason for my father to be dead that makes sense—even though nothing could justify or truly explain it.

My hospital room is full of remorse and sadness from my mom and brother. Understandably so, but difficult to breathe through. They were here when I woke this morning, their obligation to be here heavy in the air. I feel the weight of it, and it's oppressive.

Joseph is hovering…hovering…hovering.

Agitation crawls up my skin. I can't stand it. I throw back the covers, swinging my legs over the side of my bed, grimacing and biting back pain from the sutured hole in my shoulder. The hole from the same bullet that killed my father.

Fuck. That hurts.

Joseph jumps up. "Christ, what are you doing?"

He's in front of me faster than I can move, stopping my progress. "I'm going for a walk," I bark, pushing his hands away.

"Wait. Just wait." His voice softens as he kneels low enough to see my downcast face.

"Sweetness." His tenderness is unhinging, and my traitorous tears begin to fall again.

I peer at him, roughly wiping at my face, sneaking a glance at my family, who watch me with bleary-eyed despair.

"I have to get out of here, or they need to leave—or both," I whisper.

He nods. "Let's take a walk, then maybe they'll let me take you outside in a wheelchair for some…fresh air."

I sigh with relief. He understands. I need to get away for perspective more than fresh air.

Joseph talks quietly with Jace and my mom, suggesting perhaps I've had enough of visitors for a while. I escape to the restroom. When I come out, they give me gentle hugs and quick goodbyes, seemingly relieved to be leaving.

Robe and slippers donned, Joseph and I make our way out of my room.

He takes my hand, twining our fingers with a need to be in constant contact with me since I woke up last night screaming, screaming as I relived the events that stole my father's life away.

"Do you think maybe next time you need a break you could tell me instead of hurting yourself to get out of bed?" He glances sideways at me, watching, calculating my reaction and his response.

I sigh. "Yes, I suppose I could." He seems satisfied by my answer, yet I'm not. "I can do this Joseph. You don't have to stay. I appreciate you being here and all you've done for me. But I can take care of myself."

I've been doing it my whole life, it feels like.

He squeezes my hand. He's calm like he expected me to say as much. "Just because you can take care of yourself doesn't mean you have to, or that you should." He repeats his sentiments from our first dinner together.

We stop at the end of the hall. Before heading back, he pivots in front of me, still holding my hand. His free hand snakes in my hair, tugging gently to lift my face to his. "Samantha, you're not alone. I'm here. I *want* to be here. Let me."

His eyes bore into mine trying to drive home his point. I think there's more he wants to say, but he remains silent. He left me in silence for so long…but he's here now.

I nod once.

Satisfied, he presses a kiss to my forehead before we resume our walk down the hall.

It's a long day with multiple walks and visits from Margot and Joseph's family.

Margot stays to help me with a shower. The nurse offered but was convinced to let Margot and Joseph handle it once I confirmed I was okay with it. Keeping my wound dry is a challenge but Joseph is good at applying the water proof covering the nurse provided.

My robe drapes open at the collar to reveal my wounded shoulder. Joseph tenderly kisses along my neck, pausing at my ear. "Are you sure you don't want me to help you shower, Sweetness?"

I muffle a moan and shudder at the thought of him having his hands all over my wet body. My elation is marred by the pain that shoots through my shoulder. I wince with a whimper.

He grips my waist, bracing me against him, sighing. "I'm sorry. I shouldn't have done that." Turbulent green eyes meet mine.

"I'm not. It was hot." I kiss his cheek, thankful that on this day, full of so much sadness, he finds a way to make me feel desired, cared for yet not pitied.

I join Margot in the bathroom where she's been setting up, getting everything ready.

She jokes, helps me relax and not feel self-conscious about sitting naked in a shower chair as she washes my hair, alternating handing me soap and rinsing me off as I wash my body.

She ends up getting pretty wet in the process. If she weren't so tiny, she could have worn some of my clothes my mom brought earlier. But as it is, she heads home for dry clothes and a date with Bobby, Sebastian's friend.

Sebastian came by today. He was on duty in the ER this morning when he heard news of a trauma that came in yesterday, on his day off, of a father/daughter shooting. Nobody besides me had his number, and honestly, calling people was not anywhere on my list of concerns. Out of curiosity he checked the computer for notes of the trauma as a learning tool. He was shocked to find out the daughter was me. He was livid when he showed up at my hospital door, but relaxed when he laid eyes on me and saw that I was okay.

I was worried how Joseph would respond to him, given his response in January when he thought I was on a date with Sebastian. Joseph couldn't have been any nicer. They actually talked about Sebastian joining the next Six-Pack poker night. I'm not sure if I should be happy about that or be upset he's no longer jealous of Sebastian.

I'm pouting when Joseph comes back from walking Sebastian out. *Is he my friend or Joseph's?*

Joseph stops in his tracks. "What's that look for?"

"You!" I point at him in frustration, standing up from the chair I've occupied for the last hour. "You nearly mauled me at the restaurant the last time you saw me with Sebastian, and now you're…you're like best buds. Do you want to date him?"

His toothy, dimpled smile only infuriates me more, which makes him throw his head back and laugh that rich, deep laugh of his.

Ass!

He cocks his head and stalks toward me, gently wrapping me in his arms. "Sweetness, are you upset I'm not acting all jealous? Is that what this is about?"

"Hmph," I reply, picking at invisible lint on his broad, muscled chest.

He leans down. I feel his smile, even though I can't see it. He kisses my jaw, and then tilts my chin so he can see my eyes. "Do you need me to ravage you against the wall like I did last time to make you feel better?"

My insides clench in hopeful anticipation.

Jesus, what's wrong with me? I've been shot, and my father just died. "No."

His all-too-knowing smile is back. "Sebastian and I came to an agreement. Therefore, I trust him to keep things as just friends. But make no mistake, Samantha, I will rip any man's head off if he tries to touch you."

"Oh." Fuck. That's sexy as hell.

His lips brush mine. "Yes. '*Oh.*' Are we good?"

I nod, still trying to get my bearings.

"Good." He notices my still-wet hair clipped on top of my head. "Why don't you let me dry your hair, and then we can curl up on the bed and watch a movie. How's that sound?"

I rest my forehead on his chest. His hands caress my back, and I let out a deep sigh. "It sounds like heaven."

PART 8
SAVING GOODBYE

Twenty

Joseph

I LEAVE HER ON THE COUCH WITH JACE AS I HEAD TO the kitchen to get us some food. Fin and Matt are sitting at the island eating, drinking beer. The guests have all left; only immediate family remains, hers and mine. The funeral and reception are finally over. I can breathe again. It's been a hellacious week. Samantha has been a trouper through it all, pulling more than her own weight. Jace and Eleanor have been in a daze. I'm sure if I wasn't here, if my family wasn't here to help out, they'd step up more. At least I hope they would. But, I'm not willing to take the chance and leave Samantha all on her own. Plus, there's nowhere else I'd rather be than by her side in whatever capacity she needs.

"Hey," I say to Fin and Matt, wondering how they'd react if it was our father who was killed. Would they shut down or would they step up and be the men I believe them to be?

"Hey," they reply in unison.

"How's Sam?" Matt asks.

"She's okay. She's hanging out with Dad and Jace at the moment. I need to get her some food."

Fin motions around the kitchen to the assortment of foil covered to-go containers, glass casserole dishes and the like scattered around. "Take your pick."

"The lasagna is really good. There's salad too, if you think she'd like that," Matt offers.

I put together a couple of plates for her and Jace on a tray with some

165

drinks, napkins, and any other items I think they may want or need. After I take it to them and get her settled with promises she'll actually eat, I return to the kitchen to visit with my brothers.

I grab a beer and some food, then join them at the island bar. I take a couple of bites and have to agree with Matt, the lasagna's really good. Sometimes, there's nothing like good old comfort food to hit the spot.

"Thanks guys for being here today, this week. We couldn't have gotten through all of this without you both." In all sincerity, that's the truth. Beyond keeping the place packed with food, running errands, helping with funeral planning, Fin even worked with Samantha's principal, after approval from Eleanor, to get her school work sent home and organized a tutor if she needs help.

They try to brush me off, downplaying their parts.

After a few minutes of companionable silence, Fin speaks up. "She's a great girl, Joe," he says pointedly.

I meet his eyes. "Yes, she is."

"She's crazy about you," he says.

My beer stops midway to my mouth. "I'm just as crazy about her."

"She's a tender soul. Be careful there." His eyes are fierce with protectiveness for her and that gets my back up.

"Fin, is there something you want to say to me?"

"I just did," he says dryly.

"Why are you getting all bent out of shape?" I finish off my beer and get up to dump my paper plate in the trash. "You know how I feel about her. We've talked about this, probably more than we should."

He lets out a breath, running his hands over his face. It's been a hard day for all of us. "Look, I don't mean to be a dick, really. I'm just worried about her. There's a sorrow, an emptiness. I'm worried you being all *Mr. Practical*, and *it's not our time*, will break her."

"I can't fuck this up." My shoulders sag at the thought.

They both mutter their agreement.

I lean against the counter. "She needs my support now. That's why I'm here." I stare at the wall as if I can see her on the other side. "That, and the fact there's no way I wouldn't be here for her or Jace. I don't want to hurt her, but I don't want to lead her on either. I can't give her the future she deserves yet."

"Joe, I don't disagree with anything you've said. I'm just saying, her father dying makes it more complicated, makes her more apt to get hurt. Be sure, no matter what you do, she knows *why* you're doing it. It might make it an easier pill to swallow."

"Maybe you need to rethink the whole timing thing," Matt chimes in. "Isn't she gonna be eighteen soon, anyway?"

"Yeah, in a few weeks. But it's more than that, she needs to focus on college and what she wants to do with her life. I don't want to be the reason she doesn't pursue her dreams, her aspirations. I want to help her become who she's supposed to be, not be the reason she doesn't become it. She needs time to experience life." I wish I had the answers, an easy fix.

"Wherever she ends up, isn't that where she's supposed to be?" Jace's voice sounds from the doorway, his brow arched in question.

"Okay, Buddha," I tease. I take the tray from him and hand him a beer, figuring he could use it.

"Thanks," he says, making his way to the island to sit by Matt. "She went in to see Mom, in case you're wondering." He smirks at me, knowing that was in fact the next question out of my mouth.

Dad comes in shortly, and we discuss the plan for the next few days.

The weight of this day and the conversation we just had hangs heavily on my mind.

♡

Samantha

I slip into my parents' room. Mom's asleep, which I figured she would be. I need to see her, if only for a few minutes. I close the curtains and move to close the ones on the French doors that open to the backyard. Instead, I find myself standing there, admiring their semi-private garden. I sit on the chaise lounge in front of the doors, lost in thought. My father had this private area put in a few years ago, to give them privacy when their curtains were open and not feel like anyone in the pool could see directly into their room. I thought it was a really romantic gesture. Something I imagine having someday, maybe even with Joseph.

Mom stirs, and I turn to see her watching me.

"Mom?" I move closer. "I'm sorry, I didn't mean to wake you."

She frowns. "No, your father woke me." She touches her lips. "He kissed me and told me to wake up." Her sad eyes roam his side of the bed. "That obviously didn't really happen."

Oh, god. I swallow the lump in my throat and sit on the edge of the bed, holding her hand. "Can I get you anything? Fresh water? Food?"

Her eyes slip back to mine, trying to focus through the haze of her sleeping pills.

"Sam." She cups my cheek. "Your father was always so proud of you. He'll be really angry when he realizes he's going to miss seeing you grow into the woman you're destined to be, finding your way, making a life and a family of your own."

"Mom," I plead as tears begin to fall again. They seem endless these days.

She squeezes my hand. "In some way, he'll see you. I'm just sorry it won't be in the tangible way he had always planned. He was looking forward to walking you down the aisle when you marry Joe."

"That's not…you don't know if that will happen. He…just don't talk about Joseph like that. It's too painful to think about, especially if it never happens."

Patting my hand, she leans close. "Sam, life is too short. Don't let that man get away from you if he's the one you choose." Her gaze turns to the French doors. "I know what I'm talking about. I never thought I'd be a widow in my forties."

Overcome with emotions and unwilling to break down in front of her, I hurry to her bathroom, blow my nose, and splash water on my face. When I open the door, Jace is sitting on the edge of the bed where I just vacated. He brought her some food.

I put my hand on his shoulder. He snakes his arm around my waist, pulling me onto his lap. "How are you holding up?"

I nod and try like crazy not to cry. My chin starts to tremble, and I'm going to fail miserably. I quietly cry on his shoulder as he rubs my back. "It's okay, Sam. You don't have to be brave. It's okay to cry."

That makes me cry even harder, and then I hear my mom's heartbreaking sobs. *No.*

I jump off Jace's lap, moving the tray of food out of the way. He moves closer and pulls her into his arms, and then wraps his arm around me, holding us both, as I hold both of them.

It's a heartbreaking thing, to hear your parent cry with such sorrow, such loss, such hopelessness. I don't blame her; I don't think I could stand to lose Joseph, and we are nowhere in the same place that my parents were. They were each other's soulmates, their other halves. She's faced with having to live the rest of her life missing half of herself. It's frightening for me to even consider my future without my dad in my life. I can't even fathom the depth of despair she's feeling. I can empathize, but I can't truly understand the magnitude of it.

To top it off, there's my brother, who's the happy-go-lucky life-of-the-party guy, but tonight he's breaking. My older, stronger, tougher-than-me brother is crying. I don't blame him. I don't think less of him. There is no shame in his tears. It is just hard to witness. It puts the reality of the situation front and center.

I don't know how we move on from here. I don't know how we knowingly, actively move forward without my father. He wouldn't want us to stagnate, stay where we are in loss and grief, but the knowing and the reality of the action is daunting, to say the least.

I slowly pull away, kissing them both on the head, and take Mom's tray of food to the kitchen. She's not going to eat it, at least not now.

The house is quiet. Joseph's family must have left. According to the clock in the kitchen, it's only nine, but it feels so much later. I'm exhausted. I take one look at the kitchen and know I'm not going to bed anytime soon.

I turn on the water, open the dishwasher, and start to rinse and load the dirty dishes. I'm lost in thought, or maybe I'm lost in no thoughts at all, when I feel strong arms around my waist.

"Sweetness." Even he sounds sad.

He's been my rock this week, in the hospital and out. I've tried continually to distance myself from him, but he continually pushes through my barriers, knocking them down one by one.

"Don't be nice to me, Joseph, or I'll start to cry again. I don't think I can take anymore today," I warn.

He kisses my neck and squeezes me gently. "Tell me what I can do to help."

I glance over my shoulder at him and around the kitchen. "We have to find a place for all this food. Can you throw away what's nearly gone or not worth saving? Maybe make a place for things that don't need to be refrigerated. Then, when I finish the dishes, I'll start making room in the refrigerator."

"I'll make room in the fridge."

We work well together, organizing, tossing, combining food, making order out of apparent chaos. With my injured shoulder, it takes me longer than it would otherwise. I try not to think about it, ignoring the pain and weariness of my bones and aching muscles.

Of course, Jace comes in just as we finish. I start to laugh as soon as I see him.

"What?" he says, his blue eyes red-rimmed and completely confused by what I find so humorous.

With the back of my hand over my mouth, I try to stop, but I just can't. "I'm sorry, it just struck me as funny that just as we finish cleaning up such a mess, you come strolling in."

He stands there, arms crossed over his chest, annoyed. "I was actually coming to get something to eat. I'm still hungry."

I start to laugh harder.

He looks at Joseph, who only shrugs. "Hey, if you make a mess, you better clean it up."

More laughter.

Joseph captures my hand. "You're getting punchy, Sweetness." He pulls me into his side, wrapping his arm around my back with his hand resting on my hip. "How's your mom?" he asks Jace.

"She's resting now." Jace's sad smile says it all. He surveys me. "You okay, Sam? That was a little rough in there. I heard a little of what she said to you before you went into the bathroom."

"Yeah." My laughter silenced.

His eyes shift to Joseph and then back to me. "Do you want to talk about it?"

I shake my head. "No, Jace. I really don't."

"Okay," he says.

I grab his hand. "I love you." And slip out of Joseph's embrace to give Jace a hug.

He hugs me back, his head sinking into my hair. "I love you too, sis."

We stay like that for a few moments, then I ask him. "What do you want to eat? I'll get it for you."

He pulls away, a true smile on his face now. "Really?"

I chuckle. "Yes, really. Besides, we just cleaned up, and you're a bit of a tornado in the kitchen."

Joseph laughs behind me. "God, don't I know it."

Surprisingly, with all the food we have, Jace wanted bacon and eggs. I wasn't going to deny him, after all he buried his father today too. Joseph ends up wanting some. I make enough for the four of us, in case Mom wakes up and wants something later. I get the boys fed, wrap a plate up for Mom, make mine into a sandwich and leave the two of them visiting while I go shower.

Twenty-One

I SLIP INTO BED AS JOSEPH ENTERS THE ROOM ONLY wearing workout shorts. I lie on my side, pulling the covers up under my chin.

The bed dips behind me, and his warm body envelops me from behind.

I ask him the same question I ask every night, hoping I'll get a different answer. "Are you staying?"

"No." He nuzzles my neck, as his hand moves to my stomach, pulling me flush against him.

I'm turned on and disappointed at the same time.

"I can't stay in your room, Samantha. It wouldn't be right. I want to." He kisses my neck and chuckles when I shiver. "But, I can't."

I lay my hand over his. "My mom won't know. She's out of it right now."

He props up and tenderly pulls me to my back. His eyes lock on mine as he runs the tips of his fingers down the side of my face. "I'd know. And you'd know. I care too much to treat you that way." His lips graze my shoulder. "Now, roll back over and let me hold you for a while. I'll stay until you fall asleep."

I settle back on my side, wrapped in his arms, my back pressed to his front. How he can do this and not get turned on?

Slowly, my eyes get heavy, but a persistent thought keeps nagging me. "Joseph," I whisper, unsure if he's asleep.

"Sweetness." His sexy voice is so sure, so close, so comforting.

"If you're going to break my heart, please do it sooner rather than later." I clench my jaw, trying to keep my emotions from overflowing for the umpteenth time today.

He squeezes me tighter. "I'm not going to break your heart." He kisses along my injured shoulder.

"I just don't think I'd survive losing you too." My voice cracks and tears start to fall.

"Please don't think like that." He pulls me so tight, I think he'd crawl under my skin if he could. "I won't ever lie to you, baby. But I also won't promise you the moon when I'm not in the position to give it to you, not yet."

I sniff and wipe away my tears. "I think I can live with that."

He chuckles. "Good, 'cause I don't think I'd survive losing you either."

"I can definitely live with that."

"Good," he says softly.

"Good," I agree.

"Now, go to sleep. You know I need my beauty sleep."

"Goodnight, Joseph."

"Goodnight, my beautiful blue-eyed Sweetness."

Joseph

Jace catches me in the hall as I'm slipping out of her room. I run my hand nervously through my hair, knowing how it appears. He follows me into the guest room.

"So you're sleeping with her?" He's riding the edge of anger.

I close the door, so we don't wake up Samantha. I lean against it, facing him, trying to stay calm. It's been a really shitty week for him.

"No, Jace. I'm not sleeping with her." I cross my arms over my chest. "I wouldn't do that to her." Pushing off the door, I move closer to the bed. "We're not even messing around, except maybe a kiss here or there." I slump against the headboard. "She's hurting, just like you are. I want to be here for her, comfort her, be strong for her, be whatever the hell she needs me to be. But I'm not going to take advantage of her or the situation." Waving my hand. "Hence, why I'm in here instead of with her."

He sits on the end of the bed. "You'd rather be sleeping with her than staying in here?"

I almost laugh. *Is he serious?* "Is that a trick question?"

"No, I'm trying to judge where you're at. What she is to you." He runs his hands over his face and falls back on the bed. "I overheard my mom talking to her tonight. I only caught the tail end of the conversation before Sam disappeared in the bathroom, crying." His eyes fall to me. "My mom's hurting." He motions in the air. "Obviously. Who wouldn't be? She just lost the love of her life, the man she married when she was just nineteen and still in college. Just a year older than Sam and a year younger than me.

"Anyway, she was telling Sam how much our dad is going to miss watching her grow up, become who she's meant to be, and walking her down the aisle when she gets married…" His focus on me intensifies. "…to you."

"Shit. Your mom actually said that?" No wonder Samantha was upset tonight, talking about if I'm gonna break her heart, do it now and not later.

"Yeah, she did. Look, my parents love you, they love your family. They weren't blind. They saw what was happening between the two of you at Thanksgiving. And in the hospital, you stepping up to take care of her. I see it too. I think anyone who's around y'all for a few seconds can see it." He sighs and sits up, resting his arms on his knees. "The problem is, Sam doesn't believe it."

Shit.

That's ridiculous. I've told her she's mine; she knows I'm hers and that I just need more time. She knows how I feel; she has to. "What do you mean, she doesn't believe it?" My voice is eerily calm, not reflecting my inner turmoil in the least.

"I think she's *afraid* to believe may be more accurate. She told mom to stop talking about it. She couldn't stand to have those thoughts in her head, especially if they don't come true."

"She has a point, Jace." I get off the bed and start to pace, needing to move.

"Okay, now what do *you* mean?" His eyes bore into me.

"I mean…Fuck…Jace, she's a virgin, barely even been kissed. She's crazy smart, beautiful, compassionate…I could go on and on. But she's still young, not even eighteen. She's never had a boyfriend, barely any life experiences. You expect me to make a lifelong commitment to her now, before she's barely even started to live her life? Before she's who she's meant to be? It's like claiming her life before she has a chance to live it."

Awe, Christ, I'm gonna hyperventilate. I bend over, gripping my knees.

He presses his hand to my back. "Calm down, man. We're just talking here. I'm not accusing you, honest. I'm your friend, but I'm also her brother and her best friend." He laughs. "I see it now. It's destined to be, my two best friends, getting together, making a life for themselves."

"I wish it were that simple," I say, straightening up.

Studying me for a few uncomfortable moments, I notice for the first time he has the same blue eyes as Samantha and in some way, it is like I'm staring back at her.

"Joe, you're truly the nicest guy I know. You're incredibly smart too, but sometimes, you're a dumbshit. Maybe, it *is* as simple as that. Maybe what Sam is destined to be is your wife, and you her husband. Life, love, relationships, is not about what job you have. What Sam does, or will do for a living, is not who she is. And maybe, just maybe, she's not destined to be a tramp like me, but a one-man woman with you." He heads for the door. "Think about it." He opens the door and then pauses, not turning around. "Planning is all well and good, until it's not. Your life is happening right now. You're cheating yourself out of time—and no one knows how much we get. Don't miss out on what's right in front of you while you're planning for your future."

"She's not even eighteen, Jace," I whisper to his back.

"She will be in a few weeks. You and I both know she's more mature than most adults." He turns, pinning me with his stare. "If you don't want her, then don't be with her. Make it a clean break, and do it now. But if the only reason you're not taking the bull by the horns is because of her age, her inexperience, then that's crap."

I stifle a chuckle. "Are you telling me to sleep with your sister?"

He doesn't take the bait. "No, I'm tell you to grow a pair and don't fucking break her heart."

♡

Joseph

A warm body brushes against me, stirring me from sleep. I open my eyes, blinking, trying to focus. "Samantha?"

"I didn't mean to wake you," she rasps, moving a little closer, but not quite close enough.

I reach out and pull her flush against me. "If you're gonna be in my bed, at least come cuddle with me properly."

She lets out a low giggle. "There's a proper way to cuddle?"

"There is when it comes to you and me," I say with all seriousness.

"Oh yeah, and how's that?" Her voice is light with humor.

I wrap her in my arms, pulling her close to my side with her head on my chest. "As close as humanly possible." I tilt her chin up to gauge what's really going on. "What's wrong, Sweetness?"

It isn't until the words are out of my mouth I realize what a stupid question it is. *Her father's dead, and she's been shot. For fuck's sake…that's what's wrong.*

She lays her head back on my bare chest, her hand resting over my heart. "I just woke up and couldn't get back to sleep. My mind started racing, thinking about all that's happened. I…I just didn't want to be alone."

Of course, she didn't. I run my hand up and down her bare arm. "Do you want to talk about it?"

"Not really. Can I just be like this with you for a little while?" she asks softly.

"For you, my arms are always open for business." I kiss the top of her head.

176

"Business? Is that what I am?"

"Far from it," I scoff.

After a pause, she lets out a long breath. "Then what am I, Joseph?" Her voice is low, seductive even. It does things to me.

I run my hand down her back, and she arches into me, pressing her breasts against my side, letting out a small whimper.

Christ, she's going to make me hard in two seconds flat.

"You're my future, Samantha."

"What if I can't be the person you want?" she whispers, finally giving voice to her fears, letting me in.

Ridiculous. "What do you mean? You're already the person I want."

"You're the Ivy League boardroom CEO, man of the world, and well, I'm not."

"So?"

She shakes her head. "Can you picture me on your arm at company parties, fundraisers, schmoozing with the business, political, and social elite? Being the perfect wife who always knows the right thing to say?"

"No." I laugh. She tenses in my arms, but I hold fast. "You think I want that? Sweetness, I love your mind. Our compatibility. We're going to rule an empire together. Don't you dare relegate yourself to trophy wife material. That's not who I want."

"Oh." The tension leaves her body all at once as she finally understands my plans for us. I run my hand up and then down her back again. Each time I hit her lower back, she presses against me, then sighs, not in exasperation, but in pleasure.

"Please, stop doing that." Her voice, barely a whisper across my chest, makes my nipples hard and my cock stir.

I smile and do it again.

This time she wraps her arm around my waist and holds on as she squirms. *Christ.*

"Please," she says softly.

"Why? Why do you want me to stop?"

"Because."

"Because, why?" I run my hand down her back, stopping in that magical trigger spot, and trace circles across her heated flesh.

She presses against me, burying her head in my chest. "Joseph," she moans my name.

Christ almighty, my cock just got hard as steel hearing her say my name like that.

"Do you want me to stop because it turns you on?" My desire is evident in my voice.

"Yes." Her lips brush my nipple, and my cock twitches for attention.

"Does that embarrass you?"

"Yes." Her voice is barely audible.

"Do you have any idea how much it turns me on to know you're turned on?" Before she can answer, I gently roll us, taking her injured shoulder into account. I settle on top of her, my erection pressed against her.

"Is that your…" She can't even finish that statement. I have no doubt she'd be bright red if there were enough light for me to see.

"Yes, Sweetness, and it's all for you." I run my lips just barely across hers. "You're so beautiful, Samantha. You made me hard the second you walked in the kitchen that Friday before Thanksgiving break. All confidence and sass, and yet incredibly innocent and vulnerable at the same time." I press my lips to hers for a tender kiss.

As I pull away, she flicks her tongue out and licks my lips. I growl and go back for more, this time taking her tongue captive. She's going to be the death of me, I just know it.

Our lips lock together in an endless dance of need, want, and desire.

"Samantha." I break our kiss, moving to flick on the nightstand lamp, and pause to take in her heavenly face. The desire in her eyes nearly bowls me over.

"Am I hurting you?" I motion to her shoulder where her bandage is visible under her barely-there camisole.

"No. It's fine. Just don't ask me to put my hand over my head," she teases, trying to make light of her injury.

I kiss her shoulder tenderly. "I don't want to hurt you."

Her warm hand brushes my cheek. Our eyes meet and hold. "Joseph, the only part of me you're likely to hurt is my heart."

So brave. Always so brave. Facing her fears head on. *My girl.*

"Not gonna happen, Sweetness. I'm never letting you go."

I kiss her before she can verbalize what the shocked expression on her face means. I know she doubts me, my intentions to be with her for the long-term. I'll just have to prove it to her.

She moans as I deepen our kiss, holding her close.

My girl. I could have lost her.

I groan at the thought, my body at war with itself, wanting to just hold her and make her feel safe, reassure myself she is safe. And wanting to bury myself deep inside her, claiming her, making her mine.

My girl.

I stutter kisses across her face. "Do…you…want…to…stop?"

Her hands stop my kisses. I rise up to meet her gaze.

"No, don't stop." She lifts her lips to mine and plants a soft supple kiss, pulling away, sucking on my bottom lip, and then releasing it with a *pop.* "Don't ever stop."

Christ. I just got harder, if that's even possible.

I don't bother hiding my growl as I take possession of her mouth.

She moans in response, and it makes me want to please her more, turn her on more, do whatever is necessarily to hear more of those sexy as hell sounds of hers.

Her hands leave a blazing trail on my back and arms, pulling at me, urging, inciting my desire. I lay kisses down her neck. She arches, giving me free access to suck and lick my way to her ear.

"Wrap your legs around me."

My cock pulses from the sounds coming from her mouth and the feel of her glorious body beneath me.

She's only wearing panties and a camisole, and I'm in my boxer briefs. As much as I want to rip her clothes off, I'm not willing to take her virginity on the night she buried her father, nor am I willing to take it on a whim, even when most of my blood is taking up residence in my cock.

She slowly wraps her legs around my calves, rubbing her feet up and down my legs, pulling at me.

I adjust, settling my cock against the wet spot on her panties. "Look at me."

Her eyes meet mine.

I watch her face as I move my hips against her. She feels so good below me, better than I dared to imagine, and the need on her face tells me all I need to know.

"Joseph," she beckons in that sexy voice of hers.

"Let me take you there, beautiful." I grind harder, deeper, groaning when she moves her hips against my cock in rhythm with me.

"That's right, Sweetness. Show me what you need."

"Oh, God." She sounds desperate.

I ravaged her against the wall after New Years, but it was not nearly as intimate as this.

My girl.

"I got you, baby." I capture her lips, letting our bodies express how we feel for each other.

This is the beginning of something big, something important for our lives. I took to heart what Jace said earlier. I can plan the hell out of my life, her life, but if we're miserable for the next several years, is it worth it? When we can be together sooner, make a life together in the near future, isn't that a good thing? I'm not going to ask her to marry me tomorrow, but I'm done fighting what I've been fighting for months.

Her body starts to tremble, tensing with her imminent release. Her head falls back, breaking our kiss.

"Christ, you're sexy." I tweak her nipples as I grind against her. She circles her hips, bringing me along with her.

"Let it go, Sweetness. That orgasm you're holding onto is mine. Let me have it." I growl in her ear, barely managing to hold out for her.

She lets out a guttural cry, and I quickly stifle the sound with my mouth, swallowing her pleasure as she comes, quaking below me, continuing to move her hips with me, kissing me as if I'm her lifeline to her next breath. Her hands squeeze my ass, pulling me tighter against her.

The tingle starts in my balls, moving up my spine. I grind every bit of pleasure out of her orgasm as I fall into my own explosive release. "Samantha, fuck." I groan as my cum pumps across our bellies.

I don't stop grinding, and before I recover from my orgasm, she spirals into a second one, seemingly just as powerful as the first. I suck and pull on her nipples, prolonging her release as long as I can, relishing hearing my name on her lips as she comes for me.

I kiss across her face, chest, and neck as she recovers, not quite ready to break away from her to clean us up.

"You look entirely too proud of yourself," she taunts.

I chuckle. "I was just wondering if I'm the first to give you an orgasm. Obviously, not this time, but the time before." I'm almost embarrassed, thinking that I may have given her her first orgasm and in a public place nonetheless.

She rolls her eyes. "You have a thing for my firsts, don't you?"

I capture her face in my palms. "You have no idea."

"Would it make you happy if I say *yes?*"

I remember her saying those exact words when I asked if I was the first to touch her lush breasts. I give her the same smile I gave her then, one of complete satisfied accomplishment.

"Are you going to slowly claim each part of my body? Each of my firsts?" she asks.

"Oh, Sweetness, I have every intention of making every inch of you mine." I repress the desire to growl and bite her neck in total possession. I want every single one of her firsts.

My girl.

PART 9
DREAMS AND NIGHTMARES

MARCH

Twenty-Two

Samantha

JOSEPH AND I ARE OFFICIALLY SOMETHING. IT'S YET unnamed. Though he has introduced himself as my boyfriend instead of just a friend, or Jace's roommate, or Jace's friend. There are a lot of titles he could have chosen, so I guess it's something that he chose the boyfriend title. He's just never said those words to me.

He's only been gone a few weeks, but it feels like a lifetime ago he was here taking care of me in the hospital and the week of my father's funeral.

It sucks that we finally make it official—but have to be long distance. I know he wishes he were here too, and that makes it a little easier. And we talk every day, so there's no more radio silence, and that makes a huge difference. I don't know how I'd have survived the last few weeks without him.

Relying on someone like this scares me.

It feels too perfect to be real.

There's a knock at the front door, and my stomach plummets. I dread opening it. To be faced with the reality of what's out there. Who's out there.

FBI Special Agent Michael Hennessey greets me with a stiff smile. I think he might be even more uncomfortable than I am.

I step back, letting him enter. "Agent Hennessey, come in."

"Please call me Michael, Sam." His voice is gruff and curt.

"Michael it is, then." I lead him into the kitchen, offering him a drink, which he declines. I get myself a glass of iced tea and pour a glass for him, ignoring his harrumph when I hand it to him.

Surprisingly, he ends up downing half of it in one large gulp, making me laugh as I quietly refill it.

"Thank you." I'm gifted with a genuine smile. He should do that more often. He's actually really good looking when he smiles.

"You're welcome, Michael." I want to give him a hard time, but decide to let it pass. If, however, he keeps up this hard-as-nails exterior, I may have to work extra hard to break through his icy façade for no other reason than to have some sort of connection with the man who's best friends with Fin and Victor, and has come to talk to me about my father's death.

"Sam, I realize this might be awkward, given we met previously on a more personal level, but today I'm actually here on official FBI business."

He says it was personal before, but I don't believe that to be true. He came with Fin and Victor to the hospital to visit me. I got the impression he was there as a favor, to unofficially check in on me and get his impressions of the situation with my father.

"I figured as much from your phone call yesterday."

"Director Sinclair would like to speak to you in the coming days, but I asked to speak to you first as a courtesy to Joseph and your ties to his family."

That rubs me the wrong way. I understand what he's saying, but it irks me all the same that I don't qualify for special treatment on my own—I only get it because of my relationship with Joseph.

If he notices my silent disapproval, he's doesn't acknowledge it. "As I mentioned on the phone, the FBI will be taking over your father's case. We'll continue to utilize some of the local PD resources, keeping them in the loop, but I'll be your primary point person going forward."

I cross my arms, still irritated by all of this. "And why is that?"

"Why will I be your contact?" He scoffs as if I've offended him. "I told you, because of your ties to the McIntyres."

I lean toward him over the table, hardening my voice. "No. I mean why is the FBI interested in my father's murder?"

He nods, not bristling over my tone. "Because of your father's involvement with the FBI at the time of his death."

All the air in my lungs whooshes out in a huff. I clench my fists in an effort to focus on breathing. It takes me a moment before I can speak. "What?"

This time he leans forward, his voice softer when he speaks. "This information is confidential, Sam. It's important it not be repeated. If anyone else is to know, I need to be the one to vet them."

"What about Jace and my mom?"

"I'll bring them in."

"What about Joseph and his family? They're the whole reason you're even here." I sound bitter.

"I deserve that I suppose, but, for now, no."

"No?" I repeat.

"No. They don't fall in the need-to-know column," he says simply.

"But they're the reason you're here," I protest.

"The irony doesn't escape me."

"I don't want to lie to Joseph." I cross my arms. "He'll know if I'm hiding something."

"I imagine this will be difficult for you to keep from Joseph, but it's in the best interest of his safety, and in the best interest of the investigation. The fewer people who know, the better."

Safety? "Is Joseph in danger?" My heart races at the idea of any of my loved ones being in danger, especially Joseph, who's become my rock. I already lost Dad. I can't lose anyone else. "What do you mean his safety?" I shoot to my feet as if I'm going somewhere.

His hand grasps my arm. "Stay with me. I won't let anything happen to Joseph or anyone else." He pauses until I focus on him. "I'm more concerned about you at the moment. You're the one the killer was stalking. *You're* the one he shot. We're putting you under protection, but you should be unaware of their presence for the most part. For now, I want you to continue your normal activities—work and school."

"Why me? And why was Dad working with the FBI? He's a surgeon, not a secret agent!"

Michael sighs. "The less you know, the better."

With men posted outside to *protect* me, he leaves, giving me his card and cell number, telling me to call him day or night with issues or concerns. And of course, if I spot the killer, to call him immediately.

Someone shot at me once. What if he attacked again while Joseph was here visiting, or even tried to get to me through him? If he got hurt because of me, I'd never be able to live with myself.

My throat burns.

I stalk to my room and grab my phone.

"Sweetness." Joseph's soothing voice fills me with regret as soon as I hear it.

"We need to talk." I start to pace the floor, trying to psych myself up for what I'm about to do.

"Shit. What's wrong?" See, even he knows those four words never mean any good.

I take a deep breath and brace my hand against the wall, leaning forward, my head bent, my eyes closed. This is for his own protection. "I can't do this anymore, Joseph. This long-distance thing is too hard. I'm not saying never. I'm just saying not now."

Twenty-Three

Joseph

"FUCK. FUCK. FUCK. FUCK. FUCK!" I BELLOW INTO the empty house.

Thankfully I had the foresight to not throw my phone, as was my first inclination when she ended the call. I speed dial Fin.

"Hey, Bro. What's up?"

"She fucking broke up with me." I pace into the living room, not fucking believing this. It's been a rough few weeks, but I considered it growing pains. Us feeling our way, trying to make the long-distance relationship work. But, I never thought she would break up with me, not like this, not over the phone and when we weren't even fighting. Other than the distance, we've been perfect.

"Tell me."

"There's not much to tell. She just called and said she can't do this anymore. She said the *long-distance thing* is too hard." I punch the wall. "Fuck! I can't believe this." I swallow the pain in my hand. Thankfully, I didn't hit the wall hard enough to put a hole in the drywall. The pain gives me a temporary reprieve from the pain in my chest and the sickness in my gut.

I drop to the couch, my head falling into my hand.

"What did you say?" His shock is apparent.

"I didn't say much. I tried to get her to talk to me, but she said she couldn't and hung up. It was obvious she was upset. I tried calling her back, but she didn't answer—it went straight to voicemail—she must have turned off her phone."

I stand and gaze blindly out the window. "Something must have happened. I don't know what, but I'm going to find out. My first guess is something to do with her father. Jace is at work, so I doubt it has anything to do with him. The police won't give me any details about the case. Can you talk to Victor or Michael? I'd call them, but I think they're more likely to tell you."

"Agreed. I'll speak to them and call you back. Victor is off for the night, so it might not be until tomorrow."

"Understood." I let out a sigh of relief. "Thanks, brother."

"Of course. Try not to worry. I'll call you back as soon as I have any news."

I head to the bar where Jace works to see if he has any idea why Samantha would break up with me for no apparent reason.

He sets a shot in front of me, as lost as I am as to why Samantha would break up with me out of the blue. "She didn't say anything to me. I'll call her when I get off work. See if I can find anything out."

I groan in thanks and toss back the shot. I relish the burn as it slides down my throat and warms my gut.

Jace sets another shot in front of me, motioning over my shoulder. "Tiff's over there. I'm sure she'd like to take your mind off your troubles."

"Are you fucking serious?" I swallow the next shot before he can answer.

Jace's has been a fucking mess since his dad's death. All the progress he made after Thanksgiving regarding dating women instead of just getting laid left and right has all gone to hell. He's back to his old ways. Actually, he's back to his old ways times two. I walked in on an orgy last week. He and three women right in the middle of our living room. Last night, he and our friend Davis disappeared with some girl into his room, doing god knows what. I assume they were double teaming her. I've never known Davis or Jace to swing both ways, but he's not himself right now. He's heartbroken and taking it out on his body, his sex life, and anyone daring enough to get near his dick.

He sets another shot in front of me. "Sometimes you gotta do what you gotta do to get by." He shrugs and moves to the other end of the bar, filling drink orders as he goes.

I down the shot knowing I shouldn't, but welcome the numbness that dulls the pain of losing Samantha.

"Come on, Joe. You gotta help me out a little here. You're like dead weight, and you're bigger than me as it is." Jace pulls me along with my arm wrapped over his shoulder and his around my waist. I try to focus on his face and his words, but both are difficult at the moment.

I stumble over the doorjamb to our house, catching myself before I slam into the entryway wall. "You're a good friend, Jace." My tongue feels too thick for my mouth, and my words are a slurred mess. I lost count of how many shots I had after the first seven.

"Yeah, yeah. Be a good friend and make it to your bed before you pass out, huh?"

"You got it, brotha."

He laughs as he dumps me on my bed. My eyes stay open long enough to see him yank off my shoes.

$\sim\!\heartsuit\!\sim$

Joseph

"Ah sweets, that feels so good." Her tongue runs up the thick length of my cock, before circling the head with her talented tongue.

Fuck! Where'd she learn to do that?

Christ, I don't want to know that.

"Samantha, baby. Fuck." I groan as she swallows my cock, going deeper each time.

"Oh fuck. Yes." Her hot mouth consumes me over and over again. My hands fist the sheets to keep from sinking into her hair and pounding into her mouth until I come down her throat so fucking hard.

I moan at the thought, overcome by the vision in my head.

Then she's riding me, taking me deep. Her head is thrown back, lost in her own pleasure.

"That's right, baby. Make it feel good." I grip her hips as I thrust up into her, relishing her cries of ecstasy as she comes undone…for me.

She's gripping me, her hungry pussy sucking at my cock. "I'm coming, baby."

My head falls back, letting go, giving her all I have. Everything I have is hers. "Samantha."

Joseph

I wake up, my head pounding and my cock begging for attention. I roll to a sitting position, slinging my legs over the side of the bed, burying my head in my hands.

Fuck. I have to lay off the alcohol.

I stumble to the bathroom and turn on the shower, slathering toothpaste on my toothbrush and brushing vigorously while the water heats up.

As I shower the vision of my dream comes back to me, reviving my hard-on.

Christ, that dream seemed so real. What I wouldn't give for it to have been.

"Fuck."

I soap up my cock and fist it, reliving my dream. Samantha's sweet mouth and cunt all over me, eating me up. I rub one out, needing to savor the memory of my dream as the heartache of her words slams into me anew. *I can't do this anymore, Joseph…I'm not saying never. I'm just saying not now.*

"Samantha." It's a plea; it's an exultation as I come thinking of my girl in my fantasy and in my waking world where she doesn't want to be my girl. *I'm not saying never. I'm just saying not now.*

"Fuck," I grunt out as remorse fills my head and settles in my bones.

I quickly dry off, throwing on some athletic shorts, and stalk toward the kitchen in desperate need of coffee and aspirin.

"Hey, man," Jace greets me all too loudly.

I wince.

"That bad, huh?" He's amused.

Fucker.

"Worse. What was I thinking?" I swallow two aspirin and a full glass of water before tackling the Keurig.

He comes to stand next to me as I wait for my mug to fill with black gold. "So…I see you didn't turn Tiff away last night."

I huff out my exasperation, too hungover to deal with his happy ass this morning. "What the fuck are you talking about?"

He motions to my chest. "She's likes to leave her mark."

I study him for the first time today, really getting a look at his face. He's amused, but also guilty. "Jace, I know I'm hungover, but what the ever-loving-hell are you talking about?"

"Have you looked in the mirror?"

No, actually I hadn't. I kept the bathroom light off and my eyes closed most of the time. But I still don't know what he's talking about.

I stalk to the mirror in the entryway, seeing myself for the first time since yesterday.

"What. The. Fuck?"

I run my hands through my hair, pulling just enough to inflict pain. I need to be sure I'm awake. Realizing I am, I run my hand over my chest, over what I can only describe as claw marks: red vertical lines, down my chest, ending halfway down my abdomen. The skin is irritated with red puffy lines.

"Tiff likes to leave her mark," Jace says again, leaning against the wall, eyeing me. Now he looks guilty as hell.

"Christ, fuck." I sink to the floor as the realization hits me. "It wasn't a dream."

It wasn't Samantha.

It was Tiff.

And.

It.

Was.

Real.

"No. No. No. No. This cannot be happening." My head falls to my hands. "Jace, fuck, man. Please tell me that didn't happen last night."

My eyes burn with tears as I stare up at him.

He shrugs. "It's not cheating if she broke up with you."

"Are you fucking kidding me?" I bark.

"No." He backs up to the living room, scoping his options, like he needs to escape whatever's going around in his head.

Realization dawns again. "You knew."

I get to my feet and storm toward him. "Tell me you did not fucking send Tiff to my room, knowing I was completely shitfaced."

"You needed it, man." He backs up.

I press forward, pushing him just hard enough to make him fall back on the couch. "No! What I fucking needed was your sister. Not some random fuck from one of your leftovers." I loom over him, wanting to punch the hell out of his smug face.

Thinking better of it, I back up, running my hands through my hair. "Jesus Christ, Jace. What the fuck is wrong with you? Can't you see how fucked up this is? I was drunk out of my mind over your sister, so you send some girl into my room to suck me off?"

He points to my chest. "She did more than suck your dick. By the looks of it she rode you hard, holding on with her fingernails."

"Goddammit!" I can't fucking believe this. I collapse onto the adjacent couch, the grief and guilt hitting me full force. I close my eyes, letting my head fall back. "I didn't even know it was happening." I'm so fucked. How am I ever going to explain this to Samantha? Who would believe it wasn't my choice?

"You really didn't know?" His voice is almost unrecognizable and barely breaches my thoughts.

I don't look at him. I can't bear the sight of him. "I thought it was a dream. It was Samantha. The most amazing dream ever…a fantasy."

"Shit," is all he says.

"Imagine someone doing that to Samantha—sending some guy into her room when she's had so much to drink she's barely conscious. And he fucks her while she's lying there, thinking it's all a dream."

He swallows hard. "That's rape, man."

"Exactly. I didn't fucking consent to fuck Tiff. That's on her, but you're the one who sent her in there knowing the state I was in." I get up off the couch and stomp to my bathroom. I hold my breath before I look in the trashcan. Shit. I let out my breath. Thank god there's a condom and the wrapper sitting on top.

I can't believe this. I walk back to Jace, who's still slumped down on the couch. I'm determined to make this right. "Jace, I love you like a brother. But you broke something between us. I don't know if we can make this right, but I'm damn sure going to try to get Samantha back. If you can't get on board with that, then you need to stay the fuck out of my way."

I start to walk away.

"Joe."

I hear the regret in his voice. I stop, but don't turn around. "Don't. I can't deal with you now, Jace. You need to figure out your shit. You're falling off the deep end, and you have good reasons, but you have a mom and a sister who need you healthy and strong, not a lost manwhore, trying to corrupt his friends. Self-destruct by yourself. Leave me and your family out of it."

Heading to my room, I throw on a t-shirt to hide the evidence of last night.

I thought it was Samantha. I never for one second thought it was real, but the most amazing fantasy ever—that not only had she not broken up with me—but that she had given herself to me fully, completely, and without abandon.

Christ, fuck. This is a nightmare.

I can't tell Samantha Jace sent another woman in to… She's lost her dad. If she knew what Jace had done, she'd throw him from her life as well. She needs him—well, he needs to get his shit together first. But I refuse to take anything from her life. Which means I'll have to lie.

All I want is to make things right between us, but that means lying to her to salvage her relationship with her brother—if he doesn't self-destruct first.

I sit on the edge of my bed, taking a deep breath, and make the hardest phone call of my life.

Twenty-Four

I HARDLY SLEPT LAST NIGHT. AFTER CALLING JOSEPH and breaking things off with him, I called in sick to work and did the same today. I can't even get out of bed. I made my choice, but it doesn't feel like a choice, it feels more like something done to me. I couldn't put Joseph in danger. There was no choice in that. I can't have what happened to my father happen to him. I'm thankful for the first time that he and Jace are four hours away. It's not far, but it seems safer than if they lived here.

Now I need to do the same with Margo, Sebastian, and my mom. I need to distance myself from them so they aren't in danger. I guess that includes Jace too, though he's been absent since Dad died. I doubt he'll even notice.

I couldn't live with myself if anything happened to any of them.

My cell ringing startles me out of my stupor. I don't even lift my head to see who's calling—I don't care to see who it is. I let it go to voice mail. A few moments later, it rings again, and then again. I finally reach for it to see who's so persistent.

Seeing as it's Michael, I decide to answer. "Hello."

"Sam, why aren't you at work?" His gruff tone is less than welcoming.

"I called in sick."

"Why?" He sounds angry.

"Why what?" I'm feeling obstinate. He brings it out of me for some reason.

"Sam, don't play games with me. Why did you call in sick? You aren't sick." His irritation is apparent.

"You know what, Michael, I have a parent, and though I just lost my dad, I don't need another one. I'm home. I'm safe. I'm not going anywhere. I'm also ending this conversation." I hang up, and it feels damn good.

It's not like me to be so mean, but I'm raw. I'm worn out, and I can't take his judgmental shit right now.

I roll over and fight the tears that keep coming.

My phone rings again. This time I answer it on the first ring without even looking. "What?" I nearly holler into the phone.

"Samantha?"

"Shit, Joseph. I'm sorry. I thought it was…" I don't want to tell him I thought he was Michael—it'll raise all kinds of questions I can't answer. I can't have him figuring out why I broke up with him. I harden my voice. "It doesn't matter. Why are you calling?"

"I have to talk to you, Sweetness." He sounds upset. I guess he should be if he feels half as bad as I do since we spoke yesterday.

"I can't right now." I start to hang up.

"Please. Don't hang up. If you don't talk to me now, I'll just come there in person. One way or another you're going to listen." He's obviously not going to be as easily deterred as Michael was.

"Okay."

He lets out a deep sigh. "I have to tell you something."

After a few moments of silence, I can't take it. "What?" I brace myself for him to plead with me to take him back. *Stay strong. He's safer far away from you.*

A strange noise comes over the line, a noise of anguish. I panic at the thought of him crying on the line with me.

"I slept with someone." His voice is so deep and pained. "I didn't mean to. I didn't set out to cheat on you. I got drunk…and, she…well… it happened."

My stomach twists and lurches. *Don't be sick. Don't be sick. Don't be sick,* I chant to myself over and over again.

"Samantha?" His voice breaks through my mental chant.

"When?" I manage before the tears start to fall.

"Last night."

Oh fuck! I rush to the bathroom, dropping my phone, barely making it to the toilet before I lose the contents of my stomach, which isn't much since I haven't eaten. That doesn't stop my body from continuing to try.

When the heaving finally stops, the sobs start. Having barely recovered from throwing up, my breathing is choppy and strained. I fall back on my haunches, my eyes squeezed tightly shut, causing stars to appear.

I can hear Joseph's voice in the background. I'd nearly forgotten he was still on the phone. I pull myself up, rinse my mouth and splash cool water on my face. I grab the hand towel to dry off and sink to the floor.

In the quiet stillness of the bathroom, I can hear the panicked echo of Joseph's voice. "Christ, Samantha, please pick up the phone."

More expletives escape before I reach for it.

I clear my throat. "I'm here." My raw throat protests my painful rasp.

"Ah, fuck, I'm so sorry. Are you okay? I mean, from getting sick, are you okay?"

I've never heard such worry and helplessness in his voice. It nearly breaks my heart as much as the idea of him having sex with another woman does. How could he move on so quickly? Did I mean nothing to him? And why is he telling me? Is this revenge for breaking up with him, and he's trying to hurt me?

"I'm sorry, Samantha. I can't tell you how sorry I am." He continues to say it over and over again.

"Joseph—"

"Please, please forgive me.

"Joseph—"

"I'm so sorry, Samantha."

"Joseph—"

"I didn't mean to. I didn't want to. I would never—"

"Joe," I nearly scream.

He stops talking, his less formal name getting his attention. Finally.

"Don't call me that." His pain is palpable.

He fucked another girl the day I broke up with him, and he's telling me not to call him Joe? "We weren't together. There's nothing to be sorry for." The chill in my voice is unexpected, even to my ears.

"Samantha," he pleads.

I drag myself to my feet, turning toward the haggard woman in the mirror.

Please, Daddy, give me strength, I pray as streams of tears roll down my face and onto my shirt.

Squaring my shoulders and shaking the tears away, I give one last attempt to set him free. "I can't do this anymore, Joe. I'm saying never." I hang up the phone, turn it off, and set it on the counter.

"Goodbye, Joseph," I whisper to no one, as there is no one to hear me.

No one to take away my pain, my sorrow, my loneliness.

It is just me now.

That's all I need.

That's all I've ever needed.

All I've ever really known.

I should never have believed otherwise.

I knew better.

Shame on me.

I climb in bed, nearly numb to the events of the last twenty-four hours.

Nearly.

But not nearly enough.

I'll give myself tonight to feel the weight of what I've just lost.

Tomorrow. Tomorrow, I will lock it all away and begin again without my dad, without Joseph, without Jace or my mom, without everyone I have ever loved.

PART 10

HAZE

Twenty-Five

Samantha

MICHAEL WASN'T AS EASILY DETERRED AS I thought he was. He scared the crap out of me when I woke up sometime Saturday evening and found him sitting in a chair next to my bed, reading on my tablet.

"Jesus, Michael, you scared me!" I gasp, shooting up, trying to catch my breath.

He chuckles, obviously finding my distress amusing.

Asshole!

"Serves you right for hanging up on me earlier," he says pointedly.

"Really?" I sit against the headboard. "You were being an ass." I throw a pillow at him. He catches the pillow without even looking. "How did you get in here anyway?"

"I'm a trained operative. I can do lots of scary shit, the least of which is breaking into a locked house with piss-poor security." His head tilts. "About being an ass, yes, I guess I was. I'll try to curb my assholeness in the future."

He sets the tablet on my nightstand and leans forward. "I was worried about you. You didn't show up for work on Friday or today. I guess I could have been gentler in my delivery, but you could have given me a heads-up. I had people in place ready to cover you while you worked. I was angry and I let it get the better of me. I'm sorry."

Wow. I did not expect a hard-ass like him to apologize so easily.

"Apology accepted. I'm sorry for not telling you. Honestly, it never even crossed my mind."

"You're forgiven. I should have been clearer on the context of our communication. So, we'll start fresh." He sits back in the chair, lifting his jean-clad legs and feet to rest on my bed. "What's wrong, Sam? Why didn't you go to work, and why are you still in bed?"

The concern in his voice brings tears to my eyes. I close them for a moment to temper my response. "How do you know I'm *still in bed?* I could have just laid down for a nap."

He shakes his head. "I came in to see you when I first got here, but decided not to wake you. That was six hours ago. Try again."

I throw back the covers and get up. I'm only wearing a t-shirt and panties, but I refuse to feel uncomfortable in my own bedroom. If he plans to come into my room while I'm sleeping, he's going to see me in what I sleep in. I am, however, thankful I'm wearing an oversized t-shirt instead of my normal cami. I turn to face him with only the bed between us. "I'd really rather not talk about it, if it's all the same to you."

He studies me for a moment and nods, having come to some conclusion I'm quite sure he's not going to share with me. "Fine." He stands up and moves to the door, stopping to glance back at me. "Put some clothes on and come downstairs. I've got dinner on the stove."

I peer down at myself, holding the hem of my t-shirt out like a skirt. "What? You don't like my t-shirt?"

His eyes scan down the length of my body before returning to my face. "Oh, I like it just fine, but I don't think Joe would appreciate me seeing you in such a state of undress."

I cross my arms over my chest, trying to alleviate the ache the mere mention of his name inflames. "Joe doesn't have any say in who sees me in any state."

His progress stops again, and he turns to face me fully. "What did you do?" His words are quick and intimidating.

"Why do you assume I did something?" I huff in response, trying to intimidate him right back.

"Because that boy is so in love with you, there is no way he wouldn't be pissed at me standing here in your bedroom," he says with certainty.

So in love he'd punish me by sleeping with someone else. You know, 'cause he cares so much. "I wouldn't bet on that."

He studies me for a moment before he moves, stalking, backing me up to the wall. "I'll ask again. What. Did. You. Do?" He eyes me with laser beam intensity.

I raise my chin and square my shoulders, refusing to be intimidated by him. "I did what needed to be done. And he did the rest…"

"Hmph," he says as he backs away, turning to the door. "We'll see," he mutters before closing my door behind him.

❧

Joseph

My phone wakes me up early Sunday morning. My drunken hangover's gone, but has been replaced by my emotional hangover. I'm spent, wiped out, haggard as hell inside and out.

Fin's voice comes over the line before I even say hello. "The FBI has taken over her father's case."

He's got my full attention now. I sit up, shaking off my sleep fog. "When?"

"Michael went to see her Friday, late afternoon."

"She broke up with me on Friday."

"Yep."

"You don't think that's a coincidence, do you?" I'm beginning to see it's not either.

"Nope."

"Do you know why the FBI is involved?" My mind races, hoping I can turn this whole thing around. A part of me died yesterday when I heard her getting sick over the news of me cheating on her—or her thinking I cheated on her.

Actually, I think a part of me died even before then when I

realized it myself. I spent the day pissed as hell at Jace. It wasn't the truth, but I couldn't think of a better lie. I've still been plotting out how I'm going to make this right. How I can redeem myself for hurting her.

"Neither Victor or Michael are saying. Michael knows. He's the lead on the case. As for Victor, I'm not sure, but he's being tight-lipped either way."

"If the FBI is involved, it either means the killer is known to them or her father was," I surmise.

"I'm venturing it's both."

"What aren't you saying, Fin?"

He lets out a sigh, a rare sign of Fin's effort to keep his cool. "I don't know anything for sure, but a few months back when I mentioned you stayed with the Cavanaghs for Thanksgiving, Michael and Victor exchanged a look. At the time, I didn't really think much about it. Those two are always all cloak and dagger, it's par for the course with them. Then, Michael showed up at the hospital after the shooting. I assumed Victor had called him, to be there for us in case we needed him, but now, I'm not so sure."

Swinging my legs over the side of the bed, I hop up in one quick motion, reality having dawned. "She's protecting me. Michael thinks she's still in danger, which means anyone near her is in danger too." I pull on the nearest pair of jeans, placing the phone on speaker, then toss it on the bed. "She wouldn't want anyone to get hurt. She'll do whatever's necessary to make sure that doesn't happen, including breaking her own heart."

Fuck. My girl sacrificed everything for me, and I got hammered and…and everything got fucked up, but Samantha doesn't know that, and I'm not sure how to fix it.

"I would agree with that assessment."

"I'm calling Michael. In the meantime, can you put Victor on Samantha? I want her covered 24/7. He can hire guys as needed. I know he's got the contacts. I'll cover the cost. Can you live without him?" Victor is Fin's right-hand man and best friend, but I trust him to do this right. I have no doubt Michael has her covered, but they operate in the realm of the government regulations; we don't.

"I'll manage. Consider it done." I hear movement on the line. "I'm glad to see you taking the bull by the horns, brother. I was worried after our last phone call," he admits.

"To be honest, Fin, things got a whole lot worse after we spoke."

"Worse than her breaking up with you?"

"Yep." I fill him in on my drunken night and the revelations of yesterday.

"Christ, Joe. You were…Jesus. Are you okay? Do I need to kill Jace?"

"I'm…dealing. Jace is punishing himself plenty, believe me." He's been so apologetic it's getting on my nerves. Words won't make what he did better—I'm going to have to get tested because of that asshole on top of everything else. At least his orgies have stopped…for now.

"And she must be devastated."

"I'm going to make it right. I'm done sitting on the sidelines and letting life lead me by the nose-hairs. This is my party, and I'm playing the next record."

He laughs. "That is a shit-ass analogy, but I get the point. You've been trying to logic your way into and out of this relationship since you met her. I'm glad to see you taking control. What else can I do to help?"

I fill him in on a few other ideas I have, but I'm not ready to move on those. He's on board though, which is a relief. As always, he has my back.

After we hang up, I finish getting dressed and head to the kitchen for coffee. The house is silent; either Jace is still asleep, or he didn't come home last night. I'm betting it's the latter. I'm still pissed at him, so it's probably best he's not here.

I call up Michael's number. He answers before I even hear it ring.

"Michael, you're on my shit list."

He chuckles. "It's about time you woke your ass up. Open your door."

I open the front door to Michael standing there with two coffee cups and a couple sacks of groceries.

"What are you doing here, man?" I take the coffees out of his already full arms.

"Putting my job on the line," he says as he passes.

I shut the door and follow him to the kitchen, knowing he's getting ready to lay some heavy shit on me. But I'm ready.

I'm ready for anything.

I'm ready to fight for my girl and our future.

The End

…well, not really!

Samantha and Joseph's journey continues in *Until You Are Mine* Book 2 in the *Until You* Series.

This is a dream for me to be able to share my love of writing with you. If you liked my book, please consider leaving a review on the retailer's site where you purchased this book (or on GoodReads).

Personal recommendations to your friends and loved ones is a great compliment too. Please share, follow, join my <u>newsletter</u> at mckdavis. com/subscribe, and help spread the word—let everyone know how much you loved Joseph and Samantha.

Acknowledgments

Thank you to my husband for your unwavering support and quiet cheer-leading while you text everyone that your wife is a published author. It's embarrassing but it also makes my heart flutter that you're proud of my accomplishments. To my children who make me feel like I'm conquering the world with each word I write.

You are my heart—I do this for you.

Special thanks to Teddy who never gives up on me and loves me through my silence. To Tamara for hand holding me through the editing process and for not dropping me when I'm quite sure she regrets taking me on. To the *Publish or Bust Gals* (Teddy, Shelly, Gayla) and the *M&M* Ladies (Teddy, TZ, Peyton, Pinkie) who saw *Until You* in the roughest forms and supported me anyway.

And lastly, to the readers—thank you for allowing me to share Joseph and Samantha with you. They've touch me deeply and drove me to write *what only the heart hears*. I hope you will tune in for their continued story in *Until You Are Mine* (dmckdavis.com/all-books/series/until-you/until-you-are-mine).

Until You Are Mine

An Until You Novel

Book Two

Playlist

Say Hey (I Love You) by Michael Franti & Spearhead

Little Things by One Direction

Birthday Cake by Rhianna

Let me Love You by DJ Snake (featuring Justin Bieber)

Birthday Sex by Jeremiah

Then There's You by Charlie Puth

I Get to Love You by Ruelle

Kindly Calm Me Down by Meghan Trainor

I Miss you by Adele

Mercy by Sean Mendes

This Town by Niall Horan

She Will Be Loved by Maroon 5

When reality becomes too much, dream of a better future.

This is for all the dreamers looking for more than they have and
daring to reach for it. It's never too late to ask for more.
To expect more. To strive for more.
It's *never* too late.

Sometimes you have to leap
Before you now if you can fly

Until You Are Mine

PART 1
HAZE

MARCH

One

Samantha

WEEKS PASS IN AN EMOTIONAL HAZE. THE NEVER-ending stream of friends and strangers dropping in to pay their respects by bringing food or flowers has long stopped. It's just me and Mom now. Except, it truly feels like it's just me and a body that used to be my mother. She barely leaves her room. She's not handling Dad's death well. I can't blame her. I really can't, but she can't spend the rest of her life in bed. She needs to feed, bathe, and clothe herself.

It's like I've lost my mother too. Like I'm the mother, having to re-mind her of life's basic needs.

It's hard getting myself up and to school when most days I would rather just roll over and go back to sleep. Besides missing my dad, I miss Jace and Joseph. I miss Joseph oh so much, but I just can't go there. The immediacy of life is banging down my door, far too many things to worry about and stress over to think about Joseph and our future that may never be.

The reality is, I'm barely keeping it together. I'm in my senior year of high school, getting ready to graduate, intern at MCI this summer, and start at UT in the fall while also trying to keep our house running like my father was here. Like his absence hasn't left me with paying bills, keeping track of home and car maintenance, grocery shopping, dealing with the bank and lawyers to sort out my father's estate. Things an eigh-teen-year-old should not have to deal with.

There's that, too. Today's my eighteenth birthday.

I'm not up to celebrating. There doesn't seem much to celebrate.

Really, it's just another day. I've had to make an effort to be alone today. I changed my shift at work. I told Margot I was spending my birthday with my mom in a quiet celebration, no fanfare. Margot was disappointed, but I knew she understood why I didn't invite her to come over.

Then there was the text from Joseph. He asked what I was doing to celebrate, and I told him I was going out with Margot. He's been texting me every day. He wants to move back to where we were, and I'm trying to move forward without him. Most days, I don't answer. I can't give him or me false hope. Although the last thing I want is to be apart from him, my self-preservation says I should close the book on Joseph, since he slept with someone else three minutes after we broke up. I try not to think about him having sex with that woman. He doesn't mention it, and because I don't respond most of the time, it goes unaddressed.

What is there to say, really? I broke up with him. I have no right to be upset or jealous. I made my bed. Now I'm lying in it alone, trying not to think about who's been sharing his bed for the past two weeks.

Jace and Michael were my last loose ends on the whole birthday lie. I spoke to Jace a few days ago, telling him I was going out with Margot. He's been so distant lately, he really didn't take much convincing. I think he only asked out of obligation anyway. I don't think he really cares, not anymore. As for Michael, he told me he was going to be out of town but to save him a piece a birthday cake, and he'd see me tomorrow. There's always the stream of federal agents watching me, but they couldn't care less if it's my birthday.

My mom, well, she never mentioned it. I doubt she even realizes what day it is. I made her dinner and actually got her to eat in the kitchen with me. We ate in silence. I tried to smile and keep things light, but I'm just not feeling it. Today of all days, I shouldn't have to pretend things are fine, that my dad's death isn't taking a horrible toll on our lives.

Dad would be so disappointed to see us now, to see how far we've fallen from the happy family we used to be.

When Mom escapes to her room, I clean up the kitchen. After the last dish is put away, I pull out the single piece of cheesecake I brought home from work yesterday, slide it onto a plate and grab a fork.

I stare at it. Its top is bare, no birthday writing to wish me *Happy 18th Birthday, Sam.* No flickering candle for me to wish on before the wax drips down.

I wish…

What would I wish?

Impossible wish? For my father to still be alive.

Improbable wish? For my father's killer to be caught and for Joseph to show up at my door begging me to take him back.

Realistic wish? I think maybe I've had enough of reality.

I glance around the empty kitchen. No friends and family to sing me happy birthday and *many more…*

Who would have thought last year would have been my last happy birthday? If I had known, I would have made a better wish—the impossible wish—for time to stand still—for my father to still be alive.

I place the cheesecake back in the fridge. Maybe I'll eat it later, after I finish my homework. I turn off all the lights and pass through the quiet hall to the library, seeking comfort in the room I love, filled with books and possibilities of escape.

A few hours later, I indulge in a long soak in the bathtub. I don't do it often, but since being shot, hot baths soothe the ache in my shoulder better than most things.

About the time I'm ready to slip into bed, my phone rings. *Darn, I forgot to turn it off.*

I answer instead of ignoring it like I really want to.

"What the fuck, Sam?" Jace barks into the phone.

"Hi, Jace. How are you?" I say calmly, trying to delay the brewing conflict.

"I was fine until I got a call from Joe asking me why you didn't go out with Margo for your birthday."

"How does he know I didn't go out with Margot? And why's he calling you?" *It's not like you give a shit.*

"He called to see if I knew what your plans were and if they'd changed."

"Oh." That still doesn't answer how Joseph knew.

"Why didn't you go out with Margot?"

I sit on my bed, peering out the window, my heart beating in my ears.

"Sam?" he says softly.

"Yeah?" My voice tightens with emotion.

"Shit, don't cry." He exhales a deep breath.

"I'm sorry." I fall back on my bed, wiping my eyes.

"Spill." He's still pissed.

"Why are you mad? It's my birthday. Aren't I allowed to spend it as I want to?" I ask defensively.

"You mean, like *it's my party, and I'll cry if I want to* kind of crap?"

"Yes, exactly like that."

"Did you?" His voice is losing its edge.

"Did I what?"

"Sam. Did you cry on your birthday, alone?"

"These days, crying on my birthday, or any other day, is not much of a stretch."

"What's going on, Sam?" His concern is clear, but it's too little too late.

I sigh and sit up. "Nothing's going on, Jace."

"That's bullshit, and you know it. Talk to me."

"Are you mad because I lied, or are you mad because you've been inconvenienced in having to call and check up on me? I must be cutting into your fucking time."

"Sam." My name is full of regret, yet I'm not sure if it's for calling him on his shit or because I've hit the truth—he'd rather be fucking than talking to his kid sister.

I rub my forehead and squeeze my eyes shut, trying to relieve some discomfort from my growing headache. "You know what? I'm going to stretch my newly liberated eighteen-year-old wings and utilize my right to not talk. I love you, but I'm hanging up now."

He yells as I end the call.

A beat passes, and my phone rings. Does he really think I'm going to answer when I just hung up on him?

A second later, my phone chimes with a voicemail. Then a text:

Jace: *Answer the damn phone!*

Me: *I don't want to talk.*

Jace: *Too fucking bad, answer your PHONE!*

My phone rings again. I reject it.

Jace: *Sam, come on. Talk to me.*

Me: *Nope. Don't you have some tail to chase? Stretch your manwhore wings.*

Jace: *HARSH, Sam. Harsh.*

When I don't answer on his third and fourth calls, he gives up.

A few minutes later my phone rings—Joseph. It will be the same conversation. He doesn't need to get involved. I send his call, and the two that follow, to voicemail. Then he resorts to texting:

Joseph: *Sam, please talk to me. You're worrying me.*

Apparently Jace didn't give up—he just sicced Joseph on me.

Me: *I don't want to talk. I'm fine. Don't worry. Leave me alone for a while.*

Joseph: *What does that mean? …a while?*

Me: *It means, IT'S MY FUCKING BIRTHDAY AND I CAN SPEND IT ALONE IF I WANT TO AND I DON'T HAVE TO EXPLAIN IT TO YOU OR ANYBODY ELSE. See? You should have left me alone. Not a good time. Just let me be for a couple of days.*

Joseph: *Not fucking happening!*

Me: *You don't have a choice. You're not my father. You're not even my boyfriend. Go with Jace and find some college girls to fuck. I'm turning my phone off now. Bye.*

I turn my phone off and turn the ringer off on the house phone in the kitchen. There are other phones in the house I hear ringing in the background, but I ignore them. The phone in Mom's room is always off these days, so they can call all they like.

I'm sure I'll regret my texts and lies over the past few days. But at the moment, I just can't. I don't have it in me to be strong and act like everything is okay, because you know what? It fucking is *not* okay! Not by a long shot.

I turn off all the lights and climb in bed, trying to focus on the things I can control, which seems like so little at the moment.

Samantha

The doorbell startles me awake Wednesday morning—early, but not so early I shouldn't already be up for school. Did I forget to set my alarm? I roll to my back and consider just letting whoever it is exhaust their efforts and go the hell away.

The persistent ringing turns into persistent knocking and then pounding. If they haven't woken my mom, they will surely have woken the neighbors by now.

I scurry out of bed, don a robe, and tiptoe down the stairs. Why am I being so quiet? There's no way they could hear me through all that racket they're making.

I creep to the front door. The doorbell chimes again. I jump and nearly scream, but manage to keep it together so whoever's on the other side of the door doesn't hear me.

I take a deep breath to calm my racing heart, and look through the peephole.

Fin and Joseph.

Shit!

I silently bang my forehead against the door.

"Go away," I say to the crack in the door so I don't have to raise my voice.

"Samantha." Joseph's voice is muffled, but there is no way I could mistake the way he says my name for anyone else.

Fin chimes in. "Is that any way to greet us?"

"No, it's not. I'm sorry, but I don't want to talk." *And I most definitely don't want to see you.*

Silence.

I don't look through the peephole. I don't need to see them to know the cogs in their brains are clicking as they think of a way to get me to open the door, which I'm sure I'll end up doing. I can't be mean to them in person.

"How about this?" Fin offers. "You open the door. Let us in so we can truly see you are, in fact, alright. You don't have to talk to us. You don't have to say a word if you don't want to."

I peer out at them. "Not happening. You need to go. Joe, you should be at school. Fin, you have a company to run. You shouldn't be here. What's happening with me is none of your concern."

"The fuck it isn't." Joseph pounds the door. "Open this goddamn door right now!"

I actually laugh, he's so angry. To see him here in the middle of the week when he should be in Austin, and knowing he's this upset is wrongly satisfying and quite gratifying, to say the least.

"If you don't leave, I'm going to call the cops," I warn.

"That won't be necessary." Michael steps into view.

Fucking Michael.

"I'm surprised you didn't just break in like you did last time, Michael."

Joseph's head whips around to glare at Michael. *Whoa, Joseph's not happy about that.*

Michael smiles deviously. "I have a key, actually." He holds it up to the peephole. "I don't need to break in anymore."

"Then why all the pounding and racket? You've disturbed the whole neighborhood."

Displeased, he narrows his eyes at Fin and Joseph. "I just got here. Believe me, I would have handled this differently if these two schmucks hadn't beaten me here." I swear his eyes lock on mine, knowing I'm looking at him. "Now, open the door, Sam. Or I'll use my key. Your choice."

Damn. Damn. Damn. *Fucking Michael.*

I'm going to regret this. I know it.

I unlock the door. Instead of opening it, I race up the stairs trying to escape them.

Joseph's voice stops me at the top. "You'd better be going to get dressed," he warns. "You've got five minutes, and then I'm coming in there and will drag you down here to talk to us in whatever *state of dress* you're in."

My mouth falls open, and I scowl at Michael, who smiles unabashedly. "I told you he wouldn't like me seeing you in your t-shirt and panties."

"Asshole," I sneer.

He laughs and shakes his head. "You have no idea, princess."

"Michael," Joseph barks.

Michael nods and motions to Fin. They disappear into the den.

"Samantha." Joseph's voice is silky smooth, the voice I've come to know so well.

I clutch the railing as I peer down on him in his black t-shirt and jeans. Sexy as sin and as heartbreaking as ever.

"I'm serious, Samantha. Five minutes, then I'm coming to get you."

The sadness in his eyes painfully tightens my throat. I couldn't even reply if I tried.

I nod once and turn away, slamming my hand over my mouth as a sob tries to break free. *I can't do this. I can't be this close to him and not be affected by him.*

"Samantha."

The pain I saw in his eyes a moment ago is now in his voice. It pins me in place just before I manage to escape into my room. I don't know how he made it up the stairs so quickly and silently.

I wipe my tears. My face tipped down, I glance sideways over my left shoulder, hoping I'm in shadow enough to hide my tears. I remain silent.

"Please don't walk around barely dressed in front of Michael or anyone else."

Jesus. Seriously? Such a caveman. Then don't go sticking your dick in other women! I want to scream at him. But I don't. I simply nod and move toward my door.

He clasps my left shoulder, stopping my progress.

"Don't." I shrug to dislodge his hand as if it burns me.

I move past my doorway, slamming it behind me just as he says, "Samantha, please."

I only make it a few feet before I collapse into a mass of tears.

Please, God. Give me strength.

The door opens. "Christ, Sweetness." His footfall alerts me to his movement a second before he wraps me in his arms and lifts me off the floor.

I jerk violently. "Let me go, Joe. Dammit, let me go!"

His grip is firm as he carries me to my bed. "Never, Samantha. Never."

I beat at his chest, pleading with him. "Let me down."

"No." He squeezes me tightly as if he's afraid I'll disappear.

We drop to the bed.

"Jesus Christ. Stop!" He pins my arms beside my head and uses his body to stifle mine. "You're going to hurt your shoulder. Please stop fighting me." His chiseled face is stricken with anguish. "Please, Samantha."

His pleading breaks me.

I stop struggling. "If you ever cared for me, Joe. If you ever felt anything for me, please just let me go. Leave and don't look back."

The tears I've been fighting break free. I can't fight them anymore. I can't fight *him* anymore. He has to choose to leave. I can't make him, because deep down I don't want him to. I want him to stay and fight—for me—for us.

"Sweetness, it's because I do care, I'll never walk away from you. I could never leave you hurting like this." He releases his hold and wraps his arms around my back, burying his head in my neck, his entire body cocooning mine. "I'm sorry. I'm so fucking sorry." His voice cracks with anguish. "You have no idea how sorry I am. Please, please forgive me. Let me be here for you. Let me help you." He's crying. He's fucking crying.

Jesus. He's so perfect for me, it hurts to know it'll never be.

With little hesitation, I wrap my arms around him, squeezing him tightly. We hold each other as we expel all we've been through these past weeks, finding the comfort we both desperately need. Sorrow rolls off us in waves, deeply ravaging regret so palpable it's hard to breathe.

Eventually, our tears dry. He rolls to his back, taking me with him to lie alongside him. He kisses my forehead, then clears his throat and rasps, "Please stop calling me *Joe.* It's like a fucking knife to the gut every time you say it."

I knew it would bother him, rub him the wrong way. I get a small amount of pleasure in that. However, it's also a means to distance myself from him, protect my heart, or what's left of it. "I'll think about it."

He squeezes me, running his hand down my arm. "Well, think about it good and hard, because the next time you call me *Joe*, I'm going to take you in my arms and kiss, lick, and suck every inch of your body until you agree to call me *Joseph*."

Holy smokes, this man. My heart will never survive my traitorous body, which wants nothing more than for him to do all of that and more.

"Are you throwing down a gauntlet?" I tease, amazed by how easy it always is between us, at least when we're in person.

His chest ripples with his laugh. "No, Sweetness. I'm making you a promise. The first of many I intend to keep."

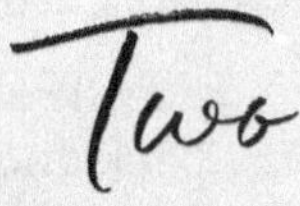

Two

Joseph

"**W**HY ARE YOU HERE, JOE?"

Fuck. She's gonna test me. Should I have expected less? I roll off the bed, pushing down my agitation, shaking my head. "I'm going to give you that one, but that's the last one." I bend down, hovering over her, looking into the amazing blue eyes I've missed so much. "The next time you call me *Joe*, I'm going to make good on my promise."

A wicked smile lights up her face, which should delight me, but it doesn't. She's not taking me seriously.

"You realize your promise is much more of an enticement than a deterrent, don't you?"

"I'm not playing games, Samantha. This is my heart we're talking about." I take her hand and hold it over my pounding heart. "You're in here, Samantha, and I'm not letting you go." I sit on the bed next to her and place my hand over her heart. "I need you to let me back in here, and you'll never do that as long as you're calling me *Joe*."

Her smirk is gone and replaced with the sadness consuming much of her life now.

"I know we have things to talk about. I know you still need time to process what I did and time to forgive me, and I'm going to wait that out. But, I'm not going to allow you to put an extra wall between us. That wall that says *I'm just some old Joe* to you. I'm not *Joe* to you. I'm *Joseph*. *Your* Joseph. I need you to respect that and call me by that name. The rest I'll be patient for, but that, I will not stand for."

Her eyes cloud with unsaid emotions and desire. She may not admit it, but she likes it when I go all caveman on her. She might even crave it, need it. Her needs have been ignored for so long, she eats up the attention and my need to claim her—to be claimed by her.

I kiss her forehead and step away from the bed. "You need to get dressed." At the door, I glance back before opening it. "I'll be downstairs. Don't take too long, or I *will* come back and get you."

Leaving her on the bed, staring after me, I follow the scent of bacon into the kitchen to find Michael cooking and Fin sitting at the island drinking a cup of coffee. I head to the coffeemaker.

"Have y'all seen Eleanor?" I blow across my mug, then taking a tentative sip.

Michael glances at me before returning his focus to the eggs he's scrambling. "She's in her room, probably still in bed. Where she always is," he says flatly.

An arched brow from Fin gets my attention before I look back to Michael. "What do you mean *always?*"

Turning the stove off, he pushes the pan to the back burner and covers it before facing us. "She spends all of her time in her room. Sam ensures she eats and showers every day, but other than that, she's pretty much a lump of useless flesh."

"Jesus, Michael," Fin castigates.

Michael runs his fingers through his short buzz of brown hair. "It's harsh, I know. But the reality is, she's not functioning. She's not taking care of Sam. She's not working. She's not taking care of the house or any other matters Daniel handled. She's lost in her grief, and Sam's paying the price. She didn't even remember Sam's birthday, for fuck's sake."

"It's okay she didn't remember," Samantha's soft voice trails from the kitchen doorway.

"Fuck," Michael exclaims. "I'm sorry, Sam. I shouldn't have said that stuff."

"Or at least said it with a little more tact," Fin interjects.

I pull her into the kitchen and hand her a cup of coffee with cream and sugar, just the way she likes it. "Is it true though, Samantha? Is she really that bad?"

"It's…she's…" She sighs, her frustration palpable.

I lean down and kiss her head. "Hey, there's no judgment here. We just want to help."

She nods. "Yes, it's bad. I'm doing the best I can, which obviously is not enough if the three of you are here during the day when you should be working or at school."

The grandfather clock in the hall chimes eight times. "Shit! *I* should be at school." Samantha jumps.

I put my hand on her shoulder. "Stop. You're not going to school today. In fact, I think you should take the rest of the week off." I nod to Fin. "We'll talk to your principal and square it with him."

Fin exits the kitchen, understanding my silent request to call her school. He established a relationship with her principal while she was in the hospital. I was too preoccupied with her to even think of her school work.

Michael, ever the voice of reason—not always calm, but always reasonable— suggests we continue this conversation over breakfast. We agree and sit down to eat in the breakfast nook.

Fin joins us shortly with a silent nod, confirming her school situation has been handled. He sits at the table, surveying the kitchen. "The place looks clean, organized, better than the last time I saw it. It was a mess after the reception."

Sam glances at him, but doesn't say anything.

"How many times a week does the maid come?" Fin continues.

Samantha leans back in her chair. "Never."

"You've been doing all the cooking and cleaning?" I ask.

"Yes."

Fin grunts in appreciation. "Well, you're doing a good job. I'd hire you, if I didn't know you have higher aspirations."

She sets down her fork and scans the three of us. "Why don't y'all just ask me what you really want to know instead of going on this fishing expedition? It will probably save us a bunch of time and allow you to get back to your own lives faster."

I reach over and squeeze her hand. "We're not in any hurry. We're here to help, but we do need some details so we can be sure we're helping in the best way possible. Tell us what's going on with the house, and don't leave any details out."

Reluctantly, she fills us in on where things stand. She's been paying the bills, grocery shopping, etc. out of her savings account. She's also been cleaning, doing laundry, and managing the yard work and pool maintenance. I'm sure there's more, but that's all she's sharing at the moment.

"Christ. You should have told someone. Asked for help," I spout.

She just shakes her head. "Who was I supposed to dump all this on? There's no one. Just me."

"There's me, Fin, Michael, Jace. My entire family," I offer.

"It's not your responsibility. You all have busy lives. I can't burden you with this. And Jace can't handle this stuff from Austin. Plus, well, it isn't his forte, nor does he seem to be in a place to offer much help."

I can't disagree with the Jace assessment.

"That may be all true, but the burden doesn't fall to you alone. Not anymore." I squeeze her hand, making sure she understands I'm serious.

This shit right here, this self-sacrificing is going to stop. Now.

The bottom line is she's a senior in high school, who will graduate with an associate's degree and probably a 5.0 GPA because of the difficulty of the classes she is carrying. She has enough going on, plus dealing with her own loss and grief around her father. She doesn't need to be running a household and taking care of her mother too.

"Let's take care of one thing at a time." I get up to refill everyone's coffee. "Your mom needs help. We can move her to my parents' home. My mom would be more than willing to take care of her. She misses having someone to pamper since I moved out years ago. It would be a good interim solution to more drastic measures. We can see how it goes and then reassess in a week or so."

I wait for the three of them to voice any objections, but none come. "Okay, agreed.

"As for the household maintenance and financials, I recommend we let the lawyers set up arrangements for your and Jace's finances and a property manager for running the house."

I look to Samantha for confirmation. "Agreed?"

She gives a soft, "Yes."

"I would like to speak to Samantha alone about the next piece. Fin, would you mind calling our parents and getting the ball rolling with the lawyers?"

"On it." He stands and strides out of the room.

"See you in a bit," I say to Michael as I guide Samantha out of kitchen and to the library.

Samantha

When I woke up this morning, I thought today would end like it did the night before, and the night before that, and the night before that. Endless nights of homework, house work, and nursemaid to my mother. Apparently, I was wrong.

I have no idea what Joseph wants to speak to me about, but it can't be good if he wants it to be done in private.

"I don't want you here alone in this big house. As much as I'd like to stay, it's just not a possibility. Plus, I still think I'd be too much of a distraction to be beneficial." He quickly gets to the point, but I can hear the smile in his voice when he continues. "Not to mention you'd be a distraction for me and my school work too."

"We're not an item anymore. It's not your place to take care of me any longer. I don't expect you or anyone else to upturn your life. You're worried, I understand, but I'll be fine here by myself. You're taking the added pressure off by getting my mom settled with your parents, and the house will be taken care of shortly. As for being alone, I am most of the time anyway. That's nothing new."

He grimaces as if he realizes how true that fact it. "I want you to stay at Fin's."

What? "Fin's?"

"Yes. You shouldn't be alone. He'll look out for you and keep you safe."

"Safe? I don't need Fin to keep me safe." I move away, pacing the room. "No. No. That's not happening." My mind races. I can't put them in danger. I have FBI protection all because my father's killer is still out there, seeking the information he unsuccessfully tried to squeeze out of my dad. The information he's willing to kill for. I can't knowingly put Joseph or anyone else in danger. The killer knows me, but I don't know for sure if he knows who's important to me. I'm not willing to take a chance on anyone else's life.

"Samantha." He moves to me, lifting me up in his arms.

"Put me down." It's more of a plea than an order.

"No, you're panicking." He sits on the nearest couch, holding me in his lap.

God, I love being in his lap, feeling his protective arms around me.

He cups my cheek, ensuring I meet his gaze. "I know why you broke up with me. You did it to protect me. And now you don't want to live with Fin because you think you'll put him in danger."

Shit.

"You're not in this alone, Sweetness. Michael and his team have been watching you for weeks, but I've also had Victor and his guys on you, as well."

"Joseph." What is he saying?

"You were never really alone. I was always there, watching, keeping you safe, and I will continue to do so. But, it'll be easier to do it in a high security building like MCI towers, where Fin and Matt live and work." His fingers slip into my hair as he pulls me closer. His lips press against my temple, breathing slowly and steadily.

His stillness centers me, and my panic begins to dissipate as I relax into him, matching his breathing, closing my eyes and feeling the sense of home he instills in me.

"I won't let anything happen to you or your family," he whispers.

I wrap my arms around him and bury my face in his neck. "It's you I worry about. If he wants to get to me, you're my weakness. That's why I pushed you away—not because I don't want you as much as I ever did."

His fingers gently move down to massage the back of my neck. "Sweetness, I appreciate you thinking breaking up with me would fix that, but I don't believe it does. The killer can't be that easily deceived. He would see through your ruse eventually, just as I did."

"You believed me at first." Seeing regret wash across his face and his demeanor change, I wish I could take back my words.

"Yes, I did. I was in hell believing you no longer wanted me. And I—"

"Stop." I push my way out of his lap, needing distance.

He reluctantly lets me go, but stands to pursue me, his face pained. "Samantha."

I can't take it. "No, we don't need to talk about this. I hurt you. I'm sorry for that. You have no idea how sorry or how bad it hurt me too." My fist beats against my chest. He'll never know how sorry I am for driving him into the arms of another woman. I swipe angrily at my tears. "But, we don't need to talk about the…" I wave my hand at him, trying to dispel the thoughts, "…the other stuff."

I back away as he continues to moves closer. "Baby, we do need to talk about it." He captures me around the waist, stopping my retreat.

I close my eyes and turn my head to the side. "Please, I can't. Not now." *Not ever.* The thought of him making love to another woman makes me nauseated all over again. I stumble back, hating my weakness, letting something I caused affect me so strongly. "Please," I say as much to him as to myself.

He pulls me into his arms. "Okay. Okay. Not now." He kisses my head. "But make no mistake, Sweetness, we will talk about it. I hurt you, and you need to give me a chance to make amends." He squeezes me tighter. "I need you to forgive me." His voice is heavy with emotion.

"There's—"

He cuts me off with a kiss. A soft, chaste kiss. "Shhh. No more." His lips return to mine, but this time they're no longer chaste, but hungry.

Wonderfully hungry.

Joseph's parents showed up a little over an hour ago. They're all treating me with kid gloves, like I might break. I won't, but I may go off on them and have another bout of emotions. So, I guess it's better they stay clear of me, or I stay clear of them.

I'm sitting at the top of the stairs. I was on my way to my room, but thought better of it, afraid they'd leave with my mom, and I wouldn't get a chance to say goodbye.

"Sam," Fin says from the bottom of the stairs. "Why are you sitting there?"

I shrug instead of answering him. I don't want to share my pathetic thoughts.

He climbs the stairs and sits sideways on the step below me. "I'm glad you're coming to stay with me. I didn't like the idea of you staying here alone."

"According to Joseph, I haven't really been alone."

He contemplates a moment before speaking. "Well, in some ways, no, but in other ways, you have been." He touches my arm. "You've *felt* alone, and we don't want you to feel that way anymore. This is a good compromise, and I get the added bonus of company too."

"I don't need a babysitter. I'm quite capable of taking care of myself." In my head, I sat up straight, and my words came out strong and with conviction. In reality, I'm slumped against the wall, and I think it came out more like a murmur.

"You are capable, and I'm not a babysitter." He moves to the top step and pulls me into his side. I don't have the energy to protest, and, frankly, I don't want to. "I'm a friend, and I think you could use one of those right now."

"Okay," I agree. There are so many reasons I should continue to fight this, but one rather handsome six and half feet of convincing man named Joseph is wedging his way back in. I'm not sure I have the heart to continue fighting on my own, so it would be nice to have Joseph and his family on my side—standing up for me—protecting me.

"I thought for sure you'd fight Joe on this. I had a whole speech planned out and everything." He seems disappointed.

"Did you have visual aids, graphs, and diagrams? 'Cause I'm a sucker for a good presentation."

"Smartass." He releases me just as Joseph rounds the corner.

He scowls when he sees us. "Are you packed, Samantha?"

My contrition is obvious. "No, sorry."

He comes up the stairs, stopping in front of us, eyeing Fin and his nearness to me. "Don't you have someplace to be, brother?"

Fin laughs, shaking his head as he rises to his feet. "Calm yourself, caveman." He winks at me. "I'll see you later for dinner at my place." He nods at Joseph with a pat on the back before trotting down the stairs.

"Come on, I'll help you pack." He offers me his hand and pulls me to my feet.

"Have you talked to Jace?" I ask as we walk down the hall to my room.

He visibly stiffens. "Fin's going to call him and fill him in."

That's odd. "Why?"

"Why what?" His hand touches the sensitive spot on my lower back, and he chuckles when I arch in response. "So sensitive." He's laughing, but his eyes look at me with yearning, like he missed me nearly as much as I missed him.

"Why is Fin calling Jace instead of you calling him?" I pull his hand away from my back, but don't release it.

"Why aren't you calling him and telling him yourself?" He sidesteps my question.

"Because I'm mad at him, and I think he's mad at me. I really don't want to deal with him right now."

He nods and follows me into my closet, pulling down the suitcase I point out on the top shelf. He lays it out on my bed, unzipping it. "My answer is kind of the same. I'm not very happy with Jace at the moment, and it's probably best for all of us if Fin deals with him right now."

I touch his arm and wait for him to make eye contact. "Do I dare ask why?"

He gives a sad smile before cupping my nape and running his thumb across my jawline. "No, it's probably best you don't."

"Okay." I survey my room, thinking of where to start.

So, Joseph's idea of *helping me pack* is him lying on my bed, perusing my panties and commenting on their lack of material. I swipe his latest acquisition out of his hand. "Joseph, are you trying to be the creepy guy who stalks my underwear drawer? 'Cause you're doing a fine impression of a creeper."

He holds up his hands up in surrender, sitting back against the head-board. "I am most definitely. *Not. That. Guy.*"

"Thank god. You were creeping me out. I was starting to think I'd turn around, and you'd be wearing a pair of my panties."

He chuckles. "Sweetness, my junk wouldn't fit in that scrap of material you call panties."

I can't help but laugh. "So, you're not saying you wouldn't wear them. You're just saying they're not big enough to accommodate your manhood."

If looks could scorch, I'd be on fire. "Samantha, the only way I'll be inside your panties is if you're still wearing them."

Holy fuck.

I need a minute to recover from his smolder. I close my suitcase and zip it up. With a sigh, I face him. "I think that's it."

We get my suitcase downstairs, and I collect my backpack and purse from the library. When I come back to the front door, my mom is standing there in a daze between Joseph's parents. I drop my things on the floor and move to her, but she just stares at me. Actually, she's staring *through* me. There's no acknowledgment, no recognition in her eyes. Those once lively, full of love, pale green eyes are now glassy and blank. There is no emotion in them at all. No sadness. No anger. No nothing.

I wipe away my errant tear and touch her shoulder. "Mom, I'll see you soon." My voice cracks. Joseph is behind me before I even see him move. One hand grips my right side, the other squeezes my left hand, his front blanketing my back, protecting me, giving me strength to see this through. With steadier breath, I give Mom a quick unreturned hug, and step back.

Before I can sink into Joseph's arms, Fiona, Joseph's mom, embraces me. "She'll be alright. Give us a few days to get situated, and then let's chat about how she's doing."

I pull away and nod, returning to Joseph's side.

Not to be outdone, Hugh, Joseph's dad, pulls me into a warm bear-hug. "If you need anything, I mean *anything*, you just call. Night or day." He pulls away, meeting his son's eyes. "Take care of her, Joseph."

I smile at the use of his full name.

"Of course." Joseph gives both his parents hugs. "We'll talk tomorrow."

As he closes the door behind them, he turns to me. "Give me a minute to double check the house is secure and then we'll go."

"I'll put my bags in my car." I pick up my purse and backpack.

"You won't need your car, and if you do need one, you can use one of mine or Fin's. Just give me five minutes, and I'll be ready."

He disappears up the stairs before I have a chance to even argue. And to be honest, I don't even want to. I'm sure I should, but at the moment, it feels good to be taken care of, including being driven around. He already shared that a car will drive me to and from school, which I'm good with. It means I get to do homework while on the road, or even just close my eyes and relax, have a moment of Zen.

Michael and his team follow us to Fin's. I wonder who else might be out there watching such a precession, or even joining without us knowing it.

PART 2
BEGINNING

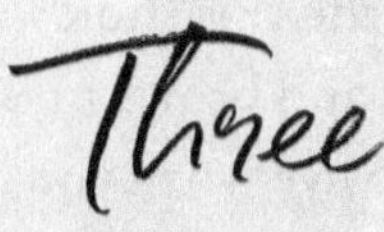

Three

Joseph

S HE'S QUIET ON THE WAY TO FIN'S, UNTIL WE ENTER the parking garage at MCI Towers.

"Why do your brothers live here?"

"It's extremely convenient." I slip into one of Fin's parking spaces.

"Do they ever really get to leave work behind? Don't they end up working all hours of the night, just because they never leave their place of employment?" The censure is clear in her voice.

I stare at her, contemplating, before getting out of the car. I'm not sure if this really bothers her, or if she's trying to pick a fight in an effort to keep herself closed off from me. "I don't think Fin working long hours would change if he lived at another location. It would just mean he'd lose those productive hours commuting. Now, Matt's a whole other story. He works hard, but he plays hard too. If he didn't live so close to where he works, he probably wouldn't be as productive."

"Joseph, how can you not see that living where you work is not a good idea?"

I move around the car, drawing her close. "It works for them. Maybe not forever, but for now they're happy." I grab her bags out of the car and motion for her to follow.

Michael and his team have already swept the place and have men positioned in front of the elevators here in the garage and on the penthouse level where Fin and Matt live. Victor and his men are a little more discreet, monitoring the security cameras and their normal positions they cover for the MCI business as a whole. Having Samantha here will make it easier on Victor and his team, with cameras everywhere except in the penthouse itself.

I enter the elevator, situate the luggage, and only then realize I'm alone. She's stopped cold on the threshold of the elevator, not moving, just staring at me, lips pursed and brows furrowed.

"Is this where you plan to live when you graduate?" She seems bothered by the idea of it, and I'm not sure why.

I nod. "Probably—it's convenient and available." The doors start to close, and I quickly put my hand out to stop them. "Samantha, please." I motion for her to enter. We don't have time for this now. We need to get up to Fin's and get her settled, not stand here in the garage debating my family's living situation.

Surprisingly, she obeys my command and enters the elevator.

As we rise from the garage level, I slip the penthouse key into the control panel and enter the code granting us access to the top floor. Stepping back, I face her. "I never really thought much about not living here. I just assumed I would. There are four more penthouses in the other Omega Tower that are currently unoccupied. They're used for business occasionally, but my dad has left them empty so I'll have my pick if I choose to live here. My parents stay occasionally, if attending a late-night function downtown. There's security, twenty-four-hour concierge service, maid service, and a fleet of cars at our disposal. Let's talk in a couple of days and see if you still think the same about living here so close to MCI."

"It's only temporary for me. Additionally, I don't work here."

"You could live here. And you do work here, at least in the summers—for now," I say matter-of-factly.

The elevator chimes, announcing our arrival. I remove the key and step out before she can reply. Once I've got the luggage out of her way, she joins me in the marble vestibule with two large doors on opposite sides.

"This one is Fin's." Moving to the door on my left, I unlock it and motion over my shoulder. "The other door is Matt's."

I stand aside for her to enter, then set her bags down and close the door behind us. The light in the foyer is on but nothing else. Fin's at the office, having left Sam's before we did. He gave up most of his morning to help me with Samantha and her mom. It's a sacrifice and put a large dent in his agenda for the day.

"Lights," I command from behind her.

She jumps and scowls at me as if I gave her a direct order. Realization dawns as the entire place comes to life. Various lamps and recessed lighting turn on, some brighter than others, but a warm glow encompasses the entire living area. Then faint music fills the air. Samantha makes her way to the wall of windows in the living room.

"It's beautiful," she says almost reverently, taking in the downtown skyline of the city we both grew up in.

It is spectacular. I take a moment to enjoy the view. It's quite awe-inspiring to be in the middle of the skyline, a part of it. Up close and personal.

She turns and does a double take when she sees me smiling at her. "Still think it's so bad to live here?" I ask.

"I didn't say it was bad to live here. I just worry Fin never disconnects from work. Or maybe that's what he likes. It's a good excuse to be a workaholic."

"Hmmm. Let me show you to your room and give you the ten-cent tour."

I leave her to unpack and shower. I putter around in the kitchen, grabbing some grapes as I text with Fin to see what he wants to do for dinner. He quickly replies he has it covered and will be home around six. It's unusual for him to be home so early, but it's good for him to take a break now and again. Having Samantha here will be good. Give him something else, *someone* else to focus on.

Samantha is right—Fin is a workaholic, though I don't believe he's proud of that fact. I think it's just the way his life is right now. He takes on a lot, trying to take the strain away from our dad and our uncles. Dad is the oldest of his brothers, who all work for MCI in one aspect or another. Eventually, our cousins will come to work for MCI, if they choose to do so. It's always our preference to keep the company in the family; no one is going to care for it or understand its roots and its importance to our family as much as we do. My dad and his two brothers started at MCI just like my brothers did, and I will in a year's time.

My cousins are younger than me. I think the next-oldest one turns eighteen this year and starts college this fall. Therefore, it will be a few years before any other McIntyre heirs join the company full-time. Most start as young as we did, at thirteen, working in various departments over the summers, getting a feel for the business and finding their niche.

I look out over the skyline, looking forward to dusk when the city lights come to life. I never really doubted the idea of living at MCI Towers once I graduate college. It made sense to live here close to work, close to my brothers, who are also my friends. I'm trying to see it from Samantha's perspective and why she objects. It seems to be more than just the idea of being so close to work, and I need to find out what it is. Maybe not tonight, but before I make this my permanent residence. I need to dwell in the head of Samantha Cavanagh to see what exactly is bothering her and making her prickly to the idea of penthouse living.

Samantha

Incredible, I think as I turn off the shower. We're not poor by any means. My dad was a doctor and my mom an attorney, after all. We're upper middle class, I suppose. We live in a nice house with modern amenities, but never have I experienced a shower like this. Besides the fact it's big enough for six people, it has recessed adjustable rain shower heads across the top and more along the sides. There's even a control panel to adjust which heads are on, the temperature, and the desired spray type. I've never been so gloriously surrounded by water and not been submerged in it. It's calming, tranquil, and surprisingly sensual. I think I'm in love.

I reluctantly exit the shower, grabbing a towel from the warmer. *A warmer! Seriously.* Then head to the closet for some clothes. I search through the drawers trying to remember where I put everything when I quickly unpacked before jumping in the shower. I grab a t-shirt and yoga pants, matching bra and panties, and make my way back to the bathroom.

My shoulder wound is healing nicely. The hot shower helped loosen the muscles and reduce the constant ache. My doctor believes it should be healed enough to start physical therapy next week. I'm actually looking forward to it and hope I can say goodbye to the sling. I still wear it to school, and if my shoulder aches more than normal when at home.

With a sigh and a shake of my head, I give up the examination and move onto the business of drying my hair and getting dressed. When I'm done, I quietly slip out of my room and down the hall toward the living space. It's quiet. I'm not sure where Joseph even is.

Stopping at the entry, I scan the room. It really is a beautiful place and not too masculine, but definitely modern with a bit of old world rustic thrown in, which helps warm up the space with the marble floors and floor-to-ceiling windows.

My perusal of the space stops as soon as I spot Joseph, stretched out on the couch, sound asleep. I continue my path to the kitchen. A bottled water I find in the fridge will have to do as I don't want to wake him up with the ice dispenser. I pad back to the bedroom to get my tablet before making myself comfortable on the opposite couch.

Concentrating on my ebook seems pointless. I think I've read the same paragraph five times. My eyes keep wandering over to the sleeping man in front of me, his dark hair disheveled from his fingers, lying on his side, facing me. His arms are crossed over his chest, causing his muscles to bunch in such a way I just want to kiss, lick, suck, and possibly bite them. He looks peaceful, the emotions of this morning washed from his features by sleep.

It's hard to believe I met him for the first time four months ago. I, of course, knew of him via my internship with MCI, but I'd never met him or even seen him in person until Jace brought him home. Even in my fantasies, I never dreamed Joseph would want to be a part of my life, watching out for me, wanting to keep me safe despite the danger to his own life and that of his family. The truth is, though, if my dad hadn't died, Joseph would still be in Austin living his no-Samantha life. He would have kept his vow to not pursue a relationship. Not now, and maybe not ever.

But here we are, four months later having not been together, then been together, then not together again after I broke up with him two weeks ago. It's been turbulent at best and heartbreaking at worst. I don't trust it for so many reasons, but the bottom line is he's here because of my father's death, and that's not a reason that'll keep him with me for the long haul. It won't be a strong enough reason to overcome the obstacles we're still bound to face.

It doesn't mean I don't believe he cares for me. I believe he does. I'm not sure, though, if his feelings for me are stronger than his need to protect me. They may go hand in hand, or maybe his protective instincts are making him believe he feels more for me than he really does, clouding his vision of what his true feelings actually are. He's a caretaker by nature, a protector. I think if we were just friends, he would still feel the need to protect me, protect anyone he feels is in danger and he has the power to protect.

Obligation.

Maybe.

That's.

What.

I.

Am.

"Hey." Joseph's husky voice draws my eyes to his waking form. He frowns and sits up, rubbing his hands across his face. "What happened? Why are you crying, Sweetness?"

Shaking my thoughts away, I jump up, wiping my face. "Nothing. I'm fine." In the kitchen, I grab a bottled water and two glasses of ice.

In typical Joseph fashion, he doesn't let it drop easily. He doesn't let me hide. He takes the water and glasses out of my hands, setting them on the coffee table. "Come here, baby." He pulls me into his arms, over his lap, and back onto the couch as he lays us both down, facing each other. My head rests on his arm that circles around, pulling me closer as his other hand does the same on my lower back. He uses his leg to pull mine between his thighs. Once we're situated the way he wants, his attention turns back to me. He runs his hand tenderly across my cheeks, his gaze never veering from my face. "What is it?"

I shake my head. I can't tell him what I'm thinking. What I'm feeling. It will only upset him, and he'll say whatever he needs to say to convince me I'm wrong. But I'm not wrong. I burrow into the crook of his neck. "I don't want to talk. Just hold me. Please."

"Sweetness." He voice is gentle and kind like I'm the most precious thing to him.

But, I'm not. I can't be.

He pulls me tighter, our bodies pressed together, not a hair's breadth between us.

"Honey, I'm home," reaches into the depths of my sleep.

My head jerks up.

"Fin," Joseph growls. "Shhh. I got you, Samantha." He cups my face and kisses my brow. "I'm sorry he woke you up like that."

Still foggy from sleep, I bury my face in Joseph's chest, his warmth welcoming me back. "Hmmm."

His chest rumbles with laughter. "Just rest till dinner gets here."

I vaguely hear their conversation before drifting off to sleep again, lost in the comfort that exists only in his embrace. His chest. His smell. His possessiveness. His heart.

His.

Only.

His.

"Sweetness." His lips feather across mine.

I fight to remain in the world of the sleeping, and yet at the same time, fight to return to the man who's calling my name.

"Dinner's here. You need to wake up so I can feed you." His lips pass over mine again, just barely there.

"Feed her?" Fin scoffs.

Joseph stiffens as his arms squeeze me gently. "Asshole."

Warm lips press to mine.

One.

Two.

Three times.

Fin's laugh resonates from the distance. "Caveman."

I respond to his kiss before he can pull away or acknowledge his brother's comment, moving my hand to hold the back of his head, pressing him to me, ensuring our kiss continues. Lathing my tongue across the seam of his lips, he opens on a gasp, and I take full advantage, delving in deeper, holding him tighter, pressing against him and rolling my hips into him.

"Fuck, Samantha. You're gonna make me come if you keep kissing me like that," he whispers against my lips, sending chills down my spine.

To say the thrill roaring through my body at his admission of what I can do to him is no small thing, would be an understatement. It's everything.

"You say it like it's a bad thing," I tease, opening my eyes for the first time, taking in his emeralds that seem to burn just for me.

He chuckles and slaps my butt. "You need to get up so we can eat."

"Killjoy," I grumble as I extricate myself from his body, standing up slowly to stretch and catch my bearings.

Fin smirks at me from the kitchen. "Good evening, Sam."

I can't help the sleepy smile and small laugh at his greeting. "Good evening, Fin." I enter the kitchen. "How was work?"

He pulls down plates from the cabinet, and I take them from him, silently asking where to place them. He motions to the dining room as he grabs flatware and tells me about his day, or at least the part of his day I'm not already privy to since he was with us for much of it.

I set down three plates but notice there's a fourth one. "Who else is joining us?"

His Cheshire Cat smile is beyond devious. "I invited a friend to dinner. I thought you might enjoy the company and even out the ratio a bit."

"The ratio?" I glance to Joseph, who shakes his head.

"Yes, the male-to-female ratio," Fin says matter-of-factly, handing me the utensils and napkins before returning to the kitchen.

I grin, catching Joseph's eye. "Fin invited a girl over. A female friend." I cock my head around the corner. "I didn't think you had any female friends, Fin."

"Sam, you don't know me well enough to make that assessment," he says simply. No animosity, just a point of fact.

"Yep, I guess you're right." I shrug and finish setting the table.

A few moments later, the doorbell rings. Fin stops what he's doing in the kitchen and disappears around the corner with that damn Cheshire smile still on his face.

Four

Joseph

DINNER IS GOOD, BUT THE COMPANY IS BETTER. Particularly the company of my girl. She kissed the hell out of me earlier, topping off the joy of holding her in my arms as she napped. I don't know what upset her, and I hope to find out later, but at the moment I'm happy to watch her laugh and banter back and forth between the four of us as if we do this all the time. It's easy. Natural. The way it's meant to be. The way I imagine it always could be.

The surprise guest is Margot, Samantha's good friend. I suspect Samantha refuses to call Margot her best friend out of respect for Jace. I would say Jace lost that slot a long time ago, though I'm not sure he truly ever earned that title in the first place. However, that's not my call to make. I'm still angry at him about Tiff. I'm definitely not the best judge of his character or his worthiness to be called Samantha's best friend.

"What do you mean you don't go in the water?" Fin reacts to Margot's dismissal of his invite to join us at the lake house this summer.

She stares at Samantha as she answers, her eyes pleading. There's a story behind that look.

"Well, I don't wear swimsuits, so I don't go in the water." Margot offers as explanation, but it actually raises more questions than answers.

"Ever?" Fin's shock is apparent on his face and in the volume of his response.

I stifle a laugh. He's getting all worked up as if it's the most ridiculous thing he's ever heard.

Samantha pokes at her food, moving it around her plate. She puts down her fork, giving Margot a quick smile. "She's sensitive to sunlight, so it doesn't make much sense to hang out at the lake or the pool."

"But do you swim?" Fin questions further.

"Uh…yes." Margot shimmies uncomfortably in her chair.

I can't figure out what's really going on here between Fin's interest in this topic and Margot in general, and Margot and Samantha's evasiveness, but I'm quite intrigued myself. I also find it funny he hasn't caught on that she obviously doesn't want to talk about it, but Fin just keeps digging.

"Do you go to the lake often?" Samantha directs the question to Fin and me.

Fin responds quickly, barely giving his brain time to process the question. "I think we could stand to go more often, particularly if you two joined us."

I think Fin really likes Margot. I gave him crap about it when we ran into her and her sister in Austin, but in typical Fin fashion he brushed it off, making light of his suspected interest in her. The fact he wanted me to invite her for dinner doesn't bode well for his supposed disinterest in her.

"Sam, we thought you and Margot might like to take a spa day tomorrow." Fin drops the surprise we've been hatching.

I take Samantha's hand. "You're off the rest of the week, and it's been arranged for Margot to go with you tomorrow if you're up for it. We thought you could use a day of pampering and relaxation." One day is not going to erase the stress of the last month since her father died, but it's a start. I want her to use these next few days to just relax and recharge, not worrying about being in control of anything. She needs to step back and just worry about herself for a while.

Samantha's wide eyes roam the three of us before landing back on me. "Seriously?" The smile gracing her face is precious. I want to do whatever I can to put that look on her face as often as possible.

I squeeze her hand. "Yes, Sweetness. Anything you want, for as long as you want."

She claps her hands, bouncing in her seat, and asks Margot, "You knew about this?"

Margot's smile matches Samantha's, and for a moment I'm not sure who's more excited about this spa day. "Yes! I was dying to tell you, but promised to keep my mouth shut until the menfolk broke the surprise." She rolls her eyes, glancing between Fin and me.

"Victor will be here at ten to pick you up, and Margot will meet you there," Fin fills her in on the details.

Samantha bounds out of her chair and gives Fin a kiss on the cheek. "Thank you, Fin. Truly. Thank you."

She then bounces over to me and kisses me on the lips. "And thanks to you, too."

"You're welcome, Sweetness."

Samantha captures Margot in a hug. "I'm so excited. This will be so fun."

The two of them get lost in conversation about tomorrow as Fin and I begin to clean up dinner.

Samantha

Margot left right after dinner, but not before I pulled her aside to apologize for lying to her about my birthday plans. She doesn't really understand, but she forgives me and knows she probably wouldn't have left it alone if I had told her I just wanted to be by myself. Just as Jace or Joseph wouldn't let it slide either. They think they want me to be upfront with them, but in truth, none of them wants to hear how much I didn't want to celebrate.

"Sam." Fin catches me as I close the door behind Margot and hands me an envelope. "Here's a key to the penthouse and the elevator, the code for the elevator, the code for the alarm system, and cardkey for the garage."

"Wow. That's a lot of information." My head spins trying to process the importance of what's inside this flat white envelope.

"You don't need to worry about any of that for tomorrow, but I want you to have it, just in case. Victor will see to it when you leave for the spa and when you come back. I'll show you how to use it all after I get home."

"Thank you, Fin. For everything." I surprise him with a hug, but it doesn't take him long to hug me back.

"You're welcome." He kisses my head before releasing me. "I'm glad you're taking a day to relax and recharge. No one could have handled what you've had to endure with more grace and dignity. You're not alone anymore. I'm here. Joseph is here, even though he won't always be here physically. Matt and my parents all want to help, as well as Michael and Victor."

I nod, not trusting my voice. I don't understand the level of commitment his family is showing me, but I appreciate it and am touched by it all the same.

I join Joseph and Fin in the living room, listening to them discuss work. Normally, I'm endlessly fascinated with the world of MCI, but it's making me uncomfortable tonight. The idea of Joseph living in a penthouse like this in a year's time drills home the point that they live in a different world than I'm accustomed to. I'm the worker-bee, not the queen. Joseph needs a queen. I know we discussed it before, but this just brings it all crashing back, reality shining brighter than the lights outside Fin's penthouse window, a beacon of the life that awaits Joseph. A high-end, fancy, busy life as a MCI VP.

Add on my doubts over his feelings being heightened as the result of my father's death, the fact he slept with someone else, and that I'm putting them all in danger by simply being here—my anxiety boils over. I hop up with the excuse of getting a drink.

Out of their sight, I pace the kitchen, trying to contain my emotions and raging thoughts. I drink two glasses of water before I decide what I need to do.

Both men stop talking as I reenter the living room. Joseph frowns when he sees me, reading me all too easily.

"I'm going to go to my room." It's only eight, so I can't really say I'm going to bed. "Uh…Fin, thank you for letting me stay. I guess I'll see you tomorrow night."

"Goodnight, Sam. Please call me tomorrow if you need anything." He watches me warily as if he can read me too.

Joseph's eyes narrow, his muscles flex, ready to pounce.

He knows.

I clear my throat, trying to gain strength. "I guess I'll see you…sometime? Thank you for everything. Goodnight."

He stands. "Samantha." His voice is pained with the reality of what I'm trying to do.

I hold my hand up, as if the motion alone would calm him and release him of his self-imposed responsibilities. "Just…don't. Let me go, Joe. It's better this way."

"Goddammit, Samantha!" He stalks across the room too quickly for me to react beyond a few bumbled words and a graceless step backward.

I yelp as he lifts me off my feet and throws me over his shoulder. "I told you." He grips my legs, holding me secure. "I warned you."

"Put me down! You can't do this!" I protest and slap his ass.

"Sweetness," he says all too calmly, "we discussed this. I told you what would happen if you called me that name again. I'm nothing if not a man of my word."

"You can't do this!" I reiterate, holding on to his hips. "Fin, tell him he can't do this."

"Joe." Fin arches a brow at his brother. Their silent exchange happens in a blink of an eye. "Sam." He addresses me now. "Do you really want me to interfere?"

Do I? He would. I can see it in his eyes. Do I want or need Fin in the middle of what's going on with Joseph and me? Isn't it complicated enough without me dragging Fin in to play referee?

Besides, I *don't* want him to stop this. I want Joseph to fight for me. Not out of obligation. Not out of misplaced feelings. I need him to want me for me, as I am now, and not who I may or may not be in the future. "No," I say softly.

Fin nods. "Fair enough."

Joseph grunts and heads toward the hall leading to my room.

"Joe." Fin's voice stops him in his tracks. "Remember who she is—who she is to *you*."

Joseph lets out a huff of air. "I know exactly *who* she is—*what* she is to me," he barks back, turning and continuing on his path. "*She's* the one who needs reminding, and that's what I intend to do."

Holy shit!

Five

Joseph

TO SAY I'M ANGRY WOULD NOT FULLY ENCAPSULATE the depth of what I'm currently feeling. I'm angry as hell and frustrated. I'm hurt by her need to pull away from me—despite the danger she'd willingly put herself in to do it—and pained knowing I'm partially to blame. I'm roaring with possessiveness and the need to mark my territory by sinking my cock balls deep into her to prove she's *mine*.

But fuck. I can't treat her like that. She deserves better. Always.

I plunk her down on the bed, placing my hand on her chest, my thumb and fingers bracketing the space between her collarbones. "Don't move." I hold her down, gently. I'm too angry. *Fuck.* "I need a minute." To calm the fuck down. I start to remove my hand, but she tries to sit up.

I push her back down. "Christ, Samantha. Fucking listen to me for once!"

She lies back, surprised by my vehemence. I brush my free hand across my face. "I won't hurt you. I swear, I could never hurt you, Sweetness. But you're pushing me away—don't deny it—and I need a minute to calm down." I stand up, moving away from the bed. "Give me that, please."

She nods. Her eyes soften as she watches me. "Okay."

I let out a long breath and move to the other end of the room. The curtains are open. Night has come alive outside her bedroom windows. It's nearly as beautiful as she is, though it can't truly hold a candle to her incandescence. Just the thought of that starts to calm me. I glance over at her. She's in the same spot, focusing on me.

I come back to her, grabbing my t-shirt at the back of my neck and pulling it off over my head. Her eyes widen as she takes in my bare chest. My cock swells to painful proportions. I'm not naked enough.

I stop at the edge of the bed. "Take your top off, Sweetness." Silently, she shifts to pull her t-shirt off, taking extra time in extricating her right arm, revealing a pale purple bra cupping her breast provocatively. Her breathing increases, and her chest moves up and down to accommodate her increased heart rate's need for more air.

"Fuck, you're beautiful," I whisper.

I quickly discard my pants and boxer briefs, and crawl up her body, stopping only to kiss up her exposed abdomen and sides.

"Joseph," she breathes.

Thank fuck. She remembers my name.

"That's right, baby. Say it again and again until you know me by no other name." I run my lips across the silken cups of her bra as my fingers trace the lace edges along the top curve of each billowing breast. "I can feel your nipples." I run my lips across each hidden peak again, baring my teeth to scrape the ridged swells. "They're hard for me, Samantha. Just like my cock is hard for you."

Her hands clasp my shoulders as she arches toward my mouth, gasping.

"Yes, baby. So fucking beautiful." I reach underneath her and unclasp her bra with one quick twist. Sitting back, I slowly trail the sexy yet inhibiting bra off her glorious tits. Her eyes blaze with heat when I bend down and flick my tongue over one taut nipple.

"Joseph."

I can't help but smile. "That's right. Say it again." I flick my tongue over her other stiff peak.

She remains silent, yet her hand laces into my hair, trying to draw me to her.

I resist. "What's my name, Sweetness?" I flick her nipple again. "What's my name to *you*?"

"Joseph," she moans.

"Yes. Again." I draw her nipple into my mouth, and this time she chants my name as I suck, pull, and bite on her luscious offerings. I don't give her any respite as I take her other one in my mouth, my fingers continue to tease, pinch, twist her wet and swollen peak I just abandoned. I continue back and forth, torturing her, loving her, making her mine in every way I can until I can make her mine in the most intimate of ways.

Her head tips back, begging me for more, my name escaping her lips over and over again with abandon.

My cock bobs against her belly, anxious to claim her, and my need to touch her roars through my body. *Make her come.*

I slip my hand into her yoga pants and inside her panties. When I touch her slick flesh, she bows off the bed.

"Yes. Please," she pleads.

I place her hand on my cock. "Touch me, Sweetness. I need you too."

Her moan as she touches me for the first time nearly has me coming like a first-time teenager. "Fuck, just like that. Squeeze and pull it, baby."

I slip between her folds, wetting my fingers and moving back to her swollen clit. "We're gonna come together."

She squeezes my cock as her thumb rubs my pre-cum around my cock head.

"And then I'm going to lick you and taste you until you're so hoarse, you can't cry my name any longer, but you'll still be saying it in your head as I drink you up."

She clenches, and her whole body trembles. "Joseph, I'm gonna come."

I press harder and watch as she detonates under me. Her skin flushes, mouth open, crying out my name as her body rocks against my fingers.

Her cries of ecstasy and her hand on my cock take me with her. "Fuck, yes. Just like that." I pump into her hand as I mark her with my cum, feeling all too proud to be doing so, and still hard as fuck.

"Joseph." She continues to grind against my fingers. I don't stop.

I suck her nipples and stroke her clit into two more orgasms. I come again on the third one. Her hand never left my cock. Her hunger for me is just as strong as mine for her.

Samantha

Joseph kisses me awake a little after midnight. "I have to go, Sweetness."

"What?" I try to sit up to focus on what he's saying, but he keeps me still, his body over mine. He's no longer naked, and I'm disappointed. "You're dressed?"

He smiles at my surprise. "Yes. They tend to frown when you arrive at the tarmac naked. I think it's some kind of FAA regulation or something," he teases.

"I don't want anyone else to see you naked." I'm not teasing. The whole jealousy thing is back, and I'm instantly inundated with thoughts of the girl he fucked a few weeks ago. Tears prick my eyes. "Why do you have to leave? I thought you were going to stay since it's just one more day of school for you. You don't have class on Fridays."

"You're right. I don't have school on Fridays, but I need to be back for class today."

"Oh." I can't hide my disappointment.

He kisses my head and then moves to sit next to me, pulling my naked body into his lap. "I need to give you your birthday present."

His sheepish smile is almost enough to chase the sadness away. "You got me a present?"

"Yes. I've had it for a while, but I wanted to wait and give it to you on your birthday."

"How long have you had it?" I'm looking around and don't see any presents laying on the bed.

"I got it over Christmas before I mauled you on your date with Sebastian."

"That wasn't a date," I correct.

"It wasn't a date for *you*. It was a date for him until he and I came to an understanding," he clarifies.

"Hmm. Well, if that's a mauling, then you can maul me like that anytime." I squirm at the memory of the way Joseph stormed the restaurant and made me come in an alcove where we could have been discovered, claiming me like I was his.

He grips my hips to still me. "You're going to make me hard if you keep that up."

I move to straddle him, his growing erection pressing between my legs. I lean forward and whisper in his ear, "Too late." I kiss his neck and suck his earlobe. "I want to taste you."

His hands grab my hips again. "Christ, Samantha." He's turned on and wants it too. But still he denies me. "I didn't make good on my promise to kiss and lick every inch of you. We'll have to save that for next time."

I start to move away. But he stops me, holding me tightly against him. "Where you going?"

"You said *no*," I say softly, keeping my eyes on his clothed chest.

He lifts my chin with a finger. "I said no to a taste test. I'm not saying no to letting you get me off again." He kisses my chin and then my lips, tenderly, before pulling way. "I don't think I could ever deny you wanting to touch me."

I see the truth in his eyes.

He motions to the bed. "Lie down."

I quickly comply as Joseph stands, stripping off his clothes. He throws the covers to the end of the bed and turns the nightstand lamp on before he lies beside me.

"I want to see you. I need to remember this moment for when I'm away from you." His eyes roam my body and settle on my face. "You're the most beautiful creature I've ever seen." He leans down and kisses my neck and then moves lower to my nipples, hard in anticipation of his touch. "Spread your legs for me. Show me that glorious pussy."

"Joseph," I gasp, loving his dirty talk but shocked by it too.

He smiles wickedly as he sucks my nipple into his mouth and moves his hard cock against my thigh.

I arch and spread my legs for him, wanting him in ways I don't understand in places I've never been touched before.

He groans as I take his hand and press it between my thighs. "Christ, that's hot." He watches as his fingers slip through my wet slit. "Show me what you need."

I move my hips against his fingers, wanting him to enter me, but he doesn't. I wrap my hand around his cock and tease his moist head before moving up and down his shaft in time with my hips.

"So fucking beautiful, Sweetness." His eyes never leave mine as our bodies soar once again.

He growls at the clock. "I'm late."

Finishing getting dressed, he comes back to sit next to me on the bed. His hand slips below the covers to between my legs. "I can't get enough of this, Samantha." He pulls back, slipping his fingers into his mouth with a groan.

OMG! That's so hot.

"Next time, I'm spending all night with you coming on my tongue and face."

How can I be turned on again? My hips move of their own accord. My hand rubs his jean-clad erection. He closes his eyes and moves his hips into my hand as his fingers slip below the covers again. "Show me." His voice is low with need.

I pull back the covers and spread my legs, no longer shy of showing him what he does to me.

"You want me, Sweetness?" One-handed, he undoes his jeans, pulling out his rigid cock, wrapping his fingers around it, stroking it hard and fast.

The sight of him pleasuring himself is nearly too much. "Yes." I arch back, needing more.

He fingers move lower, rounding my entrance, teasing but not entering me. "You want me here? You want my cock filling you up?"

"God, yes."

He moans at my eagerness. "Touch your breast for me. Make your nipples hard. Make it feel good."

I grab each breast and squeeze. My nipples harden under my palms. I pull and twist slightly, sending currents of pleasure to my clitoris.

"Slip your fingers inside your pussy, baby. Fuck yourself for me. Let me watch." He's so turned on, cum beads on the head of his cock.

I reach over and swipe it, licking it off my fingers, before lowering my hand between my legs.

"Fuck, Samantha," he groans as I slip my fingers into my virgin passage. "That right there is the hottest damn thing I've ever seen."

He continues to circle my clit with one hand as he strokes his cock with the other, watching my fingers slip in and out. "Fuck, you need to get there. I'm about to come just from the sight of you."

I can't keep my eyes off his near-bursting cock. I want to run my tongue along the tip, licking the cum as it escapes.

"Curl your fingers, baby, just a few inches in and press." His gravelly voice nearly sends me over.

I do it. A whole new sensation causes me to clench around my fingers. "Oh, god!"

"That's your g-spot, beautiful. Stroke it." He watches my fingers slip in and out. "That's right, just like that. Tell me. What does it make you want?"

"You. You inside me, filling me, rubbing me right there with the head of your cock. And yet I need you deeper too."

My words hit me more than they do him. I'm overcome. "Joseph." I close my eyes and twist my head away. It's too much.

Suddenly, he's over me. His mouth is on one nipple as his hand teases the other one. I open my eyes, and he's no longer touching himself. He's totally focused on me.

"What about you?" I grab his cock and stroke him in rhythm with my fingers. Fuck, that's erotic. I can feel it, the tingling starting in my legs.

He grunts against my breast and sucks harder, biting down slightly. That does it. The most powerful orgasm I've ever felt rips through my body. I grip him tighter, trying not to forget him as I shake and clench around my fingers, coming for his pleasure and mine.

Minutes, possibly hours later, I open my eyes to Joseph sitting next to me sucking on my fingers and wiping off my abdomen and then between my legs with a warm washcloth.

Panic hits me. "Oh, god, did you come?" I don't even remember if I let go of him or if he even came. I was too wrapped up in my own release to focus on him.

He releases my fingers with a *pop.* "All over you, Sweetness." His dimpled smile is stunning.

Taking the washrag back to the bathroom, he returns a moment later, beaming, relaxed, and satisfied. He lies next to me, fully dressed, and pulls me into his arms. "That was the hottest sexual experience of my life. I've never been so turned on or come so hard." He kisses my forehead. "Actually, I've never come that many times in one night. Ever."

I shyly nuzzle into his neck, entirely too sated and happy to even respond except to say, "Me neither. But, I suppose you already knew that."

He lifts my chin. "I could spend hours talking to you about that, but I have something important I have to do before I leave. And I really have to leave or I'll never get back to Austin."

Reaching into his pocket, he pulls something out. "This is a sign of my devotion to you. It represents my promise to you of a future I'm determined we'll have together."

He slips a ring on my left ring finger, and brings my hand to his lips and kisses it. "Forever, Samantha. This is my promise."

"Joseph—" I start to protest.

He stops me with a kiss, deepening it more than he should if he intends to leave. He pulls back, breathless, just like me. "You need time. You need to process what all has happened. Not just tonight, but over the last few weeks. I hurt you. I slept with someone else. Intentional or not, it still happened, and you need time to process that."

Intentional or not?

He squeezes my hand. "I need you to forgive me. I need you to come to trust what you are to me, and what I am to you. Not just now but in the future. Our future. Together." Kissing me one more time, he slips out of bed, tucking me in. "I'll talk to you tomorrow." Then he smiles. "Well, later today actually. I set your alarm for nine in the morning. Victor will pick you up at ten for your spa day. Take your phone and your ear buds. I'm going to send you something, and you'll need them."

I start to panic, and tears cloud my vision. "Joseph." I grip his arms tightly, not wanting to let him go. When he's here and close, all feels right. It's when he's gone, away from me, I start to crumble and begin to question everything.

As if he can read my mind, he takes both my hands in his and holds up my left hand so I can see the platinum band of solid diamonds he's placed on my finger. "Do you see this ring?" He waits for me to nod before he continues. "This ring is my promise to you, my commitment to you and our future. When you have doubts, when you're scared, lonely, or mad at me, just look down at your finger and know I'm here."

He kisses the ring, my palm, and each finger, then presses my ring-clad hand over his heart. "And know you are here. Always. Promise."

PART 3

FALLING

Six

AT EXACTLY TEN THERE'S A KNOCK ON THE penthouse door. I look through the peephole, although whoever it is needs a key in order to make it up to this floor unannounced. There's a wall of chest staring back at me. I slowly open the door, not 100% sure it's such a good idea.

"Good morning, Sam." He gives me a quick nod, his face stoic, not giving up any thoughts dancing around in his head. *Dancing* may be a little too lighthearted for this man. His thoughts probably *stomp* around in his head.

"Morning, Victor." I give him a warm smile trying to coax one in return.

"Are you ready for your spa appointment?"

"Yep."

Victor sets the alarm, and then escorts me out the door and to the elevator.

He's a striking man, late twenties and built like a linebacker, probably about the same height as Joseph.

Yes, I will probably forever compare all men to Joseph. He's my new standard of measurement, apparently.

Victor has blond hair, a square jaw, and a neck the size of my thigh. He has light brown eyes and a hard-set mouth. He's so serious, his face might actually crack if he did smile. He's wearing a black suit that has to be custom made to fit such a muscular guy.

"Victor, you're not really a driver, are you?" He's way too fit; he has to be a bodyguard, at the least. I don't know his background, but he's an ex-military type, perfect for running security.

When I met him at the hospital, Fin introduced him as his longtime friend and driver. I thought it was kinda odd, but I guess a busy man like Fin needs to be able to concentrate on other tasks while driving around the city. I wonder which came first, the friend or the driver part, but just yesterday Joseph told me *Victor and his men* have been watching me for weeks. So obviously, he's not really a driver.

"Well, Sam, I'm driving you today. So, technically I am a driver."

Smartass.

I glare at him, unblinking, cock my head, my hand on my hip, trying to stare him to death until he admits he's more than just a driver.

I almost get a smirk. "That laser-beam glare of yours won't even penetrate my thick skin. You might as well give it up before you pop a blood vessel." He has a slight Texas drawl and a steely façade I'm determined to crack.

I sigh and look away. "Fine. If you won't tell me, then I'll just have to make up my own back story and job duties for you." The elevator doors open, I step out. "You may not like some of them. Fair warning."

"Duly noted." He motions to the left. "This way."

Did I detect a hint of amusement in his voice? Am I getting to him already? *Hmmm, this might be fun.*

The ride to the spa is quiet and peaceful. Margot is meeting us there, so I'm enjoying these few minutes of solitude. Not that Margot's a chatterbox, but when we get together, we are usually anything but quiet. We've been fairly good friends since second grade, but became closer when Jace went off to college. Jace still holds the title of "best friend," and it's hard to let go. It feels like I'm betraying him if I do, but honestly, I'm not sure he'd even notice with how distant he's been lately.

While I've always considered Jace my best friend, I've never really shared everything with him. I realized this past Thanksgiving, perhaps I don't really have a best friend. The situation at the dance club, where I told Joseph my history with Jace's old hookup Veronica, made me realize I don't really tell anyone anything—not important things. I never told a soul about the shitty way Veronica treated me by seducing my then *kinda* boyfriend. Until I told Joseph, only Veronica and Roger knew what they did to me.

And while it wasn't technically cheating because Joseph and I were already broken up when he slept with someone else, part of me still feels like I've been cheated on again. I pushed him away to keep him safe, and the worst thing happened, so why am I letting him back in?

It could all go horribly wrong *again*.

Am I selfish enough to let them in and put them in danger? Or do I continue to keep everyone at arm's length and hope my father's killer focuses on me, ignoring everyone else?

"You alright, Sam?"

I meet Victor's eyes in the rearview mirror. "Yeah, why?"

He seems worried. Silently, he hands me a tissue. It's only then I realize I'm crying.

Shit. What is wrong with me? I've got to get a grip. I wipe my face. "I'm sorry. It's been one of those kinds of weeks."

"No need to apologize. You've had more than just a rough week." The concern is evident in his voice.

"Yeah. I guess you know all my dirty laundry." I lay my head back and close my eyes.

"Sam, we're here." I jump, but Victor stops me with a soft grip. "I didn't mean to scare you. I tried to be gentle." He's apologetic, like being gentle is foreign to him.

I nod and take a deep breath. "It's okay." I rub my head, trying to soothe the dull ache.

"Do you have a headache?" He's not the hard ass he wants me to think he is.

"No." I stare past him to the glass doors in front of me.

"Ms. Dubois is already here. Once you check in, they'll bring you to her." For a moment, I think he's talking about Margot's mother, but I realize he's referring to Margot. She'll get a kick out of being called Ms. Dubois.

My gaze moves back to the hulk of a man leaning down next to me in the open car door. "How long do we have? How do I get in touch with you?"

"I'm at your disposal, Sam. If you stay for an hour, or if you stay for six, it is completely up to you. Though, Ms. Dubois' parents ask she be home by eight, given it's a school night, and she's already playing hooky with you today." There— almost a hint of a smile.

"I can't imagine staying here that long. Maybe a massage and a pedicure, a few hours, tops."

I move to get out. Victor stands, offering me his hand in assistance.

"Give me your phone. I'll put my number in. You can call me or text when you're ready." I pull it out of my purse and hand it to him.

As I wait, I stretch my sore shoulder and try not to fidget.

He hands me back my phone, eyeing my bad shoulder for a moment. "No rush, no advance notice needed."

With a nod I head to the door.

"Sam." He moves closer, standing in my space so that I have to crane my neck to make eye contact.

"I do more than drive for Mr. McIntyre." He nods curtly and backs off, seemingly satisfied, as if he's relinquished a huge secret.

I study him for a beat. "No dice, Mary Poppins, that in no way equals the crap you know about me." I head toward the door. "The stakes have changed. Enjoy washing Fin's unmentionables."

I disappear inside. It takes everything I have not to turn around to see if any reaction shows on his face. Though, not knowing doesn't stop a huge smile from spreading across mine.

Game on, Victor.

After ditching my clothes and purse, I don a sumptuous white robe that's two sizes too big, but honestly, it feels amazing, and the large size is like wearing a blanket of the highest quality. It feels good against my bare skin. Decadent even. I find Margot sitting in a private lounge, relaxing on a caramel-colored chaise, reading a book. She's old school, preferring hardcopy as opposed to my ebook preference.

I take the lounger next to hers. She's lost in her book and has no idea I've even entered the room.

"I'm pretending to be sophisticated," she says quietly, her eyes focused on the page.

Well, so much for thinking I'm stealthy. "And what makes you think you have to pretend?"

Her eyes meet mine. "You and I both know that's not true." She shakes her head and smiles. "This place is supercalifragilisticexpialidocious, and I'm trying to contain my girlish desire to dance around in excitement." She straightens her shoulders and raises her chin. "Sophisticated, see?"

I study her, then nod succinctly. "Yes, I can see that. Very sophisticated indeed."

She beams, playing along, but then her face falls. "I have to ask. Don't be mad."

"You can ask me anything. I won't get mad."

She closes her book, setting it to rest beside her. "Did she ever remember?"

I stifle a flinch when I catch her train of thought. I'd wanted to spend it alone, but I can't deny the fact my own mother forgot my birthday stings like hell, despite the circumstances. That's how I know she's truly lost right now. My mom—and my dad—were amazing parents. But as amazing as they were, they were even more amazing as a couple. Awe-inspiring and everything I ever want in a mate. What my mom lost when he died was more than a partner—he was her soulmate, and I can't be mad at her or even disappointed in her. If celebrating my birthday can't bring her back, I don't know what it's going to take. "No," I sigh.

"It makes me sad to think about you being alone and Eleanor forgetting it was even your special day. She always makes such a fuss over birthdays. She even makes a fuss over *my* birthday." She's nearly in tears.

Sweet Margot, genuinely sad and offended for me.

I can't have that. I already cried once this morning, and even though we're not together, maybe Mom will snap out of it while with Joseph's parents. *That* is more important than any birthday present or fuss that could have been made. "That's why it's no big deal. If my father were still alive, it would've been a completely different day. But, the reality is—it's a new reality. My mom may never be the birthday-celebrating Eleanor again. She might be a whole different Eleanor, in every way."

Margot leans over and squeezes my hand. "I'm sorry."

I smile a smile I'm not feeling, but I'll fake it until I do. "Me too."

She swings her legs over the side to face me. "So, what are we having done today? Did you decide on a treatment?"

"Yes." I pick up the menu on the end table and point to the massage with a name I can't pronounce, so I don't even try. "I want this one. It's an-hour-and-a-half and sounds incredibly relaxing. Then I want the pedicure with the paraffin wax treatment."

"That's the massage I asked for too. Great minds think alike. I could go for a pedicure. That sounds like an excellent plan." She points to a but-ton on the wall. "They said just ring the bell when we're ready."

I push the button, and almost immediately, two women come to get us. Before we separate, Margot gives me quick hug. "Thank you for in-cluding me. I'll see you afterwards for lunch."

Samantha

The massage was everything I hoped for. It was a little awkward at first, me being naked and all. I mean, she's a professional, but still, it's the idea of being naked with a stranger's hands on me.

She went to town on my shoulders, taking special care with my in-jured one. She kept telling me I carry my stress in my shoulders and neck, and that I'm far too young to have as much stress as she was working out of my body.

Hello? I've been shot. I've lost my father. Killer on the loose. And my on-again off-again piece of man-cake drama is enough to put me over the edge. Stress in my shoulders is minor collateral damage.

After the full body massage, she cocooned me in a therapeutic wrap and started a warm oil drip on my forehead. The scent of eucalyptus, lav-ender, and vanilla wafted in the air. I actually dozed off when she began to massage the oil into my scalp.

I stir when she starts to remove the warm blankets and the cool air hits my warmed, sensitized skin.

"I'm sorry to wake you, Ms. Cavanagh." Her smile is sweet and comforting. "You looked so peaceful, it's a shame."

I stifle a yawn. "It's okay." I scan the room, wondering how much time has passed. "I'm so relaxed. Thank you, that was wonderful."

She slips a dry sheet over me before removing the last of the damp towels from underneath the sheet. "I'm glad you enjoyed it. Now, be sure to drink plenty of water. You'll need to flush out all those toxins I released from your muscles."

With my promise to do just that, and a final thank you, she slips out of the room to leave me to shower.

I'm feeling weak and a little overheated, so a hot shower is not in the cards. I stay in just long enough to shampoo the oil out of my hair. With a quick blow dry and a slathering of the wonderful smelling lotion she left as a sample, I slip my robe back on and go in search of Margot.

The spa set up a private lunch in the same lounge we were in before. Margot isn't there when I enter, so I take a seat on a lounge chair and pull out my phone. My heart flutters when I see a text from Joseph.

Joseph: *Sweetness. I hope you're enjoying your spa day. Listen to this and know I'm thinking of you. (I will deny it if you tell anyone I've even ever heard of One Direction).*

I put in my earbuds and click the link in his text. My YouTube app opens and the video of "Little Things" by One Direction starts to play. I've never been much of a One Direction fan, but I may start to love them as I listen to the song Joseph wanted me to hear, telling me he loves all these little things about me…and that he loves me.

Seriously? Did he just tell me he loves me through this song?

Self-consciously, I glance around the room, confirming I'm still alone. I hit play again and dash away the tears as they fall. No matter how hard I've fought it, I can't help falling in love with this man. I know it's too soon, and I'm struggling with the conflict of letting him go to keep him safe and keeping him close because I need him. I let my emotions run free until the end. Then, I search for the perfect song to send back in retribution.

I laugh out loud when I find it. It's scandalous, and he might not find any humor in it, but I need to stop this sentimental love train before it sweeps me away.

Me: *I promise to keep your One D obsession to myself. Here's a song for your listening pleasure. Enjoy.*

I include the link to the "Birthday Cake" by Rihanna video. It is definitely not One D. It's hot and sexy and gives a completely different idea of what I want. It's not that I don't want the hearts and flowers, I do. I truly do. I just don't want to get wrapped up in believing in the fairytale of Joseph and me. Not yet. It's too soon. I'm in danger, which means if he stays near me, *he'll* be in danger.

And he slept with someone else two weeks ago.

It's too fucking soon.

Plus, I'm not convinced he doesn't deserve better than me. I will be heartbroken when he finally figures that out. So, I'll send him sex songs to combat his romantic love songs.

That way, when he comes to his senses and realizes he's more protective over me than in love with me, maybe it will be easier because I haven't bought into the delusion from the start. Until then, until it all blows over, it's best if we—if *I*—keep things casual.

A good defense is a good offense—or so they say.

Margot and I have a salad of roasted chicken, candied walnuts, carrots, red onion, blue cheese, and heirloom tomatoes with a sweet vinaigrette that knocks my taste buds for a loop.

Maybe not all that healthy, but it was darn tasty.

"Holy nut crackers, Sam. What's on your finger?" She drops her fork and grabs my hand before I can pull it away. "Did he propose? Are you engaged?" Her voice gets louder with each word and is nearly a shrill by the time she reaches *engaged*.

"No. Calm down." I snatch my hand back, checking the room. Thankfully we're still alone, which seems odd. I wonder if it's by design.

Shit. It is.

I can't believe I didn't see it before. Joseph or Fin or fucking Michael made sure we would be alone, undisturbed, safe. I sink back into my chair and take in how that makes me feel. Cherished. Protected. Loved.

"Sam." Margot's worried voice pulls my attention.

"I'm sorry. I just realized we haven't seen another customer. They must have arranged it."

She takes in the room. It's clearly meant to be a community gathering place to wait or relax between treatments. Granted it's during the week, but still, the people who can afford to come here wouldn't be concerned about working hours as most of the women probably don't even work. Not that being the wife of a highly successful man is not work, it's just not nine-to-five work.

Margot's knowing gaze returns to mine. "You're right. I didn't think about it, but it seems so obvious now. Wow." She leans back, her awe mirroring mine. "He must really love you to go to all this trouble and cost."

"It might not even be Joseph who did this. It was probably Fin or Michael."

She shakes her head. "No. Uh-uh, it was Joe. He called my parents, arranged for the car to come and pick me up, and also invited me to dinner last night."

"What? I thought it was Fin who invited you to dinner."

"He knew about it, but Joe set it up." She's certain.

My mind is spinning between him flying to Dallas, jarring me out of bed, whisking me away to his brother's house, setting in motion all the other stuff regarding the house and my mom, and then last night. *I mean, Jesus, last night.* It was incredible and wasn't just protectiveness. My eyes fall on the ring. Could he really love me? Is that what he's telling me by actions and not words?

"Don't cry, Sam." Margot comes over and hugs me. "It's not a bad thing. Don't look so sad."

"He can't. It's too soon." I sob on her shoulder.

"He can, and it's not."

In the middle of our pedicures I get a text from Joseph. I shouldn't look. It's rude, but I can't help it. I'm dying to see what he said about my song.

Joseph: *That was quite a song you sent me. I'm not sure what to say. So, I'll just say this…*

Damn! He sent me a link to "Let Me Love You" by DJ Snake. He's persistent, I'll give him that. I have to up my game.

Me: *I'm not sure what you're trying to say. I think I'm missing the subtlety. Let me give you this to ponder. Maybe it will clear your head.*

I nearly chicken out, but hastily paste in the link to "Birthday Sex" by Jeremih before I lose my nerve. I laugh to myself; I seem to have a birthday theme going, which is apropos considering I just had mine.

His response comes faster than I anticipate.

Joseph: *I see how you're going to play this. I'm a determined man, Sweetness. I'm not giving up. For your listening pleasure, beautiful…*

Double damn! He's good. I click and listen to "Then There's You" by Charlie Puth. And before I even finish the first song, he texts me another one: "I Get to Love You" by Ruelle.

I start to cry when listening to that offering. He's breaking my heart already.

Margot touches my arm. "What's wrong?"

Stopping the song, I unplug my earbuds. "Joseph sent this to me."

I put my phone on speaker and start the song over. I close my eyes, laying my head back, and listen to the words, and just let the tears fall.

Margot clasps my hand in hers, closing the distance between her chair and mine by way of our joined hands.

The song surrounds me like a kaleidoscope of bright jewels dancing in my head, telling me the things I won't let him say. The things I'm afraid to hear—I'm afraid to believe.

How will I survive him?

He'll never let me keep my walls up.

He's gonna do everything he can to make me fall for him.

It's already too late.

Seven

'M GETTING READY FOR BED WHEN MY PHONE RINGS. I run to catch it before it rolls to voicemail, hoping it's Samantha. It's Fin. I try not to let my disappointment seep into my voice as I answer. It's some connection with her, after all.

"Hey, how's it going?"

"Is that really what you want to ask me?"

"No." He knows me too well. "How is she?" I was all confidence and bluster today during our song texting, but truthfully, I'm anxious. I don't want to push her too fast, too hard. But, I also want her to know my intentions. I don't want to leave her with any doubt.

"She'll be alright, Joe. She just needs time to unwind. She keeps everything too close to the cuff, I wonder if she was ever really a kid. Has she ever let anyone do anything for her or has she always been in such control?"

"I think, from what she and Jace have told me, she's always been independent, self-reliant," I offer.

"The question is, is she in control because she wants to be or because she has to be? Based on her level of stress, I think it's the latter. And I don't mean to insinuate she's been neglected, but sometimes, when you have one wild child, which is Jace, in this case, and one straight arrow, such as Sam, the straight arrow is left to their own devices because they seem so capable. Perhaps it's not truly in her nature to have such control. If it was her nature, she would feed off the control and gain strength from it. In this case, though, I think the weight of the control is sapping her energy.

It's taking everything she has to stay afloat, and she's come to the end of her reserves."

"You sound like a man who knows what he's talking about. Mr. Control Freak."

He laughs. "Uh, pot meet kettle."

"I learned it from the best," I say, referring to him. "I agree with your assessment. She's completely capable of being in control, but I do sense she'd rather not be, at least not always. It's been worse since her dad died, though. I'm sure feeling like she didn't have a choice in the matter makes a difference as well. When you choose to be in control, you're prepared, expecting it. This was unexpectedly dumped in her lap."

"I think the spa day was a really good idea, as well as taking tomorrow off. It'll give her a chance to recharge, refill her well, so to speak," Fin says with his typical level of confidence.

"I wish I was there." Regret fills my voice with an edge.

"You didn't have to leave."

"I did. She needs time, space. I need to give her that, and not run her over with how I'm feeling. I have a hard enough time holding back when I'm not with her, but when I'm with her, it's all consuming."

He laughs. "Yeah, I noticed that last night when you practically grabbed her by the hair and dragged her to your cave."

"I wasn't that bad." *Was I?*

"Nearly. I was hoping she'd ask me to stop you, but apparently she's fallen under your spell and actually likes your caveman ways."

I smile at the memory. "She kinda does, doesn't she?"

"Don't let it go to your head. Like you said, she needs time. I'll watch after her for you."

"Thanks, brother." I owe him one. I owe him millions by now for a lifetime of support.

"Welcome. Always."

My phone beeps, and I'm instantly pacified by the sight of her name. "Fin, she's calling."

"Go. We'll talk tomorrow." He hangs up before I can even reply.

I take a deep breath and answer.

"Sweetness." My voice is low and gruff, a voice I only use with my girl.

"Hi."

I'm happy to hear her voice, that one word holding so much emotion.

"Thank you for today. The spa, Margot, the texts, the songs. The ring. Everything," she continues quickly.

My heart fills to near bursting. "You're welcome, Samantha. Anything for you. Always."

"I miss you." She's tentative with those words, but I'm impressed she said them at all. That's not like her to be so vulnerable. I'm hoping it's a good sign in the right direction.

"I miss you too. More than you know." More than I should, or have a right to, given the state of our relationship and the distance in our future as we both finish college. I don't know how to resolve that without impacting the plans we have for our lives, our goals. I only have a year left here. Thank god she'll be here for that year. But after I graduate and return to Dallas, we're back in the same boat living in opposite cities. She has such a bright future. I can see it clearly. I can't wait to witness it. I want to be a part of it. I want to be a supporter, an encourager for her.

I take a breath. I can't solve it now. I made my choice. I'll figure it out. Make the distance work. I'm choosing to be with her now instead of waiting. "It took everything I had to leave you. I nearly turned around no less than half a dozen times," I confess. Not just because I can't stand to be away from her, but because I want to be the one by her side, keeping her safe, making her feel secure, loved, cherished.

"Really?"

She's still so uncertain about us. "Really, Samantha. Look at your finger and tell me you remember what I said."

The line is silent except for her soft breath. I picture her gazing down at her left hand, fingers splayed, admiring the ring I gave her, shining brilliantly like her beauty.

"Do you see it, Sweetness?" I wait for her to answer. I need to be sure she's with me.

"Yes." Her voice is barely audible.

"That ring of diamonds is nearly as precious as you are to me."

"You always say the sweetest things. It's hard to hear but even harder to believe." Her honesty both shocks and saddens me.

"Why do you doubt it so much?"

"God, Joseph, have you looked in the mirror? Seen what a prize you are? I've just…no one's ever seen me like you do. I expect maybe a nerd in my computer class to see me that way, but not you. Not the guy who works for my dream company, in my dream job, and treats me like I'm someone special."

"You're killing me, baby. Don't you see? I am that nerd who's sitting next to you in awe of your mind, blown away by your beauty, and kneeling at your feet asking you to love me in return."

"You're the one killing me." Her voice breaks with emotion.

"Fuck. I need to see you. Get your iPad, and I'll call you on it."

I hang up, barely giving her a chance to reply.

I power up my iPad, situating the pillows against the headboard, and get another on my lap to set the iPad on.

The moment she answers and her face appears on my screen, the air is stolen from my lungs. It's been less than twenty-four hours, and I already forgot how beautiful she truly is. I need a picture of her to remind me of that fact instead of relying on my faulty memory, which is insufficient to the task, apparently.

"God, I've missed you," I exclaim. "Look at you all cozy in bed. Sexy as hell, cute and beautiful, all at the same time."

Her smile gets bigger. "You're such a liar. I'm red and blotchy from crying. I'm a mess." She reaches out and touches the screen. "I've missed those green eyes and those dimples." Her eyes brim with tears.

"Please don't cry, baby." If she starts to cry, there's no way I won't join her when I can actually see her so full of emotions, and I'm hundreds of miles away, unable to comfort her the way I want—the way I need to. The backs of my eyes sting with the possibility of tears.

She nods. "I'm sorry. I'm a bit of a wreck." She brushes away a few tears that manage to fall. She feigns a smile, trying to mask her emotions.

"That's even more reason for you to listen to me and stop trying to fight me on this. I'm yours. You're not getting rid of me. You can fight me or you can get on board. But I'm not backing down, unless you can tell me here and now you feel nothing for me, that you don't want me to fight for our future. That you don't want me to fight for *you*."

She breaks. "Oh, god." Her sobs rip at my heart. She buries her face in her hands.

"Tell me, Sweetness. Tell me what you want. Tell me what you need and it's yours."

She raises her head, sniffling as she wipes her face. "I need you to be safe."

Christ. Fuck. That's my wish too, for her to be safe. "Do you know how scared I was when I heard you'd been shot?"

She shakes her head.

"It was like the air had been sucked from my lungs. The very life force of my being diminished with the possibility that I could lose you. Forever. No amount of planning, no amount of logical thinking could have prepared me for the vision of a life without you in it."

"But when I broke up with you…you so easily replaced me." The hurt on her face guts me.

Never. I could never replace her. How can I ever tell her the truth?

"When you broke up with me, I was right back there in that dark hole, forced to envision a future without you. I drank too much. I foolishly tried to drown my sorrow, find a reprieve from a painful reality where you married another man. Where you gave your heart to *another* man. My drinking put me in a bad place…where something incomprehensible happened."

Where I made love to you in my dream, while my body was ravaged by another.

"I can't erase what happened. I can only ask for your forgiveness and spend the rest of my life working to be the man who deserves you." One who doesn't drink himself into oblivion, putting himself at risk. I'm lucky Tiff used a condom and all tests came back negative. But I have to take responsibility for putting myself in a high-risk situation where I was not in control of my body. It's not all on me, but that part is. And that's what I have to ensure never happens again.

"It's not on you, Joseph. I'm the one who broke your heart. I started that train in motion." Her tears are back, but her eyes never waiver from mine. She's owning her part, just as I'm owning mine.

"How 'bout we share that burden? I'll forgive you, and you work on forgiving me." I suggest a compromise, as we could go all day, blaming ourselves for causing the other's pain.

She nods with a soft smile.

"Now, let's make this official. I want you to be my girlfriend. Officially. You're already wearing my ring. I want everyone to know it's *my* ring on *your* finger."

I'm so glad I can see her face. Her blue eyes stare back at me. She's biting her lower lip, and I can see her thoughts swirling around in her head.

Come on, Samantha. Say yes.

"What does that mean, exactly?" She's traded her lower lip for her thumb, capturing it between her teeth, as her eyes continue to study my face.

"It means you're mine. No one else's. It means I'm yours and no else's. Exclusive. No one touches you, and no one touches me. We make time to see each other when we can, and when we can't, we talk on the phone, text, video conference, as much as possible. It means we stop pretending this is not what it is. We embrace it and grow as a couple."

She's still just staring at me, but she's at least stopped troubling her lip and thumb. "What do you say, Sweetness? Will you be mine?"

"I think I always was, Joseph," she says softly, reverently.

A single tear streams down her cheek. I reach out to wipe it away before I realize how silly it is. "The same for me, baby. Say *yes.*"

"Yes."

My smile does not even begin to reflect the joy my heart has just exploded with. "You have no idea how happy you just made me, Samantha."

"And you're really mine? *Only* mine?" She casts her eyes downward, like she can't bear to see me if I say *no.*

"Look at me."

Tears well up as she focuses on the screen.

"Baby, why does that upset you?"

Her chin starts to tremble. "I'm sorry I keep crying, Joseph." She averts her eyes as she wipes the tears that continue to fall.

"Please, look at me."

She raises her chin, her eyes back on mine.

"That's better. I don't like it when you hide from me. You don't need to apologize for being emotional, especially not after all that's happened. Tell me why you're crying."

Her voice cracks as she replies. "Because no one's ever been mine before, and no one has ever *wanted* me to be theirs."

There it is. That insecurity of being a supposed leper. Damn, Jace.

"It's a first for me too, Sweetness. I've dated, but I've never met anyone I wanted to be exclusive with, not until you. To answer your question, yes, I'm 100% yours, only yours. Exclusively."

She smiles, and then yawns as she wipes the last of her tears.

"It's late. I should let you get to bed." I kept her up late last night.

"I don't want to let you go, not yet. Can we talk for just a few minutes more?"

That pleases me endlessly. "Yes. Lie down and put me on the bed next to you like I'm lying there with you."

We both lie down, placing our tablets in the place the other person's head would be if we were in bed together. She settles in, flipping her hair up over the pillow, pulling the covers up. I can see her from the shoulders up, sexy and adorable. It's a heady combination.

The conversation flows easily. It always has between us. Natural. Unforced.

Home.

She's my home.

Samantha is not someone who needs to be talking all the time, or have social interaction, or attention lavished on her. She's more of a loner when it comes to that sort of thing. She prefers not to be in the limelight. She's definitely not like her brother in that respect, who loves to be the center of attention.

She yawns again.

"Baby, you're so tired, close your eyes. I'll stay on the line until you fall asleep, or until your screen times out."

She smiles sleepily. "I wish you were here to hold me, keep me warm, make me feel safe and taken care of."

"I wish I was there, too. But I promise you are safe and taken care of. Now blow me a kiss and close your eyes."

She blows me a kiss and flashes me a dreamy smile. "Thank you, Joseph, for today. For my ring, for forgiving me for my birthday lie."

"You're welcome and forgiven. I'm sorry I didn't understand what you really needed for your birthday. I'll endeavor to do better. To give you what you really need and not what I think you need." I blow her a kiss back. "Now, close your eyes. Call me tomorrow."

"Okay. Goodnight, Joseph."

"Goodnight, Sweetness."

She settles further into her pillow, letting out a deep breath, fidgeting just a moment, before she stills and her eyes slowly start to close. She fights it, but eventually her body wins out, and she falls asleep. I stay on the line, watching her sleep, dreaming of the day I'll be there beside her in person every night, not just occasionally.

When her screen finally goes black and the call ends, I whisper, "Goodnight, my sweet girl." I close my tablet, roll over and turn off the lights, settling in for a better night's sleep than I anticipated getting.

Samantha

Despite having the luxury of sleeping in, I wake up at seven, which is sleeping in for me, but not as long as I had hoped. I could roll over and probably go back to sleep, but decide it's better to just get up. I'm anxious to get my day of relaxation started. I throw on yoga pants and a t-shirt, just getting myself decent enough to walk around Fin and not embarrass myself, or him.

When I open the door, the amazing smell of coffee reaches me all the way down the hall. I walk into the kitchen and stop.

Fin's there with his back to me, wearing a pair of workout shorts. Nothing else. He's fit. Really fit. Seeing him like this only makes me think of Joseph, though. Fin's good-looking with the same dark hair and remarkable green eyes as Joseph, and a body no one would throw out of bed, but he's not my Joseph. Joseph is taller, more muscular, broader, and has thicker thighs. Fin is a leaner version of Joseph. If they were athletes, Fin has the swimmer's body, and Joseph is the football player.

He turns, surprising me.

"Hi," I say before he catches me staring at him.

"Oh, hey." He stills, surprised to see me. "I thought you'd still be asleep." He grabs the towel on the counter and dabs at the sweet on his body. "Sorry, I just worked out and wanted to grab a cup of coffee before showering."

I avert my eyes. "It's your home, Fin. You don't need to apologize. I'm sorry I startled you." I point to the coffee. "Do you mind if I get a cup?"

"No, of course." He hands me a mug from the nearby cabinet. "There's creamer in the fridge and sugar is right there." He points to the carafe sitting next to the fancy coffee maker.

I still when I get a good look at the contraption in front of me. "Fin, do I need a license to operate this?"

He chuckles as he comes over to help me out. "No, but it did take me a few weeks to conquer it." He takes the mug from me. "Here let me show you."

He demonstrates how to pour a plain cup of coffee, and how to use the plethora of other functions as well. In the end, I end up with a French vanilla cappuccino that smells to die for.

I take a tentative sip, not wanting to burn my mouth. "Holy shit. This is amazing." I look back at the machine and then at him. "You should marry her. Don't let her get away."

He laughs. "Don't think I haven't considered it."

I open the fridge, taking out the bacon and eggs he showed me last night. "If I make breakfast, would you eat before you leave?"

The awe on his face makes me wish he had someone to cook for him every day. "Absolutely."

As he heads off to the shower, I think how lonely it must be up here. "Fin, would it be alright to call Matt and see if he wants to join us?"

When Fin doesn't respond, I figure he didn't hear me. Then his voice sounds from down the hall. "I'll call and invite him. Go ahead and plan on it."

"Okay." Before I do anything else I run to my room and grab my iPad. I set it on the counter and call Joseph. I want to see him before I start my day.

"Sweetness. This is a nice surprise. I didn't expect to hear from you, much less see you this morning." His voice is sexy and still gruff from sleep.

"I took a chance you'd be up." I disappear out of the frame. "I hope you don't mind if we chat while I work." I come back and adjust the tablet to angle toward the stove.

"What are you doing?" His neck cranes as if he can control the angle of my iPad just by his movements.

"I'm making breakfast for your brothers." I glance up just long enough to see him smile.

"That's really nice of you. Matt's coming over too?" He seems surprised.

"Yes, I thought it was weird me being here and not offering to make him breakfast too, given he's just across the hall."

"If he is across the hall," Joseph replies.

"Where else would he be…" Then it dawns on me. "Oh, you mean—"

"Yeah, he may have slept out." He runs his fingers through his hair.

I brush off the thought as I put the bacon on the cookie sheet for the oven. "It's no big deal. I'll eat whatever is left later." I glance up at him. "What's your day like today? Do you need to leave?"

"No class today, remember? I'm heading to a study group."

That's right, it's Friday. I've lost track of my days. "If you need to go, it's okay. I just wanted to say hi." I peer over my shoulder at his framed, handsomely sleepy face. "I wanted to see you, even if only for a minute."

His dimpled grin makes my heart race. "It's good to see you too. And I don't need to go quite yet, but I'll finish getting ready while you cook for my brothers, whom I'm jealous of right now, by the way."

I did cook him bacon and eggs the night of my dad's funeral. It would be a sad memory, except for how much he and Jace seemed to enjoy the home cooking. "I'll cook for you anytime you're in town, Joseph." I put the bacon in the oven and get out what is needed for the eggs. I hear noises but no Joseph on the screen. "Hey, are you getting naked?"

His face pops back on. "Do you want me to get naked?" I can see the gleam in his eye and his bare chest. Close enough to naked for me to appreciate what I'm missing.

"Well, I'm not sure how your brothers would feel about walking into the kitchen and seeing you in your birthday suit."

"Good point, another time then." He laughs as he disappears off the screen again. "Getting my shoes, be right back."

"Hey, is that coffee I smell?" Matt's voice precedes his appearance in the kitchen, but not by much. He smiles when he sees me. "Good morning. Thanks for the invite to breakfast, Sam."

"You're welcome. I'm glad you could join us." I break eggs in a bowl.

"What can I do to help?" Matt offers.

"How about plates and silverware?" I suggest.

"On it." Matt moves with determination to complete the task at hand. All of the McIntyre men seem to have a single-minded focus of slaying whatever tasks lies ahead of them.

"Hey, Matt."

Matt jumps. I stifle my laugh in my shoulder. I guess I should've warned him we weren't alone.

Wide-eyed, Matt scans the kitchen. "Joe?"

"Here, man, on the island." Joseph's voice fills the kitchen again.

Matt turns the iPad to face him. "Hey. Shit, you scared me. I wasn't expecting to hear your voice."

They chat for few minutes as I cook the eggs and get the bread in the toaster. Before too long, Fin joins us in the kitchen, dapper in his well-tailored navy slacks and white button-down with his tie and jacket in hand. He joins Joseph and Matt in conversation as I plate up breakfast. Matt is dressed similarly, except in dark charcoal pants. Matt and Fin's suit jackets and ties are slung over the back of the couch, waiting to be donned to finish out their business armor for the day.

I set the plates on the breakfast bar and hear my name. I turn to the three of them. Matt and Fin face me, shoulder to shoulder, the same height, and Matt's holding my iPad displaying Joseph's grinning face. Three sets of identical green eyes staring back at me. "Samantha, let me have a minute with you alone before you eat."

I take my tablet from Matt and excuse myself, exiting to my room. "What's up?" I ask on my way down the hall.

"I just wanted to say goodbye to you in private, without my eaves-dropping brothers around."

I close the bedroom door and sit on the nearest chair, holding Joseph on my lap. "Okay, we're alone."

His eyes scan my face like he hasn't seen me in years. "Thank you for calling this morning. I don't think I realized how much I needed to hear your voice and see your lovely face today."

My heart skips a beat. "Joseph, you're going to make my cry if you keep being so nice to me."

"Well, then I guess you'll just have to cry, because I'm not going to stop telling you how much you mean to me or how I'm thankful you thought to call me this morning."

I'm glad such a simple thing makes him happy. "It's good to see your handsome face too, but honestly, I think it makes me miss you more."

"It's a good thing I get to see you soon then, for spring break."

"What do you mean?" I'm shocked. "Are you coming home for spring break? I thought you and Jace were going on a trip."

"I'm coming to see you, Sweetness."

"Joseph." I have to close my eyes to stop from crying.

"Open your eyes, beautiful. Let me see those baby-blues I love so much."

He loves my eyes?

I open them. His gaze is soft. "There they are. You don't have to try not to cry with me, Samantha. I'm not Jace. I'm not going to call them your *girly emotions* and make you feel bad about them. Whatever you feel, I want to know it. I want to see it."

I nod and wipe away my tears. "When will I see you?"

He thinks for a moment. "I'm not sure yet, the Saturday before the break, for sure."

"I'd like that."

"Me too." He flashes his watch. "I gotta go. I'll call you later. Enjoy your day and know I wish I was with you."

"Me too. Bye, Joseph."

"Bye, Sweetness."

Eight

Samantha

AFTER A DAY OF NO SCHOOL OR WORK, I'M GOING stir crazy. I can't sit around Fin's place one more minute. Yesterday's spa day was alright as I was busy doing something, even though it was relaxing and not work or school related. But after Fin and Matt left for work, sitting around Fin's not knowing what to do with myself is a feeling I'm not comfortable with. I'm not good with idle time, and too much time to think is not a good thing for me, at least not right now. I don't want to focus on my father's death, the school work I'm missing, or how much I miss Joseph. It's only been two days, and it feels like weeks.

My options are limited. Everyone is either at work or school. On a whim, I call Sebastian. Maybe he's off today or has a late shift.

"Hey, how's the prettiest friend I have?" his silky voice oozes over the phone.

"Bash, you know I hate it when you lay it on thick like that. Who talks like that, really?"

"I do, babycakes. If you hung out with me more, you'd know that," he admonishes.

"If you're available, we could remedy that over lunch."

"Done. Where?" He jumps on that idea rather quickly.

"Um, I'm downtown. Any place you recommend between here and wherever you are?"

He laughs. "Why are you downtown? And why aren't you in school?"

"I'll tell you all about it over lunch."

"Are you playing hooky? Are you going to ask me to forge a parent note?"

"Seriously?" I'm not really upset, but it's fun to push his buttons. He always comes circling back quickly with his comforting, flirtatious way of his. He wouldn't dare let me go a minute without knowing he's 100% behind me, whatever it is.

"I can't think of any other reason you'd be out of school and still be okay to have lunch. You're obviously not sick, at least not physically."

"Oh gee, thanks."

"I'm kidding, beautiful. I know you're physically sick too." He busts out laughing, and I can't help but join him.

We agree on a place to meet. What should I do from here? Do I go on my own, or do I call Michael or Victor? I decide to text both of them and see what they say.

I toss my phone on my bed and quickly get ready. When I come out of the bathroom, there's texts from both of them informing me that Victor will be up shortly to collect me.

Collect. Me.

That cracks me up, like I'm garbage or laundry to be collected and carted away.

"Enough of the pleasantries. Fill me in, Sam. What's going on?" Sebastian discreetly motions to the guy who walked in with me and then proceeded to sit two tables over from us, looking like he's studying the menu, but I'm sure he's actually checking out the room behind those dark shades he's wearing.

"Just ignore him. I doubt he's the only one in here. I'm not supposed to notice them, but I can feel 'em watching me."

He gives me a stern glare. "Spill it, babycakes. What the fuck?"

"Do you talk to your patients with that mouth?" I smile and try to make light of the situation.

"I do lots of things with this mouth, the least of which will be to unleash its full verbal potential on you if you don't start talkin." He's not kidding. Nice, laid-back Sebastian has taken a backseat to overprotective, concerned Sebastian.

"Okay…" As I start to fill him in, it dawns on me, perhaps we shouldn't be discussing this in public. It would have been a better idea to have him come to the penthouse. I imagine Joseph would prefer a public meeting—and I needed to get out of the house.

I wrap up the drama of the last few weeks, feeling bad we haven't spoken, but it was part of my plan to keep everyone I care about safe. Bash is no exception. Though we haven't been friends long, he's become important to me. He doesn't have any preconceived notions of who I am. He doesn't let me fall into my self-doubt, and he most definitely can't go more than a few minutes without reminding me how beautiful and special he thinks I am. I love that about him.

He may wish we were intimately involved and not just friends, but he cherishes our friendship too. He doesn't really have any female friends. He's the typical sex god with tons of macho male friends, and the only women in his life are either related to him or date him. I'm the first woman to turn down his overt flirtations, and I stand out in his mind, in his life because I'm not the typical pushover who falls for his charms. I see to the heart of who he is under all his boastful confidence and preening.

He reaches out and takes my hand. "Fuck, Sam. Seriously? You should have called me sooner. I would have been there for you, especially after the Joseph thing." He squeezes my hand gently. "That must have broken your heart. I can't believe he slept with someone else."

My stomach churns. "I shouldn't have told you that. It's not fair to him. He didn't do anything wrong. I'd broken up with him. He was…" I look away nearly in tears.

"Heartbroken." Bash gives voice to what I can't bear to say.

"Yeah, and apparently really drunk." I wave the vision away. "Anyway, we both have regrets, and we're working through it." I take a long sip of iced tea.

His hand brushes my cheek. "Do you want me to talk to him?"

I shake my head adamantly. "God, no. I doubt he'd be happy I told you. I really shouldn't have. I'm sorry." This learning to share thing is hard. I don't want to betray Joseph's confidence, but if I don't talk about it, how do I learn to let people in? How can I share my life without any details? It's obviously a fine line I'm going to have to learn to navigate.

"You don't need to apologize. You were telling a friend in confidence what's been going on with you, and that's a pretty big chunk of your news. I'm not happy with what he did, but I'll reserve my judgments based on how you're handling it. And right now, you're telling me he didn't cheat on you because you were broken up at the time, so I'll accept it until I know otherwise."

"Thanks. I don't want to impact your view of him—your relationship. It's important to me that you two get along."

"It won't, but I'm your friend first. So, if there are sides to pick—"

"There aren't." My eyes search out his. "But, if there were, you should pick his side. I was the one who hurt him first. It's my fault what happened."

"Sam," he castigates, getting ready to admonish me for my self-deprecation.

"Don't. Please. Let's just drop it and enjoy our lunch. Okay?"

He stares at me for the longest time. I wait patiently for him to come around to my way of thinking or at least acceptance of it.

"Okay." His soft acquiescence is nearly lost in the din of the restaurant.

"Thank you."

He gives me a curt nod. "Welcome." He points to my food. "Eat. I can tell you haven't been taking care of yourself. You eat, and I'll entertain you with my latest patient escapades." The mischief in his eyes and playful smirk make me relax.

All at once I'm thankful for having met Bash and his easy way of lightening my load. He's a gift. A true gift, and I can't wait till he finds the woman who's strong enough to love him. I nearly get lost in my rumination of what this woman will be like and if she and I will get along, when he brings me back with his next line.

"I finally convinced him to drop trou and show me the problem." I can tell by the gleam in his eye this is going to be good. "I kid you not, Sam. He had a fucking eel attached to his johnson."

I spit the mouthful of tea I was foolish enough to take a drink of mid-story. I manage to turn my head just enough to only spew it across the side of the table and over his left arm.

"Oh, crap! I'm so sorry." I start to mop up the table and him, mortified by the looks the other customers give me.

He's laughing so hard, he doesn't even care I spit sweet tea all over him, or at least a part of him. He swishes my hands away. "It's fine, baby-cakes." He uses his napkin to wipe himself off. "I'm an ER doctor. I'm used to being covered in other people's bodily fluids.

I nearly gag. "Bash! Uh, that's just gross."

He chuckles. "Tell me about it." He settles back in his chair, checking me out. "You okay?" Ever the doctor, needing to be sure I didn't hurt myself choking on iced tea.

I dab my mouth, clothes, and my side of the table. "Yeah, you just took me by surprise. I wasn't choking." He glances in question at my shoulder. "It's fine."

He drops the concerned look and gets back to his story. "You think you're surprised? I yelled in horror when I saw a long black thing just hanging from his…dick. I thought it was a huge leech at first."

I lean forward. "Please tell me it wasn't still alive." Poor eel.

"That's what you want to know? Not how it got there in the first place?" His face is lit with amusement.

"I already surmised why he wanted an eel on his… So, my next thought was, was it alive when it happened, and did you have to kill it trying to get it off?"

"Baby, I did not get the man off." His hands cross in a motion as if he's an ump calling a runner "safe." "In fact, just the vision of it is enough to make me sustain from getting off for some time to come."

I think he's totally serious. "You're joking, right?"

He smirks. "Well, partially. But, it's a vision I'm gonna have to work to wipe from my mind every time I touch my cock." He cringes. "Sorry."

Bash doesn't talk sexually to me. *Ever*. He's succeeded at keeping our friendship as, well, just that…friends. He's naturally flirty, but rarely mentions sex or sexual body parts. Though, I'm not sure if it's the whole friendship thing or him trying to protect my innocence.

"You know I'm an adult, right? You don't have to shy away from talking about sex or penises and vaginas. I can handle it."

He shrugs. "I'm trying to be good here and not go into dangerous territory not covered by the friendship clause."

So, he's not protecting my innocence, but our friendship. "Bash, really?

Even friends talk about sex. Are you telling me you don't talk about sex and body parts with your male friends?"

He leans closer. "That's different, and you know it. I don't want to have sex with them."

"Bash—"

His hand goes up, stopping me mid-thought. "I cherish our friendship, Sam. But you know I don't see you as a sister. I never have. I never will. We may never be more than friends, but it doesn't mean I'm not still attracted to the sexy, smart, witty woman sitting across from me." He raises his eyebrow in emphasis, waiting for my acknowledgment. Once again, he wants me to accept his compliment without brushing it off.

I grab his hand and squeeze, trying to hide the tears in my eyes. This man is too sweet to me. "You honor me with your words. Your reverence of our friendship, and your respect of my relationship with Joseph." I hold his gaze momentarily, but I can't keep eye contact if I have any hope of not crying. "You're an amazing man, Sebastian Cole. I can't wait to meet the woman who's worthy of your heart."

"Sam." His voice is heavy with emotion now.

The room is bustling around us, but there's a moment of peace and quiet between us. We know where we stand. We respect it and each other enough to be honest. I meet his eyes. I see the beautiful man behind his model-handsome face. "I *see* you, Bash. Don't ever forget that."

His eyes glisten, making my tears overflow their confinement. "I see you too, beautiful. And don't *you* ever forget that."

As I dab my tears, he proceeds to tell me the eel was alive when it became attached, but had long since died from lack of oxygen. Sad, so sad for that poor eel.

"Where in the hell did he get an eel?" PETA should be called in to investigate. It's a travesty. *Okay, maybe I'm over reacting a little, but seriously. A fucking eel?*

"He wouldn't tell me. He was afraid of getting fired from his job. So, I did *my* job and removed the appendage from his gnarled and heinously unimpressive man-meat."

A horrendous thought hits me. Bash doesn't miss the flash of disgust on my face. "What?"

"Please tell me he wasn't planning on…uh…having sex with that thing still attached to him."

He frowns. "You mean as in a slip-on eel dildo to enhance his size?"

"Yes." I shudder at the thought and the poor recipient of such a gift.

"Fuck. Jeez, I surely hope not. Thanks for that visual." He shakes his head to dispel the thought. "We didn't talk much more after he clammed up about where he got the eel in the first place. Psych came and talked to him. I pretty much just focused on the immediate issue of removal and salvage."

A whole-body shudder takes over at the thought. "I think your story just may have ruined sex for me."

He laughs.

I point at him. "You won't be laughing when Joseph calls to ask why you filled my mind with such horrible imagery and ruined any chance he had of popping my cherry."

His head falls back, and a deep, full-body laugh escapes. "Like you'd ever be able to resist him for long. I see the way you two look at each other. It's a miracle you've lasted this long."

"It is, isn't it?"

We near the end of our meal, and I know he has to get back to the hospital. He's working a split shift today, so he only had a little time to spare. I'm thankful he wasted it on me. I excuse myself and head to the restroom before we leave.

I do my business and head back to the table.

And then I see him.

The man who shot my father and me, and tore my family apart.

I nearly miss my chair as I stumble back into my seat. I take a long drink and try to calm my nerves, hoping I look casual, natural instead of completely terrified. Did the security team fail, or was this man here already, the universe conspiring against me to make this moment happen?

"Sam?" Bash sees there's something wrong. "What…"

I stab at my food. "Don't look around. I need you to make a phone call for me."

"You're scaring me, Sam."

I reach across and squeeze his hand. I'm the world's biggest asshole for putting my friend in danger because I selfishly thought I needed a day out of the penthouse. It's been days, not months. Why didn't I stay there where it's safe? Where everyone else was safe—far away from me. "Please," I whisper so softly I'm not sure Bash hears me.

With a squeeze in return, he asks me the number. I automatically dictate the number Michael forced me to memorize. He was insistent I know his number by heart. I guess this is a perfect example as to why.

"Why aren't you using your phone?" Bash asks as he puts the phone to his ear.

"I don't want him to know I saw him."

Bash starts to say something, but stops when Michael answers. I can hear his voice coming through the phone. "Sebastian. What's wrong?"

I dig through the packet of sugars as if I'm trying to find the magical one I need. "He's here," I simply say.

Bash starts to repeat, but I guess Michael can hear me too and cuts off Bash's reply. "Where?"

"Back left corner of the bar." I purposely focus in the opposite direction, pointing at a paining on the wall as if I'm telling Sebastian something about it.

"Don't move," Michael orders before he hangs up.

If anything happens to Sebastian because I invited him to lunch, I'll never forgive myself. My heart pounds, and I meet Sebastian's steely gaze for the first time since returning from the bathroom.

"I'm sorry," I softly impart, barely two seconds before all hell breaks loose.

PART 4

HEAR ME ROAR

APRIL

Nine

Samantha

I N A FLASH, EVERYTHING CHANGED. I WAS YOUR average girl-next-door who studied too much, worked too hard, and rarely had any fun. The only notable male interaction in my life was with my father, my brother, or my co-workers, none of whom wanted to date me. I then watched my father die in my arms, survived being shot, dated, lost, and then again dated the hottest man I've ever seen.

To say he's hot is not even fair—and doesn't do him justice. It makes him sound like a one-dimensional Ken doll with nothing between his ears whom I only appreciate for his physical beauty. While it is true I do appreciate every inch of his body, he is, in fact, the smartest man I know. His brain, his heart, and even his caveman ways are all a part of the man I've grown to love.

I said I wouldn't fall in love with him. But it was a lost cause from the moment I laid eyes on him that Friday Jace introduced us. I was a fool for believing I could resist his charm, his steady green-eyed gaze, and all-consuming presence. I thought he would leave me heartbroken and devastated.

Well, I *am* heartbroken. I *am* devastated. But, not from Joseph. I am broken from losing my father, my mother, and my brother in one fell swoop. Though I haven't physically lost my mom and brother, their absence in my life is just as true as the loss of my father, with one exception. My mom and brother *chose* to shut me out of their lives. My father didn't have a choice.

Joseph is the one picking up the pieces, holding me together, comforting me, giving me strength, and giving me a safe place to land. He's been my saving grace.

My godsend.

My protector.

My healer.

My teacher.

My confidant.

My rock.

My heart.

My breath.

My soul.

He picked me up when I didn't deserve it. He healed my brokenness and set me free.

"Sam!" Michael snaps at me.

I whirl around and face him. "What?"

"Where the hell were you?" He sighs, exasperated with me as he wipes sweat off his face and arms. "Are you ready to go again?"

I take one more long drink of water and then head for the center of the mat. "Bring it, asswipe."

He chuckles. "You only cuss at me. Why is that?"

I love it when I can make stoic Michael—always serious Michael—laugh. I shrug. "I don't know. You bring out the best in me, I suppose."

He assumes his fight stance opposite me. "Well, let's see if you can take me down this time."

"If I do, you have to answer any question I ask you honestly, and not a one-word answer. You have to give me a complete, truthful, no-bullshit answer."

His eyes narrow as he gives me the evil, take-no-shit glare of his. "And if you don't take me down? What do I get?"

"What do you want?"

A mischievous smirk reduces his glare to a decisive squint as his eyes sweep up and down my body. "A favor."

I step back and cross my arms over my chest. "What kind of favor?"

He laughs again, reading me like a book. "Not *that* kind of favor. Get your head out of the gutter."

"What kind, then?"

He shrugs. "I don't know yet. But I kinda like the idea of you owing me something. Something I can collect on at anytime, anywhere, and you can't say no."

It's a sobering thought of how much I already owe this man. He's doing his job, protecting me, keeping me out of harm's way. He's gone above and beyond to help Joseph and me. I don't know all the facts, but I see the looks, I hear bits and pieces of conversations. He's fully invested in me and my family's safety, and that's a debt I can never repay.

And if that wasn't enough, he and Victor have been working with me for the past month teaching me self-defense moves based on kick boxing and jujitsu techniques. Michael is a fourth-degree black belt. Victor never went the formal route. What he learned was from his years in the military and as MCI's head of security. He may not have black belt status, but he can kick ass all the same.

"Michael, I already owe you. I couldn't possibly owe you any more than I already do. If you ever have anything you need from me in the future, you don't have to collect a favor. I owe a debt to you I can never repay. So, whatever you need, it's yours. Pick something else for our wager."

He steps close enough to touch my arm, just grazing it, before letting his hand fall to his side. "You don't own me a damn thing, princess. It's my job, my honor, to protect you and keep you safe." He moves back into position. "The wager stays the same. You won't owe me for protecting you, but you'll owe me one favor, anything, for not taking me down. Now, come on, show me what you got, little miss bookworm."

Thirty seconds later, I'm flat on my back, Michael is hovering over me with a totally satisfied smirk.

"Crap!"

He shakes his head and gives me a hand up. "Again."

Fifteen minutes later, I'm completely winded and only managed to knock him off balance, but not off his feet. "Jesus, what are you, a weeble-wobble?"

"As in *weebles wobble, but they don't fall down?*" he chuckles.

"Yes! Fuck. Seriously. I almost had you, but you refuse to fall down!"

I stomp toward him and push him hard on his chest. He doesn't fucking budge.

His face softens. "You've done really well, Sam. Don't get discouraged. I've been at this for a long time. What kind of ex-military, FBI agent would I be if you could take me down after only four weeks of training?"

"A damn good instructor! That's what you'd be." I sigh and grab my water. "Are we done?"

Glancing at the clock, he nods. "Yeah, take a breather. Let me clean up here, then I'll take you home."

I swipe my towel and my gym bag as I head out front.

We're in an unmarked gym across town from Fin's. I have no clue what goes on here during the day, but whenever we come to train in the evenings, it's completely empty except for Michael, me, sometimes Victor, and the other agents assigned to me. It's fully equipped with treadmills, ellipticals, free weights, punching bags, dummies, wall-to-wall mats, and three boxing rings dispersed throughout. I've asked questions, but Michael's not giving up any details. It's like it's a secret society or something.

I've learned to choose my battles. I'm safe here, the doors are locked, security system is engaged, and there are more agents roaming around than I could possibly need. I'm not complaining, though. I remain thankful for the feeling of security it affords me. That security has been extended to the rest of my family and Joseph's as a precaution. I've agreed to stay away from Margot and Sebastian, especially after what happened the last time I saw Bash.

It's been four weeks since the scare at the restaurant with Sebastian and seeing my dad's killer there. Michael and his team came in like SWAT, ready to take down the place, but somehow the weasel managed to slip away. I felt guilty, like maybe I imagined the whole thing. I was thankful when Michael told me later, after watching the security tapes, the killer had, in fact, been there. I was relieved until I realized how much danger we were in and what could have happened. He was mere feet from me when I went to the restroom. He could have grabbed me or hurt Sebastian to get to me.

"You ready?" Michael stands near the door, his gym bag slung over his shoulder. His gun is holstered, secured at his hip once again.

"Yeah." I roll my shoulders, trying to release the tension.

On the way home we stop for food from a drive-thru. One thing I really like about Michael, is his love of Jack-in-the-Box monster tacos. He has a serious addiction that rivals my own. He ordered eight monster tacos to my two, onion rings, and two large cokes.

Food in hand, we step off the elevator. He drops our gym bags outside Fin's door, but instead of going inside, he moves to the door around the corner I'd assumed was a closet or storage of some sort. Apparently, it's a stairwell.

He holds the door open, motioning me through.

"Where are we going?" I start to climb the stairs.

The door shuts behind him with a soft clasp instead of the echoing boom I expect from most stairwell doors. "You'll see. Come on, slowpoke," he teases as he races up the stairs ahead of me.

My legs wobble like rubber as I make the ascent to the roof. The rooftop pool, that is. "Holy shit. This is incredible."

"I'm surprised Joe hasn't brought you up here."

"Me too." After the restaurant incident, Joseph couldn't fly home to my side fast enough. It took me a week to get him to go home to Austin with a begrudgingly made promise to stay away, at least for the interim. I'm not sure if it was me or Fin, Michael, or Victor who finally talked some sense into him. Whatever it was, he finally went home with his own security team in tow—that was for *my* peace of mind.

His absence is hardly bearable, but I need that extra knowledge he's hundreds of miles away. I've been keeping to myself, barely working, only going to school and home to Fin's. I can't stand the idea of getting anyone hurt because of me, and that includes those whose job is to protect me. It's not forever. The solitude is temporary, and really, other than Joseph, it's not any great sacrifice. It's in my nature, and I'm feeding that lone beast quite regularly.

I move closer to the pool's edge. It's beautiful and tranquil with the shimmering light just below the surface. I resist the urge to jump in.

Michael sets down our food and drinks at a table surrounded by blooming potted plants.

Spring. I forgot it was spring already.

We eat in companionable silence. I wasn't always at ease around him, but over the last month, Michael has pretty much become my daily companion. Except when I'm in school or working, one of the other guys is stuck to me like glue, but any other time, it's Michael at my side. We eat together. We watch TV together. We even read together. I never pictured him a reader, but he enjoys pretty much anything as long as it's not a romance. He learned to appreciate a good book in the military. There was a lot of down time, waiting for orders, or waiting for someone or something to happen. He always has a paperback on him, either in his bag or in his back pocket.

I swipe an onion ring from him. He chuckles and pushes them between us. I finished my tacos in record time, starving after our training session and my physical therapy I had before that. I'm thankful it's Friday. I can't wait to shower, my new guilty pleasure thanks to the penthouse's decadent showers, then crawl into bed and not wake up until my eyes open on their own, sans alarm clock.

Michael draws a napkin across his mouth, wipes his hands, then collects our trash and disposes of it in the nearest trashcan. He comes back and sits in the same seat, but his focus is now on me instead of slaying his mound of monster tacos.

"What?" I wonder if I have food on my face, but I'm pretty sure I managed to wipe all the greasy goodness off.

"Ask me."

My brow furrows as I try to surmise what the hell he's talking about. "Ask what?"

"Your question. Our wager." He states it so simply, like I should have known what he was talking about.

"But I didn't win. You did. You get your favor, which you didn't need in the first place." I roll my eyes in mock dismissal of his claiming "it's his honor" to protect me. *Shit.* It's enough to make me cry. He's a good man. Tortured, but good.

"It doesn't matter. You earned it." He tips his chin. "One question. One full disclosure answer."

"Seriously?"

"Seriously." He clasps his hands behind his head and leans back in the chair. "Ask."

I don't have to even think about *what* I want to ask, but I do have to think about *how* to ask it.

His arched brow and the rocking of his chair balancing on two legs tell me he's nearly done waiting on me.

"Okay." I take a deep breath and decide to go for it. "When I look at you, Michael, I see a strong man who's seen his fair share of bad things, probably horrific things. I see the soldier you used to be, the agent you are, the loyal friend, the protector, the guy who wants to have a beer and watch TV, and the quiet guy who likes to get lost in a book. I've seen many sides of you, and I'm sure there's more. The one thing I want to know is what happened to put that longing in your eyes? The memories that steal your smile. The devastation that damaged your spirit."

His smug look disappears as his chair slams down on the cobblestone patio. "Fuck." His hands wash across his face. Leaning forward, he plucks a flower from the pot near his foot, before his arms come to rest on his knees.

I'm not sure he's going to answer me. The longer I wait, the more likely it is he'll brush off my question, or maybe it's a good sign he hasn't blown me off yet. A sign he's contemplating an answer instead of formulating a lie.

"I should have known it wouldn't be an easy question." His voice is heavy with emotion. His sad eyes measure mine, wondering if I can take what he's about to say. "I'll tell you what I can, but I can't tell you all of it or give you specifics. Not because I'm lying to you, but partly because I can't legally, and mostly because it's not my story to tell."

Jesus. This is gonna be heavy. Maybe I should have asked him my cop-out question: *What's your favorite sexual position?* It would have been an easier question for sure, but not nearly as meaningful. I have a feeling this is a burden he needs to share, and I'm willing to listen. I want to know more about the man I've spent so much time with lately and is such good friends with Victor and Fin. He's more than his gruff façade—that I know for certain.

He sits back in his chair, his hands gripping the arm rests and his eyes boring into me. "I was undercover a few years ago. Investigating a real scumbag. The kind of guy whose death would be too kind a punishment. He was dirty in a lot of ways, used people, manipulated innocent people who lost their way. If you can imagine the things a charismatic low-life, morally corrupt, pompous asshole might enjoy, he did it and worse."

His eyes cloud as he gazes out over the pool. "Sometimes—actually most times—when you're undercover, you have to do things you wouldn't normally do to maintain your cover and get closer to the suspect. This job was no different. I'm not proud of what I did, the compromises I made, but I wouldn't do it any differently. I wouldn't change a damn thing as it brought me my Gracie, and it put him away for life."

My Gracie. Jeez. I'm gonna cry.

"She wasn't supposed to be there. If I'd known what he had planned, I would have intervened, but it all happened so quick." He closes his eyes and shakes his head as if to dispel the unpleasant memory.

"Anyway, I ran interference. I tried to distract him. I did everything I could to keep him away from her for as long as I could. But…" His voice cracks, and a beat passes before he continues. "I couldn't jeopardize the investigation. If I hadn't been in so deep, if we weren't so close to making an arrest, I would have just left and taken her with me. But I couldn't. I had to choose."

He clears his throat. "I chose my job. I chose the greater good over her. The sacrifice of one for the many."

"That's what you were trained to do. To sacrifice for the greater good." I'm sure it's little solace for the guilt he feels.

"Yes." He nods. "A good soldier follows orders, doesn't rock the boat. Doesn't put the needs of an individual over the needs of the masses. But I should have put her needs over all else. I should have taken her and slipped away in the night. I could have saved her. Protected her innocence."

Shit.

He eyes lock with mine. "What if she was meant to do amazing things and because of this horrible incident, she doesn't do it? Aren't the masses impacted anyway? Maybe the needs of the one should take precedence over the needs of the many because the future masses are impacted if the one is derailed in some way."

"Michael, you don't know that. Nobody does. All we can do is make the best decision we can at the time based on the facts we have at that moment. You can't spend your life second-guessing yourself. It won't change the past, and it may, in fact, change your future because you're too busy looking back to look forward."

He seems to contemplate for a moment. I want to know what happened to her, but I'm afraid to ask. I don't want to dredge up more pain than he's already feeling.

"You loved her."

"Yeah."

Then I realize. "You *still* love her."

His eyes meet mine. "Yeah, I do."

Michael. He's breaking my heart. "How'd she get away from him?"

"I snuck her out." He sits back in his chair, washing his face with his hand again and lets out a long breath.

"In the end, I did choose her. Better late than never, I guess." He shrugs. "I snuck her out early in the morning and hid her on the grounds far from the main compound. I had to go back and collect evidence, set a smoke screen to keep her escape a secret for as long as possible. What I had no way of knowing was that her boyfriend and his family connections got the FBI to raid the place about an hour later."

He lets out a bitter laugh. "She would have been saved anyway. In the end, what I did didn't mean crap."

"I don't believe that. You chose her. She knows that. She might've been hurt in the raid if you hadn't gotten her out. What you did made a difference. It kept her safe." *What if she did get hurt?*

"Yes, she was safe and out of danger. I was making my way back to get her, when her boyfriend and other agents found her."

Oh shit! "What'd ya do?"

"The only thing I could. I sent her home with the man who could love her better than I could."

"Michael, that's heartbreaking." I quietly wipe away an errant tear.

He peers out over the night sky, and I think he's done talking. Then he surprises me. "You have no idea."

I do actually. I have some idea what it's like to let go of the one you love because you believe they're better off without you. Safer without you. I did it, and it broke my heart, and it sent Joseph into the arms of another woman.

I know what heartbreak is.

I know that sacrifice.

I know the emptiness that follows.

I. Know.

Ten

Samantha

"HEY, SAM," MICHAEL GREETS ME AS I STEP OFF THE elevator, having just gotten to Fin's from school.

"Hey." I walk through the front door, setting down my pack and purse. "I thought I wasn't going to see you today."

"Yeah, plans changed. When do you leave to see your mom?"

I plop on the couch, less than enthused by that prospect. My last visit, she cried the entire time. Fiona, Joseph's mom, says she really is making progress, but believes seeing me reminds my mom how much things have changed and how far she's slipped away from the life she used to have. She's at least started seeing someone to help her work through her grief, both one-on-one and in a group setting. But the idea of seeing her tonight…I'd rather not.

"About that. I don't think I'm gonna go. It only upsets her, and I end up feeling like crap afterwards." I glance up at him. "What's the point? She could care less if she sees me." She and Jace have written me off. I can only assume they blame me for my father's death, and they may be right. If I hadn't been there, the killer wouldn't have been able to use me as a pawn against Dad.

The cushion dips as Michael takes a seat next to me. "I could see how you'd feel that way. Give it more time, but don't think she doesn't care. I actually think she cares too much, and that's why it hurts so badly."

His normally closed-off eyes are warm and comforting. "I'm not making excuses for her. She's been a shit mom since your dad died. She's having a hard time coping, and that's her weakness, not yours. You haven't done anything wrong to warrant her treatment of you, or her lack of effort to make things better."

He takes my hand and holds it between his large, callused ones, turning it over, examining it. "You never know what you're made of until the shit hits the fan, then you truly know if you're made from strong stock or not."

His eyes narrow as he focuses on me. "You. You're made from some strong stock. Your mom and Jace, not so much, unfortunately. I still have hope for them, but you and I both know Jace was a mess even before all this stuff with your dad and you getting shot. I think it pushed him over the edge to crazy-whoring-town, and he can't seem to find his way back." He places my hand back on my lap. "He's always been a self-absorbed asshole who thought with his dick instead of his brain most times." He gets up and paces to the window. "I'm sorry. I really am. You deserve better."

I manage to hold in my bitter laugh. I probably deserve exactly what I've gotten. I won't debate it with Michael. There's no point. He would never agree with me, even if a part of him believed it to be true.

"We need to talk about the investigation." He turns, his face in shadow with the sunlight behind his back.

I squint to see his face, but it's no use. "Tell me."

"I wasn't at liberty to tell you these things before." He moves to the nearest chair, getting comfortable before he speaks again. "Your father worked with the FBI for many years. I only became aware of him in the last few years. By then, I had already met Jace through Fin and Joseph, so I pretty much had a conflict from the get-go with your father. However, my director believed I could keep my personal connection to Jace separate from my work with Daniel…your dad."

"You…you knew my dad? You actually worked with him? What was he?" I clasp my knees as I sit forward on the couch. "There's no way he was a spy. What did he do, perform surgeries on injured agents?"

"You're right. He wasn't a spy. It was his medical skills that interested the FBI." He moves to the edge of his seat, leaning closer, speaking softly. "And maybe other branches of the government too. I can't confirm, it's just a gut feeling."

My shock continues as Michael fills me in on the history of my dad's involvement with the FBI. Apparently, he came to their attention after his impressive work with the military in helping soldiers injured in service to their country. He performed procedures ranging from simple skin grafts to complete facial reconstruction. The latter was of primary interest to the FBI, where my father performed complete identity-changing facial reconstruction surgeries, allowing the patients to arrive pre-surgery looking like themselves, and leave looking like somebody completely different.

"Who were these people receiving new faces? Were they criminals? People in witness protection?"

"Majority of the time, it was agents, those you might consider spies, who needed to get lost, disappear, either for a job, or after a life-changing assignment forcing their retirement. I'm not going to lie to you and say some of your father's patients weren't unsavory, but he was not allowed to know their names, their circumstances, or why they were having surgery. He only knew what was pertinent for his job, which was all medical-related. Everything else was on a need-to-know basis, and your father did not need to know those facts to perform his job, nor was it safe for him to know those details. He trusted his government was making the right call. He felt he was being called to service his country by using the gifts he had."

Michael's hand encapsulates mine and squeezes. "He helped so many military men and woman have better lives because of his surgical skills, including his regular patients. Your father never took a frivolous job for vanity's sake. He could have made a killing as a Hollywood plastic surgeon, catering to the wealthy who sought and paid premium dollar for bigger boobs, smaller noses, and skinnier waistlines. But he didn't. He had a higher calling to fix what was broken either by birth, chance, or war."

I swipe at a tear. "You make him sound like a saint, Michael."

He gifts me with a rare smile. "To his patients, he was a saint, a godsend. To the government, he was a highly sought-after practitioner of healing what many thought could not be fixed, including the occasional identity-changing surgery. He didn't do many, only a few a year. His main involvement, his true gift, was simply fixing what had been broken by circumstance or fate."

I collapse back into the couch, closing my eyes, trying to comprehend the depth of my father's skills and the number of lives he impacted in a positive way. It makes me proud. It also makes me terribly sad that he never got to share this amazing part of himself with us. He was a hero, a bigger hero than any of his family knew. He'll no longer be able to help anyone ever again.

I slowly open my eyes to the reality of this conversation. "Why are you telling me this? What does it all have to do with his death?"

After another slight smile and knowing nod, I think I passed some secret test. "I'm glad you see the correlation, Sam. I want you to remember all the positive things he did as we talk about the man who brought death and mayhem to your door."

Joseph

I miss my girl. It's hard not to fly home every weekend, not to spend every night with her safely tucked in my arms. I want to. Christ, I want it more than I need to draw my next breath. But I promised her I'd stay away, for a few weeks at least.

I'm on a countdown. She graduates next month, and come hell or high water, I'm going to be there. I don't give a flying fuck what Fin, Michael, or Victor think about it. *I'm going.* There's no way I'd miss my girl graduating and giving her valedictorian speech.

The only positive thing about me staying away is it gives her the space she needs to come to terms with what's happening between us. Not that she has any choice in the matter. I have no intentions of letting her go. I don't want to steamroll her, though. She needs time to absorb it, live with the idea, let it ruminate without me hovering over her, breathing down her neck both figuratively and literally. If I were there, there would be no break from my physical need to be near her, touch her, woo her, love her, and most definitely protect her.

If it were up to me, we'd be living in our own fortress by now where no one would ever get inside to hurt or scare her again. But that's not a life. That's a prison.

Victor is still watching her, which has become much easier with her living at Fin's. Michael is as communicative as he can be without putting his job in jeopardy. He's already broken too many rules by coming to see me after Samantha broke up with me. He knew something was wrong as soon as she didn't go to work for two days and didn't get out of bed until he made her get up the following day. It took my remorse to a whole new level to hear she'd taken to her bed and didn't get up for two days after she broke up with me and after the news of me cheating on her, so she thinks. I understand that level of devastation and sorrow. I felt it too, deeply, inexcusably.

And being apart from her now is even worse when I know she's in danger.

Sometimes life gives you just what you need when you need it. So when her face pops up on my phone, a warmth floods my chest, and I feel forgiven, though we still have obstacles to traverse. The truth. Will she ever know the truth?

"Samantha, baby."

"Joseph."

The sadness in her voice sets me on edge. "What's wrong?"

She takes a deep breath, and it seems like an eternity before she speaks again. "I just…needed to hear your voice. I miss you. I know you're staying away because I asked you to, but I wish you were here. I just want to feel your arms wrapped around me, telling me everything's going to be alright."

If she asked, I would drop everything and fly, drive, walk, and even crawl to my girl. "Sweetness, I miss you too. You're making it hard for me to stay away. Tell me what happened. Aren't you seeing your mom tonight?"

"I canceled. I couldn't take another visit, feeling like it doesn't matter if I'm dead or alive. So, I copped out. I didn't even have the guts to do it myself. Michael called your mom for me. I don't know what he'll tell her, but I doubt it'll be the truth."

"Don't feel bad about it. Sometimes you have to put yourself first—and you rarely do so. Take a few weeks and see how you feel. But,

Samantha, your mom cares you're alive. It does matter to her, even if she's doing a piss poor job of showing you. I'm not defending her. No one is under the illusion that how she and Jace have pulled away from you is okay. It's not. I think you stepping back is completely understandable. Maybe you should stop trying. Let her be the one to reach out to you."

She lets out a long sigh. "Thank you for your support. I think you're right. It only hurts me and makes me mad every time I open up to her and try to be there for her. I'm so tired of trying to make it better, make *her* better. If she was making an effort, it would be different. But she's not, so I'm done, at least for now."

"I don't know if you need to hear it or not, but I, for one, am damn happy you're alive, Samantha. And anyone who doesn't relish that fact doesn't deserve to be in your life. Step away for a while. Let me handle it. I'll talk to my parents. I think it's time to put her in a facility where they can take care of her 24/7, give her the psychological help she requires. It might be the wake-up call—or boost—she needs." I make a mental note to call my dad as soon as we hang up.

"God, I feel nearly as guilty as I feel relieved. I should be the one to handle it, but I can't, or don't want to. I'm not entirely sure which, to be honest."

"No guilt. I've got this. It's my honor to do this for you. Anything. Anytime. Always."

"Thank you."

"No thanks needed, but you're welcome all the same." I settle back on my bed. "Now, tell me what happened today. What's going on?"

My sweet girl fills me in on her conversation with Michael and the details behind her dad's murder. Michael didn't give her any names, rightly so. It would only put her in more danger.

"That's some crazy shit. So, your dad performed facial reconstruction surgery on a guy your dad's killer has been trying to find for years, and he thought your dad had information about the guy's new identity?"

"Yep. It makes sense. That day in the parking lot, he told my dad to go to his office and get the information he wanted, while he kept me as collateral."

"The idea of you being held at gunpoint, Samantha. I…want to kill him. For scaring you, for taking your father from you, for shooting you. If I ever see him, I won't hesitate. Not for a goddamn second." My blood boils at the thought of him hurting my girl, using her to get what he wants.

She surprises me by laughing. "Sometimes, I really love the caveman in you."

Love. Christ, please say those three little words to me.

"Yeah?" I say, instead of what's in my heart. She's not ready to hear me say those three all-important words. She's opening up to me more and more each day, learning to trust that I'm not going anywhere, that she can count on me. I'm not like Jace—dumping her at every turn, and I pray I'm not leaving her like her father did. I don't want to scare her off, shut her down by saying them too soon. Too soon by her standards.

"It's hot."

Aaaaaand my dick is hard.

"Samantha." I don't even try to hide my growl.

"See, just like that. It's hot as hell, Joseph. It makes me feel cherished, special."

Jesus. And just like that it goes from sexual to intimate. "Sweetness, you are special and beyond cherished." I need to see her. I need to hold my girl.

"Keep talking to me, Joseph. I need to hear your voice."

Anything for my girl.

Anywhere.

Anytime.

Always.

Eleven

Samantha

MY HEART IS GONNA BEAT OUT OF MY CHEST. HOLY *crap!*

But wait. What if it's nothing?

What if it's something?

Shit!

"What was that, Sam?" Victor looks at me in the rearview mirror, his eyes hidden by his sunglasses, jaw tight. His demeanor gives away nothing, as usual.

Did I say something? "Uh, is Michael around? Do you know?"

He glances at Smith, Michael's man, my bodyguard for the day, sitting in the passenger seat. I'm pretty sure *Smith* is not his real name. He shrugs.

Victor's attention is back on me. "I'm not sure, but I can find out."

My knee bounces in rhythm with my heart. I don't want to make a big deal of this. "It's okay. I was just wondering."

I focus out the window, but I can still feel Victor's eyes on me. "You sure?" he presses.

"Yeah." *Is he buying my nonchalance?*

I'm lost in thought when the car comes to a halt, and I'm confused as to why we're not in the garage of MCI towers. "What are we doing?"

Victor frowns and motions to the building to my right. "It's Thursday. You have physical therapy today."

Oh shit! I totally forgot. Maybe it will be good to work off some of this nervous energy.

I glance at my backpack and back at him. "Are you waiting? Should I take my stuff with me?"

He turns around, gauging me. "What's going on, Sam? I can smell your nerves from here."

What the fuck? "Are you saying I stink?"

He laughs. "No! I'm saying you're nervous as fuck, and if I were a predator, I could smell your fear. Now, what's going on?"

"Nothing." I open my door and hop out before he can stop me or question me further.

Smith is at my side with my gym bag in hand. I glance back at the car and the back door where my backpack sits on the floorboard along with my purse and cell phone. I want to go back and get them, but Victor will be more suspicious than ever since I usually leave them in the car during therapy. I glance at the front seat where Victor's removed his shades and is eyeballing me with a fearsome gaze.

Shit. Why do I think I can hide anything from him?

Smith's hand on my shoulder stops me from smacking into the glass door. I kept walking, even though my attention was on the car and not where I was going.

Cool move, dipshit. I have to get a grip on my nerves.

I enter through the double doors fully expecting Victor to follow and start interrogating me. Thankfully, after I've changed into my workout clothes, he's nowhere to be seen. I relax. Maybe, just maybe, I got away with my evasiveness.

Agent Smith assumes his pillar impression against the nearest wall, close but not so close that he'll be a hindrance to my therapy.

I'm always surprised when no one asks me about the security following me around. I've started to think Michael, Victor, or maybe even Joseph calls ahead to warn people, asking them not to acknowledge or mention them to me. Even at school, rarely does anyone say anything to me about my stream of larger-than-your-average-guy protection following me around everywhere I go. I do mean everywhere. The first few days, they cleared the restroom before I entered to be sure it was safe. It only took a few screaming female students for the principal to grant me access to the teachers' restricted bathrooms. Their one-occupant facilities allow my protection to open the door, scan the room, and then stand outside while I do my business like a dog on a leash. I'm not complaining, not really. It's just an interesting position to be in and see how people react to them, or in this case, do not react to them.

My hour therapy session is over before I realize, and I'm more than happy to be heading home. I've got less than a month of school left and lots of projects to wrap up before graduation. Though, tonight I'm going to be sidetracked with the envelope in my bag.

Victor doesn't say anything to me on the ride home other than to ask how my therapy went. Once in the garage and escorted to the elevator, I'm allowed to ride up by myself, which is unusual. Normally, Michael or one of the other guys escorts me. With the elevator key in place, it's an express ride to the penthouse floor, so it's not like I'm in danger from the garage to Fin's apartment. However, if I'm right about what I suspect is in my bag, I doubt even this small reprieve from security will be allowed again.

As the elevator slows, so do my thoughts and my rush to get inside to find the answers I seek. The doors open, and I step out slowly, debating about heading up to the pool level for a moment of true peaceful solitude.

Yes. That's what I'll do. The envelope's not going anywhere.

I turn toward the rooftop stairwell.

With a click of a door down the hall, my heart jumps into overdrive as thoughts of my father's killer cloud my vision. Someone's here.

Without even a moment's hesitation, I take off for the stairs, and as I breach the doorway, I realize my fatal flaw.

Where will I go once I'm on the roof? Jump? Not likely. There's nowhere to go.

Sweat beads on my forehead.

Damn! What the fuck am I going to do now?

A strong hand lands on my left shoulder, stopping me in my tracks.

I grip that hand, bending the thumb back, and I spin around to face my attacker.

"Sam!"

"Jesus, fuck, Michael!" I step back and release him, but not before noting the pain on his face. *Shit.*

"Sam, what the fuck?" He's not angry like I expect, which throws me off even more. I move back, stumbling on the first step.

He's there, lightning fast, pulling me upright before I hit any hard surface of the stairs or wall, and instead crash into him, a solid wall of muscle.

"Breathe, Sam. What the fuck's going on?"

I cling to him, my knees weak and my head spinning. "I…you… scared me."

He scoops me in his arms and storms out of the stairwell, rounds the corner, and heads into Fin's apartment.

I don't struggle. I can't get my bearings. I can't even get enough air.

He sits me on the couch, pushing my head forward. "Put your head between your knees. That's it. Breathe, princess."

"Michael—"

"Shh. Just breathe. Give yourself a moment to calm down." He pats my back. "Stay here. I'm going to go get your stuff. You dropped it in the stairwell."

His voice trails from behind me as he heads out the door. "Better?" He kneels beside me a moment later, holding out a glass of water.

I push back into the couch and try to take the glass from him, but my hand shakes.

His hand clasps over mine, helping me take a drink. "It's the adrenaline. Take another sip, finish it if you can." As I drink, he scans my face. "You're still white as a ghost. You sure you're okay?"

I finish off the water, and he sets the glass on the coffee table before I can answer him. "Yeah."

He settles in the chair next to me. "Good job on taking me down, by the way."

I roll my eyes. "I didn't come anywhere close to taking you down."

"You would have if you hadn't pulled back as soon as you realized it was me. I was on my way to my knees with the vise-like grip you had on my thumb and arm." He nods. "It was quick thinking. You did good."

"No. It wasn't." I move to the end of the couch, slipping off my shoes and curling my feet under me. I search for the blanket that's usually behind the couch.

"Here." Michael tosses me the blanket. "Cold?"

I wrap it around me, pulling it up under my chin. "Yes."

"That's to be expected too."

Great. Shaky. Cold. And Emotional. Fun times.

I return to his comment from a moment ago. "I shouldn't have gone to the stairwell, but it was too late by the time I realized my mistake. I should have gotten back in the elevator."

He shakes his head. "The doors had already closed. You made the right move for where you were and for where I was. It was good self-defense even if you don't feel like it was. You had limited options, and your instincts chose correctly."

I guess I'll take that. He is the expert, after all.

"Why were you loitering out in the hall, anyway? And what happened today?" He points at me. "And don't even think of trying to blow me off like you did Victor. He knew something was up, but he didn't want to push you. He called me, and I came straight here, waiting on you to get home."

"I was thinking of going up to the pool and taking a swim."

He frowns not liking that idea. "What happened at school?"

"Where's my backpack?"

"I'll get it." He heads to the entryway. "Victor said you were weird about leaving your stuff in the car during therapy. I can only assume there's something in there you need to show me, and that's why you were asking for me."

He sets my pack down next to me. "You could have called me, you know."

I unzip my pack but don't touch it. I glance up at him. "I didn't want to bother you. Especially if it's nothing."

He sits on the coffee table in front of me. "Sam, you're upset. Something got under your skin today, enough to spook you, make you nervous, secretive, and paranoid. When you stepped off the elevator and heard the door open, you feared for your life. Did it feel like nothing?"

"No." I crack. "It felt like the farthest away from nothing it possibly could be."

"Exactly." He brushes a tear from my cheek. "Next time, call me, even if it's during school. Even if you know I've got something important going on, you can still call me. If I can't answer, one of my guys will call you right back. But you could've called Victor or talked to him in the car. You didn't need to carry this fear around all day, letting it grow and fester. It may have started out as nothing, but it most definitely is not nothing now." He glances at my backpack and then back at me.

"It's an envelope. It's addressed to me. It was sitting on my desk in my macroeconomics class when I arrived." I hold open my bag so he can see inside. "I didn't open it. There was something about it, setting off red flags. I only touched the right-hand corner getting it into my pack."

He leans forward, straining to see the envelope without touching it. "Stay here." He takes my pack to the kitchen.

I don't argue with him. This is his area of expertise, and whether I see what's in the envelope first or last, he's still going to see it, so there's no point in making a fuss. Besides, I'm actually relieved to no longer be responsible for it being in my possession.

I hear him talking on the phone. I can't make anything out, only the murmur of his voice. A few minutes later my phone rings just as Victor walks in the front door, nods at me, and heads to the kitchen.

I round the couch to get my phone from my purse, eyeing the kitchen to see what they're doing in there. "Hello?"

"Did you get my letter?"

My vision narrows, and a scream rips from me as I drop my phone. That voice. I'll never forget that voice. Not as long as I live will I forget that accent I can't place, or the steely calm of his overly pronounced words.

My knees buckle, and somehow Michael catches me in a huff as my dead weight takes us both to the floor.

"It was him." I gasp. "He wanted to know if I got his letter."

PART 5

HIGHS AND LOWS

Twelve

Joseph

AFTER AN URGENT CALL FROM VICTOR, I HOPPED on the first flight I could get and flew home. It's been two days since I've spoken to my girl. We've texted. Lots. But no phone calls. I miss her voice. I called her earlier today, but she didn't answer. Now I know why.

One of Victor's men picked me up from the airport, so I'll have to wait to get any further details once I'm at the penthouse. Samantha will probably already be asleep when I get there. It won't stop me from going to her as soon as I'm done talking to Michael and Victor.

We pull into the underground garage, and I hop out barely before the car is in park. My bag in hand, I head toward the elevator. I'm a man on a mission, no time for bullshit.

I open the door to Fin's penthouse. It's late and quiet, except for the low murmur of voices I hear in the distance. The lights are dim, giving the illusion of calm, but there's nothing calm about what went down here today. I find Fin, Michael, and Victor in Fin's office.

"She'll be happy to see you," Fin says, not even looking up from his desk.

"Probably not as happy as I'll be to see her." I acknowledge Victor and Michael. "Is she sleeping?"

Michael surprises me with a hug and a smile. He must be drunk. "She should be. I put her to bed over an hour ago."

I stop in my tracks. "What do you mean you *put her to bed?*"

Fin finally lifts his head. "Calm, caveman. He was just looking out for her."

"I trust Michael, bro. I'm more concerned that she needed assistance. Is she okay?"

"She's fine, just tired is all," Michael assures me.

Fin leans back in his chair and motions to the bar. "Do you want a drink?"

I set my bag down. "Just some water. Do you want anything?"

Fin holds up his tumbler of amber liquid and turns back to his computer. "I'm good."

Michael and Victor indicate they're fine too.

I put ice in a glass and grab a bottled water. I plant myself in the closest wingback chair, allowing me to see all three of them. Fin glances up from his computer when he hears the ice crackle as I pour water into my glass.

"Will you be working very late?" I ask Fin, wondering how many nights he stays up late in his office.

"Not very. I left a little early tonight because of the situation here, so I have a few things to finish up before calling it a day," he says, then takes a slow sip of his Macallan scotch.

I'm not much of a whiskey man, but I could grow to love my brother's stockpile of vintage 1939 Macallan. It has a sweet toffee undertone that's hard to resist.

"So. Fill me in, Michael. From the beginning." I'm anxious to get to Samantha, but I need to hear this to help me gauge her state of mind.

Michael finishes off his whiskey with a deep sigh. I can almost feel the sweet burn he must be experiencing. He nods to Victor. "He noticed Sam acting nervous and distracted as soon as he picked her and Agent Smith up from school."

"She was a bundle of nerves, but downplayed it without much success," Victor adds.

"Well, she couldn't have been too much of a basket case or Smith would have noticed. Or he *should* have noticed," I point out. Smith needs to move on to another assignment.

"Agreed." The censure in Michael eyes conveys he's on the same page about Smith.

The two of them fill me in, with the majority of the details coming from Michael.

"Fuck, she thought you were the killer?" I stop Michael as he gets to the part in the stairwell.

"Yeah, by that point her nerves where so amped up, and she didn't have protection in the elevator, her imagination got the best of her. Plus, she wasn't aware of me waiting for her. We thought it best not to tell her, so she didn't have time to come up with an excuse not to tell us what's going on. In hindsight, probably not the best move on our part. On a positive note, she responded to the perceived threat like a champ. I'm proud of her."

That is something to be thankful for. I let him continue retelling the events as they unfolded. My gut clenches when I hear about her reaction to the killer's phone call. I can barely stand another minute before going to her.

"Can I see the letter?" I debate getting a glass of whiskey, but I need to stay sober and strong for Samantha. I don't need my senses dulled by alcohol.

"The original has already been sent for forensics analysis, but we have a copy." Michael grabs a piece of paper off Fin's desk and hands it over.

I take a moment to read through it once, then again.

Sam,

I can't express to you how sorry I am for what happen in the parking lot that day. I had no intention of shoot you or your father. It was just a convincing threat to get what I needed from him. You can still help me. You can make all of this go way. You can make me go way by helping me get what I need. No one else need get hurt.

I'm reasonable man. I know I hurt you deeply. I don't expect you to forgive me, but I am sorry. Please, help me make right a wrong done to me by help me get the information I seek. It's not too late. Then, I promise to disappear. You will never hear from me again.

Rod

"Rod?"

"His name is Roderick Hoffman. He's German," Michael advises.

"German? Huh. Samantha said she couldn't place the accent, familiar, yet not."

"That's because he's German but was raised by his mother in Johannesburg until his teens. His accent is a combination of the two, according to our intel." Michael looks at all three of us, pointing to the letter. "This is good news. We've needed a break in the case. Him reaching out to her means he's desperate. He's also putting himself out there, which makes it easier for us to catch him. But mainly, it means we have a way to get to him, to set him up."

I set the letter back on the desk. "You mean to use Samantha as bait."

"We're throwing around ideas." Michael moves closer. "She's the only connection we have to him. He reached out to her in the letter and the phone call. He used a burner cell. He could have called from a public phone, but instead he left a way for her to contact him. We mean to take full advantage." He runs his fingers through his hair and pops his neck. "I won't pretend it's not dangerous for her." He and Victor exchange glances. "We're working on a secondary plan as well, one that does not involve the FBI. It's another layer of protection. She won't go out there unprotected or unarmed."

"Unarmed? You plan to arm her? Christ." I pace to the window.

Fin stands to refill his drink. "It's a precautionary measure. A third redundancy, if you will. Victor and Michael have been working on her fighting skills, and, as she proved tonight, she's a quick study. She's Texas born and raised, no stranger to firearms. Daniel made sure both his kids knew how to shoot. Victor's guys will work with Sam on brushing up her skills." He nods to Michael. "Michael will be out of the loop. Plausible deniability since Sam carrying a gun is not a government-sanctioned practice."

Christ almighty. "When?"

Victor stands and joins us in the middle of the room. "We're thinking her graduation ceremony. She can convince Roderick it's the best choice because of the amount of people in attendance. She'll tell him she's under surveillance 24/7, but certain she can slip away in the midst of all those people. From our side, the crowd gives us better cover and allows us to bring in more manpower. She'll also have trackers on her, some of them FBI trackers and some of them ours. They'll be on her body and hidden in her belongings/clothing."

"What if he searches her?" I interject.

"We'll have a few in obvious places we're sure he'll find. It's normal protocol for a subject to have trackers and not know it. Sam won't be aware of where they are, so she'll have plausible deniability." Victor's confidence in this plan is comforting.

"You already have trackers on her, don't you?" I glance between Michael and Victor. They simply nod in confirmation. Figures.

Fin, ever the peacekeeper, suggests we let it rest for tonight. "Come on, caveman. I'll walk you to her room. I assume you're staying with her?"

"Yep." I've never been awkward about being with a woman before, but admitting I'm planning on sleeping with Samantha seems different. Not wrong, just more intimate, and not something I want to share with anyone, even Fin. Talking about it feels like I'm breaking a sacred trust.

"Do you need anything? Protection?" He almost seems embarrassed to ask.

I stop in my tracks. "Fin, I'm not having sex with her."

He scoffs. "Well, in case you change your mind, there's a box on condoms and some other stuff in the other guest bath. I didn't think she'd appreciate me putting them in her room."

"Jesus, Fin, you bought condoms for us? I'm not sixteen. I know how to have safe sex." I should probably be mad, but I'm actually finding it quite humorous.

He shrugs, seemingly uncomfortable. "I know. I know. I just…well… fuck. It's Sam. I just wanted to be sure you were safe. Prepared."

"She's gotten to you, hasn't she? She hasn't just been working on Victor and Michael. She's been working on you too."

"Joe, it's not like that. I feel protective of her. I care for her. I've been watching over her while you and Jace have been away. I'm like her surrogate parent, her adopted brother, and her friend, all rolled into one."

I back down. "I'm not accusing you of anything. I'm just jealous you've gotten to spend all this time with her. She seems to really respond to you, to like you. I, on the other hand, haven't spoken to her in two days, and I'm worried she won't be happy to see me."

He squeezes my shoulder. "Joe, she's scared. She's worried you're gonna find someone older, more experienced, more of what she thinks you need in a life partner. She's lost so much. She's afraid of losing you either to your career path or the killer. She needs reassurance she's the one, and that both of you are safe."

"That's shit, Fin. I couldn't find anyone better than her. Ever. I could scan the globe for the rest of my life and not find anyone half as amazing as she is."

"You don't have to convince me. You have to convince her."

I sigh, rubbing my hand across my face. "I know."

"So why are you still standing here with me?"

"Fuck. Alright, I'm going."

He stops me before I open the door. "Oh, I got her out of school tomorrow. You're welcome." He laughs as he disappears down the hall.

Fucker.

Thirteen

Joseph

I GET READY FOR BED IN THE GUEST ROOM ACROSS the hall so as not to wake her. Well, not to wake her until I'm ready to wake her. Since she doesn't have to get up in the morning, I'm most definitely waking her up. I need to see her, to touch her, to lose myself in her scent, to connect with her in a more tangible way than text messages. But, mostly I need to be sure she's okay after the events of today.

I set my phone on the nightstand and hit play. The volume is low, and it only takes a moment for my love song to her, *I Get to Love You*, to fill the stillness of her room.

She doesn't stir until I climb in bed behind her, blanketing her body with mine, and whisper ever so softly against her ear, "Sweetness."

"Hmmm," she responds, pressing her body into mine, still asleep, but knowing I'm here, at least on some level.

I cradle her with my body, her back to my front. She's so warm, tucked in under the covers, it's like rubbing up against warm silk. I bury my nose in her hair. "Christ, you smell good." I run my nose along the curve of her neck and kiss up her shoulder. "Like spring flowers and you."

"Joseph, you're here," she murmurs, reaching her arm up, stretching, and rolling slightly onto her stomach.

I roll with her, pressing into her back, not letting any distance come between us. "Of course, I'm here." I wrap my arms around her. "Tell me you're okay, Sweetness."

"I was so scared." Her soft, hoarse words shoot straight to my heart. It pains me I wasn't here for her, but then she rubs her face against my cheek. "I'm okay, Joseph. And you're here. You came."

I unfurl from around her and move so she can see my face. "Always. I will always come for you."

She sighs and gives me a sweet smile, soothing me. I kiss along her back as my hand caresses up her outstretched arm, entwining our fingers, and press into her, swiveling my hips.

"Joseph," she gasps as her body moves with mine.

"I love to hear my name on your lips." I move lower, rubbing my face, my lips, my hand down her back until I reach the bottom of her camisole. I slowly start to work it up her body, kissing and caressing as her bare skin is revealed. Her skin is so soft, every inch of her perfection. When I've lifted her cami as far as I can, she rocks gently, allowing me to pull it off over her head.

She tries to roll over, but I stop her. As much as I want to be bare chest to bare chest, I'm not done exploring her back. I start at her head, losing my fingers in her mane of brownish red locks, sweeping the silkiness aside. My mouth settles on her neck, kissing behind her ear, nipping and then licking her earlobe. She squirms, mumbling like she meant to say my name, but she wasn't quite capable.

It makes me smile. She's still trying to wake up, and I'm inundating her with my body, full force, not giving her a chance to settle and get used to my presence.

I kiss down her back and relish every squirm, sigh, and moan. "You're so beautiful, Samantha." I nip at her side. "Tell me how you can ever allow anyone to call you Sam?"

"Joseph, please," she whispers.

"Please what?" I stop my journey southward and return to hover near her head, needing to hear what she is pleading for.

"I don't want to talk about that." Her voice is sexy and seductive, and she doesn't have a clue how it affects me.

"What do you want then?" I probe.

"You. I just want you," she says.

My lips return to her shoulder, kissing along her arm and then back to her neck as I reply, "And I you, baby. Tell me what you don't want to say. I need to understand, as I don't see how someone as gorgeous as you can be called by anything other than Samantha, goddess of my heart."

"Joseph." It's a plea, of what, I'm not sure. Maybe it's for me to continue my exploration of her body, or for me to stop this line of questioning. Perhaps it's both.

"Tell me, and I'll give you anything you want." I'll give her anything she wants anyway.

She buries her head in her pillow and turns the other way, trying to hide. "When you hear the name *Sam*, what do you think of? Who do you picture?"

"That's easy." I shrug and move so I can see her face over her other shoulder, my body still covering hers, straddling her hips, my hard cock pressed against her ass. "I picture some guy, non-descript, but definitely a guy."

She nods. "And what do you picture when you hear the name Samantha?"

I smile. "That's even easier. I picture you, Sweetness."

She shakes her head. "Nope. Before me, before you even knew I existed."

"I guess I pictured a woman. A woman with silken hair, curvaceous curves, graceful and seductive. Beautiful."

"Exactly," is all she says, not a word more.

I don't understand. I rise up and roll her over. "Exactly what?"

She sighs in exasperation. "If I meet you for the first time and you're expecting a Sam, then in most cases you'll be pleasantly surprised to see me. But, if you're expecting a Samantha, I can't live up to the ideals men conjure in their heads." She brushes her hand across my forehead. "As Sam, I rise above the curve. As Samantha, I fall below."

"Christ, is that what you think?"

"It's what I know to be true." She sounds so sure. She truly believes that crap.

"Either you're hanging out with idiots, or someone's sold you a load of crap. Who put this idea in your head? Who made you feel you didn't live up to your name?"

She shakes her head. "It doesn't matter. It's true. Sam fits me better. No one calls me Samantha except you. Not even my parents, who named me, actually ever called me by it. That means something."

She moves to get up, but I stop her from pulling away. She falls back, locking eyes with me. "Everyone calls you Joe. Why is Joe good enough for you, but Sam isn't good enough for me?"

Capturing her hands beside her head, our fingers lock in an embrace. "Only you and my grandmother call me Joseph. As for everyone else, you're right, they call me Joe."

I kiss across her cheek and stop at her lips. "It's different, though. I don't insist people call me Joe because I don't feel worthy of Joseph. I couldn't give a fuck if they call me Joe or Joseph, it doesn't change my opinion of myself." I run my nose along hers. "Except you. I like it when you call me Joseph because it seems special, to hold more meaning." I press my lips to hers in a slow, tender kiss. Pulling away momentarily, I study her face. "Tell me who hurt you, Samantha. Who boxed you in, keeping you hostage to a boy's name?"

"I like you calling me Samantha. It irritated me at first, but then I understood you weren't making fun of me. It meant something to you. It's special when you say it, and now I don't want anyone else to call me Samantha. Only you."

"It is special." I kiss her, capturing her bottom lip, pulling slightly. "Now stop trying to distract me. Tell me who hurt you?" I'm not giving up, I'm like a dog with a bone, and this bone needs to be buried.

Even in the dim light I can see her studying me, contemplating her next move. "Jace," she says so softly, I would have missed it had I not seen her lips move.

What the fuck? Jace, man. Christ.

I roll onto my back and pull her into my arms. "What'd he say, Sweetness?"

"We were young, Joseph. Don't be mad at him. He has no idea what he said made a lasting impression."

"Samantha." I'm losing my patience, not with her, with Jace. He's impacted her so much, and he has no idea. Now I have to hear how he's stifled her opinion of herself with her name on top of the fact he already made her feel unwanted when no one would date her due to him putting out a moratorium on her.

"Okay. Okay. I was twelve or so. I got a wild hair and starting asking everyone to call me Samantha. I thought it sounded more glamorous, more grown up. But when Jace heard me tell someone my name was Samantha, he started laughing and said, *'Sam, you're too much of a tomboy to ever be called Samantha. Those are shoes you'll never fill.'* So, I dropped it and went back to being Sam. I've been Sam ever since."

Christ, he's a fucking idiot. He and I are going to have words. Again.

I nudge her. "Samantha, look at me."

She props up, her chin resting on her hands splayed across my chest.

"We've already established your brother's an idiot on a good day. I have no doubt, if he thought you would take what he said to heart, he never would have said it. He was being flippant and irresponsible, and a kid. He was only what, fourteen? He didn't know jack-shit about life." I cup her face. "You more than surpass your name in beauty and intellect. Maybe you were a tomboy and Sam seemed to fit when you were a kid, but you're all woman now, and *Samantha* you will always be to me. If you continue to request people call you Sam, do so because you only want *me* to call you *Samantha*, and not because you feel unworthy of such a name."

I roll over, pressing into her, only this time we are chest to chest. I cup her face, running my thumb down the line of her cheekbone. "Samantha, you are the most beautiful woman I have ever seen. From the moment I saw you, you captured my mind, my body, and my heart. You are a goddess. You are my goddess. My *Samantha*. Tell me *my* words carry as much weight as Jace's words did when you were just twelve. Tell me your mature eighteen-year-old ears hear me now, beautiful."

Her eyes continue to study mine. Her hands travel to my

shoulders, holding me close. "I want to be what you see, Joseph. I want to be your *Samantha*."

"There's no *want*, Sweetness. You *are*." I lower my head, brushing my lips across hers. "Let me love you. Let me show you what you mean to me." I tear my gaze from hers and move down to her breasts, smiling up at her. "I'm going to get lost in these beauties." I settle lower, between her thighs, her glorious breasts staring back at me. "Anything you don't want me to do, just say so. I'm not rushing this. We're not having sex, but I'm going to explore every inch of you, Samantha. Every inch of you is going to be mine by the time I'm done."

She arches, wiggling below me. "Joseph."

"Christ, I love how you say my name when you're all hot and bothered. Don't hold back, baby. Don't ever hold back. I always want to hear how much I please you." With that, I'm done talking, done analyzing anything except how to read her body, how to make her feel good. I capture her taut nipple in my mouth, sucking deeply. My hand continues to tease the other one, pinching and pulling gently.

She nearly bows off the bed. "Oh, god."

I lose myself in the clasp of her arms holding me in place, her round breasts to sink my face into, and hard, sensitive nipples beckoning for my mouth to suck and lick. I'm so turned on, my cock aches for relief, but I don't care. This is all about her, and I'm in the haze of her arousal, pulling me to her, begging for more.

She clasps my face, forcing me to release her. She's breathless and has a pained expression.

Pained? Shit, have I been so wrapped up in her body I didn't notice I was hurting her?

"Joseph, please," she pleads.

I move up her body. "Christ, have I hurt you? What's wrong?" I scan her face, her breasts, and run my hand over her injured shoulder for signs of trauma.

She cups my cheek, bringing my face back to hers. She's still panting, crazed, maybe confused. "I ache, Joseph. I can't take any more."

Realization dawns. "Sweetness, you need release." My hand travels down her body and slips inside her panties. She's soaked. "Fuck, baby."

I sink my fingers between her folds and back up to her clit. "Kiss me. Show me what you need."

She lunges and nearly knocks me back. I quickly recover my position over her. Her tongue flicks across mine as my finger circles her clit. She moans and sucks my tongue. My cock twitches, eager with the idea of her sucking on it.

Christ, I'm gonna come in my underwear if I keep thinking like that.

I adjust, lying half on her, using my leg to open her thighs to me more. I sink my tongue in past her lips, making love to her mouth as I wish my cock could do to her pussy. She cries out, her nails biting into my back, turning me on even more. Her hips undulate, teasing and begging for more, more of the things I can't give her. Not yet, anyway.

I pull on her bottom lip, releasing it as my fingers pinch her nipple, rolling it, teasing it along with her clit. "Come for me."

"Joseph," she cries out, arching back, legs shaking as her orgasm takes flight.

"So fucking beautiful. I can't wait to be buried inside you, feeling you come undone around my cock."

She lets out a long moan, and I almost come, knowing how my words affect her. I suck on her breasts as I continue to circle her clit, prolonging her orgasm, extracting every bit of her pleasure.

When she loosens her grip on my back and starts to relax, I trail kiss down her body. I'm on a mission of a different kind. The destination is the same, but the journey much different.

"Lift up." Without hesitation, she lifts her hips, allowing me to pull off her panties.

She's laid out, completely naked before me. "You're exquisite, Samantha. The most beautiful creature I've ever seen."

Her hand snakes in my hair. "What are you doing, Joseph?" Her face is languid, beautiful without a stitch of makeup on.

"Exploring." I run my nose along her closely cropped landing strip, guiding me to my destination. "You smell so good." I spread her legs, burrowing my shoulders under her knees.

"Joseph," she screeches. "I'm not sure…" Her words are lost as my tongue sweeps her folds. "Oh, god!"

"Christ, you taste even better than I imagined."

She jumps as I lick her clit.

"You'd better settle in, Sweetness, this is going to take a while. I imagine two to three orgasms, at least."

Samantha

"Joseph, I can't possibly. You don't need to do that. I just had a quite spectacular orgasm. I don't need more." I rise up on my elbows, gazing down at the most handsome man I've ever seen looking up at me from between my thighs.

My thighs! Never in my wildest dreams did I picture him there, like this. Well, I did picture him, but honestly, my imagination is poorly lacking, as the reality is so much sweeter.

He flashes a devious smile. "Sweetness, you have no idea what your body can do." His tongue licks across my opening, pushing, but not breaching my virgin passageway.

My insides clench, wanting him to enter me, wanting him to be the one to take my virginity, to claim me in all ways.

My head falls back. "Please."

"Please what?" His tongue does it again. "Do you want me inside you? Do you want me to fill you up, take your virginity, make you mine?" He echoes my thoughts.

I push up on my hands, my eyes finding his. "Don't fuck with me, Joseph."

He frowns. "You're right. I'm sorry. I'm teasing you, but I'm not trying to make light of the situation. I want to explore you, but I won't enter you. I won't take that precious gift. Don't get me wrong, Samantha. I will be your first and last lover, but we're in no hurry. I want to savor every inch of you, cherish everything you give me. I won't take your virginity until you're ready to be mine. Forever."

He rises to his hands and knees, climbing up my body to hover over me, forcing me to lie back down. His face is mere inches from mine. "In case you don't know it. I love you. I'm in love with you."

In love with me? *Oh, shit.* This man. He takes me places I feared to imagine but hoped were possible.

"I will kiss you. I will suck your nipples. I will touch you. I will eat your pussy and explore every inch of you, making you come in every way possible. But I won't take your virginity until you are ready to give yourself to me. Fully. Endlessly. Forever."

"Joseph, I'm willing to give you my virginity now. You don't have to wait." I touch his erection through his underwear. He hisses and closes his eyes. "Let me touch you and give you pleasure. It isn't just about me."

He bends down and kisses my neck and then bites me. I yelp, and he soothes it with his tongue. "Samantha, you can touch me, you can lick me, you can suck me, you can do anything you like to me, anytime you like. But, you still don't fully believe in our future. Together. You don't fully trust me not to leave you, abandon you. I won't take your virginity and leave you with the idea that there could be another. I will be your first and your last. You will have no other lovers than me. I will have no other lovers than you. You will not be my first, but you will be my last, my most precious, my most cherished. My forever love."

He's killing me. He's breaking my heart, but he's right. I'm not fully there yet. I'm afraid of getting him killed. I'm afraid of him leaving me for someone better suited for his VP stature. I'm afraid I'll come to fully rely on him and when I need him most—he'll be gone. I don't know how to trust like that. To give with abandon. To trust without limits.

His soft caress brings me back. "You're thinking too much. Let's give you something else to concentrate on." He straddles my stomach, then pulls his boxer briefs down, setting his amazing cock free. He places my hand on his shaft, moving it up and down as he slowly moves his hips. "Christ, I'm so fucking hard for you, Sweetness. I won't last long. Make me come, and then I'll get back to exploring your incredible body with my mouth."

I grip him harder.

"Yes, baby, just like that."

He's so beautiful in his raw need for my touch. It's heady to see the desire in his eyes and know I put it there.

I cup his ass. "Raise up, closer to me."

He moves closer and before he can settle back down, I lick the head of his cock, capturing a drop of cum on my tongue and swallow.

"Christ. Fuck, that's hot."

If he thinks that's hot, he's gonna love this.

I rise up and capture the head between my lips and suck as my hand pumps his shaft. I can't get all of him in this awkward position. But I manage as best I can, as best I know how, considering I've never done this before.

"Fuck, Samantha. You don't have to…ah…yes," he exclaims as I suck him deeper. He leans back, his hand finding my clit. "God, you're even wetter than before. I want you to come with me, but I'm not sure I can wait for you."

That only encourages me to make him lose his ever-loving mind, to make him as lost and overwhelmed as he made me a few minutes ago, sucking my nipples until I thought my head was going to explode.

He slowly pumps his hips as I suck and stroke him. His hands explore me, tweaking my nipples and playing with my clitoris. I'm not sure what's hotter, watching him come undone, or the words coming out of his mouth. When he starts to talk about wishing he could finger fuck me while he fucks my mouth, I lose *my* mind and come.

"Christ, look at you, sucking me even harder as you come."

I buck under him, overwhelmed by my release, but still trying to focus on him.

"Fuck, yes. I'm coming," he warns, watching me to see if I release him, but I don't. I just suck him harder, determined to taste him, to swallow everything he has to give me.

He cups my face. "Sweetness." He calls out over and over again as he shoots cum down the back of my throat.

"Holy shit, baby." He breathlessly pulls his still-hard cock from my mouth. "That…" He collapses beside me. "…was incredible."

He wraps me in his arms, and I rest my head on his chest. "Tell me again," I say softly.

He kisses my forehead and runs his hand up my back. "I love you. And not because you just sucked my cock."

I let out a sigh of contentment. "I love you too, Joseph." I may be afraid to commit to our future, to believe in forever. But one thing I know for certain—I will love him till the day I die and probably beyond. Nobody has ever seen me, or treated me like he does. I doubt anyone ever will.

He squeezes me tighter. "Say it again, Sweetness."

I smile against his chest. "I love you, Joseph."

"Those are the sweetest words I have ever heard." He rolls me over. "I love you."

He nuzzles into my neck and then moves lower, sucking on my nipples, before making it back down to my body. "Now, let me taste you. I need to feel you come on my tongue."

"Oh, Jesus, Joseph."

He laughs. "You love my dirty talk. It makes you hot." He checks out my breasts. "It made your nipples even harder. Let's see if it made you wetter."

Fourteen

Joseph

I MADE HER COME TWO MORE TIMES WITH MY MOUTH. It was quite spectacular. Really.

Now my cock is painfully hard, again. I had to ditch my underwear. I roll on my back, my cock bobbing against my abdomen. She eyes it, not missing a thing, even in her sex-drunk state.

"Come sit on my face, Sweetness, and take my cock in your mouth. I need you again."

"Joseph, you're insatiable. I don't need any more. I can just take care of you." She moves to take my cock in her mouth.

I'm not having it. I lift her by her hips and laugh at her yelp as I swing her around, placing her knees on either side of my chest.

Her ass sways as she peers back at me.

"When I said I needed you again, I meant I needed *you*." I lick her wet swollen pussy. She shudders and instinctively opens her thighs to me. "I meant, I needed to taste you again. I need to feel you come. I need it more than I need you to suck me off."

"God. Joseph, the things you say." She takes me in hand and licks my cock, tip to base and back.

Christ, she's gonna kill me. Abso-fucking-lutely kill me.

I take her cue and lick her from her clit to her asshole. I run my fingers in her wetness and back to her untried rosebud, over and over again. Then circle it with my finger.

She stops sucking me. "Joseph?"

"Baby, I'm trying to be good here, but Christ, you push me. I'm gonna finger fuck your ass while you suck me off." I feel her clench against my fingers. "You like that, don't you, beautiful?"

She's silent, her head lying on my hip, my cock lost in her soft hair. "Sweetness, it's nothing to be ashamed of. Does it turn you on to think of me taking your ass?"

"You taking any part of me turns me on, Joseph."

"I'm happy to hear it. So, it's a yes to the ass play?"

"I want to do it to you too."

"Oh…wow…uh, I've never done that." I've thought of it.

"Me either, obviously." She giggles.

I pat her ass. "Get up a sec. I'll be right back."

She rolls off me, and I jump up, heading to the guest room to see if I can find what we need. I come back a minute later, my search successful.

I'd long since turned on the table lamp in her room, tired of not being able to see her. She's lying on the bed, not a hint of shyness left in her. I think I've sexed it out of her tonight. It's hard to hide when someone's buried between your thighs. I've never been shy about my body, but with her I've never felt this comfortable, this relaxed. I've also never been this turned on either, even after I come, I'm still hard and aching for her. I'm starting to think the only thing that will quench the beast is to sink my cock deep into her sweet pussy and feel her squeeze my release from me, one slow, tight clench after the other until we're both so wrung out we can't see straight.

She props up on her elbow. "Joseph, are you sure you don't want to call it a night? We've been at it for hours. I could just take care of you. Honest, I don't mind."

I sit beside her and run my hand down her hip and back up to cup her face. "Are you tired? I guess I got a little wrapped up in discovering you. I didn't stop to think you might be worn out."

She sits up, her breasts pressing into me. "I am tired, but that's not it. I have to get up in five hours for school." She glances away, blushing.

I lift her chin. "What's with the embarrassment? If we were in Austin, I'd be the one getting up for class. It's not a mark of your maturity to have to get up for school." She nods, and I kiss her nose. "However, I do have some good news. Fin got you out of school tomorrow. You don't have get up early. But, if you're having second thoughts about the ass play, we don't have to do it. Remember what I said, all you have to do is tell me you're uncomfortable, and it stops. There's no pressure. Ever. We're both all in, or we aren't. There's no sacrificing for the other person's pleasure. It's both of us 100%, or it's not happening. Clear?"

"Clear." She smiles widely. "No school?"

"No school." My smile meets hers.

She motions to the bed. "Shall we resume then?"

I pull her into my lap, skin to skin. How easy it would be to simply move her to straddle me and sink into her wet, welcoming pussy. I look in her eyes. "I don't know what I did to deserve you, Samantha, but I'm deeply grateful. I only pray I'm the man you need—that I'll grow to be all you'll *ever* need."

She lays her head on my shoulder. "I'm the lucky one. I pray I'll be woman enough for you and for your job."

"Sweetness, you are. Just as you are right at this moment. I will never need more than you are. I only need you to believe in me and our future."

"I'm trying."

"I know you are." I raise her face to mine. "Now kiss me, Sweets. Show me what you need."

Her lips perk up into a smile. "I think you know what I need better than I do."

I agree. "Then give me those lips and let me show you."

She presses her mouth to mine, and for a moment I just let our lips linger. But when I pinch her nipple and she gasps, I take the kiss deeper, showing her what we both need. What we both want.

♡

Samantha

"Joseph," I pant, finding coherent thought difficult at the moment. He's kept me on edge for so long, trying to get me ready. If I'm ever going to be ready, it's now.

"Stop sucking me. Don't touch me until I tell you. Otherwise I'm going to come the second my finger slips inside you." His strained command nearly sends me over the edge.

I release him and glance over my shoulder. "Okay. What do I do?"

"Lay your head on the bed next to me. Can you do that, or is it uncomfortable?"

I move into position, my ass still in the air, as I straddle his face. *God, who would have ever thought I'd be doing this today?*

"You alright, Sweetness?"

"Yes. What's next?"

"Just relax and try not to come." His tongue runs up the length of me. "Christ, I love how you taste," he growls. "Okay, this might be a little cold."

I hear the pop and assume it's the lube he found when he left my room a bit ago. I'm not sure I want to know why he has it or where he found it. It was too quick for him to have borrowed it from Fin. Plus, Joseph was naked so I doubt he went in search of Fin. I feel Joseph's warm fingers moving over my ass a second before I feel the cold lube. His finger circles my hole, it's not uncomfortable, it actually feels kinda good, but I'm nervous about what's going to happen next. "Joseph," my voice quivers.

He kisses the inside of my thigh. "It's okay, baby. Just relax. You tell me to stop, and it stops. But give it a chance." He starts to rub my clitoris in the same motion as his finger on my ass.

It doesn't take long for my arousal to come back to life. It never left, just waited in limbo for him to touch me again. I can't help the need building in me, the need for him to fill me up, the need to have him sink his cock inside me. Now, with him teasing my ass, I have the need for more there too. I push back on his finger.

"That's it. Push again."

"Joseph, I'm gonna come." I start to shake, trying to hold it off.

He stops rubbing my clit, but continues the manipulation of my ass. My orgasm drops away but my desire is still high.

"Relax, baby." He pushes harder, and then he's there. His finger breaches my opening. I let out a moan, and he stills. "Are you okay?"

"Yeah." I try to steady my breathing, relax my muscles. I tensed up the moment he entered me, feeling both pleasure and pain.

I feel more lube, and then he pushes in again, this time the progression is much smoother and all pleasure. I moan into the bed. He's gonna make me come just from this.

"So damn sexy." He runs his lips along my thigh. I hear a plop next to me where the lube landed. "Your turn, go gentle."

I grab the bottle and move slowly to hover over his cock, so I can get to his ass. I can't help but snicker. I'm moving carefully so as not to dislodge his finger in my ass. "This is awkward." I laugh again.

"I know, it's a bit clinical at the moment. But I'm still hot as hell for you."

"It's weird. You've got your finger in my ass." I giggle. "Will I be able to look you in the eye again?"

He moves his finger, in and out. I still, experiencing the sensation of what it might feel like to have his cock inside me. I clench around him.

"You're squeezing me. Does that mean it feels good?"

"Mmmm."

"That's right. It's gonna feel even better when I'm touching your clit and you're sucking my cock, imagining it's my cock buried deep inside you."

A small moan escapes my lips, and his cock bobs against his stomach. I don't think either of us it going to last much longer.

"Then add in the fact you're going to be fucking my ass at the same time. It's kinky as hell." His voice is strained as he tenderly caresses my abdomen. "Now, get moving before I come all over myself."

I get lubed up, have him spread eagle, so I can reach his ass. I start at his perineum and work my way back. His cock twitches. With gritted teeth, he reminds me not to touch it. He's hanging on the edge, much like I am. I start to massage his ass. His moans encourage me to push harder, making his cock bob as if it's begging for attention. My insides clenches as if my vagina is begging for his cock.

I clench again, and Joseph moans, "Fuck, baby, when you squeeze me—it nearly does me in. Push harder, before I come all over us."

I'm pushing. "I'm afraid. I don't want to hurt you."

"Suck my balls, Sweetness, and then push through. I'll tell you to stop if it's too much."

I do as he asks, and before I know it, I'm sucking his cock deep and finger fucking him as he sucks and licks me, finger fucking my ass. I thought I was overwhelmed before, that was nothing compared to this act of unadulterated hedonistic decadence.

My body's on fire. I'm gonna come. I think about releasing him, to warn him. But reading my mind, he squeezes my ass cheek and sucks my clitoris without pause. As the tingle starts in my legs and works its way up, I fuck him harder and suck him deeper as I come undone. I can't scream his name, but I moan around his cock right before he unleashes his desire and comes deep in my mouth. I swallow everything he gives me and only release him when I feel his cock finally soften.

He doesn't let up on me though, he continues to lick me, his finger going deeper in my ass, and his other hand moves over my vaginal opening teasing me, raising my desire again. He squeezes another orgasm out of me, and I come so hard I actually pass out, black out, or zone out.

I come to with him carrying me to the bathroom and sinking us both into a hot bath. I can't move. I'm catatonic. Every muscle in my body feels limp and over used. I'm done. I can't even help as he bathes me, and then himself. He talks softly in my ear, soothes me, comforts me, and doesn't makes me feel like the lump of useless flesh that I am.

He gets us out, dries us off, props me up at the sink, and hands me a toothbrush with toothpaste already on it. He steps away to brush his own teeth in the sink next to me, watching me all the while to be sure I don't fall over. I'm not convinced I won't.

He finishes first and runs kisses along my neck and shoulders as his hands caress up my back and sides. The moment I'm done, he sweeps me up in his arms and carries me back to bed. After I'm settled under the covers, naked and clean, he disappears out my bedroom door with only a towel on. He comes back a few minutes later with two glasses of water. Helping me sit up, he holds the cup as I drink down the entire glass of water. He takes a few drinks of his, then offers me as sip, but I refuse and lie back down. He finishes his, placing both cups on the nightstand before crawling in bed next to me.

He spoons me from behind, our legs and limbs intertwined. He kisses my neck, caresses my hip before his hand settles on my abdomen. "Good night."

"Joseph. Love. You," I manage to eke out before I close my eyes.

"I love you too, Samantha. I'm sorry I wore you out, Sweets. But that was the most amazing night of my life."

I hum in response. He merely chuckles and pulls me closer.

I start to drift, never having felt such love in my life, either emotionally or physically. He has absolutely ruined me for all other men. If he leaves me, it will more than break me, it will devastate me.

It.

Will.

Crush.

Me.

Fifteen

Joseph

I AWAKE ALONE IN HER BED. IT TAKES ME A MOMENT to realize what happened last night was not a dream, but reality. A fantastic reality at that. I search for the clock on the nightstand. It's only a few minutes past seven. I think it was around two when we finally went to sleep. Even after all the sex play, my morning wood makes its usual appearance. I listen to see if Samantha is in the bathroom, but everything is silent. I guess this erection is going to go unsatisfied.

I sit up, swinging my feet over the side of the bed, stretching. I rise to my feet after a few moments and make my way to the bathroom. After slipping on a pair of basketball shorts and grabbing a t-shirt, I open the door and immediately hear laughter. I hear *her* laughter, specifically, and I can't help the smile occupying my face or the warmth in my belly as a result. It's good to hear her laughing and happy. I endeavor to hear more of it in the coming days.

I enter the living room and see my brothers and my woman laughing and carrying on, having a good ole time in the kitchen. I smell bacon, and can only assume she's cooking breakfast—for them. Jealousy smacks me in the face until her eyes lock on mine, and the sizzle that cracks between us is purely ours. The heat I see in her eyes and the flush moving up her chest and face is for me. Only. Me.

As if in some synchronized move, Fin and Matt look at Samantha and then turn to lock eyes on me.

"Hey, did we wake you up?" Matt says as he walks toward me.

"No. I didn't hear a thing until I opened the bedroom door," I reply as I slip on my t-shirt, still staring at Samantha, who is quickly making her way to me. My arms wrap around her the minute she's by my side. I kiss her head and relish the smell and feel of her. "Good morning, Sweetness," I softly say into her hair.

"Morning. Hungry?"

"Starving, actually." For her and for food.

"Good." She pulls back. "Let me go finish, so we can all eat together." She stands on her tiptoes and kisses my mouth all too quickly before returning to the kitchen.

I'm loving this public display of affection. I've never been much for PDA, but with Samantha, I want everyone to know she's mine. Plus, I'd never survive trying to keep my hands to myself. I can't resist her, not since I've gone full in, and especially not after last night.

Matt moves closer and gives me a hug. "So, you finally bit the bullet, huh?" He nods to Samantha. "I'm happy for you. She's the best." He pats me on the back as we walk toward the breakfast bar. "And she makes a killer breakfast."

I smile at that. "Yes, she does. I'm a little jealous you two get a home-cooked meal every morning."

Fin hands me a cup of coffee. "It's the good life. I won't deny it. I'm not going to let her move back home. My stomach would revolt."

She bumps his hip as he comes to help her. "I think you'd manage, Fin. You've survived all these years without a cook. Perhaps it's a sign you need to find a woman. Someone to fill your bed *and* your stomach." She eyes me before she continues. "And your heart. That goes for you too, Matt."

"You had me at bed and stomach, but lost me with the love stuff," Matt grumbles.

Matt is the die-hard manwhore, just like Jace. Well, maybe not like Jace anymore, who's taken it to a whole new level. But Jace is gonna have to clean up his act and focus more on school and his future career aspirations, which just might bring him to MCI to work with Matt. They are two peas in a pod in more than just their womanizing ways. They're PR twin gods and would make a remarkable team, taking MCI to a new level of marketing and public relations.

If Jace would pull his head out of his ass.

"Someday, you two will find the woman who will knock you off your feet. You won't know what to do with yourself, how to function without her." She turns and gives Matt a wink. "And more so, you won't even want to survive without her."

My stomach twists with her words. She believes Matt and Fin will find someone they can't live without, yet she doubts she is *it* for me?

She stops mid-step. My face must reveal my thoughts. As realization dawns, she sets down two plates and returns for the others, her smile and lightness of step gone.

Once we're seated and conversation flows easily, I notice she's just pushing the food around her plate, not eating, and not joining in on our conversation. I softly nudge her shoulder. She gives me a placating smile, one I don't believe for a second.

A moment later, she hops up and says quickly, "Excuse me. I'm going to shower." She turns away before I can see her face. "Leave the dishes," she says before disappearing down the hall to her room.

I glance between my brothers, embarrassed and not sure of what to say.

"What happened?" Fin asks, his fork stopped halfway to his mouth.

I shrug and scratch my head. "I think it was my reaction to what she said to you two, about finding the *one* and never letting her go."

"What? You don't think that's true for us?" Matt asks.

"No, that's not what he means," Fin interjects. "Sam thinks you and I will find the one," he says to Matt. "But she doesn't believe she's the one for Joe." Fin looks at me. "Right?"

"Yeah, basically. She either believes I won't find the one, or when I do, it couldn't possibly be her." I let out a sigh. "But fuck, it is her. She's it for me. I've told her that as recently as last night." I run my hand through my hair and then get up, taking my empty plate to the sink. I grip the counter and meet Fin's gaze. "I told her I love her. She even said it back to me."

"But, she doubts it's forever?" Fin asks, already knowing the answer.

I nod. "She doubts she's *my* forever. I don't think she doubts her feelings for me. She still thinks there's someone else out there for me, and when I find her, I'll break Samantha's heart." I lean back against the island facing them.

"Motherfucker." I close my eyes and scrub my face with my hands.

"Shit," Matt says. "I thought it was mutual with you two. It seems so obvious you're made for each other."

"We are."

"They are," Fin says at the same time.

"I have to prove it to her."

"How?" Fin asks skeptically. I swear that man can read my mind. We're so much alike.

"I could ask her to marry me."

"No," Fin says almost angrily, getting up and coming around the bar to stand in front of me. "It reeks of desperation. You already gave her a promise ring, don't mess it up by pushing before she's ready."

"I need her to believe in my commitment to her."

"Then prove it to her, day in and day out. Don't tie yourself to her with a marriage license, where she might think you're just obligated to stay with her. Convince her by being committed, through your schooling, through the distance of living in different cities. Show her you're committed in the face of no commitment. Meaning you aren't married, and you could easily cheat or go find someone else, but you won't. You don't. You stay with her because you *choose* to stay with her, not because you're tied to her through marriage."

"You're right," I agree.

"Damn straight I'm right. This is the long game, brother," Fin says.

"It's a marathon, not a sprint," I reinforce.

"Exactly," Fin nods.

"A marathon," Matt repeats with awe in his voice. I have to smile, he seems dazed and confused by all of this.

Fin laughs. "I'll explain it to you on our way to work." He pats Matt on the back. "Let me grab my laptop, and I'll be ready to go."

Matt stares at me for a minute. "So, she's the one for you?"

I nod in the affirmative.

"But, you're not going to ask her to marry you?"

I shake my head no.

"You're going to be committed with no commitment?"

"Yes."

"Alright." He gets up and surprises me with a big hug. "I'm happy for you, brother. She's perfect for you." He releases me, but keeps his hands on my shoulders. "Don't let her fuck it up."

More poignant words have never been spoken.

PART 6

UNTOUCHABLE

MAY

Sixteen

Samantha

I DON'T KNOW HOW MICHAEL, OR ANYONE WHO HAS to go undercover, pulls it off. I've only had one phone call with Roderick, my father's killer, and it made my stomach churn. I immediately felt dirty, in need of a shower. I didn't have to pretend I was only agreeing to meet him under duress, or keeping it a secret, as it is both those things. Only Joseph, Fin, Michael and his team, and Victor and his team are aware of the plan. I'm not an actress by any stretch of the imagination, and though it's still weeks away, the stress of it weighs on me daily.

There's an extra layer of secrecy between Victor and his team's involvement in areas the FBI are being kept in the dark, except Michael, who's fully vetted and in the know. I think. Honestly, Victor is probably the only one who knows everything. I'm sure he's keeping some things from Michael just to lessen the blowback when the FBI hears of Joseph, Fin, and Victor's involvement.

Per the plan they've cooked up, I'm supposed to slip away at my graduation ceremony using the massive crowd as cover. I thought for sure I'd have to convince Roderick to wait till then, figuring he'd insist on meeting sooner. He didn't take much convincing at all. I didn't even have to tell him about my 24/7 protection. He already knew. No surprise there. As much as he watched me before that fateful day, it makes sense he would continue to watch me afterwards, especially since he hasn't yet obtained the information he seeks.

I don't trust him. I would be a fool to believe he intends on letting

"

me go. A part of me hopes there is honor even among thieves, crooks, murderers. That his word is worth something, but I don't believe that to be the case. It's a risk to meet him, to agree to be alone with him, to put myself out there, vulnerable. But I don't have a choice. Not if I want the people I love to be safe. Not if I want a chance at a normal life, not looking over my shoulder for the rest of it. And not if I want justice for my father's death.

Michael and Victor are planning on nabbing him before we even make it to the parking lot. They're not planning on me actually disappearing with him.

But I am.

I've got plans of my own I'm putting into place, as a backup of the backup of the backup. Triple redundancy. A girl can never be too prepared, especially when dealing with a man with no scruples who is an expert at evading capture.

I've pulled Scott, the head chef at work, and Sebastian into my web of lies. I elected to keep Margot out of it. She'd be more than willing to help, but I can't bring myself to put her in danger. She's got enough going on with her family troubles, and she's just a little wisp of thing. She couldn't fight a flea if she had to.

I met with Scott at work a few weeks ago. He still cooks me dinner on my breaks, so it's not unusual for us to hang out during our shifts. It didn't raise suspicion, and my protection stayed out of the kitchen, watching the doors and diners instead. I slipped into the freezer just before it shut behind Scott.

"Shit, Sam. You scared me." He glanced to the closed door. "What are you doing, girly?"

"You're ex-military, right?" I said in quick succession, afraid I'd lose my nerve.

His arms folded over his massive chest as he squinted, scrutinizing my every word. "What are you up to?"

I looked around the freezer. It seemed like such an easy idea, so simple, but now that I was standing there in front of this huge guy, who probably knew more about clandestine schemes than I could ever think to dream up—I felt downright ridiculous.

His face softened, and he cocked his head. "Tell me, Sam. What's got you all twisted up that you had to sneak in here away from your protection to ask me such a question?"

"I need your help."

His arms dropped to his sides. "Anything. What do you need?"

I took a long, steadying breath. "I need you to help me survive meeting my father's killer."

He let out a punch of air. "Fuck, baby." His head fell forward, shaking slowly side to side. He cracked his knuckles, muttering to himself.

I wasn't sure if he was contemplating helping me or contemplating throwing me out on my ass.

Suddenly, he straightened, cracked his neck and met my eyes. Decision was written all over his face. "What'd you have in mind?"

I nearly broke down and sobbed in relief. *He's gonna help me.*

Each shift we used my break to scheme, get status checks. He pulled Sebastian in, with my urging. Scott was the one to contact him, though, so Sebastian and me were never seen in direct contact with each other. During the day, they scouted out what was needed, and we finalized the plans each time I worked. We've not left any electronic trail of our interactions. Everything was in person, and anything written down was only done by Scott, as he is the most unlikely suspect since we've never associated with each other outside of work. I trust him and Sebastian explicitly.

A horn blares and jolts me in my seat.

"Sweetness?" Joseph's hand grips my leg, concern written all over his face by my overreaction.

I smile and lean against his shoulder. "Sorry. I guess I'm a little on edge after shooting practice."

His arm wraps around my shoulder, tucking me in securely at his side. His warm lips brush my temple, once…twice…three times. "I'll have to find a way to help you relax, then."

I try not to squirm in my seat. His eyes are molten green gems of desire. "How?" I feign ignorance.

His scans my face. "Christ, I love the way you blush when you're turned on." His warm lips press against mine, slowly, tenderly. I sigh, and he ensnares it, presses forward, his tongue flicking and teasing mine before his mouth captures my lips, sucking and pulling one and then the other, retreating and then going back again for more. Savoring me like a sweet wine or a cherished delicacy.

"Sir." One of Victor's men interrupts our splendor.

On a groan, Joseph pulls away, his eyes scorching me. "Hold that thought, Sweetness."

I try to catch my breath as he directs his focus to Victor and the muscle-bound guy in the passenger seat. I can't remember his name. Michael's team is behind us somewhere, never far behind. The FBI haven't sanctioned my right to practice shooting a gun, but they also haven't put a stop to it. Michael is notably absent whenever we go, which is intentional.

"Yes." Joseph's deep voice rumbles in his chest.

"We're here, sir." Huge Guy's eyes dart between the two of us. "Do you still want to go in, or do you want to pick up?"

I glance at Victor in the rearview mirror, and his knowing smirk makes me blush further. He's warmed up tremendously over the months, showing me he's actually human. Not so scary, at least with me. If he barked orders at me like he does his men, I'd pee myself. Seriously.

Joseph's hot gaze eats me up. "I believe we'll take it to go." He raises his brows in question.

I nod, nuzzling into his chest. "Yes, to go sounds perfect."

We make a picnic on the floor in my room, sitting face to face, eating out of the Chinese takeout containers. He's feeding me more than I'm feeding myself.

"Open." He holds lo mein noodles above my head, dangling from his fingers.

I open like a baby bird, taking it all in. He flicks his tongue at the corner of my mouth, catching the yummy drippings before I can swipe it away, then sits back and sucks his fingers clean.

"No need for napkins when I'm around." He arches a brow playfully. "I'll lick you clean, Sweetness."

I groan as I pop a shrimp in my mouth to accompany the noodles, more from the visual of him licking me than from the taste of the food. "Sounds delicious," I manage through my bite.

He smirks, giving me a closed-mouth kiss, his lips warm and sexy as hell.

I dangle a snow pea in front of his mouth. He holds my hand in place as he closes his lips around the end and sucks it in, in one slow, steady suck. Then, he nips my fingers before pulling them into his mouth to clean.

My insides contract. *Jeez, he's serious about the no napkin thing.*

He feeds me another bite using chopsticks this time. "Samantha, I want to talk to you about something."

"Uh oh, sounds serious," I tease.

His stoic face not giving anything way, he tilts his head. "It's a serious topic...rather intimate." His eyes light up at that admission.

Oh. It must have to do with sex for him to consider it *intimate.*

"I don't want to embarrass you, so I'm just going to ask it straight out."

"Okay," I hesitantly reply, unsure I want to hear his question.

"We haven't talked about it, and we aren't together enough for me to know for sure without asking."

So much for him asking straight out. He always says that, and then he eases me into it. He rarely just blurts out whatever the question is.

"You're on the pill, right?" His expression is uncharacteristically bashful.

"Yeah." I put down my food. I can't think about food anymore.

He's not having it, though, and holds up another bite of chicken. "Eat," my caveman commands.

I comply but ask, "Why?" before I do.

"Because you're not eating enough."

"No! Why do you want to know about me being on the pill?"

He winks. He knew what I meant. "I think you're close to trusting my commitment to you, to our future. You're not there yet, but soon, and I want to be prepared. Because when you are there, when you fully believe in me, in us, I'm making you mine." He cups my cheek and leans in, running his lips down my neck.

I tremble from the contact and the idea he's conjuring in my head.

His lips press to mine, sucking my bottom lip as he pulls away. "I don't want anything between us. I want you bare."

"Joseph," I nearly moan, closing my eyes, nipples tightening, my breath shallowing, waiting for his next move.

He runs his nose along the side of my face, nuzzling into me. "I'm clean. I was tested recently, but I've never had unprotected sex." A full body shudder has me gasping at the thought of having sex with him. *Real* sex. *Penetrating* sex.

He chuckles and kisses the corner of my closed eyelid. "Open." I open my eyes as he presents a shrimp. "Bite."

I sink my teeth in, maybe a little too aggressively, and I'm slightly disappointed it's food instead of his cock.

He smirks and pops the other half in his mouth, then kisses me. "You like that, Sweetness? The idea of my cock inside you? Bare, nothing between us, feeling me hard and needy, moving in and out of your wet heat. Making you tremble with need until you come for me, squeezing me, pulling my cum from me, filling you up."

"Jesus," I mumble, panting, heart racing, and wet as sin.

He moves the food and pulls me sideways onto his lap. Our lips crash together, and our soft, slow kisses from earlier are replaced with hot, devouring ones.

In a flash, I'm naked, stretched out across the floor, and he's buried between my thighs, his mouth devouring me in a whole other way. He's giving me pleasure, but he's taking it too, enjoying it nearly as much as me. When I finally come with an arch in my back and a scream echoing in my ears, he growls and laps up my desire as if it is his sustenance.

"I love you, Joseph," I whisper into the cavernous bliss of my orgasm.

"I know, Sweetness." He kisses my thighs. "Now, show me again how much."

His mouth returns to the warm sanctuary he insists is his new home.

Seventeen

Joseph

"**C**HRIST, JOE. SIT THE FUCK DOWN. YOU'RE EVEN making me nervous," Michael's gruff voice interrupts my thoughts. I stop in front of the window, my hands buried in my pockets and my shoulders raised to my ears, taking in the skyline from Fin's penthouse.

"I'm gonna go crazy today. I hate her having to do this. It's like a knife to my heart that I can't be by her side the whole time. It's killing me." The anger in my voice is unmistakable.

A large hand grips the back of my neck, hard. I relish the discomfort.

"We'll be watching her, Joe. Nothing will happen to her. You have to act the part of the calm, cool, proud boyfriend, not the anxious, up-tight, out-for-murder, protective caveman you are at this very moment. If you can't do that, then you need to stay the fuck home. Your behavior could put her in jeopardy if Roderick notices. And believe me, he'll be watching you as much as he'll be watching her." Victor pats my back before stepping away.

"I got it." Over my shoulder I survey Victor and Michael's teams, the ones not in route or at the coliseum already. They're all staring at me.

Turning to fully face them, I square my shoulders, hands by my side. Solid. In control. "I won't fuck it up."

I point to every one of them. "But if she gets hurt, if one hair on her beautiful head is messed up, I'm coming after every one of you. I don't give a shit how strong, smart, and well-trained you all *think* you are. She. Is. My. Life. I will take you all down if you jeopardize that."

They could have laughed in my face. The protective boyfriend lashing out, making idle threats. But there is nothing idle about my threat. I mean every word, and if it takes me to my dying breath, I will make good on it. Maybe it's my size, the power in my voice, or the determined set in my stance, but not one of them laughs, smirks, or dismisses my threat. I get curt nods or *understoods* from each of them.

After a quick word and disbursement of his team, Michael saunters over. He stands shoulder to shoulder with me as I peer out the window once again. "You would have made an excellent commander, Joe. I think you missed your calling."

I think he's being a smartass, as usual, but his earnest gaze surprises me. He's looking at me with admiration, maybe. My anger dissipates instantly. "You won't let her out of your sight." Not a question.

"Not for a heartbeat," he replies with the confidence I need to hear.

I glance at my watch. "Let me have a minute with her before we leave."

He nods. "Fifteen."

"Knock when you're ready." I don't wait for his reply. I disappear down the hall.

I rap on the door before entering to give a heads-up, not to ask for permission to enter. I'm in no mood to be turned away. I need my girl.

She's standing in front of the full-length mirror. The mirror I had her stand naked in front of only last night as I brought her to orgasm, twice. Once with my fingers and then again with my mouth.

Her eyes catch mine in the mirror. The blush creeping up her skin tells me she's thinking of last night too.

I stalk closer, bracketing her back, my lips graze and suck gently at the nape of her neck. "You look beautiful, Samantha." All dressed in black: black dress, black pumps. Simple, classy, and sexy as hell.

She sighs and leans into me. "Thank you." She hugs my arms encircling her waist, her eyes wary as she studies my reflection. "What is it, Joseph?"

Buck up, asshole. She needs you strong and confident.

I turn her around so I can see the face of the woman I love beyond words. I cup her cheek and kiss her rosy lips before answering. I don't want to rehash my concerns, my fears over her being used as bait.

"Be careful. Focus. Be smart. Be strong." I close my eyes as I wrap her in a tight embrace, pressing my lips to her forehead. "Come back to me." I say it as much as a command to her as a prayer to God and the universe at large.

She squeezes me tightly, not letting up. "Always."

♡

Samantha

I grip my hands to stop their shaking. I've got to get a handle on my nerves. I was doing alright until Joseph had to leave to take his seat with the rest of his family. I'm thankful for the McIntyres and all they've done for me, my mom, and even Jace. They're my second family, but honestly, I feel more a part of their family than my own.

What would it be like to *truly* be in their family? It's a thought I've become more comfortable with and one I've allowed myself to dwell on more and more. It doesn't seem so a farfetched any longer, the idea of Joseph and me together for the long haul.

He's been my steady rock since my dad died. We've had our ups and downs, many self-inflicted by me and my meager attempt to squash our relationship before it took flight. I'm beginning to believe we were always destined to be from our very first breathtaking hello. I've been a fool for trying to stop it, such wasted time and heartache.

"Sam."

That familiar voice makes me jump. I turn, surprised to see Jace standing at the doorway.

My mom's not here. She's still at are center she's been in for months now, trying to find herself in the midst of her sorrow over living without my dad. I didn't know if Jace was coming today. He's been his normal-since-dad-died distant self.

"I didn't think you were coming." I don't try to hide my anger. It's been hard not having him around, and I resent the fact he's even here now, pretending he wants to be.

He frowns and steps in the room, glancing at Michael and then back at me. "It's your graduation. Why wouldn't I be here?"

"For the same reason you haven't been around for the last three months. You don't care."

He steps closer, hurt etched along his face. "I do care. Jesus, I've really fucked things up with us, haven't I?"

You think? Asswipe. "What do you think?"

He runs his hand nervously through his dark hair. "I think you're mad at me and have every right to be."

"Well, now that we're in agreement, you can leave. I've got a speech to get ready for, and I don't need you in here undermining my confidence and making me more nervous," I spew in one heated breath, sick to my stomach for having said it so harshly.

His wide-eyed shock tells me my words hit home, exactly how I intended them to. "I'm sorry, Sam. I truly am. At the risk of making it worse, I've got something I need to tell you."

I pace away from him, glancing at Michael, hoping he'll throw Jace out.

Michael's raised brows confirm he'll in fact do just that if I want him to.

I stop. *Do I want him to?*

"Michael, can you give us a minute?" Jace asks.

I don't glance back at Jace, but it's obvious there's unsaid tension between the two of them by the contempt on Michael's face.

"Actually, Jace, I can't," Michael bites out a little too happily as he crosses his arms over his chest, standing in front of the closed door. He's playing the protector to the hilt with no plans to give an inch.

Maybe not to Jace, but he might for me. "Can you wait in the hall?" I ask softly.

Michael sighs. "Fine. But you only have about twenty minutes before this dog and pony show commences."

I thank him as he slips out the door, giving a menacing scowl to Jace.

"What's that about? You piss off Michael too?"

He shrugs. "Apparently, but really, how can you tell? He's always got his panties in a twist over something."

I can't help but smile—it's true. Michael is intense and brooding, and seems pissed off about something most of the time. Though, I have seen a softer side of him, one I don't imagine many get to see. Things have been different between us since he shared his heartache over losing his Gracie, but I'm not about to betray the trust he's afforded me by mentioning to Jace that he's not always hard as nails.

I sit down on the lone couch in the room. There are two other chairs, but they don't look all that comfortable. I wonder if any famous people have stayed in this room while waiting to go out on stage. I guess this is a dressing room. There are a few others in this hall, but this is the one Michael sequestered to keep me separate and safe from all the hustle and bustle going on behind the scenes as they ready for our graduation ceremony. I'm just a small player in the ceremony, and imagine I wouldn't have such accommodations if I wasn't in the situation we're in now.

"Congratulations on Valedictorian, by the way." Jace's voice brings me back to him.

"Thank you."

"Are you nervous?"

"Very. You know I don't like being the center of attention. I'd rather be home right now than walk across that stage to get the diploma I've worked so hard for, much less getting ready to make a speech." Maybe I'll just skip it altogether and move up the timetable in meeting Roderick. It'd be a good excuse to not have to give my speech or stand up in front of all those people.

"You'll do good. I have every confidence in you, Sam."

I nod but don't respond. If he wants to talk after all this time, he's going to have to make the effort.

He sits in the chair closest to me. His leg bounces with nerves. "I've been a shitty brother since dad died. I plan to make it up to you. We can talk about it whenever you want to. But right now, I need to tell you how I was a shitty friend to Joe and in turn an even shittier brother to you."

That sounds even more ominous than those four dreaded words, *we need to talk.*

His hands squeeze the armrest until his fingertips are white. Not a good sign.

I glance at the clock. He's running out of time. "You'd better move it along."

He follows my motion to the clock and nods in understanding. Taking a deep breath, he proceeds to remind me of one of the worst nights of my life, the night I broke up with Joseph.

"He ended up at the bar in the middle of my shift. I didn't have a clue why you would break up with him. And to be honest, I didn't really care. I was too deep in my own shitstorm to see beyond myself. All I could think about was who I was gonna fuck after work." He looks chagrined and unsettled as he continues. "Tiff was there, one of the chicks I've been with in the past. More than once. I knew if Joe said the word, she'd be all over him, more than willing to help him forget his troubles."

My chest tightens, and my stomach lurches. "Stop." I hold up my hand. I can't hear this. I can't hear how Joseph and *Tiff* got together. I could have died happily never knowing her name.

He moves to sit on the coffee table in front of me. "No, I can't stop. You need to hear this."

No, I really don't.

"He wasn't interested, Sam. He chastised me for even mentioning another woman to him, for thinking he would even be interested in fucking another woman."

I close my eyes. "Please, stop saying that word."

"What? Fucking?" He seems confused.

"Yes! You talk about it like it's no big deal, like it doesn't mean anything. Yet for some of us, it means…everything." Shakily, I wipe the tears from my cheek.

He leans forward, his arms braced on his thighs, his face buried in his hands. "I wish I knew what that felt like. For me, it doesn't mean anything. Not anymore…if it even ever did."

"Jesus, Jace. What happened to you?"

His hands fall away, the weariness in his face and eyes so apparent. He's lost.

"I wish I knew." He sits up and squares his shoulders. "We're getting sidetracked. I'll try to curb my language." His small, sweet smile reminds me of the boy I used to know, which makes my heart ache for him all the more.

"The bottom line is, he blew off my suggestion. All he wanted from me the rest of the night were shots to drown out his misery. Once I got off work, I got him home and into bed. He could hardly walk or speak clearly, he was so drunk. I knew he was gone, out for the count."

Shit. Here comes a *but.*

"I asked Tiff to follow us home driving his car, and I'd get her a cab home. Ended up, one of her friends drove her car to our house. One thing led to another and me and her friend disappeared to my room, but before I closed the door I directed Tiff to Joe's door telling her to make him forget."

"Oh my god, Jace! He told you he wasn't interested, and yet you sent her into his room knowing good and well he was too drunk to probably even say no." I push away from him, needing distance and motion to calm my raging anger and racing heart.

Joseph didn't choose her. He didn't purposely seek out another woman to have sex with.

"I told you I was a shitty friend. The thing is, the next morning, he had no recollection of what happened. He didn't remember Tiff at all. He thought it was a dream. A dream of you, Sam. Not Tiff. When he saw evidence of what happened…that it was real…that it wasn't you, he was devastated and angry as fuck at me."

I stop my pacing. "Evidence?"

He stands and faces me. "Tiff likes to scratch. Leave her mark."

Jesus.

Joseph let me think it was his choice, but he didn't choose her. He thought it was me and that it was just a dream. Why? He lied to protect Jace? All this time he's been carrying this around, apologizing to *me* for something he didn't do. Apologizing for something that was done to *him.*

Speechless. I'm speechless and angry as fuck.

"Get out."

Joseph

I'm beyond tired of waiting for this day to be over. I see Jace making his way to our seats a moment before the ceremony begins. I'm not happy to see him, but I am happy he pulled his head out of his ass long enough to be here for her. It's bad enough her mom couldn't make it. Him being here is some consolation, I suppose.

My phone vibrates in my hand. I didn't bother to put it in my pocket. I don't want to chance missing a call or text from Samantha, Victor, or Michael.

I'm elated to see it's a text from my girl.

Samantha: *I'm all in, Joseph. I choose you. All of you. Always. I'm yours today, tomorrow. Forever.*

My heartrate increases as pure joy spreads to fill every empty crevice, secret dream, and distant visions of our future. *Our* future. Together. That revelation, momentarily soothing the anxious beast in me.

Me: *You have no idea how happy I am to hear that. I'm all yours too. Today. Tomorrow. Forever. My love. My Sweetness.*

She doesn't text back, and I don't expect her to as everyone is filing onto the stage. I'll see her any moment taking her position with the other officiates. As much as I hate not being by her side, I at least get to see her beautiful face sitting on that stage and know she's safe while she's up there. Mere moments pass and those on the stage finally settle.

I scan the stage, starting to get that tingle on the back of my neck. Something's not right. I don't see her. Everyone's seated, and there's an empty chair on the stage. A few of the staff look around, conversing, trying to figure out where she is, I imagine.

Dread fills me.

Something's wrong.

I glance to the nearest FBI agents and see a few are already on the move. I make eye contact with Victor's man, my man, and he motions to me one second before I get another text.

Michael: *She's gone.*

PART 7
HIDING IN PLAIN SIGHT

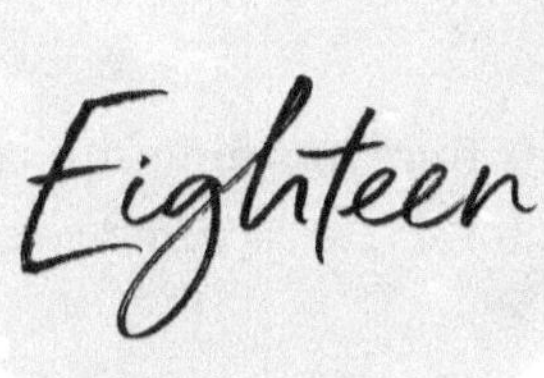

Eighteen

Joseph

I STORM TOWARD MICHAEL. "WHAT THE FUCK DO YOU mean she's gone?"

Michael squares his shoulders, braces for the shit storm I'm about to unleash. "She was talking to Jace. Then I escorted her to the stage with the others. She passed behind a curtain, following in the order they would sit on stage. Two seconds later, she's gone." He runs his hand nervously through his hair, actually pulling hard at the end of the motion. I know that move. It gives a little twinge of pain and lets you know if you're not dreaming.

Fuck. I wish this were only a bad dream.

"Calm, Joe. She needs you calm and collected." Fin's soothing voice comes from behind. I turn and see Fin on his phone. He raises his pointing finger to me telling me to wait just a second.

Fuck!

I scan the area. It's total chaos with FBI agents scrambling around backstage checking every door, nook and cranny. I move to start to search myself, but I stop when I realize it's only Michael's men searching. Where are Victor's men, my men?

A second glance at Fin has him motioning me to follow him.

We make a few turns backstage. I stop cold when I see he's leading me out a door marked EXIT. I'm not leaving if there's a possibility she's still in this building.

Fin drops his phone in his pocket. "We need to go. She's not here."

He says it with such certainty, my solidly planted feet move quickly to close the distance between us.

"How do you…the trackers?"

"Yep." He looks back over his shoulder before pushing me through the door.

The bright light of the mid-morning sun blinds me momentarily.

"There," he shouts as he starts to run down the long alleyway heading toward a ramp.

Without a second thought, I follow, reaching the top a few seconds behind Fin and stop in my tracks when I see a black SUV with Victor at the helm. Fin dives in the back, leaving the door open for me. I climb in. I need to know what the hell's going on and why the men I'm paying aren't in the coliseum searching for Samantha along with the FBI.

Victor speeds off before I even get my door closed.

"She's with Sebastian," Victor advises, then turns his attention to his man in the passenger seat who's looking at his laptop.

A few quiet interactions later, Victor's attention is back on me. "Your sweet innocent Sam has been hatching her own plan. She has no intention of falling prey to Roderick. She's been in cahoots with Scott, that chef from her job, and Sebastian."

"What? For how long? And how the fuck do you know this?" I bark, my patience long gone.

Victor glances at me in the review mirror. "When you asked me to protect her, I investigated her co-workers and found out Scott is ex-military. I approached him, got him on the payroll. His job was to keep an eye on her at work. It wasn't much of a stretch for him. He'd already been doing that—he and the other big guy there, Bruce. They watched out for her after Roderick started showing up and displaying stalker-type tendencies. They walked her to her car each night, basically already playing the job of protection. I just made it official. And it let Sam think she had one place with a little extra slack—the illusion of freedom from her security team. Nothing interesting came of it until Roderick reached out to her."

"The letter?" I ask.

"Yep. That and the plan to use her as bait sent her self-preservation skills into overdrive. She got Scott and Sebastian on board early, but the plan didn't fully come to fruition until Michael put today's plan in motion. She knew we'd have protection everywhere. I suspect she feared Roderick would bring in extra men and it could turn into a blood bath. She set up her own plan to meet with Roderick on her terms, on her timetable."

I lean forward, close enough to bite his ear off. "Why the fuck am I just now hearing about this?"

❧

Samantha

I slip into the back of the car, my head down. "Any trouble?"

"Nope. All's smooth in the world of Operation Babycakes." Sebastian chuckles at his pet name for our plan.

"You know, it doesn't sound very foolproof, or well-planned, calling it 'Operation Babycakes.' Why not something more menacing?"

"Because it needs to seem innocent and not all clandestine cloak and danger type shit." He takes a sharp right out of the parking lot heading onto the main road.

I let out a deep breath of relief. Phase One, complete.

Pulling out my phone, I quickly text Roderick.

Me: *Change of plans. Meet me at Micky's Burger Joint. 20 mins.*

Instead of replying in text, he calls me, as I anticipated he would. "Hello."

"What the hell are you trying to pull, Sam?" His accent is thicker and still unrecognizable to me.

"I'm not trying to pull anything." I let out a sigh and hope he buys my exasperation. "I got spooked, okay? It's not like I do this every day. There were too many of them. You never would have been able to get to me. I saw an opening, and I took it. I ditched my detail. I'm on my way to Micky's now. Are you coming or not?"

After a long beat and two heavily exaggerated sighs, he finally agrees. "I'll be there."

I hang up without a goodbye. I look up at Sebastian and shrug. That's what they do in the movies. There's no pleasant goodbyes when talking to bad guys.

"Why aren't you using your burner phone?" Bash asks.

"Because I don't want Roderick to think I'm smart enough to get a burner phone. Plus, I want my guys to track me and listen to the calls. I'm not hiding anything from Michael and Victor. I just needed to be in control of how this goes down, be a few steps ahead of them. Roderick thinks I can get him what he needs, and as long as he keeps believing that, I have the advantage. But I need Michael and Victor to be there when my advantage runs out." Which it will. It's just a matter of time.

"But you don't have a clue where the information is, do you?" Bash asks over his shoulder.

"I actually do. I have a feeling. I'm not sure, but I suspect." I stare out the window and my mind races to Joseph. "It doesn't matter, though. I just need to give Michael a chance to catch up to us. My goal is not to give Roderick what he wants. My goal is to get justice for my father's death." And keep Joseph and everyone else safe.

My phone still in my hand, I send Joseph a text.

Me: *Find me, but stay out of sight. I will run if I see you. I can't lose you. One of us in danger is enough. Trust me. I love you.*

Joseph: *If the roles were reversed, would you let me do this on my own?*

Me: *Yes, if you felt it was the only way. I wouldn't want to distract you worrying about me while doing something so dangerous. Besides, I'm not alone, am I?*

Joseph: *No, Sweetness, you're not. Never alone. I'll do it your way for now, but I'll come for you when the time is right.*

Me: *I'm counting on it. Tell me you love me. Tell me I'm yours.*

Joseph: *Sweetness. I love you more than life. I'm Yours. You're Mine. Don't get hurt.*

Me: *Same goes. Keep this number 555-563-6726*

"Pull over, Bash. This is where you get out." I collect my purse and backpack from the backseat and set them in the passenger seat.

"I don't like the idea of leaving you alone, Sam. It's not my car I'm worried about. It's you."

I grip his shoulder. "I know and I appreciate it, I do. But I have to do this without distraction. If you're with me, I won't be able to solely focus on what needs to get done. I'll be worrying about you. You're helping me in the way I need you to."

He pulls over.

I hop out. "Call Scott. He'll come get you."

"Wait. He doesn't know I picked you up?" He's surprised, but I had to keep them in the dark on some things.

"No. He's working for Victor. I had to be sure I could get out of there without an entourage." I squeeze his arm and give him a quick kiss on the cheek. "Hopefully, this will all be over soon."

Not one for quick goodbyes, he pulls me into a hug. "Be careful, baby-cakes. Don't get dead."

"I'll do my best." I hand him an envelope with Joseph's name on it.

He furrows his brow, confused.

"Just in case." I quickly move around to the driver's door.

"Sam." His worry is nearly more than I can bear.

"Don't, Bash. Please." I can't afford to get emotional now. I gesture to his hand. "Just hold on to it. You can give it back to me when I see you again."

"Go get 'em, Sam," he says with renewed determination.

With a nod and a parting wink, I hop in his car and drive off.

Joseph

I'M STILL PISSED AT VICTOR'S RESPONSE WHEN I asked why I didn't know about all of this.

Instead of being threatened by me, Victor just chuckles. "Because you're too emotionally invested. I couldn't take the chance of you pushing her to tell you her plan or trying to stop it. She needs that confidence, believing she has a leg up over Roderick. He'll never suspect what she's done. It's not much. It's basically a bunch of redundancies. Scott and Sebastian did the leg work, since she couldn't get out from the eye of her protection, so she had to rely on them. They set up different touch points between the coliseum and her father's office and then seemingly random locations around town just in case she needed a place to go. In each location, they drafted two employees to keep an eye out for her today. The watcher's job was simply to send a text message to a burner phone with the time and location she was spotted and if someone else was with her. She also had them stash weapons, so she could arm herself after Roderick ensured she wasn't armed. But to be honest, I wasn't aware of her plan to escape today on her own. Scott was in the dark too, or he's playing double agent. For his sake, I hope that's not the case."

I can't believe she pulled this off on her own, or nearly on her own. I slip my phone in my pocket, knowing I won't be hearing from her anytime soon. She's made her move. Now she just needs us to follow her, keeping an eye on her movements, keeping her safe from a distance.

I'm not crazy about it, but we don't have much of a choice if we want to catch this guy.

Victor pulls into a parking space across the street and down from Mickey's, the location Samantha's numerous trackers are showing her to be. We sit in silence, all four of us watching the laptop screen for any sign of movement.

"Do we have eyes in there?" I ask.

"Yes, two agents. Michael and his team are on their way," Victor responds. "And he's pissed off, thinking we knew about her plan to disappear today. I tried to tell him it was as much a surprise to me too, but he's not buying it." He shrugs a shoulder, blowing off Michael's accusations.

"Do you think Roderick has any additional people working with him?" Fin asks.

"I doubt it. He's managed to evade capture primarily because he's kept such a low profile since the shooting. I'm sure he could use the help, but it makes it harder for him to fly under the radar if he starts hiring goons. He's burned most of his bridges over the years, and the FBI aren't the only ones looking for him. Anyone he brings in now is a huge unknown for him. Not worth the risk, if he's smart. He's a lone wolf kinda guy. I think this is a one-man operation." Victor holds up his hand, stopping any further conversation as he answers his phone.

I continue to watch the laptop screen. Immediately one dot disappears, and before I can question it, another one disappears, and then another one. I start to panic, but Victor's man whispers over his shoulder. "We expected this. It's a good sign. He searched her and found the trackers we thought he would, but he didn't find all of them." He points to the remaining blips. "We're good. We only need one."

My phone vibrates. As I dig it out of my pocket, I see it's a call from Michael. I answer, but don't get a word in before he lets loose on me.

"Did you fucking know?"

I can't help but smirk. Shit's gonna fly before this day is over. "No, man. I had no idea. You think I would've been freaking out if I had? I wouldn't have even wasted any time with you. I would have been following her. You know I'd be with her if I had my way, and not let her put herself in further danger with her secret plan."

I can feel the waves of fury rolling off him. "I can't believe she fucking did this. Have you heard from her?"

"She sent me a text a about ten minutes ago." I fill him in on the gist of our text exchange as it applies to the case, not about the stuff related to our personal relationship. I also give him the new number she gave me, though I don't think it's trackable, assuming it's a burner phone.

"I guess her planning on us coming for her when the time is right is something. Now we just have to wait and see when that is and where they'll be heading next." He's calmer. Thinking instead of reacting.

"If I had to guess, I think they'll go to her dad's office," I suggest. "But why wait? Why not just go in there and get him? It's a public place, but I have no doubt one of your guys could get close enough to put a gun to his head before he even knows you're there."

"I've considered it. What if he has a gun pointed at Sam under the table? You don't think he anticipates we're following them? He may not know we're here now, but he knows we'll find her eventually, and when we do, you better believe he will use Sam however he sees fit to ensure his own survival."

"Then why the fuck did you put her in this dangerous situation?" My heart is pounding so badly, my head is starting to hurt.

"Because we need to catch him. Because she was in danger long before her father was shot. Because he never would've let this go. He's hellbent on revenge, and he sees Sam as the key. She either helps him, or he'll eliminate her and move on to Jace or Eleanor. Whoever is closest and likely to be the most useful."

"Fuck."

"I know, man. I made you a promise, and I'm gonna keep it. She's not going to be harmed. I'll do everything in my power to keep her safe." He means within his job description or not. He's already proved he's more loyal to us than to the U.S. Government. "Stay with Victor. I'll be in contact with him from here on out. When I see you next, this will be over."

God, I sure hope so.

Samantha

You can do this. Be strong. This is about getting revenge for Dad and keeping everyone safe. This guy can't read your mind. Act cool. You can do this.

I take a cleansing breath and continue the running dialog in my head, if for no other reason than to not think about how scared I am or how badly things could go wrong.

I park in the back, taking a minute to delete all my text messages from my phone, closing out apps, and then slip it into an outside pocket in my backpack. I'm sure he won't let me keep it, hence deleting all recent activity, but I want him to think I don't have a clue. If I leave it in my car, it shows I knew he wouldn't let me keep it. If I have it on me, and he's the one to take it from me, then I come across as a dumb girl who doesn't know any better. I need him to believe the latter.

I slip my driver's license and some cash into my backpack, then slip the rest of my cash in my bra along the side band, hoping he won't search me in great detail. I'm fairly certain he'll take my cash from the backpack. I grab some lip balm, gum, and a bottled water and tuck them into the backpack. I then put my purse on the floor board in back, throwing a jacket over it. I hope it won't raise suspicion if I don't bring it with me. I think he'll buy I just didn't want to carry both.

I'm sure Michael and Victor have trackers in my purse, but I'm sure they have others in my backpack, or my clothing, or shoes. If not, I'm screwed for them being able to follow me. They wouldn't tell me where the trackers are in case my reaction while being searched gave anything away and made Roderick suspicious.

As much as I'm relying on my guys to be able to track me, I'm also prepared to go this alone. That's why I've taken all the precautions I have. If all else fails, I have to be able to save myself.

The door closes behind me, and I blink a few times before my eyes adjust to the darkened interior of Mickey's. I scan the dining room, spotting him where else but at the bar, his gaze boring holes into me. I take a deep breath and head over.

You can do this, I chant, ignoring my racing heart.

"Sam." He nods and pulls out the barstool to his right. "Nice of you to join me." He's all cocky grin and confidence. He thinks he's got this in the bag.

"I wish I could say the same." I don't have to pretend to like this guy. He would be more suspicious if I did. I sit next to him and start to place my bag in the seat next to me.

"I'll take that." He nabs my backpack and starts to rifle through it. He pulls out my phone, setting it on the bar and then pockets my cash. "We'll need this shortly." He ignores my lip balm, hair tie, and loose change in the outer pockets. "What's in here?" he asks as he starts to go through the main compartment.

"A change of clothes. I'm not running around with you in this dress and pumps."

His eyes rove my body, then he hands me my pack. "Change."

It only takes a moment before I realize he's following me to the women's restroom. Right before I get to the door, I whip around and face him. "You are not coming in here with me."

His momentary surprise disappears in a smirk. "No, I'm not. But, there is something I need to take care of first." He steps into my space, pulling the backpack from my shoulder, dropping it on the floor.

"Arms out," he demands. He runs his hands along my upper body. I close my eyes and turn my head to the side. "I'm not going to hurt you, Sam. I just need to be sure you're not wired or carrying a weapon." His hands cup my breasts, pausing a little too long to be merely searching me.

I open my eyes and face him.

He's openly smiling at me. "Nice."

Jesus. I'm gonna be sick.

I leer at him. "If you're done feeling me up, can I go change now?"

He scans down my body. "Not just yet." His hands move down, across my abdomen and my legs.

"Turn," he orders.

I sigh and quickly turn around, facing the wall—the quicker I obey, the quicker this will be over.

His hands begin moving back up my legs, which is completely unnecessary since I'm wearing a dress, and he can plainly see I don't have any weapons or wires strapped to my legs. But it doesn't stop him from moving in closer as he runs his hands between my thighs and then up over my ass.

"Nearly done." His hot breath over my neck causes my stomach to convulse.

I manage to stay still and not show any reaction.

His hands move over my back, up to my shoulders, and I wince when he squeezes my right shoulder just a little too hard.

"Still sore?" I'm surprised to hear remorse in his voice.

"What do you care?"

He harrumphs. "I know you don't believe me, but I truly never meant to shoot you or your father."

I push back and turn around, facing him. "Enough!" I step into the bathroom, holding the door open. "Here." I lift up my dress to above my waist, revealing my bare legs and panties, then turn around, pausing, closing my eyes and swallowing, giving him time to see I'm not wired or armed.

Dropping my dress, I turn to face him. "Satisfied?"

He backs up, his hands in the air. "Yes." He nods and actually manages to look chagrined.

I grab my backpack off the floor and let the bathroom door close behind me. I lock myself in the large stall on the end and quickly get to the business of changing clothes and securing my safety. I take the opportunity to use the bathroom while I lift up the large trashcan in the stall with me. A small bag falls free from the bottom. Pride wells up seeing my planning pay off.

I quickly take out my change of clothes, slip off my shoes and dress, and put them in my backpack. I slide on my jeans, socks, tennis shoes. But before I put on my shirt, I open the hidden bag and take out what I really need: the burner phone, a small pocket gun that fits in my bra, another that straps to my ankle, and extra cash. I'm most nervous about the ankle strap, hoping he doesn't try to search me again.

I turn on the burner phone and quickly text Joseph. "I love you." And another text to Scott and Sebastian's burner phones. "Phase 2 complete." I then put the phone on mute, not vibrate as I don't want it making any sound. I slip it in my bra. It's a tiny phone and sits in the opposite cup of my bra than where I placed the gun, evening out the additional bulk on both sides. Thankfully, the padded cups easily hide the unusual shaping. Plus, I'm wearing a loose-fitting black shirt doing little to show off my figure.

After stowing the now-empty hidden bag back under the trashcan, and the extra cash and my ID in my jeans, I check my watch and see only seven minutes have passed. I quickly wash my hands.

When I step into the hall, I'm surprised Roderick isn't there waiting. I start toward the bar, but I'm grabbed by the arm with a quick jerk in the other direction. "This way, Sam."

Outside the back door, he demands, "Ditch the backpack."

"What. Why?"

He pauses a moment before answering. "Less baggage." He takes it from me and readies to dump it into a large trash bin.

"Wait!"

He scowls, and I plead my case. "I need a couple of things. My keys, lip balm, and sunglasses."

"You don't need your sunglasses and lip balm."

"Okay, but if you want to get into my dad's office without setting off the alarm I need my keys."

He shoves the backpack at me. "Fine. Be quick about it."

Joseph

"They're on the move," Victor advises his team via the ear bud and mic hanging from his ear. His eyes are on the laptop as we see two trackers head off, leaving three behind.

"She only has two left," I whisper.

Fin's hand grips my arm as Victor replies, "I doubt she'll lose those two."

While I appreciate his confidence, I'm not feeling as sure as he is. "Why are we just sitting here? Shouldn't we be on our way, for fuck's sake?"

"We don't want to spook him. My guys are on them. The three of us are too recognizable to stick close." I assume he's referring to himself, Fin, and me, since I don't even know this other guy's name. "We have to let mine and Michael's team handle the close game."

My head hits the back of the seat. This waiting is killing me. I want to get out and run after her and beat the shit out of Roderick for what he's done to her. It's already been over an hour since she escaped by herself. Every minute I'm away from her, my need to be near her grows.

Fuck me. A horrible thought comes to mind. "Is he…what's his MO? Does he have a history with sexual assault or anything like that?"

Victor's eyes meet mine in the rearview mirror. "No. No history," he says firmly. "He's actually known for being good to his wife before she died. He was raised by his mother and two older sisters. He has a daughter nearly Sam's age. I don't think he'd hurt her in that way, Joe."

Well, that's a relief. Roderick might not hurt her in *that* way, but that doesn't mean he won't hurt her, as he's already proven by shooting her.

I close my eyes and focus on my girl, willing her to be safe, strong, and brave, and most of all, to come back to me.

Fuck this.

"I'm going to go crazy if I just sit here." I lean up, talking to Victor. "Let me go to the bank where her father has a safety deposit box. If they don't find anything at her dad's office, the bank will be the next stop. Let me go there with one of your guys. We'll give the manager a heads-up about what might be coming their way. Let me be there for her if they show up." I'm not really asking for permission. I need to be in motion. Give my brain something to focus on, something proactive to do.

He glares between Fin and me. "Okay, but no heroics. My guy will have the name of who you need to speak to. We had a feeling Roderick might end up there, so this won't be news to them."

After one of Victor's men drives up, we have a brief rundown on how this is going to play out. The decision is made—Fin will accompany me, which I'm sure is only to keep me calm and stop me from doing something stupid.

I hop out of the car with a quick, "I'll call you with updates," from Victor.

"I'm counting on it. Every step, Victor," I confirm as Fin and I get in the back of another car, and make our way to the bank to ease the path Samantha may need to take to get back to me.

PART 8
RECKONING

Twenty

Samantha

LIFE CAN BE SURREAL SOMETIMES. THE WAY I SAW this day going was more cloak and dagger and not so much shopping for clothes with the man who killed my father. He's not hurried, nervous, or even seemingly concerned about being followed. It's like this is an everyday occurrence for him.

I'm still in a daze by the time we exit the store with every piece of my clothing down to my socks and shoes completely new, even my bra and panties. If shopping for underwear with my father's killer isn't icing on the weird-cake, then I don't know what is.

Thankfully, he didn't insist on going in the changing room with me, therefore, I was able to re-secure all of my hidden paraphernalia. Doubly thankful, he hasn't searched me again. Maybe he feels safe now that my clothing's been replaced with items that couldn't have been tampered with.

He insists I drive his car since I'm more familiar with the roads to my dad's office. Somehow, I doubt that. His stalking skills would ensure he knows the route backwards and forwards. I don't argue, though. Holding onto the wheel gives me a sense of power, like I control where we're going, even though I don't, and the gun in his waistband ensures I remember that.

"Why are you after this man?" I blurt.

His sad eyes meet mine for a moment before I focus back on the road. "He killed my son."

Woah. "I'm sorry. How old was he?"

"He was twelve, nearly thirteen. Now it's just Rebecca and me." His sorrow is palpable, making me feel sorry for him.

"Is Rebecca your wife?"

"No, my daughter. My wife is no longer with us."

I silently question what '*no longer with us*' means, like divorced and moved away, or no longer alive.

He seems to understand. "My wife is dead."

Jesus, this just keeps getting sadder.

"I'm really sorry for the loss of both your wife and your son." I mean it in all sincerity. I can sympathize.

"Thank you. I know you have some idea of what it is like to lose a loved one." He catches my eye when I stop at the next light. "I honestly had no intention of killing you or your father. I am deeply sorry for what happened. You must understand this man took my son and my wife from me. I will not stop until I have justice." His demeanor quickly changed from sorrow and remorse to angry and vengeful.

This angry, vengeful man is the one I need to remember is there, just below the surface. Some part of him may truly be sorry for killing my father and shooting me, but the greater part of him is what I see before me. He's the one who won't hesitate to squash me or anyone I love standing in his way. I see the depth of his despair is what drives his revenge, its fuel a never-ending furnace feeding the flames of vengeance.

I.

Cannot.

Forget.

That.

Samantha

This is the hard part, convincing Roderick I have some idea what I'm doing. Looking for something I'm quite sure is not here. I don't know how much he knows about me, so I can't play the dumb card too much, but it doesn't stop me from trying to sidetrack him with a wild-goose chase.

There's no way to distinguish the government surgeries from his normal ones. It's not like they're stamped TOP SECRET. We spend an hour separating out the male patient files within the last year—that's when Roderick believes the surgery took place on the man he's looking for. I make a stack for him to review while I move onto the reception area to go through the computer files.

My father's laptop isn't here, and I can only assume the authorities have it as evidence. However, under the office manager's desk is a hidden server I installed for my dad years ago to make backups of his files whether he was in the office or at home.

I turn on both the receptionist's computer and the server.

As I'm waiting for the computers to boot up, I realize Roderick's sequestered in my dad's office, and I'm out front, out of his eyesight. There is nothing to keep me from running out the front door and the FBI coming inside to get him. It would probably be a battle to the death, as he'd be a caged animal. Maybe that's what he deserves, but I don't want him to get suspicious.

"The computer is taking forever to boot up." I don't tell him about the backup server in case I actually find something. I have no intention of actually handing over the patient's file and putting another person's life on the line. I stick my head in my dad's office.

Roderick is sitting on the floor going through file after file.

"How did your wife die?" He didn't say the man he's after killed his wife, but he mentioned blaming the man for both deaths.

In his frustration, he doesn't even look up. He hasn't even acknowledged me, and for a moment, I think he's going to ignore me, which may not be a bad thing. I start to head down the hall to check on the computer when his voice draws me back.

"She was never the same after our son's death."

Rightfully so. Losing a child is traumatic. Losing a child in a tragic way, even more so.

I stand quietly in the doorway, not moving, not distracting him from his thoughts.

"We tried to have another child, but she was too old to conceive. We tried fertility treatments, which didn't work, and the extra hormones made her sorrow even greater." His eyes close as he continues to speak. "In the end, Rebecca and I were not enough reason for her to want to live. She couldn't get beyond the loss of our son to see the two people who loved her and were still alive standing right in front of her."

Jesus, I can relate. His wife and my mom must be cut from the same cloth.

"She took her own life on the two-year anniversary of his death."

Shit. Such loss and devastation. "Why?"

He frowns and huffs in irritation.

"Why did this man kill your son?" I clarify.

"Ah, yes. You want to know how it all started." He stands, stretching. I can hear his back crack from across the room. He takes a deep breath, sliding easily from the heartbroken father and husband to the detached, angry killer I understand him to be. He leans back against my father's desk with his casual demeanor, but there is nothing laidback about this man.

I watch him wearily as he crosses his arms over his chest, his eyes scanning me in contemplative study. After what seems like forever, he begins to speak. "The man I'm searching for, my son's killer, upset a lot of bad people. People I owe, people I could not say no to. I was sent to make an example of him, show him and others like him there are far worse things than dying."

Shit. This is not good. This man is showing me who he really is, and I need to pay attention. I cannot afford to mess this up.

"He had two kids. A boy and a girl, almost the same age as mine. He had to choose one," he says in a cool tone.

"Choose one?" *Please don't say what I think you're going to say.*

"One of his kids was going to die. He had to choose which one. In front of his wife and children, he had to make a choice or they all died."

No.

"It wasn't easy, but finally he made his choice. He chose his daughter to die."

Fucking assholes, both of them, the one who chose and the one standing before me.

"You see, this was supposed to be a punishment of the greatest kind. He chose his son to live. Therefore, he was the one I killed."

Jesus. I grab onto the doorframe to steady myself, my knees weak and my stomach trying to convince me to throw up.

"No," I groan.

"In reality, he lost his whole family. His son died. His wife left him, and his daughter could never forgive him for choosing her to die. It was the worst kind of punishment. A living hell."

I swallow the bile rising in my throat. "He came after you. Made you make the same choice?"

He nods. "Yes, but I tried to outsmart him by choosing my son to die, thinking he would do the opposite, as I did, and kill my daughter. But he outsmarted me, and killed my son in front of my wife and daughter."

"Jesus, you all are a bunch of sick fucks. Using kids as chess pieces to get what you want, to manipulate the situation to your liking." I step into the room and pull the gun from my bra. My arm is steady, my aim is true. "No more. This ends here. I won't let anyone else die in the name of your sick game or those sick bastards you work for. I won't help you any longer. I'm not a pawn. I'm a living human being who has just as much right to live as you do, as your sons did."

If he's surprised I have a gun, he shows no hint of it. "Your father would be proud of you."

"Don't," I warn.

He just smiles and shakes his head. "I'm serious. I told him that day he should be proud of the strong woman you are."

"Stop! You won't manipulate me with your words."

He nods in understanding. "I want you to know, no matter how this ends, I meant what I said. I never meant to kill your father or harm you. What I have done in this life will haunt me into the next. I have made peace with that. But you do not want to taint yourself with the stain of taking another's life. You're too good for that."

"Sam." Michael calls from down the hall.

I don't take my eyes off of Roderick.

"Ah, good they're here." He motions to my gun. "You can put your gun down now. Let the professionals handle it from here." His voice is full of condescension, like I'm a good little girl, and I should run along home and let the adults handle this.

"Sam." Michael steps into the room, his weapon drawn and pointed at Roderick. "I've got this. Put the gun away and step down the hall."

I don't move. I don't look at Michael. I don't trust Roderick. It's too easy. He has something up his sleeve.

In a blink of an eye, Michael moves toward me, and Roderick reaches for the gun tucked in the waist of his pants.

"Look out!" I scream and squeeze the trigger just as Michael fires his gun.

Both shots hit Roderick square in the chest in a one-two punch, slamming him back against my dad's desk.

Blood stains the front of his shirt as he gasps for air.

The hand holding his gun falls slack at his side as he slides to the floor, landing on a thud and slowly keeling to one side.

I focus on his eyes that never seemed to leave mine, the life slowly draining away, reminding me of my father when he died. Even as the room fills with agents, and Michael puts his arm around me, guiding me from the room, Roderick's eyes stick to me like glue.

Twenty-One

Joseph

'M HAVING MY OWN GROUNDHOG DAY MOMENT HERE, getting a call telling me shots have been fired. My girl's in danger, and now I'm rushing to be by her side, not knowing if she's okay. I'm reliving the day her dad was killed and she was shot. And just like that day, nothing can keep me from her or my need to take her away from all this craziness.

I need her by my side, on my lap, in my arms, beneath me, however the fuck I can get her.

I. Need. Her.

The selfish caveman in me will not relent until that happens.

We pull up in front of her dad's office. Police cars, two ambulances, and a parking lot full of black unmarked cars—the FBI and Victor's team—clog my path.

Victor's on me before I make it ten steps and braces his hand against my chest. "She's fine. She's not hurt." He hedges as his hand drops from my chest. "At least not physically. Mentally, I would expect some residue."

Residue?

He grips my shoulders. "Joe, look at me. Focus."

I stop scanning the parking lot like a heat-seeking missile to concentrate on him.

"Roderick is dead," he says.

"Thank God." I let out a breath and relax. "What else?" I'm sure there's more, or he wouldn't be stopping me to tell me now, at this moment, when he knows all I want is to get to my girl.

"Both Michael and Sam shot him." His stern voice gentles.

"Fuck." I run my hands over my face and then through my hair. I'm filled with pride and sorrow. Pride for my girl kicking Roderick's ass and sorrow for how she might be feeling about it. I, for one, am happy he's gone and that she had something to do with it. A karmic *fuck you* to the motherfucker who killed her father.

I look back to him, but he's no longer watching me. I follow his sightline to Samantha sitting in the back of an open ambulance.

Mine, is all I can think as I make my way to her.

As soon as she sees me, she pushes the EMT aside and stands. "Joseph," she exclaims as she starts to run toward me.

It's like a fucking movie, her getting closer to me as though in slow motion. It's an eternity before her body crashes into mine on a leap, and she wraps her arms and legs around me and buries her head in my neck.

"Sweetness." I hold on to her, tightly. "Christ almighty, baby, I was so fucking scared. Never. Never do that to me again. No more guns, no more bad guys. Okay?"

"Joseph." She shakes as her sobs take over.

"Shh. It's okay, Sweetness. I got you." I close my eyes and sink into her neck, breathing her scent, her warmth. "God, I love you."

"I…I…looove…youuuu…too," she sobs.

My heart breaks for my girl. I can't ever let this happen again. Never. Ever.

Michael places a blanket over her shoulders. He nods at me, full of emotion himself, which only bodes for how heavy this whole thing is probably weighing on her.

"I want to talk to you," he says softly, glancing over his shoulder. "But I have to finish up here first." He looks at her and then me. "Maybe I can swing by, bring dinner. She's done what she needs to for now, anything else can wait. I'll get one of my guys to drive you home."

She relaxes in my arms, her sobs turning to sniffles. She's got to be as relieved as I am to not have to stick around.

He calls out to someone and then turns back to us, touching her back lightly. "You did good, Sam. I'm proud of you."

She slowly lifts her head, taking a second to wipe her nose and face with the blanket. She's disheveled and cute as hell with her red nose and pouty lips. Her legs release from around my waist, and I slowly lower her to the ground, holding her steady.

She surprises us both by barreling into Michael nearly as hard as she did to me, wrapping him in a hug. He quickly reciprocates. I stand there watching as they hug in silence.

They've spent a lot of time together. She trusts him with her life—she's had to. Luckily, that trust paid off. I clasp his shoulder. "Thank you for taking care of her, for all you've done for us. If you ever find you want a civilian job, come work for me at MCI. You'd work with Victor, but you'd be my man."

He gifts me with a rare smile. "You might regret that offer." He takes a second to examine the scene surrounding us. "It might be time for me to move on."

He squeezes Samantha and then steps back, meeting her eyes. "You need to get going. You'll crash soon. Have some food, lots of water, and then a nap. I'll see you later."

Samantha moves to my side, but her eyes stay on him. "You're a good friend, Michael. Thank you for protecting me."

When her gaze locks on mine with such love in her eyes, I could cry. *I'm a totally pussy when it comes to this girl.*

To Michael she asks, "Can you tell Scott and Sebastian too? Maybe y'all should come over for dinner, get it over with. I think once I go to bed tonight, I'm going to want to sleep for a week. I'd rather see everyone tonight and then have a few days with just Joseph." Her lovely face returns to me. "Are you okay with that?"

I kiss her temple. "Sounds perfect."

"Why don't we do it at my place, that way you two can leave when you feel like it." Fin's voice of reason comes from behind me.

"Thanks, Bro." That's a fucking fantastic plan.

With quick goodbyes and a promise to see them later, we make our escape.

I settle her in my arms in the backseat of a black SUV as Michael's man drives us home.

PART 9

MINE

Samantha

I FALL ASLEEP ON THE WAY THERE, ONLY WAKING UP at Joseph's gentle prodding once we're parked in the garage. We step into a different set of elevators on the wrong side of the building.

Home. When Joseph said home, I assumed he meant Fin's home. But apparently, he meant *his* penthouse in the adjacent tower of MCI, opposite from Fin and Matt's penthouses.

Noticing my confusion, Joseph hand circles my waist and tugs me into the elevator. "We're in the other tower. You're not staying with Fin any longer. You're staying with me." His expression is one of pure satisfaction.

"I need my things." I pull back, meaning to go to Fin's to collect them now instead of waiting. I'm starting to shut down. Once I stop moving, I'll crash. Hard.

He smiles and pulls me to his side as he secures the key and code to the penthouse level. "It's all taken care of, Sweetness."

"Oh." I'm relieved. Maybe I should be upset he just assumes I'll stay with him, but truly, I couldn't be happier.

As much as I pretend I don't, I like his caveman ways. He's an in-charge, take-charge kinda guy, and he suits me just fine. I feel cherished, seen, and appreciated. He wants me with him all the time. How could a girl not love that?

We step out of the elevator and into a vestibule identical to Fin and Matt's.

"How can you tell the difference?" I have a vision of being drunk and not having any idea which tower I'm in or which penthouse is his. I don't drink, but if I did, this could be a nightmare.

He laughs. "Well, besides the fact we came up a different set of elevators in a different tower, you can tell by the 2A next to our door. We're in 2A. The other building is the same except they're 1A, 1B, 1C, 1D. Fin is in 1A."

"How have I not noticed the numbers before?" I study the number at his door and then glance across the hall. Have the numbers been there the whole time? "I didn't know there were four more penthouses. Does this tower have a roof pool too?"

"Yes, and then two floors down is the fitness center." He frowns before he puts the key in the lock. "Did Fin never show you around?"

"No, I only knew about the pool because of Michael. Does the other building have a fitness center too?"

He smiles. "Tell you what. I'll take you on a tour tomorrow or the next day as soon as you feel up to it. I'll show you all the secret passageways and hidden doors this little key can get you into." His smirk is playful as he wags his brows at me.

I lean into him. "Sounds like fun."

He opens the door, and I'm momentarily brought back to the first time I entered Fin's penthouse. The lights turn on, seemingly on their own. These must be motion sensitive. I step through the entry and down into the living room. The space is exactly the same as Fin's except it has a different feel. This is homier, more laidback, more like Joseph. The same floor-to-ceiling windows take center stage as well as the wall-to-wall marble floors. I slowly approach the windows and notice this tower's penthouse faces the opposite direction. We have a more tranquil view of Reunion Tower, the Margaret Hunt Hill Bridge, and the Trinity River Corridor.

His warm body blankets me from behind as he wraps his arms around me. "What do you think?"

"It's beautiful, Joseph. I think I like this view better."

"Me too. I've always loved staying here. This one has the best view in my opinion."

"I would agree wholeheartedly." I lean into him, relishing this moment. I let out a long sigh when his lips press against my neck.

"Why don't you go take a hot bath and let me rustle up some lunch."

My stomach growls at that precise moment. We both laugh. "I think that sounds like a great plan." I kiss his cheek and start to head down the hall.

"Sweetness," he calls me to a halt.

I turn and face him. "Hmm?"

He smiles and saunters over to me, taking my hand and leading me in the other direction. "We're in the master suite."

"Oh." The thought never even crossed my mind. I was heading in the same direction as the guest room I occupied at Fin's.

If I wasn't so tired and sinking quickly, I would be totally impressed by the massive bedroom. The bathroom is larger than the one I used at Fin's, but the shower and bath fixtures seem to be identical, which is a good thing as it took me a while to master them.

Joseph starts the tub, dropping in a bath bomb, and turns to kiss me tenderly on the head. "Don't fall asleep, baby. I'll be back in a few with lunch."

After I'm settled and getting sleepy, he appears in the bathroom door holding a tray of goodies. "Nuh uh, don't fall asleep on me, Sweetness. I need to get you fed and to bed."

I sit up, hoping it'll revive me. "Sorry."

He sets down the tray and bends down to kiss my cheek. "Don't be. You've had a hard day."

Grabbing the vanity stool, he places it next to the tub. He sits down and begins to feed me bites of sandwich and fruit with sips of water in between. While I'm chewing he takes a bite and then feeds me more while he's chewing. *I think he likes to feed me.*

The whole interchange is quiet and relaxing. "You're a good caretaker, Joseph."

The entire time he stayed with me in the hospital and out, after I was shot, I don't think I ever said that to him. "You've always taken such good care of me. I'm sorry I've never told you before or said thank you. That was selfish of me. So, thank you."

"Samantha, it's my pleasure to take care of you." He brushes his cold watermelon lips across mine and pulls back with a smile. "Are you ready to get out?"

"Yes, I'm getting pruney."

He helps me out, wrapping a warm towel around me. He kisses my shoulder and leaves me to finish up as he jumps in the shower.

I finish drying off and slip on a silk robe, not bothering with panties. I don't know what Joseph has planned, but anytime I'm near him like this, intimately, not even necessarily sexually, my panties get soaked anyway, so what's the point? I quickly brush my teeth, avoiding his reflection in the shower or I'll never get out of here.

I grab our lunch tray and take it to the kitchen, cleaning up and then refilling our ice waters. As I pad back into the bedroom, it feels strange, like I'm going to Fin's bedroom. I'm sure I'll get used to it in time.

Joseph steps out of the bathroom as I enter the room. He frowns. "Why aren't you in bed?" Not chastising, just a question.

"I would have fallen asleep before you were done. I cleaned up lunch and refilled our waters." I hold up the glasses in my hands as evidence.

He walks over, taking them from me. "Thank you. Now get in bed." He's *Mr. Serious*.

I can't help but snicker as I drop my robe where I stand and walk to the bed buck naked. He merely groans behind me, and my smile only widens. I do manage to stifle it as I climb under the covers.

He sets down our waters and flicks off the lights before climbing in bed. Since it's early afternoon, some light creeps in through the curtains. They're blackout curtains, and it only took me one time to learn that when you close them completely, *blackout* means blackout. I couldn't see a damn thing. It was a little disconcerting and reminded me of visiting Carlsbad Caverns as a kid, when they turned off all the lights for three of the longest minutes of my life. I was scared shitless and never wanted to go back. I appreciate the light and don't mind when some streams in, even when I'm trying to sleep.

"Come 'ere, Sweetness." He scoots closer, drawing me to his side, where I rest my head on his chest. He continues to situate me until we are completely touching down the length of our bodies.

I could do it myself, but it's kind of fun letting him. It thrills me that he wants me this close to him when we sleep. He's a cuddler, and he's not ashamed of it, not one bit. I love that about him.

He sighs and kisses my forehead. I know what's coming. What he's wanted since he found me at my dad's office. He needs me to unload on him, share the details of what happened, not leaving a single solitary thing out. It's as much for me as it is for him. He won't let me carry the burden of what I know alone. He wants to share it with me. He *needs* to share it. It kills him he couldn't be the one to be by my side, that it was Michael who was there in the end and not him. It was Michael's job, though, what he's trained to do. Joseph's guilt is misguided, believing he's lacking in some way, or worse—that he's let me down.

In my eyes, he wasn't lacking at all. He was where I needed him to be. Away from me, where he was safe, and I could concentrate on what needed to be done. I never could have kept my cool if Joseph had been there for me to rely on. I would have deferred to him and probably gotten us both killed. I needed to stand on my own two feet, and even as much as I did, I also knew he, Victor, and Michael's teams were there to back me up.

"Tell me, Sweetness. Tell me all of it." His voice deep and soothing, and I know I will never make it through this without more tears.

"I need you to forgive me for conspiring without you." I move back so my head rests on the pillow. I need to see his face. This incredibly handsome, masculine face showing how much I hurt him by keeping it from him. "I need you to forgive me for doing such a huge thing without you."

I touch his cheek. "I was so scared, Joseph." My tears start, and he wipes them away as they fall, one by one, and then a flood that is too copious to keep up with. "If things could have been okay without confronting him, I would have taken that path. But I knew, as all of you knew, that was never going to happen. He was never going to leave us alone as long as he held out hope we could give him the information he sought, or could use us to obtain it from someone else." My heart squeezes. "And that's why I pushed you away, distanced myself from you for so long. I couldn't bear the thought of anything happening to anyone else I love. I saw my dad…I couldn't bear to see that happen to you as well. I thought I was protecting you, but—"

"I know, Samantha. I'm not angry or disappointed in you. I know why you did it. I wish you'd let me help, but I understand why you thought you had to do it yourself." He presses his lips to mine. I close my eyes as his breath catches and his voice breaks. "I'm so fucking proud of you." He closes his eyes, and I break when tears streak down his face. It's my turn to wipe them away, kiss, and comfort.

"You couldn't do this for me, Joseph. I know you wanted to. You wanted to protect me from all of this, but you couldn't. I had to do what I needed to, to feel safe. I needed to be in control and not just a puppet. That's where Scott and Sebastian came in, and don't be mad at them. If they didn't help me, I would have done it without them. They didn't really have a choice. I didn't give them one. I suspected Scott was working with Victor because of a look I saw exchanged between the two of them, but they never thought I knew. That's why I had to keep my plan to disappear before the ceremony a secret. I wasn't even completely sure I was going to leave before my speech. I saw an opportunity and took it. Plus, I was impatient to get it over with. And not thrilled to be giving a speech in the first place," I confess.

I go on to share all of it with him, the details, my thoughts behind my actions and the horrible truth of why Roderick was after the guy who killed his son. When I finish, we both just lie there in silence. We'd long since switched to lying on our backs as I laid out what happened from the moment he left me behind the stage at the coliseum to when he found me sitting in the back of the ambulance.

"Christ, he was one messed up sonuvabitch. The whole situation was a nightmare. Do you think Michael knew the story between those two, about killing their sons?"

I shake my head. "I don't know. I would like to think he didn't, but

I have no idea. You can ask him. I really don't want to think about it anymore. Once we meet with our families and everyone else tonight, and finish whatever needs to be done with the FBI, I just want to put it all behind me. Behind us."

He smiles. "I like that plan. Now, come 'ere. You need to rest, and I need to hold you."

He'll get no arguments from me. I cuddle back into his side, half-lying on him as his fingers lazily trace up and down my arm and hip in a slow, steady motion.

His tender touch and rhythmic breathing lull me to sleep, where I am safe and protected in the arms of the man I love.

Twenty-Three

Joseph

W E SPEND THE EVENING AT FIN'S, WELL, A COUPLE of hours at least. Samantha didn't seem up for more. All the hugs, congratulations, and emotions coming from everyone was a lot for her to take in. Even Jace was there to give his better-late-than-never support and love. I'm proud of him for that. He and I are nowhere near where we need to be, but I can see after today there's a good chance we'll get there.

Fin, Matt, and my parents, along with Michael, Victor, Scott, Sebastian, and Margot were all there. The guys joked with Samantha and Margot, telling them they needed to bring more X chromosomes to the next get-together. I would agree. There was entirely too much testosterone in that room. Though, the two of them did seem to eat up the attention, but I could see on Samantha's face they're a lot to take at one time.

Samantha and I say goodnight and make our way back to our penthouse via the elevators and crossover bridge.

Once inside, she lets out a deep sigh and rolls her neck and shoulders. The stress of today has gotten to her. I need to see what I can do to alleviate it.

I take her hand. "Let's get you to bed."

"I don't want to go to sleep."

"Who said anything about sleeping?" She gives a small squeal as I pick her up and make our way to our bedroom. "I believe I made you a promise, and I intend to keep it."

Her beautiful blue eyes are full of innocence. "Promise?"

I lay her down on our bed. "The promise that the moment you gave yourself to me, believed in our forever, believed in me, I was going to make you mine."

She shudders, and her warm palm captures my cheek, pulling me toward her. "I meant it when I sent you that text. I didn't say it because of what Jace told me about Tiff. I was all in before then."

I settle over her and kiss along her jaw to nuzzle her ear. "I know, Samantha. I read the letter you left for me." She shakes her head, so I clarify, "The what-if letter you left with Sebastian."

"Oh." Her forehead puckers. "You read it? I didn't mean for you to read it. Well, not unless something happened to me."

"Well, you addressed it to me, so I figured I had the right to read it either way." I study her remarkable face. What this woman does to me. "You wrote it before you talked to Jace." My voice cracks with emotion. "You gave yourself to me, not even knowing what really happened with Tiff. You forgave me thinking I had turned to another woman on the same night you broke up with me. You forgave me anyway."

Her letter was heartfelt, full of love and compassion and forgiveness for me. Believing I had chosen to sleep with someone else, she forgave me anyway—wanted to set me free of any guilt I may harbor. It wasn't long. It didn't hash out everything. She simply explained why she went behind my back to meet up with Roderick. She went on to apologize for leaving me in such a way and telling me how much she loved me and would haunt me until the day I died if I didn't mourn her sufficiently before I found my true love, married and had babies. She closed her letter telling me that I was the love of her life, and she only regretted not having a forever with me.

She smiles and kisses me softly. "I forgave you anyway. Always. That's what you do when you find your other half. You do whatever is necessary to be with them. Forgiving you was a small thing—you did nothing wrong. Forgiving myself?" She crinkles up her nose. "I'm working on it."

She touches my cheek. "Forgiving Jace. Not so much." She sighs and tries to sit up, but I stop her. "I'm so sorry, Joseph. What you went through, how you felt you needed to lie to protect Jace after what he did to you. I'm so upset with him. And you…you didn't know." She buries her face in my neck, sobbing. "I'm so sorry, Joseph. Please forgive me."

Christ. "Forgive you?" She feels guilty, like it's her fault. "I know I should be upset with Tiff, but honestly, I don't remember it, not in that way. What I remember is my fantasy of you. In my head and in my heart, it was you. No one else. She took advantage of the situation, and that was awful, but Tiff probably didn't know how gone I was. With Jace's encouragement and my body's reaction to her, she had no reason to believe I wasn't coherent enough to realize what was happening. It's disgusting, but the blame is on Jace for setting it all in motion. I don't know if Jace and I will ever overcome this, but no part of that is on you."

"But if I hadn't pushed you away—"

I pull back, needing to see her face. "You did nothing wrong. You were trying to keep me safe by keeping me away from you. We've both learned that together is where we're strongest. We know better now."

We stare at each other in silent communication, and then she nods, accepting my word as truth.

I bend closer. "Now, give me those lips, Sweetness, and let me make my fantasy a reality."

"Joseph." Her voice is so soft and reverent. I want to do everything I can to earn that from her every day of our lives.

"My beautiful girl, let me make love to you. Show you how it is between us, how it will always be." I steal a quick kiss before pulling away, needing her answer. "Be mine, Sweetness."

She sucks on my bottom lip, pulling slightly, and my cock draws to full staff. "I've always been yours, Joseph. From the first moment you laid eyes on me."

Christ, I love hearing her say she's mine. "Then let's make it official. Say yes."

"Yes," she says with the best smile and twinkle in her eyes.

"That's my girl," I groan seconds before my lips take hers.

We've kissed before, we've had months of kissing and touching, and even groping and sucking. But this right here, this first true kiss since she's agreed to be mine, is different. It's more precious than any kiss that has come before, even more than that very first one where she so impatiently told me she would burst for the waiting. This is the kiss marking she's truly mine. I will be the last man to ever kiss these sweet, luscious lips.

Mine.

Mine.

Mine.

I let it free, the caveman who needs to claim her for himself.

Breathlessly, I pull away. "I need you naked." She simply nods, and I stand up and start to strip. "I promise to go slower next time where I unwrap you like a present. But this time, I need to save my patience for when I'm actually inside you. I need to go slow, be gentle. I won't hurt you. I just don't have patience for clothing today."

Christ, I need to calm down. My heart is racing a million miles a minute. I need—want—this to be good for her. I want it to be everything.

She gives me a sweet smile as she stands up and starts to peel off her clothes. Once I'm naked, I pull back the covers and then turn to help with her bra and panties. She steals glances, but won't keep my eye contact. She's tentative, and I can't have that.

"Samantha." I cup her cheek and guide her eyes to mine. "I won't hurt you. I promise. If at any time you want me to stop, just say the word, and I will." I kiss her lips and all along her makeup-free face. I love her all made-up, but I love her all-natural best.

As she settles in our bed, I rein in my caveman who's screaming *take her* and decide on a new course, a slower one. I lie beside her, my body trembling with desire that's amped up due of the emotions of the day and the fact that this will be our first time—*her* first time.

I kiss her softly. "We're going to take this slow, okay?"

"You don't—"

"I do. I won't *take* your virginity. This is not about me *taking* anything from you. I want this to be about *giving.* I want to give you something no man ever has. I want to give you a part of me I've never given anyone. You're my heart, Samantha, and I need to cherish you, worship you, make love to you."

Her breath catches.

I kiss her pulse point on her neck, feeling her blood race. It's hot as fuck knowing how turned on she is. Chin tilted, she gives herself to me. "So sexy."

She moans as my fingers trace along each breast, circling but never touching her nipples. I kiss along her neck and make my way back up to her lips. "My beautiful girl."

Every time I speak she lets out a sigh. I love how I affect her. For every squirm, moan, sigh, arch, and shudder, I feel it too. Her pleasure is my pleasure. Her racing heart and heady desire meets my racing heart and heady desire. She gives back to me in every breath of her being, in every touch of her warm, needful hands, and in the wanton haze in her eyes.

My girl.

As I play with her nipples, her arching back tells me what she really wants. With a lingering kiss, I slowly nip, suck, and kiss my way down her neck and chest to her stiff, succulent peaks. "So fucking beautiful."

She cries out as I tease and suck on her nipples. My cock, painfully hard, rubs against her thigh.

Her hands have free rein and alternate between imploring, guiding, and exploring.

"Joseph," she begs.

"I know, baby." I know what she needs, where she needs me.

My hand makes a path down her body, taking time to enjoy every inch of her silky skin. She nearly jerks off the bed when I graze over the soft spot just above her hip bone.

She catches herself and giggles. "Sorry." Her smile is sheepish and embarrassed.

I grin and kiss her swollen lips. "Don't be." My hand continues down, down, until I reach my destination. I watch her face as I slide my palm over her mound. Her mouth opens as a sigh escapes, and her body rocks into my touch. Her head tilts back, but her eyes never leave mine as she continues to glide slowly against my hand, back and forth. "Christ, Sweetness. I think I could come just from watching you rub against my hand."

"Yeeeessss…come." She groans, and I nearly fucking do.

I don't know how much more of this I can take, but I'm lost in her, lost in her pleasure, lost in her seductive shyness and the way she gives herself over to me. I'm so lost that I'm found.

My middle finger slips between her folds, easily slipping through her wet heat. Her hips call me, beckon me, draw me into her. And I do, I go where I've never gone before with her. As soon as I'm inside her, she arches back, and her inside contract around my finger, pulling at me, drawing me in. Beautiful and…tight.

Christ, so tight. I'm going to die when I finally get my cock inside her.

I realize now I shouldn't have waited to do this. I should have been doing this all along, getting her ready, stretching her to accommodate my size. I don't want to hurt her.

I freeze.

"Joseph, what's wrong?"

"You're tight. I'm afraid I'll hurt you."

She pulls my face to hers. "It might hurt at first, but it's okay. It's to be expected, right? You didn't really think my first time would be pain-less, did you?"

I shake my head. "I'd hoped it could be." I see the disbelief on her face. "I've never had sex with a virgin. I've never been anyone's first choice." I didn't realize how much that meant to me until I said those words out loud.

"Joseph, you are my first choice for everything, but especially this." She pulls my hand away and pulls me on top of her. "Now kiss me and make love to me. Enough waiting. I think I will surely burst if I have to wait for you any longer."

Her playful pouting is adorable. "God, I love you."

She nods. "I know. Now show me." She wraps her legs around mine and swats my ass.

I chuckle. "You're going to be the death of me, aren't you?"

"I sure hope not." She smiles deviously. "Kiss me."

My fear of hurting her has taken the edge off my urgency. I can do this. Our lips meet in a heated caress, just as my cock rests against her pussy. As I slip my tongue inside her mouth, she arches and rocks her hips against me, and the tip of my cock slips inside her. She gasps, not in a painful way, but in an oh-my-god-that-feels-amazing way.

With the catch of her breath and the arch of her hips, I slip in further.

Tight. So tight.

I rest my forehead against hers. "You okay?" *Please, be okay.*

She rocks against me, again. "Yes, Joseph."

She arches back. "Please," she moans.

Fuck. That's it.

I push in further. Slowly, with each rock of her hips I sink deeper until I am fully seated inside the warmest, tightest, most succulent pussy I've ever felt.

She will absolutely be the fucking death of me.

"Oh god, Joseph." Her sexy voice reaches my ears right as she squeezes my cock and comes.

I've barely even moved, and she's coming all over me. I groan as I watch, feeling her tremble and moan my name. The most beautiful sight and sound I've ever witnessed.

"Fucking spectacular, Sweetness." I kiss along her neck and face, and gently peck at her lips until she comes back from her orgasmic high.

Her eyes open, and a radiant smile spreads across her lips. "Wow."

I nod. "Yeah, wow." I suck her bottom lip and then pull back. "Now, let's do that again, and this time I'm coming with you."

"Yes, please."

I chuckle at my sweet sexy girl. So full of wonder and passion. Will I ever get my fill?

Not.

A.

Fucking.

Chance.

Twenty-Four

Samantha

JESUS, THERE'S BLOOD EVERYWHERE. I CAN'T GET IT to stop. "Daddy!"

"It's okay, pumpkin." His hand cups my cheek, grounding me. Breathe. Don't think about the blood.

His eyes shine with tears, and his skin pales—fading. "Don't be afraid," he whispers through a wisp of a smile. "Love. You."

"Daddy," I sob. "I love you, too." My words fall on deaf ears.

"I love you, too." I cry to the heavens because that's the only way he'll hear me.

I bolt awake, a sob on my lips, a knife in my heart, and gasping for air. "Fuck." I exhale as I realize it was only a dream. A nightmare. A memory.

His arms surround me on my next breath. "Sweetness." His warmth draws out the painful memories and combats my sorrow.

"Joseph." I bury my face in his neck. "My dad…" is all I manage before my tears take over, any semblance of composure gone.

"I know. You cried out for him." He squeezes me tighter. "Shh. I got you, Samantha. It's over. It's all over." His gravelly voice, sexy and calming, covers me like warm memories and happily-ever-afters.

Daddy, I'm not afraid anymore. I wonder if he can hear me.

I peer up at Joseph. His beautiful face is distorted with sympathy and eyes glistening with tears. I wipe my eyes and sniffle, trying to find solid ground through the latent haze of my dream and the reality staring me in the face.

"That day, he told me not to let fear stand in my way of seeing what's right in front of me. To not let my mature ways squash what remains of my childish hope and belief so I could see the life I could have with you."

A single tear falls from his soulful green eyes, watching me, waiting.

"I'm sorry it took me so long to see it, to believe in it, to believe in us."

"Sweetness." His lip trembles and tears fall, and my heart races, pounding with need to make this right.

"I believe, Joseph. I believe in you. I was just afraid." My voice cracks on the last word as his lips press to mine.

"No more fear, baby. Not about us."

"No more," I agree, kissing him back.

Our mouths make peace with the turmoil that's been between us, on and off since we met.

"No more," I breathe against his lips.

He smiles and kisses down my jaw to my earlobe, nipping it gently before rasping in my ear. "I need more of you."

His breath sends a shudder through my body and moisture to my core. "Yes," I hiss, and latch on to his shoulder as he rolls us to my back.

Hot kisses traverse my body, licking and sucking in rapturous consumption of every inch of my skin. I'm on fire with desire and arching with need, aching for him.

"Joseph." It's a plea, an exultation, a demand.

Tight, hot, and shaking with restraint, Joseph, enters me on a groan so feral, goosebumps ripple across my body. I wrap round him, consuming his scent, his sounds, his beauty in motion.

"Fuck, yes," he chants on every pump of his hips, not gentle, not rough, just achingly perfect.

I try to concentrate on him, watch his single-minded focus as he makes love to me, but it's a lost cause. With every thrust, I cry out, lost in my own pleasure, rising higher and higher.

"So beautiful, Sweetness," he murmurs against my mouth, before sucking on my bottom lip as he pinches my nipple.

"Oh." *Jesus.* I clamp down as the jolt of pleasure sears to my clit. "Again."

He growls as he does it again.

"Oh, god. Joseph…I'm gonna—"

"Come," he finishes for me.

That jolt of pleasure turns into an outright explosion, my words lost on the moan that rips through me as my body takes flight.

"Fuck." His arms wrap around me. His hips surge deeper, grinding round and around, pistoning through every tremor. "Christ, Samantha, I love the way you squeeze me when you come."

His words and the groan he lets loose as he comes send me into another orgasm even stronger than the first. I'm lost, soaring above, tethered only by his hold on me and the sensation of him coming inside me.

"Sweetness," he coos against my neck as I come down from my blissful high and the last of my orgasmic contractions wane.

Kisses rain across my face, my body going limp, still holding on to him, but just barely.

"God, I love you." I breathe out on a sigh of release.

I had no idea sex could be this good.

This spectacular.

He's a god.

And he's *mine*.

He chuckles, brushing my hair from my face. "I love you too, sweets."

Rolling to his side, he situates me the way he likes. "Now, go to sleep, Samantha." He kisses my temple. "You're keeping me from my beauty sleep."

I swat at his chest as he chuckles, thinking he's so funny. *Ass.*

He captures my hand and presses it to his lips. "What? You don't need beauty sleep, Sweetness. There's nothing on this earth that could make you any more beautiful to me."

Shit. Okay, he's a sweet ass.

I cuddle into him and let out a sigh of contentment, the stress of the day leaving on that puff of air. My body relaxes further with every soothing stroke of his hands, beat of his heart, and brush of his lips.

"Sleep, baby," he whispers before I finally let go and succumb to the night.

Joseph

I made love to her three times last night, and she came multiple times, each and every time. My inflated ego was undaunted by her teasing me over breakfast, telling me it was the best sex she's ever had. Of course, I'm the *only* sex she's ever had, and I plan to keep it that way.

I tell her she's the best sex I've ever had, hands down. Sadly, she's not the only sex I've ever had, but she wipes all others from my mind. With her, I have a clean slate, and I intend to fill up every inch of that slate with her pleasure.

I kiss her softly. "Are you sore, Sweetness?" My cock hardens as to the why she'd be sore.

Her sweet smile warms my heart as she leans her head on my shoulder. "Only in the most delicious of ways."

After she finishes her last bite of breakfast, I whisk her back to our bedroom. I can't keep my hands off her or my dick out of her now that I've had her. Maybe it was the waiting, maybe it's the love, maybe it's her. Actually, I'm quite positive it's her. I've never loved anyone like I love her, nor have I ever wanted someone like I want her, not just sexually either. I need her in my everyday life. I need a life partner, and she is it for me.

If I didn't think she'd freak out, I'd ask her to marry me right here, right now while I'm inside her. But, she's not ready for that. She just got on board the Joseph and Samantha Train, and I'm not doing anything to derail it. Though, I'm going to do all I can to keep us on the same track, heading in the same direction. Together.

After, I kiss her head, cuddled into our post-coital position, her back to my front. "You know I'm never going to let you out of this bed, right?"

She giggles. "I'm starting to see that." She squeezes my arm around her waist. "I'm not complaining. I love being here in your place, in your bed. I had misgivings about you living in a penthouse, but I'm beginning to see the appeal."

"Not my place, not my bed. This is *our* place, *our* bed. Unless you'd rather we live someplace else?" I nuzzle into her neck. Her softness and scent are making me hard, again.

She sighs. "No, I love it right here."

I grind my erection against her ass. "I'm going to make love to you all summer."

She shudders in my arms, and her nipple hardens under my palm.

"Mmm, you like that, Sweetness."

I tweak her nipple, and instinctively her ass presses into me. "Joseph."

My lips run up the curve of her shoulder as I continue to taunt her with my hands. "We may never even make it to MCI this summer. I don't think I can stop wanting—needing—to be buried deep inside you long enough for either of us to go to work."

I pull her top leg over mine and push into her slowly from behind. She arches and gasps, making my cock harder than ever. "It feels better every time. How is that even possible?" I snap my hips and fill her completely.

"Oh, god," she moans and reaches down, grabbing my ass, sinking her fingers into me with every thrust.

"Then when we move to Austin, you're gonna live with me, Sweetness. I'm not ever going to let you out of my bed. I don't care if we live in the same house with Jace or find someplace new, but you and me are it. There's no more living apart from each other, not for a night, not for a week. Not ever."

My right hand moves down her body, slipping into her wet folds, finding her clit swollen and ready. My cock pushes into her over and over from behind, the motion rubbing her clit across my fingers.

She's close already, her warm pussy squeezing me so tightly. "Tell me you want that, Samantha." Her walls clench around me, letting me know she does, but I need to hear her say it.

"Yes, Joseph. All of it, yes."

Thank fuck. "Now come for me, my sweet. Take me with you."

I bite into her neck, sucking and licking the spot that sets her off and fulfills my caveman need to mark her. A need that will probably continue until she is mine in every sense of the word.

When she detonates, I hold on for the ride of my life as I take her pleasure and give her all of mine, pumping my seed deep inside her. "My Sweetness."

My girl.

My love.

My life.

My forever.

The End

Acknowledgements

Thank you to my husband for his unwavering support. It means the world to me that he's proud of me and my accomplishments. To my children who make me feel like I'm conquering the world with each word I write. You are my heart—I do this for you. To my mom, thank you for loving me when it wasn't easy and for supporting me in my passion.

Special thanks to Teddy for sharing this writing journey with me. I truly don't believe I would have made it this far without her undying support, knowledge, and sisterhood-of-the-traveling-pants type of connection we have.

To Tamara, who kicks my ass when my story needs it and for sticking with me as my editor. I live for her praise, like the needy little writer I am.

To my follow writerly peeps: Teddy, Shelly, Gayla – thanks for all the support and putting up with my Thursday Inspiration, Friday Humor, and Hottie McHottie emails. I enjoyed each and every one nearly as much as I enjoy you.

And lastly, to the readers—thank you for sticking with me through the cliffhanger in book 1, *Until You Set Me Free* (dmckdavis.com/books/until-you-set-me-free). I promise to *try* not to have any more of those, but sometimes the characters have so much to say, it's hard to get it all in just one book. I'm even more in love with Joseph and Samantha by the end of book 2. I pray you want more as their love story continues in *Until You Say I Do* (dmckdavis.com/books/until-you-say-i-do). That is the last from them, at least for now, but you will continue to see them in Fin's story— Until You Believe (dmckdavis.com/all-books/series/until-you/uybelieve).

Until next time, I will continue to write…

"What only the heart hears…"

An Until You Novel

Book Three

Playlist

Welcome To The Jungle by Guns n' Roses

Never Be the Same by Camilla

One Woman One Man by Magic

Crazy Love by Aaron Neville

Have A Little Faith by Michael Franti & Spearhead

I Won't Give Up by Jason Mraz

You Are the Reason by Calum Scott

I Will Wait by Mumford and Sons

Still Yours by Jamie Lawson

Say You Won't Let Go by James Arthur

Perfect by Ed Sheeran

I Get to Love You by Ruelle

You Are the Reason - Duet Version by Calum Scott & Leona Lewis

To the readers who love Joseph and Samantha and wanted more.
This is their more. Their everything.
Their Forever. Always. I Do.

Will you *Dance* in my *Darkness?*
Or *Relish* my *Light?*
Will you *Come* to me *Sweetly?*
Or *Take* me in the *Night?*

Will you *Add* to my Abundance?
Or *Grow* my *Shame?*
Will you be the *Fuel* to my *Fire?*
Or *Extinguish* my *Flame?*

D.M. Davis

Until You
SAY I DO

One

WELCOME TO THE JUNGLE

AUGUST

Joseph

WHEN I WAS A KID, I BEGGED MY PARENTS TO TAKE the training wheels off my bike so I could ride around like the big kids—like my older brothers. I was tired of feeling left behind, like the runt of the group, not so much in size but in ability. My dad was uncertain, sure I would hurt myself and damage my confidence.

"Let him try," Mom said.

"He's only four, Fiona. He's too young. He can't even tie his own shoes yet," Dad protested, ever my protector.

"Take 'em off, Hugh. He'll fall and come crying for you to put them back on." She was so sure.

With a sigh of resignation, and as I bounced on the balls of my feet in nervous anticipation, my dad removed my training wheels.

It took one good push with my left foot, while my right pressed down hard on the pedal, to get enough momentum to place both feet on the pedals. It was a millisecond, a mere beat of my heart, a gasp from my mom, and *yes!* from my dad, and I was off, tearing down the street. My balance improved with every steady pump of my legs and the fierce support from my brothers as they ran beside me—not in front to lead me, or behind to push me—but *beside* me to guide and encourage.

That's been the story of my life, all twenty-three years of it. My need to prove myself before it was time, my family's ability to let me do it, and my brothers being by my side the entire time.

My proverbial training wheels as VP of Products and Technology for McIntyre Corporate Industries are off. Uncle Max is officially retired. I'm on my own. Only I'm not. My brothers are here, sitting in the chairs facing my desk, in my executive office at MCI's corporate headquarters in downtown Dallas. They're eyeing me expectantly, waiting for my next words, for my agreement, for *my* approval.

"Do you really think he's ready? That he's right for the job? Right for MCI?" I know the answer. I've always known the answer, but what happened a year and a half ago put a damper on my enthusiasm in bringing Samantha's brother, Jace, on board.

"He's changed, Joe. He's really trying. He had an impressive start at Solengers. They'd be fools to let him walk away, but I know he wants to be here as much as I want him here." Matt glances at Fin before his identical green eyes flash on me. "Jace won't accept our offer unless you okay the deal."

I pace to the wall of windows, not that I have to get up to see the view. I could have just turned my chair as two of my four walls are windows. But I need a break from their expectant stares. "You don't need my approval. Marketing is your baby." Matt doesn't need my approval, but he *wants* it.

He laughs. "Apparently I do."

A knock at the door brings a reprieve. "Mr. McIntyre." Lydia pokes her head in without waiting for my reply. Her face lights up when she sees me. "I…er." She looks between Matt and Fin as she enters the office.

I scowl at Matt, who's eyeballing her a little too appreciatively. When he sees me notice, he simply shrugs and looks away.

She throws her shoulders back, bringing her all-too perky breasts front and center. Her eyes lock on my crotch, and her tongue sweeps across her lower lip.

Christ, really? Have some self-respect. I internally sigh and roll my eyes. What to do about my new overly eager assistant, who spends entirely too much time staring at my dick and playing with her hair? Mary, my regu-lar assistant, is on maternity leave, and I fear she may decide not to come back. I need her now more than ever. Lydia makes Mary look like a god-dess among admins.

I clear my throat, and Lydia's eyes dart to mine without a hint of em-barrassment, more like a dare. "Your two o'clock rescheduled to tomorrow."

I glance at my watch, noting the time, and wonder what Samantha's doing for lunch. Hands in my pockets, scowling, I clench and unclench my jaw, tempering my response. "You could have told me that between meetings."

She nods. "Yes, well…I thought you would want to know, given you'd requested it be set up for today."

True. I did. "Thank you for being thorough. I'm fine with tomorrow."

She smiles as if my thanks means more than it does. "I like to be hands-on and thorough." Her gaze darts to my crotch again, only this time she bites her lip.

Christ. She's trouble. "Thank you, Lydia." I usher her out of the office and all but slam the door.

I turn, letting out a punch of air.

"Brother, you have a problem," Fin states the obvious.

"I'm well aware." I return to my seat and run my hand through my hair as I call Michael.

"Boss," he answers before it even rings.

"Lydia. She needs to be gone today, before my wife sees her."

"She's not your wife yet." The humor in his voice is unmistakable.

I don't need the reminder. It was my brilliant idea to have the big wedding, talking Samantha out of the elopement she wanted. Or said she wanted, but deep down she really wants the full-blown affair: white dress, wedding cake, reception, first dance, and family. It's the *family* part that makes her think she doesn't need the fuss. Her family, not mine.

Four months. I have to make it four more months, then she's mine. Forever.

"Just…fix it."

"I'll talk to HR," Michael assures me before hanging up.

He's been a great addition to MCI's security team. Though he reports to Victor for all things security related, he's my man. My number one in security and getting things I don't necessarily have the time or tact for done. Not that Michael is full of tact. This is one thing he truly lacks, except when it comes to my wife. He and Samantha formed an unbreakable bond over the death of her father and his subsequent protection over her. After he and Samantha both shot her father's killer, he retired from the FBI, took some time off, and has since started working for MCI.

"What about Jace?" Fin brings me back to the topic at hand.

Jace. He's spent the best part of a year apologizing to me and Samantha in every way possible for bringing Tiff into my bed, and for all but abandoning his mom and sister when their father died. He's remorseful. I believe that. But has he truly changed? Am I the one to judge whether he's groveled enough to warrant a reprieve? Maybe. On the Tiff thing, yes. But on the family abandonment issue, no. That's all Samantha. It's her place to let him back in. She's trying, but trust doesn't come easy for her. Their relationship is vulnerable. I can sense her waiting for him to screw up, to prove she's justified in her doubt and mistrust.

I, on the other hand, still have no memory of Tiff and our drunken encounter. Rape. I was raped by Tiff. Samantha is outraged for me. I only remember my drinking-induced fantasy sex dream with Samantha. I can still see and feel her as if it were real. But it wasn't Samantha, it was Tiff. Samantha hates that I'm not more upset by it. I'm pissed at what Jace did and feel like something was taken from me that I did not offer or knowingly give. But because I still have a sweet memory of Samantha, I won't let it be tainted by dwelling on the Tiff aspect. I choose to focus on all that is Samantha Cavanagh. The fantasy of her, the reality of her, and the blessed day she becomes my wife.

Until Samantha is ready, though, I can't fully get on board the Jace bandwagon. I'm following her lead as Jace has caused enough damage to last her a lifetime. "Here's the thing." I steeple my hands, resting my elbows on the edge of my desk. "I think Jace has potential. The potential to be highly successful at MCI and bring our marketing to the next level with you, Matt. But, he also has the potential to break my wife's heart, irrevocably."

"She's not your wife," they both chime in. Fin smirks, and I can hear his silent *caveman* in my head.

I raise my hand dismissively. "Semantics." She is my wife—my life—in every way that matters. "I'm remaining on the fence. It's Jace's game to win or lose. I won't disagree with bringing him on board, but I'm not going to champion him, either." I meet Matt's gaze. "That's the best I can give you."

He nods and rises to leave. "Fair enough."

Fin stays behind and waits until the door closes behind Matt. He crosses his leg, playing with the seam of his slacks. "And Lydia?"

"You want her?"

"Fuck, no." He chuckles. "She's a lawsuit waiting to happen. HR needs to have a serious discussion with her, and then place her with a female boss."

"Or leave MCI."

He laughs again. "Yes, or leave." He stands and buttons his suit jacket. "That would make your life way too easy if all of your challenges simply up and left, brother."

"We're planning a wedding, I'm new to this VP gig, and my wife is getting ready to live apart from me for the next year while she finishes college in Austin. I could use fewer challenges."

"She's not your…" He stops mid-protest when he sees my scowl. "Fine. Fine. Call her your wife. You're already like an old married couple anyway."

"There's nothing old about us."

He laughs. "No, I suppose there's not, but you do have that couple thing about you. I don't think you'll survive a year apart from her."

I scrub my face. "Fuck. I can't ask her to stay. I can't ask her to give up her dream of graduating from the same college as her parents."

He shrugs. "She'd do it for you, you know."

"I know. That's why I can't ask."

"I hear ya. Regarding Lydia, I'll talk to Michael and Victor. We'll ensure she gets a job, somewhere outside of your organization and the view of your crotch."

I slump back in my chair in relief. He'll make it happen. "I owe you one."

He heads for the door. "I'll add it to the growing stack of IOUs." He looks back before opening the door. "Consider it done."

Samantha

"I'm sorry, ma'am, but you can't go in there without an appointment." The buxom blond darts around her desk to stop my progress to Joseph's office.

"I don't need an appointment." I try to walk around her, but she throws her arm out to stop me. I suppose I should have called first to let him know I was coming, but that would have ruined the whole idea of me surprising him.

I never had this kind of trouble with Mary. Sighing, I take a step back and don my friendliest smile. "I'm sorry. Let's start again." I stick out my hand. "You must be Joseph's new assistant. I'm Sam Cavanagh, Joseph's fiancée."

She wrinkles her nose, looking at my hand as if it's covered in something truly nasty. *Seriously?* I arch a brow, waiting expectantly.

She doesn't take my hand. Though, she does manage a stiff smile. "Miss Cavanagh, while I can appreciate you *feel* you have the right to barge in on Mr. McIntyre without an appointment"—she grabs my arm and begins to turn me away from the executive offices—"you will have to make an appointment like everyone else."

Oh no, I don't think so. I slip out of her hold, pivoting around her. "Why don't we ask Mr. McIntyre how he feels about me barging in." The snottiness in my voice is undeniable. She's a piece of work. I hope she doesn't treat clients with the same condescending attitude. I barrel through Joseph's closed door, only stopping once I'm well inside and away from Miss Attitude.

"You can't—"

"Samantha?" Joseph stands, ignoring his assistant's protest. His eyes meet mine, and my insides clench at the sight of him in his black body-defining designer suit, looking ever the part of a corporate bigwig. It never gets old.

Oh my. My heartbeat goes into overdrive, and I strain to stop myself from fanning my face as heat creeps up my cheeks.

"Gentlemen, can you excuse us?" He escorts the men he was meeting with to the door, grabbing my hand as he passes, pulling me along.

After the men exit, he tucks me to his side and faces his assistant. "Lydia, cancel my afternoon." He releases me, and then he leans back through the door. "Oh, and Lydia, my wife takes precedence over all else. Don't try to stop her from entering my office again." He closes and locks the door without acknowledging her stammering reply.

"How'd you know?" My anger diminishes with his prompt admonishment of his assistant and claiming me as his priority.

He chuckles. "You walked in ready to decimate anyone standing in your way. I simply assumed you didn't arrive that way, but had a run-in with my new assistant." He steps closer. "Now, what brings you here?" He touches my cheek, studying my face. "You've got that look."

I lean into his touch. "What look?"

"That look that says you need me to show you how much I love you." He steps closer, his body pressing against mine.

I look away, feeling a bit foolish. "I know you love me," I softly reply.

His emerald eyes shine with understanding. His arms wrap around me as he nuzzles the side of my face, running his mouth along the curve of my ear.

He always knows.

I relax into him with a deep sigh. "I need you."

I squeal in delight as he sweeps me into his arms and heads to his adjoining bathroom. "I need you too, Sweetness."

Samantha

I think I could stay right here, in the arms of the man I love, for the rest of my life and be perfectly content. Forget sleep, food, school, or a career.

This man is all I truly need. I burrow deeper into his chest. We haven't moved or spoken since he carried me from the bathroom to recover on the couch, wrapped in each other's embrace.

He traces circles up and down my back, lulling me further into the calm sanctuary of our post-sex haze. My eyes flutter closed, though I try to resist, to remain present and mostly conscious. His lips skim my forehead as a sound of pure satisfaction rumbles through his chest. A purr, nearly. I press in further to keep from laughing. He truly is such an animal at times, usually when he's extremely turned on or extremely relaxed. Both states he managed to hit in the mere thirty minutes since my arrival.

Heaven.

Home.

"Tell me. What got you out of sorts? Why'd you need the caveman?" His deep timbre makes my lady bits ache for him all over again.

"I came to surprise you with news, but the run-in with your assistant threw me off my game." I pull back enough to see his eyes. "I made a decision…that…well, I now realize maybe I shouldn't have made without you."

He kisses my nose. "Sweetness, I'm sure whatever decision you made, I'll be happy with, especially if it makes you happy."

I frown and sit up. "But you don't even know what it is. It's a really big decision. I shouldn't have made it without you."

His brow furrows. "Are you *wanting* me to be upset with you?"

"I…" Huh, do I? "No. I wanted it to be a surprise. You'd never ask it of me, but it's something I wanted to do. For us."

He sits up fully, his front to my side with his legs around me. "Now you've got me really curious."

I wait, wondering if he'll guess. Save me the drama of having to tell him.

He runs his finger down my nape and through my cleavage, which is fully exposed in his dress shirt I confiscated off the bathroom floor before he picked me up and settled us on the couch. "Tell me, Sweets. Don't make me play twenty questions." He cups my breast, running his thumb over my nipple.

I bite my lip to suppress a moan. "You're gonna have to stop that if you want me to talk."

"Hmm." He pulls me onto his lap as he leans back, his eyes caressing my exposed breasts, watching his fingers tease my hardening tips. "Maybe you could make it quick?"

Quick? Does he mean sex or my secret? "Oh!" His hips thrust, pushing his erection against my bare ass. I grab onto his shoulders as he swings my legs so I'm straddling his cock, pressing intimately against me.

He nibbles across my chest as he lowers his shirt from my shoulders. My hips sway, moving on their own, needing the friction. "Tell me, Samantha," he groans before his mouth consumes one lucky nipple, sucking it deeply.

"Joseph." I latch on to his hair. Jesus, I love it when he sucks my breasts as if he's starved for me. I reach between us, lifting up, and lower myself onto his hard shaft, groaning over every delicious inch.

"Fuck. You're so wet." He thrusts, burying himself deep, then holds my hips securely, ensuring I can't move. His eyes meet mine. "Tell me, before neither of us can speak with anything other than our bodies."

I arch back and contract around his cock, needing him to move, to take me, to make love to me.

His hand wraps around the back of my head, sinking into my hair, and he pins me with his gaze. He means business. My caveman has come out to play. I contract around him again. I love Joseph gentle, and I love him hard, but I think I love my protective caveman most of all. The one who needs to see me safe, happy, and, most of all, thoroughly fucked.

"I…I'm not going back to Austin." I close my eyes, afraid of his reaction. I'm met with silence, and when his hold on me softens, I open my eyes. My heart flips when I see such adoration in his eyes, though I also see a mix of concern. I cup his face. "I can't imagine a day, a night, without you. I tried to be brave. I did, I swear. I just can't leave this weekend and move back to Austin without you."

His hand drops from my neck and settles on my hip, mirroring his other hand's hold. His fingers knead at my flesh, making my hips jerk with want.

"More," he manages to rasp.

I'm not sure if he means my hips or more of my secret. So, I give him both. Leaning forward, placing my forehead against his and my hands braced on his shoulders, I start to move, slowly, with my words. "I transferred to SMU."

He cups my ass, helping me, guiding me as he begins to thrust into me. "Oh!" God. "I start in two weeks."

His lips find my breasts. "Tell me why, again." He bites my nipple and then sucks the sting away.

"Oh, yeesss." I wrap my arms around his head, pinning him to me. I move faster, urgently. "Because I know what it's like to live without you, and what it's like to live with you. And I don't ever want to be without you again."

"Fuck." He groans, encapsulating me, his arms and hands pressing me closer, controlling our thrusts, meeting our need to be one. "Look at me, baby." He tips my head, and our eyes lock. "You. Make. Me. So. Damn. Happy." He punctuates each word with a thrust. He sucks on my bottom lip and kisses me tenderly despite our urgency.

My body begins to tingle and reach for that pinnacle I've only ever known with him.

"Now, come for me, Sweetness. I'm gonna come so fucking hard for you."

His words send me spiraling. "I'm…"

"Ah, fuck. Yes, you are." He looks at me. "That's right, squeeze me, baby. Make me come."

"Yes. Yes. Yes." My vision blurs as I shatter around him, gripping and holding on as he continues to pump into me.

"So fucking hard!" he moans as he pulses and comes deep inside me. "Christ!"

I cry out again as he sucks on my nipple, driving me into a second orgasm.

"Fuck, yes. Just like that," he rasps before latching back on.

Once our bodies still, we collapse onto the couch, panting, him still buried inside me. "Never pulling out," he mumbles.

I sigh into his neck. "It might be hard to get any work done like this."

"I think *hard* is the relevant word in that sentence." He emphasizes his point by thrusting into me and growling. "Still hard for you, Sweetness."

Two

RELISH MY LIGHT

Joseph

THE AROMA OF DINNER ENTICES ME FROM MY HOME office. "Damn, woman, something smells incredible." I stride into the kitchen, grab her from behind, and bury my nose in her hair, taking a deep whiff. *Christ, she smells even better.* I latch on to her neck.

She giggles and squirms, pressing her ass into me. "Joseph," she moans as I tweak a nipple.

I'm hard. Instantly.

I had her three times at the office this afternoon. *Three* fucking times, and I'm rock hard again like a sex junkie on Viagra.

I groan and slip my hand between her thighs, cradling the gift that has been bestowed on me. The greatest gift I've ever received, besides that of her heart. Her moist heat permeates the thin fabric of her barely-there panties. "You're killing me, baby."

She squeezes her legs together, locking me in place. "I think you're the one trying to kill me, Caveman." Her hand caresses my arm. "You're the one who insisted I wear your shirt and only my panties after we showered."

On a sigh, I slowly disengage. "You're right. I'll try to behave, but you can't blame a man for admiring his woman."

Her sweet smile nearly has me throwing her over my shoulder and heading for the bedroom or couch. Shit. This counter right here would do just fine.

She cocks a hip, swinging her hair off her shoulder as she swivels to face me.

Stunning. Standing there in my shirt, hanging off her shoulder, and bare legs, looking like the siren she is. *My* siren.

"What's the deal with your new assistant?"

Visions of Samantha riding me on the couch in my office are derailed by the mention of my heinous ex-assistant. I swipe a hand across my mouth and down my neck as I think of the best way to approach this topic. Honesty. That's what we've promised each other. No more secrets that needle their way between us, filling in any gaps with doubt and darkness.

Honesty lets the light in, keeping the darkness at bay.

"Lydia is no longer my assistant. She's been reassigned."

Samantha's arched brow, smirk, and twinkling eyes have me grinning back at her. "What? Didn't she start recently?" She grabs the oven mitt, preparing to open the oven.

"Here, let me do that." I quickly maneuver around her to take over. We'll never eat if I see her ass peeking out from my dress shirt.

She giggles, knowing full well the effect she has on me.

I fill her in as discreetly as possible as we plate dinner and make our way to the dining room. She listens intently, not commenting, barely showing any reaction at all. It's making me a little nervous. My baby is usually so easy to read, but at the moment, she's playing it close to her chest. I'm worried this whole thing will upset her—allow old doubts to seep in.

"You…what? Had her replaced"—she snaps her fingers—"just like that?" She smiles, finding this humorous, surprisingly.

"Yeah, pretty much. I asked Michael to take care of it. Fin was in my office when I spoke to him about it. Fin followed up to ensure Lydia was moved to another department, far away from me."

Chuckling, she takes a bite, shaking her head, looking amused and disbelieving. "Poor girl. She thought she was gonna snag her a VP, and she ends up getting shipped off to Siberia."

"Marketing is not Siberia."

She laughs again. "It is if that's not where you want to be." She continues before I can protest. "I'm not questioning your tactics or motives. I'm thankful a shark like that won't be around you every day, causing you undue stress and putting ideas in my head." She slips onto my lap, wrapping her arms around my neck. Instinctively, I kiss her warm lips and pull her closer. "I forget sometimes how powerful you and your brothers are. You say *'jump'* and your employees ask *'how high?'* You each wear your power so effortlessly, it's easy to forget you run a multi-billion-dollar company."

Christ. She makes it sound like I leap tall buildings in a single bound. It's nowhere that glamorous nor fun, but I'll take her compliments any day. I live for her adoration, and right now the light shining in her eyes is nearly my undoing. I couldn't stand it if Lydia caused any further problems for Samantha. I'd endure heaven and hell for this woman. My. Woman.

"I'm glad you're not upset." I keep checking her eyes to be sure we're on the same page.

She pats my chest and returns to her chair. "I'm not that easily undone, Joseph; I can take a little flirting. But she was downright rude, and I worry who else was subjected to her wrath. I'm glad she's gone, but I do feel a tiny bit bad for her."

"That's because you have the heart of a saint."

She scoffs. "A saint would have forgiven her brother by now and worked harder to make amends with her mother." She glances out the penthouse windows into the lit-up downtown around us. "I'm no saint."

Her lightness of heart from a moment ago is gone. Her damn family and the heartache they bring her. I hate to even broach the next topic, but I can't keep it from her. Honesty—our motto—the string that ties our souls together, forever tethered, forever forged, forever one.

"Matt brought up the Jace thing again. He feels the time is right to bring him on. He believes Jace is ready."

Her focus returns to me. "What do you think?"

"I think I don't want to do anything that will bring you a single moment of unhappiness." *Shit, I should have talked to her before I gave Matt my answer.*

"Joseph." She cants a brow. "That's not realistic, and you know it. I saw the news report about Solengers. They're saying their latest product campaign could triple their profit margin by first quarter next year. That would be an impressive feat for a three-year plan, much less a target that's not even seven months away. If Jace had even one percent of impact on those numbers, you'd be silly to pass him up."

I pull her out of her chair and into the living room as I command the house computer to play *our song*. "Dance with me."

She slides into my embrace, the yin to my yang, fitting me with such precision it's hard to believe we are not one and the same.

"So, it wouldn't upset you?"

Her blue eyes meet my green ones with open vulnerability. "I would never ask you to make a business decision based on my personal preference." She lifts on her toes, leaning into my ear. I pull her tighter, supporting her. "Jace has caused both of us pain, and if you can look beyond it, then so can I." She kisses my cheek and gives me a squeeze before lowering to her normal stance. "I'm not saying it will be easy seeing him more often, or that we're best buds again. But I made a promise to him and myself: that I would stop purposely avoiding him. He can't make amends if I never give him the chance." She shrugs. "I guess this is life's way of telling me the time is now."

"Are you sure? Nothing's been confirmed. I told Matt I wouldn't stop him from hiring Jace, but that I still have my reservations."

"Are your reservations about his work ethics or his abilities?"

"No."

She smirks. "I didn't think so. You're a VP, Joseph. You have to lead with your head, not your heart."

"I prefer to believe there's a place for both. I will never let my head lead me where my heart is not willing to go. I nearly lost you by trying to use only logic. I won't let that happen again with you or MCI."

She nods and wipes away a tear. "That's why you're the man I love. You're not just one thing. You're so many wonderful things wrapped up in this amazing man I'm lucky enough to call mine."

My heart swells, and as our song starts again, I pull her close. "Enough talking, Sweets."

Our song and everything else is drowned out by my pounding pulse and her sweet gasps as I consume her mouth and ravish her body.

Mine.

Samantha

I climb into bed after having showered for the third time today. Thank god, I do so love our shower. It's the only competition Joseph will ever have to worry about.

"What's that smirk for?" Joseph asks over my shoulder.

My smile grows. "I was thinking how much I love our shower, which is a good thing considering your libido has me using it more and more."

He snuggles in close. "My libido?" He sounds incredulous as he wraps himself around me from behind. "I do believe your sex drive is as strong as mine."

I burrow back into him on a sigh. "You bring it out in me, my caveman. I can't resist your gentle heart and Neanderthal ways."

"Caveman is one thing. Neanderthal is quite another. I am a well-educated man, with couth and manners, who happens to enjoy his wife's mind, body, and soul."

I chuckle at his mock indignation.

He squeezes my breast. "Did I mention rockin' body?"

"Yes, Caveman, you did."

His lips grace my shoulder, paying special attention to my scar. The scar is all that remains of the hole made when the bullet that killed my father exited my body. I shudder at the memory.

"Are you sure about this school thing?" He presses into me. "I don't want to live apart, but I'm willing to do it. I don't want you to regret giving up that dream."

I roll to my back and touch his cheek. "Life has a way of putting things in perspective. Things that used to seem so important-—like graduating from the same school my parents did—aren't really important at all. If my father were here, he'd tell me to do what makes me happy and not to fear the unknown."

Joseph kisses my palm and holds it over his heart. "And what makes you happy, Sweetness?"

Joseph is not a man short on confidence nor conviction, but some-times—when it comes to me—he needs reassurance. Not so much in how I feel about him. He knows I love him. It's more about him giving me what I need. Loving me the way I need to be loved. I pull him to me and kiss him soundly before I answer. "You."

He smiles against my lips, his eyes searching mine. "That's it?" He seems shocked.

How can he ever doubt he gives me more than I need? "Yes, just you. Here. Not four hundred miles away from me. We could survive the year apart, but why? At what cost? And for what purpose? So that I can stick to some old goal I made for myself when I was a kid? We grow up and our goals should change with us, otherwise, we'd all be ballerinas, cow-boys, and astronauts."

His laugh tickles my ear as he holds me close. "I love your mind, baby. I love how it works. I love how you meld your philosopher's soul with your intelligence." His lips graze across mine. "But, mostly, I love how you love me." He licks across the seam of my mouth before diving in with deep, penetrating precision, curling my toes and making me gasp for more.

Shifting, he settles over my naked body, nestling his hardness be-tween my thighs. I open for him, always open to my Joseph and what he gives me—mind, body, and soul.

"Sweets." He pants, rubbing the tip of his cock against my clit. "But I also love that you're not leaving me." His voice cracks with emotion as he surges, filling me in one swift motion. "You chose to stay." He groans.

I contract around him, speechless, pulling him to me with each and every thrust. Telling him with my body how much I love him. Reassuring him that I'm here, and I'm not going anywhere.

"Fuck, yes. Squeeze me."

All sense of reason and words leave me as he takes me higher, rock-ing me into oblivion.

"You chose me," he chants with each thrust, with each gasp of air between kisses, with each glorious touch of his hands.

Ignited, I burst into flames, grounded only by his voice in my ear. "I'll always choose you, Sweetness."

Locked in my embrace, he grinds in deep and stills. "Always." He shudders with his release.

Joseph

"You alive?" She lies limp in my arms, so still and quiet I'm not even sure she's awake, but I'm pretty sure she's breathing.

"Mmm…barely," she murmurs and settles in further, rubbing her face in my neck, like she's scenting me.

I relax, knowing I haven't sexed her to death. I have to rein it in. She's not going anywhere.

This has been an emotional day. I didn't realize how anxious I was about her leaving for Austin until she told me she wasn't. Then all those pent-up feelings and anxiety over living apart from each other came crashing in and took over, making me need to claim her over and over again. Too much and yet, still not nearly enough. Never. Enough.

"I was gonna suggest something, but now I'm not sure it's such a good idea. We can't seem to stop having sex."

I laugh and relief floods my body. She can at least joke about it. And she said *we* can't stop having sex, so she doesn't think I'm mauling her.

"I'm just overwhelmed with relief that I won't have to live without you for the next nine months." I stretch and scratch my stubbly chin. Jeez, I need to shave. I probably gave her beard burn all over her body. She never complained, though. "Ignore the fact that I can't seem to keep my dick out of you. What was your suggestion?"

"You know you don't have to try to fit in a year's worth of sex."

I smile at that. "It seems my body hasn't caught up with my mind telling me you're not leaving."

She rests back on her pillow, allowing me to see her eyes. The blue eyes I love so much. "I was thinking that since you're out an assistant, and my internship is over for the summer..." She bites her lip.

I lean over and tug it free, giving it a quick suck. "That's mine."

She smirks and rolls her eyes. "You're like a two-year-old, thinking everything is yours, or the birds in Nemo: *Mine. Mine. Mine,*" she mimics.

Stifling a laugh, I take her mouth, keeping my kiss as chaste as possible. "I don't think everything is mine, Sweets. Except when it comes to you, then yes: *Mine. Mine. Mine,*" I parrot as I quickly kiss all my favorite parts of her.

Samantha squirms and giggles. "Forget my idea. We can't even have a conversation without your hands and mouth all over me."

Hands up in surrender, I flop back on my pillow. "Ok, no touching. Tell me."

She sighs as if she's frustrated with me, but I can see by the mischievous gleam in her eyes. "You need an assistant. I don't have anything to do for a few weeks, besides plan a wedding, get ready for school, and ensure my big strong man gets enough at home that he can keep his hands to himself in the office."

I scowl. "Keep my hands to myself? What does that mean?" Surely, she doesn't think I'd cheat on her.

"I mean I could be your assistant for a few weeks or until you find a suitable replacement. But none of this funny business in the office." She emphasizes with a nod of her chin and arms crossed over her luscious chest.

She's fucking adorable.

"You'd do that? Be my assistant?" I thought she was teasing, but she's serious about helping me out. I'm touched.

She softens. "Of course. You need help. I may not be fully qualified to be an assistant, but I'm sure I can manage to get you coffee, answer phones, and keep your schedule on track."

"You're more than qualified. You're *over*qualified. But I'd love to have your help. I could relax and find someone who really fits instead of taking the first person because I need someone."

"Good. You let Michael and Fin know. I'll contact Angela in the morning. I'm sure she can give me a few pointers. She manages to keep Fin on task, and I'm sure he's more difficult than you are."

"I wouldn't count on that. I'm the newbie, remember. I need a more hands-on approach than Fin does." I waggle my eyebrows.

This is gonna be fun.

Three

FUEL MY FIRE

Joseph

EARLY THE NEXT MORNING, MY FATHER KNOCKS ON my office door, entering without waiting for my response. He doesn't need to, he's the CEO. He chuckles as he closes the door and sits facing my desk.

"Good morning, Dad. What's so funny?"

He shakes his head. "You're either crazy stupid or crazy brilliant, and honestly, I'm not sure which."

I follow his meaning as he motions to the door. "Brilliant." Having Samantha here with me day in and day out for as long as I can is pure genius. Too bad it wasn't my idea.

"I don't know how you talked her into it, but just remember to treat her with respect above and beyond how you would your normal assistant. Because you know each other so well, it will be easy to take advantage and let simple niceties slip. *'Please'* and *'thank you'* go a long way. Remember, you go home to her every night. Make it a good experience for you both— you're crazy brilliant. Make it miserable—you're batshit crazy stupid."

I laugh and bow to the master. "Noted. Thanks for the advice."

The intercom buzzes. I pick up the line instead of using the speakerphone. "Sweetness."

"I'm sorry to interrupt, but you have ten minutes until your nine o'clock meeting in the executive conference room."

"Is the team here?"

"They're setting up. Do you need something before the meeting, coffee or water?"

You are what I need. "I'll grab a water from the refrigerator in there. You'll be joining me, right?"

I'm met with silence.

"Samantha?"

"Is it expected that I join you as your PA?"

She's hesitant. This is her old team. She worked closely with them over the summer. This was her project, and she had to let it go to return to school. Now, I'm asking her to join me in a lesser capacity as my assistant.

"We don't have to tell them you're my PA—no one knows yet. Join me in an advisory capacity. One who knows the product backward and forward."

"Okay."

I hang up and look at my father. "I can see this could be challenging." I hadn't considered Samantha's role here in the past. Her tenured internship allowed her to work on highly sought-after projects. Appearing now as my PA could be considered a step down and be seen as preferential treatment, seeing as she's engaged to the VP of Product and Technology. It's a fine line we will have to maneuver, not only now, but in the future when she comes to work for MCI permanently.

Dad stands, buttoning his suit jacket, reminding me of how similar he and Fin are in their mannerisms. "I'm sure you're up for it." With a swift pat on the back, he follows me out.

Samantha

I settle in at the conference table, next to Joseph. He insisted. I'd rather disappear in the back in one of the chairs lining the walls. You know, for *observing*, and not so much *participating*.

Clasping my fidgeting hands, I force myself to breathe deeply and relax.

You know these people. You've worked with them for months. So what that you said goodbye to them last week, and—surprise—here you are sitting next to the VP of their department.

Ugh, these people are gonna hate me. Think I'm the teacher's pet.

And I thought I was doing a good thing by helping Joseph out.

Under the table, Joseph squeezes my leg and says, without looking at me, "It'll be fine. No worries." He squeezes again, leaving his hand in place. He turns and leans in as if to kiss me, then freezes, catching himself.

Shit. That was close.

He whispers in my ear. "It'll be fine. We'll find our way." His dimpled smile has me relaxing instantly.

I can do this. He's here, and he won't let anything bad happen. He's in charge. This is his meeting. I'm only here to observe…and probably take notes since I am his PA, after all. I focus on my laptop and begin taking notes as the presentation begins. There are no introductions; everyone here knows each other. I get a few quick glances, but for the most part, all eyes are on Joseph and Alex, who's the project manager.

Halfway through the demo of the mock-up application, it freezes up. As Alex works to reboot the system, I flip over to the server where the coding is stored. Thankfully, I still have access. I jump to the section I'm more than familiar with and spot what I'm looking for, unfortunately. I glance up at Todd, the head programmer on the project and not my favorite person. He's glaring at me with daggers in his eyes, daring me to say something.

Joseph leans over to look at my laptop. "What is it? Do you know what's wrong?"

"I'd rather not do this in front of all these people," I whisper and send a silent plea, hoping he can read my expression.

His eyes search mine. I know he wants to talk about it now. He wants it solved. With a small nod, he turns his attention to Alex. "Let's give it another minute. Then if it's not up, we'll reschedule."

That minute turns into five minutes with little-to-no progress. I'm embarrassed for them and frustrated at the same time. This could have been avoided.

Joseph stands. "Alex, let's reschedule. Fix the problem then contact me to see where I can squeeze you in." He doesn't wait for Alex's reply. Joseph looks at me expectantly.

I hop up, close my laptop, and head out the door with him hot on my trail. As we near his office, his hand presses to my lower back. "My office, please."

He closes the door and paces to me.

"I'm sorry," I blurt and fall into a chair at his conference table.

His brow furrows. "What do you have to be sorry for?"

"I knew there was a problem. I told them how to fix it, but I guess they decided against my recommendation."

He sits beside me. "Show me."

We spend the next half hour reviewing the code on the version Alex demoed, comparing it to the fixed version on my laptop, and then run the program from my code. The app works perfectly—as I knew it would.

"When did you discover the problem?"

"A few weeks ago. The app kept failing. I kinda went around Todd and took a look at the code myself."

He sits back, crossing his arms over his chest. "Did you report it?"

"Of course."

His pensive look has me concerned. I don't want to get any-one in trouble. "Who did you tell? And do you have a record of that communication?"

Oh god, they're all going to hate me for sure. I slump in my chair. "Yes."

"Show me."

"I'm starting to hate those two words," I grumble.

He kisses my cheek. "Don't. You didn't do anything wrong."

"Then why do I feel like I did?"

"Because you're about to show me how my employees dropped the ball and weren't smart enough—man enough—to take direction from someone younger and smarter than they are."

My head drops to his shoulder. "They're going to hate me."

"Shh. Stop. I'll handle it. I just need to have all the facts first."

I show him my email communication, my notes on the app, when I found the problem, and that I reported it immediately, starting with Todd, the lead programmer. Then followed up a few days later when I saw it still wasn't fixed. I followed up again asking if he could help me understand why he felt the outdated coding was better. I'd even appealed to his ego, saying he's more experienced, and perhaps there were details I didn't understand.

"Do you really think there are valid reasons for keeping the old coding?" Joseph asks after reading my last email to Todd.

"No, not really. But he's more experienced. I was trying to be open to the idea as well as not offend him outright. He dislikes me enough as it is."

He chuckles. "I think the mere fact you exist offends Todd. I saw the glare he was giving you in the conference room. He was not happy to see you when he walked in and even less so when the app crashed. I didn't really understand what his attitude was about. Honestly, I wanted to reach over and smack him for even looking at you with such disdain."

"Oh, god." My head falls forward.

"Hey. Don't do that." He tugs my arm. "Come 'ere." He pulls me into his lap.

"This is not proper boss/employee behavior," I chastise.

He pulls me closer. "No. This is boyfriend and girlfriend, husband and wife behavior." His lips press to my forehead. "I'll fix it. I promise." He pulls my laptop in front of him. "Now, show me the rest."

Secure on his lap, I click the remaining emails. The final communication is to both Todd and Alex, where I again stress the importance of considering the new updated code statements. This will make the program run 50% faster, making it that much more efficient on system resources, increasing reliability, and reducing cost.

"Those assholes. I can't believe they completely ignored your insightful recommendations. Did they even respond to you?"

"Todd basically told me to mind my own business. Of course, not in writing. Alex never replied. I don't even know if he saw my emails."

He pats my butt. "Get up a sec."

I slip off his lap and take a quick glance at his calendar on my laptop. "You're going to be late to a meeting with Fin if you don't hurry."

Joseph punches a button on his desk phone. A second later it dials on speaker.

"Hi, Joe," Angela, Fin's PA answers.

"Can you reschedule my eleven o'clock with Fin? Something's come up."

"Sure. Oh…uh, hold a moment, please."

There's a click, and Fin's voice comes on the line. "It had better not be your dick that's *come up*."

"Fin, you're on speaker phone, and Samantha's in my office," Joseph says flatly.

"Shit. I'm sorry, Sam."

I stifle a laugh. "It's okay. Really."

"Fin, can you hold on a sec?"

"Sure."

Joseph puts him on hold and hands me a pin drive. "Can you call Michael and ask him to come up? Then copy your files to that drive."

"No problem."

He looks chagrined. "I hate to ask, but would you mind getting me some lunch? I'm starving."

I smile and walk around his desk. "Joseph, it's my job to get you lunch or whatever else you need during the workday."

He pulls me close, kissing me softly. "I'd like a blowjob later. Can you pencil that in?"

"I'll see what I can do, Mr. McIntyre." I pull away, grabbing my laptop. "Your next appointment is at two. Try not to be late. It's with your father and uncles."

"Yes, ma'am." He smirks. Before I reach the door, he calls me back. "I love you."

"I know, Caveman. I love you too." My smile doesn't nearly match the megawatt one blazing back at me.

Samantha

The MCI cafeteria is a familiar place. I've eaten here often with my co-workers and sometimes alone during the course of my two summer internships. This summer, though, was the first I never ate alone. If I wasn't dining with co-workers, then I was eating with Joseph. He would have preferred it that way every day, but he has a tight schedule, and lunch away from his desk isn't always possible. We'd eat in his office if we needed to, allowing us to spend time together. I feel at home there. It no longer feels like the huge powerful office of one of MCI's Vice Presidents. It feels like my fiancé's office.

As I wait in line, I shoot off a text to Margot. She's not happy about my decision to remain in Dallas instead of returning to the University of Texas with her. I don't blame her. I wish I could pay for her to join me at SMU, but she has a full ride to UT, and it doesn't make sense for her to blow that. Luckily, my financial situation is different. My dad set aside money for our college, and since I'll graduate after only two years instead of the normal four, I have the extra funds needed for Southern Methodist University, which is a private school.

Besides the fact that going to SMU allows me to remain with Joseph, it also affords me the convenience of being close to our wedding venue as the planning progresses. We're getting married at a church on campus. The Highland Park United Methodist Church is one of the prettiest churches I've ever seen. It has a small chapel as well, but now that I've given in to the whole "big wedding" ideal, I really want the large church with its wooden pews, stone floors, arched wooden cathedral ceiling, stained-glass windows, and a magnificent Dobson pipe-organ that encompasses the entire wall behind the altar.

We're getting married the Saturday before Christmas, not necessarily the best time for a wedding as everyone is already so busy with the Christmas and New Year's holidays. It was the best time for us, though, to be able to take a honeymoon immediately after the wedding since I'll have nearly a month-long break between the Fall and Spring semesters.

I order us lunch and wait. I never really felt out of place here at MCI until today. Now, I feel like I'm an interloper. I have to get over it. I love MCI and don't want this one project blip to color my feelings about working here, even as Joseph's temporary PA.

My phone chimes after I pay for and collect our to-go boxes. Grabbing a chair at an empty table, I respond to Margot's text. She leaves this weekend to return to Austin, and I'm hoping I get a chance to see her before she goes. Sadly, we didn't spend much time together over the summer, both of us busy with our summer jobs. We thought we'd have all year to catch up once school started, but that's all changed.

As our texts bounce back and forth, negotiating the best day to meet up, my ears prick up at the mention of Joseph's name somewhere behind me.

"He'll never marry her. She's just his plaything. Have you seen her?" one woman asks.

"No, but I hear she's quite pretty. But Joe's a hottie. There's no way he'll tie himself down to one woman. Even if they do get married, he'll be getting some on the side. Guaranteed," another woman responds.

Are they talking about me? Us?

"I hear the pool's reached a thousand dollars," yet another woman chimes in.

A pool?

"I bet fifty they won't make it to Halloween."

"I said they'd make it through Thanksgiving and call off the wedding the first week in December."

Wow. I'm in shock. I stand to slip away. It's obvious they don't know who I am, or, if they do, they haven't seen me yet. I hate slinking away with my tail between my legs.

"I hear she got Lydia fired."

Shit. Now I'm getting blamed for that too? I can't. I can't walk out of here and not at least set *that* straight.

They never see me coming, too engrossed in their hateful gossiping.

"That's simply not true. What happened to Lydia was her own doing. And for the record, she was transferred—not fired."

Four heads turn toward me.

"What—"

"Who are—"

"Shit. You're her."

"Yep, I'm *her*," I respond.

"Who her?"

"The fiancée."

"Shit."

"I recommend the next time you decide to talk smack about your bosses' boss's boss, you remember who signs your paychecks and works hard to ensure you still have a job to come to each day." I lean forward, looking each of them in the eyes. "But *if* I were a betting person, I wouldn't bet against Joseph and me. That's a sucker's bet, right there." I turn on my heel and strut away, leaving them wide-eyed with mouths-agape. I grab our lunches off the table on my way out.

I make it to the executive elevators before the implications of what I did hit me. Thankfully, a keycard is required for access, so I'm alone on the ride up. I hold on to the railing for support, feeling like I might pass out.

Hold it together.

What was I thinking?

Joseph

I'm fuming. Michael confirmed, through system logs, that Alex did in fact read Samantha's email and even sent a response to Todd. But there was no action taken to fix the code, at least none that I can see. I can read code, but I'm not nearly as proficient as Samantha. I trust her instincts. I trust her brainpower, her integrity, and her desire to see something succeed over her desire to be recognized for that success. She's not in it for the glory, at least not the individual glory. She's in it for the success of the company as a whole.

I've just gotten Alex on the phone when Samantha sets my lunch on my desk. She's pale and avoiding eye contact. I go on alert. She halfheartedly smiles and slips back out as quietly as she entered.

That won't do.

"Ten minutes, Alex. My office."

I call my Managing Director. "Ron, could you be in my office in ten?"

He sighs. "Yes. Is this about Project Nemesis or a new issue?"

I shake my head, disliking that project name. *Nemesis* sounds so combative, nefarious. "Yes. I've asked Alex and Michael to join us."

"Michael from Security? Is that necessary?"

"It is. I'll see you shortly." I hang up, not willing to address nor justify my decision to have my head of security join us. I have many reasons, none of which are Ron's business.

Opening my office door, I see Samantha isn't at her desk, and her lunch is in the trash. *What the fuck?*

I pull it out and examine the contents. Her chicken salad sandwich is untouched.

Samantha returns looking noticeably better, but still not her vibrant self. She glances at the container in my hands and down to her trashcan. "It must have fallen," she offers.

Really? If she knew it fell in the trash, why wouldn't she pull it out? *Samantha, why are you lying to me?*

"What's wrong, Sweets?"

"Nothing. It's been a trying day." She maneuvers around me. "You'd better eat." Her eyes hit my chest as she sits and starts clicking her mouse. "I've got some resumes to look through. And don't forget your two o'clock," she dismisses me.

"Michael, Ron, and Alex will be here momentarily. Please send them in."

She visibly swallows. "Of course." Her response is clipped.

My glare would tell her I don't believe a word she's said if she'd only look up and meet my eyes.

Dismissed? We'll see.

My meeting is wholly uneventful and not nearly the tongue thrashing I anticipated giving. Once everyone is seated at the conference table in my office, Alex jumps to apologize before I can even voice my findings. A preemptive strike to my planned attack.

"I was wrong not to give Sam's concerns the due diligence they deserved. I should not have taken Todd's word that the issue had been resolved. Obviously, by this morning's failed demonstration, the program has not been fixed as I was led to believe." Before I can respond, he continues. "It's not an excuse. I'm the project manager and should have confirmed for myself the app was working as designed."

Ron jumps in. "We appreciate your candor, Alex. I would like one of our other programmers to take a look at the code and make the required changes." He looks to me. "I know Sam could do this, but since she's returning to school, I'd rather have a permanent employee who will be around to support it going forward and understands the changes needed. Would you agree?"

"Yes." I do agree, but it chafes me that he doesn't consider Samantha a *permanent employee*. She'll probably be his boss someday soon—at least if I have my way about it. "However, Todd needs to move on. An honest mistake is one thing, but purposely letting a project fail out of pride or misplaced resentment is unacceptable. MCI is a business that thrives on new blood, new ideas with fresh perspectives. There's no room for ego in product and development. If we need a little housekeeping to ensure our team remembers that, so be it. I expect this to be fixed by tomorrow morning. And Ron, I want a plan by the end of the week to ensure this type of talent subterfuge doesn't happen again."

I glance at Michael, who gives a stiff nod, acknowledging the topic we discussed earlier. I'm concerned Todd may be a problem for Samantha if he stays, and even more so if he goes. There is a darkness in his eyes that makes me uncomfortable.

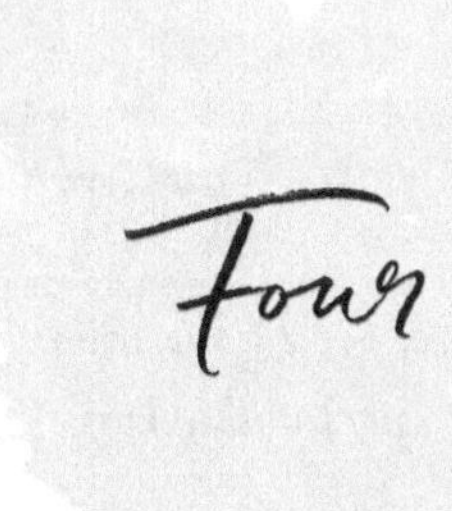

COME TO ME SWEETLY

Samantha

HONESTY. THAT WAS THE TEXT I RECEIVED FROM Joseph before he left for his last meeting of the day.

I've avoided him most of the afternoon, uncertain how, or even if, I should address what occurred in the cafeteria. I allow my head to fall back, and flex and stretch my shoulders. I need to work out. The stress of the day has taken its toll on my old shoulder wound. It aches, every throbbing pulse reminding me how precious and fleeting life can be.

Honesty. I have to tell him.

I make it through the last of the PA resumes HR sent up. I pick a handful I think will make a good fit and block time on Joseph's calendar to review with him in the morning. I can set up interviews from there.

At five, I pack up and shoot Joseph a quick text.

Me: *I'm heading home. See you at the bar?*

We have a standing Wednesday night get-together. It's primarily the Six Pack: Fin, Matt, Joseph, Victor, Michael. Jace used to be a part of the pack, but he's keeping his distance. Then there's me, Sebastian, and sometimes Margot. The attendees always vary, depending on schedules and who's in Austin at school. But since summer, it's become regular for the whole lot of us to make it. The guys, besides Joseph, don't usually bring dates. It's not a *date* kind of atmosphere. It's a hang-out-shoot-the-shit-give-each-other-crap-I-know-you-better-than-most kind of atmosphere. And it's a blast.

My phone chimes.

Joseph: *Michael will drive you. I'll meet you there.*

My protective man.

Me: *I'll take a cab. Or walk. God gave me two good legs for a reason.*

Joseph: *Yes, he gave you 2 spectacular legs. Fuck, now I have visions of them wrapped around me.*

Good. Maybe that will sidetrack his thoughts of me walking.

Joseph: *Don't walk. Michael is on his way to the penthouse.*

Me: *Caveman!*

Joseph: *Always, when it comes to my girl.*

I reply with a heart emoji and give up on trying to assert my independence. Michael is going anyway, so it's not like I'm a hardship.

As I push the button for the elevator, it dings and the doors open.

Michael. Standing there with a shit-eating grin. "Princess."

"Do I even want to know how you knew I was still here instead of on my way home?"

"No." His smile warms as I join him. "I'm sorry you had such a shitty first day as Joe's assistant."

"Thanks. It was one for the record books, I think."

He tilts his head. "What else happened?"

I hedge, not sure whether to temper my feelings about what happened today with Michael, or wait and unload it all on Joseph.

"Hey." He touches my arm. "You know you can tell me anything. I've always got your back."

I nod and blink away impending tears. I wish it didn't upset me so. "Did you know there's a betting pool on whether Joseph and I will get married?"

He scowls. "Who the fuck would make that wager? They obviously don't know you two very well."

"Maybe."

He sighs like a gale-force wind. "Please tell me you're not letting this get to you. It's crap."

"The pool's up to a thousand dollars."

"Maybe I'll bet against all those schmucks, then when you marry, I'll be a grand richer."

The doors open on the crossover bridge floor. I move to exit, but Michael grips my arm. "Wait." He steps out, placing his hand on the elevator door to keep it from closing and scans the area. Satisfied, he motions me forward.

We fall into step, Michael to my side with his hand on my back. "You know protocol," he softly admonishes.

"Why are you in protective mode?"

"Precaution."

We pass through the open double doors leading to the crossover bridge to MCI's Omega Tower. He stops me again to determine if it's safe to proceed; only then do we move on.

The hairs on the back of my neck prick. Visions of my father's killer flash before me. I take a cleansing breath and push them aside. I've spent too much time dealing with my self-doubt and fear to let it get the best of me now. "Precaution against what?"

"Todd, that asshole programmer, was fired today."

I stop in my tracks, halfway across the glass-enclosed bridge. "What?" I'm shocked, and yet I probably shouldn't be, given what he did and the menacing way he glared at me. Joseph wouldn't have taken any chances, not with MCI, and not with my safety.

Michael wraps his hand around my arm, looking around. It makes me nervous, so I start looking around—like *I* know what I'm looking for.

"Princess, you're making my job harder if you stay here in broad daylight in a glassed-in enclosure. We need to move."

"Precaution, huh?"

He smiles down at me as we walk to the elevators that will take us to the penthouse level. "Like I said, whoever bets against you and Joe getting married is an idiot. That man is not taking any chances with your life, and there is absolutely no way in hell he would ever break up with you."

"You would never assume I'd break up with him?"

He looks stumped like I just said something in a foreign language he doesn't understand. "No, of course you would never break up with him either."

"But that's not what you said."

"It's what I meant."

"You think, like those people betting against us, if anyone was going to get dumped, it would be me." Of course he does. Why wouldn't he? Everyone thinks that—even me.

I rush into the apartment, knowing good and well Michael will follow. Grabbing a water in the kitchen, I head to our bedroom, hollering over my shoulder, "Can you tell Joseph I'll see him later? I'm not going tonight." I slam the door behind me and lock it, knowing if Michael wanted to come after me, a locked door would not stand in his way.

"Dammit, Sam. Don't do this." He hits the door. "Please, I'm sorry. I didn't mean it the way it came out. You know I'm no good at this touchy-feely crap."

I stop. It's not his fault. I open the door. The big lug is nearly pouting. "Michael, it's been a really…difficult day. I'd like to punch the hell out of something, take a bath, and go to bed."

"Punch me," he eagerly offers.

He'd let me too—that is something Michael understands—how to punch, how to work out your frustrations on a punching bag or a willing sparring partner. "I appreciate the offer, but I'd really like to be alone."

"Please, Sam," he softly pleads.

I slip my arms around his waist and give him a hug that he quickly returns. He's been a great friend over the last nearly two years that I've known him. He's Fin and Victor's best friend, and Joe's good friend. He's essentially adopted me as his little sister, but one you treat well and take care of—not one you call names and dismiss. "Michael, I'm really not feeling up to it, and it's not really what you said. It's a culmination of all of it. I need time to unwind, clear my head, and distance myself from the emotions of it."

He tries to talk me into watching TV with him, or keeping each other company while we read our separate books. He's a book lover like me. He offers to spar with me, to pick up dinner, to even talk if I need to. But I finally convince him to go. I'm safe in the penthouse. There are no threats here, except for the negative voice in my head, threatening to undo all the progress I've made with believing I'm good enough for Joseph—that I'm enough for a man like him.

Joseph

The penthouse is quiet when I enter. Dropping my laptop bag and jacket at the entry, I make my way to our bedroom and quietly slip off my clothes, moving closer to the bathroom. The sound of water sloshing and the smell of vanilla tantalize my senses before I even see my girl luxuriating in a bubble bath. She slowly rotates her neck and stretches her shoulders on a deep sigh. The stress of today has taken its toll. As much as I want to absorb this moment of seemingly blissful relaxation, I know she's like a duck under the water—paddling and paddling to stay buoyant. She's not nearly as relaxed as the ambience suggests.

"Sweetness." I slip off my shirt as I enter.

"Joseph." The weight of my name, full of emotion, confirms I made the right choice to come home—to her.

"Is your shoulder giving you trouble?" It's rosier than her other one, telling me she's been rubbing it, trying to alleviate her discomfort.

"A little." She sits forward, her fingertips rimming the edge of the tub.

"Mind if I join you?"

She shakes her head but remains silent.

My boxer briefs, the last piece of clothing, hit the floor. I step in behind her. The water is nearly as hot and seductive as she is. I pull her close, wrapping around her like a barrier between her and the outside world.

She buries her head in my neck, whispering my name in sweet veneration.

"I'm here." My lips press to her cheek, her temple, anywhere I can reach without disturbing our embrace. "I'll always be here."

A tremor sends goosebumps rippling across her body with a small whimper. I turn her sideways on my lap, and her chest presses against mine. I hold her tightly, whispering to her as she slowly lets go and starts to cry. "You are the air in my lungs, the beat of my heart, the genius in my every thought."

She moans as if my words wound her, but I can't stop. She has to know.

"You are the moon to my night. The sun to my day. The fuel to my fire. There is no me without you." I kiss her bad shoulder, wishing my kiss—my love—could heal her shoulder and everywhere else she hurts. "Don't you know that by now? There's no one who can hold a candle to you. The world is a blur to me with my focus fully on you."

My hands find her shoulder and slowly go to work to loosen the strained muscles tightened with stress. She melts into me, holding me with more than her arms, every inch of us bonding to the other more deeply than the physical, more powerfully than the mind, more abundantly than the emotions. In this moment, we are untethered, yet bound only by our love—eternal.

As her tears wane and the water cools, I help her out of the bath, wrap a towel around myself, and tenderly begin to dry her off.

Her fingers snake in my hair as I kneel to run the towel down her legs. "How do you always know?"

Her trembling voice has me looking up into her water-cast eyes. "Know what?" I place a soft kiss on her stomach before standing.

"The right thing to say." She drops her hands to my shoulders, watching me intently as I continue to run the towel over every lovely inch of her.

I cup her cheek, my thumb grazing her bottom lip. "I tell you what's in my heart." Discarding the towels, I carry her to bed, lying down with her in my arms. "I don't want you to doubt the depth of my love. There is no time limit, no expiration date, no cause for termination. It is a permanent—beyond *death do us part*—soul-binding kind of love, Samantha."

She nods, her eyes welling up again. "It's the same for me." She kisses me sweetly. "It's always been forever for me," she breathes across my lips.

"Shh, no more tears." I press my mouth to hers, wanting to draw out her passion to still her emotions.

Once we're panting, and there's no sign of tears, I speak again. "Why didn't you tell me about what happened at lunch?"

"I wasn't sure how to proceed." Her head rests in the crook of my arm, and her eyes search mine. "I don't want to get anyone else in trouble. And it's entirely possible I'm blowing the whole thing out of proportion."

"If it upsets you, I *want* to know about it. No matter how small or inconsequential you may think it is. I don't want to hear from Michael how upset you are. He's a mess, by the way. He wanted me to apologize again for his careless remark." I smile, thinking of him storming in the bar, upset. It wasn't funny then, but the idea of my girl getting him so worked up was a sight to behold. The stoic Michael, brought to heel by my girl's hurt feelings.

"I told him it's okay. I know he didn't mean to hurt me with what he said. I'll talk to him tomorrow."

"You might want to call him tonight. I left him drinking at the bar with the gang."

"Lord. That man. He can't stop beating himself up," she mumbles as she reaches for the phone by the bed. She hits his number and puts it on speaker.

The phone only rings once before he answers. "Princess."

"Michael, what are you doing? I told you I wasn't upset with you, yet you send Joseph home to apologize for you like a pussy. What's up with that?"

He groans. "Why do you always cuss at me, Sam? And I'm no pussy. I was worried. You know I'd never mean to hurt you."

God, he's groveling. She's got him so wrapped around her finger, I think she could say *"jump"* and he'd ask *"how high, Princess?"* I'm not jealous. Michael's a stand-up guy and would never hit on another guy's woman. Plus, I'm pretty sure he sees Samantha more like a sister.

"I know, you big lug. And you know my insecurities around Joseph. You hit a sore spot that was already irritated. Okay?"

"Yeah, okay." He clears his throat. "We good?"

"We're good. Except I could use a good workout." She winks at me.
"Your shoulder?" he asks.
"Yeah."

"I'll be there at seven in the morning. Eat breakfast, drink lots of water, and be prepared to bring it. 'Cause you know this Weeble's not going down," he teases.

"It doesn't mean I won't try."

"I'm counting on it. G'night, Princess."

"Goodnight, Michael."

He hangs up, and she looks at me. "Satisfied?"

"Satisfied? Me?" I take the phone and set it back on its base. Rolling her to her back, I settle between her legs. "There are lots of things I love about you, but the fact that you don't let Victor, Fin, Matt, and especially Michael, intimidate you—turns me the fuck on." I flex my pelvis, rubbing my cock against her moist heat. "But as you can feel, no, I'm not satisfied."

"What do you need, Joseph?" The light in her eyes shimmers with mirth.

I run my nose along the column of her neck, breathing in her sweet scent. "I need to make love to you, Sweets." The hitch in her breath has me hardening further. "I also need you to promise that you'll come to me next time when you need support and validation of what you're feeling."

Her hand slides up my back and into my hair. "I'm sorry. I really was planning on talking to you, but I didn't want to do it at the office, especially after the day you were having with Project Nemesis. But you're right. I should have come to you sooner, or waited. I shouldn't have talked to Michael, at least not until discussing it with you first." She kisses my shoulder, her legs wrapping around mine. "Forgive me?"

"Forgiven. Always."

My adoring words from before are replaced by my desire to show her how much I love her and my need to connect with her—I let my body do the rest of the talking.

Our Yin and Yang.

Fire and ice.

Dark and light.

Feed and devour.

Mine.

Hers.

One.

Joseph

The next morning, I find myself staring out my office window, contemplating the resumes Samantha left me to peruse before we meet later this morning. When I left the penthouse, she was seriously working hard to take down Michael. If I didn't have such a busy day, I would have hung around to see how it played out.

My office phone buzzes. It's Fin's admin. "Good morning, Angela."

"Good morning, Joe. Fin would like you to come to his office."

Why didn't he call me himself or text? "Sure. Now?"

"Yes, please."

"I'll be right there."

"Thank you."

I freshen my coffee on my way to his office at the end of the hall. Angela smiles and motions me to go on in.

Fin's on his cell phone when I enter. He glances up with a grimace and turns his back to me. "It was great to see you." His voice is low, hoping I won't hear, I'm sure. He's quiet, listening to the other person talk. "Me too. I'm sorry I won't get to see you again before you leave. But…I'd like to…check in…see how you are from time to time." He laughs. "Yes, I'd like that." He clears his throat. "Joe just walked in." Silence. "I don't think that's wise… No rush. Take your time… Yes… Soon… Goodbye." His last words seem hopeful.

When he turns, I don't miss the wistful look in his eyes. I'm more than intrigued, but I need to move this along. "So, your phone's not broken, then?"

"No." He looks confused as he sets his cell on his desk and takes a seat.

I sit across from him. "Why the summons from Angela? A text would have sufficed."

"Sorry. My phone rang as I was getting ready to text you. I quickly asked Angela in my stead."

Sounds reasonable. "What's up?"

"I heard about the bet going around MCI. Is Sam okay?"

All these guys protective of my girl warms my heart. "She is now." I'd already filled him in on the project issue and firing yesterday, even though it's my department. We always share challenges, especially firings, across business units to keep us informed, consistent on best practices, and to stay on top of trends.

He nods. "I'm glad. Let me know if I can help."

"Is that it?" I stand.

"No." He glances to his open door and back to me. "Who's the blonde?" he asks matter-of-factly.

With a scowl, I sit back down. "What blonde? Where?"

"At the bar. Last night. There was a blonde all over you before Michael pulled you away." He's full of censure.

"Brother, are you accusing me of something?" Agitation courses through me as I stand, leaning forward, matching his glare.

He slowly rises and walks around his desk, leaning his hip against the side and sliding his hands in his pockets. "Do I need to?"

"No!" I step back, thinking about last night. "There was a group of British tourists. A few of the women got a little tipsy. They asked for selfies with me. You know…" I stand up straight and pose like a GQ cover model with smoldering sexuality. "Pics with the good-looking American to show their friends back home."

He laughs. "Fuck. Don't ever do that shit-ass pose again. You look like an asshole."

I punch his arm. "You're just envious 'cause I'm better looking than you."

"Whatever." He pushes away from the desk. "I'll walk you back to your office." I join him as he strides past Angela's desk. He's pensive. "It looked like more than that."

I stop, forcing him to turn and come back to me. "Fin, they were drunk. Maybe a little too touchy-feely. The whole thing lasted like two minutes. It was a blip in my crazy day yesterday. Was one of them a blonde? Yeah, maybe. I really couldn't tell you what any of them looked like. It was so inconsequential, I barely remembered it happened." He nods. "The wager about Samantha and me, please tell me you're not buying into that crap about me not being able to be faithful."

He steps closer, placing his hand on my shoulder. "I don't." His eyes reflect the truth in his words. "It looked bad, though. The blonde was hanging on you, and you had your arm around her waist. I didn't see any selfie action, or much attention from the other girls. I might have missed it, but if Samantha had walked in at that moment, it would not have been good. You're a friendly guy, Joe. You're no longer the college kid who's everyone's best bud. You're a Vice President of one of the largest companies in the US. You have an important, prestigious job. There will be women who will seek you out because of it. You need to be prepared to respond to it quickly, efficiently, without drawing undue attention."

"Shit. You're right." I should have stepped away. The minute their hands touched me, I should have removed myself from the situation. I shake my head and look to my PA's desk, not fifty feet away, where Samantha will be sitting shortly. "I wasn't thinking. I was trying to be nice, accommodating. It seemed harmless, but I can see from an outsider's perspective it was anything but."

We move toward my office. "I'm glad you understand. Next time you'll be prepared." He stops at my door after I enter. "And make no mistake, Joe. There *will* be a next time. Lydia and the chick from last night are only the tip of the iceberg. Some will be innocent, others calculating. And the fact that you're taken, and not interested, will only make you more of a challenge."

"You're a ray of sunshine today."

"Do that pose you did earlier—you'll scare them off." On a chuckle, he heads back to his office, leaving me with visions of women chasing me down the street trying to get selfies.

"Fuck," I mutter, shaking it off, and get back to work.

ADD TO MY ABUNDANCE

Samantha

THE FIRST WEEK AS JOSEPH'S PA IS BEHIND ME. I managed a little wedding planning with Joseph's mom, Fiona. We finalized everything for the rehearsal dinner, wedding ceremony, and only a few things remain in flux for the reception. Joseph is handling the honeymoon. It's coming together more quickly than I thought and more easily than anticipated, but I know that's because of Fiona and Jackie, our wedding planner.

As for my replacement as PA, thank God, we narrowed down the prospects, interviewed potentials, and…WOOHOO…he picked one. I tried not to give my opinion when it came down to the final two. Joseph is the one who has to live with the decision, not me. I had influence over the applicants, but I didn't want the burden of the final choice. Thankfully, though, he picked the one I wanted. The one I would want as *my* assistant should I ever need one.

I knock on Joseph's open door before I enter.

"Baby, you don't have to knock. I told my last assistant my wife has precedence above all else. Do I need to reiterate that fact with you too?" The edges of his mouth twitch, trying to suppress a smile.

"Yes, Mr. McIntyre, I believe I do need a refresher on the importance of your *wife* in the hierarchy of your priorities." I close the door behind me, locking it.

He raises his brow at the sound of the click. He slowly rises from his desk. "Is there a reason we need privacy for this discussion, Miss Cavanagh?"

"I thought it best, given the nature of the topic."

He stops directly in front of me, as close as he can get without touching, his hands buried in his pockets. "I see. And what topic are we discussing, exactly?" His green eyes gleam with possibilities.

"You requested an item be added to your schedule last week, and given that I begin training my replacement tomorrow, I believe today is the last day I have full control over what items appear on your calendar." I trail my finger along his abdomen above his belt. His muscles contract, and his breath hitches.

"It appears we have two items on the agenda then? The priority of my wife—"

"Yes." I love that one. I can never hear that enough.

"—and the other item, Miss Cavanagh?" His eyebrow arches. "You'll have to remind me." He presses closer, his erection fully present now.

"Perhaps you'd like to sit in your desk chair? This is your office, after all. You should have the seat of authority for this agenda item."

He grabs my hand and pulls me behind him as he moves to his chair. "I believe that position of authority applies to both agenda items. Please remember that. I am the utmost authority when it comes to my wife and the importance she holds in my life."

"Joseph." I break our role-playing personas. Even playing, my caveman holds me in such reverence.

He turns and cups my cheek tenderly, leaning forward and whispering against my lips, "You are my world, Sweetness." His eyes search mine, and with a slight nod, he waits for my confirmation.

I nod and swallow around the knot in my throat. "Sit," I whisper, having trouble slipping back into my role. I really just want to sink into his lap and let him love me.

He does as I ask, and also what I want, by pulling me down with him. "How long do we have, baby?" His voice is strained with need.

"Not long enough." I kiss his cheek and take a moment to relish the feel of being in his arms. On a sigh, I stand.

He reluctantly releases me, his hands grabbing onto the arms of his chair.

I clear my throat and square my shoulders. "Mr. McIntyre, we don't have time for more than this."

"Perhaps something could be rescheduled." He's serious.

My man. He knows me so well, better than I know myself. I will my love to show in my smile—he lightens me. I kneel before him. "Oh, no, Mr. McIntyre, that won't be necessary. It won't take me that long to bring my agenda item to conclusion." I smirk, thinking I'm so clever.

"Miss Cavanagh, I hope it will be a very happy ending." He shakes his head in amusement. He's as silly as me sometimes.

I rise, trailing my hands up his thighs, butterflies fluttering in my stomach. I want to make this good for him. Memorable. "I hope so too."

His fingertips trail along my jaw, and he tenderly lifts my chin. Green eyes overflowing with love stare back at me. "Always," he whispers, sensing my uncertainty. His warm lips press to mine. "You don't have to do this. It's okay."

I don't want him to think that. "I want to." My hands find his belt and get to work freeing his erection from its confinement while my eyes stay on his. "I'm nervous. Ignore me."

He chuckles. "Miss Cavanagh, rule number one of *my wife takes priority*, is I never ignore her." His breath catches as I stroke his freed cock.

"I never ignore her needs…" He groans as I lick his length. "…her wants and desires." He struggles to speak as I wrap my lips around its head and suck.

"Christ," he exclaims as I take him deep.

His hands white-knuckle the arm rests as his head falls back. "Fuck. Yes," he chants as I increase my tempo. His words give way to moans and sighs of pleasure.

Watching him fall apart, giving himself to me so completely, turns me on and makes me want to please him all the more. I stroke him in time with my mouth. His hips flex and still, fighting his desire to thrust. He's letting me give him this pleasure instead of taking it from me—from my mouth.

"Fuck, baby, I'm gonna…ah!" He groans as his body jerks, and he comes. "Yes, Sweets…fuck."

Languid and satisfied, he collapses in his chair. I sit back on my heels, out of breath and throbbing with need. A dimpled smile spreads across his face. "Miss Cavanagh, you surprise me. You're timid one moment and a succubus the next."

"Are you complaining, Mr. McIntyre?" I wipe my lips and under my eyes, fearing I look as undone as I feel.

"Hell no." He finishes tucking himself in his pants and pulls me into his lap. "I'm the luckiest man alive." His hand trails up my thigh.

I swat at him. "We don't have time."

"Nah uh, this is not a one-sided deal here. I come. *You* come." I struggle, but he stills me with a single look. "My wife takes priority." His lips graze my neck. "Now spread those sweet thighs and let me in."

I shudder and suck in a breath as anticipation tingles through my body. I comply as he situates me so that I'm sitting on his lap, my back to his front, my head on his shoulder, and my legs dangling over his—spread wide—my skirt up to my hips. "That's better." His lips trail up my neck as his hand slips inside my panties. "Fuck, Sweetness. Always so wet for me."

I moan.

"Shh. I know. We're in no rush remember? You're my priority." His finger enters me, and I instinctively thrust to take him deeper. "My creed." Another finger slips inside and begins to move in and out. "My heaven."

I can't stay still or stop my sighs of pleasure. His words as much as his body are going to make me come.

The hand around my waist slides up my body, slipping inside my blouse and bra, and squeezes my breast, tantalizing my nipple. Shamelessly, I roll my hips, riding his fingers, and push my breast into his hand.

His warm breath skates my ear. "You're making me hard, Sweets, watching you make love to my hand." He bites my ear lobe and squeezes my nipple, sending pleasure straight to my clit. I cry out, and he does it again. "As soon as you come, I'm burying my cock deep inside you and we're gonna do this again. I want to watch you writhe in my arms as you ride my cock."

"Oh, god."

His palm presses on my clit as his fingers increase their tempo. "I need you to come for me, baby." He squeezes and pulls on my nipple, sending me over the edge with explosive force. His arms hold me as I shake and tremble. "My girl." He kisses the side of my face and down my neck. "My beautiful girl."

I'm spent. Somehow, Joseph maneuvers us to the couch, slips his pants and underwear to his feet, and his cock inside me in one quick motion.

I shake and clench around him with aftershocks of my orgasm.

"Christ, you feel good." He was serious—he wants me in the same position—my back to his front.

He sets the pace, grinding his hips, his finger on my clit, a hand on my breast, and our mouths captured in a deliciously slow kiss as if we have all the time in the world—but we don't. I sever our kiss and glance at the clock. "Joseph, you've got to pick up the pace. You have ten minutes."

"That's plenty of time, baby."

No. No it's not. "Harder." I brace my bare feet on the edge of the couch—*Bare? When did he remove my shoes? And hell, where're my panties?*—and my back against his chest, lifting my lower half, giving him room to move. "Harder."

His growl tells me he's not happy, but as he pounds into me, the growl that follows tells me how very much he likes the idea. "Fuck." He pants.

Each thrust hits that magical place inside, and I cry out, biting my lip to stifle my outburst. He places one hand under my thigh, helping me meet each thrust in counter motion. His other hand snakes around to rub my clit.

The smell of sex, the sound of our bodies joining, our combined groans of pleasure, and the feel of him pounding into me sends my mind whirling and my orgasm climbing. "Joseph," I call out, my legs shaking with fatigue.

"Go, baby. I'm right there with you," he rasps in my ear, increasing the pressure on my clit. "Take it."

And I do, in a cataclysmic explosion that makes me lose all control of time or space. All I feel is Joseph's arms around me, protecting me, soothing me as I violently contract around him, taking him with me, hearing him moan his release in the recesses of my mind.

Minutes, hours, millennia pass. I come back hearing Joseph on the phone. "Charles, I need to reschedule."

I try to lift off the couch, but it's of no use. I'm like a cracked egg on a hot Texas sidewalk in August—fried. What the hell was I thinking?

"I'll get you rescheduled… I appreciate it… Thanks." He hangs up.

I hear the padding of bare feet and manage to look up. Joseph comes into view in his boxer briefs, nothing else.

"Where are your clothes?"

He grabs a bottled water from his minifridge. "I was burning up. I had to strip before I passed out." He kneels next to me. "Here, baby, drink." He helps me sit up and slides in next to me, pulling me against him as I guzzle half the bottle. He finishes the rest.

"What the hell happened?"

His chest rumbles with a chuckle. "I wore you the fuck out—correction—we wore each other out."

"Oh, god. We can't keep doing this in your office."

He sighs. "Sadly, you're right."

"Shit. Your meetings," I panic.

His hold on me tightens. "Cancelled."

"All of them?"

"Yep."

I relax into him. "We really can't keep doing this."

"Nope." He kisses my brow. "But I wouldn't trade this for anything."

An hour later, the sun is setting, and we're still lying on his couch. The last part of his afternoon is a bust, but it's been nice stealing these precious hours alone, the two of us, before his new assistant starts tomorrow, and I start school next week.

"I'll miss this." I turn to face him. "It was nice having this last week and a half with you, even though we were working. It felt like we were a team."

His hand caresses my hair. "It was nice. We work well together." He presses his lips to my forehead. "We're still a team."

"You know what I mean."

He smiles. "I do. It gave us an idea of what it'll be like once you graduate. You by my side—*not* as my assistant," he clarifies adamantly. "We'll be an unstoppable team."

"I think I like the sound of that."

I'm graced with his sexy dimpled smile. "Really? Because I'm serious. I want you by my side, not working four floors away from me, where I only get to witness your brain at work during staff meetings. I want you. By. My. Side."

I lift up and kiss him softly. "I got it, Caveman. You want me by your side."

"You're okay with that?"

"Joseph, you know I love watching you work too, and I'd be honored to work for you in whatever capacity you feel I'll most benefit MCI. And if that's by your side or in the mail room—I'm all in."

"Christ, I love you, Samantha." His lips crash over mine. "So…so fucking much."

"I'm glad it's mutual. I'd hate to be in this alone."

"Don't even jest." He frowns.

I laugh and touch his cheek. "I'm not kidding. I'd be lost without you. I'm the luckiest woman in the world. You love me mind, body, and soul. And I'm honored to be the recipient of such love."

"Sweetness." His voice cracks.

With a quick kiss and a moment of staring into the green eyes I love so much, I pat his chest and sit up. "Now, take me home and feed me. I'm starving."

"Miss Cavanagh, you're awfully bossy on your last day as my PA."

"You'd better get used to it. I have a feeling Teddy is gonna whip your ass into shape," I tease as I start to get dressed.

"Hey, I think my ass is in fine shape."

I swat it as he walks by. "Yes, Mr. McIntyre, that is a mighty fine ass."

Hand in hand, we make our way home. Luckily, it's only two private elevator rides and a crossover bridge away. Why did I ever think I wouldn't want to live so close to work? This is a dream. I need to apologize to Joseph for being such a baby about it when I first came to stay with Fin.

"Have you talked to Margot since she's returned to Austin?" Joseph brings me back to the present.

"Oh, shit! I forgot to tell you. I saw her. Here. Leaving MCI twice last week. I can't believe I forgot to tell you."

"When?"

"Thursday morning—the day after happy hour and my meltdown." I blanch at the memory. "I was late that morning because I worked out with Michael." I stop on the crossover bridge and point down to the curb, past the main entrance of Alpha tower, the tower we just left. "She was there, getting in the car with Victor."

"Victor?" He's surprised.

"I thought maybe I was imagining things, that it was someone who looked like her, until I saw her again on Friday afternoon. She was walking to her car. I know it was her because it was loaded down for her drive back to Austin."

"Shit."

"What?"

"Fin."

"Fin?"

"Yes, Fin." He pulls me along as we continue home. "I knew it!"

"You knew she was here?"

"No, Sweetness. I knew he had a thing for her. He has since he met her nearly two years ago."

"Really?"

He looks at me sideways. "Don't say anything. Let them tell us. Maybe it's merely a hookup."

"Maybe it's love. Oh my god!"—I tug on his arm—"She could be my sister-in-law."

"Don't get all worked up. It could be nothing."

"Or it could be something." My smile nearly cracks my face.

He pulls me into the elevator that goes directly to our penthouse floor. "You're so cute." He kisses my nose. "You want everyone to find a love like ours, don't you?"

I throw my arms around his neck. "I do. I really, really do."

His arms wrap around me, pulling me close. "So fucking cute," he breathes across my lips.

Joseph

I'm wrapping up a conference call when Samantha knocks on my door, slipping inside and closing it behind her. I want to chastise her for knocking, but I'm struck dumb by the goddess in front of me in a black fitted skirt that flares at the bottom and has a ruffle that cascades down the right side. If she's wearing a shirt, I don't even notice as I can't get past the come-hither sway of her hips and the sight of her gorgeous legs in black pumps with a little strap around the ankle.

Fuck me. My dick gets hard.

"It's a damn good thing Teddy's here. If you wore that skirt yesterday, we would have lost more than the afternoon fucking in my office."

She giggles as she rounds my desk. "We wouldn't have been able to do what we did yesterday in this skirt." Her skin pinkens at the memory.

I stand and press her to me, my hand gripping her ass as I trail a finger down her cheek. "Believe me, I would have found a way." Her eyes flicker with want—want that I cannot satisfy—at least not now. On a sigh I step away, returning to my chair. "Sadly, that will have to wait."

She bends, holding on to the arms of my chair, and presses her lips to mine, softly, tenderly, pulling away all too quickly.

"Fuck it." I grab the back of her neck and pull her back to me, consuming her delectable mouth, urging her into my lap. But she resists, pushing away and stumbling back. I grab her hand to steady her.

"Shit," she sighs.

"Yeah," I groan.

She motions to the door. "Uh, I really came in to tell you that Teddy is here. I…uh." She runs her hands down her skirt, her blue eyes searching mine. "Shit, Joseph, you've scrambled my brain."

I throw my head back in a laugh. "I know the feeling. At least you don't have a raging hard-on."

She shakes her head. "No, but I may have to run home to change my panties."

With a growl, I stand, hovering over her. "You're killing me, Sweetness."

Her hand presses to my chest. "I'm sorry. Think of baseball and puppy dogs or whatever you men think about that is totally not sexy."

My girl is cracking me up. "See, the problem with that is, I think of baseball—I think of you in a baseball jersey, little shorts, and a baseball cap on your head. You're cute as fuck, and I just want to sink into you."

Her breath catches, and she whispers my name.

I fall back into my chair. "Now, puppies. That should be a safe topic, but then I see you on the ground, laughing and playing with this little fur ball that's jumping around and licking your face." I sigh and rearrange my junk to make room in my pants. "You're cute as fuck—aaand I just want to sink into you."

Her soft giggle has me smiling. "I love you, baby, but you've got to get out of my office, and don't tell me about changing your panties while I'm working."

She's still laughing as she heads to the door. "Oh!" She snaps her fingers. "-I remembered. Do you want to meet with Teddy before I start training him?"

"Yes, but not with you." I point at her, motioning her out of my office. "Go change your panties or whatever you need to do. I don't want to see your sexy ass before lunch." My firm voice softens as I remember. "We *are* still having lunch together today, right?"

A mischievous smirk overtakes her face. "Meet me at home." On that, she exits my office, closing the door as she goes.

Great, I'll never get rid of this hard-on, thinking about what she has planned. I adjust my pants and command my body to heel.

Teddy knocks on my door a few minutes later. "Good morning, Mr. McIntyre. Sam said you wanted to see me?"

"Good morning, Teddy. Yes, please come in." He closes the door behind him, which pleases me that I didn't have to ask.

Once he's seated, I get right to the point. "I know Samantha will show you the ins and outs of the job and how I like things to work, but she won't tell you these things."

He nods slowly and opens his tablet to take notes.

"It's important to me that you and I work as a team. What happens in this office, stays in this office. No gossiping about what you hear, see, or presume. Respect, trust, loyalty, and diligence are key in your role as my assistant. I will, in turn, grant you the same. This team,"—I gesture between us—"this partnership, if you will, can only succeed if we both hold up our end of the bargain." I pause, letting his fingers catch up to my rambling. Once he looks up, I continue. "This is a family business— *my* family's business. We are vested heart and soul in this company, our employees, and the success of both. However, because we are related, the normal family dynamics do seep their way in occasionally, and you will be privy to things you might not otherwise know. Discretion, Teddy, is very important to me."

"Of course. Absolutely," he responds while still typing.

"Good. Any questions so far?"

"No, sir."

"When it's only us, you can call me Joe, if you like."

"Thanks, I'd like that." He smiles and his shoulders visibly relax.

Am I making him nervous?

"Now, for the main reason I asked you in here alone." I glance at the door, envisioning Samantha on the other side, or maybe she did run home for that change of panties. *Damn! Now, I'm getting hard again. Shake it off, man.* I stretch my neck and stand, pacing to the window. "Samantha is my life. She is my number one priority. If she calls, you put her through. If she shows up, you let her in. There is no reason, ever, to keep her away from me or my office. If she asks you for something, you do it." I face him, meeting his gaze. "She. Is. My. Priority. Understand?"

His eyes are wide with surprise. "Wow."

I chuckle. "Don't get me wrong, this job, my family are important too. But none more so than my wife."

His brow furrows. "I thought you weren't married…yet."

I wave him off. "Semantics."

He laughs. "Okay. I get it. I'm on board."

I think he'll work out just fine. "Excellent."

Samantha

I ring Joseph's office line. "Sweetness." The warmth in his voice spreads all over my body, and my skin ripples with goosebumps.

"Hey, Caveman," I whisper, my heart reacting to the mere sound of my lovename on his lips.

"Don't start," he gently growls.

I shiver and shake my head. "I'm not. Honest. I hate to interrupt your meeting with Teddy, but your nine o'clock is here."

"Thanks. When Teddy comes out, you can send them in."

"Great. Thank you."

"Always." His animal magnetism comes through the phone line and wraps around me, heating me to my core.

I hang up on a sigh. *My man.* I can't laze around in the visions he sparks. I've work to do. Movement in my peripheral reminds me I'm not alone. I walk over to the gentlemen waiting. "Mr. McIntyre will be with you in a moment. Can I get you something to drink while you wait?"

The tall, lanky one jumps to his feet, awkwardly sticking his hand out. "H…Hi. I'm Gregory…from…from robotics."

I take his proffered hand, my brain lighting up. "Robotics. Wow. It's great to meet you. I'd love to come down and see your lab sometime. That is, if it's not an inconvenience. I wouldn't want to stop the progress of genius."

"Really? You're welcome anytime." The other guy in the ill-fitting suit and friendly smile offers his hand. "I'm Jackson."

It's funny they think they have to introduce themselves, like I don't know who they are. When it comes to next gen robotics, these guys are *it.* They're famous—at least in the tech industry. Their combined brain power could probably light up both MCI towers alone. I stop fangirling long enough to shake his hand.

"You're Sam Cavanagh, right?"

"Yes." I'm shocked. "How'd you know?" The thought that they know me from the rumor mill/betting pool has me wanting to slink away.

"Samantha." Joseph's voice shivers up my spine. He's walking toward us with Teddy in tow. Joseph shakes Gregory and Jackson's hands with a warm greeting. "I'm sorry to keep you guys waiting." His eyes lock on mine as he places his hand on my lower back. "I see you met our robotics team." His smirk tells me he knows how much I loved meeting them.

Gregory speaks up. "I was about to tell Miss Cavanagh—"

"Sam, please," I insist.

"—uh, yes…Sam…" He looks between Joseph and me, finally settling on me. "We know who you are because you wrote an integral piece of code last summer that breached the gap in the robotics program, allowing it to become fully integrated into 1025D."

I'm both delighted and confused. "1025D?"

Jackson jumps in. "That's the name of a confidential project we can't really talk about." He smiles in apology.

"Huh, and what happened to 1025A, B, and C?" I tease, knowing they can't tell me.

Jackson and Gregory exchange a knowing look. "That's confidential," they chime.

"Anyway, we'd be honored to have you visit our lab anytime." Jackson looks to Joseph. "Pending your approval, of course."

"Approved." Joseph advises without hesitation. "Email Samantha the NDA beforehand." His hand slips around my waist and squeezes lightly. "Gentlemen, please have a seat in my office. I'll be right there."

The robotics twin gods say their goodbyes and head off to Joseph's office.

"Teddy, would you mind heading down to Starbucks and getting us two iced coffees? Get anything you want, as well. Oh, and one of their cinnamon crumble muffins." He flashes me a smile. It's my favorite. I guess I'm in for a treat. "Charge it to our MCI account. Call Samantha if you have any trouble."

"Sounds good. I'll be back." Teddy dashes to the elevators.

"You cleared the floor rather effectively, Mr. McIntyre. Any particular reason?" I tease.

He pulls me into his arms, his forehead resting on mine. "To tell you I love you." He kisses my head and smiles. "And to tell you I love hearing my robotics guys fawn all over your brain."

I can feel the flush creeping up my neck. "Please. Those guys make me look like a kindergartner."

He shakes his head. "Still. They were impressed with you. You have to come see me after you visit their lab. I don't want to miss the all-cylinders-firing-lightshow look you'll be bursting with."

I giggle. "That's quite a look. Deal."

"I gotta go. Love you, Sweets."

"Love you, Caveman."

He moans and kisses me quickly before pulling away. "Have Teddy bring in my drink when he returns. Enjoy your muffin." He backs away.

"Do you want me to save you some? And why don't you want me to bring you your drink?" I frown.

He rakes my body as if I'm standing before him gloriously naked. "Baby, if you come into my office looking like that, sashaying like you do, neither I nor the robotics twins will be of any use. And no, I plan to eat my favorite muffin later." He winks and leaves me throbbing in his wake.

Shit. Now I really need that change of panties.

NEVER BE THE SAME

Samantha

I HAD A NIGHTMARE LAST NIGHT. I HAVEN'T DREAMT about my father and Rodrick, his killer, in a long time. I'm not even sure when the last time was. A heavy weight lingers like a cloak of darkness. As if my injured shoulder is truly bearing its weight, the ache is more prevalent today. A constant reminder of my waking with a scream ringing in my ears and Joseph wrapped around me like the safe vessel he is. My constant, my barometer, my guiding light showing me the way home—to him.

When he proposed six months ago, I was shocked and yet surprised he'd waited so long. I knew he wanted to ask sooner, but he gave me the time I needed to grow into our love and come to truly trust him as *the man* in my life who would never leave me. Who would never abandon me for something better. Who didn't think there were greener pastures than the one he's cultivating with me. *I'm* his greener pasture, and he's my horticulturalist. *I'm* the one he wants. The one he desires. The one he looks at with love and reverence. As remarkable as it still seems to me, I'm the *one*.

And he is, most definitely, the one for me. But he always was. From that breathtaking moment when we first met to every moment that followed, he is my other half, my protector, my champion, my caveman.

He tugs on my hair as he passes the dining room table where I'm supposed to be studying. School started a week ago. "What's got you lost in thought?"

I meet his gaze over my shoulder. "You."

His dimpled smile says he's pleased. "Oh, yeah? What about me?" He pivots and joins me at the table.

I blush at the memory. "Your proposal."

He lights up like the beacon he is, proud and confident. "You liked that, huh?" He scoots closer, leaning in, his arm over my chair, his fingers running along my nape. "What was it you liked best? Jumping from the waterfall hand in hand? Sailing the Caribbean at sunset? The moonlit dinner on the beach? Or making love in our oceanfront cabana?"

My dreamy mood lingers as the memories come flying back. "Those were all amazing. Each and every one." I lean into him, take a deep breath, and allow the tantalizing smell of him and the memories of our trip to swirl around me like a warm ocean breeze. "It was a great vacation." I squeeze his thigh under the table. "You've set a high standard, Caveman. Do you think you can top that for our honeymoon?"

"Abso-fucking-lutely."

I laugh and stand, holding out my hand. "Come." He takes it without question and follows me to the couch. We sit side by side, me tucked under his arm, looking out over the brilliantly lit-up downtown skyline. "All of that was amazing. But none of those are my favorite moment."

His hand runs up and down my arm. "No? What was?"

"Do you remember at the airport when that guy bumped into me, scattering my purse and all its contents across the floor?"

"Yeah," he says with confusion.

"You grabbed me, ensuring I was steady on my feet before kneeling down, handing me my purse, and then you carefully picked up and handed me each expelled item, giving me time to place them back in my purse where they belong—instead of simply scooping it all up in your big hands and dumping it in my purse like a trash bag."

"Okaaaay."

"Then each and every day you carefully, dutifully, covered my body with sunscreen to ensure I didn't burn. You kept a water bottle by my side and fresh fruit within arm's reach to ensure I didn't get dehydrated or hungry."

"Rubbing your body with suntan lotion was purely selfish on my part." He winks when I look up at him.

"And then there was that fateful day we tried street food, against your better judgment." I shudder at the memory. "I was so sick. Luckily, you weren't, but you didn't write me off to go play in the sun and sand. You stayed by my side. Held my hair when I threw up. Carried me back and forth from bed to bathroom when I was too weak to do it myself. Bathed me. Tried every trick in the books to keep me hydrated. Held me through my fever and clammy night sweats. You gave me everything I could ever need without even having to ask."

"Who would leave you to be sick on your own?"

I chuckle. "I can think of more than a few I'm quite sure would've been out snorkeling or jet skiing—any place other than stuck in a hotel room with their sick girlfriend."

"Fiancée," he corrects.

"I wasn't your fiancée yet."

"You've been my fiancée since I slipped that promise ring on your finger." He kisses my head and squeezes me. "You just didn't know it."

I laugh and adjust to face him. "My sweet Caveman, you've had it all figured out from the beginning, haven't you?" He nods with certainty. "You've been waiting for me to catch up?"

The back of his hand sweeps the side of my face, anchoring at my nape where his thumb continues to caress my jaw. "And I would wait for an eternity, Sweetness."

I lean into his touch, believing he would. "And that brings me to my favorite moment of our trip." His eyes light up as if he can't wait to hear it. As if he doesn't already know, but I'm not sure he knows *why* it's my favorite moment. "You could have proposed in any of the amazing places we visited: the sunset sail, the romantic dinner on the beach, the waterfall before we jumped."

I smile at the memory of him diving under the water, after we jumped, to find me. I hadn't come up right away. I'd gone deep, pulled out of Joseph's grasp by the impact of our plunge. I wasn't hurt as he feared, I was simply enjoying the peaceful moment—the elation of jumping and then the feeling of weightlessness as I slowly rose to the surface—that is, until Joseph grabbed me by the waist and hauled me up, as fast as he could, with a look of pure panic on his face when we broke the surface.

"But you didn't do it in any of those places. Instead you took me to the highest peak, on the highest island, where we met the dawn and ushered in a new day by you getting down on bended knee, pledging your love for me and endless days of sunrises and sunsets—together. Where you said it didn't matter where in the world we lived, where we worked, where we traveled, whether we had kids or not, whether we were rich or not. All that mattered to you was that I was in your world—for I *was* your world. Your. World." My voice cracks. I'm still amazed.

He tenderly wipes away my tears as they fall. His lips kiss along their trail. "You are my world. I breathe for you. My heart beats for you. My every thought, every emotion, every action, are with *you* in mind."

I nod, wiping at my tears as my chin quivers. "But I didn't truly believe it until that moment. I knew I would love you forever, Joseph. I knew it to the core of my being, with every fiber of my body—I knew you were *it* for me." I hold his open palm against my cheek, cradling it with my hand. "You told me over and over again how you felt. But it was something about that moment, the stillness of the morning, the purity of the new dawn breaking, the earnest sincerity of your words, and the light shining from your eyes. It finally clicked—you love me, truly, deeply, eternally—just like I love you. It wasn't one-sided. I didn't imagine it, or embellish it. Your love is true, honest, and pure. And that was the moment I knew I was *it* for you."

"Yes, Sweetness." He pulls me into his lap. His lips find mine before raining kisses all over my face and neck, burying his head in my shoulder. "Why didn't you tell me? I would like to have known, to experience that epiphany with you."

I shrug. "I needed to live with that revelation a bit, let it take root and grow." I pull away, finding his face streaked with tears. "Oh, Joseph. I'm sorry. I think mostly I'm ashamed it took me this long to get where you are." It's my turn to wipe and kiss away his tears. "We were always on the same page, on the same journey, except my self-doubt kept me from seeing you right there—next to me—at the same point in time that I was. We were always in sync. I was too blind to see it."

"But now you see me?" His soul, his heart is wide-open for me.

"I see you, Joseph. I see the love reflected in your eyes is the same as mine. We are one hundred percent in this together."

He smiles mischievously. "One hundred and fifty percent, Sweets."

I press my forehead to his. "Yes, one hundred and fifty percent to infinity."

"Infinity," he breathes.

"Infinity." My love.

Joseph

The days that follow come and go quickly, with a natural rhythm I haven't found before. I'm lighter: an unrecognized weight has been lifted by the knowledge that Samantha knows I'm not going anywhere. It's more than that, though. It's that there is an equality now. A balance has been reached where she knows she's the one for me, just as I've always known she was it for me. I'm sorry it took her six months to tell me, but I believe that for her, it took that long for the knowing to work its way to the surface, fully vested and indestructible.

Teddy, with his cock-sure way about him, has been a godsend. He's working out better than I could have hoped. Samantha comes in a few days a week after class to touch base, answer his questions, and fine-tune any processes he doesn't fully understand or believes could work better.

I step out of my office when I hear her laugh. She's early. I still as I spot her leaning on Teddy's desk, her face lit up with amusement, her shoulders shaking with laughter.

Teddy spots me and stiffens. "Sir."

"Relax. I never said you can't have a little fun," I respond to Teddy. With a nod and a smile, I move to my girl. "You're early."

She slides to my side as my arm wraps around her waist. "A little. My last class ended early. My professor had to be somewhere, and his TA didn't show up." She shrugs. "Lucky for me."

I kiss her temple. "No, lucky for me." Her smile widens, and I feel it in my cock.

"Actually, it's lucky for me. I need your help on that spreadsheet I mentioned. I'm hoping you'll have time to look at it." Teddy brings us back to reality.

Samantha gives me a quick wink before turning her attention to him. "Of course. Does he have a few minutes before I get started?"

"Don't talk about me like I'm not here," I grumble.

"Hush. Let Teddy do his job, which is to handle you and keep you on track. I don't want to mess that up."

I shake my head and walk to my office, knowing I have seventeen minutes before I need to leave for my next meeting.

"He has seventeen minutes," Teddy confirms.

"Great. I'll be right back." She enters my office and closes the door.

I'm leaning on my desk, my arms crossed. "You could have asked *me* how much time I had."

Her smile softens as she sashays toward me in black jeans, boots, and a sweater. My girl loves her black. "Don't pout. You only have a few minutes." She throws her arms around my neck, forcing me to uncross my arms. "Wouldn't you rather spend that time kissing me hello?"

I grip her waist, brushing her lips with mine. "For the record, I don't need anyone '*handling*' me, except for you."

"Duly noted." Her eyes crinkle with mirth.

Enough teasing. I need these few precious moments with my girl. I kiss her slowly and tenderly, savoring her taste, the feel of her in my arms, and her sweet sighs.

With a heavy sigh of my own, I pull back, resting my forehead against hers. "Tell me you'll go home after helping Teddy and get all your homework done. I'm going to need a bit of your time when I'm there."

She smiles. "Only a bit?"

"Okay, hours. I'm going to need hours of your time." I slip my hand between her jean-clad thighs. "Fuck, I can feel your heat." She grips me tighter as my hand slides back and forth. "I'm going to need hours loving you, Sweets."

Her head falls against my chest. Her breathing increases, and I have visions of her nipples hardening in anticipation of my touch.

"Ah, fuck, baby, I can't wait."

"Wha…" her response is lost in the sound of me undoing her jeans.

I slip my hand inside, cursing the tight fit of her sexy-as-fuck jeans, but manage to slip two fingers inside her.

"Oh god," she moans.

"Look at me." I grip the back of her neck. Her face rises to meet mine with eyes shining with need. "There's my girl." I pump my fingers in and out, my palm rubbing her clit. "Do you hear that?" I breathe against her lips and then move to her ear. "Your wet pussy pulling my fingers back in."

She moans, her breath licking at my ear.

"You make me so hard, baby. I want to sink into you and feel you squeeze my cock like that, sucking me back in over and over again."

"Joseph." She trembles and tightens her hold on me.

"I want to feel you come all over my fingers." I pump faster, my breath quickening, my heart pounding. If she touches my cock, I'll come like a teenager in my pants. "When I get home, I'm going to take you against the wall, bent over the couch, on the kitchen counter, on the floor, pressed against the penthouse windows. Wherever I find you, that's where I'm taking you, Sweets." She shudders and clenches. "I want to give this to you, but you make me so fucking hot, I want to tear your clothes off and fuck you right here."

"Yes!" rips from her lips as she comes undone.

I wrap my arm around her, holding her up. "My girl, how I love to see you fall apart for me."

My desk phone intercom beeps. "You have ten more minutes. Your father's meeting is running late." Teddy's voice sends a reprieve.

Thank fuck, we have more time.

Before I can respond or stop Samantha, she's on her knees,

unleashing my cock. "Baby." I try to tell her that's not necessary. I need the ten minutes to calm the fuck down.

"You're so hard." She looks up at me, all eyes and innocence, her cheeks flushed from her orgasm.

And fuck if I don't want her mouth on me more than my next breath. "Make it hard and fast, Sweetness." I touch her cheek. "I won't last long." With a sweet smile that belies the act she is getting ready to perform, she licks the cum off the tip. "Ah, fuck." When her mouth consumes me, I lean against my desk, gripping its edges, and let my head fall back. "Fuck, yes, like that."

She takes me deep, so fucking deep. Her hand pumps my shaft as her tongue flicks over the underside before she sucks me back in, over and over.

I look down, my hips thrusting, her head bobbing, her hand pumping. It's all too much, and yet it's not nearly enough. "Stop."

I lift her off the floor and swivel, pressing her to the wall, her back to me. "Hands on the wall." I push her jeans and panties to her ankles. I spread my legs and bend my knees, position my cock. "Hold on."

"Yes." She gasps as I fill her up.

Her wet heat swallows me, squeezing me like I knew she would, like she does every time. "Fuck, Samantha, my love. This is gonna be fast and hard. Are you okay with that?"

A tremor runs through her body. "God, yes."

Thank fuck.

I grip her hips and thrust. The feral groan that escapes my mouth is sure to be heard down the hall, but at this moment, I can't give a fuck. My girl calls my name, and I do it again and again, pounding into her, relishing the sound of our bodies joining. Mating. Doing what we were meant to do, becoming one. The perfect design of yin and yang. My cock to her pussy.

Pounding.

Pounding.

Pounding.

She tightens and grips, squeezing and milking me as she comes, sending me over the edge with her.

I groan as I pump into her, leaving my mark, my soul, the very essence of who I am. All for her.

With a quick kiss, I leave Samantha recovering on my couch, locking the door behind me. I send Teddy on an errand to give her more time. I catch up to Fin and Matt on my way, which is no great feat considering we work in the same wing.

"Did I hear you're flying to Austin tonight?" Matt asks Fin as we wait outside of Dad's office.

I perk up at that notion. "Austin?"

"And where did you hear that?" Fin deflects. He glances at me and does a double take, his eyes squinting, giving me a once-over.

Shit. Can he tell I just had sex? I fight the urge to squirm under his scrutiny.

"From Monica," Matt affirms.

Fin frowns but looks away. I silently sigh in relief. *Have to stop having sex in the office.*

"And who did Monica hear that from?" Fin glances at his phone before looking at Matt.

"From Angela." Matt smirks at me with a wink. He's messing with Fin, like I would if I had heard that news first.

"Hmm. I would think our PAs have more important things to do than gossip about my travel plans."

"So you're not denying it?" Matt pushes.

"No."

"Would your visit have anything to do with a slight brunette who's been spotted visiting MCI before returning to Austin a few weeks ago?" I can't resist pushing him a little. Though, I can't push him too hard, or he might call me on my shit I'm quite sure he's aware of—or suspects.

Fin's eyes widen momentarily before he regains his composure. "I'm not sure who you're referring to." He scowls at me again for good measure as censure for conspiring with Matt.

Deny. Deny. Deny. He's not ready to talk about it. That's obvious. With a shrug and a quick glance to Matt, I change the subject, focusing on the topic at hand—second quarter earnings and third quarter projections. This is in Fin's wheelhouse and a much safer topic by the way he jumps right in and visibly relaxes into the discussion.

We're an hour into our two-hour earnings meeting when I get a text from Samantha.

Samantha: *Can you let me know when you're out of your meeting?*

Me: *Anything wrong? I can step out.*

Three dots bounce on the screen, disappear, start again, then disappear again. Either she's distracted or she's contemplating her answer, which means it's *something*. Finally, she responds.

Samantha: *No, don't do that.*

She didn't say there wasn't anything wrong—which means there is.

Me: *Where are you?*

Samantha: *Finish your meeting. I'll be home when you get there. It's not urgent.*

I can barely concentrate the rest of the meeting. Fin keeps eyeing me, which brings me back to the here and now. The moment the meeting is over, I head to my office, picking up my laptop and a few reports before advising Teddy I'll finish up at home.

"Goodnight, Joe. Enjoy your evening." His smile is bigger than it should be, making me think he knows what happened earlier in my office. Well, he'll have to get used to it. I'm sure it won't be the last time, despite my best intentions.

Samantha is coming out of the bathroom, wrapping a towel around her body, head down, when I enter the bedroom. Her wet hair is clipped up high. Drops of water cascade down her shower-warmed skin. She's beautiful, all undone, not a stitch of makeup, only her angelic face, tender curves, as beautiful on the outside as she is on the inside. My Sweets.

She stops cold when she sees me, eyes and lips puffy. She's been crying.

"What's wrong?" My instincts were right, I should have come home the moment she told me not to. Dammit!

Her eyes dart to my dresser. "That came today. Addressed to me." Her voice shakes with emotion, ripping at my heart.

I step closer, pulling her to my side as I reach for the piece of paper sitting on top of the dresser.

He's mine. You'll never make him happy.
Leave now and I'll play nice.
Stay and you'll wish you'd taken my advice.

Sincerely,
The ONE Joseph really loves

What the fuck? Anger rages through me. "Where did you get this?"

She pulls back, reacting to my anger, her eyes big, scanning my face, trying to read my thoughts. "It was in the mail. Teddy handed it to me before I left."

"Did he see it?" That came out way too accusatory. Fuck!

"No!" She steps back, extricating herself from my grasp. "I didn't read it until I came home." Her head tilts, piercing me with her glare. "I texted you right after."

"Fuck." My head falls forward, and I grab the back of my neck. "I'm sorry." I look up to see tears staining her cheeks. I rush to her, wrapping her in my arms. Thankfully she doesn't resist. "Christ, you know it's bullshit, right?" Her whole body sags against me. "I'm sorry. I'm not angry at you. I'm angry at the situation." I cup her head to my chest and kiss her wet hair. "I'm not angry with you," I whisper, my lips still pressed to her hair.

She simply nods and squeezes me tightly.

"It's probably some jackass trying to win that stupid bet. Trying to get you to break up with me by a certain date so he or she can win," I offer the first solution that pops into my brain.

"Maybe it's Lydia," Samantha pipes in.

Christ. "Maybe it is." I lift her chin. Her eyes lock on mine. "It's not true. Tell me you at least know that much."

She nods. "I don't believe you'd cheat on me."

I sigh in relief. I knew she knew that, but I had to be certain. "Why the tears then?"

Eyes cast down, her shoulders rise and fall. "It makes me question if I'm enough."

The sorrow in her voice squeezes my chest. "Samantha."

She pulls out of my embrace. "I know." She sighs, starting to pull clothes out of drawers. "It's old news. It's *my* old news." Clothes gathered in her arms, she looks at me pleadingly, sad. "It feels like the world is conspiring against me, against *us*, continually ripping off the scab of my insecurities as soon as I start to heal and feel confident."

After the events of the past few weeks, I'm not surprised. First it was Lydia, then the bet against us, and the overheard discussion about me never being satisfied by only one woman, and then Michael's poorly worded comment making her feel like she was the one who would be dumped- if it happened—not me.

I open my arms. "Come here, baby."

She doesn't hesitate. She drops her clothes and walks right into me, wrapping herself around me as I do the same. "We'll figure out who sent it." I kiss her swollen, soft lips. "I don't want you to give it another thought." My lips brush hers again. "I need you to listen to me, focus on my words— the *only* words that matter."

Her lips curl in a seductive smile. Her eyes shine with love as she waits patiently.

I walk her backwards. "You own me. Heart and soul. Mind and body. Everything I have, everything I am, everything I will be—is yours. There is no *me* without *you*. No other women even exist for me. They are monotone shades of gray compared to your shining, all consuming incandescence."

Her smile falters when the back of her legs hit the bed, startling her.

Slowly, I release her towel, letting it fall to the floor. "I will love you to the end of time, Samantha." My arm around her back, I gently lower her to the bed. "Every inch of you inside and out is my heaven, my sanctuary."

"Joseph," she gasps, bowing off the bed when I draw a taut nipple into my mouth and suck deeply.

I repeat my ministrations on her other succulent peak as I work to remove my tie. Her nimble fingers work to free my shirt from my pants. In moments, it's discarded, and I settle myself over her, bare chest to bare chest, my hard cock straining against my slacks, pressed between her legs. "My world, my life, is yours."

With racing breath, her lips find mine, her tongue pressing for admittance. I gladly let her in, taking all she has to give and returning it with equal vigor.

"Mine," she growls, coming up for air.

"Fuck, yes," I agree with relief to see the sadness gone, replaced with desire and possessiveness, making my steel-hard dick throb with the need to claim her as mine, too. I want to claim her, love every silky inch of her with my mouth, but my need to mark her with my cock wins out.

"Finally," she exclaims when I'm naked and pressing into her.

"My greedy girl." I sink in to the hilt, reveling in her gasps of pleasure, and still. Our gazes lock, her panting breath wafting over my face. "This, Samantha, is my favorite place. I love you in all things, in all ways. But here—buried deep inside you—is where I find my solace, my home, my respite. When we make love, I'm not a McIntyre, an heir to a Fortune 500 company. I'm not a VP. I'm not a son, a brother, a friend. All I am at this moment is a man, *your* man, making love to *his* woman, trying to express with my body the depth of my love and devotion."

"Joseph." She trembles below me, squeezing me tightly with her legs, her arms, and her pussy as tears stream down the sides of her remarkable face. "You make me feel like I could fly." Her chin trembles, and tears continue to fall into her wet hair. "Like I'm somebody special."

My heart bursts. "Christ, Samantha, you *are* somebody special. You're *my* somebody special." I grind my hips, pressing into her slowly and deeply.

She cries out, already so close. My words, my love, taking her faster than my body can alone.

"Fly for me, Sweets. I'll be here to catch you when you land."

Seven

DANCE IN MY DARKNESS

SEPTEMBER

Samantha

'M UNRAVELING. JOSEPH HAD TO LEAVE TOWN FOR four days for a tech conference in Las Vegas of all places. Sin City. Before he left, it had been three weeks since that fateful letter arrived. We'd moved beyond it, quickly falling into our normal stride, the letter all but forgotten. Michael is looking into it, but other than that, I haven't heard any further news. Joseph didn't want to leave, not because of the letter, necessarily, but because neither of us wanted to be apart for four days. In the big scheme of things, it seems silly. It's only days, not weeks.

In Austin, I had Joseph and Margot to hang out with. Jace was there, but we only saw each other occasionally. Being back in Dallas, going to school at SMU, has been an adjustment without Margot. And now that Joseph is gone, I'm feeling lonely, but it's good for me to re-member what it's like to hang out by myself. I used to do it all the time. Four days is no big deal. Plus, I have Michael if I need anything, and

I could always call Sebastian, though he's been picking up extra shifts and hasn't had much time to hang out lately.

The day after Joseph left, I received a package. There's no return sender, but I assumed it was an early wedding present. A few have been trickling in now and again. Inside the box was Joseph's blue tie. The one he bought to match my eyes. It was such a sweet, thoughtful gesture, and then there it sat in a box.

I pushed it aside and found a note.

This is as tame a package you will receive.
Leave now and I won't be forced to take this any further.
He's mine. Leave.

Sincerely,
The ONE Joseph thinks about when he's fucking you
P.S. Loving Vegas!

I gripped the kitchen counter, my stomach churning. I tried not to give its words life, meaning in my head, but it was hard to ignore.

How do I know it's Joseph's tie? I rushed to our closet to see if his was still there.

I didn't find it in our closet.

Like his father and brothers, all of Joseph's ties are handmade silk with his initials stitched into the back. I turned over the tie in the box, praying I didn't find what I was looking for, but right there in perfect calligraphy stitched letters was JPM. Joseph Patrick McIntyre. How did she get Joseph's tie? When was the last time I saw him wear it?

P.S. Loving Vegas.

He's not cheating on me. She's not there. She wants to put doubt in my head. Play with me. She's succeeding!

All those thoughts swirled in my head, and when he called that night, I feigned a headache so he wouldn't know something was wrong. I can handle this. I trust him. It can wait. If he knew another package came, he'd screw up his trip to fly home to make it right, to ensure I know it's not true. My heart *knows* it's not true, but it's his tie—his tie for *me*. How did *she* get it? Whoever the hell *she* is.

True or not, someone is fucking with us. And this someone is capable of getting hold of such a personal item and knows Joseph is in Las Vegas. This is not good.

For the next few days, I go to school and back. Bury myself in my studies and help Teddy when he needs it, but with Joseph out of town, he doesn't seem to need much help. When I talk to Joseph, I make it short and sweet, trying not to give anything away, keeping the conversation on him and what new technology caught his eye. It's not hard for either of us to get lost in tech talk.

"Are you sure you're okay, Samantha? You seem a little distant." His low voice makes the ache in my heart that much worse.

"Yeah, I'm just busy with school and tired. I haven't slept well with you not here." All of that's true. I don't tell him that the thoughts racing around in my head are contributing to my lack of sleep.

"I miss you."

"I miss you too." Madly. Deeply. Truly. Heart-wrenchingly miss him.

"I can't wait to see you tomorrow. I'm going to devour you as soon as I see you."

"I can't wait." I squeeze my eyes shut, tapping my forehead, trying not to think about the letter. *Signed, the one Joseph thinks about when he's fucking you.*

No! He's not interested in anyone besides me. I won't let her get under my skin.

"Oh, I have that thing with my mom tomorrow. So, I'll see you when I get home." I'd completely forgotten about it. Jace and I are supposed to join my mom for a family counseling session. I'm dreading it nearly as much as showing Joseph the package.

"That's right. Do you want me to meet you there? I could cut out of the afternoon session and catch an earlier flight so I can go with you."

"No. Don't miss the end of the conference. I'll see you when I get home."

"Are you sure?"

"Positive." No, I'm not sure at all. But it's the right thing to do, to say.

"Okay. I love you, Sweets."

"I love you, Caveman."

"Bye, baby."

"Goodbye, Joseph."

The silence that hangs in the air after I hang up is stifling and eats away at my confidence to remain silent. I can't tell anybody about this. I promised Joseph I would come to him first, but I can't tell him now and mess up his trip. It can wait. I'll survive.

I combat the loneliness with working out. After I change, I head to our ensuite gym. I could go to the Omega Tower Gym two floors down, but I don't need fancy equipment. I only need the treadmill and blaringly loud music to beat the thoughts out of my head and exhaust my body so I can sleep.

Tomorrow.

He'll be home tomorrow.

Joseph

My intuition is screaming at me. *There's something wrong.* But I choose to listen to what Samantha is telling me. She's not being distant. She's tired and missing me. I can relate. I haven't slept well since I've been gone either. I miss *her*, but I also miss her sexy body pressed against me all night long, reminding me what my dick was made for. I head home tomorrow, and I can't wait.

It's the last full day of the conference. Tomorrow morning, we have meetings scheduled with a few tech companies that have promising products I'd like to acquire. These are not the products we saw during the dazzling expo. These are the little-known hush-hush products that are not quite off the ground and might be a few years away from the marketplace. Now is the time to secure and foster them to fruition.

Whether that means partnering with them or full acquisition remains to be seen.

I meet Charles and the rest of my team for a strategy planning breakfast before we tackle today's full agenda.

Securing my seat at the head of the table, I address the team. "I won't be in the main session today, so I'll rely on you to be my eyes and ears." I get a few questioning looks, but I go on to explain. "I'll be attending a break-out session with other leaders in the technology industry, brainstorming what we can do to reduce our carbon footprint by minimizing the fallout when our new tech becomes legacy."

"Everything is about becoming green," Jackson mirrors my thoughts.

"Exactly. We need to leave the world a better place than how we found it, which includes not leaving our new inventions to be shipped off to other countries to be burned, scrapped, and piled into already overflowing landfills when they become outdated," I recap.

That leads into ten minutes of them giving me their ideas, which ends up giving me some great feedback to take to the session. Once these guys get going and their free thinking is set loose, it's hard to wrangle them back in. Their neuropathways ignite as ideas are tossed back and forth to each other like a technology round of hot potato, moving faster and faster until they're all lit up like a nuclear Christmas tree.

I love my job.

By the end of breakfast, everyone understands their mission for the day and what needs to get done in preparation for tomorrow's meetings. As my phone vibrates in my pocket, I grab my stuff, say my goodbyes, and head out to find a quiet place to take this call.

"Tell me." My mind is going a million miles a minute, racing with thoughts of Samantha mixing with those from my stimulating breakfast.

"Morning to you too, boss."

I sigh, knowing I need to reel it in. "Good morning, Michael. What did you find out?"

"She received a package a few days ago."

My heart sinks. *Samantha, Samantha, Samantha. What are you doing, baby? Honesty. Remember?*

"What kind of package? Do you know what's in it? Did you talk to her?"

"From the security footage it looked to be the size of a shoe box. She didn't mention the package. Therefore, I don't know what's in it. I assume you don't want me to ask her about it."

"No. I'll address it when I get home tomorrow. I don't want to upset her any further by discussing it over the phone." I slip back into my hotel room, deciding I need a few minutes to regroup before continuing my day. "Did she seem upset when you talked to her?"

"We didn't really talk much. You know how she is when we spar. She gets pissed she can't kick my ass. So, yeah, a heart-to-heart wasn't likely to happen." He lets out a punch of air. "But she did seem a little somber. I'll see if I can get her to hang out with me tonight if you want."

"Everything else on the security footage looks okay? Nothing out of the ordinary? Nothing suspicious from Lydia? No Todd? She's safe?"

He chuckles. "Man, how much coffee did you have today?"

"It's not that…I just…" I pace to the window and look out over the Vegas strip, wishing more than ever I could have convinced her to come with me. "I hate being away from her. Her inner demon gets the best of her when she has too much time to think."

"And you're not here to ground her, reassure her."

"Yeah, that too." Most definitely that. If I could touch her, hold her, look into her eyes, I could chase away those evil demon, self-doubting thoughts of hers.

"She's safe, Joe. Nothing seems out of the ordinary, except for possibly the package. But even that could be nothing. It could be wedding stuff. It could actually be a pair of shoes."

"Maybe, but my gut is telling me otherwise. Plus, she wouldn't have shoes delivered to the office."

We talk for a few moments more before I have to head downstairs. It's going to be a long day. I was excited after my breakfast, but reality is bringing me back to the here and now.

And the here and now is telling me to get my ass back home.

Samantha

A horn blast startles me. I look around to be sure I'm not the offending party. The light is still red, and I'm not the only one not moving. So, yeah, I don't know what the honking was about. I can't even determine who it was that honked in the first place.

I check the clock on the dash and sigh. *Come on, come on, come on.* I urge the light to change. I'm late to meet Joseph's mom for an early dinner before meeting Jace and my mom for our joint therapy session. Now, that appointment I wouldn't mind being late to, but I don't want to cut my visit with Fiona short. She's been more than supportive during this whole drama with my mom and Jace. Not to mention her guidance and support during the wedding planning process.

At the time of my high school graduation last year, I'd finally realized I wanted nothing more than a future with Joseph. A future that would eventually make me an official member of Joseph's family. The support they all showed me after my father's death astounded, humbled, and endeared them to me. Though I was still trepidatious, I think if Joseph hadn't asked me to marry him, I would have asked him. The idea of not being in his family for the rest of my life was unbearable. They became my family. Joseph's dad, Hugh, could never replace my father, but he's come pretty darn close. Fin and Matt are like brothers to me. And Fiona, well, she's more than my future mother-in-law. She's become my confidant and strongest supporter, besides Joseph.

A break in traffic gets me to the restaurant only a few minutes late. I spot Fiona the moment I enter. "Ah, Sam, aren't you a sight for sore eyes." Fiona gives me a warm smile and an even warmer hug. Pulling back, she grasps my shoulders, taking me in. "You look beautiful, but tired. Are you working too hard and not getting enough sleep?"

I laugh. "Are you saying I look like crap?"

"No!" she adamantly exclaims. "Tired. That's all." She sits, motioning me to do the same. "You have a beauty that comes from within, so no matter how tired you are, you'll still shine like no other."

Jeez, she's gonna make me cry. "Fiona, now you're going overboard." It's obvious where Joseph gets his silver tongue from.

Thankfully, the waiter interrupts us for my drink order, and, since I'm short on time, we order dinner as well.

Once he leaves, her focus is back on me. "How are you, really?" The tenderness on her face and in her voice allow for nothing but the truth.

Not all the truth, though. I can't tell her about the letters. If Joseph wants her to know, that's up to him to tell her, but I can't imagine he'd want his parents to know. I'm not even sure if anyone besides Michael knows. I take a sip of water and reply as openly as I can. "I'm tired, and I miss him." My eyes start to well up with tears.

"It's hard to sleep when he's not there beside you, isn't it?"

"How'd..."

She merely smiles and pats my hand at my surprise. "I can't sleep when Hugh is away either. Honestly, once the kids were old enough, I started traveling with him whenever I could. It was easier on both of us." She looks off as if remembering something fondly. After a moment, her gaze meets mine. Her eyes are dancing with memories. "I think it was good for our marriage too. They say absence makes the heart grow fonder. And in some cases, I'm sure it's true. But for us, the quiet time we had together, away from our normal routine, was far more valuable to our marriage."

Fiona and Hugh have a great marriage, much like the one my parents had. She's blessed, and I know she values it even more after seeing how my father's death has impacted my mother.

"What else do you know was good for your marriage?" I'm anxious to hear all the sage advice Fiona has to share. After all, hers is a living example of what a successful one looks like.

She lights up, welcoming the opportunity to share. Before Joseph even proposed to me, Fiona told me how much she and Hugh enjoyed having me around. I was the daughter they never had. I doubt any of her sons would ask her for such advice, and she's relishing every moment as much as I am in hearing it.

The dinner with Fiona was wonderful, relaxing, and filled up those empty holes in my heart left by my mom's absence, as well as my dad and Jace's.

On the other end of the spectrum, this session with Mom and Jace only seems to deplete the warmth Fiona instilled and replace it with dank, darkness.

"Sam, I'd like to start with you this time. Give you a chance to voice how you're feeling, tell your story since your father passed."

I open my mouth to speak, but nothing comes out.

"Why don't you start with your relationship with Jace?" Dr. Weston gives me an encouraging smile, looking between Jace and me.

Dr. Weston isn't messing around. We didn't ease into the issue of my own flesh and blood cutting me off at the knees when my dad died. I thought we'd only be dealing with my relationship with my mom since he's her therapist and not mine or Jace's. Apparently, he feels differently.

Jace is as flustered and as surprised as I am to be the topic of discussion. "I thought we were going to focus on Mom and her recovery," he asks.

"This is part of Eleanor's healing process. She needs to understand how your father's death impacted the two of you. She needs to hear it from your perspective, in your words." Dr. Weston types on his tablet before looking at me expectantly.

"How can she not know how his death impacted us?" My eyes dart to my mom. She's silently looking out the window as if I'm not even here. "Our father died, and you abandoned us too." I thought I'd cry, but anger seems to be the driving emotion at the moment. "It doesn't take a genius to figure out that it sucked."

Dr. Weston doesn't bat an eye. "That's a good start. Let's narrow down the *sucking* and discuss specifics. Tell me about you and Jace."

Jace's sorrowful blue eyes meet mine. I don't look away, I don't hide. It's time to give him a chance. A *real* chance. "Jace has apologized. Many times, in fact. He wants to make amends, but I haven't really been open to him." I face Jace on the couch we're sharing. "I want to make things right with you. I'm afraid. I don't want to get hurt again." I hastily swipe at my tears. Next to Joseph, Jace is the most important person in my life. He's my family, and based on the fact that my mom hasn't even acknowledged my presence—he's going to be my *only* family.

He grabs my hand and pulls me into a hug. "I'm not going anywhere. I swear, Sam. I'm here to stay. I'll do anything to be a part of your life again. Give me a chance. I won't let you down. Not this time."

The anguish and sincerity in his voice knock down my defenses. "Okay."

He pulls back with a hopeful smile on his face. "Yeah?"

"Yeah."

Dr. Weston is pleased with our interaction and encourages us to be patient with each other, as reconciliation doesn't happen overnight. It's a process that will have hiccups along the way, but open communication and forgiveness will make it a smoother road to travel together.

He moves on to the topic of my mom. "Jace, I'll ask you the same question in a moment, but I'd like to continue with Sam." He motions to me. "Please tell your mom what this last year and a half has been like for you."

I really don't want to go there. I've worked hard to push down these emotions of inadequacy, of not being enough for my mom to want to stick around and be a parent. Mom sits across the room, facing Jace and me. Her gaze hasn't left the window since I walked in the door. Jace was already here when I arrived, so I have no idea if she speaks to him when I'm not here.

"I feel like an orphan. Abandoned by my family. Dad didn't have a choice when he died." That's not true. "I guess he did have a choice. He chose to protect me, and in doing so, he was shot. His choice was selfless." I've tried so hard not to think about that day, not to second guess what I could have done differently. *If* I had done anything differently, would it have made a difference? "But, Mom, your choice to leave me was selfish. You left me alone to deal with the fallout of Dad's death, not only emotionally, but everything. The money. The house. Bills. Everything fell on my shoulders. Even taking care of you."

"Eleanor, how do you feel about what Sam's shared?" Dr. Weston asks.

"Sam, I'm so sorry." Jace takes my hand and holds it tightly as both he and I wipe at our tears.

Mom, on the other hand, can't even look at me. She wipes at her tears with a tissue, but remains silent. That's all I've gotten from her for over a year now. Not. One. Word.

I wait, glancing at the clock, and when five minutes have passed and her tears have ceased, I reach my breaking point. I squeeze Jace's hand and give him a nod and a quick smile. "Jace, I'm willing to talk with you whenever you want. Call me, come over. Whenever."

More tears slip down his pain-ridden face as he looks at me with regret. "I'd like that. I'll call you tomorrow."

I turn my focus to my mother for a moment before looking to Dr. Weston. "I'm sorry, but I can't do this anymore. If my mother truly wants to make amends, then I'll come back, but until then, I'm done."

With a succinct nod, he replies, "I understand. I appreciate you trying." He shakes my hand as I stand to leave. "I'll be in touch," he says before turning his focus to my mom.

Jace and I hug, and then I slip out the door. I don't know if he'll stay. Perhaps she'll talk to him. At the moment, though, I'm finding it difficult to even care.

Tears block my vision, making it nearly impossible to find my way. I manage to exit the building, only progressing a few steps before I hear him.

"Sweetness."

"Oh, God, Joseph." I all but crumble to the ground. Joseph's quick reaction saves me as he sweeps me into his arms.

"I got you." He holds me tightly, one arm below my legs and the other around my back, anchoring me to his chest.

I hold on to him for dear life, giving in to the grief, and let go.

His lips press to my head as he whispers, "Christ, baby. I got you. Shh, I got you."

Joseph

I don't know what the hell happened in there, but I'm angry as fuck to see Samantha hurting so deeply. I cut my meetings short, leaving my team in Vegas to do what they've been trained to do: seek, find, acquire. I've never been so thankful that I listened to my gut and came home to meet her at the care facility where her mom has been staying.

Once we're sitting in the back of the SUV with Victor at the helm and Michael in tow, driving her car, we head home. I hold her for the entire ride with no desire to ever let her go. Her crying has stopped, and I can feel her drifting off to sleep.

The forty-five minute drive feels like a lifetime. I don't try to wake her once we pull into the garage. Victor grabs her purse that I leave on the seat as I slip out with her cradled in my arms.

Michael parks in her space and grabs her belongings from the car. I stop cold when I see a box tucked under his arm.

"What the fuck is that?" I whisper with clenched teeth, determined not to wake Samantha.

"It was on the hood of her car," Michael replies with concern written all over his face.

I tremble with rage at the idea of her being alone, coming out in the condition she was in, and finding that box sitting on her car. A person can only take so much. I'm worried she's reaching her tipping point, and this box might put her over.

"Fuck," is all I can manage.

With a knowing look to Michael, Victor hands over Samantha's purse and leaves us to head up to our penthouse. I have no doubt Victor is heading to Fin's for a tumbler or two of Fin's cherished 1939 Macallan.

I manage to settle my girl on our bed without waking her. I turn on a lamp in the sitting area of our suite, in case she wakes up and is confused about where she is. Shutting the door behind me, I head back to Michael, whom I know is waiting.

I find him in the kitchen, eyeing the package and drinking a beer. Without even looking, he hands me an opened bottle of Heineken. He pulls a knife out of his front pocket.

"We can't open it." I move toward him, placing my hand over his.

He scowls. "Why not?"

"Because it's not addressed to you or me," I state the obvious. "But also because she needs to trust us not to hide anything from her." I take a long pull on my beer.

He sets his knife down and leans back against the counter. "What if it's a bomb?"

I grimace at the thought. "Do you think it's a bomb?"

"No." He drinks his beer, his eyes studying me. "She needs 24/7 protection." He points his bottle at the box. "Whoever delivered that followed her tonight, left it, and I imagine they stuck around to be sure she found it."

"Shit."

"It's escalating. The first two came to the office, but this one was delivered personally."

"You know about the box?"

We both whip around to see Samantha standing in the living room.

"Wait? *First two*? That sounds like there's been more than two." She moves closer and stops, waiting for a reply.

I close the distance between us. "There was a box on the hood of your car tonight. That makes three."

"What?" She steps back, fear written all over her face. "No, that can't be." Her head shakes. "No."

"Baby." I pull her into my arms, hold her tightly, and kiss her temple over and over again. She's shaking. "It'll be okay, Samantha. I've got you. Michael's got you. We won't let anything happen to you."

Calmer, she looks up. "So, you know about the first box, the second delivery?" Her eyes bounce between Michael and me.

I cup her cheek. "I knew something was wrong. You've been off for days. Michael checked the security footage and saw Teddy hand you a box."

"Oh." She steps out of my arms. "That makes sense." She turns and walks down the hall toward our bedroom.

I glance at Michael, who simply raises his eyebrow at me, but remains silent.

Samantha comes back a moment later, stopping in the living room with an identically sized box in her hands. "I didn't want to tell you about this over the phone. I didn't want to ruin your trip. That conference only comes once a year, and I know you had big plans for it."

"I understand that, but you should have gone to Michael. That's why I left him here, to be sure you remained safe and had someone to rely on if you needed it."

"We agreed I'd tell you first." She glances at Michael, who's still in the kitchen watching us, before meeting my eyes. "You didn't like it when I went to him first about the office betting pool."

I grip the back of my neck and squeeze. "You're right. I'm sorry. From now on, if you can't tell me, you tell Michael. What matters is not who hears it first, but that you tell someone and don't have to deal with this on your own."

"Okay." She glances between me and Michael. "Where's the other box?"

She's calm, no longer upset. Is it because she's truly okay, or is she only worn out from earlier? I point to Michael. "It's in the kitchen."

With a nod, she gives me the box in her hands. "I guess you'd better open this first."

I take the box from her, grab her hand, and join Michael in the kitchen.

"Before you open it," she says. "I want you to know that even though I'm confused on how the item in that box could be there, I don't believe what the letter says."

Fuck. What the hell could be in this box? "Okay." I kiss her forehead. It's good to know her faith in me hasn't been broken.

I start to open the box, but freeze when Michael hollers, "Stop." He looks around the kitchen. "Let's be smart about this. Sam's fingerprints are already on the box and its contents, right?" He looks to Sam, who confirms it with a single nod. Michael finds what he's looking for and pulls out box of Ziploc baggies. "Put this on your hand before you touch anything on the inside."

With the box on the counter and my right hand in a large baggie, I awkwardly open the box, revealing my blue tie. "Hey, I've been looking for this."

"You have?" Samantha's worried eyes meet mine.

"Yeah, I haven't seen it in weeks. I can't even remember the last time I wore it."

"You're sure it's yours?" Michael chimes in.

"It has his initials on the back," Samantha says. "And his is missing from the closet. I checked."

I turn it over, and sure enough, JPM is stitched into the back, like all of my custom ties. "Yep, it's mine." I drop it and look at Samantha, her blue eyes locking on me. "I bought it because it matches your eyes. I only have one this color, like I only have one of you."

A single tear drops down her cheek. "Joseph." She snuggles into my side.

"Only one of you, Sweetness."

Michael clears his throat. "That's really touching and all, but could we move this along? I'd really like to get this other box opened sometime this century."

He's right. "I'm sorry your tie got tainted by all of this," I say to Samantha as I reach in to pull out the note. Her response is lost on me as I fume at the words on the page. "What the fuck?"

"It's worse than the first one, huh?" Samantha says.

I read it again before showing it to Michael. As he reads it, I finger her chin, guiding her face to mine. "It's total bullshit. You know that, right?"

"I know."

"There's nobody but you."

"I know."

"There sure as fuck wasn't anybody with me in Vegas."

She places her hand on my chest, soothing the beast in me. "I know."

"You know?" I need her reassurance.

Her smile is unexpected but wholeheartedly welcomed. "I know, Joseph." She pats my chest. "I trust you. I believe you. I don't know how she got your tie, but I'm sure there's a logical explanation. We just haven't thought of it yet."

"God, I love you." I hold her against my chest, ignoring Michael's eye roll. "Are you okay if Michael opens the other box?" I ask Samantha.

She waves her hand. "Please, have at it."

We exchange a quick look in agreement, then watch as he slowly opens it. Michael dons two baggies, one on each hand, and lifts out a pair of black Mack Weldon boxer briefs.

I recognize them instantly as the brand I exclusively wear. I grip the counter. *What the hell is going on?*

Samantha gasps.

Michael scrutinizes me. "I take it you recognize these?"

"I recognize the brand and style, but I have no reason to believe they're actually mine." I point to the crusty-looking white stuff along the front. "What the hell is that?"

"Oh my god!" Samantha exclaims.

Michael turns them around so he can see, then looks back to me like I'm an idiot. "Really?"

Realization dawns. "Even if those are my underwear and even if that cum is mine, there is no way that proves anything other than someone managed to get a pair of my dirty underwear." I point to the other box. "And my favorite tie. Whoever the fuck this is has proven themselves to be quite resourceful, but none of this proves I know them or have ever had sex with them."

Michael agrees. "It's cir-*cum*-stancial at best."

"Seriously? Tell me you did not make a cum joke at a time like this?" I suppress a smile, nearly giving in to it.

"Hey, if not now, when?" Michael retorts.

"Grow up, you two," Samantha barks. "It's entirely too soon for cum jokes."

I groan at my stupidity. "You're right." I motion back to the box. "What's the note say?"

Michael places the underwear back in the box and carefully slips the piece of paper out from under it, holding the note so we can all read it.

This is proof of what I do to him.
He comes for me like he'll never come for you, Sweetness.

Sincerely,
The ONE Joseph calls "Baby"

I catch her right before she goes down. "Samantha!"

TAKE ME IN THE NIGHT

Samantha

A RMS, LEGS, BODIES INTERTWINE. NEEDFUL MOANS, *gasps, and cries for more.*

"Joseph, you're mine." An unfamiliar voice cackles in the air.

A deep, "Baby," in response scrapes against my skin like sandpaper.

No! I protest, but nothing comes out. I am silent. Mute.

A sultry "What happens in Vegas, stays in Vegas" runs on repeat.

Silence it. I need to silence—her.

"Samantha," he calls.

It's not true. He's mine. Not hers.

More moans. More gripping and pulling. More—

"Baby, wake up!"

I bolt up, nearly tumbling from the bed before a tight embrace stops my downfall. My heart pounds. My throat is dry. I frantically look around the room for something…anything. I lock on him. His familiar green eyes melt my fear. "Joseph."

"You were dreaming." He nuzzles into me. His lips caress my face as comforting arms pull me tightly against his strong body. His warmth and smell surround me like a soothing cocoon. "Are you okay, baby?"

Baby?

Visions from my dream flash before my eyes. Arms. Legs. Bodies intertwined. *His* body. But not with *mine.*

I pull away on a groan, shaking my head, rolling over to extricate myself from this bed and his arms. "Don't call me that." I stumble to my feet, swaying slightly, catching on to the corner post at the end of our bed.

Joseph slowly rises from the bed. "Don't call you what?" He cautiously moves toward me, his hands flexing at his sides, concern written all over his face.

I step back as he moves forward until I bump into the couch in our sitting area. Joseph quickly steadies me with a hand on my hip, shifting forward, allowing no room between us. His naked body presses against mine. "What don't you want me to call you, baby?"

My head shoots up to meet his worried gaze. "*That.* Don't call me *that.*" But as soon as I say it, I realize how stupid it is. I slump against him. My forehead hits his chest. *What the hell am I doing?* "Oh, god, Joseph. I'm letting her in my head."

His arms wrap around me. "I know it's hard to read such words and not let them affect you." His voice is gravely, tired.

I hug him back. My hand captures the back of his neck, trying to get him closer.

He runs kisses along my neck and shoulder. "But that's *my* word for *you.* No one else. I've *never* called anyone else 'baby.' Only *you.* It's *your* word."

A whimper escapes at his claim over that one simple word, making it ours again. I lift my head needing to feel his love. "Kiss me."

"Baby," he moans as our lips touch, gently, tenderly at first. His tongue sweeping, prodding, asking for admittance, which I gladly grant on a gasp of air, intensifying our kiss with penetrating need.

His hands sweep down my body, firmly holding me against him, grinding his hard cock between us. Our moans mirror the other's in need and intensity. Hands grasping and pulling, my pulsing desire demanding more. Demanding everything.

With graceful precision, Joseph lifts me off my feet and onto the back of the couch. My legs wrap around him as he buries himself deep inside me in one long, hot thrust of his hips.

"Christ, Sweets." He stills. Our eyes lock. "This is always, ever, just you and me."

He pulls out and pushes in again. "There's no room for anyone else."

His hands hook under my knees and pull my legs over his forearms as he locks his hands around my back. With each thrust he goes impossibly deeper, impossibly harder, and impossibly tenderer—all at the same time. His words, his face, his mouth, his hips, his entire body, filling me with his love.

Each thrust is punctuated with "baby," "oh, god, baby," "fuck, yes, baby" to take back the word she tried to steal from us.

I hold on. I hold on so damn tightly, I don't even know if I'm breathing. If I *can* breathe. The tingle starts at my toes and slowly glides up my legs. My nipples harden, my insides contract, and a moan that must have come from the depth of my desire blasts from my lips as that tingle reaches my core. My head falls back as ecstasy erupts, consuming me in wave after wave of tremors.

He thrusts and thrusts, then grinds out his release as I continue to shake and tremble in his arms.

Over and over again, we make love throughout the night. One or both of us wakes and reaches for the other, igniting our passion, our need to reconnect. I feel powerful. I feel loved. I feel solid in our commitment. By the time the first morning light streams through the bedroom windows, I am sore, spent, languid, and more confident than ever in our future.

Joseph is mine. He's not going anywhere. I give him what he needs as he so intuitively gives me what I need. We are a team, a unit, a rock-solid force that won't be put asunder by a few letters and items of clothing that any maid could have picked up.

Dreamily, my head falls to the side, finding Joseph watching me with a mischievous grin. I roll toward him. "What's that grin for?"

He props up on his elbow, leaning over me. "I was watching you wake up. It's like I could see the light radiating from you. And when you smiled, I knew in that moment that my girl was going to be okay."

I run my fingers through his sex-wrecked hair, my smile growing with every second his gaze lingers on me. "I'm going to be okay, because *we're* going to be okay."

"Damn straight." He kisses me softly, then rolls out of bed, throwing me the TV remote. "Don't get up. I'm bringing you breakfast in bed. We're playing hooky today." He pulls on a pair of pajama bottoms, and with a wink, he disappears down the hall.

I guess I'm playing hooky today.

Surprisingly, it doesn't stress me out about the schoolwork I'll be missing. That's what study partners are for, right?

With a yawn and a noisy stretch of my well-sexed body, I turn on the TV and welcome the day at home with my man.

Joseph

The first time I saw her, I knew she would be mine. Clichéd? Yes, but that doesn't make it any less true. We've come so far and only have three more months until that premonition comes to fruition. Three months, then no one can give me crap about calling Samantha *my wife* before she actually is—because she will be- my wife—and I will be her husband. She'll even be that much closer to coming to work for MCI as a full-fledged employee and not as an intern or as my PA.

I can't fucking wait.

That is my end game, my ultimate goal, my telos. But before that happens, I have to figure out who the fuck is messing with us. It's not only her they're targeting. Hurting her may be *their* end goal, but they're using me as a means to achieve it. I can't help thinking of what Fin told me weeks ago, after my happy hour slip up of letting those drunk tourists get a little too close for comfort. There are women who will want to get close to me because of my job and may enjoy the added challenge because I'm not interested in anyone except Samantha.

A week has brought little to light on who is trying to get Samantha to leave me. We haven't brought anyone else into the fold, besides Michael. For now, it's best to play it close to the vest as we don't know who could be watching, who could inadvertently let information slip in front of the wrong person. The fewer people who know the better. Besides, someone claiming I'm cheating on Samantha and providing "proof" in the form of soiled underwear is not something I relish sharing with anyone—especially not my family.

My cell phone chimes with a message.

Michael: *I'm coming up.*

I request Teddy hold my calls as Michael enters my office and takes a seat, letting out a telling sigh.

"I don't like it when you're stressed, Michael. It means I should be worried."

He smirks with a shake of his head. "I think you'd worry no matter how I'm feeling."

True. But I would feel a little more at ease about it if he wasn't concerned.

"I heard back from my contact at the forensics lab. He's emailing me a complete report, but I figured you'd want to know his initial findings."

I nod, not sure I can speak over my pounding heart.

Leaning forward, his eyes lock on mine. "The first letter has yours, Sam's, and a third set of fingerprints. There's no match in the system. I'll reach out to a different contact who has access to additional databases. If this person is in the system, we'll find him or her."

"Okay. And the second letter?"

"The second and third letters only have fingerprints from Sam and the same unknown contributor. So that's good that they match. Maybe we're only looking at one person here."

I sit back waiting for more.

"The tie came back with DNA matching the sample you provided. No other contributors were found. It's safe to say it's your tie."

No surprise. I was fairly certain it would come back with my DNA on it. "And the boxer briefs?"

He shifts in his seat. "There were two individual contributors to the fluids found on the underwear."

"Two?"

"Yes. Male and female."

Ah, fuck. My head hits the back of the chair, and my eyes lock on the ceiling. "It's mine, isn't it?"

"Yes." That's as solemn of a yes as I've ever heard.

I lift my head. Waiting. *Say it's Samantha's DNA. Please, God, let it be hers.*

"The female contributor is unknown."

"Fuck!" I lean forward, my head resting on the edge of my desk.

"Have you been with anyone else besides Sam?"

I shoot up out of my chair and round my desk as he stands, rock solid, no give. "What the fuck?" I bite, ready to take his head off.

He glares at me. "I have to ask. It's my job. I need all the facts to be able to help you, to find out what's really going on here. I also need to be sure you're not being a dick to Sam."

I back down. He'll protect Sam to his last breath, and I wouldn't have it any other way. "I haven't looked at or touched another woman since the day I met Samantha nearly two years ago." I sigh in resignation. "Except the Tiff thing."

His brow arches. "Not even before Sam was shot? When you were trying to leave her alone, let her graduate from college?"

Moving to the leather couch, I plop down. "No one. I wasn't interested."

Michael sits in the adjacent chair, surprise written all over his face. "What were you going to do all those years before she finished school, become a monk?"

I shrug and hold up my right hand with a smirk.

He relaxes back in his chair. "Jesus, that's a long time to go without pussy, man."

"She's worth it. I'd still be waiting for her, if that's what she wanted." And that's the truth of it. If I can't have her, I don't want anyone else.

"Then I guess I'm adding Tiff to the list of suspects. She could have easily snagged your underwear while you were smashed out of your gourd." Michael stands.

"You think so?"

"I don't know, man. It's possible. I'd rather start with her than dig up older partners." He pauses before he gets to the door. "But you'd better start thinking who else in your past might have a reason to want to hurt you or Sam. The female DNA may have been added later. It could be anyone's."

"I assume you mean sexual partners."

"Start there, but anyone who had access to your house in college could get a pair of underwear—male or female—so, I wouldn't limit your thinking to only women you had sex with."

"Jace." It's out of my mouth before I even have a chance to think on it.

Michael stops in his tracks and turns. "Really?"

"No, not really. But he, more than anyone else, had the easiest access over the past four years." I sigh on that thought. "No matter what's happened with his family—with me—I don't think he'd do something like this. But he had a lot of women coming and going. I never had a negative run-in with any of them." I tug at the seam of my pants. "Except Tiff."

"Then I say we start with her, but not rule anyone else out just yet."

With that he exits my office, closing the door behind him.

And opening up a whole other can of worms.

Nine

ONE WOMAN ONE MAN

OCTOBER

Samantha

WALK INTO THE LOBBY OF THE CRESCENT HOTEL where I'm meeting Jace for lunch. It's not a normal hangout for either of us, but it's close to home, and he had business in the area. This will be our second meeting since the failed counseling session with Mom.

Michael accompanied me the first time. Today it's William, his hand barely touching my back, not guiding me, just sticking close. Both Michael and Joseph insisted he remain in constant contact with me when out in public and on the move.

We reach the hostess, and William takes over, ensuring the proffered table meets our security needs. Luckily, once he's comfortable with our lunch accommodations, he'll back off and sink into the background, observing from a safe distance.

"Sam?" Jace's familiar voice comes from behind me. I turn to see him giving William the once-over and extending his hand. "I'm Jace, Sam's brother. I assume you're keeping my sister safe?"

528

William shakes his hand. "William. And yes, sir, your sister's safety is my only priority."

Only priority? *Only?* That strikes me as an overly pointed reply, as if to say he'd throw Jace in the line of fire if it would save me.

"I'm glad to hear it." Jace's face softens as his gaze lands on me. "Hey, sis."

"Hey."

He kisses my cheek and wraps me a quick hug. "It's good to see you."

"You too," I respond and look to William. "Are we ready to sit?"

"Yes," he replies, then nods to the hostess, letting her know we're ready.

We sit, order drinks, peruse the menu, and talk about nothing in particular. William long forgotten, I look at the man sitting across from me. He's changed over the last few years. His black hair is shorter, definitely more GQ-business-man-of-the-town kinda style. His features are more chiseled, more defined. But there's still a hint of sadness in his eyes, particularly when he thinks I'm not looking. He's matured, in a good way. He seems more…manly…more grown up—more like Dad.

My heart pangs at the thought. *God, I miss Dad.*

After we order, Jace scans the restaurant and stops where I believe William has taken up residence. "What's really going on, Sam? Why do you have protection? Michael was with you last time, and I assumed he drove you and decided to come in and eat, but now you have a complete stranger guarding you."

"He's here to be sure I'm safe." That's probably more than I should say, but Jace knows I haven't had protection following me around since my dad's murderer was killed—by Michael and me.

His blue eyes look into my matching pair, pleading for more—asking me to trust him. "You can't tell *me*, or you're not telling *anyone?*"

"No one." Shaking my head, I open my mouth to say more, then close it. There's nothing more I can say, really.

With a gentle smile, he drops it. "Fill me in on the wedding. Is there anything I can do to help? Either planning or paying?"

"Paying?" I never would have expected that offer.

"I know Joe and his family are loaded." He lays his hand across mine, resting on the table. "If Dad were here, he'd be paying for the wedding and the reception. I'd like to help."

I'm not sure Joseph would have let Dad pay for anything. Maybe something as a token of respect, but when it comes to money, my family can't hold a candle to the McIntyres. "I appreciate the offer, but it's covered."

Disappointment spreads across his face. I swallow around the lump in my throat, unsure if I'm ready to be this vulnerable with him. "There is one thing, though."

"Yeah?" He looks hopeful. So hopeful.

"I need someone to give me away." The lump in my throat bites as my eyes sting with impending tears.

His hand squeezes mine; his jaw clenches, and his eyes mist as he fights his own emotional battle. "Are you asking me to give you away?"

The rawness in his voice undoes me, and tears start to fall. All I can do is nod as I swipe at my face, clear my throat, and try to keep the flood of emotions at bay.

"God, I'd love to." His voice cracks on his reply. He bows his head for only a moment, and then sits up straight with a huge, beaming smile. "I would be honored to give you away, Sam."

I'm flooded with relief. I wasn't worried he'd say no. I was worried I wouldn't have the courage to ask, or that he wouldn't realize the importance of me asking *him*. I'm beyond thankful because he gets it. He didn't make light of it, and he said yes. With a teary smile, I manage a simple "Thank you."

We both work to fill the next few minutes with light-hearted conversation in order to get our emotions in check. What I really want to know is if he's happy. Food arrives, and after a few minutes I bite the bullet. "Sooo, tell me what's going on with you? I know you're looking to move to MCI. Is that what you really want? Are you not happy at Solengers?" I don't want him to make the move in an effort to get closer to me and Joseph. I want him to love where he works.

"I like Solengers. It's a great firm. I've learned a lot in my short tenure, and I'm sure I could learn a lot more from them." He fidgets with his silverware, lining it up, smoothing out the tablecloth, and positions his water glass precisely so. I don't know if he's stalling, or if this is a new idiosyncrasy he's developed. The old Jace never cared where his silverware was placed on the table, as long as he had the means to get the food from his plate to his mouth as quickly as possible.

Satisfied, he looks up. "I want to work at MCI. It's something Matt and I have been talking about for years. You know, before Dad died." His shoulders rise, and he tilts his head. "It would be nice to be back with the guys. I've missed them." His eyes pin me. "I've missed you."

Yeah, the waterworks are back. "You know you don't have to work at MCI to be a part of our lives, right?"

"It would help."

I can't deny that. He'd be right in the thick of things with his old buddies, working day in and day out with Matt, Fin, Joseph, Victor, and Michael. "The Six Pack reunites!" I tease.

He lays his hand next to mine, our fingers barely touching. "If it will make you uncomfortable, I won't, though. Making things right with you and Joseph is my top priority. I don't want to push, and I don't want to fuck it up." The depth of his words shines brightly in his eyes, and I know he means them.

I move my hand to link our pinkies. It's a little awkward with him sitting across from me, but I manage. Just as I used to manage when we were kids. He didn't always want to hold my hand, but he'd let me link pinkies with him, giving me that little boost of connection I often needed from him. He was my big brother, my protector from a world I often found moved too fast and was a little too loud for my liking.

He smiles at our joined hands. "I'm sorry, Sam," he all but whispers.

His heartache is too much. I can't take any more crying. I cup my hand over our joined ones and squeeze. "I know." My voice is low. "I forgive you, Jace. Let's move on from *I'm sorry*, okay? I need time to get to know you again, to learn to trust you."

That's going to be harder than forgiveness, as I don't think I've ever truly let anyone in besides Joseph. All those years I thought of Jace as my best friend, my confidant, he truly wasn't. I kept him and everyone else at arm's length, not relying on anyone except myself. "Baby steps. And this right here is the first of many to come."

"Baby steps," he agrees.

I pull my hands back and pick up my fork. "I think you coming to MCI is an excellent step as well."

"Yeah?" He's relieved.

"Yeah."

Baby steps.

One foot in front of the other.

One pinkie-hold at a time.

Moving forward.

Forgiveness.

Trust.

Family.

Joseph

I hang up with Samantha—the joy and hope in her voice was contagious as she imparted the details of her lunch with Jace—when Teddy comes on the line. "Mr. McIntyre, there's a Jace Cavanagh here to see you."

"Really?" Did he come home with Samantha? She just arrived. I'm sure she would have told me if they had returned to MCI Towers together.

"Is he related to your wife?" Teddy whispers.

Pride wells in my chest each time he calls her my *wife*. "He's Samantha's brother."

"Oh. I…didn't…never mind." He's obviously surprised.

There's been no mention of Jace or their mother to Teddy. No reason to, really. Maybe if it wasn't such a fresh wound for Samantha, their existence would be more common knowledge.

"You can send him in, Teddy."

"Of course."

I rise to meet Jace as Teddy opens the door and steps inside, allowing Jace to pass. "Can I get either of you a drink?" Teddy offers.

Jace crosses to the sitting area. "None for me, thank you." He seems happy. Maybe he felt their lunch was as successful as Samantha did. I can only hope, for her sake.

"Thanks, Teddy. Please hold my calls." I shake Jace's hand. "This is a surprise. Everything okay?"

"Yeah." He takes a seat on the couch, and I sit in a chair facing him. "Actually, no…or I don't know…that's why I'm here. I want to know what's going on. Is Sam okay? Is she in danger?"

I cross my leg over my knee, pulling at the crease of my slacks—a Fin tactic all the way—giving me time to consider how to respond. "Why do you ask?"

Jace leans forward, his arms resting on his knees. "Seriously, Joe? Don't bullshit me. I know I've fucked up in the past. I haven't been around, but I'm here now, and I'm not going anywhere. Is she in danger? Has something happened? Why does she have a bodyguard sticking to her like glue?"

I smile, and that only seems to piss him off. I hold up my hand to stop whatever he's about to say. "I'll tell you." I chuckle. "It's good to see you getting all protective over your sister. It's a good sign."

He relaxes and sits back on the couch. "I've been an ass to you both, but even at my worst, I never wanted anything to happen to either of you. Learning about the kind of danger she was in from our father's killer was hard to hear after the fact. I don't want to miss out on anything, even if it's bad news. So, tell me what's going on, and what can I do to help?"

It only takes me a second to decide whether to bring him in or not. He is Samantha's brother, after all, and he also knows Tiff. Maybe he can be of help in that regard. Put some feelers out and see what he turns up. I'm not stupid, though, so I call Michael and ask him to join us. From a strategic perspective, when it comes to catching bad guys, Michael is the pro.

After Michael joins us, I fill Jace in on what's been happening. Even though I'd rather keep the details private, if we expect Jace to be able to help, he needs details to work with.

Jace finishes reviewing the photocopies of the three packages received. He holds the latest letter in his hand. He's been quiet most of the time. He hands it back to Michael and chugs the rest of his bottle of water before he speaks. "Has Sam seen all of this?"

Michael and I both nod.

"And the underwear? She's seen it? Knows the DNA results?" he asks.

"Yes. Unfortunately, all but the last package she opened up on her own. And I've shared the DNA results with her as well. We don't have any secrets between us."

Jace runs his hand over his face. "I can't imagine how she must be feeling." He looks at me. "How would you feel if some guy was sending you these things about Sam? Items of her clothing with her…DNA on it. Letters telling you how sex with *him* is so much better than sex with you? How would you feel? I'd be pissed and hard-pressed to listen to reason."

I can't deny the same thought hasn't crossed my mind. If the roles were reversed, I'm not sure I would be as open and supportive as she's been. I like to think I would be, but the thought gets my blood boiling to the point where all I see is red. "Jace, I'd rip his head off."

He looks at me and laughs. "Yeah, you would." He sobers. "But she's not the one being accused of cheating. You are."

"Yes, I am." I square my shoulders, waiting for the accusation.

Jace waves me off. "Relax, man. I know you're not cheating on Sam."

"You do?" It's my turn to be surprised. I thought for sure his over-protective instincts would accuse first, question later.

"Joe, I know you, man. You've never been a horn dog. Even before you met my sister, you were never one to sleep around. Your career was more important than chasing pussy. But after you met Sam, your grumpy ass didn't even know other women existed." His eyes meet mine for a moment before he looks away. "And I saw the look on your face when you realized what happened with Tiff wasn't a drunken dream about the girl you love, but the harsh reality of what I did to you both." His eyes close for a beat or two, then his shame-filled eyes lock with mine. "I saw the devastation in your eyes, the pure remorse as it ate you up. You, Joe McIntyre, are not a cheater. You are a one-woman man, and like I told you after my dad's funeral, Sam is a one-man woman. You were destined for each other. I know you would never cheat on her."

I let out a shaky breath, emotion tight in my chest, as I look at my future brother-in-law sitting across from me. "You have no idea how much that means to me." Maybe there is hope for me and Jace to move past the

Tiff thing after all. I reach out and pull him into a hug. "It's good to have you back, brother."

He pounds on my back. "It's good to be back, brother." He pulls away and rubs at his eyes, shakes his head, and laughs at his emotions. "You have no idea."

No, I don't have any idea. But I can see his self-imposed exile has been difficult, probably in ways we can't even imagine.

We spend the next thirty minutes or so discussing how Jace can help narrow down the suspects, starting with Tiff. By the time they both leave, we have a plan of action that gives me a sense of peace I haven't felt since the first letter arrived.

Now I need to head home to the only true peace I know.

My girl.

Joseph

Silence greets me as I enter our penthouse. The lights are dim, but I can smell food cooking. I relinquish my armor—my jacket, tie, and briefcase—in the entryway and grab a water in the kitchen. I check the oven and the timer—all good—and go in search of Samantha.

I'm not surprised when I find her asleep on our bed. She hasn't been sleeping well since all of this began. Her nightmares are back, but they've morphed into a combination of her father's death and me with another woman. I cringe at the thought. It'll never happen. I'd never cheat on my girl. It's more than that, though. It's not even a battle. It doesn't even cross my mind. I truly see no other woman in a sexual way. I only have eyes for her. My dick only wants *her.* I know she knows it, but deep down her insecurities still linger. Her subconscious is struggling and beating her up in her dreams.

Toeing off my shoes, I slip into bed, curl up behind her, wrap her up in my arms, and revel in the warmth and peace that engulfs me.

Warm, soft hands traverse my body as I slowly come awake to the realization that I'm hard as stone, and Samantha is lying naked beside me. She's managed to get my shirt unbuttoned. Her hot, wet mouth is sucking on my nipple, and her hand inside my unzipped pants strokes my cock. I flex into her greedy hand. "Christ, Sweets." What a way to wake up.

I shuck my clothes. Her hands and mouth never leave me. I'm shaking, on edge, ready to blow.

I'm not going alone.

She squeals when I lift her on top of me as I roll to my back, finding heaven in her mouth before I slide my way home. Slow thrusts as she grinds against me, her moans and gasps challenge my control. My name on her lips nearly has me blowing like a rocket.

I'm not going alone.

Rolling us over so I'm on top, still buried to the hilt, I grind against her, hitting the spots that send her sailing. Her hands grasp and pull. Her head, thrown back, allows my mouth to ravish her delectable neck. She chants my name over and over again. My heart is pounding, pounding, pounding in time with my cock. Deep. Deeper. And deeper still.

She squeezes, contracts, and moans. And when her release wraps around me, and her fluids coat my cock and seep down my balls, I shoot over the edge, growling, filling her. Filling her. Filling her.

Spent, I collapse and roll to my side, gripping her ass to stay inside her. My mouth finds hers, and we kiss, our bodies entwined, connected, until we are both out of breath and ready again.

Never enough.

Over dinner we catch each other up on our days. Her lunch with Jace, details she didn't share earlier, a phone conversation with Margot that gave no hint of a relationship with Fin, much to Samantha's dismay, and plans with Sebastian to join our next happy hour. He's missed the last few due to his schedule. I fill her in on a few business meetings, and then the unexpected and very productive meeting with Jace.

"Wow. He really is trying, isn't he?" Her surprise matches mine.

"Yeah, he is. Are you okay with this?" I try to read any emotions that play along her face, but she seems okay.

"What? You meeting with him, him knowing our dark, dirty secret, or him helping out with our dark, dirty secret?"

I try not to flinch. "I'd rather you not call it our 'dark, dirty secret,' but, yeah, all of that."

Her brow bunches on a head tilt. "But it *is* our dark, dirty secret, Joseph. We're not sharing it with your brothers, whom you share everything with."

I grab her hand, lacing our fingers, my lascivious stare eating her up. "Not everything." I've never shared details of our sex life. They know the extent of my love for her, but the rest is none of their fucking business. A blush creeps up her neck. She fidgets in her chair and bites the corner of her bottom lip. So fucking sexy.

"I'm glad to hear you don't share *those* details." She sits back, pulling her hand from my grasp. "But that's not what I meant. We're in trouble, someone's after me—"

"Us. They're going after you through me. *Us.*" We're a unit, my tone holds no leeway.

"Okay, *us.* My point being, we're keeping it a secret from the people you trust the most. If I were being threatened with kidnapping or bodily injury, would you hesitate to confide in them?"

She has a point. "I prefer to keep it secret because of its malicious sexual nature."

"I know." Her voice so soft. "I don't disagree with your desire to keep it private, nor do I disagree with you bringing Jace on board."

Thank God. My shoulders relax, and the knot that was forming in my stomach unwinds. "Good."

"What's the plan?"

"Jace is going to reach out to Tiff. Play up the whole falling out with us over your father's death and what happened between her and me. He's going to work on getting a DNA sample, but of course, a confession would be good too."

"Well, if anybody can charm the pants off a woman, it's Jace." She takes her half-eaten plate of food to the kitchen, setting it on the counter.

"He's working with a bit of a disadvantage, though." I join her in the kitchen, pointing to her plate. "You need to finish that."

"I'm done." Her intonation is flat, not open for debate. "What disadvantage? He's sworn off women?" she teases, scraping her plate into the trash.

"Yes."

"What?" Her head whips up.

I take the plate from her hands before she drops it. "He's been celibate for a year. He feels it's what's giving him his clear head and edge in the office. He's written off women for the immediate future, at least."

"Wow. I never saw that coming."

I chuckle. "You and me both."

CRAZY LOVE

Samantha

'M LATE. I'M NEVER LATE. I'M ABSOLUTELY ALWAYS ON time or early. Never. Late. I throw the box at William, "Hold this," and slip into my Creative Coding class, knowing William will either follow or stand sentry at the door. I can't think about which, and I most definitely can't think about the box that was delivered to me moments ago as we walked to class.

William nearly tackled the guy as he approached me. After the third degree, checks of the delivery guy's credentials, and pictures taken of all of it, I was left holding the box. I stared at it as if it might give its secrets away by the mere fact I was giving it a death glare. When nothing happened, and with William's quiet reminder of the time, we jogged the rest of the way to class.

I settle at a desk near the door, easy in, easy out. My professor gives me a nod and glances at the door as if she's waiting for William to follow. When he doesn't, I get a questioning look before she turns her attention back to the projector and her lecture. As it was when I had FBI protection my last few months of high school, nobody asks me about my protection, but it's obvious someone gave my teachers a heads-up. This time, I'm sure it was Joseph or Michael.

I pull out my laptop and wake up the screen, thankful I turned it on earlier. Soon, my brain focuses on the images, formulas, and statements on the professor's projected screen, and all thoughts of the box waiting for me fade into the background.

After two more classes and lunch, I take the box from William as we sit at a table in the commons area. Turned so he can't see the contents, I unwrap it to reveal the same type of shoebox I've received two times before. I lift the lid and set it aside. I don't have to touch the contents this time to see what is inside. Side by side, possibly affixed to the bottom of the box to ensure maximum effect, is a picture of Joseph. Next to it is a letter. The same type of letter I've received before, but this time the punch is a little deeper seeing his face right next to *those* words.

"Sam?"

I look up into the blurry face of Michael standing over me. I blink a few times to clear my tears. The sadness in his eyes is too much. I place the lid on the box and hand it to him. "Take it to Joseph." I brush away my tears and look at William. "I'll be late for class."

He nods and collects our trash, disposing of it while Michael keeps watch.

"Come with me." It sounds like a plea, but coming from Michael it can't be. I can't stick around and watch tough-as-nails Michael go soft on me.

Shaking my head, I stand and gather my things. "Tell Joseph I'll see him at home." I walk away before I change my mind and melt into his concern and the idea of finding comfort in Joseph's arms.

Joseph

My two o'clock meeting is interrupted by a text.

Michael: *We have another package*

Luckily, I'm not the one presenting, nor am I key to this meeting.

I make my excuses and exit the meeting with Teddy in tow. "Clear my afternoon."

"Yes, sir." He heads to his desk as I enter my office to find Michael standing at my desk, his back to me, looking down.

I stop and close my door. "Samantha?"

He turns. "She's still at school. She said she'd see you at home later." The Grim Reaper look he's sporting tells me this is worse than the others. How can it possibly be worse?

"How bad?" I set my laptop down on my desk, giving wide berth to the box, catching only a glimpse of the letter inside.

"Bad."

"Are you gonna make me look, or can you just tell me?"

His eyes lock on mine. "You need to see it the way she saw it."

"Fuck." I close my eyes, like I need the reminder that my girl is being inundated with this shit over and over again. I steel myself and move around to stand next to him.

Inside the box is a letter on the left and a picture of me on the right. It's close-up from the mid-abdomen up, looking down on me, like whoever took it was sitting on me. I'm in a bed, my head on a pillow, white sheets. It could be my college bed or any hotel bed—any fucking bed— it's impossible to say. It can't be too old of a picture. I look the same age, maybe a tad younger. My hair is a sticking out as if I, or someone else, has had their fingers in it. And my face…Jesus, my face…has a look of pure ecstasy. I'm coming—hard, by the looks of it. "Fuck me," I sigh.

"Yep, that's pretty much what it looks like." I'm getting no sympathy from him. He seems pissed. "Read the note."

I know this face well.

It's the one he makes when he fills me with his cum.

Sincerely,
Joseph's baby girl

"Goddamnit!" I'm about to lose it.

Michael grips my shoulder. "Calm down. I need to ask you some questions before you go all caveman."

I pace to the window, close my eyes and breathe slowly in and then out until I feel calmer. "Okay."

"Come look at the pic again, and tell me what you see."

I stomp to my desk and scrutinize the box's contents. "I see me. In a bed. White sheets. I've got fucked-up hair. And…" I clench my jaw as I look up, meeting Michael's gaze. "…and I'm having an orgasm."

He smirks. "Yeah, that's one sight I'll never get out of my head. Your come-face."

"Fuck off." I try not to, but he makes me laugh. "You're just envious."

Ignoring my comment, he continues. "Do you know where this was taken? When it was taken? Who you were with?"

The questions go on and on like an interrogation until my emotions have settled, I'm feeling numb, and his queries are exhausted. My best guess is this pic is from college and may or may not be my bed. I have no idea whom I was having sex with, but I'm positive I wasn't alone as I've never taken a sexual selfie in my life—plus, most of the time I jerked off in the shower, not in bed.

Thankfully, my sex life with Samantha leaves me with no need or desire for self-gratification. I want all of her pleasure, and I want to give her all of mine.

"Are we done? I'd really like to get home to my girl."

Samantha

I'm not a drinker, but after today, I need something to help me quiet the voice in my head. The one that shouts *he's cheating on you, and you're stupid enough to believe he's not when the evidence is staring you in the face.* It's a mean, nasty voice. I take a glass and an open bottle of wine to the balcony. I'm on my second glass when I hear the door open and Joseph step out.

His eyes roam over me and then the wine bottle. He sits next to me on the chaise, finishes off my glass, refills it, and then holds it to my lips. I take a sip, my eyes glued to him. His tongue licks across his bottom lip as he watches me, heat flaring in his eyes, causing wicked thoughts of his tongue to take flight. I nearly groan when he takes a deep drink and sets it aside.

His jacket, shoes, and tie are already discarded somewhere inside. His shirt is untucked and lies open, his every movement highlighting his taut chest and abdomen. "Samantha," he breathes as his lips brush mine. It's just my name, but it sounds more like *I'm sorry… I love you… Don't believe what you see.*

My sob is consumed by his mouth, tender and passionate, pleading and demanding. He tantalizes my senses, and my body explodes with need to consume and be consumed. I'm famished, starved for something my body knows only he can provide. My hands dwell under his shirt, pulling him closer, but when his bare chest comes into contact with my clothed one, he groans his disapproval, pulling away enough to remove the sweater I put on when I came home.

"Fuck, yes," he growls when he sees I'm braless.

His head dips, pushing me down on the lounger, his hands and fingers squeezing and pulling at my breasts. His tongue flicks over my nipples, making them hard before sucking them deep. With a pop, he releases one before he moves to the other. His hands grip the waist of my leggings, and in one clean motion, he relieves me of them, my panties, and my socks. I'm naked, and the cool October breeze sends goosebumps rippling across my skin.

Green eyes of fire look up at me with a quirked brow, asking *too cold to say outside?* When I don't object, his hands and mouth continue to lave me in his love. His kisses move lower, and my moans of pleasure merely feed his fire. He lifts my legs, pushing my knees to my chest, spreading me wide, and he dives in. There's no slow buildup of kisses down my thighs, around my pussy, teasing my opening. No, he dives tongue first, slipping inside me and kissing me like it's my mouth—long, deep, and probing.

"Oh, god, Joseph." I try to buck my hips, but I'm locked in place, only able to take what he gives.

The more I thrash, the hungrier he gets. His forearms rest on the back of my thighs, holding me open. His hands tease my clit and play with my breasts, working me into a frenzy. My cries echo around the balcony, turning me on even more thinking someone could hear us. I doubt they can see us, but my excitement ratchets even higher.

"I can't. I can't," I cry out, needing more, needing less, needing *him*.

"Yes," is all he manages before his entire mouth covers me, his tongue fucking me, his sucking on my clit in time with his fingers pulling on my nipples. In a move worthy of wrestler pinning his opponent to the mat, Joseph holds me down as I buck and shatter around him, crying out to him, to God, for mercy, for more, for *him*.

As my contractions abate, Joseph releases his cock, rubbing his head over my clit a few times before sinking inside. "Sweets," he groans. Kneeling on the chaise, my legs over his arms, his eyes latch on to mine, feral and hungry as he thrusts.

For leverage, I hold on to the sides, but it's of no use, I can't hold back my caveman. He needs this. He needs to claim me. He needs me to know I'm his, and he's mine.

"Look at my cock, baby."

My eyes break from his and lower to where we are joined. It's so hot watching him slide in and out of me.

"I'm covered with your sweet juices. This cock belongs to you. It only fits your hot and hungry pussy, only yours."

I clench around him. "Joseph." He's gonna make me come again.

"Watch, Samantha. Watch what you do to me. I only come undone for you." He wraps his arms tightly around my thighs, adjusts his thrusts, and when he hits that magical spot inside, I'm the one starting to come undone. "Fuck, I can feel you. You're so ready, baby." He presses his thumb to my clit, and I spiral out of control. "Yes, Sweets. Fuck, yes, take me with you."

On a scream I don't recognize as my own, I come so hard as he pistons deliciously in and out of me with quickening strokes. My mewling mixes with his as his orgasm overtakes him. My eyes never leave his as I relish the look of ecstasy on his face, the look of love in his eyes.

He has *that* look. My heart sinks.

The. Look.

That matches.

The one.

In the picture.

The look that was for somebody else.

Not me.

Eleven

GROW MY SHAME

NOVEMBER

Samantha

I HAVEN'T BEEN TO THE OFFICE IN WEEKS. IF TEDDY needs me, I talk to him over the phone or desktop share if he needs more guidance than words alone. But, honestly, I don't have much else to teach him. It's all just my opinion now. We've moved beyond my expertise as to what's best as Joseph's PA. Teddy is making his own rulebook now. I only guide when asked, and it's usually application-related. It's really my Microsoft Office skills that are needed. I'm his personal helpdesk, I suppose.

My life consists of going between school and home now. Fiona has been handling all wedding-related tasks, dealing with our wedding planner, Jackie, as needed. School is the perfect excuse as to why I'm too busy to deal with it properly. The reality is, as much as I try to deny it, I'm avoiding everything wedding-related. If I can't brush it off and change the subject, then I make any excuse to separate myself from the person asking.

We're six weeks away, and that means Thanksgiving is only a few weeks off, which also means tonight is our couple's wedding shower. I insisted that we keep the festivities down to only one. I don't have any family to invite or to host a shower. I don't have enough female friends to attend a non-family shower, and Margot can't afford to throw one, plus she's in Austin. It doesn't seem fair to put that kind of pressure on her. Therefore, Joseph and I requested that we have a couple's shower with family and friends. So, no girly, all white, tea and finger foods shower for me, which I'm totally fine with. Especially since I have no desire to be the center of attention, which goes against the whole bridal tradition of being doted on. I don't want that. At. All.

"Why are you frowning?" Joseph's voice startles me.

I turn from the bathroom mirror. He's watching me from the door, his brow hard-set in a line. I grab what I need for my clutch and skirt around him. "I can't shake the feeling we shouldn't be doing this."

"What? Having a wedding shower?" He follows, hot on my heels, his gaze hitting mine in my dresser mirror.

I slip my cell phone into my small purse as I step into my pumps. "No. Yes, but not just that."

His steps, never far behind, as I walk to the kitchen. "I'm not letting this bitch, or whoever it is, stop me from marrying you." His voice is hard and chockfull of emotion.

Grabbing a bottled water, I hand it to him before getting one for myself. "Maybe you should."

He hates this discussion. We've had it many times over the last few weeks, since the last letter and picture arrived. I can barely look at him without seeing that picture. I can't get it out of my mind. I haven't even let him touch me since that night. He's pissed and frustrated. "Don't fucking do this."

His anger grows, and I just become silent, resolved, and distant. I'm pushing him away, preparing for the worst. Each letter said it would get worse until I finally left him. Maybe it's time to heed that warning, at least until the person is caught.

Do I believe he's cheating on me? No, not really. But the doubt is so tangible, it's like a third person in the room. It sours everything. It's turned his touch into flinches of pain. It's turned his look of love and desire into a mask I can only see him using on someone else. He's pissed at it getting to me, and I'm helpless to see anything else but his face in that come-shot.

We silently board the elevator and meet Michael in the garage. He's driving us to Joseph's parents' house for the shower. William will be outside, along with a few other guys keeping watch, but they have orders to stay in the shadows since our friends and family don't know what's going on. Michael opens the door and stares at me when I remain mute, barely making eye contact with him.

I slip into the back of the SUV, and the door closes behind me as Joseph and Michael converse in voices too low for me to make out. But I don't miss the shortness in tone from either of them as they make their way around the car to get in.

Michael's penetrating glare in the rearview mirror does nothing to ease my nerves. "Sam," he says softly, too softly, with too much concern. He thinks I'm an idiot, too. I'm surrounded by testosterone-laden men who can't see that perhaps it's best to delay the wedding and lie low until things blow over. God forbid it make them appear weak by giving in to the threats. I, on the other hand, would like to get married without the threat of unspeakable packages already received, and those yet to be delivered, tainting everything in my path.

My path to the altar is littered with nasty letters saying how much Joseph loves another woman, fucks her better, comes for her harder, leaves articles of clothing covered in their sexual secretions as proof of their joining. And yes, let's not forget the lovely picture of Joseph in complete and utter rapture as he has sex with *someone else.* Nothing says *joyous wedding* like the proof of your betrothed's sexual exploits that don't include his bride.

Do I believe he's cheating? No.

Do I believe this whole episode is tainting our wedding? Abso-fucking-lutely.

Joseph squeezes my hand, and I fight to keep it securely ensconced in his. *This is the man you love. Let him hold your hand, for God's sake.* I take a deep breath and close my eyes.

"Please, Samantha. Let it go." His lips brush my cheek. "Let's just enjoy tonight with our friends and family as we celebrate." He tips my chin, and I open my eyes to meet his warm green ones. "I love you. Don't think about anything else but that."

I curl into his side. "Okay." I can do that.

He loves me.

He loves me.

He. Loves. Me.

Joseph

I can't stand how much this is affecting her, affecting our relationship. I thought it was tough after her dad died, but this arbitrary line she's drawn between us, keeping me at a distance, keeping me from touching her intimately, makes that time look like a walk in the park. She can't look at me without seeing that picture. I don't know how to fix that. I don't know how to wipe it from her mind. How to make her see me as I am now and not how I looked while having sex with some woman I can't even remember.

"You look tired, son." Dad claps me on the back and motions across the room. "Your bride doesn't look much better."

"There's just a lot going on, Dad."

"She looks like she'd rather be any place else but here." Fin hands me a beer.

"Thanks." I take a long pull, watching Samantha talking to Margot, Mom, and two of my aunts. "She hates being the center of attention."

Fin chuckles. "Then she's gonna love opening gifts in front of everyone."

"Gifts? We said no gifts. We don't need anything." And if we do, we can buy it for ourselves.

"Your mother is a traditionalist. You have a wedding, you have wedding gifts. It's not about whether you can afford to buy it for yourself or not. It's about everyone expressing their happiness for you—by buying you gifts." He shrugs with a laugh, his look telling me *get used to it.*

I wonder if Samantha knows there will be gifts.

Jace joins us, greeting my dad and Fin before eyeing me. "You look like shit," he teases, but I also see deeper meaning in his gaze.

"Thanks."

"You're welcome. How is she?" He scans the room until he finds Samantha.

"Distant." A single word that sums it up.

He looks to my dad and Fin, who are deep into MCI business, oblivious to the two of us. "I'm sorry, man. I know this has to suck. I'm making progress." He glances around and whispers, "Next week. She'll be in town."

I know exactly who the *she* he's referring to is, and I hope that means he'll be meeting up with Tiff when she's in town. A raised brow is all it takes for confirmation.

"Yes, we have plans to meet up."

"That's great news." Maybe we can get this wrapped up before Thanksgiving. That will give me nearly four weeks to make Samantha forget all about it before we say *I do.*

Damn, that day cannot come soon enough for me.

Samantha

"Babycakes, what's going on? I don't think you could look more miserable if you tried." Sebastian pulls me from a group of Joseph's family members I've never met before.

"Shit, Bash, I'm trying. I really look that bad?" I thought I was doing a pretty good job of faking it. I actually meant many of the smiles and thank yous I've given in the last hour and a half.

He nudges me with his shoulder as we continue moving away

from the crowd. "No, I can just read you. It's my job to pick up on patient cues even when they don't want me to see what's really going on."

I sag in relief. "I really don't want to be here. Can you just act like you're me, but be all friendly and social like you, which is not like me at all, but it's the me that needs to be here?"

He laughs. "I think you've cracked." His hand presses to my forehead, then he feigns taking my pulse. "Nope, nope no fever, heartbeat normal. Yep, you're all good."

If only he knew how *not good* I really am.

His stare pins me in place, waiting for an explanation. I sigh. "I'm just tired. School is busy, life is…busy. You know I don't like social situations."

"Psh, that's not true. You're great at social situations." He looks around the room. "You just don't like this big of a crowd." He wraps an arm around my shoulder and squeezes. "You like smaller, intimate gatherings like our happy hours, where you know everyone."

I nod. "And where I'm not the focus."

"Ah, yes. I hate to break it to you, but you're going to have more eyes on you than this at your wedding. You'd better get used to it."

"I wished we'd just eloped," I whisper more to myself than him.

He turns his concerned look on me. "Do you really?"

"Yeah, I think I really do." There's no *thinking* to it, truly. Maybe if we were already married, the office betting pool wouldn't have had a chance to even start. The woman trying to get me to leave maybe wouldn't have even tried. All this heartache could have been avoided.

I look around the room at Joseph's family, our mutual friends, and Jace—my only family—and I'm hit with guilt. Would I really want to do this without all of them by our sides, cheering us on, congratulating us, supporting us every step of the way? "No." I turn to face Bash. "I wouldn't want to do this without you…" I motion haphazardly over my shoulder to the rest of the room. "…or them."

His devilishly handsome smile is enough to know I'm right. "I would have been really mad at you if you'd run off. You deserve the big wedding."

I don't know about deserve, but I'm getting it whether I do or not.

"Come on, let's go see my husband-to-be." Joseph needs a little reassurance that I don't hate him.

Joseph

My girl curls into my side, and my chest nearly collapses into itself, tight with emotion. She came to *me*, seeking *my* touch, *my* comfort. Sebastian smiles at me, standing with her between us. I don't know what he said, but I'm thankful that whatever it was prompted this. I smile and shake his hand. "We've missed you at happy hours."

He nods. "I got a suck-balls rotation this round. I'm trying to swap a few shifts to see if I can make it next week."

"Maybe we could swap days, occasionally, to something that works for you. We'd at least get to see you a few times a month," I suggest.

"That'd be great. Let's see if I can make the next one, then we can discuss it with everyone."

Samantha looks up and presses into me. She likes that suggestion, and that I'm working to fit her *Bash* into our tight-knit group. But really, everyone loves Sebastian. He's a great guy. He cares for my girl—in a way I'm not threatened by—and he's funny as shit with hysterical stories from his ER patients. We'd do the same for anyone else in our group if they had a continual schedule conflict.

I steal a kiss and relish the fact that she doesn't pull away from me.

It's not long before my mother calls the two of us to take a seat in the chairs placed in front of the fireplace, facing the room filled with our guests. *Shit. She's gonna hate this.* I squeeze her hand, letting her know she's not in this alone—I'm right here beside her—not letting her go. Ever.

Fuck. Now I just want to take her to my old room upstairs and see if she'll let me kiss and hold her some more. I don't even care if we have sex—I just need to reconnect with my Sweets—feel her safe, secure, and at peace in my arms.

Fuck me running backwards with a dog in my arms, this is gonna be a long-ass night.

Margot kneels beside Samantha, writing down each gift and who it came from. I guess that's the job of the maid of honor? Or maybe it's just a best friends thing. My brothers take turns handing us gifts that Mom has stashed in some other room, hence why we didn't know there were gifts—even though we agreed there wouldn't be any. Samantha and I take turns reading the cards, telling Margot and the room whom it's from, and opening the gift.

To my complete and total shock, we have a china pattern and thus far, we've received twenty-four complete place settings. Who the hell needs twenty-four place settings of china? We can't even seat twenty-four people in our penthouse. We can seat sixteen at our dining room table and four at the breakfast bar. I guess four lone diners could sit on the couches or eat at the coffee table. Huh, maybe we do need twenty-four. Who'd have thunk it?

Fin, being the ass he is, even though we have a completely good cof-feemaker, bought us the exact same contraption he has. Great, now I'll have to get a second degree just to run the damn thing. Samantha, on the other hand, is ecstatic, jumping up to hug Fin so fast she nearly trips over the monstrosity. Christ, that thing is ugly. *I wonder if it does dishes?*

I'm so busy giving Fin a hard time, I miss what the next gift is or who it's from. I simply hear a gasp from beside me, and when I look to Samantha, she's turned as white as her sexy bride-ish looking blouse. "What—"

She slams the box shut, clutching it to her chest like it's a bomb about to go off, protecting everyone as she nearly hurdles over any obstacles or guests in her way. She runs out of the room—and I mean runs—flat out, as fast as she can, fifty-yard-sprint kind of run. I catch sight of Michael's back as he rounds the corner and barrels up the stairs after her. Without a second thought for our guests or any explanation as to what happened, I bound up the stairs behind them in time to see Samantha slam the bathroom door shut. Michael skids to a halt as he grabs the doorknob, only to find it locked.

He looks at me solemnly, glancing over my shoulder. "Let me know if you want me to break it down." He pats my shoulder as he passes. "I'll keep everyone away." He stops at the top of the stairs, blocking Fin, Jace, and I don't know who else from coming up.

Ignoring them, I turn to the door, checking again to be sure it's really locked. It is.

I press my forehead to the cool surface. "Samantha, please let me in. Let me see what's in the box. We're a team. Remember?"

In response, all I hear are her soft sobs. Fuck. "Please, baby, let me in."

The sound of running water fills my ears, muting any other noises. She must have turned on the faucet. I press my ear to the door, closing my eyes to concentrate on what's happening on the other side. A deep, muffled voice fills the void, but I can't make anything out. Then it's gone, only to come back a few seconds later. Another sob, loud enough to breach the water barrier she's erected. Then the deep voice again. A loud clang has me pulling away momentarily before I catch myself and resume my listening stance. Only this time, over the din of the water, I hear the worst sound imaginable—the sound that sends me back to that day I told her I slept with someone else—the sound that fills me with so much regret and helplessness—the sound of the woman I love retching.

I look to Michael. "I have to get in there."

With a quick nod, he's by my side. He stills and listens. "Is she—"

"Yes." Fuck. Yes, that's the sound of my girl vomiting over whatever is in that goddamned box. "I have to get to her, Michael. Now."

I move aside, giving him room as he prepares to kick the door in.

"Stop!" Fin elbows his way past William, who took Michael's place as guard. "Did it even cross your mind to pick the lock? Aren't you the ex-FBI-military-extraordinaire?"

Michael pats his pockets. "Didn't come prepared to pick locks at a wedding shower."

"Then it's a good thing one of us is prepared." Fin hands me the master key.

I move to insert the metal key into the hole to pop the lock, but stop. "Fin, I need you to stay back."

He looks offended but nods and steps back.

"Michael, I need you to get that fucking package and ensure no one sees it."

"On it."

That's all the confirmation I need. I pop the lock, push the door so hard it bangs against the wall and hits me on the rebound, but I move on, not letting it slow me down. Samantha is slumped over the toilet, still throwing up. I glance at the open box lying on the floor and get a glimpse of a video and the sound of my voice coming from inside the box. Motherfucker!

Michael picks up the box. I turn my attention back to my girl and block everything else out, knowing he'll take care of it.

I kneel beside her, gather her hair in my hands, relieving her of her valiant attempt at keeping it out of her way. I hold it with one hand and gently pat her back. "It's okay, Samantha, I've got you."

She vomits again and again.

Her body finally gives out—gives up—and I'm able to get her cleaned up and tucked against my chest on my old bed, in my bedroom. The one I wanted to bring her to earlier, under totally different circumstances. She's cried herself out and has fallen asleep. I text Michael and ask him to send Sebastian to meet me in my room.

With a soft knock, the door opens and Sebastian peers in. I motion him forward. He quietly closes the door behind him and walks silently to my side of the bed. His eyes rove over Samantha.

"I need you to watch her. Stay with her. I need to step across the hall, and I don't want her alone if she wakes up while I'm gone. Can you do that?" I ask, knowing he would never say no.

"Of course. Is she sick?" His concerned doctor eyes study her face.

I slowly extricate myself from her grasp. She moans and frowns in response but doesn't wake up. I move us away from the bed and quietly explain. "We've been getting disturbing mail. I don't know what was in the box she opened, but it was enough to upset her to the point of making her sick." I look at her resting peacefully on the bed. "If she wakes up, call for me." I move to the door, not giving him a chance to ask questions. "I'll only be across the hall."

I step into the adjacent room, not surprised to see Fin and Michael standing there arguing. Once I get the door closed, Fin is all over me. "What the fuck is going on?"

I hold up my hand. "Fin, I need to talk to Michael, alone."

He flinches as if I slapped him. It's not like me to keep secrets from Fin. "I can help."

On a sigh, I sit on the bed. "I know you can. And you will, but right now, I need you downstairs getting rid of all these people. Tell them Samantha is sick, thank them for coming, smooth over ruffled feathers, and get them the fuck out of the house. I'm gonna take Samantha home soon, and I'd rather not have to carry her through a house full of guests."

"And then we'll talk?" he confirms.

"And then we'll talk. Tomorrow."

He wants to protest. I can see it in the tension of his body and the bite in his jaw, but he simply nods. "Tomorrow, brother."

"Tomorrow." I stand and hug him, fighting to keep my emotions in check. "Thank you, brother."

As soon as Fin leaves, I turn to Michael. "Show me."

He hands me a note.

Why haven't you left yet?
Is this not proof enough?
You'll never be able to satisfy my Joseph, not the way I can.

Sincerely,
Joseph's cock riding baby

Rage courses through my body, and my fists clench, needing to hit something—someone. Michael grips my hand, forcing me to release the note before pushing me down on the bed. "If you think that's bad, you're really gonna hate the video."

"Michael." I don't even have the words.

He grips my shoulder. "We're gonna find this motherfucker, and when we do, we're gonna take them down, rip them apart limb from limb. Whatever it takes."

"Show me."

Sitting beside me, he pulls out an old iPhone. There's a still of me on the screen. He hits play.

I come alive on the screen. My eyes are closed, and from the movements, it's obvious I'm having sex with the woman taking the video.

"That's right, baby. Make it feel good." My voice echoes in my ears—so familiar.

The me in the video moans and thrusts in time with the woman who's moaning too.

Then I open my eyes, staring into the camera with pure pleasure on my face. *"I'm coming, baby."*

The video ends.

Fuck me and my life.

I stand abruptly. "I need to get Samantha home."

"I'll have William pull the car around back. We can go down the back stairs and through the garage."

"Fine. Let me know when we're ready." I open the door and stop. "Michael, I'd like you to move into the penthouse. I know that's a hardship, but I'd feel better having you close."

"Not a problem, brother," he says with conviction, and he means it. He'd die for Sam.

It had better not come to that.

"Thank you, brother."

I slip across the hall to collect my girl and take her home. Tomorrow we will face this shitstorm together, but tonight I need to hold her, comfort her, and love her in any way she will let me.

HAVE A LITTLE FAITH

Samantha

WARMTH SURROUNDS ME AS I SLOWLY WAKE. HIS hand skims my hip, his breath on my neck, and the tender graze of his lips across the bare skin of my neck and shoulder has my nipples hardening.

"Keep your eyes closed. Stay in half-slumber. Don't think." His raw voice sends chills skating down my body.

A soft kiss behind my ear.

"Let me love you."

Kiss on my neck.

"Don't turn me away."

Kiss. Kiss along my shoulder.

"I need you."

Kiss on my ear.

"I miss you."

His tender words lull me in and keep me in a peaceful place, not asleep and not fully awake. I linger, welcoming that space where nothing exists but the two of us.

"I love you."

He moves over me, whispering across my skin his words of love and comfort. His hard, heated parts, rubbing, seducing my softer, needful ones. Warm breath and hot tongue soothe and tempt in sync with his knowledgeable hands, pulling and teasing, opening and filling. His body surrounds me, cocoons me, fills me and fills me, taking me flying—higher and higher.

Our love. Our souls. Our bodies burst like a phoenix, consumed in flames, fed by the hunger of our passion, our sorrow, our need, our joining. Burning and burning until we are reduced to ash and are reborn.

I leave the thoughts of yesterday and the vision of that video where it belongs, in the past. Showered and dressed, I head to the kitchen to start breakfast. Peace and calm is my motto for the day. It's Sunday, after all. If peace can't be found on a Sunday, then there is no hope.

"Princess." Michael's presence halts me in my tracks.

"Michael?" It's not that unusual to see him here early in the morning, but it is on a non-working day.

He chuckles. "It looks like we're gonna be roomies for a while."

"What?"

Joseph ensconces me from behind, nuzzling into my neck. I can feel his smile against my skin. "I asked Michael to move in. Temporarily."

"Temporarily?" I repeat, turning in his arms.

My Caveman nods with a shrug, not wanting to elaborate.

Peace and calm.

"Okay." It's not like it's a hardship. I love Michael, and it's not the first time we've spent more than our fair share of time together. It's too bad it always seems to be when I'm in danger, which they obviously feel I am. "Pancakes?"

"Hell, yeah!"

Joseph

Michael and I meet with Jace before the others show up. It's family meeting day. It's time to bring in the big guns and stop fucking around. Privacy be damned, except for the picture and video. They'll be aware of their existence, but they don't need to see them.

Jace is pacing the floor, having finished viewing the video. "Jesus, I can't unsee that."

"Welcome to my world," Michael mutters.

"Hey, this is no cakewalk for me. It's humiliating as fuck," I bark.

They both turn to face me, stunned.

Jace is quick to make peace. "Sorry, man."

"Yeah, me too. I know how hard this is on you and Sam," Michael replies with sincerity.

Now that that humiliating show and tell is out of the way. "Anything we need to discuss before Fin and Victor get here?"

Michael grabs a seat across from my desk. "We may need to let Victor see the copies of the picture and video. He has expertise in this area. He may see something we don't." Michael's already overnighted yesterday's package to his forensic buddy.

"I leave that up to your discretion, but under no circumstances are my bothers to see them. The letters are bad enough."

"Matt's still out of town. I can bring him up to speed when he returns," Michael offers.

I nod my agreement before ushering them out of my office to wait for the others' arrival. My need to check on Samantha is strong, more than normal. She seems fine, better than fine. I'm not complaining, but I don't think she's dealing with the events of yesterday, and I don't want to leave her alone too long.

We find her in the kitchen, making lunch for everyone. She may not like social gatherings, but she sure enjoys feeding the Six Pack when we're all together. Sebastian is coming over too; he's going to keep her company while I fill in Fin and Victor. I'm not looking forward to it. It's a total clusterfuck, and I'm quite sure neither of them will fail to remind me of that fact.

"It smells good, Sweets." I kiss her cheek and then her temple, giving her a side hug as she stirs the large pot of gumbo on the stove.

"I hope it tastes good."

I tip her chin, searching her eyes for any signs of sadness. "I have no doubt it'll taste even better." A slow kiss on the mouth with a suck on her bottom lip has her leaning into me like she hasn't done in weeks. "God, I've missed you." I breathe between our lips.

She drops the spoon, letting it stand in the pot, turning into me, wrapping me into a welcoming hug. "I'm sorry," she whispers against my chest.

"Shh, none of that, Sweetness. You're with me now. That's all that matters." With my cheek pressed to the top of her head, I hold her tighter, never wanting to let her go.

A throat clears from behind us.

Fuck off. I don't give a shit who it is, and I don't bother to turn to see.

Another "ahem" has Samantha pulling away, but I stop her. "I'm not ready," I say, my voice low, only for her to hear.

She looks up, a sweet smile lighting up her face, and I'm lost in her blue eyes. She pats my chest, nodding behind me. "I think we have an audience."

On a groan, I turn to see Fin, Victor, Jace, Michael, and Sebastian staring back at us with stupid grins on their faces. *Fuck me.* "Can't you see we're having a moment here?"

Fin laughs. "When *aren't* you having a moment?"

I try to smile back, but if he only knew how rare this was lately, he'd leave us the fuck alone.

Samantha kisses my cheek. "Do you want to eat or have your Boy Scout meeting first?"

Fin and Victor say, "Eat."

Michael, Jace and I say, "Meeting."

"We need to get this over with," I say to them. A nod to Michael has him prompting them to follow him to my office.

Sebastian comes around the breakfast bar. "I guess it's just you and me, cupcake."

My girl smiles. "Now you made me want cupcakes."

"Damn, that does sound good," he agrees.

I'm quite sure he means an actual cupcake and not *my* Samantha, whom he calls *cupcake*. But either way, it sure as hell puts one delectable image in my head of losing myself in my Sweets' pussy. *Shit. Concentrate.* "You two don't have to wait for us to eat, if you don't want to." I kiss her quickly—trying not to think of her other parts I'd like to be kissing—and thank Sebastian for keeping her company with a silent nod, then leave to apprise Fin and Victor on the crap that's been consuming much of our lives for the past few months.

"Why in the hell did you keep this to yourself?" Fin steams as Victor glares daggers into Michael and me.

Yep, pretty much the reaction I expected.

"What could you have done differently that we haven't already done?" I challenge.

Fin steps forward. "Supported you." He clamps on to my upper arm. "Make sure you knew this was bullshit, and we don't believe a word of it."

"Is this why Sam hasn't been to the office?" Victor seems to have calmed down a tad.

I turn on a silent nod, running my hand down my face, not able to admit she can't look at me without seeing that damn photo, and now that fucking video making it even more ominous, more real.

"Brother?" Fin's concern pulls at my gut.

"She's been pulling away, wanting to delay the wedding," Michael steps in.

"What? She can't possibly believe it's true. You'd never cheat on her." Fin's outrage and the depth of his unwavering belief in me tightens the vise in my chest.

"She won't… We haven't…" I turn to face them, avoiding Jace, as I know this is awkward for him, being Samantha's brother. "She can't see me without seeing that fucking picture, and now she has a video to remind her." I stare at the door, like I can see her on the other side. "Today was…unusual." She's her old self today—my girl.

"And we interrupted your moment." The sorrow in Fin's voice is evident.

A curt nod is all I can manage.

"Does she believe you're cheating on her?" Victor asks.

The weight of the last few weeks hits me hard, and I slump down into the couch, my head back, and press my palms over my eyes. *Keep it together.* I still can't find my voice to answer them.

Jace steps up this time. "She doesn't believe it. She trusts Joe." I can feel his eyes on me. "She can't get the images of him with someone else out of her head. She's never been confident in her ability to hang on to him—"

I growl and lean forward, my arms resting on my knees, my hands buried in my hair. "Fuck!" It's one thing to know it. It's another thing to hear it from someone else's mouth. "I'd never cheat on her. She's my world." My voice cracks. It's killing me how much this is hurting her—hurting us—bringing these fucking doubts to the surface that have long since been buried.

The couch dips as Jace and Fin take a seat on either side of me, their hands clasping my shoulders. "We know," they chime in unison.

I look at them, surprised, not so much that they believe me—that is huge, trust me—but that they're so in sync. Jace has been apart from us for a long time, it's good to see him slip back into our fold so seamlessly, as if he never left.

I clear my throat and hope I can keep it together. "Yeah, so she feels we should delay the wedding until things blow over. Not because she believes I'm cheating, but because she believes maybe the threat of even worse packages will stop if we don't get married." I stand at the windows with the image of Samantha walking down the aisle to marry me. "All of this is ruining the wedding for her, 'tainting it,' she says. I won't lose her. I won't let them win by delaying the wedding." Pure menace rages through me for whomever is behind this emotional blackmail.

"We won't let that happen, brother," Fin says, always so sure of himself and his ability to fix my problems.

A soft smile and moment of peace, believing what he says is possible. "Let's talk strategy, then."

Michael takes over, laying out our plan. I glance at the door again, hoping, praying the warm, open woman I left a few minutes ago will still be there when I return.

Samantha

"You're such a troublemaker, Bash." I push his shoulder, and he falls over on the couch laughing.

"I can't help it. If you don't want people knowing you're having sex in the on-call room, then don't have sex in the on-call room." He shrugs. "It's fair game. We may eat at the hospital and sleep there, but that doesn't mean it's okay to have sex there. Seriously, it's our place of business. You don't have sex where you work."

God, if he only knew.

"What? Why are you blushing?" He sits up, looming over me. "Cupcake, is there something you need to confess?"

I push against his chest, laughing. "No. I don't have anything I'd like to confess."

He squints at me. "*Like to confess?* That means you do, but you're not saying." His eyes widen. "Oh my God! You've totally had sex at MCI!"

"No!" I jump up and head to the kitchen. "That would be so wrong." I can't keep a straight face.

Bash follows me. "But kinda hot," he murmurs behind me.

"Really, really hot." I sigh as I stir the gumbo and turn off the rice.

"Holy fuck, Samantha Lilian Cavanaugh, you've totally had sex at the office." He leans against the counter, facing me.

Shaking my head, I suck in my lips. I'm not admitting anything. But I can't keep a smirk from spreading, despite biting my lip to keep my mouth closed. I bang the spoon on the pot, place it in the spoon holder, and close the lid. "I wish they'd hurry. I'm really hungry."

"I can't believe you're not going to answer me. After all the stuff I've told you." He feigns indignation.

I scoff. "Uh, you're the one who says sex talk is off limits. It goes against our *friend-agreement* or some shit like that."

"That was when you were still a virgin, and before I knew you were having sex at the office."

"I never said that."

He chuckles, his face all handsome and lit up. "Babycakes, you don't have to say it. Your body is telling plenty."

He's enjoying this way too much. "Oh, hush. Stop looking, then." I can't get away with anything. All these men around me read me like an open book, like I have a digital banner running across my forehead, advertising my inner thoughts. It's frustrating. Except when Joseph does it, it's kinda hot that he can read me so well.

Bash leans in, whispering in my ear, "Okay, I'll stop. Don't be embarrassed. It's great you two have such an adventurous sex life. I never would have thought of you taking such a risk." He kisses my cheek and pulls away, his teasing gone, but his eyes still twinkle—enjoying this way too much.

"What risk? He has a lock on his office door." I wink as I leave him gawking at me from the kitchen.

The guys finally come out of the office. Joseph looks worn out and leery as he approaches. I meet him halfway. His hands grip my hips like he needs me to ground him. I rest my arms on his shoulders as his forehead touches mine.

"Sweetness," he says so softly it sends chills across my skin.

One hand sinks into his hair, and my other cups his cheek. "I'm here, Caveman."

His eyes close on deep exhale. "Say that again."

Oh, Joseph, you're breaking my heart. I brush my lips across his. "I'm here, Caveman." Kiss. "I love you." Kiss. Kiss. Kiss.

He pulls back, his eyes red-rimmed, but sparkling green. "Besides your orgasms this morning, that's the best sound I've heard all day."

"Well, then, I guess I'll have to be sure to tell you again and again." I kiss his cheek and take his hand. "Now, let me feed you so you have the stamina to pull more of those sounds from me later."

He pulls me back around. His lips crash into mine with a deep rumble in his chest. "Fuck, you made me hard."

I press against him. "You're making me wet."

"Christ, I've fucking missed you." He breathes across my lips.

"The sooner we feed the guys, the sooner they'll leave."

With a gleam in his eyes and a panty-dropping smile on his lips, he pulls me to the kitchen. "Come eat, you assholes, so you can get the fuck out of our house. The caveman needs his woman."

Well, that's one way to call people to come eat. Too bad he doesn't remember he's asked Michael to live with us. Though, I don't think that will stop Joseph from throwing me over his shoulder once his belly is full.

My Caveman needs me. How can I say no?

Thirteen

EXTINGUISH MY FLAME

Samantha

TWO YEARS AGO TODAY I WAS HAVING Thanksgiving with Joseph and my family, our little budding romance not much more than pure attraction and burning lust. My father was still alive and deeply and endlessly in love with my mom. Jace was still a manwhore, and my best friend and overprotective brother.

In a blink of an eye, a shot of a gun, a strike of a single bullet—everything changed. My father was dead from the bullet that tore through his heart and into my shoulder. And, as if that very bullet continued to ricochet through my life, it tore my brother and mother from me too. That one action took everything from me, yet it also gave me everything. It gave me Joseph, though we admittedly had a rather rocky and unconventional start. It also gave me my second family in Joseph's brothers— Victor and Michael fall under the umbrella of *brothers*—and his parents.

Even without Mom, I feel at peace today. Jace is back, full force, one hundred percent in my life. It's a work in progress, but I'm hopeful our relationship will be better than it was before. We're more honest with each other. I don't pretend I don't need anybody, and he doesn't disappear on me.

He's making strides with Joseph too, not only because he's back in my life, but because he believes in Joseph's fidelity and is sticking by him to help figure out the Tiff angle in the emotional blackmail scheme we're in the middle of.

Jace is joining us for Thanksgiving at the McIntyres', but he called Joseph a few minutes ago, sending Joseph striding out of our bedroom to talk to him. "Sweetness," Joseph calls from the living room.

"Coming." I'm running late. I have to stop and pick up a few last-minute items from the grocery store. I rush from our bedroom. "Sorry. I'm ready."

Joseph motions to his cell phone. "Jace has an update. I've got Michael on the line, as well."

"Hey, guys."

Their voices greet me via the speaker on Joseph's cell.

"Jace would you mind repeating what you just told me?" Joseph pulls me down to sit beside him on the couch.

"I met with Tiff," Jace shares.

My eyes lock on Joseph's. He nods as if I need the confirmation that Jace's words are true.

"I only had to push her a little. She folded like a house of cards." Jace clears his throat. "Joe, are you sure want to talk about this with…"

Me. He doesn't want to talk about Tiff with *me* on the phone. I squeeze Joseph's hand. "It's okay, Jace."

A few beats pass before he continues. "Someone named Lydia reached out to Tiff."

"Lydia? MCI's Lydia?" I ask.

"Yes," Michael chimes in.

Wow. She really did hate me.

"Tiff doesn't know how Lydia found her, but Lydia convinced Tiff that you two needed your lives turned upside down—that you didn't deserve to be happy. Lydia played the bitch card, and Tiff bought into it hook, line, and sinker, providing the boxer briefs and video from the night she raped Joseph."

"No. No. No," I whisper. This can't be happening. All of this is from his rape.

"Can you guys give us a moment?" Joseph puts the call on hold. "Samantha, look at me."

My blurry gaze locks on him.

"This is good news." He seems so happy, and I'm devastated.

"What? How can proof of your rape be good news?"

His beautiful smile reveals the dimples I love so much. "Because we know where the underwear, pic, and video came from. We know who's behind this. It's all a scam concocted by Lydia."

I touch his face. "Joseph, you amaze me that you can see the positive in such devastation."

He kisses me quickly before taking the call off hold. "Okay, we're back.

"Everything alright?" Jace's concern is evident and so very welcomed. It's good to have him back.

"Yeah. What else?" I don't want to dwell on the details around Joseph's rape, at least not with Jace and Michael on the line. It makes me sick to my stomach to even think about it.

"I didn't let on that I was in cahoots with y'all. I figured it would be better to keep her on the hook in case Lydia contacts her again. We don't want her to give up that we're on to them." Jace pauses for a second before he continues, a bit sheepishly, I might add. "I, uh, was able to get a DNA sample."

I don't want to know how he accomplished that without making her suspicious.

"I sent the DNA sample off to my guy, but we're going to assume that it's her DNA on the boxer briefs."

Lovely. My stomach rolls at the thought.

"Fin, Victor, and I tracked down Lydia late last night. She no longer works for MCI—Fin was more than happy to fire her ass." Michael chuckles.

"So, it's done then? It's over?" Joseph's hope is contagious, but I have doubts.

"How did Lydia even know about Tiff?" I ask.

"That's a very good question." Michael goes on to advise after threatening Lydia with charges being brought against her, she admitted she was not the mastermind behind all of this. "Supposedly a woman named Bonnie was the one who approached Lydia after she was transferred to Accounting."

"Bonnie? Who the fuck is Bonnie?" Joseph's happy bubble just broke.

I give him a consolatory smile and kiss on the cheek. It was too good to be true. Nothing this nasty wraps up this easily.

Michael continues. "Lydia was out drinking with a few coworkers the evening she was removed as Joseph's PA. She was complaining about not working for Joseph any longer. This Bonnie chick approached her in the bathroom after overhearing Lydia's bitch session. Bonnie convinced Lydia the two of you needed to be taught a lesson. Lydia was all too willing to help."

"I'm sure she was." I don't like to hate people, but I'm pretty sure what I feel for Lydia right about now is hate, pure and simple.

"I should have fired her for her lecherous behavior instead of giving her a second chance." Joseph's happy bubble is definitely gone.

"I doubt it would have made any difference. She would have been bitching about being fired instead of transferred. Whoever Bonnie is probably had her sights on MCI employees, waiting for an opportunity. I doubt her finding Lydia that night was a coincidence," Michael interjects before continuing to share the details of his Lydia discovery. "Lydia was the middle man dealing with Tiff. Lydia swears she has no idea what Bonnie did with the underwear or the video. She said she partied more with Bonnie than anything else."

"Any idea who Bonnie is?" Joseph asks.

"No, but we'll work to get video footage from the places Lydia said she met Bonnie and see if anything comes of that. We also have her cell number. Victor's looking into that, but we assume it's probably a burner phone. I'd also assume Bonnie is not her real name. I'll let you know when we have more." Michael sounds confident we'll figure this out. I find some level of comfort in that, at least.

We hang up with the promise of seeing them later at Joseph's parents' house.

"I guess that's both good news and bad news." I get up from the couch. Despite this latest news, we really need to get going, otherwise we're going to be late for Thanksgiving dinner, well, lunch.

My caveman rakes over my body from head to toe. "I think it's all good news. It's not resolved, but we know more now than we did a few days ago." He stalks closer. "Maybe we can skip Thanksgiving dinner this year." He pulls me into his arms. "Have a little feast of our own." His mouth latches on to my neck on a growl. "Yes, I could savor you for hours, Sweets."

All but panting, I pull back. "Nuh-uh, we're not missing Thanksgiving." I pat his chest. "You'll have to cage the thought. Until later."

On a sigh, he releases me. "Okay, but I'm not swearing I won't whisk you off to my old room for a little dessert afterwards."

My heart leaps. "I look forward to it, Caveman."

Joseph heads to Fin's and will meet me at their parents' house in a few hours. William and I take the elevator to the basement. "Why aren't you spending the holiday with your family?"

He smiles sheepishly. He's a nice-looking guy, tall, big—like Victor— brown buzz-cut hair and pale green eyes. "My family's in Tennessee. I promised Mr. McIntyre I'd see this job through until we catch whoever is threatening you. I mean to keep my word, even if it means I miss a few holidays."

"I hate that you have to work today, but I'm grateful to have you here, protecting me."

"It's my honor, Sam." He opens the door to the SUV, helping me in, before he rounds the front of the car to the driver's side.

Joseph's not crazy about it, but I've asked all the guys to call me Sam. Maybe once we're married, I'll be okay being called Mrs. McIntyre, but I haven't earned that name yet, and being called Ms. Cavanagh only makes me think of my mother. She's the last thing I want to think about today, or most days, for that matter.

We hurry through the store, picking up the last minutes items Fiona needs. The crowd is not bad, but they don't have many cashiers working, so the checkout line is taking a while. I pivot from foot to foot, like I have ants in my pants.

William eyes me with a raised brow. "Problem?"

"I, uh, need to go to the bathroom."

He looks around, trying to hide his smirk. "Okay, we'll find the restroom." He starts to pull out of line, but I stop him.

"Look, we're next. You check out, and I'll run to the bathroom and meet you back here." I squeeze my legs together.

"No. I'm not leaving you unprotected."

I grab his arm, trying to communicate with my eyes that I'm in dire straits here. "I don't have time to argue. I'm gonna pee my pants." I fidget, glancing behind me. The lady next in line only smiles and points to the back of the store. I give her a silent thank you and turn back to William. "Okay, I'm going."

I take off in a near run, having no idea if he's following me. Why is it that the closer you get to a bathroom, the more urgently you have to go? I barge through the door, find the nearest stall, lock it, and barely make it to the toilet.

As I finish and sigh in total relief, a manila folder slides under the stall door.

Holy shit! In my haste to see Bonnie or whoever the hell is stalking me, I stumble over my panties, still down around my ankles, and slam into the stall door. By the time I get situated and out of the stall, the bathroom door closes. I rush out the door, only seconds after whoever was in there with me, but all I see are shoppers and their carts, busy finding what they came for, not paying me any mind, having no idea of what went down in the bathroom. I scan their faces, looking for anyone familiar, but it's to no avail. Whoever it was is gone.

I reenter the bathroom and wash my hands, peering over my shoulder to the envelope lying on the floor behind me. I keep staring at it as I dry my hands and collect my purse. With a resolved sigh, I pick up the envelope.

It's addressed to me, no surprise there.

I have two options. I can wait to open it with Joseph at his parents' house—not my favorite choice—or I open it now, so I can be prepared.

I open it.

And nothing could have prepared me for what I find inside.

Nothing.

There's three pictures.

And a note.

Jesus, those pictures.

I force my emotions down. I can't afford to get upset now.

My hands are shaking, making it difficult to put it all back into the envelope and stuff it in my purse.

Don't think. Move.

I exit the bathroom.

Don't think. Move.

I head to the nearest exit, glance over and see William busy checking out. He doesn't see me.

Don't think. Move.

Outside, I hail a cab.

Breathe. Close your eyes and breathe.

The cab stops at my destination. I pay and get out. I don't have long.

Don't think. Move.

I ride the elevator, unlock the door. Quiet. Empty. Hurry.

Don't think. Move.

I grab an overnight bag, haphazardly throwing items inside. Hurry. Keys.

I run to Joseph's office and grab the keys I need. Hurry.

Don't think. Move.

With a final look around our penthouse, I close the door and take the elevator, sending Michael a text.

Me: *I need you. Don't bring Joseph. Find me like you always do.*

I unlock the door. Cold. This doesn't feel like home. I drop my bag at the entry and walk to the nearest couch. My phone chimes.

Michael: *Fuck, Sam. Why'd you have to ditch William? I'm coming. Don't move.*

Me: *I'm safe. I'm not going anywhere. No Joseph.*

Michael: *I heard you the first time. I understand.*

I turn my phone off. Even if Michael succeeds in leaving Joseph behind, there is no way Joseph won't call me. I'm not sure I'm strong enough to reject his call—but I need to.

The envelope in my purse is taunting me. I take it out and throw it on the coffee table. Maybe the taunting won't be as loud over there.

There's no knocking; only Michael opening the door alerts me to his presence. Of course, he has a key. He always has a key.

"Princess." He approaches me slowly, assessing. His eyes land on the coffee table. "When did that arrive?" He stops in front of me, standing between me and *it*.

My chin starts to quiver. *Dammit, I was doing so good too.*

"Oh, Sam." He's at my side before my first tear falls. He pulls me into a hug. He's big and strong, but he's not Joseph. He's not my home, and that makes me cry even harder. "Shit," he murmurs into my hair. Feelings are not Michael's favorite thing.

I pull myself together enough to speak. "Someone slipped it under the bathroom stall at the grocery store."

He doesn't seem surprised. William must have told him about my pee emergency. "Did you see who it was?"

I shake my head.

"Did you open it?"

I nod.

"It is worse than the last one?"

My tears start to fall again.

"I'll take the fact that you ran away as a yes."

"I didn't run away. I ran home." I look around. "Well, almost."

He smiles. "Thank you for that. It's easier to protect you at MCI than anywhere else."

I don't have a death wish. "That's why I came here."

He eyes the envelope. "I need to open it."

Taking a deep breath, I sit up, allowing him to extricate himself from my side.

He pulls plastic gloves from his pocket and slips them on. "I came prepared." He opens the envelope and tips it up, letting the contents slip out. "Fuck."

"Yep." I can't look away as he picks up the first picture—I should—but I can't.

It's a picture of a woman lying on her back, legs spread wide, held open by strong, powerful hands. A beautiful man with dark hair and emerald eyes feasts on her with a look of pure desire in his eyes—my Joseph's eyes.

He picks up the next picture. This one is basically the same—same woman—except it's from a different angle where I can see the woman's face, smiling at the camera, looking into my soul—laughing at me—as Joseph eats her out with his eyes closed, and I can nearly hear him growling in pleasure. The window is open behind them with a beautiful view of the Las Vegas strip all lit up at night. *Loving Vegas!* Rings in my ears as an echo from the second letter.

I point at the pic. "That's Veronica Hamm." I can't believe it as I say it. I'd hoped the face I saw in the pictures in the bathroom was a mistake, but now that I see them again with the shock worn off... It's her.

"Who's Veronica Hamm?" Michael points a gloved finger at the woman's face. "Her?"

"Yep."

"How do you know her?"

"It's a long story. She used to date Jace, and now she doesn't, because of me." I laugh, but it's humorless. "Jokes on me, huh."

"It looks like we found our Bonnie." He sets it down and pics up the last picture. "Holy shit."

"Yep."

"That's Lydia."

"Yep."

The third and last offering is a picture of Lydia on all fours with Joseph fucking her from behind. Again, Vegas is in the background, and if you look closely enough, you can see Veronica's reflection in the window flipping me off as she snaps the picture.

Michael points it out as he notices Veronica's reflection.

"Yep. It's icing on the fuck-you cake she's worked really hard to deliver."

"Fuck. This girl has to be crazy."

"Nope. She really doesn't like me. She never has, and I don't know why." I'm not sure it matters anymore. She's obviously gotten what she wanted. To take away the man I love—to leave me feeling like I'm noth-ing. Nothing at all.

"Sam, I'm so sorry."

The pity in his eyes is more than I can take. "Read the letter."

He loves my pussy.

He can't get enough of my taste or the way I feel around his cock.

He's mine. LEAVE. NOW!

Sincerely,

Joseph's favorite meal

P.S. I let Lydia get a feel of his massive cock as he pounded her from be-hind, watching me the entire time. See, I'll share my Joseph—just not with you.

Michael puts everything back in the envelope, sets the discarded gloves on top, and slumps back into the couch. "I don't know what to say. I want to tell you it's all bullshit. That those pictures aren't real. And there's a very good chance they aren't. But given that it's this Veronica chick and Lydia, both of whom have a connection to you and Joe, I really don't know anymore."

"You understand why I don't want to see him, then?"

He huffs. "Oh, I understand, and I don't blame you. But, I also know Joseph. I believe in my gut he would never cheat on you. I can't explain anything in that envelope, but I promise, I will work night and day to find the truth. Not what Joseph says is the truth, but the *actual* truth. I can promise you that."

Fourteen

I WON'T GIVE UP

Joseph

IT'S BEEN AN HOUR SINCE MICHAEL DROPPED everything to find Samantha. I don't know how he does it, but he always seems to know where she is. I assume he still has a tracker on her after all this time. He's not taking any chances. I'm thankful for that.

I'm home, pacing. I told my family to proceed with Thanksgiving without us. I made Fin promise to stay there and make sure we don't ruin dinner for them. The last thing I need is Dad and Mom up here in my business—my sexual business—my love life, my future, my world.

"William, sit the fuck down. Or better yet, go to Fin's and get a bottle of his Macallan," I bark, pointing to the front door like he doesn't know where it is.

It's okay for me to pace, but his pacing only agitates me further.

"Yes, sir." He exits quietly. These ex-military guys move with such stealthy precision—it's unsettling at times.

I text Fin so he doesn't freak out about one of his precious bottles missing. I'm sure he has his stash plotted out to the ounce on some multicolored spreadsheet somewhere. His reply is instantaneous, "Take what you need, brother."

Always there. Always supportive. Always has my back. That's Fin.

My phone dings again.

Michael: *Sam is in penthouse 2C. Another package was delivered. Send William down, and I'll come up as soon as I get her settled.*

Relief floods me knowing she's safe and close, but not nearly as close as I want her. I promised Michael I'd give him time to deal the situation before I barged in, possibly making it worse.

Me: *I sent William on a Macallan run. I'll send him over as soon as he gets back. Tell her I love her. She's not answering her phone.*

Michael: *Good, you're gonna need it. Have a couple of glasses to calm yourself down. I can hear your pacing from here. She turned her phone off. I'll tell her.*

Me: *I'm dying here. I need my girl. I need to know she's okay.*

Michael: *You're gonna have to trust me. This is bad. Really fucking bad. She's not okay, but she's safe. I'll always keep her safe.*

"Fuck!" I set my phone on the breakfast bar before I throw it across the room. How can anything be worse than that video? I can't imagine what's in this next package, but if Michael says it's bad, then it's probably horrific—like worst nightmare horrific.

I change into a t-shirt and workout pants. It's gonna be a long day, and I need to run to work off some of my agitation. In the living room I find Jace and William pouring tumblers of the only scotch whisky that passes my lips, thanks to Fin's good taste.

"I hope one of those is for me." I flop down on the couch facing the door. I don't want to miss a second of scrutinizing Michael when he enters.

"They both are, if you need it, but I was hoping to join you." Jace hands me a glass before sitting across from me. "Have you heard anything?"

"William, Michael is with Samantha in penthouse 2C. He'd like you to go down there so he can come here to fill us in."

"On it, sir." He swiftly departs.

"Your mom sent over food. I left it on the counter, not knowing if you'd want to eat it while it's still relatively warm." Jace takes a sip of his whisky.

I, on the other hand, swallow it in one sweet-burning gulp. "Thanks, but I think I'm good with this for right now."

He refills my glass. "Don't get shit-faced, brother. You're gonna need a clear brain when Michael gets here."

"Funny. Michael told me I needed to get a couple of drinks in. Do you know something?"

He laughs. "No, I know my sister. She never would have asked for Michael instead of you unless it was something really bad and incriminating against you."

"Fuck," I hiss and take a slow sip this time.

"You don't have any idea what's happened?"

"Another package was delivered. Samantha ditched William at the grocery store and came here, and asked Michael to meet her, sans me."

"That completely blows."

My sentiments exactly.

Except for the calming music Jace turned on a few moments ago, we sit in silence while we wait for Michael.

We both jump up when the door opens. Michael looks worn out, like he's been up for two days straight instead of the five to six hours it's actually been. It's still early afternoon. His white button-down is rumpled and untucked, and I don't miss the smear of mascara on his chest.

"She's been crying?" I point to his shirt as I sit down on unsteady legs.

He pulls at his shirt, examines it, and then shrugs. "Yeah." In the kitchen he grabs a beer and then joins us in the seating area.

I wait. Impatiently.

He opens his beer, tossing the lid on the coffee table, and sets a manila envelope on his knee. After a long drink, he looks at me. "This was delivered to her in the women's restroom at the grocery store."

"Fuck. Is she okay? Did she see them? Did they hurt her?" Questions charge from my mouth like a runaway train.

He holds up his hand. "How 'bout you let me tell you, then you can ask questions?"

Testy. A testy Michael is not good. I simply nod. Otherwise, I might have to punch him.

"She's fine. Physically. She didn't see anyone. No one hurt her."

"Why did she ditch William?" Jace asks.

"I think once you see what's in this envelope, you won't ask that question." Michael looks to me. "I need to show you these in private." He points at Jace. "I'll explain why after." He gets up, taking his beer and the envelope, and heads to my office.

I finish off my scotch and follow, dread eating me up as I go. I close the door behind me and face Michael.

"You're going to need to sit down." He motions to the couch.

After I sit, he hands me a set of gloves that match the ones he's already wearing. I slip them on as he pulls something out of the envelope and sits on the coffee table in front of me.

"There's no way to warn you, other than to say it's bad. Really, really bad."

I nod my understanding. What is there really to say other than let's get it the fuck over with!

He was right to warn me. There's no way to prepare for what I see. I stare at it in disbelief. "I see it, but I don't believe it. There is no way that's me." I point at the woman's pelvis. "I've never been with a woman with a tattoo. I have no idea what that one says, but I'm pretty sure I'd remember, with it staring me in the face in that position." I hand it back to Michael. "Don't look so fucking pissed. It's not me."

Silently, he hands me the next picture. Same position, same woman, except her face is showing. "I've never…wait." I stand and then sit again. "Son of a bitch! That's the woman from the happy hour. The one Fin was questioning me about. She's a British tourist."

"Do you know her name?"

"No." I shrug and hand him back the pic. "I only talked to her for a few minutes. She and her friend wanted a selfie with me. That's the night Samantha stayed home, upset because of the whole betting pool thing. Remember?"

He groans. "Don't remind me. That's the day I stuck my foot in my mouth and hurt her feelings."

"It's a sensitive issue for her. And this shit right here is not helping." I catch his gaze. "She thinks I've cheated on her, doesn't she? Because of these pics."

"Let's finish with the contents before we jump into what she's thinking. I need both your and Jace's feedback on these pics. It's quite a puzzle, and it seems each of you may have input to help pull it all together."

I hold out my hand. "Hit me."

He lays the third pic on my hand. "Ah, Christ." I close my eyes and turn my head. "That's Lydia." I try to hand it back to him.

"I'm sorry, man, but I really need you to look at these pics in detail and tell me what you see." He pushes my hand away.

Drawing a deep breath, I look at the pic again. But instead of looking at Lydia, I look at the guy. "That's not me. That's not my body. It may be my face, but this dude is skinner than me."

"What else do you see?"

"Uh…shit is that Vegas?" I look up. "Holy fuck, Samantha thinks I cheated on her in Vegas." I drop the pic and storm out of the office.

"Jace, don't let him go," Michael yells.

Jace jumps in front of me, holding me back. "Joe, just wait. Wait." He looks behind me at Michael.

"I've got to see her, Jace. She thinks I cheated on her."

"Joe, we need to finish this. It's going to take the three of us to figure this out. Until we do that, she's not going to see you. I promised her I'd find the truth. I intend to do that, but I can't do it without your help. Don't make her suffer longer than she has to. Come back to the office, and let's finish this. She's going to need real proof this time."

My head falls forward. He played the Samantha's suffering card, knowing there is no way I'd knowingly cause her any more pain. I back down.

"Jace, grab the Macallan and join us." Michael squeezes my shoulder as I reenter my office.

Michael collects the pictures, gives Jace some gloves, and repeats the same process he did with me, handing Jace one photo at a time.

Jace glances at the first one and then at me, his brow raised.

"Jace, I swear to you. *That* is not me." I point to the guy in the photo.

He shakes his head. "This is taking our relationship to a whole different level." His gaze bounces between Michael and me before landing back on the pic. He squints. "This guy is too skinny to be you."

"See, I told you," I say to Michael.

"Hey, do you have a magnifying glass?" Jace asks, looking closer at the photo. "That tattoo looks familiar."

"I think I have one—" I start to say.

"I don't think you'll need it once you see the next picture." Michael hands Jace the second photo.

"No fucking way." Jace looks at the photo, to me, and back to the photo. "Joe, do you know who this is?"

He says it like he knows who it is. "Who?"

"You don't recognize her?" He holds up the pic to my face.

"Wait." I look at Michael. "How does he know who it is? I only met her that one time at the bar. Jace wasn't there."

Michael smiles. "Now we're getting to the meat of it. Jace, tell Joe who it is."

"You really don't recognize her?" Jace asks me again.

"No! I saw her that one time in the bar, but you weren't there. She's a British tourist, but I never got her name, and I sure as shit didn't do to her what those pictures lead you to believe." This is insane. What the hell is going on?

"British tourist?" Jace frowns at me. "I can't believe you don't recognize her. You gave me such shit for dumping you and Sam to go home with her." He shakes his head, staring at the picture. "I can't believe it's her." He looks up at Michael. "Why would she do this? Besides the shit that happened with Sam, she's the sweetest girl I know."

I'm crawling out of my skin. "Who the fuck is she?" I nearly scream.

Jace's big blue eyes look at me with pure sadness. "It's Veronica. My Veronica."

The name takes a moment to come back to me. "Veronica Hamm? The one who hurt Samantha?"

He nods. "Yeah."

"Fuck. Wait. So, you're saying the British tourist isn't a British tourist at all and was Veronica? How did I not recognize her?"

He shrugs. "Even back then you only had eyes for Sam. I guess what she looked like didn't really register for you, only what she did to Sam made a lasting impression." He sets the photo on the table and looks at Michael. "Is there more?"

Michael hands him the last pic.

Jace studies it for a second, not even flinching. "Who is this?"

"It's Lydia, my old temp PA."

"The one you fired? You fucked her?"

"Christ." I stand up and pour myself three fingers of scotch. "Fin actually fired her since she was transferred to his department. And no, for the hundredth time, I didn't fuck anyone. I haven't had sex with a single solitary person in over two years except Samantha and that bitch Tiff. Which I still don't remember, but we're being technical here, so there." I set down the bottle harder than I should and take a large gulp from my tumbler, when I'd rather drink it from the bottle.

I turn to them. "Look at that guy in the picture. You've both seen me practically naked. That guy is not me. He's a different body type than me, close, but smaller and probably shorter, but my thighs are bigger. My chest is wider, and my guns are definitely bigger than that guy's."

Jace looks at the picture again. "Shit. Did you see the reflection?"

Michael nods.

I lean against the wall, not really wanting to look at Lydia getting nailed by some guy who's been digitally altered to look like me. "What?"

Jace holds up the pic and points to the window. "Veronica is there, taking the pic, and giving us the finger."

"Sam thinks she's giving *her* the finger," Michaels speaks up. He's been rather quiet.

"Michael, what do you think?" I resume my seat on the couch.

"I think Veronica Hamm is Bonnie. I think she's the mastermind behind all of this. What I don't know is why or how she got ahold of Joe's blue tie, or if these pictures are doctored." He holds up his finger. "We'll get back to that. Here." He hands me the note that came with the photos. "You need to read this before we get into the other details."

"Motherfucking bitch from hell." I hand the paper to Jace. My eyes lock with Michael's. "You don't believe me. That those pictures aren't me."

The look of guilt tells me all I need to know.

"Actually, I believe you, Joe." His response is not what I was expecting. "To be honest, I didn't initially. At first glance, those pics are awfully incriminating. The photo from the fourth package was you. The video from the fifth package was you. The underwear and tie are yours. This next set of photos are good—whoever doctored them is really talented. But mostly, when I look at you, Joe, I see a man who's so in love with one woman, that there is no way in hell you'd cheat. I know you, man, and even if you did cheat, you wouldn't keep lying about it. You'd fess up. Shit, man, you even fessed up to sleeping with Tiff, and she's the one who raped you. You don't even remember it, yet you still owned up to it like you cheated."

He stands before me, his hand outstretched. I take it, and he pulls me to my feet. His hand holds mine tightly, and his other grips my shoulder. "You listen to me." His brow is pinched, and his eyes stare at me like he's pissed off, but his words tell me otherwise. "You did not cheat. You. Were. Raped. Whether you remember it or not. That's the truth of it. I don't know if you still harbor any guilt about it. But you need to let that shit go. Understand?"

"Yeah." I nearly choke on my reply. That's the most Michael's ever said to me about the Tiff incident. He's always made it clear he believed me, but still, the level of his support is moving. "Thanks, brother."

"Don't mention it, brother." With a squeeze of my shoulder, he releases me, moving back to his chair.

"All this stuff doesn't help, does it?" Jace motions to the photos and letter on the table.

I sit back down. "No, it doesn't help having it thrown in my face over and over again. The worst part, though, is how it's impacted my girl. I'll endure any hardship if only to save her from all of this."

"You need to remember that, Joe. She's really upset. I know she wants to believe in you, but her self-doubt and lack of confidence in being able to compete with all of this is eating her up. She doesn't want to see you. She made me promise that if she remained at MCI Towers, where we can keep her safe and under our watchful eye, then I have to keep you away. If you force her to see you, she'll run. She's proven herself to be quick on her feet and calculating. I have no doubt if she wanted to, she could evade our protection like she did today, or before when she plotted to meet up with Daniel's killer. She's smart. We all know it, and she's not afraid to put herself in danger if she believes it's for the greater good."

"Okay, I'll agree to it for now, but I don't know how long I can go without seeing her. I also have one condition. I need to go to her tonight. Even if it's only to talk to her through the door. I *have* to speak to her. I *need* to do this."

Thankfully, he agrees, and we spend the next few minutes filling Michael in on why Veronica hates Samantha so much, and what Veronica did to her in high school.

"Jace, you had no idea?" Michael asks in disbelief.

"No. You know I'm a self-absorbed prick. I had no idea any of the girls I hung out with were bitchy to Sam. Joe filled me in. I still can't believe it. I was so oblivious. Veronica has always been so sweet and quiet, maybe a little standoffish with the other girls. But I had no idea she was plotting against Sam. Veronica was never catty like that in front of me. But the whole blowjob set-up thing—that's a level of spite I couldn't ignore. I cut off all ties with Veronica that Thanksgiving. The last time I saw her was at Dad's funeral."

"You didn't tell me she was there." I'm not too happy about that.

"She didn't approach Sam or me, so I figured it was harmless. Plus, I didn't want to upset Sam by bringing it up."

Understandable. "What are you thinking, Michael?"

He collects the evidence and puts it back in the envelope. "I think I need to get these to my forensics guy, but I want to show Victor first. Then we need to find Veronica and get a confession out of her, or prove it's not you in these photos." He stands. "We need concrete proof to show Sam."

"We'd better fucking hurry. We get married in less than four weeks." I glare at them both. "Don't even think it. There is no way in hell I'm not marrying my girl."

YOU ARE THE REASON

Joseph

MY ALCOHOL-INDUCED CALM HAS PASSED, AND now the need to see my girl is overpowering. I'm done waiting. I send Michael a text telling him I'm on my way. I take a couple of Advil, grab a water, and head to the penthouse below ours.

She's only one floor away, but it feels like a continent at the moment. A floor, a door, the width of our clothing, a single breath between us seems too great a distance.

I knock, knowing it won't open, praying she'll at least listen if nothing else. There's shuffling on the other side, a few murmurs. Then I hear Michael. "She's here. She can hear you."

On a thankful sigh, I lean against the door and speak into the crack that separates us. "Sweetness." My voice breaks, and I have to take a couple of deep breaths to keep my shit together.

With steadier emotions, I try again. "Those pictures…the guy in them. It's not me. I know all the evidence tells you otherwise. But it's not me, and I'll prove it to you. Don't give up on me—on us. Give me time to find Veronica and get to the bottom of it."

Her sob breeches the barrier between us, and it guts me.

"Sweetness, please let me in. Let me hold you. Comfort you."

More sobs.

"I'm sorry. I'm so fucking sorry."

She wails.

Shit! "No. I'm not apologizing because I cheated. I didn't. Those photos are not me. I understand why you think they could be real, but I promise you they aren't. I'm sorry for hurting you, for making you doubt me, for everything that Veronica's done to you."

"Us," she croaks from the other side.

I gasp on my own sob. "Yes. Us. What's she's done to *us*."

She spoke to me. She thinks we're still an *us*. There is hope, and I'm not letting go of it. "I'm here. I'm not going anywhere. You cry, and I'll sit here and comfort you." I slide down the door, sitting sideways, my lips pressed to the crack, and I swear I can feel her breath slipping through and feeding my soul.

"Joseph," she cries with such anguish. Her voice is even with mine, confirming she's on the floor too.

"I'm here, Samantha. I promise you I'll always be here. Until my dying day, I'll always be here."

Her crying stops only to start up again. Hours pass and eventually she falls silent as do I, afraid if she's fallen asleep, my voice will wake her up.

My ass is numb, and I'm sore from sitting in the same position, but I don't dare move. Her cries, her words, her silence are the only company—only comfort—I need.

I start to doze. My head falls forward, and I catch myself. I've ignored offers from William to get me something more comfortable to sit on. I'm not going anywhere. I'll sleep right here on this cold hard floor. It's as close as I can get to her. I need to be here if she needs me.

At some point, I must have fallen over. I open my eyes and blink at Michael, who is staring down at me. He throws me a pillow and comforter. "She fell asleep. I put her in bed, but she insisted I give you those if you're going to stay out here all night."

I sit up, smiling. "She still cares."

Michael laughs. "Of course she cares, jackass. You don't cry your eyes out over someone you don't give a shit about." He throws something at

William. "The key to 2D. He's gonna have to go to the bathroom eventually. Maybe you can drag him inside once he falls asleep."

"I'll fire you if you do." I crack my neck and smile at my comforter and pillow. My girl is looking out for me. It's a good sign.

Day 2

Joseph

I wake on the hard floor, wrapped in the comforter, my head on the pillow and a smile on my face. Things don't seem so bleak today. My girl spoke to me last night. She made sure my camping out at her door was as comfortable as possible, and she still considers us an *us*. That's huge.

Stretching out my aches, I get to my feet and spot Victor in a chair outside the other penthouse door. "Good morning, lover boy. Breakfast and coffee are inside, if you'd like some." He stands as I approach.

I shove the comforter and pillow at him. "Take care of these, will you? I'll need them later."

"Yes, sir." He chuckles, finding this way too humorous.

First stop, the bathroom, then breakfast, and then attacking my plan to woo my girl and prove my innocence.

Samantha

When my father died, I thought I knew what darkness was. When I broke up with Joseph, believing he slept with someone else that same night, I didn't think I could sink any lower. I was wrong. I should know better than to tempt fate, believing it couldn't get any worse. It can always get worse.

I'm not going to say this is the worst—that I can't go any lower—the whole fate thing has me skittish. So, I'll just say—it sucks. I'm feeling emotionally hung over, and in desperate need of my Joseph fix.

He couldn't have been any sweeter last night. He didn't force his way in. My Caveman honored my wishes, my request that he not try to see me. He kept his word, comforting me from the other side of the door in a way that only Joseph can do with a simple turn of a phrase. He might be a caveman, but he's a romantic beast.

Flowers. He sent me the largest arrangement of flowers I've ever seen. There have to be six dozen roses, at least. William sets it on the coffee table and hands me the card.

My Sweets,
I love you more with every passing moment.
Don't let the doubt in.
Check out the newest song in your music library.
You are the reason for everything I do, for everything I am,
for everything I will be.

I love you,
Joseph

I pull up my music on my phone, and there in my library is a new song, "You Are The Reason" by Calum Scott. I hit play, and by the end of the first verse I'm crying.

I send him a text as I continue to listen.

Me: *You break my heart in the most amazing ways.*

Joseph: *If I'm breaking your heart, then I'm doing something wrong, Sweets.*

Me: *You're doing everything right, Caveman.*

I wipe my tears and lie back on the couch, his card held to my chest. As I listen to his song again, my phone chimes.

Joseph: *I'll be at your door after dinner. I'll bring my blanket and pillow. You don't have to say a word. I need to be close to you. To feel you near.*

That night and the two that follow, Joseph shows up after dinner. He sits outside the penthouse door, talking to me through the crack. Sometimes I answer, but most times I don't trust myself to not break down. I love him, and I know he loves me. I don't know how we move past this. How can I marry him after seeing those pictures? Those pictures that don't make any sense to me. How could he cheat on me with Veronica, of all people, and that bitch Lydia?

He wouldn't! But…I don't know what to believe. My heart and my eyes don't agree, and I can't bear to look at those pictures again—to study them—to pick them apart—to see if I can tell truth from lies. So, I don't. I stay sequestered the Friday after Thanksgiving through the weekend. The only time I feel alive is when Joseph is sitting outside my door at night, telling me he loves me and that he'll prove his innocence.

Proof. I need proof, and that's what he's promising. So, I wait each day for him to show me he's not a cheater—that it's all a scam—concocted by one of my brother's ex-sluts and my fiancé's bitter ex-PA, all in an effort to get back at me for a wrong they believe I've done them, when in fact, I've done absolutely nothing.

But sometimes life and people don't care much about truth or what's right. Sometimes life throws a tantrum, and those in its wake just have to hold on, ride it out, and pray—pray—for mercy.

Sixteen

I WILL WAIT

DECEMBER

Joseph

DAY 5

MONDAY. THANK GOD. THE WEEKEND WAS torture without my girl. I welcome the distraction of work and an office full of people and meetings. I've avoided my parents for as long as I can, with Fin running interference. Matt is finally back in town. I don't know where the fuck he's been, but I've been a little busy with my own shitstorm to worry about him.

I enter Dad's office and close the door, finding Dad giving Matt the third degree. Fin sits on the couch, busy on his phone, but it's a ruse. Taking a seat next to him, I silently ask what's going on with a single look. All I get is a shrug and a raised eyebrow.

Matt looks uncomfortable, like he'd rather be anywhere else than here.

"You requisition a company plane to fly to Sin City for a week and don't even bother to call your mother to let her know you won't be home for Thanksgiving!" Dad's voice is getting rougher the redder his face gets.

I feel like I'm fifteen and about to get grounded, waiting for my turn on the chopping block.

"Actually, we only spent two nights in Vegas. We went skiing for Thanksgiving," Matt tries to clarify, like that's going to make a difference.

But then it registers—what he said. I elbow Fin. "Uh, Vegas?" I ask loud enough for them to hear me.

All eyes zoom to me.

"You have something to add, Joseph?" Yeah, Dad using my full name is not a good sign.

I stand and clear my throat. "Who were you in Vegas with?"

Matt scowls and looks away. "What difference does it make?"

"Bear with me." I look at Fin to see if he's caught on to my train of thought, but the crease in his forehead tells me he hasn't. "Who were you with in Vegas?" I ask again with an edge to my voice.

Matt avoids eye contact like his life depends on it.

In a heartbeat I'm in his face. "What's. Her. Name?" My body hums in agitation for what I believe is coming.

Dad steps forward, pushing us apart. "What's going on, Joseph?"

Ignoring my father, I glare at Matt.

"Spit it out Matt, before he pummels you." Fin joins me at my side, facing Matt.

"Lydia." Matt steps back as if I'm going to attack him.

But that's not the case, not at all. I'm filled with elation.

"Who else?" Fin asks, finally catching on.

"Some chick you don't know." Matt frowns at us walking to the sitting area, putting the couch between us.

I nearly laugh. If I wanted to get to him, that couch would not stop me. "Her name?"

"Joe, what the hell is going on?" Dad moves toward Matt, looking between the three of us like he doesn't know who he needs to protect and who he needs to scold.

"Just…" I hold up my hand to the man who gave me life. "Give me a second, then I'll explain."

"Matt," Fin barks.

"Bonnie. Her name was Bonnie, for fuck's sake. Jeez." Matt looks at us like we're crazy.

I try to catch my breath. "Thank, God." I collapse on the couch, my head in my hands. "Someone get Michael and Victor in here. Now!"

Samantha

The bed seems particularly empty this morning. Melancholy oozes from my pores. The sun coming in from the bedroom windows is entirely too chipper. But I'm glad it's Monday. I need the distraction of school to eat away the hours between now and when Joseph comes this evening.

William escorts me to the car. I'm in a daze. I can't get my mind off the last thing Joseph said to me last night, and every night since those damn photos showed up.

I'll prove it to you. I'll prove my innocence.

Proof. I keep saying I need proof.

But what does that mean?

What kind of proof do I need?

Do I need some sort of forensics report stating the pictures are fakes?

Couldn't that be doctored as well? Who's to say Victor or Michael won't have one of their contacts provide a fake report? I'd never know the difference. It's not like I'm an expert in photographic forensics. I don't know what I'm looking for. I don't know what verbiage on the report would satisfy my need for proof.

How far am I willing to take this until I'm convinced Joseph didn't cheat on me?

How long am I willing to live without him? A month? A year? Forever?

Am I going to cancel the wedding? Why? Because some bitch sent me a photo that may or may not be real? I know Joseph. *His love* for me is real. *That's* what matters.

Dizzy with a wave of nausea, I grip my stomach and lean forward.

What the hell am I doing?

"Stop! We have to go back."

"Are you okay? Are you going to be sick?" William's concern is evident.

"No. Turn around."

Damn downtown. It takes three rights to make a left with all these one-way streets. Finally. Finally, we pull into the garage. As soon as we're parked, I jump out and run to the Alpha Tower elevators. "Come on."

"Sam?" The sound of William's pounding feet get closer until he catches up with me.

I glance over. "Don't tell him I'm coming."

He smiles. "No, ma'am. I wouldn't dare."

I walk laps in the elevator. William simply stands back, watching me in amusement.

When the doors open, he steps in front of me. "At least let me get out first."

I nod. I've broken all kinds of protocols already. And if I have my way, I'm about to break some more.

With his okay, I rush to Joseph's office.

Teddy stands when he sees me. "Sam. God, he's going to be so happy to see you."

I hope so. "Hi, Teddy." I motion to the door. "Can I?"

He smiles. "I wouldn't stop you for the world."

I return his smile, but a rush of fear stops me from opening the door.

"Go on," Teddy whispers from behind me.

I subdue my emotions on a deep breath and slow exhale, and then open the door and step inside.

Joseph rises to his feet. "Samantha."

As soon as I see him, my emotions crash into me. Tears prick my eyes, and I cup my mouth to stop a sob from escaping. Five days. It's been five torturous days.

What the hell was I thinking?

Joseph rushes to me. "What happened?" He collects me against his chest as soon as I'm within reach.

I can't answer him. The dam has broken free, and there's no stopping it now.

"Nothing. Nothing happened. She… needed to see you," William says.

A mass of noise and shuffling pass by us, and then silence. Except for my sniffles and stunted breaths, I hear nothing else.

Joseph whisks me off my feet and sits with me on his lap. "Christ, it's good to see you, to hold you in my arms." His lips brush my forehead as his warm breath skirts my face. "Tell me what's going on."

"I believe you." I look up, meeting his eyes. "I believe *in* you."

"Thank fuck," he sighs, his relief palpable. "What changed?" I start to pull back, but he stops me. "Please don't. I need to hold you."

I cup his cheek. "I'm not going anywhere. I just need to see you."

He situates us so he's holding me as close as possible while still making eye contact. "Better?"

I smile my reply, but when I see his fatigue-worn eyes, my chin starts to quiver. "I've missed you so much."

He runs his hand down the side of my face. "I was there. I was always there."

"I know." I bite my lip and close my eyes to stop from crying.

"Hey." He taps my cheek, and I open my eyes. "Don't hold it in. If you need to cry, cry. I'm not going anywhere. I'll wait forever to hear what you have to say."

"I'm so sorry. I feel like I'm always apologizing for being a step behind, for not being confident enough in our relationship to trust you without proof." I run my fingers through his hair. *God, I've missed this hair.* "But you know what? I had proof all along."

"You did?" He truly seems perplexed.

I nod. "Your love. Your commitment to me for the past two years, even when we weren't together. Your eye never strays from mine. You don't ogle women when you think I'm not looking. You don't tolerate threats. You simply remove them—hence, Lydia. You've never been a playboy even in your most single of days before me. You're a one-woman man—and I'm *it*."

"Yes, yes you are." His smile, even tired, is still devilishly handsome.

"I don't know if you can forgive me, but I pray you will. And if you'll still have me. I'd like to marry you in three weeks."

His lips crash into mine. *Oh, god, I've missed these lips.* But he pulls away on a groan, ending the kiss too soon. "Sweets, there was never any chance of you not marrying me in three weeks." His desirous stare and growled words send a chill through my body.

"God, I've missed you, Caveman."

Seventeen

STILL YOURS

Joseph

WE MANAGE TO MAKE IT TO THE PENTHOUSE before we launch at each other. Five days. Five fucking days without my girl. "Never again," I hiss as our mouths collide in a needful, hungry kiss. She moans, latching on to my hair and the back of my neck, trying to consume me, keep me from pulling away. No way am I stopping. Not now. Not ever.

I lift her off her feet, and she wraps her legs around my waist as I cup her bite-worthy ass. To the soundtrack of our moans and lustful kisses, I make my way to our bedroom and drop her on the bed. She giggles on a bounce as I free my cock and relieve her of her panties. "Thank god for skirts."

She squirms as I gather the material over her hips and settle between her thighs. All thought of removing shoes or any other articles of clothing is lost in a single thrust, sheathing my rock-hard cock in her warmth. "Fuck." My eyes lock on hers, telling me everything I need to know.

"Kiss me," she pleads, lifting her legs, spreading, welcoming me to sink in deeper.

And I do. I anchor my forearms under her shoulders, and my hands are lost in her hair. My lips brush hers tenderly as I grind my hips,

595

burrowing as deeply as I possibly can. She clutches me to her, pulling, as if she's trying to absorb me into her body. "Kiss me," she repeats, but I know what she really means is *fuck me*.

"Sweetness," I breathe before the caveman takes over, consuming her mouth as I drive my cock into her over and over again, setting a relentless pace.

Ravenous, my girl asks for more. "Harder. Faster."

"Fuck." She's gonna unman me with her moans and need for me to claim her, to take her, to love her even in this heated mania.

My phone starts ring.

"Ignore it," I command myself and her, kissing her harder.

Her phone starts to ring.

I growl and pound harder. "Stay with me…"

A door slams as shuffling feet and low murmurs come from the entryway. "Joe!"

"Christ. Fuck. We're not done. Don't move." I pull out on a groan and stalk to our bedroom door. "Fifteen minutes. You better be dying!" I bellow and slam the door, locking it.

Samantha giggles from the bed, closes her legs and starts to pull down her skirt.

"No. No fucking way are those assholes stopping me from making love to you." I climb back on the bed and still her hands.

"It's okay. We can do this later."

"*Do this later?*" I hover over her on all fours, my eyes searching hers, watching her trying to calm her breathing. "No, Sweets. You came back to me, and not even the end of the world could stop me from being with you." I settle between her thighs, rubbing my cock through her wet folds. "Now, where were we?" I pull back and push into her deliciously slowly.

Her back arches. "Oh, god."

I pull out and push in again slowly, ever so slowly. "Was this where I was?"

"Nearly," she mews.

Out and in a little faster, a little deeper. "Here?"

"Almost," she moans, her eyes begging for more.

Ah, fuck, my sexy girl. I thrust. Deeper. Harder. Pumping. In. Out. In. Out.

She moans, clutching me to her. Her whole body shaking, begging for release.

"How about now, baby? Is this where I was?"

"Yes! Oh, god, yes!"

My mouth consumes hers, plunging, teasing, sucking as my body rides her like the best damn seesaw I've ever been on. Back and forth. Our hips rocking together. Back and forth. Her knees come up. Her feet lock below my ass and squeeze with each thrust.

"Fuck. Just like that, my Sweets."

Harder. Deeper.

Faster. Faster.

"Joseph." She's warning me, praising me, telling me she's coming.

"Yes. Come for me, baby."

And she does. Christ Almighty, she does. Gripping my cock with the most glorious pussy I'll ever know, she shatters, calling my name, begging me not to stop—like I'd ever stop. She comes undone and takes me with her.

I groan my release with quick thrusts, bury my face in her neck, and nearly weep—so thankful to have her back in my arms, in my life—asking me to fuck her and never stop.

Never stop.

My girl.

Samantha

I'm panting, trying to recover with Joseph's dead weight pressing me into the mattress, or maybe it's me still clutching him to me—with my arms and legs—like he'd float away if I let go. A deep breath, a steady exhale, I slowly loosen my grip—not completely—but enough for him to lift his head.

His lips and warm breath kiss along my jaw, nip my chin, and down the other side. "You okay, Sweetness?"

"Yeah. You?"

The green eyes I love so much come into view. A slow smile ticks across his lips. He thrusts his hips, reminding me we're still joined. "I couldn't be any better." His mouth moves lovingly over mine with slow brushes of his tongue pushing my lips apart, languidly kissing me until he starts to harden and twitch inside me. He pulls back on a groan. "I guess I need to go see what the guys want."

Dazed, I simply nod.

He smiles, then presses his mouth to mine softly. "Hurry, come join me."

I whimper when he pulls away, sliding out of me.

Before I can close my legs, he dips his head and lays a gentle kiss above my clit, his tongue sweeping out and pressing ever so tenderly.

I gasp and nearly bow off the bed.

He does it again and again, holding my legs open, pinned to the bed. His fingers plunge inside slowly, caressing that tender spot that makes me want him even more.

I clutch the comforter, close my eyes, and pray he doesn't stop.

He doesn't.

Thank god.

Thirty minutes later, we walk into the living room. Joseph sits on the couch and pulls me next to him with my legs flung over his, one arm behind my back, while the other rests over my legs. Michael, Victor, Jace, Fin, and Matt are scattered around the room, talking, getting drinks from the bar, food from the kitchen, and completely oblivious to us joining them.

Fin quirks a smile when he spots us. "Nice of you to join us. Enjoy yourselves?"

Joseph squeezes my leg. "Fuck off."

"I'll take that as a *yes*," Fin teases, offering to get us drinks.

Once everyone has settled, all eyes focus on Michael, who looks to me and then Joseph. "So, you told her?"

My love's hand kneads my leg as if to soothe his response. "No, not yet."

Michael's eyebrows arch as if to say *why the fuck not?*

I meet Joseph's gaze, his eyes hopeful, if not a little sad. "Right before you came to me, we discovered that it was actually Matt in the pictures with Veronica and Lydia."

Holy shit! I seek out Jace and then Matt to see how they're handling this news. "Matt, you were in Vegas?"

He simply nods, obviously embarrassed.

"But how…your face?" I stumble, looking to Joseph.

"They were doctored," Victor speaks up. "With Matt and Joseph looking so much alike, it's easy to do."

"Not you?" I whisper to Joseph's blurry face.

He swipes at my tears. "Not me, baby."

"Oh, god. I'm so sorry," I bawl.

Joseph pulls me to his chest, my face buried in his neck. "Shh, Sweetness. None of that. You believed me before you had proof. There's nothing to be sorry for. Anyone would have doubted with the evidence stacked against me."

That only makes me cry harder.

"Asshole! I can't believe you fucked her!" Jace's voice breeches my meltdown.

Matt backs up, hands in the air, not wanting to fight Jace. "I didn't sleep with her, brother. She wasn't interested. I didn't even know who she was. If I'd known Bonnie was actually your Veronica, I never would have done anything with her. I swear."

Jace halts his advance. "You didn't sleep with her?"

"I swear. The only thing that happened is what you saw in that picture. She didn't even touch me. I thought she had some crazy kink and only wanted to watch, take pictures." Matt lowers his hands and slowly moves toward Jace. "I swear, brother, I didn't know it was Vee. *Your* Vee"

Vee? *His* Vee? "Jace?"

He glances at me. "Leave it, Sam." He's hurt, really hurt.

"I swear," Matt reiterates.

Jace simply nods, grabs his glass full of what I assume is Fin's favorite indulgence, and sits in the nearest chair, brows drawn, not open to further discussion.

We take a break and devour the Chinese food Fin ordered. Jace joins in, alcohol having mellowed his anger. Matt, a little self-conscious, is quiet but not closed off. Michael and Victor keep exchanging glances like they have a secret, which they usually do. Fin watches everyone, calculating who is gonna freak out next. Me? I keep looking at Joseph, finding him looking at me with a beaming smile. My heart soars but flutters a little each time I think about how I doubted him. Reading me like he always does, he simply touches me, gives me a squeeze, or a kiss—each time telling me he forgives me—he loves me—and to stop beating myself up.

Once dinner is cleaned up, we reassemble in the living room. I reclaim my seat next to Joseph, who can't keep his hands off me—not complaining.

This time it's Victor who speaks. "After the revelation this morning, Matt agreed to call Lydia and ask that she and Bonnie meet him for an early lunch under the ruse that he had gifts for them as a thank you for their time in Vegas."

None of us misses Jace's scoff from across the room.

Victor gives him a sympathetic glance before continuing. He points to Matt. "Needless to say, Matt didn't show. However, the ladies did."

Joseph leans forward. "Tell me you have them."

"We have them."

"Holy shit," Fin says.

"No. Fucking. Way," Joseph punctuates before meeting my gaze. "We have them," he whispers, pulling me closer.

"What does this mean?" I ask.

Michael moves to sit on the coffee table in front of me. "It means it's over, Princess."

I lean forward. "But we can't hold them. It's not legal." I glance around the room. "Have they broken any laws?"

Joseph takes my hand, moving closer. "Lydia broke her Non-Disclosure Agreement by sharing information she acquired while employed at MCI. Her NDA applies while she was an active employee, and for three years after she leaves the company either of her own accord or released. She shared information with Veronica that breached that agreement. Additionally, though Veronica did not blackmail us to extort money, Lydia and Tiff colluded with Veronica in acquiring defamatory information with the sole purpose of causing emotional distress to a VP at MCI and his fiancée. We may not be able to bring criminal charges against them, but we can sue the three of them in civil court for emotional distress and defamation of character. Even if we don't win, we could tie them up for years and bankrupt them for life."

Holy shit. Joseph as a hot lawyer nearly trumps Joseph as a hot VP— nearly. My panties just got wet.

He smirks as if he can read my mind.

"But…w-we can't hold them," I stutter, overwhelmed by Joseph's hot lawyer persona.

"We're simply providing accommodations for them while we negotiate their surrender," Victor offers.

I look to Michael, the only one in this room with recent law enforcement experience. He simply smiles. "We have it handled, Sam. We need to know how you want to move forward."

"How *I* want to move forward?" I look at the men in this room. All of them are watching me as if I have jurisdiction on how this should play out.

"Michael, you should share the additional information you have on Veronica before any decisions are made." Victor looks at me, Jace, and then Joseph, trying to impart some secret meaning that I don't understand.

Michael scowls. "I wanted to know what she wanted to do first before this information skews her decision." He's looking at me, but I know his bark is for Victor.

"What information?" Joseph asks.

Silently, Michael refills Jace's glass of Macallan, pours one for Joseph, and hands the bottle to Fin, then pours me a glass of FAT Bastard Merlot. "You're gonna need this, Princess."

His sad eyes have me on edge. I sit back, curling into Joseph's side, and take a sip of my wine.

Michael resettles on the coffee table. It's disconcerting he feels he needs to be this close to me. I grab Joseph's hand, take another drink, and wait.

Fin refills his glass. Victor and Michael stick to beer, which I don't think either have touched. Another reason to be concerned—they feel they need to keep their faculties sharp—which should be comforting, but it only means things aren't as *wrapped up* as they want me to believe.

Michael leans forward, his muscular arms resting on his knees, his hands steepled, and his eyes on me. "Do you remember those unidentified fingerprints my forensics guy found on the evidence?"

"Yes, you were going to send them off to another contact who has access to additional databases. Did he get a hit?" I reply.

He smirks. "Yeah, he got a *hit*."

My pulse ramps up, and Joseph must sense it as he squeezes my hand and pulls me closer.

"We didn't find the contributor because we were looking for perps—someone with a criminal record. When no match could be found, we broadened our search to include victims." Michael glances at Jace.

Shit.

"We found a match in a closed case from a few years ago. Three years to be exact. The perp was a single father who abused his kids when he got drunk—and he was drunk a lot."

Victor clears his voice.

Michael looks down for a moment before straightening up, squaring his shoulders. "Abuse is too kind of a word for this scumbag. He raped his kids. The daughter from the time she was eleven to sixteen, and the son from the age of ten to thirteen. The abuse stopped when the young girl fled from their home, taking her younger brother with her. They were homeless for a year. Living out of her car, working odd jobs, and going to school. No one knew they were homeless. Not teachers. Not friends—though they had few of those."

With each passing moment—each excruciating word—my heart breaks for these kids. "Who are they?"

Michael takes a deep breath before answering, "Veronica Hamm and her brother Spencer."

"Holy shit," I gasp, glancing at Jace. He's as shocked as I am.

"They were eventually caught stealing food from a local grocery store. One thing led to another, and charges were brought against the father. He was found guilty and is currently serving time. Veronica turned eighteen shortly after her father was sentenced and was released from the system.

Her brother ran away shortly after Veronica was removed from the foster home they resided in and before she could make arrangements to be his guardian. He hasn't been heard from since."

Jesus.

Jace sinks into the chair as if he wishes it would swallow him whole.

Michael turns to him when he continues. "When reading her file, I noticed something interesting. Veronica was interviewed by a social worker when she was first taken into custody. The social worker asked why she didn't go to live with her grandparents in Oklahoma or go to the authorities to report her father. Veronica said she couldn't bear to leave the only person who showed her and her brother any genuine kindness. The social worker surmised Veronica was probably in love or highly infatuated with this person to the point where she was willing to endure her father's wrath, and then homelessness, in order to remain close to this special person in her life."

"Don't say it," Jace pleads.

"I'm sorry, brother." Michael genuinely looks upset. "The name the social worker wrote down was Jace Cavanagh."

I gasp. I should have seen it coming, but that was one surprise I didn't anticipate. I thought Veronica was only an easy lay to Jace. But it looks like she meant more to him than he ever let on, spending time with Veronica and her younger brother, obviously doing things other than just sex. And he meant more to her. "I took you away from her."

Jace sits up. "No, Sam. She hurt you for no reason, and I cut her from my life. *I'm* the one who took me away. You didn't do anything wrong."

I stand up, handing Michael my wine glass. "Then why does it feel like I did?" I feel dizzy, like I can't breathe. I walk to Joseph's office before anyone can stop me. I need a minute to think.

Eighteen

SAY YOU WON'T LET GO

Joseph

JACE AND I FOLLOW SAMANTHA INTO MY OFFICE. The news of Veronica's past is unexpected. It's hit all of us hard, but none harder than Jace and Samantha.

"I took you away from her, so she wants to take Joseph away from me." She's facing the window and doesn't even turn around as she speaks. "I'm so sorry, Jace."

"Fuck. *You're* sorry? I'm the one who hung out with them. I had no idea." Jace plops down on the couch.

I stand close to Samantha, wanting to comfort her but getting the feeling she needs a minute to process this before I overwhelm her with my need to make this right, to make it better for *her*.

When she finally looks at me, the sadness in her eyes draws me to her. I cup her cheek, moving in close. "Tell me what you need." It's a simple phrase, and by the way her shoulders relax, it's what she needed to hear.

"I want to help her. She's had enough heartache in her life. Maybe she needs someone to give her a break." She glances at Jace before returning her focus to me. "Give her some money. Find her a place to live. Pay for her to go to college—if she wants—get her help, but let's not take anything else from her. She's endured enough."

I may have suspected she'd want to let her go, but I didn't anticipate her wanting to bankroll her. "Are you sure?"

"Jace, are you okay with that?" She wants to make this right for Jace, too.

His head comes up. "We need to find Spencer. He was such a great kid." His voice breaks as he looks away.

"We can do that. We can do all of that," I confirm. "What about Tiff and Lydia?"

On a humorless laugh, Samantha steps back. "Sue them, or threaten to sue them. Make them sign something that's legally binding keeping them from doing anything like this in the future. Do whatever it takes to make it go away." Her hand waves in the air. "Just make them go away."

We rejoin the others in the living room. No one is surprised to hear Samantha and Jace want to help Veronica and her brother. Though, I'm not sure they were prepared for the level of support we're suggesting.

"We could fund Veronica and her brother through MCI's scholarship program," Fin suggests, much to Samantha's delight.

"She needs to sign the same legal document, saying she won't try something like this again in the future or try to get more money out of you," Victor steps in. "Helping her is one thing, but making a dependent out of her is another."

Samantha nods. "She's obviously smart, smart enough to stay under the radar for a year while living out of her car, taking care of her brother, working, and still going to school. She's a survivor. I think she needs an environment where she can do better than merely survive. I want her to have the opportunity to thrive and make a future for herself and her brother."

"Veronica was smart enough to pull this whole emotional blackmail scheme together too. Don't forget that." Michael brings us back to reality.

Samantha's smile grows larger. "Even more reason to give her something productive to focus on. A bored, under-utilized brain is a dangerous one. Let's give her a chance to find a better use for her talents."

Michael nods. "Okay, Victor and I will talk to them and make the deal."

"I want to talk to them." I have things I need to make one hundred percent clear.

"Is that smart, brother?" Fin sets his glass down and moves closer. "It might be better to let someone less emotionally impacted by this situation handle it."

I chuckle. "You think I'm going to go all caveman on them?"

Fin's smirk tells me he understands my need to confront those who have caused us so much pain. "Don't say or do anything that will give them cause to sue *us*."

"Understood." I'm capable of keeping my emotions in check, particularly when it comes to protecting my girl and our future.

"What about you, Sam? Do you have something you want to say to them?" Michael asks.

She shakes her head. "No, I trust Joseph to say what needs to be said to Lydia and Tiff. As for Veronica, her past doesn't excuse what she did to me, but it changes the way I see her, and I want to help. I doubt she's in a place to hear anything I have to say. Maybe someday she'll be more open to it. But for now, giving her a chance is all the closure I need."

With a kiss, I leave Samantha with Fin as the rest of us leave to wrap up our loose ends; and give Matt, Jace, and me a chance to find closure with three women who have impacted our lives in substantial, yet different ways. I don't envy these women the shitstorm of testosterone they're about to encounter.

Samantha

While Joseph is gone, Fin helps me move my stuff from my temporary penthouse lodgings back home. I didn't have much, so we manage to get it done in one trip. Afterwards, we sit on the couch and watch one of my dirty little pleasures—okay, not so dirty, but definitely a pleasure—*Outlander*. I got Fin hooked on it when I was living with him for a few months after my father died and before I graduated high school. It could have been awkward living with the brother of my kinda boyfriend at the time—now my fiancé—but it wasn't. Fin reminds me enough of Joseph to make me comfortable. Add in protectiveness like a brother, a heart like a lion, and a wicked sense of humor and, well, I plain love the guy.

We've finished two episodes and started another when Fin pauses the show. It takes me a second to realize he's not getting up to go to bathroom. He's sitting here staring at me.

"What?" I resist the urge to wipe my nose to check if I have a bat in the cave.

"Are you sure you're okay? Do you want to talk about it?"

Talk about it? "Hmm…other than feeling bad for doubting your brother, I'm not sure what else there is to talk about." Is *he* wanting to talk about it, or maybe he wants to talk about Margot? "Do *you* have something you want to talk about?"

"Me?" He frowns. "No, I want to be sure you're really okay and not hiding from us."

I smile. "Us? Are we an *us* now?" I can't resist teasing him.

He shakes his head and laughs. "'Us' as in your family. Us."

It never gets old or fails to shock me how Joseph's family has adopted me so fully into their lives. It's as if they've known me my whole life, like I was always their little sister—well, except for Joseph, of course—that would be wrong.

"I need time to let everything settle, sink in, and I need time with Joseph to be sure he forgives me. As hard as this all was on me, it had to be even harder on him being accused of such things. Especially when the one person he's supposed to be able to rely on—above all others— doubted him." I shrug my shoulder like it's no big deal, but the depth of my shame is immeasurable.

"He knows. He doesn't blame you. You haven't had many people stand by you no matter what. He understands. We all do."

"Shit, Fin, you're going make me cry." I blink my eyes, and an idea takes root. "Fin? Would you help me do something?"

He perks up. He likes tangible things he can do, conquer. "Anything."

I hop up. "We need a tattoo parlor."

"A tattoo parlor? What? Now?"

"Yes, before he gets home."

"Fuck." He stands. "If I get punched for this, you're gonna owe me big. And I mean B-I-G, big."

I smirk. "You mean like keeping a certain brunette a secret?"

He narrows his eyes at me. "I used to like you, Sam. Now, I'm not so sure."

That makes me laugh so hard, I have to sit back down until I compose myself. "Oh Finley, you crack me up. You love me. You know it. I'm the sister you never had."

"I never wanted a sister. They're too much trouble," he says dryly.

My eyes round on a pout.

"Ah, fuck, Sam. I'm only kidding. Of course I love you. You're the best damn thing that's ever happened to my family—to Joseph. Don't cry. Please."

I smile deviously. "See, now *that* is much better."

He chuckles. "You're evil, Sam, pure evil."

"Nah, I like to give my fiancé's brothers a hard time, especially when they take naked pictures with women who try to blackmail me to leave Joseph, or when they sleep with my best friend and don't bother to let me know."

"Fuck, Sam." He's all pouty now.

"You don't have to talk about it, but if you break Margot's heart, I'll break you. Understand?"

"Fair enough."

"Excellent. Now, let's go get me a tat."

Joseph

I get home to a quiet house and a note from Samantha letting me know she had to run an errand. Fin and William are with her, and she'll be home as soon as possible. I text Fin to confirm she's alright. His reply was quick and cryptic, but didn't set off any alarm bells.

Heading to my office, I use the time to catch up on emails.

Two hours later, I'm getting out of the shower and find her standing there watching me with love and want in her eyes. My cock twitches with the idea of getting her all wet with my dripping body before getting her all wet where it matters most.

"Hey, Caveman." She bites her bottom lip, trying to hide her smile. She's up to something.

"Hey, Sweetness." I casually dry off, taking my time, watching her watch me. It's hot as fuck seeing her antsy with anticipation as her skin pinkens and her eyes roam my body like she wants to lick me from my toes to my head. She doesn't even focus on my cock, which I might find disappointing if she wasn't burning my abs, chest, and face alive with her wanton gaze. "How was your errand?"

She licks her lips before her eyes lock on mine. "Good. It was good." She fidgets with the material of her skirt, rubbing it between her thumbs and fingers.

She's definitely up to something. But it's going to have to wait. "I need to show you something." I hang up my towel and kiss her quickly as I pass by to slip on workout pants. I run my fingers through my damp hair, turning to find her staring at my ass. "Are you hungry?"

She swallows. "Yes." Her eyes still roam my body like she's never seen me bare-chested before.

"For food?" I try not to laugh; obviously the three orgasms from earlier were not enough to satisfy my hungry girl.

"What?" Her eyes lift to mine.

"There you are." I smirk. "Are you hungry for food?"

She crosses her arms, feigning indignation. "What else would I be hungry for, Mr. McIntyre?"

My brow arches. "You seem to be eating me up with your eyes, Ms. Cavanagh. I want to be sure it's food you're wanting."

Her blush is fucking adorable. "I…uh…both."

I chuckle and take her hand. "Come on, let me feed you. Then I'll show you what I need to. Then I can feed your *other* hunger."

"Okay," she whispers.

So fucking cute.

She sits on the kitchen counter as I feed her leftover Chinese and tell her about my visit with Lydia and Veronica. "Lydia was a total bitch, not an ounce of remorse. I left her in the hands of Matt, Michael, and Victor. They'll scare the pants off her. She'll sign what she needs to and be out of our lives."

"I'm surprised she didn't play all nice, still trying to get in your pants." She sucks a noodle from my fingers. "That's what I'd do."

"No, you wouldn't." I kiss her Peking Duck-flavored lips.

"No, I wouldn't. I don't have the balls to hit on someone. I could never." Laughing, she takes a bite of my pancake.

I'm struck dumb by the truth of her statement. I put down the food and wipe my hands. I wait for her to finish her bite before cupping her face as I stand between her knees. "I'm a lucky man." My voice hitches on the power of what I feel for her.

"What? No. I'm the lucky one," she insists.

I smooth out her furrowed brow with my thumb. "You're the sexiest woman I've ever seen, the way you come undone for me, the way you look at me, the hunger in your eyes, and the shyness of your blush—so fucking sexy. But you wouldn't have made a move on me if I hadn't sought you out first, would you?"

"No. Never." Her eyes beseech me.

"Even if you knew how much I wanted you, if you were positive I wouldn't turn you down?"

She adamantly shakes her head. "No."

"Why?"

"Because if you really wanted me, you'd make a move. If you don't, then it's only an idea you're toying with in your head. I don't want to be anybody's toy. I want to be somebody's everything, the somebody who compels you to make the first move. Not a knee-jerk reaction where you give in to being hit on, not a compromise, not a second choice, not an 'oh, why not' decision. I want you to know without a shadow of a doubt that you want me and are willing to take a chance, make an effort. I want a man with the confidence, the will to go after what he wants, not wait for it to come to him."

Fuck. Me. "I came after you."

She beams. "You did."

"But you weren't an easy catch."

"No, I wasn't. I'm still not. You have to work for me, Joseph. Not because I'm confident and believe I deserve it. But because I don't."

"Samantha." I press my forehead to hers. "It kills me when you say stuff like that."

"I need to be sure you understand what you're getting into with me. I don't know if I'll ever be that confident. I may always have doubts, and it's not a reflection of your character, but of mine. I couldn't love you more, Joseph. I don't ever want you to doubt that."

"I don't doubt it, baby. I've got confidence enough for both of us. If you run, I'll chase. I'll always come for you, because I know you're worth it."

She closes her eyes, nodding her head over and over again as tears slip free.

My lips brush her cheeks. "I'll always come for you, Sweets."

"I'm counting on it." Her voice is tight with emotions. She wraps her arms around my neck. "Please forgive me for my doubts. I know we said it earlier, but I need to hear it again."

I pull her closer. "I forgive you. I'll always forgive you. I'll always come for you."

"Don't let me go."

"Never. Never letting you go, Sweetness." I kiss her warm lips. "Come on."

It's now or never.

In his office, Joseph pulls me into his lap. "I need to show you something."

"You keep saying that. You're making me nervous."

"I'm a little nervous myself." His fingers tip my chin so that I'm looking him in the eyes. "We need to finish this thing with Lydia, Veronica, and Tiff. I need you to trust me, give it a chance, let me show you what I see."

I have no idea what he's wanting to show me, but the knot in my stomach tells me it's not good. I can't speak. I simply nod.

Joseph wakes up his laptop, and a large monitor on his desk comes to life with a still of Joseph. "Shit. No." I try to get up, but he won't let me. "I can't watch this, Joseph."

His grip on me tightens. "Michael obtained the full video from Tiff. What you've seen is only some of it. This is the last copy. The only copy, and once you've seen it—I'll destroy it."

"So, the video and the come-face picture are for sure from when you were with Tiff?" Holy shit. I can't watch this. I can't watch him being raped.

"Watch it, and then ask me that question again."

"Joseph, please. Don't make me watch this."

His hand cups the back of my neck as his lips crash over mine, licking and sucking tenderly, passionately.

I know what he's doing, but I'm helpless to resist him. I don't want to watch her take advantage of him. I want to be what he needs. When he needs it.

He pulls back, both of us breathless. "I need you to trust me, Samantha. I need you to see this through my eyes, see what I experienced. We need this closure." He pulls me into a hug, whispering into my ear. "Please give me this. Trust me."

How can I not? This man gives me everything, forgives me for doubting him. I can do this for him. "Okay."

As the video starts, it's obvious Tiff is on top looking down on Joseph taking the video. They're in the throes of it, moaning, thrusting. Joseph tightens his hold on me. We watch for another minute before he pauses the screen—his face frozen with a look of pure ecstasy.

"You know that look, Samantha."

"Yeah, that's you having sex."

"No, not just sex. And not sex with just anyone. That's *me* making love to *you*."

"What?" But he's having sex with Tiff. Even though I can't see her, I know it's her. They got the video *from her*.

"Watch." He resumes the video.

We watch in silence the most difficult thing I've ever witnessed—the man I love having sex with someone else.

He looks and sounds like my Joseph, the way he looks and sounds when he's with me. His moans become more coherent. He's talking to her, telling her to *make it feel good*. Shit. He's said those words to me. Tears slip down my cheek. I blink to clear my vision.

Then I hear it: "Samantha." The Joseph on the video called out to me. *Me.*

Joseph squeezes me. "That was you and me, Samantha. There was no one else in that bed with me besides you. Watch."

All of a sudden, I don't feel like a voyeur watching Joseph have sex with someone else. I'm watching with his eyes, seeing his moves, his face, his sounds he makes with me. *Me.*

In the heat of his desire, he looks into the camera. "I'm coming, baby." The look on his face is the one in the still photo—his come-shot. But the video doesn't end there. It continues, and he comes undone. "Fuck, Sweetness, I'm coming so hard for you."

The video ends.

Silence. The room is full of silence and my ragged breath.

"It was only ever you and me, Samantha. That's my drunken fantasy sex dream I had with you. I don't remember Tiff. I don't want to remember her, because what you saw is what I remember—what I cherish—you and me—making love."

He carries me to our bed, lowering me down gently like I might bruise. I sit in the middle of our bed and watch him undress. He's not giving me a show, like a strip tease, he's simply undressing—for me. When he's gloriously naked, his cock at full attention, bobbing against his tight abs, I'm in awe of him—as I am every time I see him—that he's mine.

Kneeling next to me, he slowly undresses me, his eyes caressing every bit of skin as it's revealed. My shoes. Gone. My blouse and bra. Gone. My skirt. Gone.

"What the fuck did you do?" His concern alarms me until I see his eyes are on my panties. Well, actually on the bandage sticking out from under my panties.

"Shit. I forgot about that."

"How the hell did you hurt yourself there?" His fingers gently glide over the top of the bandage. "Does it hurt?"

I lie back on my elbows. "It does hurt, to be honest. But Bowser promised it'll be better in a few days."

"Who the hell is Bowser?" Anger flares in his eyes, his jaw clenched tightly, staring daggers at me and then the bandage.

"It's supposed to be a surprise for you. But based on your reaction, I'm afraid to show you."

He takes a cleansing breath or two—okay five. His eyes soften. "What did you do, Sweetness? Please don't tell me you marked this beautiful skin with a tattoo."

Oh, no. He hates tattoos? Tears fill my eyes.

"Baby, please tell me you didn't."

I shake my head, unable to answer.

He sighs in exasperation. "Fin took you to a goddamned tattoo shop?"

I roll away, kneeling at the top of our bed, covering myself with a pillow. *He hates it. What was I thinking? So stupid.*

"Fuck. I'm sorry. Come 'ere, baby. Let me see." He moves toward me.

"No." I jump off the bed, pillow securely covering my front. "I'm sorry. I thought…I wanted to do something for you. To show you my dedication to you."

"Baby, please."

"No. It was stupid."

He stops in front of me. "Show me."

I shake my head. "You hate it. I'm never letting you see it."

"How do you think I won't see it?" He pulls the pillow out of my grasp.

"I'll get it lasered off."

"The fuck you will," he growls. He cups the back of my neck, tipping my head back. "I'm an idiot, Samantha. I'm sorry. I didn't…it's a shock that's all." He runs his hand down my neck and shoulder, watching as if he can see the trail it leaves behind. "You have such beautiful skin, unblemished, untouched, pure."

I scoff at that. "Untouched? Pure? Not anymore."

Anger flashes again. "You will always be pure to me, because your body only knows *my* touch."

"Caveman, that's exactly why I wanted to get this tattoo."

His nostrils flare. "Show me, Samantha. Let me see your gift."

He tenderly carries me back to bed, lays me down, and swiftly removes my panties. I'm naked except for the bandage. His lips reverently kiss around the dressing. "Show me."

"Okay, but don't touch it. I have to keep it clean and covered for forty-eight hours."

"I'll clean it and cover it back up after I'm done examining my present." His smile is earnest and gives me hope that he won't hate it.

"If you don't like it, they can turn it into something else, or I can have it removed."

"No fucking way. Show me." His impatience grows.

"Close your eyes."

"Samantha."

"Close your eyes, grumpy."

Finally, he does, but his hands remain on my hips, his thumbs caressing back and forth. I lift the corners and peel off the dressing, placing it on the nightstand. I look back at my man, his eyes closed, his jaw lax, his lips full and begging to be kissed.

"You're staring." He grumbles.

"No, I'm not."

"Can I open my eyes?"

"Yes." I take in a sharp breath, waiting.

He opens, zooming in on it before I exhale.

"It's green for your eyes."

He nods, staring. Then he slowly traces the tips of his fingers directly below the writing in a delicate, ornate green script highlighted in black, not too big, just big enough for him to read. Only *him*. "You did this for me?"

"Yes."

"I don't know what to say." His gaze is still locked on, examining, his fingers caressing circles around it.

"You don't like it." I grab the bandage.

His hand covers mine. "No. Don't cover it. I'm not done." The longer he stares, the deeper he breathes. Then I notice he's hard again, after having lost his erection, thinking I was hurt.

If he's turned on, he must not totally hate it. "Say something. Anything."

"I can't believe you did this—for me."

Yeah, that's not helping. I still don't know if he hates it or not.

But then he bends down, trailing warm kisses from hip to hip. He continues, moving lower until he's right over the tattoo. He blows across it, and I squirm, unable to remain still. His flicks his tongue below it, ever so close to where moisture now pools.

"Joseph."

His tongue flicks over my slit, delving in, finding my clit, and sucks.

"Oh, shit." I fist the bedspread.

"Does the tattoo mean this belongs to me?" His tongue rubs up and down over and over again.

"Yes." I want to spread my legs, but he has them pinned.

"Do you know how much this turns me on? To see you mark yourself with my name—the name you call me?"

"No, tell me."

"Fuck, Samantha. To taste you and see my name on you, like a brand, telling me you're mine. I think I could come right now if I look at it much longer."

I moan at the thought.

"I can't wait until I can touch it, kiss it, lick it."

"Oh, god, Joseph."

"I can bury my cock, balls deep, and see who you belong to."

"Yes."

He pushes my legs apart, kneeling between my thighs. His fingers slip inside. "Fuck, you're so wet." His fingers glide in and out. "Say it. I want to hear you say it out loud. Whose pussy is this?"

"Caveman's."

"Fuck, that's right. I never thought seeing a tattoo on you would make me want you even more, but the fact that you tattooed *Caveman's* right above your pussy is the hottest fucking thing I've ever seen." He pumps faster. "Are you gonna come for me, Sweets?"

"Yes."

"That's right. Whose pussy is this?"

"Caveman's."

"Fuck, my balls tingle every time you say that and I read it on your body. Come for me, baby, because I need my cock inside you. Now."

He bends down, his tongue lapping at me, focusing on my clit, his fingers working that magic spot. He sucks and licks me into a frenzy until I come undone around his fingers. It only feeds his hunger for more. His groans and sucks continue, taking me into another orgasm.

Before I recover, his thighs are spread, my legs swung over his thighs, his cock rubbing my folds, then he slides home. "Dammit, you feel so fucking good." His hands grip my hips, his thumbs on either side of his *Caveman's* tattoo. His eyes are glued to it, watching himself slide in and out of me.

"Do you like your gift?" I manage through choppy breaths as he pumps into me.

"Fuck, yeah. Tell me again whose pussy this is?"

"Caveman's."

"That's right. You're mine, Sweets. You have the tattoo to prove it, and in three weeks you're gonna have my ring and name." His eyes lock on the tattoo again. "So fucking hot, baby."

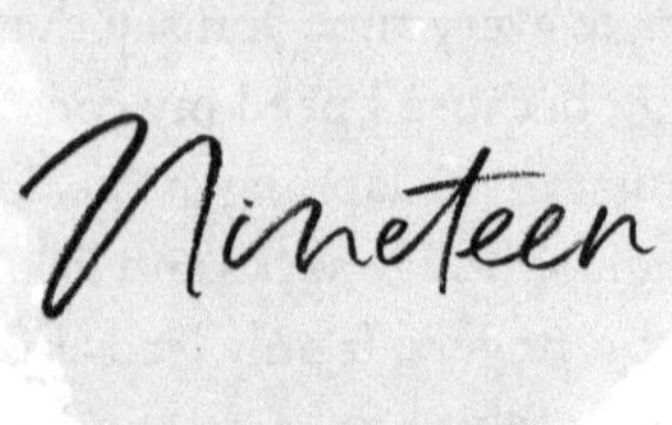

Nineteen

I GET TO LOVE YOU

Saturday Before Christmas

Joseph

MY HEART IS POUNDING, THUNDERING LIKE A champion racehorse at the starting gate, biting at the bit for the race to begin. It's been two years, four weeks, three days, and seventeen hours since I first laid eyes on Samantha Lilian Cavanagh. It was the Friday before Thanksgiving, my family out of town for the holiday. I took the standing offer from my then-roommate, Jace, to spend the holiday with his family. I'd met his parents before, many times, in fact. But the illustrious Samantha was known to me only through Jace's words and actions when he talked to her or about her.

Even then, she stood out in my mind as someone important. Important enough to be spoken of in awe by a man who chased women like a stud working for his next meal. Jace revered his sister, and though his actions didn't always equal his love for her, it was obvious, even to me, that she was the most important person in his life.

He wasn't wrong.

As soon as I saw her, my heart flipped. My jaw clenched. My cock sprang to life—but so did my soul. It's as if it recognized its other half, yawned and stretched from a long slumber, and jumped to attention. She was it. The one I had unknowingly been searching for, bettering myself for, making a future for.

She. Was. It.

My. Future.

My. Everything.

Now, I stand at the front of the church, my brothers next to me. Fin as my best man and Matt standing next to him. Margot as maid of honor stands across from Fin, who might possibly be his other half by the way he's staring at her. I want to scream at him that *this is my fucking day—pay attention.* But I don't have it in me, and it would be pointless if he feels even a miniscule amount for Margot what I feel for Samantha—it's a lost cause. He couldn't change his focus even if he tried. He's a goner.

The wedding march pipes through the biggest damn organ I've ever seen. The center doors at the back of the church open—and there—standing next to Jace—is my girl. My breath catches, and I have to fist my hands to keep from running to her. I told her I'd always come after her, but this once, I have to let her come to me. This one time.

She's all in white, her shoulders bare, her veil perched on her head like a crown, cascading around her as she walks, arm in arm with her brother—to me. Her dress hugs her curves like my body wants to do, flares at the bottom, and trails behind her.

Her face, dear lord help me, that face. Angelic and innocent, blue eyes I want to swim in, pouty lips I want to devour, bone structure I'd want as my muse if I was any kind of an artistic fuck. And that silken mane of auburn hair, curled and flowing around her, making my fingers twitch to sink in and hold on tightly, while I set those abundant breasts free from their confinement.

Holy fuck, I've got a hard-on the size of Texas for my girl.

Movement to Samantha's right has me meeting Jace's gaze. His brow is hooked with a smart-ass grin on his face. *You're a fucking pussy,* I hear his voice in my head.

Yeah, I am. And only for *her.*

They stop next to me, Jace impeding me from taking hold of my girl. The minister asks, "Who gives this woman to be married to this man?"

With a smile and dancing eyes, Jace looks at Samantha and then me. "I do." He then places her hand in mine and steps back. He grips my elbow. "She's all yours, brother. Be good to her." His eyes shine with tears.

I swallow around the lump in my throat. "Like my life depends on it, brother."

He nods, pats my back, kisses her cheek, and takes a seat.

Finally. I step closer, taking her in, that lump in my throat trying to steal my voice, but I manage to say, "You look beautiful, Sweetness."

Her face lights up like she thought I might possibly think otherwise. "You look like pure heaven."

I lean in to kiss her cheek, but she turns, facing me.

"Kiss me, Caveman." She tips her chin to me. "It's the last kiss you'll ever get as a single man."

Fuck me. Is it against protocol? I shrug at the minister and do as my soon-to-be wife requests and kiss the hell out of her. Clapping and catcalls erupt. The minister clears his throat, but I don't give a shit. This is a very important kiss, nearly as important as the one right after he pronounces us man and wife. This is my final goodbye to all that came before her, all that happened before this day, any doubts and fears she has for our future—I need to kiss out of her. And kiss out of her. And kiss out of her.

I pull away with a wicked grin. "That was *your* final kiss as a single woman."

She blinks, trying to catch her breath, and wipes at her lipstick—which must be magic as it didn't smear—and smiles. "I don't need any other kisses as I've only ever had yours. Single, married, pregnant, young, old, they're all yours."

Fuck. Me.

I'm the luckiest damn man around. I take her arm in mine and turn to the man of the cloth, who's watching us with brazen surprise. "You need to make this woman my wife, like yesterday," I command.

He simply smiles and begins…

Samantha

"I Get To Love You" plays through the ballroom speakers. Our friends and family surround us, but I only see my man—my husband—turning me on the dancefloor like Fred Astaire for our first dance.

Did I envision this day? Did I dream of my wedding as so many little girls do? No, I never did have that wedding fantasy of finding my prince in shining armor or being whisked away to his castle where we live happily ever after. I didn't have *once up on a time* kind of thoughts as a kid. I was never your average girl—I suppose I'm still not. I'd rather code than shop. I'd rather see a sci-fi movie than a romantic comedy. And I'd rather fall in love with one man—and only one man—than play the field, notching my belt with romantic dalliances before I found the one, or Mr. Good Enough.

I'm lucky. I know. I've hit the romantic jackpot. A jackpot I wasn't even looking for, longing for, or even knew was possible until Joseph Patrick McIntyre came into my life like a storm, turning it upside down and sweeping me off my feet.

"Do you take this woman to be your wife?" The minister asked Joseph.

"I do," he replied with tears in his eyes.

"Do you take this man to be your husband?"

"I do." I really, really do.

When the minister pronounced us *"husband and wife"* and told Joseph, *"You may kiss your bride, again,"* everyone laughed, except Joseph and me. The intensity of his stare, the need in his eyes, and the possessiveness of his embrace left no room for anything other than my love for this man—my husband. He kissed me like a new beginning, a breath of fresh air, a promise of happily ever afters, and a lifetime of hot, delicious sex. How can this be? How can I have come so far in two years and still feel like the same determined, ambitious girl who saw stars in her eyes, computers in her future, and didn't dare to dream that the VP of Product and Technology at McIntyre Corporate Industries would even know who I was, much less want a future with me?

"Mrs. McIntyre, I believe it's time to cut the cake." My dreamy Mr. McIntyre draws my thoughts back to our reception and our duties as the bride and groom.

I take his proffered hand, my smile blazing a path across my lips. *I can't believe I'm his wife.* "Husband, I don't think I'll ever tire of hearing you call me that. Though, I do so love *Sweetness, Sweets,* and *baby.* I hope you won't retire those."

He stops and pulls me close, our hands joined at my side. The back of his fingers caresses my cheek. "I have no intention of retiring any of those, Sweetness. I'm simply adding *Mrs. McIntyre* and *wife* into the mix. I believe my repertoire of lovenames is now complete."

"Hmm, and which one will you get tattooed on your cock?" I whisper.

His devious smirk has me blushing. "I've got it all planned. When I'm not hard and ready to fuck you senseless, it will simply say *Sam's.*" He kisses the corner of my mouth. "But when I'm hard as steel and aching for you, it will say *Samantha Lilian McIntyre's.*"

I snort on a laugh. "Oh God, I walked right into that, didn't I?"

He leans close and whispers into my ear as his erection pokes me in the stomach. "I need to bury myself inside my wife—soon. I've been hard since I saw you walking down the aisle."

"Joseph," I groan, my head falling to his chest. "You sure know how to wind a girl up."

His chest rumbles with a laugh. "Come on, Sweets. Let's eat some cake. We've only got an hour before we leave for the airport."

"Really?"

His emerald eyes flare. "It might not be what you want, but our first time as husband and wife will be a mid-air collision. I can't survive hours until we make it to our destination."

"You're not teasing me." *Please, can't we leave now?* I really want to ask.

"Mrs. McIntyre, I would never tease about a thing like that. Soon, Sweetness." His succulent lips take mine for too short a ride before he pulls away, leading me to cut our cake.

We transition from cutting the cake to bouquet and garter toss. Margot catches my bouquet, and Fin catches the garter. Now if that's not a telling sign, I don't know what is. They're still keeping their relationship a secret, but they do manage a dance or two beyond the wedding party's obligatory ones. Love is in the air, and I pray they get sucked in deeply, endlessly, and most definitely happily.

I don't bother with changing. Whatever I wear will only end up on the bedroom floor of MCI's corporate jet anyway. So, what's the point? I'll change on the plane, that is if I can manage after hours of mindless sex with my husband.

My husband. How long will it take before the novelty wears off?

Never.

Like my love for Joseph. It's endless. Timeless. Immeasurable. And steadfast. The latter sealed and made true by his unfathomable faith in me. He says I'm enough for him.

And.

I.

Finally

Believe.

It's.

True.

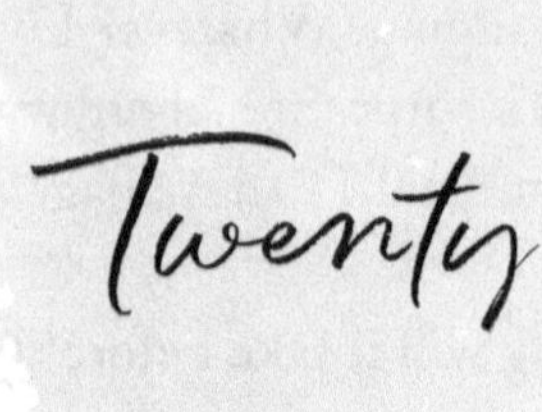

PERFECT

Samantha

A WEEK ON A SECLUDED CARIBBEAN ISLAND HAS done wonders for my tan, not to mention my sex life. My husband's unquenchable desire for me is only matched by my limitless desire for him. If this wasn't a private island, we would have been arrested by now. I thought impromptu sex in Joseph's office was our thing. Apparently, we've progressed to beaches, the ocean, sun loungers, jet skis—yes, we fell in—hammocks, sail boats, catamarans, palm trees—yes, I have the bruises to prove it—and of course every room, surface, and piece of furniture in our cabana.

I use the term cabana loosely. It's more like a beach-front mansion made to look like a hut and blend in with its surroundings. It comes complete with full-time, very discreet—never see them unless you need something—staff. Our every meal, need, whim, desire, is fully provided for by little mice I've only seen twice.

Oh, and did I mention this very private secluded Caribbean island is now ours? Yeah, so Joseph was researching honeymoon destinations and ran across this gem that happened to be for sale. So, he bought it and plans to lease it to MCI for its executive employees to enjoy—namely Joseph's family. It's like a high-end timeshare for the rich. The very rich McIntyres.

Pinch me. Seriously. Pinch me.

As if my Adonis can read my mind, he rises from the water like Poseidon. His abs glistening like cut diamonds, mask and fins dangling from his hands, water dripping from his torso—though, reluctantly, I'm sure—he whips his hair out of his eyes and blesses me with a panty-dropping smile. "Hi, Sweetness."

"Hey, Caveman. How's the water?"

"Lonely without you." He plops beside me on the double lounger. "How's the book?" He places a cool wet kiss on my shoulder and then my lips.

"Disappointing compared to our romance." Truly.

"Yeah?" He seems surprised.

"Yeah." I run my fingers through his hair. "No book boyfriend can compare to you."

"I'm glad to hear it." He shakes his head, spraying me with cold droplets.

I giggle and screech, but honestly, it feels amazing on my sun-heated skin.

"You were napping earlier when I spoke to Michael. Let's grab some lunch, and I'll fill you in."

Sitting on the covered veranda, the cool ocean breeze keeps the heat at bay, and Joseph, seated next to me feeding my body and soul, is nearly as perfect as it gets.

"As you know, everything is wrapped up with Lydia and Tiff. They've signed the papers. Tiff is still in Austin, and Lydia has moved home to Connecticut. Michael feels certain those two won't be a problem in the future."

"That's great news. I wish them well, but hope never to see or hear of them again." Though, I never did meet or see Tiff, and I'm perfectly fine with that. If I ever do see her—I'll punch her—no doubt in my mind about that. She raped my man. He may not remember it, but we all know it, and I will never forget or forgive her. She had better keep her ass in Austin.

He kisses my hand and feeds me a slice of mango followed by pineapple. "Oh, and I have news on how Veronica obtained my blue tie."

"Really? How?"

"Remember I told you about her pretending to be a British tourist that night you didn't make the happy hour?"

"Yeah."

"Michael checked the video feed from the bar. It turns out that was the last time I wore that tie. It was rolled up in my jacket pocket, hanging on the back of my bar stool. Veronica snagged it when I wasn't paying attention."

"Wow. So that's it, right? There's no more outstanding questions."

"Yep, that was the last loose end." He looks relieved. I know he has to be glad to have this behind us. I know I am.

"Did he have any more news on Veronica?"

"They've got some leads on her brother, Spencer. They haven't found him yet, but feel they're close."

"God, I pray they find him."

"Me too. As for Veronica, she's settled in her new place and has registered at UTA for the Spring semester. She's also going to counseling twice a week. Michael and Victor have been checking on her weekly and feel she's making progress, positive changes toward working through her past and making plans for the future. She wants to be a counselor for abused children."

"Wow. That's amazing. She'll probably be really good at it." I tear up at the thought of where she came from and the potential of where she can go if she chooses. "She'll be great for kids going through what she did. No one will understand them like she will. And she's smart and devious— they won't be able to pull the wool over her eyes. She'll know their tricks and help them navigate to their own healing."

"Sweetness." The look on his face has me turning toward him.

"What?"

"You."

"What about me?"

"Do you hear yourself?"

I frown, not understanding what he's saying; of course, I hear myself. I'm the one speaking.

He pushes his chair back and pulls me into his lap. "Do you not see how amazing you are?"

"What are you talking about? We weren't even talking about me. We're talking about Veronica."

His look is indulgent and tender as he tips my chin to look in my eyes. "Veronica did lots of nasty things to you to hurt you, yet you don't hold it against her. You've gone out of your way to ensure she has a future. A future that you're rooting for, like a proud parent or a good friend. You don't think that's remarkable?"

"What kind of person would I be if I couldn't see past the hurtful things she did? Accurate or not, from her perspective, I took away the only light in her life when Jace cut her off. Was that my fault? No. Would it have happened if she had been nice to me? No. But she felt threatened and acted out the only way she knew how to protect what was precious to her. Jace." I touch Joseph's cheek. "I would do anything to protect you, my husband. Love is fierce and territorial."

"But *you* wouldn't have used your body to get what you wanted."

"No. But I also wasn't raped when I was eleven by the man who was supposed to protect me, keep me safe, and show me how a woman should be treated. She doesn't know how to use her body except as a weapon. I'm hoping through therapy she'll learn."

He pulls me into his chest, holding me tightly. "You're remarkable, Samantha. You make me want to be a better man, a man who deserves you and deserves to be a father to the children we'll have—especially a daughter." His teary eyes lock on mine. "Our daughters will know how a man should treat them. And our sons will know how to treat a woman, starting with their sisters and their mother. I promise you that."

I swallow my emotions. "Daughters? Sons? Plural? Exactly how many children do you want, Mr. McIntyre?"

His hand slides up my leg as his eyes move down my body. He fingers his tattoo hidden under my bikini bottoms. "As many as this sweet body will give me."

My arms wrap around his neck, and I run my nose along his. "Maybe we should practice, to be sure we've got it down when we're ready to start trying."

"Fuck me," he hisses under his breath.

"Yes, please."

Joseph

The sun reaches through my sleepy haze. It's early, too early. The warmth cuddled against me urges me to wake up and seize the day—or at least her ass—as I burrow my way deep inside her sweet pussy. My hand roams over her body as I stretch and blink against the morning light, fully opening my eyes for the first time.

She stretches and moans, pushing her ass into my awaiting erection—morning wood—gotta love it, especially when you have someone to share it with. And lucky for me, I have someone for the rest of my life.

"Good morning, Sweetness." I kiss along her neck.

"Morning, Caveman." She turns in my arms, her plump breasts nestled against my chest, her eyes locked on mine as her face tips upward.

"Do you know I could spend the rest of my life like this, with you in my arms?" I cup a breast and bend to lick and suck her nipple, relishing her gasp and thrust of her hips toward my cock. "Except I'd be cock deep inside you at all times."

"Hmm." She moans as I slip down to take care of her other breast. "It might be hard to walk like that."

"Who needs to walk? We'll have people bring us what we need. We can take bathroom breaks, but other than that, I don't see why it's not possible."

"I don't know that I can find any fault in that plan." She rolls to her back on a stretch.

I settle between her thighs, continuing to dine on her breasts. Her hands knead and pull at me as her legs run up and down mine. It's a slow and gentle build. A lazy morning of gasps and sighs, caresses and exploration, moans and beckoning. As my mouth moves to claim hers, my cock slides inside, nestling in its rightful place, what it was made to do—who it was made for.

"Joseph," she moans, wrapping her legs round me.

"My beautiful girl." My tongue delves deeper as my cock rocks home over and over again.

When she chants my name mixed with "oh god," I know she's close. My balls tingle in anticipation, holding out for that final signal that presents itself when she squeezes my cock as she comes undone and milks me, taking my seed, leaving me in a state of bliss.

On a groan, I roll to my back, pulling her close. From our bed, we can see the aqua blue of the ocean with sailboats floating across the horizon. It's heaven here. I can't believe I bought this island—a fucking island— for a steal. It was pure luck—preparation meets opportunity.

My Sweets slips out of bed and into the bathroom. I wander out on the deck and pee out over the side, watering the green bushes.

"You're such a boy." My girl giggles from behind me.

"You'd do it if you could."

She laughs again. "Yeah, I probably would."

I go inside to wash up and brush my teeth. I join her at the railing— where we've found ourselves every morning of our two weeks' stay—kiss her shoulder and nuzzle up to her naked backside. "What do you want to do on our last day?"

"I think I'd like more of what we just did." She looks over her shoulder and kisses my cheek. "If it's all the same to you."

My hands travel around her front, finding a nipple and slipping into her wet heat. "Sweets, didn't I make it clear I could spend a lifetime inside you and it wouldn't be near enough?"

She arches into my hands, her ass pushing back on my balls, my cock hard against her back.

"Spread your legs for me," I whisper in her ear.

She widens her stance and sighs when I run my fingers through her wet pussy, spreading her juices to her ass.

"Oh, god," she moans.

I nibble on her ear, lick the shell, and suck on her lobe. All while my thumb rubs her rosebud. "I want in here today, Sweets."

"Joseph."

"Shh, only my finger, baby." We've never gone further than that. Eventually, I'd like to claim her ass, but for now, I'll take this. I kiss her cheek. "I'll be right back."

When I pull away, she slumps against the railing, her body already revved up, ready to take me, ready to go off.

Returning, I trail kisses along her back, working my way down to her ass and then to her pussy. Nudging her legs apart, I lick her until her legs are shaking and she's begging me to fuck her. I love my girl and how hot she gets.

Standing, I lube up my finger and her ass. My other hand plays with her clit, slowly, enough to keep her on edge but not enough to send her over. Taking her ass gets easier each time, soon she's pushing back, ready for me, begging for me to fill her up. My cock bobs, doing its own begging. "That's it, Sweets. Push again and let me in."

"Oh, fuck!" she screams as my fingers breeches her ass and slip inside her pussy.

"Your ass is so hot and tight, baby. And your pussy is so wet and succulent, clenching my fingers with need." Fuck. I'm so turned on.

"Caveman, I want you inside me."

I alternate my fingers, in her ass, out her pussy. "I am inside you."

Squeezing the railing, she thrusts her pelvis like she's aching for more. "I want your cock."

She whimpers when I suck on her neck. "You'll have my cock soon enough, but I want you to come like this first."

I pick up the tempo, massaging her clit with my palm.

"Oh, god." Her head falls back, resting on my chest.

"I'm desperate for you, Samantha. Come for me, so I can sink inside my heaven."

"Joseph." Her hips gyrate, grinding against my palm.

"Fuck, yes. Just like that. Come all over my hand, baby." I increase the pace, suck and bite on her neck, shoulder, ear—anywhere I can reach.

Her whole body is trembling, and I worry her legs will give out, but before they do, she takes flight. "Oh, my god."

I hold onto her, slip my finger out of her ass, continue finger-fucking her pussy until her contractions subside. I kiss and nuzzle her neck, telling her how amazing she is and how fucking sexy she is.

Cradling her in my arms, I take her back to bed, lay her down, then wash my hands and grab a warm washcloth to take care of her.

I'd planned to have her ride my cock on a balcony chair. But truly, I want her in bed, underneath me, face to face, so I can see her, kiss her, and make love to her in my favorite way—with her arms and legs wrapped around me, holding me like she can't get me close enough.

I'm horny as hell and could pound away at her, but I don't. I kiss her tenderly, pulling her back from her orgasm-fog. I want her with me. Always with me. Always beside me. Never behind me. Not in front of me, but beside me—*with me.*

Partners.

Soul mates.

Husband and wife.

The yin to my yang.

My *Sweetness* to her *Caveman.*

I sink in slowly, she arches to meet me—pulling me in—welcoming me home.

My girl.

My love.

My *Sweetness*

My *Sweets.*

My *baby.*

My wife.

Forever.

Always.

I do.

The End

Bonus Scene

9 MONTHS AFTER WEDDING

HE TAKES MY BREATH AWAY. STILL. THE CUT OF HIS jaw. His dark hair that's grown to be a little unruly—just like him. His perfect mouth, not just its shape, but the words that come out of it, the things he *does* with it. The dimples that reach inside me and squeeze when they're aimed at me. The command in his voice, in every step he takes as he rounds his desk, his eyes, on his phone. He exudes confidence. Pure, unadulterated confidence of a man who knows where he belongs, does what he loves, and has the world at his fingertips.

This is the man I fell for, married nine months ago, and get to work and live with every single day. I'm one lucky girl. I bite the tip of my pen, my eyes, trained on him as he moves with the grace of an athlete, every step bringing him closer…

"Sweetness?" The husk in his voice does dirty things to my girly parts.

I flash to his emerald eyes that see me in a way I never will. "Yeah?" I pluck the pen from my mouth, realizing I was sucking on it.

He stops before me, his crotch at eye level as I sit on the couch in his office—our office. He insisted I have a desk in here even though I have an office down the hall and my own assistant. He prefers me close. The impressive bulge in his pants, not really the reason, but not to be negated either.

Tipping my chin with a finger, he leans down till we're face to face. His crook of a smile with a barely-there dimple, alludes to his amusement and a knowing that my mind has drifted into a personal arena that has nothing to do with the new tech we were discussion moments ago as he read the latest update from one of our industry scouts. "Did you hear any of the recommendations?"

Hear? *Yes.*

Remember? *No.*

"How can I concentrate when you look like that?" I motion to his suit he wears like a second skin, a body armor decked out to slay the day, take no prisoners, securing the future of MCI and its employees. He's dedicated, but does he have to be so damn hot while he's doing it?

He drops his phone on the couch beside me and sits on the edge of the coffee table, sequestering my knees between his long, powerful legs. He grips my thighs as he leans in. "Did you notice the bulge in my pants, Sweets?"

I nod, swallowing the saliva that's pooled in my mouth.

"Then you know it's no walk in the park for me. You in heels, a pencil skirt, and blouse…" He motions to my head. "Your hair up, looking like the hottest fucking librarian I've ever only seen in my fantasies." He eases closer, his hands slowly sliding my skirt up as he goes.

Newsflash. "You fantasize about librarians?"

His chuckle does nothing to quell the need building in me. "I fantasize about *you* as a librarian. A teacher. A secretary. A flight attendant. Any stereotypical female role that makes me an asshole to think it, much less say it, has you in the starring role with my dick, my mouth, and my fingers."

I shake my head. "Not *my* mouth?" I'm poking the bear, knowing he's as turned on as I am. And that knowledge only makes me hotter.

His growl is immediate. His lips nearly to mine.

Put me out of my misery, Caveman. Kiss me. Then fuck me.

But he doesn't. He licks his lips and whispers his thumb across my mouth, barely a touch. "Always about your beautiful lips on me in any way you damn well please."

My heart hammering against my chest and erratic breaths seems so loud, I'm sure Teddy will hear from his desk on the other side of the door. "I want that."

"I know. So do I." He sits back, pulls my skirt down to a respectable position. "But we can't." He captures my hands. "We've managed to avoid office sex for four whole months since you started working here full-time."

I arch a brow.

His jaw ticks before he breaks into a full-fledged smile. "Okay." He stands, adjusting himself. "We've managed to avoid office sex during *business* hours."

"I should just work from my office. Why are we putting ourselves through this day in and day out?" I stand to collect my laptop, but he stops me.

"I need you here." Leaning on the edge of my desk, he pulls me between his legs. "I *want* you here." A punch of air cascades down my blouse as he leans his head against mine. "This beautiful brain of yours works in a way mine doesn't. We complement each other. If you weren't here, I'd be walking down to your office continually or booking you for hours upon hours of meetings. It would be no different. We've got this." He kisses me softly. Passion simmers, but this is a kiss of love and a promise: I'm his wife, and I'm also as his partner at MCI. He's not my boss. I'm an equal. At home *and* work.

"We got this," I affirm his conviction.

"Yeah, we do." He kisses up my jaw to my ear where his breath sends chills down my spine. "But I'm going to fuck you senseless when the clock strikes five."

I wouldn't want it any other way. Joseph and I have a connection that goes beyond our love for each other and flows into our love of MCI and all things techy.

He steps back, collecting his phone, and walks back to his desk. "Now try to pay attention when I read the update this time." He winks before his gaze lowers to his phone and he starts to read. His voice pulls me to him like a siren song, but this time, I am listening.

When I sit on his lap, he wraps an arm around my waist, and I cuddle close. We may not have a typical working relationship. But what we do works for us, works for MCI.

I get to see him day in and day out at home and in the office. For some that might be too much. For us, it's just right.

He's always been the yin to my yang.

My husband.
My Caveman.
And now, my co-worker.
Life is good, especially when I get to work from his lap.

1 WEEK LATER

She's crying. My wife, my everything, is crying, and it guts me. She left work early. Meeting Margot for some girl-time.

I'm going to rip someone's head off if they hurt my girl.

"Baby." My anguish is clear, but it's my presence that has her head popping up, her eyes wide. She didn't hear me come in because she was *crying.* Sobbing. "Sweetness, what's wrong?" I charge across our apartment, scoop her onto my lap before she can even hide the evidence of her tears or reply to my question.

Her curling into me gives me a peace I don't deserve, given she's so broken up over something I'm oblivious of.

"I thought I was ready. I thought I was over it. Over her—" her last word comes out on a sob.

I rack my brain, trying to figure out who *her* is. "Ready for what? Over what? Who's *her?*"

Samantha sniffs and takes stuttered breaths as she tried to calm down. I hand her a tissue from the end table and wait. She needs a second. I've promised her forever. I've got time.

Composed, she adjusts in my arms to meet my eyes. Her blues, so full of love with an undercurrent of hurt. She palms my cheek, like I'm the one upset. I guess I am. Her pain is mine. I wipe at her tears, unconvinced that's the last of them. My girl feels things deeply. Happy or sad, her tears are never far away. She was made to believe it made her weak. But it's her strength, her courage that allows her to be vulnerable enough to shed the emotions bubbling inside her. Not everyone gets that. I do, and I love that about her.

On a productive breath she licks her lips and begins. "I thought I was over my mom. I was fine without her at our wedding. I'm fine without her in our lives. I'm over it. I've accepted it. But…" Her chin trembles.

"But?"

"I didn't think I'd feel this way. I should be happy, but instead, here I am crying over *her*. Still." She hops off my lap, grabbing a few more tissues, and blows her nose with one hand and pats her face dry with the other. She begins to pace. "And I'm angry that after all this time, she's still hurting me." She stops at the window. "She's tainting my good news."

I stand and meet her reflection in the floor to ceiling window, wrapping my arms around hers crossed over her chest. "What news?"

Her chin starts to tremble again, and I swear I'm about to join her. "Baby. Fuck. You've got to tell me. Please, you're killing me." I can't help if I don't know what I'm dealing with.

"*Good* news, Caveman. Calm down." She turns in my hold, her hands landing on my chest, searing me through my dress shirt. "I'm pregnant."

I nearly buckle.

I smack a palm against the glass behind her, leaning in, my head next to hers. "Say that again."

I suck in air.

In.

Out.

In.

Out.

"I'm pregnant." She cradles my head on her shoulder.

Her touch is everything. Wrapping her in my arms, I take us to the floor before I fall.

We've been trying for six months, and once a month for every six months my girl cries when she finds out she's not pregnant by either starting her period or by a negative pregnancy test. It's three weeks of bliss as we fuck like rabbits, and a week of sorrow when her period comes… All tinged with sadness that it hadn't happening *yet*.

For six fucking months.

We said we were going to wait a few years, but once we got married and her graduation date neared, all bets were off.

"Are you sure? Were you late? Are you feeling okay?" Did I miss the signs like a selfish asshole?

She cups my face, her calmer state helping me find my center. "I'm good." My pleading stare gives her pause. "Really, Joseph. I'm good. I've felt a little off in the mornings. The smell of coffee makes my stomach churn. That, and the fact that I'm late, prompted me to take a test today when I got home."

I move us back to the couch, positioning us with my girl's legs across my lap and her back to the armrest. "And your mom?"

Twisting her lips, she shrugs a shoulder. "Yeah, my mom."

I bring our joined hands to my mouth and kiss her fingers, the back, the palm, her wrist, imbuing my love into every touch. "It's her loss. But I know it hurts to know she won't be here for you. If it helps, my mom will be excited enough for two moms."

My girl smiles, her eyes filling with tears. "She will. She'll be a wonderful grandmother. Your dad is going to have to love enough for two granddads too." A tear slips free and then another, and another.

This isn't just about our kids missing out on her parents. I know she loves me and my family as if we were her blood. But it's moments like this that are another level of disappointment. Another life event she has to face without her birth family by her side—the absence that much keener. The pain that much deeper. I'm thankful Jace has come around and their relationship is that much stronger for all the hardship they faced.

I pull her to me, hugging her as close as I can and not choke her out. "With Jace, Fin, Matt, Michael, Victor, and Sebastian, our kids are going to have lots of men who will love them like their own. Margot and whoever the guys end up with will love our kids too. They won't even realize they're missing a set of grandparents. I promise, Sweetness."

She nods. She knows. The hurt is still real, though. "Our family is big and will only grow bigger with each wedding, each baby born. I just need a minute to come to terms with my parents not being here. It's a reality check that sideswiped me. That's all."

"Take all the time you need. I'm not going anywhere." I kiss her forehead and sigh over the top of her head. She settles in close, and I relish every second of it.

She's pregnant. The thought fills me with a peacefulness I never thought was possible. "Thank you," I murmur against her brow.

"For what?" Her glistening eyes meet mine.

"For being mine. For marrying me. For loving me. For making me a daddy."

"You're making me a mommy." Her smile is the sweetest fucking thing ever.

I return it. "I am, aren't I." Pride wells as if I got her pregnant just by being in the same room with her.

She laughs and my heart soars. "You're such a caveman, Caveman."

"I am, but only for you, Sweets." I kiss her softly. "Only ever for you."

7 MONTHS LATER

Her pregnancy body is going to kill me. Downright give me a heart attack. I can't get enough of her new curves. I can't get my fill. I can't get deep enough. And when our son moves and stretches in her tummy like a scene from Alien, I get rock hard.

My Brady is a big baby. They think our son is ten pounds. The doctor is going to induce Samantha in two days if she doesn't go in to labor before then. Yeah, I'm a sick motherfucker to find pride in my woman carrying around a baby big enough to rip her to shreds on his way out.

I pray, *pray*, my girl will be alright. She has to be.

I'll remind Brady every damn day how much his mother sacrificed to bring him into the world—when he finally fucking comes.

"Here." My Sweets waddles toward me where I'm sitting on the edge of our bed. She holds out a tub of lotion she wants me to rub on her belly to save her from scarring stretch marks. And she's naked—completely—and ready to *pop*, as she likes to say.

"You want to lie down?" She won't, but I ask anyway. The sight of her makes me hard and so damn guilty for doing this to her. Every step hurts, she can't get comfortable, false labor is kicking her ass, she's barely eaten today, and she pees more than she drinks, if that's even possible.

She rubs her ginormous belly in circles and moans, "No," just as Brady's foot pushes in the spot she's rubbing.

Dipping my fingers into the tub, I come out with a heaping handful, rub my hands together and start massaging it into her taut skin. Brady moves from side to side like he's trying to mirror my movements from the inside. This kid, if he doesn't kill his mommy, is going to be my pride and joy. I can't wait to see the beast of a man he'll be one day. But for the moment, he's the source of my woman's discomfort.

I move lower, my eyes locked on her *Caveman's* tattoo below her bikini line. It's vibrant and shines from the liberal application of lotion, the top a bit distorted from stretching to accommodate Brady.

"What if they have to cut me there?" My Sweets worries her bottom lip as she holds my shoulders for support.

"They won't." I'm certain.

"But what if they do?" I catch the fear in her voice and it has nothing to do with her tattoo.

I continue to caress her silky skin as my eyes catch on her abundant breasts before locking on her troubled, blue eyes. "If they do, then our son will have a round head instead of a cone, and my girl will have a scar to brag about." I cup her breasts and squeeze, teasing the stiff peaks that are sensitive enough to make her come if given enough attention.

She gasps, her fingers digging into my shoulders.

"Whatever happens, Samantha, we've got this. I can't do this for you—and even if I could, I'm not sure I would. You're amazing. You're tough. You take everything in stride and giving birth will be no different. I'll be there the entire time, before, during, and after. I've got you. I promise."

A deep breath and a slight smile are all I get.

"And I will love your body in every stage of our lives. Scars and stretchmarks are nothing compared to the miracle you're giving us." I don't put lotion on her stretchmarks because I care about her having them. I put it on her because she asks, and any chance to get my hands on my girl is reason enough.

"Joseph," the wisp of her reply tugs at my heart.

I capture her cheek, keeping her eyes on me. "Don't you know by now, baby? I want you pregnant, not pregnant, scars, no scars, young, old. You get my cock hard, my heart racing, and my blood pumping. I'm the man I am because of you. The way you love me. The heat in your eyes and the swoon in your step when you catch me looking. Fuck, Sweets it's only you. Always has been. Always will be."

She leans in for a kiss, maneuvering around her tummy that hits me way before her mouth does. "The things you say," she whispers across my lips before she presses her mouth to mine.

I hold her close, supporting her pregnancy weight with my body, and suck her bottom lip, tugging lightly. Her moan has my cock dancing in my boxer briefs, and my hand sliding between her legs. I growl with satisfaction. "You're so fucking wet, Sweets."

"Your mouth—"

"Do you want my mouth on you, or—" I slip a finger inside her and then rub her clit. "Do you think you can stand while I make you come?" I flick her nipple and fill her with another finger as I suck on her plump peak. She clenches around my finger, her moans ratcheting up as if she's ready to come. She probably is. My girl is hot when she's not pregnant but amp her up with hormones and she's purring and ready 24/7.

"Joseph," she warns.

"Can you stay on your feet, baby?"

"Yes. Just—"

"I know. I got you." Her head falls back as I suck and bite her nipples, her hands holding on like we're on turbulent seas.

Her trembling starts with gasps and sucked in breaths, her hips moving, her pussy gripping my fingers in an effort to keep them in as I pull out. "God, Sweets. You're so fucking sexy." I tug on her nipple, releasing it with a pop.

She cries out, begging me for more.

"You gonna come for me?"

"Yes."

"I need to bury my cock balls deep in you."

She shutters. My cock fights to rid itself of its clothed cage.

"But not before you come on my fingers." I suck on a nipple, tweak the other with my fingers, strum her insides, and press on her clit until she's shaking so hard, I'm sure she'll collapse.

"I'm…" she cries out. Moisture pools a second before she comes.

"Jesus, yes. Just like that, Sweetness."

Tremors rack her body. I wrap an arm around her back, suck a nipple till I'm sure I'll draw milk that's meant for my son. I hold my girl as she falls apart for me, one clench, one scream, one erotic shudder at a time.

Before she can come down, I've got her lying on her side with me kneeling over her, straddling her bottom leg and holding her open. Her other leg is cradled against my abdomen as I sink my aching cock in her an inch at a time. Taking it slow. I may have finger fucked her hard, but this close to giving birth, she's tender inside and my cock is bigger than my fingers.

I delve in, swivel my hips. Pull out and do it again, and again. She gasps and moans, clutching the covers and my thigh, moving her hips into me. Her belly moves, her tits bounce, and her eyes stare straight into my soul.

"Joseph?"

A shiver runs up my spine. "Yeah, Sweets?"

"I'm gonna come again." She arches. "I need to come again."

"Fuck." I'm not ready to blow. Not yet. But her body is talking to mine in a way that's too familiar and hard to resist.

I wrap my arm over her top thigh, holding her flush to me and rub her clit and use my other hand to tease her breasts in just the way she likes it—the way she needs it.

As she gets closer, I switch it up, giving up on her breasts and tease her ass, squeezing and kneading, my thumb rubbing over her tight ring that's so wet from her juices.

I thrust a little harder when a soft, "More," seeps out between her moans. My thumb slips through her rosebud, my balls tighten, and my girl asks for more.

"You want my cock here don't you, Sweets?" The idea has me gritting my teeth. I don't even need her answer, her body tells me all I need to know. I push a little farther, moving my finger in and out of her ass as my cock fills her pussy. So tight. Fucking heaven. I lean over her, careful not to squish her belly. I don't need it, but I definitely want to hear her say it. "Tell me."

She captures the back of my neck and pulls till we're nose to nose. "Yes." She licks across my lips.

"My dirty girl." I kiss her hard, possessively, as I rub her clit, surging inside her. "Soon, Sweets."

"Yes," she chants as I sit back, my abs clenching as I thrust, holding off what I can't wait to give her—my cock in her ass, my fingers in her pussy, riding her hard as she screams my name and begs for more. Everything.

On a moan that starts with the pointing of her toes and the shaking of her legs and works up her body, my beautiful, pregnant wife comes so hard, she rips my orgasm from me, pulling it right along with her own release. My groan is deep and savage and so fucking full of love and awe for the woman I've been blessed with.

I fall over, kissing her thoroughly as I pull her close and hold her as we catch our breath.

Life is never boring with my Sweetness.

The sex is off the charts.

She challenges me. She fulfills me. She's my partner in life—in good times and bad.

And our life is about to get even fuller with the birth of our son.

She snuggles in as close as her belly allows, throwing her leg over me, her wet heat tempting my cock. Her hips flex and that's all it takes to convince me we're not quite done. I push inside her with languid strokes, growing harder as she clenches around me. I lean over her and suck in a nipple and find her clit.

Stroking and sucking until she comes, and comes again.

Stroking and sucking until I come.

Stroking until she comes again and falls asleep in my arms.

My cock still inside her.

My son inside her.

My world is complete.

Thank you for reading the Until You Trilogy, the first three books in the Until You Series. If you're not ready to say goodbye to Joseph and Samantha, scan the QR code below to access bonus content for them as well as further reading recommendations.

If you have any questions or concerns, please feel free to reach out to me: dana@dmckdavis.com

Did You Enjoy This Novel?

This is a dream for me to be able to share my love of writing with you.
If you liked my novel, please consider leaving a review on the retailer's
site where you purchased this book (and/or on Goodreads).

Personal recommendations to your friends and loved ones are
a great compliment too. Please share, follow, join my newsletter
(dmckdavis.com/subscribe), and help spread the word—let
everyone know how much you loved Joseph and Samantha's story.

About the Author

D.M. Davis is a Contemporary and New Adult Romance Author.

She is a Texas native, wife, and mother. Her background is Project Management, technical writing, and application development. D.M. has been a lifelong reader and wrote poetry in her early life, but has found her true passion in writing about love and the intricate relationships between men and women.

She writes of broken hearts and second chances, of dreamers looking for more than they have and daring to reach for it.

D.M. believes it is never too late to make a change in your own life, to become the person you always wanted to be, but were afraid you were not worth the effort.

You are worth it. Take a chance on you. You never know what's possible if you don't try. Believe in yourself as you believe in others, and see what life has to offer.

Please visit her website, dmckdavis.com, for more details, and keep in touch by signing up for her newsletter, and joining her on Facebook, Twitter, and Instagram.

Acknowledgements

Thank you to my husband, my children, my mom, my sister, and the rest of my family for their unwavering support. I do this for you because you believe I can.

To my follow writerly peeps: thank you to the MP group for your support and early critiques of *Until You Say I Do*. Thank you to Teddy—I could not do this without you by my side. You're my cheerleader, my confidant, my sister from another mister.

To my bulldog editor, Tamara, for putting up with my emotional, grammatically-challenged self. I wouldn't want to do this without you.

And lastly, to the readers—thank you for your kind words and support. It means so much to hear how much you love Joseph and Samantha. I hope their book three will fill all those gooey romantic parts of you with their love. It is a rather epic love story. One I have loved writing. I will miss them so much. But don't fear, Joseph and Samantha will continue to be integral players in the *Until You* series which continues with Fin and Margot's story in *Until You Believe*.

Until next time, I will continue to write…

"What only the heart hears…"

Additional Books by
D.M. DAVIS

Until You Series

Book 1—Until You Set Me Free

Book 2—Until You Are Mine

Book 3—Until You Say I Do

Book 4—Until You Believe

Book 6 – Until You Save Me

Finding Grace Series

Book 1—The Road to Redemption

Black Ops MMA Series

Book 1—No Mercy

Book 2—Rowdy

Book 3—Captain

Book 4 - Cowboy

Book 5 - Mustang

Ashford Family Series

WILD Duet

Book 1 - WILDFLOWER

Book 2- WILDFIRE

Standalones

Warm Me Softly

Doctor Heartbreak

Vegas Storm

Stalk Me

Visit www.dmckdavis.com for more details about my books.

Keep in touch by signing up for my Newsletter.

Connect on social media:
Facebook: www.facebook.com/dmdavisauthor
Instagram: www.instagram.com/dmdavisauthor
Twitter: twitter.com/dmdavisauthor
Reader's Group: www.facebook.com/groups/dmdavisreadergroup

Follow me:
BookBub: www.bookbub.com/authors/d-m-davis
Goodreads: www.goodreads.com/dmckdavis

d.m. davis
SEXY WITH HEART
CONTEMPORARY & NEW ADULT ROMANCE AUTHOR

www.ingramcontent.com/pod-product-compliance
Lightning Source LLC
Chambersburg PA
CBHW030905300726
48970CB00001B/13